M. R. James'
Dark Choices
Volume 1

M. R. James'
Dark Choices
Volume 1

A Selection of Fine Tales of the Strange and
Supernatural Endorsed by the
Master of the Genre

Including Two Novels 'The Forest House' and
'Featherston's Story,' Three Novelettes 'The
Mysterious Stranger,' 'The Mysterious Lodger,'
and 'Green Tea,' Nine Short Stories and
One Ballad

LEONAUR

M. R. James'
Dark Choices
Volume 1
A Selection of Fine Tales of the Strange and Supernatural
Endorsed by the Master of the Genre

Including Two Novels 'The Forest House' and 'Featherston's Story,'
Three Novelettes 'The Mysterious Stranger,' 'The Mysterious Lodger,' and
'Green Tea,' Nine Short Stories and One Ballad

FIRST EDITION

Leonaur is an imprint
of Oakpast Ltd

ISBN: 978-0-85706-445-5 (hardcover)
ISBN: 978-0-85706-446-2 (softcover)

http://www.leonaur.com

Publisher's Notes

The opinions of the authors represent a view of events in which he
was a participant related from his own perspective,
as such the text is relevant as an historical document.

The views expressed in this book are not necessarily
those of the publisher.

Contents

Introduction

An introduction in a Leonaur book is so rare as to be noteworthy. The Leonaur Editors believe that the text—and the reputation of most authors—is usually enough to alert the non-academic reader as to the value of the contents of the book about to be read. Not all our readers agree (and we have the correspondence to prove this), but our view remains that if the promise of a dessert with a cherry topping was never made then no one has justification for bridling at the absence of the cherry—the same principle obviously applies to our books and introductions. So having clearly established our deep conviction in this broad principle—conceived after hours of serious and sometimes fraught consideration—what follows is an *introduction*, the proverbial exception to the rule.

The presence of an introduction here is, however, a matter of necessity rather than a general change of policy on our part. The book you are now holding is part of a five volume anthology, a collection of tales by a diverse collection of authors. Anthologies must have a *raison d'être* and it is incumbent on us, as the editors, to explain what that is—so much is only fair. The idea for this anthology occurred to one of the Leonaur editors as he was working on the recently published Leonaur edition of *The Collected Supernatural and Weird Fiction of M. R. James*. For the sake of brevity your editors will assume that any reader who is about to embark upon reading this anthology, having presumably been drawn to it by its title, will not need to have anything about the biography and works of M. R. James recounted to them. For those yet 'in the dark,' if the pun is excused, it is enough to point out that in the echelons of authors of supernatural fiction James' name is at the forefront. His work is timeless, unmistakable, of the highest literary order, emulates none but is sufficiently well regarded by his peers among other fine writers of the genre to be stylistically adopted for their own excursions into the story-telling of the other worldly. As a consequence this style became known as 'Jamesian' which as far as we know is not a distinction accorded to any other author of chilling tales.

What struck the Leonaur editor working on the James collection was that M. R. James not only wrote supernatural fiction but that he also wrote about it quite extensively. Unsurprisingly, given his academic status, it was also a subject about which he knew a great deal and given his own abilities it seems reasonable to expect that his opinions and verdicts carry an indisputable weight of authority—despite the implied subjectivity of critical examination and assessment.

In letters, articles and introductions M. R. James gave his views as to which authors and which stories he regarded most highly. Irrespective of the medium we are fortunate that his opinions remained consistent. The Leonaur editors have principally drawn upon James' article 'Some Remarks on Ghost Stories,' written by him for the December 1929 issue of *The Bookman*, as their inspiration for bringing together this *M. R. James' Dark Choices* anthology series. This article references many writers and their works—approvingly and otherwise—and encapsulates James' assessment of the genre; other of James' non-fiction on the subject of supernatural fiction has been occasionally referenced by us to illuminate the opinions and preferences established in this principal article.

In the main, James dealt with the stories he discussed in 'Some Remarks on Ghost Stories' chronologically by date of publication. We have not followed his example in arranging the tales in our anthology series. In order to create volumes of similar length some consideration had to be given to the extent of each of the pieces, which range from novels to novellas to short stories and it was equally necessary to give some regard to the balance of each book. Where James extolled the merits of several works by the same author these have been distributed throughout the five volumes—as far as possible—to avoid over-emphasis on a single author in any one volume and for the sake of variety of style and ultimately for the enhancement of reader enjoyment. We have given very careful attention to James' words in 'Some Remarks on Ghost Stories,' because the citing of an author or tale is not necessarily an accolade—and on at least one occasion James' praise is decidedly faint.

Simply put the Leonaur editor thought that if one was in search of a good ghost story, it was not possible to go far wrong with the spirit hand of M. R. James as a guide. The word 'spirit' is, of course, applied advisably because the five volumes of this anthology were *not* actually compiled by James whilst he was on this side of the veil and the Leonaur editors are claiming no special powers with which they might elicit information and help from him from beyond the misty curtain. In short this anthology series is a 'bit of fun,' and such a motivation seems entirely appropriate to us because, at most levels, the writing and reading of spooky stories—with a few notable exceptions is also about the fun and frisson of a good scare—followed by a broad smile.

Readers may be reassured that M. R. James really did make written reference to the authors and stories that comprise *M. R. James' Dark Choices*. There is no author or story within the pages of these anthologies that M. R. James did not endorse to one degree or another; so is M. R. James the editor of this anthology? 'No' is the short answer, the Leonaur editors have compiled these anthologies. James simply approved of the stories included and left us his views on them in his own writings on supernatural fiction.

It is our belief that as many anthologies are edited by those who owe their renown to being nothing more than the editors of anthologies this one has much to recommended it; it is different because these are the 'dark choices' of someone who was himself a *master* of the genre. We hope you will agree and enjoy every spine chilling tale.

About This Book

This volume opens with an extended tale from the French writing partnership of Erckmann-Chatrian. Emile Erckmann (1822-1899) and Alexandre Chatrian (1826-1890) wrote almost exclusively as a team until their eventual falling out. Their writings are singular among those that James regards since they are the only authors who did not write in English, and James makes it clear that, in the main, he thought supernatural fiction was at its best executed by those who hail from the British Isles. One suspects he would not wish to split hairs over the nationality of his favourite supernatural fiction writer the Irishman J. Sheridan Le Fanu, his female counterpart Mrs. Riddell or indeed of Henry James who although born American, died British.

Erckmann-Chatrian specialised in fiction based in the places they knew best. Their homeland, the north eastern part of France close to the Vosges Mountains and the impenetrable forests of central Europe were a ready-made gothic backdrop. The novella, 'The Forest House' is one of several stories by the French partnership cited by James and indeed he favourably compares the influences of this border region of France and Germany with the benefits Le Fanu enjoyed by his ability to blend French and Irish sentiments.

Another Erckmann-Chatrian story, 'The Crab Spider,' is a highly successful and early example of 'creature-horror.' Modern readers are now very familiar with all kinds of creatures—from giant sharks to huge spiders like those in this story—that feed on unsuspecting humans. (Who can forget the monstrous Shelob from Tolkien's *The Lord of the Rings*?) James himself acknowledged the influence of this story in the writing of his own chilling spider story, 'The Ash Tree.'

James writes, 'I own to reading not infrequently 'Featherston's Story' in the fifth series of Johnny Ludlow, to delighting in its domestic flavour and finding its ghost very convincing.'

This delightful tale, the second in this first volume, is the work of Mrs Henry Wood (1814-1887) the author of East Lynne, and is the only story by her selected by James.

According to James, E. F Benson's collections of short stories 'rank high, though to my mind he sins occasionally by stepping over the line of legitimate horridness.' It could be that modern perceptions have been irrecoverably altered as to what is now considered 'horrid,' much less what would now be considered as 'stepping over the line.' However, there has been little or no criticism of E. F Benson's talent as an author of supernatural fiction, which might be at odds with James' qualified approval as readers and pundits alike acknowledge Benson's work to be of the highest order. James agrees to the degree that he was prepared to give a blanket endorsement to three volumes of Benson's stories, though regrettably without highlighting any specific titles. We have therefore considered this a *carte blanche* to make selections ourselves on the understanding that James might agree that we could not, in the circumstances, wander far astray in our judgements.

E(dward). F Benson (1867-1940) was one of three brothers, the others being Arthur and Robert (known as Hugh), all of whom wrote ghost stories. James was less impressed by the writings of the youngest, Hugh, who had a tendency to utilise his fiction as a vehicle for Catholic propaganda—a faith to which he was a convert—describing his work as 'too ecclesiastical.' This volume contains two stories by E. F. Benson, 'The Room in the Tower' and 'Bagnell Terrace' though more stories appear in other volumes of this series as warranted by both the author's abilities and James' acknowledgement of them.

Today there can be few people who have not heard of Bram Stoker's book about the fictional vampire Dracula; both the author and his character have become icons of horror, with Dracula repeatedly presented to us in all forms of media. It seems strange now to come across a critique that makes it clear the critic is less than impressed with Stoker's book. Yet James describes Stoker's book as 'with very good ideas, but the butter is spread far too thick. Excess is the fault here.' He goes on to state that the work 'leave(s) little impression on the memory.' The tough verdict continues: 'I fancy by the way, that it must be based on a story in the fourth volume of Chamber's Repository, issued in the fifties (1850's).' The Leonaur editors felt that this was too good an opportunity to pass by, so that story, 'The Mysterious Stranger,' is included for both enjoyment and evaluation in this volume. The story begins as a group of travellers make their way through the snow covered Carpathian Mountains. Beset by threatening wolves they take refuge in the castle of an eerily strange person who sleeps by day. This is familiar literary territory indeed! It was common for magazine stories of the period to be published without attribution, although the author—who remains anonymous to us—was thought to be German and the original publication date was believed to be as early as 1823. Certainly, whoever conceived it did so over half a century before Dracula saw 'the light of day'—or not in his case!

Irrespective of whether or not you agree with James that 'Dracula' is unmemorable there can surely be little dissention regarding James' choice of F. Marion Crawford's (1854-1909) outstanding and horrid story, 'The Upper Berth' and his verdict of it as 'the best in his collection of Uncanny Tales, and stands high among ghost stories in general.' The pitch of the story is just right. The claustrophobic nature of the metal walled cabin promotes a nightmare like restriction of movement when in the upper berth, immediately above the recumbent figure of the narrator in the lower berth, an unseen entity stirs—fantastic and eerie stuff, to be sure.

James leaves the reader in no doubt as to where he stands on J. Sheridan Le Fanu (1814-1873): 'absolutely in the first rank as a writer of ghost stories. That is my deliberate verdict, after reading all the supernatural tales I have been able to get hold of. Nobody sets the scene better than he, nobody touches in the effective detail more deftly.' James could not make his view clearer and this is why, in recommending Le Fanu's most highly regarded genre tales, there are more of his stories cited in James' article than those of any other author. This volume contains, 'The Mysterious Lodger'(which James considered a rival to the work of Mrs. Oliphant as the best of 'religious ghost stories'), 'Green Tea'(possibly the first appearance in print of that type of character soon to prove very popular—the supernatural sleuth) and 'Dickon the Devil,' which James thought only slightly less of than his top three Le Fanu stories.

James finds Mrs H. D. Everett's (1851-1923) *The Death Mask* to be a collection of tales 'of a rather quieter tone' yet with 'some excellently conceived stories.' That cannot be truer than of the title story itself, in which the image of a dead face reappears contoured by everyday objects. Even though 'Mrs H. D. Everett' was itself probably a pseudonym, her real name possibly being Henrietta Dorothy Huskisson, the author also wrote novels under another pseudonym, Theo Douglas, including some with distinctly uncanny themes; however she remains best remembered for the collection *The Death Mask*, which also includes the highly regarded 'The Crimson Blind.'

While James drew his readers attention to the talents of a number female Victorian authors, he did so with little more than an allusion to the high quality of their work in general and left little to indicate his specific preferences. So we are left to decide which stories to include by Rhoda Broughton (1840-1920) and Irish born Mrs J. H. Riddell (1832-1906). Rhoda Broughton, the daughter of a country parson, was born in Denbigh, north Wales and was a fairly prolific and often controversial novelist. Charlotte Riddell was the daughter of the high sheriff of the county of Antrim who went on to become one of the most influential Victorian writers and part owner of *St James' Magazine* one of the most prestigious literary magazines of the 19th century. We trust that our readers will approve of our choosing 'The Man with the Nose' by Broughton and 'The Last Squire of Ennismore' by Mrs Riddell, both distinctively haunting tales that we believe James would have enjoyed.

James has given us the rare opportunity to include the supernatural writings of authors whose names may not appear quite so readily in anthologies of ghostly and weird fiction but whose fame and talents are widely known and regarded by many. One such author is Sir Walter Scott (1771-1832). His novels including *Ivanhoe*, *Rob Roy*, *Redgauntlet* and many others are well known literary landmarks, though today not to everyone's taste particularly in terms of style. The influence of their storylines has however been undeniable. James draws his readers attention to two Scott short stories which he considers 'classical specimens,' one of which, 'The Tapestried Room' appears in this volume.

Finally, in his analysis of the genealogy of the supernatural tale James does not neglect the influence of verse. He points out that, 'we must not forget that the ballad is in direct line of ancestry of the ghost story.' James gave us a number of examples and these appear throughout this anthology series. In this volume we have included 'The Wife of Usher's Well.'

The Leonaur Editors

The Forest House

A.K.A. THE WILD HUNTSMAN OR THE HOUSE IN THE FOREST

By Erckmann-Chatrian

1

In those happy youthful days, said Theodore, when the sky seems bluer, the leaves greener, when the rush of the mountain streams sounds sweeter in the ear, and the waters of their lakes seem glassier and more transparent, when all nature is clothed in our eyes with a mysterious charm, when every object we behold speaks to us of love, of art, and poetry—at that happy age I was wandering alone through the great forest of Hundsrück.

At that time I had not learned to reason on my impressions: I welcomed happiness wherever and however it presented itself, without discussion. Everything around me seemed instinct with life and sentiment—everything, the stones, the trees, the moss, the flowers. And if, at a turn in the road, some old oak had suddenly addressed me, I should not have been greatly surprised. 'Mr. Oak,' I should have said, 'Theodore Richter, landscape painter of Dusseldorf, salutes you. He sees with pleasure that you have deigned to break your long silence in his favour. Let us talk of this sublime nature around us, our great earthly mother; you must have stored up a whole host of ideas on this important subject. What do you think of the soul of nature, Mr. Oak?'

Such was my simple faith, my childlike confidence and enthusiasm; and as for the rest, the Almighty had favoured me with one of those wiry, vigorous, sober constitutions which bid defiance alike to privations and fatigue.

I wandered on from hamlet to hamlet, from one forester's house to another, whistling, singing, making my observations at random, without any fixed aim, led onwards by my fancy, always in search of some retreat still more remote, more secluded, more embowered in foliage than any I had yet seen, where no sound should meet the ear but the rustling of the leaves and the murmur of the stream over its pebbly bed.

One morning, long before daybreak, I had left the hostelry of the Swan, at Pirmasens, intending to cross the wooded heights of the Rothalps, and thus reach the village of Wolfthal. The *garçon* had wakened me at two o'clock, agreeably to my directions, for in that region of country, towards the end of August, it is much pleasanter to do your walking by night. After nine o'clock in the morning the sun's rays, reflected from the almost perpendicular sides of the deep valleys, become insupportable

Behold me, then, tramping on through the shades of night, my short shooting vest tightly buckled round my waist, my knapsack strapped on my shoulders, and my stick in my hand. I walked at a brisk pace; vineyard succeeded to vineyard, hemp-field to hemp-field, till at length the pinewoods began to appear, intersected here and there with steep paths or glades, down which the pale moon threw long tremulous lines of light.

The exhilaration produced by the rapid walk, the deep silence which reigned around, the chirp of a bird startled from amid the foliage, the quick patter of a squirrel over the fallen leaves on its way to drink at a neighbouring spring, the stars twinkling over the tall tree tops, the distant murmur of the stream at the bottom of the gorge, the occasional halt to take breath, to listen for a moment and light one's pipe, then the fresh start, the increasing sound of the torrent, warning you that you must soon cross its waters on some prostrate trunk, or leap from stone to stone amid the foaming current, the first notes of the thrush whistling from the top-most branch of a lofty pine as if to announce, 'Yonder, far away, I see a light—the day is breaking!' and at last the pale dawn, the first ruddy blush on the horizon, against which the dark outline of the wood stands out so sharply—all these thousand varying impressions led me on insensibly to the dawn of day.

Towards five o'clock I emerged on the other side of the Rothalps, about three leagues from Pirmasens, into a narrow winding gorge, which ought to have been called the Gorge of the Water-wagtails, so much did this little bird, with its bluish gray wings, black head, and long white tail, abound in it.

I shall never forget the feeling of freshness and delight which I experienced at the sight of this secluded spot. Down far below, a little mountain stream, as pure as crystal, galloped over its bed of greenish pebbles; on the right, the face of the declivity was clothed with a dense forest of birch which stretched upwards as far as the eye could reach; on the left, underneath the dark canopy of pines, wound along a sandy road, or rather track, now hollowed into deep ruts, and again dotted on the surface with projecting masses of rock, polished to a silvery brightness by the heavy wheels of the mountain carts. Many a time have I said to myself, when travelling between Creuznach and Pirmasens, that the little oxen with their curly heads, slobbering mouths, drooping necks, and haggard eyes, whose task it is to drag the enormous trunks of oak or beech which have been felled by the wood-cutter, must have often felt their sturdy spines bend like a whip before they carved out such furrows in the solid granite.

Below the road the slopes were clothed thickly with heather, interspersed with beds of broom in full flower; lower down a few brambles made their appearance; lower still a tiny spring darted out here and there from the hill-side and made its way downwards amidst a thick carpet of fresh tufted watercress.

Those who, in their youthful days, have had the good fortune to meet with such a spot in the forest depths, at the hour when nature emerges from her dewy bath and drapes herself with sunlight; when the golden rays penetrate through the foliage and dart their tongues of fire even into the deepest recesses of the woods; when the moss, the honeysuckle, and the whole tribe of climbing plants, send up a light cloud of vapour as the heat reaches them, and blend their perfumes together beneath the leafy dome of the forest; when the blue and green titmouse wheels and flutters around the branches in his search for the tiny insects on which he feeds; when the thrush, the bullfinch, and the blackbird fly down to the streamlet and drink with swelling throats, as they hover on quivering wings over the foam of the tiny cascades; when flocks of plundering jays flap their way in Indian file over the lofty tree tops with noisy caw, directing their flight to the wild cherry-trees—at the hour, in a word, when every object is radiant with love, with light, and life—those, and those alone who have seen nature in such a garb can understand the ecstasy of delight I felt.

I sat down on the projecting root of an old moss-covered oak, with my stick between my knees, and for a full hour I gave myself up, childlike, to aimless and endless reveries.

Sometimes, stretching myself at full length on the ground, with my elbow resting on the mossy cushion, and my eyelids closed, I listened to the vague, widespread murmur of the universe around me. The hum of some early bee or the chirp of a grasshopper, at distant intervals, were the only sounds which broke in on my endless daydreams.

Sometimes, half opening my eyes, I saw above me the gnarled branches of the oak with their leafy drapery standing out in fantastic shapes against the blue sky. Something moved amidst the dark foliage—it was a squirrel with bushy tail twisting and turning amongst the branches, and spying with his little bead-like eyes in all directions; or else a woodpecker, with his great yellow claws buried in the worm-eaten bark, attacking the old tree with rapid and vigorous blows of his horny bill; or some other marvellous spectacle of the like kind.

Then I closed my eyes once more, quite dazzled, and saw all these things over again in my mind's eye as if reflected in a mirror.

Far off, in the extreme distance, the bleating of a doe could be heard calling her fawn, and I pictured her to myself bounding along the lofty peaks of the Rothalps, stopping at times to listen and snuff up the breeze.

As the sun mounted higher in the heavens, the hum of the insects grew louder, whilst the melancholy cry of the cuckoo, repeating incessantly to the echoes his two unvarying notes, marked the time as it were for this grand concert.

In the midst of these reveries, a shrill note, very slightly modulated, and evidently a long way off, struck incessantly on my ear. Ever since I had halted at the foot of the old oak I had heard this sound occasionally, but had paid little or no attention to it; by degrees, however, I began to distinguish it from the other confused murmurs of the forest, and said to myself, 'It is the whistle of a bird-catcher; his cottage can't be far off. There must be some forester's house in the neighbourhood.' I rose and cast a glance around at the surrounding heights. To the right of the glen no object of the kind was visible; as far as the eye could reach nothing was to be seen but a succession of peaks and valleys, wooded crests, and deep ravines, heaped together in inextricable confusion; but on the left, near the summit of the hill, I speedily discovered an overhanging roof, the little dormer windows and white chimneys of which glanced brightly out between the innumerable spear-like tops of the pines. It was a full half-hour's walk to the spot, but this did not hinder me from uttering a hearty ejaculation of thankfulness to God for all His mercies.

For, let me tell you, it is no light matter in the depths of the forest to know where you can sit down comfortably before a morsel of bread and a flask of *Kirschenwasser*. I therefore buckled on my knapsack again, and set out in high spirits, following the path which seemed to lead to the welcome resting-place.

For some minutes longer the bird-catcher continued his insinuating appeals, then suddenly the sounds stopped altogether. Towards seven o'clock the smaller birds have finished their morning repast, and the daylight, becoming stronger every minute, enables them to discover their enemy even through the thick foliage of his bower of branches. It is time for him to lift his lime-twigs and be off.

I was making these reflections as I proceeded on my way,

and regretting that I had not set out earlier, when, about fifty or sixty yards to the right, at the further end of a sort of opening or glade in the forest, the bird-catcher came into view, a benevolent looking old forester, tall, thin, and wiry, dressed in a short blue linen blouse, his large game-bag slung over his shoulders, his metal plate or badge on his breast, and his little pointed cap with upturned peak over one ear. He was busily occupied in taking up his twigs, and at first I saw nothing but his great round shoulders and long muscular wiry legs cased in high gaiters of brown linen fastened with a row of bone buttons and mounting up till they met his blouse; but after a little, as he turned round, I had a view of his strongly marked profile, resembling somewhat that of an old pointer, with the gray eyes half concealed beneath their heavy lids, the drooping eyes, great white moustache, and snow-white eyebrows. It was eminently an honest face, a little grave perhaps, a little dreamy, a little childish even; but something about the thick neck, covered behind with silvery hair, and the flash of the eyes from out of their deep orbits corrected what might , have been deemed at first sight the too weakly good-natured expression of his face. And if his great back seemed too rounded for strength or symmetry, the shoulders appertaining to it were so broad that an observer could not help feeling a sort of respect for the old forester.

He moved now to the right, now to the left, without suspecting in the least that he was observed, sometimes in the broad sunlight, sometimes in the shadow of the foliage, stooping and stretching—in short, perfectly at his ease. As I stood looking at him from below, leaning on my stick in the middle of the forest path I was climbing, I thought what a capital picture he would make seen thus under the luminous canopy of branchwork overhead. In the society of our fellow-men there is always more or less of constraint or affectation. Even in a village inn, with his elbow on the table and the glass in his hand, the labourer or artisan to some extent acts a part; but in the solitude of the woods, when we feel ourselves alone—completely alone—then for the first time we are really ourselves.

After taking up his twigs, he wrapped them carefully in a piece of oiled linen, and then, with one knee on the ground, began to string together his tomtits, redbreasts, bullfinches, blackbirds, and thrushes by their bills, the larger birds at the bottom and the smaller at the top, in a sort of garland or festoon. From time to time he held up the chaplet to see if the birds were properly arranged, smoothing their plumage and adjusting their tails with evident satisfaction, actuated no doubt by an inherent love of symmetry and the harmonious distribution of colours.

At last, after carefully arranging his chaplet of singing-birds, he half opened his game-bag and dropped it in; then, rising from, his knee, he gave a glance at the sun to see how the day was progressing, hitched his bag round over his shoulders, and picking up his thick holly stick which was lying beside him, he directed his steps towards the path where I was standing.

Then for the first time he perceived me, and for a moment his features assumed an expression of watchfulness and distrust, suggested doubtless by his function as guardian of the forest; but insensibly the knitted brow relaxed, and his gray eyes twinkled good humouredly.

'Hallo!' cried he in French, but with a funny German accent, 'I didn't expect there was any one just so near me. Glad to see you in the Hundsrück, sir. How goes it with you?'

'Oh! tolerably well, thank you,' replied I in the same language.

'Ha! ha! ha!' laughed the good man, 'you are French, I perceive. I saw that at the first glance.'

And bringing his hand up to his little cap with an air that smacked of the old soldier:

'Am I not right? Aren't you a Frenchman?'

'Not altogether. I am from Dusseldorf.'

'Ah! from Dusseldorf. No matter,' said he, felling back into the German dialect, 'you are a fine hearty young fellow all the same.'

Then, laying his hand on my shoulder with a kindly gesture, 'You haven't a light about you, have you? I left my flint and steel at home, and I shouldn't be sorry to have a smoke just now.'

'With pleasure, sir.'

I handed him the flint, steel, and tinder. He brought out a little black clay pipe from beneath his blouse, and clenching it between his teeth, began to strike a light.

'You must have been early on the road this morning,' resumed he.

'Yes, I have come from Pirmasens.'

'It's three good leagues from here to Pirmasens. You must have started about three o'clock.'

'I left at two; but I stopped for an hour in the valley yonder.'

'Ah, yes, near the source of the Vellerst. And, if I may make so free, you are going to—'

'Oh! I go everywhere—I am only strolling about, seeing anything that is to be seen.'

'You are not in the timber way?'

'No, I am a painter.'

'A painter? Ah! good—a capital trade that; a man can earn three or four crowns a day by doing nothing but walking about with his hands in his pockets. We have had painters in this country before now. I have seen several during the thirty years I have been here. It's a good business. Thank you, sir, it will do very well now.'

He was sending great clouds of smoke into the air, and had resumed his stick which he had leaned against a tree.

We pursued our way together towards the forest house, he striding along in front with measured step and rounded back, and I following behind, full of cheerful anticipations of rest and food.

The sun, which had risen above the tree tops, was now blazing down on us in full force, and this, with the steepness of the path, made the ascent no trifling matter. Now and then immense *vistas* opened on our left, disclosing valley after valley in endless succession, interspersed with deep gorges and bluish mountain peaks, the whole sinking away gradually to the banks of the Rhine, beyond which the dusty plains stretched backwards until they met the sky.

'What a magnificent country!' exclaimed I, stopping in front of one of these superb landscapes.

We were on the summit of the hill, buried up to the middle in the tall heather, while millions of insects hovered about us.

At my exclamation the old forester stopped, and fixing his piercing gaze on the distant view, replied gravely:

'Yes, that's true, sir. I have by far the best district of the whole mountains up to Neustadt. Everyone who has seen the country, even his honour the forester-in-chief, says it is very fine. See, look yonder—that is the Losser running over the bed of rocks. Do you see that white line? That's foam. You should see that near at hand, sir. You should hear the noise it makes at the melting of the snows towards the end of April; it's as grand as the thunder among the mountains in a great storm. And then look up yonder at that height covered with flowering heath and broom—that is the Waldhorn. At this season the flowers are beginning to fade, but to see it in spring you would say it was one great nosegay reaching into the skies. And then there is the Birckenstein; if you are fond of curiosities you should not forget to take a look at it; all the learned folks, and we have one or two of them here every year,. never fail to pay it a visit on account of the old inscriptions on the stones.'

'Then it is a ruin?'

'Yes, an old wall or two built on the solid rocks, and half buried amongst nettles and briars—a regular owl's nest. For my part, I prefer the Losser, the Krapenfeltz, the Waldhorn; but, as the French say, everyone to his own taste and his own colours. We have all kinds here, forests, groves, copses, thickets of brushwood and bramble, rocks, caverns, waterfalls, rivers.'

'Then you have no lakes?' said I to the honest fellow.

'Lakes!' replied he, as if astonished at my question: 'yes, we have one behind the Losser, a real lake a league round, deep and dark, surrounded by the lofty rocks and tall pinewoods of the Veierschloss. We call it the *Lake of the Wild Counts*.'

His head sank on his breast, and he appeared to reflect for a few seconds, then suddenly shaking his head, and without adding a word, he proceeded on his way. It seemed to me that the old forester, but just now so proud to do the honours of his mountain region, had all at once become thoughtful and melancholy, and, as if infected with this change of mood, I plodded on behind him in a meditative frame of mind. Meanwhile, with stooping shoulders, and assisting himself with his thick holly stick, he strode onwards with a pensive air, taking such immense steps that his long legs seemed to split up beneath his blouse half-way up his back.

The forest house now began to come into view between the trees, situated in the midst of a green meadow on the slope of the hill. Down below in the valley the river could be seen following all the undulations of the mountain side. Higher up the glen was an orchard of fruit trees; then came a few fields of arable land, with a little garden surrounded by a dry stone wall; and lastly, placed on a sort of terrace, with its back resting on the forest, the old forester's dwelling, neatly whitewashed, so as partially to conceal the ravages of time and weather. On the ground floor there were three windows and the door; four on the first floor with little hexagonal panes of glass; and above them four attic windows standing out from the steep roof of brown tiles.

On the side next the forest, in the direction in which we were coming, projected an old worm-eaten wooden gallery with carved balustrade, access to which was obtained by an exterior flight of steps resting against the wall. On either side was a trellis covered with long creepers of vine and honeysuckle, the foliage of which was trained in graceful festoons underneath the projecting roof. Peeping through this leafy wall the little black window panes glittered in the shade. On the wall of the kitchen garden was perched a cock surrounded by his hens; the moss-grown roof was covered with a dense flock of pigeons; on the river a flotilla of ducks was sailing proudly; while from the threshold of the old dwelling the eye took in at one sweep the sloping side of the glen, the entire valley beneath, and, beyond, an immense extent of forest, which stretched away until lost to view in the distance.

A little beyond the house and resting against it was the barn, seen in profile, with the grain-loft above and the large waggon entrance below. In the centre of the folding doors a sparrow-hawk was nailed up, the fleecy plumage of which was carried away piecemeal by the passing breeze. It seemed to have the effect of banishing the tribe of petty winged plunderers, especially the sparrows, an intelligent race that understand right well the language of symbols.

Farther on still, in the same line, were the stables and pigsties, forming a row of low sloping sheds. To the right of the house was the fountain with its weather-stained watering trough; and, behind it, the large projecting oven and bakehouse. Nothing can be conceived more quiet or peaceful than this woodland abode, thus lost as it were amidst the solitude of the mountains; its very look had a sort of charm about it that cannot be described; you felt as if you could spend all your life there.

Two old sporting dogs, the one a terrier of a foxy colour, bandy legged and fat, with snub nose and large hanging ears, the other a sort of stag-hound, tall, wiry, and thin, bounded forward to meet us. A young girl who was hanging out clothes to dry in the gallery, seeing the dogs scampering off, looked up.

The old forester smiled at her and quickened his pace.

'This is your house then?' said I.

'Yes, this is my home.'

'Can you allow me to break a crust of bread and drink a glass of wine under your roof?'

'Why of course I can! If woodrangers sent away travellers from their door here in the forest, what inn could they go to? You are heartily welcome, sir.'

We had now reached the wicker gate of the little garden. The dogs were capering and jumping about us, and the young girl waved a welcome to us with her hand from the gallery. Having crossed the garden, a second gate admitted us into the farmyard, and the forester, turning towards me, said in a hearty, cheerful tone:

'You are now at the house of Frantz Honeck woodranger to the Grand Duke Ludwig. Walk into the sitting-room; I have but to lay aside my bag and take off my gaiters, and I am at your service.'

As he spoke we were passing along a little hall, and the good man pushed open the door of a low square whitewashed apartment. Banged around the walls were a number of beech chairs, the flat backs ornamented with a heart cut out of the solid wood. A tall cupboard of walnut wood, with polished steel hinges and lock, and supported on four rounded knobs, a Nuremberg clock at the farther end, a pyramid shaped metal stove in a corner to the right, and a deal table, with cross legs in the form of an X, opposite the little shady windows, completed the furniture of the apartment. On the table were already placed a loaf of bread and two goblets.

'Sit down and make yourself comfortable,' repeated the old ranger; 'I shall be back in a moment.'

And he left the room.

I heard him entering the adjoining apartment. Thus left alone, I proceeded to disencumber myself of my knapsack, delighted to find myself in such comfortable quarters. The dogs snuffed about under the tables and benches.

'Louise! Louise!' exclaimed old Frantz from the next room. I heard his heavy shoes creaking on the boarded floor. The young girl passed in front of the windows, and her pretty rosy-cheeked face pushed aside the branches of the honeysuckle to look into the apartment. I bowed, and, blushing, she withdrew her head hastily.

'Louise!' repeated the old man.

'Here I am, grandfather; here I am,' replied she in a sweet musical voice, running along the hall.

Then I heard the whole conversation.

'There is a traveller, a fine young fellow, to breakfast with us. You had better draw a pitcher of white wine and lay two plates.'

'Yes, grandfather.'

26

'And get me my woollen vest and my *sabots*. I had a good take of thrushes this morning, and of tomtits too. They are for the Swan Hotel at Pirmasens. When Kasper comes back send him in.'

'He is on the hill herding the cattle, grandfather; shall I call him?'

'No, it will be time enough in an hour.'

Every word reached me as distinctly as the notes of a bell. Outside the dogs were barking, the fowls cackling, the foliage rustled against the little windowpanes—all was light, freshness, and verdure.

I laid my knapsack on the table and sat down, thinking how happy it would be to live there always, without any care but that of earning one's daily bread. 'What a delightful life!' I said to myself; 'how one drinks in this delicious air, how the heart swells, and the chest expands! This old Frantz now is as stout and hearty as one of his own oaks, in spite of his seventy years. And how pretty his granddaughter is!'

I had scarcely time to make these reflections when the old man, in his knitted vest and great fur-lined *sabots*, entered the room laughing and exclaiming:

'Here I am, you see! My work is over for this morning. I was afoot before you, sir; at four o'clock I had already made my inspection of the cuttings. We shall now rest ourselves a little and have a glass of wine and another pipe together. Ah! there is no end of those pipes! But, tell me, would you like to change your clothes? I can take you to my room.'

'No, thank you, Father Frantz,' replied I; 'I require nothing but a little rest and food.'

This title, Father Frantz, seemed to delight the good man. His eyes twinkled.

'It's quite true that my name is Frantz,' said he, 'and that I am old enough to be your father, and even your grandfather. If it's no offence, may I ask your age?'

'I shall soon be twenty-two.'

'Twenty-two! At twenty-two I was making my first campaign against the republican General Custine. At one blow he passed over us like a whirlwind and fell upon Mayence. Then we made our way into the mountains. They sent Hoche, Kleber, and Marceau against us, and the end of it was that they divided us into four departments, and we all set out together arm-in-arm to conquer Italy. We had become Frenchmen without knowing why or wherefore.'

The old forester gave a quiet laugh, his eyes twinkled, and glancing up at three muskets which was suspended above the door:

'There!' said he, pointing to a cavalry carbine, close to the ceiling, 'that is what I may call my first sweetheart; we roamed about the world together from the year—'

But at this moment the little Louise entered the room, carrying in one hand a pitcher of white wine, and in the other a homemade cheese on a handsome China plate ornamented with large red flowers. Father Frantz stopped suddenly, thinking perhaps that it was not becoming in him to talk of his old sweethearts before his granddaughter.

Louise might have been sixteen. She was exquisitely fair, with hair of the lightest auburn, of middle height, and beautifully formed. She had a high forehead, blue eyes, straight nose, slightly turned up at the end, delicately shaped nostrils, full red lips, in form like a Cupid's bow, and as fresh and dewy as two ripe cherries, and a timid and artless expression. She wore a skirt of blue linen with broad white stripes, supported by shoulder-straps, the usual dress of the women of the Hundsück. The sleeves of her chemise came down no farther than her elbow, displaying her plump rounded arms, a little embrowned by the sun and air. It would be impossible to imagine a more gentle, artless, innocent creature, and I felt that the actresses of Vienna or Berlin who play the parts of village maidens might have taken a lesson from her with advantage.

Father Frantz seated himself at the end of the table, looking quite proud and gratified, Louise placed the jug and plate on the table without saying a word. I sat silent and thoughtful. Going out for a moment, she returned again with two snow-white napkins and two knives. Then she was again leaving the room, when the old forester, raising his voice, said:

'Stay here, Louise, stay with us; one would think you were afraid of this gentleman. And yet I'm sure he would not like to frighten you. By the by, what is your name? I never once thought of asking you before.'

'My name is Theodore Richter.'

'Well, Mr. Theodore, if you feel peckish, take a knife and let us eat a morsel together.'

Louise had seated herself shyly beside the stove, giving a stolen glance now and then in our direction.

'Yes, he's a painter,' resumed Father Honeck, plying his jaws evidently with a good appetite. 'And, now that I recollect, there was a captain in our regiment—the 6th Dragoons—by the name of Pfersdorf, who was a painter also. He painted battles chiefly. The balls might whistle about his ears, the cannon might roar, but he painted away quietly all the same. And when the order was given to advance, Pfersdorf slipped his paper into a long tin case, seized his sabre, and mounted his horse. I saw that myself. He was an Alsacian from the neighbourhood of Wissembourg. I fancy he was made a captain in the *gendarmerie* afterwards. But that's a long time ago. It seems like a dream. Your health, Mr. Theodore.'

'And yours also, Father Frantz.'

'If you would kindly show us some of your paintings,' resumed the old forester, 'we would take it as a great favour; would we not, Louise?'

'Oh, yes, grandfather,' said the young girl, 'I never saw any paintings.'

For some minutes past the idea of taking up my abode in the forester's house, and making studies in the neighbourhood, had been passing through my mind, but I was uncertain how to broach this delicate subject. The opportunity now offered itself.

'Why, Father Frantz,' I exclaimed, 'I shall be most happy; but I warn you beforehand that I have very little worth looking at.

I have nothing but some sketches and studies. I would require a fortnight or three weeks to put them into shape. Mine are not paintings, but only drawings.'

'No matter, show us what you have.'

'Certainly, with pleasure.'

I unbuckled my knapsack.

'What I am going to show you is the neighbourhood of Pirmasens; but what is the neighbourhood of Pirmasens compared with your mountains? Your Waldhorn, your Krapenfeltz, that is what I should like to paint—that is scenery indeed!'

Father Honeck at first did not say a word. He gravely took the drawing which I handed to him—the high town, and the new church, with a background of mountains. I had tinted it slightly with water colour.

The worthy man, after looking at it for a few minutes with raised eyebrows and strained features, holding it near the window in order to catch the light, said gravely:

'That, sir, is wonderfully handsome. That will do! That will do!'

And he looked at me with a kind and fatherly air.

'Yes, that is very like. It is right well done. I would know every place in it. Louise, come this way—take a look at that. Stay, look at it from this side. Isn't that exactly the old market-place, with the old fruit-seller Catherine at the corner? And see, there's Froelig the grocer's, and there's the principal front of the church, and there's Spieg the baker's shop! In short, everything is there—everything: he hasn't forgotten a single thing. That blue mountain behind is the Altenberg—I fancy I can see it! It's beautiful!'

Louise, who was standing on tiptoe behind the good man, and peeping over his shoulder, seemed struck with wonder; she did not utter a word, but when the old forester asked her:

'What do you think of that, Louise?'

'I think as you do, grandfather,' said she in a low voice, 'it is very beautiful!'

'Yes,' exclaimed the good man, raising his head and looking me full in the face; 'I never believed you could do anything like that. I thought to myself, this young fellow is only roaming about to enjoy the fresh air. Now I see you know something. But houses and churches, do you see, are much easier to paint than the woods. If I were you I would only paint houses. Since you have hit the thing so well, I would stick to it always. It is surer.'

Then, smiling at the simplicity of the good man, I handed him a little oil painting which I had finished at Hornbach, representing a sunrise on the outskirts of the Hôwald. If the sketch had pleased him, he now seemed fairly enraptured, and it was only after a few minutes of rapt contemplation that he looked up from it and said:

'Did you do that? It is a miracle—a perfect miracle. You can see the sun behind the trees, you can see the trees themselves, and can tell quite well whether they are birch trees, beeches, or oaks. If you did that, Mr. Theodore, I respect you.'

'And if I were to propose to you, Father Frantz,' said I to him, 'to stay here for a few days, paying you of course for my board, in order to see the neighbourhood and paint it, would you show me to the door?'

The old man coloured up.

'Listen,' said he: 'you are a fine young fellow, you require to see this country, which is the finest part of the whole mountains, and I would consider myself a churlish hound to refuse you. You shall take share of whatever we have: eggs milk, cheese, with now and then a hare: you shall have his honour the chief forester's room, as he will not be here this year; but as for anything else, you will understand that I cannot possibly take any money from you.'

'And why so?'

'No, no, it can't be; if you were Rebstock the contractor, or Evig the timber merchant, or any other man of that kind, it might do well enough.'

'But, Father Frantz—'

'No, no, I won't receive a *sou*. I am not an innkeeper. But—'

Here the worthy man appeared to hesitate.

'But,' continued he, 'you could perhaps—no, I dare not ask that—it is too much.'

'Come, tell me what you are thinking of.'

He glanced towards Louise, colouring more and more, and at last he said:

'That child, Mr. Theodore, would she be very difficult to paint?'

At these words Louise lost countenance.

'Oh, grandfather!' stammered she.

'Stop!' exclaimed the good man, with outstretched arm, 'don't imagine that I mean a large picture; no, no, on a little piece of paper, say about the size of my hand. Listen, Louise: in thirty or forty years, when you are quite gray, it will be very nice to see yourself as a young girl again. For my part, I won't make any secret of it, Mr. Theodore, if I could see myself once more as a dragoon, with my cap on one ear and my sabre by my side, in my green tunic and long boots, I would feel very proud.'

'What, Father Honeck, is that all?' exclaimed I. 'Why that's a very simple matter.'

'Then you accept my offer?'

'Accept it! Not only will I paint Miss Louise on a handsome canvas, but I would like to paint you too, in this armchair, with your fowling-piece between your knees, and wearing your long gaiters and thick-soled shoes; Miss Louise standing, and resting her hand on the back of your chair; and, to make the thing more complete, we will put that old fellow into the picture too.'

And I pointed to the stag-hound lying stretched at full length on the floor, his muzzle between his paws, and his eyelids closed.

The old ranger looked at me with moistened eyes.

'I knew right well you were a good young fellow,' said he, after a moment's silence. 'It will please me greatly to be along with my granddaughter; then she will see me always as I am now, and if she ever gets married and there are any little children she can say to them: "See, there is grandfather Frantz—that is just how he looked.'"

At this instant Louise left the room. The old forester, turning his head towards the door, made as if he would have called her back; but his voice was husky and he gave up the attempt. A few moments afterwards, having given one or two coughs behind his hand, he resumed, pointing to the dog: 'That's a good hound, Mr, Theodore; I don't say anything to the contrary; he has both scent and speed. But there are many as good as he. If it is all the same to you, we will put the other one into the picture.'

He gave a call on his whistle; the terrier bounded into the room from the passage. The other dog had risen also at the summons, and both came forward, wagging their tails, and laid their muzzles on their master's knees.

'Yes, they are both good dogs,' said he, stroking their heads. 'Fox has many good qualities; he holds the scent well notwithstanding his great age; I would wrong him if I said otherwise. But if you want to see a rare animal, look at Waldine. She has as fine a nose, and even finer than the other; she is biddable, she never gives up, she is everything that a good sporting dog ought to be. But all that is a mere nothing, Mr. Theodore; what we should look for in animals is good sense, reason.'

'How do you mean? Good sense?'

'Yes, that's the principal thing in animals as in men. When a dog allows himself to be deceived by the cunning of a fox or a hare, when he follows his nose blindly, when he hasn't judgment enough to see and know a double or a false scent, or any other such trick, when he doesn't profit by experience but always commits the same faults, then you may have a good enough dog, but after all he is only an animal. Now, you think perhaps that Waldine is listening to us without understanding a word of what we say? Well, you are quite mistaken. If I said anything bad of her, instead of wagging her tail and looking up at us joyfully, she would trot off at once, and you would have to whistle more than once before you could get her back.

'Fox, on the contrary, would lie there quietly and wag his tail, as if I was paying him all sorts of compliments. Provided I don't scold him, he is quite content. So you see, Mr. Theodore, that if there are many men, and even women, with little more sense than the beasts, there are some animals with nearly as much sense as men. And this is the reason why, if it is all the same to you, that I would like better to have Waldine in the picture with me than Fox; for all true sportsmen, when they see it, will think, "That old ranger knew something about dogs; he knew how to choose a good one from a bad one, and among good ones to pick the best. I'll wager he didn't often come home with an empty game-bag," which would be much more agreeable to me than to know beforehand that they would think just the opposite.'

'Make your mind easy, Papa Frantz,' said I, 'we will put them both in.'

'No, that would give too much work. One good dog will be enough, two would take up too much room. Remember, you must leave plenty for Louise and me. But we will talk of that afterwards. Come with me now and I will show you your sleeping chamber.'

I took up my knapsack again, and we left the room, directing our steps towards the wooden gallery. The linen was still drying there in the sun. Two doors opened off this gallery; we passed by the first, holding aside the bunches of ivy that had made their way through the balustrade, and Father Honeck opened the one at the farther end.

I cannot describe the feeling of delight that came over me at the thought that I was to spend a fortnight, or perhaps a month, or even the whole summer, amidst this magnificent scenery, far from the cares and noise of the town.

The jalousies of the apartment we entered had not been opened since the departure of the Superintendent-General in the latter end of the preceding autumn. A sort of faint perfume of ripe fruit pervaded the room; the fruit-loft was probably just above it. Father Honeck walked towards the windows, and, pushing back the shutters against the thick mass of foliage which covered the wall outside:

'There, Mr. Theodore,' exclaimed he, 'look round you.'

By the greenish light which made its way through the leafy screen outside, I saw that we were in a tolerably large and lofty apartment, the two windows of which looked directly towards the valley, and at a great height above it. Thus, in spite of the close environment of the forest, the air and light of these lofty regions entered in floods, throwing sharp reflections of the tendrils of the vine and honeysuckle on the walls. Between the two windows was one of those old cabinets of carved oak, with rounded front, inlaid with steel, which are frequently to be met with even in the most secluded hamlets since the great dispersion of art treasures in the year 1792.

To the right, under a sort of canopy, was the bed, furnished with three mattresses. Four chairs, in the same style as the cabinet, occupied the recesses of the windows, and on the wall to the left, in an old black frame, was an engraving of Frederick II., a three-cornered hat perched on one side of his shoulder, and a cane in the hand in the bearing of a *schlague* corporal. There was on the chest of drawers a carafe and two Bohemian glasses.

'Why, you lodge me like a prince, Father Frantz,' I exclaimed enthusiastically.

'You are pleased?'

'Am I pleased? Why a prince could not be better treated. Yes, yes, I am pleased, very pleased, I have never been better lodged. I am completely in the seventh heaven!' I exclaimed, as I seated myself at one of the windows, and let my eyes roam from the courtyard to the garden, from the garden to the orchard, from the orchard to the meadow, and the river endlessly. What a view! Ah! How well I *could* work, how well I could breathe, how truly I could give myself to your woods, your dales, your mountains!

'Very well,' said the old man; 'all right; so much the better if everything is to your liking; but just see that you have all that you require.'

'What more can I require? Everything seems as if it had been made for me. But—one moment—wait—is there—?'

'Well—out with it!'

'Devil! It is not easy to find here.'

'What then!'

'An easel.'

'What is that?'

'A sort of desk to rest my pictures.'

'I have never seen one,' says the good man anxiously.

'After that, Father Frantz, at a pinch one can do without it; only it is not so convenient.'

'If I had known—if I had seen it—perhaps—'

'I am going to give you an idea of the thing.'

Then opening my knapsack, in four strokes of a pencil I drew him an easel. The old *garde* understood immediately.

'Is that all?' said he laughing; 'Rest assured, you will have one in the morning. You must know I am something of a cabinet maker, Mr. Theodore, something of a carpenter, and something of a turner—in fact, a little of everything. A man requires to be all that in the woods. The little one gives me many a job of that kind. Leave it to me. I shall set to work with my saw and plane, you will give me your assistance, and, depend upon it, between us both we shall manage the affair.'

'Very good—it is a bargain.'

And, full of ardour, I began at once unpacking my colours, my brushes and palette, explaining to the good man the use of all these implements, which excited his wonder and curiosity, and which he was evidently impatient to see me make use of. I also unrolled my canvas in order to settle the size of the picture I was about to execute, Father Honeck undertaking to provide the stretcher.

All these explanations and details took us fully two hours, and we were still busy talking, discussing, and making our arrangements, when the sound of a horn announced the return of little Kasper.

'Hallo! the time doesn't hang heavy in your company,' said the old forester, rising. 'Here's twelve o'clock already; the cattle are coming home. We had better go downstairs now, and after dinner we shall begin our work.'

'All right!' replied I.

And we left the room together in high spirits.

2

Just as Father Honeck and I stepped out again on the old gallery, the clock struck twelve. A stifling heat overspread the whole mountain. At this hour every living thing seeks the shade: the cattle beneath the branches of the tall trees, their legs folded under them, and their eyelids closed; the foxes in their holes and dens; and the birds in the thickest recesses of the foliage. All sounds are hushed: the insects alone keep up an incessant hum, as they rise and fall in countless swarms amongst the heath and brambles; but the vague murmur caused by the myriads of tiny wings only seems to increase the general silence.

Little Kasper—his yellow hair tossed about his forehead like ragged tufts of grass, his face burnt to the colour of gingerbread, his little thin wiry arms bare from the elbow downwards, and protruding from his scanty linen vest, which had once been blue, and his tattered gray linen trousers hanging in fringes round his legs—little Kasper, with bare feet and head thrown back, marched proudly on, blowing his horn, whilst behind him five or six she goats with hanging udders, an old buck, and three kids, plodded slowly along the dusty path. It seemed as if they must all have been burnt to tinder with the heat; nevertheless Kasper evidently took the greatest pleasure in prolonging his flourishes, without once drawing breath, until the whole mountain side echoed again.

'Hi! Kasper,' cried the *garde* from the top of the wooden staircase, 'first put your goats into the house, and then you may blow away on your horn till evening if you like.'

The little herd made no reply; he passed the back of his hand underneath his nose, opened the wicker gate of the farmyard, and, glancing at me with the corner of his eye, he watched his goats defile into the yard and trot off bleating and capering up to the door of the stable. Then Father Frantz, looking at me with a smile, said:

'These children! You must always be shouting at them.'

We descended the steps, then turning the corner, we entered the dark cool sitting-room, shaded with its overhanging creepers. Louise had spread a little white cloth, with red fringe, at one end of the table. In the centre of the cloth was a little soup tureen, and three plates were laid at intervals around. I could not repress a feeling of satisfaction at the thought that Louise was to dine with us.

'One wants plenty of air at dinner,' said the old forester, opening the shutters; 'I would rather be a little too warm than not be able to breathe freely. Take your seat there, Mr. Theodore; as long as you are with us that will be your place.'

I seated myself with my back to the wall. Almost immediately afterwards Louise appeared with a *carafe* of sparkling water, all covered over with tiny transparent globules, and a pitcher of white wine

When placing them on the table, she raised her eyes timidly towards me, and, seeing that I was looking at her, she blushed to the ears. By a strange sympathetic feeling I was conscious of colouring too.

'Well, Louise, what are we to have for dinner?' inquired Father Honeck.

'You know, grandfather, we have no flesh meat in the house,' replied Louise, with a slight tremble in her voice. 'I have made an omelette.'

'An omelette? And you had no bacon?'

'Yes, there is bacon.'

'Oh, very good—I thought that—In short, Mr. Theodore, you see what we have; another time we shall give you a hare, or some vegetables. By and by we shall—'

'Why, Father Frantz, do you take me for a *gourmand*, after all that I have said?'

'No, no; nor am I a *gourmand* either; but a good dinner doesn't frighten me for all that.'

He took the cover off the soup tureen, and the smell of an excellent soup *à la crème* filled the room. The soup being served,

Frantz and I discussed it with an excellent appetite.

'What capital soup!' exclaimed I, laying down my spoon.

'Yes, it isn't bad,' said the good man, passing his tongue over his moustache.

Louise having left the room, a few minutes afterwards, to fetch the omelette, he leaned over towards me, and said in a low voice, 'She makes a soup *à la crême* as well and better than Mother Gredel of the Swan Inn at Pirmasens; it's a perfect Godsend. But, look you, Mr. Theodore, it doesn't do to praise young people too much. Flattery puffs up the heart with vanity and pride, as Pastor Baumgarten at Pirmasens says, and it's as true as the gospel; we must always—'

Louise just then entered the room, and he stopped. After the omelette, we had cheese for dessert, and a good pull at the pitcher of wine terminated the repast.

'I have dined right well,' said the forester, rising. 'How have you got on, Mr. Theodore?'

'Uncommonly well, Papa Frantz; I never dined more heartily.'

'Well, we'll have a pipe together now. Kasper! Kasper! Come this way!'

Little Kasper, with his shock of hair standing on end in the wildest disorder, made his appearance at the door of the kitchen. 'Listen,' said the good man; 'you must start at once for Pirmasens. I promised to send some thrushes and small birds to the Swan Hotel. You will be back again at six o'clock, remember.'

The urchin made no answer. They went together into the next room, and, a few minutes afterwards, Kasper passed out through the hall, holding in his hand the string of thrushes and redbreasts which Master Frantz had snared that morning. Once clear of the house he bounded down the path, capering like a young kid. Father Honeck and I looked after him, laughing, till he disappeared in the wood.

'That little monkey,' said the forester, 'cares about nothing but running wild; you couldn't please him better than to keep him on the road from morning till night—he, he, he!'

Then he went into the kitchen, lit his pipe, and came out again, exclaiming—

'To our work!'

It was now near one o'clock: the shadows were beginning to lengthen in the farmyard, the two dogs were sleeping on the threshold of the entrance door, and the fowls were huddled close against the walls underneath the trellis.

In crossing the yard we passed by the kitchen, and, glancing in through the little hexagonal panes, I saw Louise washing our plates at the sink, and could not help giving her a little friendly nod of recognition. The old forester marched on in front. Underneath the wooden staircase of the old gallery, a low doorway gave access to a sort of cellar, sunk three or four steps beneath the surface of the ground. In the centre of this stood one of those massive benches or tables used by carpenters at their work, and round the walls were hung a number of saws, planes, mallets, and other implements of the craft.

Father Frantz threw off his vest, tucked up his shirt sleeves, and, seizing a pine plank, adjusted it on the bench, saying—

'I think this will answer our purpose. Will you give me the measurements, Mr. Theodore.'

Then we both set to work.

And this is how it was, my dear friends, that, in the year 1839, during the loveliest days of August, I found myself installed in the house of the old forester Frantz Honeck, in the midst of the immense forests of the Rothalps.

3

Even now I remember with delight the first few days of my sojourn at the forest house. Father Honeck came to my bedside early in the morning to awake me.

'Come, Mr. Theodore,' said he, putting the lantern on the cabinet, 'the day is breaking. It's time to get up.'

Then, stretching my arms and yawning, I stammered out—

'Oh, Father Frantz, if you knew how sleepy I am!'

'Sleepy! At your age! Bah! you told me the other day not to

listen to you when you said that—that you were only joking. Come, get up, it's a lovely morning.'

Then, making a desperate effort, I jumped out of bed, slipped on my trousers, passed a wet towel hastily over my face, and, still shivering, leaned out over the trellis, to cast a glance down the mountain side.

The dew was falling heavily, causing a vague soft murmur amongst the foliage. Everything looked gray, undefined, confused. The old forester had gone down stairs, leaving his lantern on the cabinet. I dressed myself quickly, pulled on my high boots of reddish leather for walking in the wet, and five minutes afterwards Waldine and Fox bounded up the stairs, jumping against my legs, and wagging their tails as if to say 'Make haste! make haste! the master is waiting for you.' Then I pulled my great felt hat down over my ears, stole past Louise's little room on tiptoe, descended the stairs to the farmyard, where Father Honeck was standing underneath the projecting roof of the cart shed, with his carbine slung over his shoulder.

'Ah! you are there,' said he; 'now we are off!'

He opened the wicker gate of the garden, and we took the path leading to the Grindelwald. We walked on at a rapid pace. Father Frantz in front, with rounded back, but with as firm a step as if he had been only twenty, I following, my head still a little confused and my eyes heavy; but very soon the fresh morning air, the rapid motion, and a feeling of satisfaction at having conquered my laziness, put all these disagreeable feelings to flight. In a few minutes I felt a calmness of mind and physical strength which I cannot describe. I could have walked forty miles without feeling fatigue. Oh, that night march in the solitude of the woods!—inhaling the fresh dewy air, the aromatic perfume of the pines, and the subtle odours of a thousand unseen plants and flowers—what strength it seems to give you, what clearness and vigour of thought, what superabundant vitality in all the springs of life!

How many souls, as it were, of flowers, of mosses, of ivy and brambles, did we not drink in during that long descent to the

Grindelwald! No tongue could tell. But all these subtle essences floating in the soft moist air seemed to warm themselves at our hearts as at a blazing hearth in winter. They whispered a thousand things in our listening ears which cannot be rendered in words, but which mounted to my brain in the shape of vague poetical imaginings, and then floated off in bluish vapour and lost themselves in a soft murmur amongst the foliage around.

Yes, Father Honeck was right to awake me, to force me as it were to follow him; for these that I have described are to this day the pleasantest memories of my life.

Meanwhile we did not utter a word, but walked briskly on, absorbed in our thoughts, without feeling the necessity of communicating them to each other in words. We were on our way to the distant cuttings of the Grindelwald, a purely woodland district inhabited by the rude and primitive population of the forest.

Have you ever heard, my dear friends, in the early morning, the axe of the woodcutter dealing its measured and ringing blows at the root of some lofty oak? Have you ever heard—far, far away in the distance, on the hill-side—the clear sharp strokes prolonged and multiplied by the mountain echoes until they gradually died away in silence? Then the cracking of the tree bending to its doom—the cry of 'Look out! there it comes!'—the crash of the branches—and the heavy thundering fall of the giant, measuring its length on the ground and crushing the brush-wood beneath it. Have you ever chanced to see the fire of the charcoal-burner crackling underneath the dark canopy of the forest, lighting up the heath and mosses, and even the tallest pine-tops around, with its ruddy glow; then dying away by degrees until it shows only as a heap of dull red embers, and anon blazing up brighter than ever as fresh logs are thrown on?

And the dark outline of the man of the woods himself squatted near the flaming logs, his broad-leafed felt beaver reaching half-way down his back, as he smokes his short pipe, and turns the potatoes that are roasting amongst the red ashes—has that ever startled you, seen suddenly through the intervening brushwood? Well, it was to such a region as this, buried amidst the vast forests of the Rothalps, that Father Honeck and I every day directed our steps.

Often we chanced, at some turn in the path, to meet Frantz Sepel, the clog-maker of Rheinthal; Nickel Biger, the cartwright of Pirmasens; Hans Aden, the cabinet-maker; Mayer Fischer, the carpenter, all coming to choose for themselves amongst the cuttings the particular log, or plank, or beam, which they required for their work; besides a number of other decent hard-working folks—pedlars, letter carriers, tinder sellers, both Christians and Jews, always on the road in the exercise of their various callings. Then there was a halt, a hearty shake of the hand, a lighting of pipes, and friendly inquiries for Mother Orchel or Father Kasper of such and such a village, of whom nothing has been heard for two or three years. 'Is she dead? Is he still stout and hearty? He ought to be getting old by this time? And little Gredel, who got married last year, how does she and her good man get on? Is he as good a workman as the people said?'

Then they chatted about the new cuttings, the prices of grain, of rape seed, and cattle; nothing was uninteresting to Father Honeck, and naturally enough, for when you have nothing to read from year's end to year's end but Silbermann's *Limping Messenger*, you have to add a little to your stock of information from other sources when you have a chance.

Thanks to these early walks, at the end of three weeks I knew the whole district thoroughly—rocks, streams, glens, cuttings, coal-mines, sledge paths, in short everything worth seeing in the mountain range, with the one exception, however, of the Lake of the Wild Counts, which the old forester would not hear of my visiting.

I shall ever remember one morning, when we were on our way to the Grindelwald, the fancy seized me for the twentieth time to question Father Frantz about this famous lake. 'But, by the way, Father Honeck,' exclaimed I, suddenly, 'what about the Lake of the Wild Counts? When are we going to visit it?'

He was walking on in front, and as I spoke he turned round

43

slowly, and looking at me for a few seconds with a strange expression, he pointed in a northerly direction, and said in an abrupt, harsh tone:

'The lake is there, Mr. Theodore, between those three lofty peaks. You can visit it, if you have a fancy.'

'How! Will you not act as my guide?'

'Act as your guide to the Lake of the Wild Counts? No, no. Everyone is free to act as he likes. I don't hinder you from going there, since the devil urges you to it; but Frantz Honeck has no love for that side of the mountain.'

These words of the old man, and still more, perhaps, the mysterious manner in which they were spoken, excited my curiosity in no ordinary degree, and as a matter of course only increased my anxiety to see the Lake of the Wild Counts. A sort of deference which I felt for the wishes of my host prevented me, however, from going there alone, and I determined therefore to wait for some more favourable opportunity.

But to return to our excursions to the Grindelwald. After our tour of inspection, which generally lasted the whole day, we got back to the forest house in the evening about seven or eight o'clock. Louise had laid the cloth, and the omelette and bacon, and the pitcher of white wine were duly waiting our arrival. We sat down in high spirits, eat heartily, took a good pull at the wine jug, and, then, lighting our pipes, leaned our elbows on the window-sill to look at little Kasper opening the stable door, and, with loud cracking of his whip, mounting the hillside, followed by a long straggling group of cows and goats. We watched the sleek handsome creatures defiling slowly through the gate of the farmyard, turning their heads from time to time and filling the mountainside with their plaintive bellowing as they plodded on their way.

It was perhaps the pleasantest hour of the day; one of those peaceful country scenes which the memory always recalls with pleasure. Sometimes also I went out alone in the mornings to the outskirts of the Hôwald, or the banks of the Losser, to sketch a rock, a clump of oaks, or a forest nook; or, from the opposite mountain top, to make studies of the scenery on a larger scale. Never in my life did I work harder or with better results.

All this, however, did not prevent our portrait from making progress, and even assuming a very respectable appearance; but Heaven knows it was not the fault of Father Honeck that it did either. Just in proportion as the honest fellow showed himself simple-minded, modest, and conciliating in everything which concerned his calling—the valuation of a cutting, the measurement of a tree, the laying out of a track through the forest, matters with which he was thoroughly acquainted, and about which he never boasted—so was he opinionated and dogmatic on the subject of painting.

I think I see him now, sitting bolt upright, in his handsome green uniform with yellow facings, his little pointed kepi inclined over one ear, carefully buttoned, well brushed, very grave and solemn, his carbine between his knees, his powder horn and shot belt on one side, his game bag on the other, and his great bushy gray moustache turned up at the ends; Louise standing behind, as red as a cherry, her beautiful fair locks neatly arranged under a little black head-dress of horse-hair embroidered with scarlet carnations and gold spangles, a little handkerchief of sky-blue silk crossed over her bosom, and her pretty plump arms resting on the back of the armchair.

It was in vain that I begged Father Honeck to put on his every-day brown shooting coat, to hold himself less stiffly, to lean forward a little after his usual fashion, and to assume a less determined expression of countenance; my recommendations were entirely disregarded.

'I am the head forester of this district, Mr. Theodore,' said he, gravely, 'and, saving your favour, I would despise myself if I didn't wear my uniform. People would say: "That's some old poacher, or trespasser in pursuit of game; that man never held rank in the Corps of Royal Foresters!" Now that's quite contrary to my way of thinking. I would rather not be painted at all than not have my rank in the picture. I know very well that green is more difficult to paint than the other colours, but if it shows my rank that is the principal thing.'

'You are quite mistaken there, Father Frantz; green is not a bit more difficult to paint than yellow, brown, or black.'

'Well, that's all the more reason for painting it,' exclaimed he in a determined tone. 'If it is not more difficult, why put on my old shooting coat in place of my handsome new tunic?'

I met with the same opposition on the question of attitude.

'A forester,' said he, 'a thorough forester ought to be as up-right as if he was on parade. If he was to lean to the right or left, everyone would think: "That's a slovenly fellow now, a man who does not know his duty." You can understand, Mr. Theod-ore, that a man like me, who has always borne a good character, would not like people to think so about him. In my young days, when I was in the 6th Dragoons, I would have fought fifty times rather than allow such a thing to be said about me. But even that would be nothing to having it in my picture, for people soon forget a man when he is dead, but a picture, you see that remains. If I stoop a little when I am walking, age is the cause of that, and the habit of climbing the mountains; but, thanks be to God, I can still hold myself straight in the presence of my superiors.'

It was impossible to shake his ideas on this point. The slight-est remark to the contrary immediately made him look grave, and it was evident he thought his personal dignity wounded. But, besides this, Father Honeck, generally so calm and equable in his manner, could not keep himself at rest for ten minutes together when the picture was in question. An extraordinary curiosity seemed constantly prompting him to look at my work. He invented a thousand pretexts for this purpose:

'And now, Mr. Theodore, shall we have a pipe, eh?' Or else:

'If we had a glass of wine together, Mr. Theodore, it would refresh us both. It's pretty warm this afternoon, I can tell you.'

And without waiting for a reply, he would start up from his chair and come over and plant himself behind me, saying with a giggle of satisfaction:

'Ha, ha, ha! very good, very good indeed. But stay, are not you putting too much red here, and a little too much gray there?

I haven't as red a nose, or as red cheeks as that. Some people, to injure me, have spread the report now and again that I drank too much; now I think nothing worse could be invented against a man than that. If I had found out who they were I think I could have wrung their necks about. Yes, there is too much red in the nose.'

'Make your mind quite easy on that score, Father Frantz, it's not to remain that way. This is only the ground; we shall cover it over by and by; only, for Heaven's sake, don't be so impatient.'

'Oh, grandfather,' said Louise in a low, agitated voice, 'I beg of you, listen to what Mr. Theodore says.'

'Well, well, since the red is to be covered over it's all right; I have nothing more to say. You needn't be uneasy, therefore, Louise. That dog can't keep steady for a moment. If he puts you out, Mr. Theodore, I'll give him a dance over the hill to teach him to lie quiet.'

'No, no, he will do very well. Turn yourself a little more to the light—yes, that's it. Now, don't stir. If you can have patience for another quarter of an hour, I shall not require you again till tomorrow.'

In spite of all these cross-purposes, the portrait made progress. The likenesses came out better every day. I was especially favoured as regards the light, which came in cooled and softened by the foliage which half covered the windows. The ivy-wreathed window to the right, with its little leaded panes; Louise's sweet, gentle face, rounded arms, and little plump hands, set off by her fresh, picturesque mountain costume; and the sunburned, wrinkled features, and gray piercing eyes, half hidden beneath their white shaggy eyebrows, of the old forester, harmonised admirably, seen by the cool green light.

And then I put my whole soul into the work. My dawning attachment for Louise, my youthful enthusiasm for my art, the exhilaration produced by the fresh mountain air, and the calmness and peace of mind resulting from this quiet life in the recesses of the forest, all these had their reflex in the picture, the most deeply felt and best executed of any I had yet painted.

The more the picture progressed, the higher I seemed to rise in Father Honeck's esteem and affection. Often, when returning in the evenings from my long excursions, I found him in my apartment, contemplating himself in a sort of ecstasy.

'Ah! you are there, Mr. Theodore!' he would say; 'I am just taking a peep at myself.'

'Do you think the likeness better now? Are you satisfied with it?'

'Ah! Mr. Theodore, you don't want the opinion of a poor old fellow like me on such a matter. You are a painter and I am just an old forester who knows nothing. I see now that you were quite right to put in all that gray, and brown, and red, that I didn't at first understand. You are a true painter. Although it's the portrait of old Frantz Honeck, and his granddaughter Louise, I tell you plainly it is not in a poor forester's house it ought to hang, but in some grand *chateau*.'

'Oh, Father Frantz, you are too enthusiastic about it.'

'No, Mr. Theodore, no; it's not the first time I have seen paintings. I have seen them of all countries; in France, in Germany, in Italy, in Flanders. Only at that time I was young, and paid little or no heed to such things. But now all that comes back to my mind. I remember I liked the Flemish paintings far the best; they represented things one sees every day—village dances, cock-fights, hunting parties, country merry-makings, burgo-masters, and such like. In their pictures you have the home, the little garden hedge with the goodwife's linen bleaching in the sun, the dove cot, the bowling green, the old gray horse eating his scanty pittance of oats at the inn door, the winding road, a group of women spinning—these things rejoice the heart. What a pity that those men knew nothing of our mountains! How they would have painted the rocks, the valleys, the woods, the mountain streams, the forest paths! But they had nothing but windmills and duck ponds before their eyes, and here and there a few cows in a square field, with a hollow tree and a ditch full of frogs by the roadside.

'In Italy again, Mr. Theodore, they paint nothing but saints, both men and women; the little infant Jesus in the manger, with the ass standing beside it. It is very beautiful, no doubt, but one gets tired of it in the end. The worst of it is that in one church you see St. Catherine or St. Magdalene with fair hair, and in another with black or brown, so that you can never tell which is the right one.'

So spoke the old forester, with an air of thorough conviction which delighted me. His judgment had as much weight in my eyes as that of Dr. Everbach, of Tubingen, the most famous critic in matters of art in all Germany. It was Louise's opinion, however, that I wished especially to ascertain; but although most anxious on the subject I dare not ask her for it.

'Just think of the good sense of that little thing,' said Father Frantz to me one day. 'Yesterday morning, when we were returning from the Grindelwald, I was thinking all along the road of our portrait, and asking myself how a little green, yellow, or red colour, on a gray ground, could represent people so well that you could imagine you saw them long after they were dead. The more I thought of that, the less I understood it. When I reached home, on opening the yard gate, I saw Louise preparing to feed the fowls. "Hey! Louise," said I, "will you oblige me by telling me, if you can, why our portrait is handsomer than the one of St. Catherine, in the church at Pirmasens?"

'"Why, good gracious, grandfather, it is because ours is living."

'"Living?"

'"Yes, to be sure! It is not your face, nor mine, that Mr. Theodore wishes to paint, nor the leaves of the vine over the window, nor the daylight behind them, it is our minds." Could you believe such cleverness?' exclaimed the good man; 'she understood the thing at the first glance. Ha, ha, ha! there are no children now-a-days, they are all born men and women!'

And Father Frantz gave a hearty laugh. I felt delighted. At last I knew what Louise thought of my handywork.

The old forester had not the least suspicion of my growing attachment to his granddaughter. Was I quite aware of it myself?

I am not sure. One thing is certain, that Louise's image became blended every day more and more with those that I held dearest on earth. In the house, I could not hear the sound of her light footfall in the passage, the rustling of her dress against the balustrade of the old gallery, or her comings and goings in the farmyard, without feeling my heart flutter. Outside in the open country, I fancied I saw her walking before me in the sandy path; her graceful figure, golden locks, and quick gliding step seemed to waylay and haunt me in every forest nook; and in the evenings, when, quickening my pace, the moss-grown roof of the forest house at length appeared through the foliage, it was not Father Honeck's upright figure that first met my inquiring gaze, but always Louise's, sometimes in the old gallery, sometimes in the little garden, or peeping through an attic window, where she was tying up a stray tendril of honeysuckle or ivy.

'Well, Mr. Theodore, have you found any fine views in the forest?' she would cry in her clear, sweet voice. 'Are you satisfied with your excursion today?'

'Yes, Louise, yes; I feel as happy as a king. Your mountains are so beautiful!'

I longed to say more, but the pure, limpid, untroubled look of the old forester's grandchild inspired me with even more respect perhaps than love.

Nevertheless, one evening when we were standing together on the old gallery, watching the magnificent autumnal sun sink in a fiery ball behind the distant mountain peaks, and when, motionless and almost awe struck, we both remained silent in presence of the glorious spectacle, all at once, as if moved by an irresistible impulse, I exclaimed in a voice quivering with emotion:

'Oh, heavens, why cannot I remain here always? Why must I quit this lovely country?'

Louise looked at me quite surprised.

'Are you thinking of leaving this, Mr. Theodore?' said she, a slight tinge of red mounting to her forehead.

'Yes, Louise, yes, I must go! They are expecting me yonder, at

Dusseldorf, and besides—the picture is finished!'

My voice trembled. Louise, who had looked at me earnestly as I spoke, bent her eyes on the ground without replying. After a long silence, she murmured, as if speaking to herself:

'Oh, dear! I had never thought of that!'

For more than a quarter of an hour we stood perfectly silent, leaning our elbows on the balustrade of the gallery, and not daring to raise our eyes. I heard an inward voice whispering: 'Speak! speak at once—tell her you love her!' But another and more powerful voice said to me: 'No, Theodore, do not do that; think of the hospitality Father Honeck has shown you—remember that the old man has treated you like his son. What you are about to promise Louise, you are not sure you can perform.'

But while I listened to these two voices, not knowing which course to follow, little Kasper appeared on the edge of the forest, followed by his long string of goats. Louise, starting as if from a dream, said:

'There is seven o'clock, Mr. Theodore; my grandfather will be home shortly now. I must go and see after matters in the kitchen.'

. She descended the steps, her head drooping pensively on her breast. When she was out of sight I entered my chamber, and leaning my elbows on the window-sill, and burying my face in my hands, I sat reflecting on what had just passed, until the cheerful voice of Father Honeck was heard shouting:

'Hey! Mr. Theodore, won't you come down?—the cloth is laid.' Then I went downstairs and took my seat at the table. Father Frantz had that day shot a superb blackcock, and purposed to carry it himself to the Forester-General at Pirmasens. He also told us that in returning from the cuttings a herd of wild boars had trotted across the road, and that one of those fine mornings he meant to beat up their quarters, and let me taste what a boar's head dressed with white wine was like. All this put him in high spirits, and he even drank a glass or two more than was his usual custom. Then, passing his hand over his moustache:

'Child,' said he to Louise, 'the night is beautiful; suppose we

51

take a seat on the bench outside and sing the hymn—*Lord, thou Father of the pure in heart.*'

Louise coloured, and said she did not feel quite disposed to sing that evening.

'Bah!' said the good man, taking her by the arm, 'you must try. I'll engage you will get on very well. Mr. Theodore, you never heard Louise sing. She has a voice that—that—but I'll say no more, just come with me.'

And we went out.

Little Kasper was busily occupied cutting a handle for his whip from the garden hedge. We took our seats on the old moss-grown stone bench, resting our backs against the thick mass of honeysuckle which covered the wall, and Father Honeck, in a deep solemn voice, began: '*Lord, thou Father of the pure in heart.*' Louise's sweet, clear voice, rising gently after her grandfather's, swelled out by degrees on the evening air with such purity and feeling, that every fibre of my frame thrilled with delight.

His grave, manly voice harmonised and blended so wonderfully with her pure, youthful one, that I never remember to have heard anything so beautiful or touching. It was like some ivy plant twining its tendrils in graceful festoons round a giant oak of the Grindelwald. And then, to heighten the charm, the evening was a most lovely one. The sun had set, and the long horizontal lines of purple stood out pencilled against the background of deepest gold, shedding a sort of unearthly glory over mountain and valley, whilst now and then a gentle breeze stirred the foliage. Absorbed in thought, I listened with rapt attention, and at last, carried away by some secret influence, I joined my voice to those of the old forester and his grandchild. That night the all-seeing and all-loving Father, I humbly venture to think, must have looked down with approbation and pleasure on His children at the forest house.

Little Kasper, who had thrown himself at full length amidst the adjoining underwood, listened with outstretched neck, and his large brown eyes, opened to their fullest extent, gazed at us in a sort of ecstasy. When we had ended, Father Honeck cried out:

'Well, Kasper, what think you of that?' The little fellow, as his only answer, wiped his cheek with the back of his hand.

Never will this lovely evening be effaced from my memory. We all three sat there, singing, talking of paintings, chatting about the chase, about future excursions, and beautiful scenery, until ten o'clock.

The sky was studded with myriads of stars, when at last the old forester rose, saying:

'Tomorrow morning at three o'clock I must be on the road to Pirmasens. We had better go to bed. Goodnight, Mr. Theodore.'

'Goodnight, Father Frantz; goodnight, Miss Louise;' and I mounted the stairs to my bedroom, thanking God for His innumerable blessings.

4

When alone in my chamber, on thinking over the events of the day, a deep and yet softened feeling of melancholy took possession of me. I felt no desire to sleep, and seating myself at the window I leaned my head on my hand, and looked out underneath the shadow of the broad vine leaves, now silvered by the moonlight.

All the sounds in the forest house died away one by one; the old forester retired to bed, the dogs coiled themselves in their several nooks, and silence, that deep silence which is scarcely broken by the passing murmur of the night wind, settled down on the scene. I thought to myself:

'In a few days from this you will be standing on the threshold of this house, with your knapsack on your back and your stick in your hand. Louise will say in her gentle voice: "*Adieu*, Mr. Theodore, *adieu!*" Father Honeck will accompany you a few hundred yards along the hillside, to where the river branches off, then he will give you a hearty shake of the hand, exclaiming: "Well! we must part here. I wish you a pleasant journey, Mr. Theodore; may Heaven guard you!" and then all will be over. These happy, peaceful days will be nothing more than a dream.'

And thinking of these things, my heart swelled almost to bursting.

'Ah! if you could only support yourself by your profession,' said I to myself; 'or if your Aunt Catherine would make you a handsome allowance, you could then know how to act. But as it is, there is nothing for it but to go; and since your voice trembles whenever you speak to Louise, you must carefully avoid being alone with her, so that Father Frantz, in thinking of you, may always be able to say: "He was a fine young fellow that, and as true as steel!" and, what is better still, that your own heart may not give the lie to his words.'

I resolved, therefore, that I would go the following morning to the Lake of the Wild Counts as soon as Father Honeck should be on his way to Pirmasens, and I went to bed about eleven o'clock, satisfied with the line of conduct I had marked out for myself.

But other events were destined to take place that night, events so strange that they will never be effaced from my memory.

Many of the learned, or those who think themselves so, maintain that there exists nothing except what falls within the cognizance of our senses, and yet these same men, on their death-beds, will often be found gazing into the darkness with an awestruck look, as if they saw some frightful object there, and the expression of their eyes is something terrible to see. Then everyone asks himself: 'What are they looking at in that fearful way? Are there, then, other beings amongst us, who come and go, and whom the dying alone can perceive?'

The fly, when fluttering in the sunlight, does not perceive the spider watching it from its den; it only becomes aware of the presence of its enemy when struggling, too late, in its velvet claws. On these subjects it does not become us to dogmatise. Are beings of our own race permitted to return again on earth? We shall know one day, but let us not seek to anticipate that knowledge.

For my part, I shall limit myself strictly to relating what I have seen, thinking it better not to add to or diminish anything on such serious subjects, lest I might have cause to reproach myself for it afterwards.

I had been sleeping, then, as nearly as I can calculate, for about an hour, when the plaintive howling of Waldine and Fox awoke me with a start. I leaned up on my elbow in bed, listening attentively. The moon was in full splendour, and shining directly into my window, and against her brilliant disc the trellis with its rich mass of foliage, the little diamond-paned casement, and one or two dark pine tops in the distance, stood out in strong relief.

Roused thus suddenly from sleep, the dazzling contrast of light and shadow struck me at first with wonder and delight; but this feeling was soon banished by the barking of the dogs, which had in it something weird and unnatural, and consisted of a series of slow, prolonged howls, commencing in a low key and gradually rising until they ended in a shrill wail.

I immediately remembered that Spitz, my Aunt Catherine's old dog, had howled in this way on the night my poor Uncle Mathias died, and the recollection froze the blood in my veins.

Very soon the lowing of the cows, the bleating of the goats, and the deep grunting of the pigs, which were endeavouring to raise up the gates of their sties with their snouts, chimed in with the howling of the dogs, and formed a tumult impossible to describe. Then I heard Father Honeck jumping out of bed, the window was thrown open hastily, and, soon after, my ear caught the rapid tic tac of a gun being put on full cock. I waited to hear the report burst out in the night air, the expectation meanwhile sending a cold thrill through me; but the dogs continued to howl and the cattle to bellow without cessation, and at length, just as I felt the blood slowly retiring from my cheeks, the loud voice of the old forester was heard, shouting in a harsh tone:

'Fox! Waldine! stop that noise, will you?'

It was a great relief to my overstrained nerves to hear this voice; and, shall I confess it, the superstitious terrors that were taking possession of me were dissipated immediately. It seemed to me as if the evil influences around were put to flight, and I jumped out of bed full of courage.

Going out in the old gallery, the first object that met my eye was Father Honeck, standing in the bright moonlight, close to the low garden wall. He was dressed merely in his shirt and trousers, his head was raised defiantly, his gray hair tossed about in wild disorder, and he seemed to be listening for something.

I ran down the steps hastily.

'In the name of Heaven, Father Frantz, what is all this?' I exclaimed in a low voice.

'Ah!' said he, without turning his head, and pointing in the direction of the Losser, 'it's that rascal, with his hand, passing. Hearken yonder!'

I listened attentively. Not a sound save the distant murmur of the river over its rocky bed was audible in the whole mountain. This surprised me.

'Why, Father Frantz,' resumed I, after an instant's silence, 'I hear nothing.'

Then the old forester, as if awakening out of a dream, turned round as pale as death, and fixing his eyes on mine, said, with a strange expression:

'It's a wolf! Yes—it's the old she-wolf of the Veierschloss with her whelps. Every year the old beggar comes prowling about the house. The dogs scented her—they were afraid!'

And going up to the dogs, he stooped down and patted them on the head to quiet them, saying:

'Come, come, Waldine, go and lie down, the cursed beast is gone; she won't come back again.'

The dogs, trembling in every limb, rubbed themselves against their master's legs. The bleating of the goats and the lowing of the cattle began to grow quieter.

Father Honeck, rising to his feet again, uncocked his gun, and said, endeavouring to smile:

'I'll wager you were frightened, Mr. Theodore? To hear dogs howling in that way in the night time gives you a queer sort of feeling. A thousand ideas come into your head. But after all it's very natural. Dogs are like men; when they get old they begin to dote. One poor wolf is enough to frighten them, and instead of falling on him, they shout like very cowards, and would be glad to make their escape through the hole in the barn door. But see, they are getting quiet at last. I hear no noise now in the stables. Come, let's go to bed again, and try and get some sleep.'

So saying, Father Frantz opened the door of his room, and, still nervous and trembling, I mounted the stairs to my apartment.

All that I had just seen and heard seemed to me strange and unnatural. The tone of the old forester's voice, his deathlike paleness, the singular expression of his gray eyes when speaking of wolves and their whelps, all produced a strange and mysterious impression on me. My nerves were irritated to the highest degree. Was it the cold night air, the interruption of my rest, or what other cause that had put me into this excited state? I cannot tell; but for the first time in my life, ideas of invisible powers, of supernatural beings, coursed each other through my brain.

At last I got into bed, pulled the coverlet up to my ears, and, with my eyes wide open, I lay gazing at the little window panes, and thinking over all that had happened. The moon had now passed the window, but her rays were still shining full on the hillside and the pine woods below. Absorbed in thought, I listened to the low growling of the dogs, muttering at intervals like the sounds of a storm dying away in the distance. These animals' nerves were excited like my own.

At last all became still, and, worn out by the strange experiences of the night, I fell into a profound sleep.

5

It was broad daylight when I awoke. The fowls were cackling in the yard, the dogs were gambolling about on the hillside, everything was calm and peaceful about the forest house. I dressed myself leisurely and descended to the large hall. There, Father Honeck, in his brown woollen vest, was walking up and down with a disturbed air. The gaily-coloured plates, the Emmenthal cheese, and the pitcher of white wine, shone bright on the red-striped cloth which was laid at one end of the table.

'Still here, Father Honeck!' exclaimed I, quite surprised; 'I thought you were on the road to Pirmasens.'

'Kasper has gone to take the blackcock yonder, Mr. Theodore,' replied the good man.

Then, after a moment's silence, when we had taken our seats at the table, he added:

'I was obliged to stay at home. Louise is not quite well. She will not get up today.'

The events of the preceding night immediately recurred to my mind in full force. I remembered that Louise had not made her appearance during the sudden alarm, and this now seemed strange. I longed to speak to Father Frantz on the subject, but during the whole of breakfast the old forester seemed buried in thought. He appeared much less communicative than usual, and as he was evidently concealing something from me, I did not think it becoming to question him.

'Oh, well, I trust it will not signify, Father Honeck,' said I, rising, when breakfast was over.

'We must hope so,' said he in a grave tone. 'Are you going anywhere today, Mr. Theodore?'

'Yes, I am going to sketch the Thrush Rock in the Hôwald.'

'Very good,' said he, as if relieved to get rid of me. 'If you are hungry about midday you can step down to the saw mill at the Three Beeches, and break a crust with old Rheinhart.'

I bowed and left the room. A few minutes afterwards I was on the path leading to the Hôwald, with my portfolio under my arm.

'It is time you were taking your departure,' said I to myself, sadly. 'The portrait is finished, the little thing is ill, Father Frantz has something on his mind, and you are becoming an annoyance to them. Everything must have an end in this world. You have been kindly received and well treated, and that ought to content you. So now goodbye to you, Mr. Theodore, and a pleasant journey.'

My heart was very heavy.

The image of Louise, with her sweet, gentle smile and soft blue eyes, sat close to my heart. The rather dry tone of the old forester when speaking of his granddaughter also gave me much food for reflection. Was Louise really ill, or did Father Honeck suspect my dawning affection for her? How many conjectures did I not form on this mysterious theme! Meanwhile I wandered on at random. A distant opening in the underwood, the decayed trunk of some old tree, the gray outline of a mouldering rock overgrown with mosses and draped in ivy, arrested my steps from time to time. I longed to employ my pencil, to carry away with me a last souvenir of the mountain, but I could not fix my thoughts on anything. That fair, sweet face haunted me everywhere.

Towards three o'clock the weather became misty. Until then I had never seen the great woods except bathed in sunlight. A fine bluish rain began to fall. I descended the mountain to the saw mill, and the old miller, pointing to the sky, exclaimed:

'There is the autumn coming fast upon us, Mr. Theodore; six weeks or a couple of months more and we shall have winter. I feel it already in my old bones.'

For a long time we stood under the projecting roof of the shed, watching the rain falling in slanting lines through the air, and the trees assuming their dense mantle of fog; but as the rain still continued, Rheinhart had to lend me his great gray woollen cape to enable me to return to my quarters.

When climbing the hill path, down which the water ran in torrents, I came to the final resolution to inform Father Honeck of my intention to return to Dusseldorf forthwith.

Towards six o'clock I came in sight of the forest house, and perceived the old forester in the distance, standing on the threshold awaiting my coming. He waved his hand, and seemed glad to see me, bat it was only for a moment, and his features almost immediately assumed their former serious expression.

'Have you any change of clothes, Mr. Theodore?' said he, as we were crossing the yard.

'Yes, I have everything I require.'

'Well, make haste, I was waiting for you; the table is laid.'

'Very good; I shall be with you in five minutes.'

He disappeared in the passage. I climbed the stairs of the old gallery, and having changed my clothes from top to toe, I came down and took my seat at the table. As the fog had settled down deeper than ever, Frantz Honeck had lighted the candle. We ate our supper, *tête-à-tête*, without exchanging a word; he apparently absorbed in thought, his eyes fixed on his plate, while I felt puzzled and annoyed at his silence, so different from our usual relations towards each other.

This lasted nearly half an hour. The old Nuremberg clock with its monotonous ticking, and the steady drip of the rain on the foliage outside, seemed to drag out the minutes to an unendurable length, by thus forcing you, as it were, to count them second by second. That evening will never be effaced from my memory. How was I to announce my approaching departure to the forester? It was apparently quite a simple matter, I had only to say, 'Father Honeck, I leave you tomorrow.' Yes, but what would he think of such a sudden resolution? Might he not attribute it to discontent at his change of manner, to annoyance at not seeing Louise, perhaps even to my discovery of the secret he evidently wished to conceal from me? I was terribly puzzled. When uncertain how to act, everything seems an obstacle.

I looked at the old forester, who was sitting with knitted brows, and seemed to have completely forgotten my presence. However, when, pushing back his chair, he rose and took his pipe from the hook beside the window, which was his habit always after supper, suddenly breaking silence, I said:

'Father Frantz, here is the rainy season upon us; it may last like this for several days perhaps. The portrait is finished—my Aunt Catherine expects me at Dusseldorf. I may as well out with it at once: I leave you tomorrow!'

He fixed his gray eyes on me, as if he would read to the very bottom of my heart, and then, after a moment or two, he replied:

'Yes. Yes—I was expecting that. You are going away—and you

will carry with you a bad idea of Frantz Honeck and his grand-daughter.

'A bad idea! Why, I never in my whole life experienced such hospitality and kindness as I have received from you, Mr. Frantz, such—'

'Yes, yes, that's not what I mean. You cannot conceal your thoughts from me, Mr. Theodore—your face is too open and sincere for that. I saw plainly last night, and I see it in your eyes now, that you have discovered something. You suspect Frantz Honeck of keeping secrets from you.'

I could not help colouring, and he, still continuing to fill his pipe, added:

'Well, you don't deny it; you see I was right. But it shall never be said that an honest-hearted young fellow like you, a true painter, left this house with injurious suspicions of our conduct. No, no, that cannot be. You shall know all. You shall know why I refused to guide you to the Lake of the Wild Counts—why the dogs gave the death howl last night—why Louise is ill; in short, you shall know everything. I have reflected well upon it. I have been thinking of nothing else all the morning. It is not to the first comer that I would disclose family affairs which are sacred in our eyes, and concern our religion and honour. No, one must know and have an esteem for people before taking such a step.'

'Master Honeck, your esteem and friendship touch and grat-ify me more than I can express; but if you see the least objec-tion—'

'No, there is none, there could be none unless you were a scoundrel. Stay, Mr. Theodore, I am going down to the cellar for a pitcher of wine, and since you mean to leave us—well! we will drink a glass together to your safe journey.'

And without waiting my reply, he disappeared in the direc-tion of the cellar. My astonishment may be imagined. The seri-ous tone in which Father Frantz spoke portended grave disclo-sures. The strange scene of the preceding night, the lugubrious howling of the dogs, Louise's sudden indisposition, the refusal of the old *garde* to be my guide to the Lake of the Wild Counts—

how could all this be explained? What mysterious story could account for facts so disconnected and unusual? I must confess that all these things had aroused my curiosity to the highest degree.

When Father Honeck made his appearance again, his features seemed to have undergone a total change: the preoccupied look he had worn ever since the previous evening had given place to a sort of feverish excitement. He placed the pitcher on the table; then, seating himself, and filling the glasses:

'Light your pipe before I begin,' said he; 'it will be a long story. But when friends are about to part, it may be forever, they do not grudge a night spent in each other's company. Your health, Mr. Theodore.'

'And yours too, Master Frantz.'

We drank. The old forester rose, and, leaning his elbows on the window-sill, looked out. Night had come on; the rain was over, and no sound was heard but the regular drip of the rain-drops falling from leaf to leaf. He took his seat again with a sort of thoughtful air, and began as follows:

'You must know that, about four hundred years ago, there lived in this country a family of wolves. When I say wolves I mean a race of fierce men, who loved nothing but war and the chase, and who fancied that plants, animals, and men were created for no other purpose than to be devoured by them. These men were called the Wild Counts, and in our ancient forest charters they are called by no other name. They themselves claimed to be the descendants of the old stock of the Burckar kings of Swabia. To say whether they were so or not is not in my power; but one thing is certain, they were all hairy men, thickset and broad-shouldered; all, from father to son, had low, flat fore-heads, tawny eyes, beak-shaped noses, wide mouths, furnished with two rows of large firmly-set white teeth, and square mas-sive chins, covered with a mass of reddish beard that extended upwards nearly to their temples. Their arms and hands were so long that they could untie their garters without stooping, and this, of course, gave them a great advantage in wielding the sabre, the battle-axe, or any such implement of destruction, in the use of which they found their chief pleasure.

'As regards the rest, to give them their due, there never was seen on either bank of the Rhine, from Strasbourg to Cologne, better cavaliers, or more famous hunters, than these Wild Counts. They passed their days and nights on horseback, either in hunting the stag, or in pillaging, robbing, burning, and sacking the smaller *chateaux*, the convents, the churches, and villages in the neighbourhood.

'This race of robber nobles had ensconced themselves from time immemorial in a fortress built on the solid rock, on the borders of the lake that bears their name. The smallest stones of this fortress measured at least ten feet every way; all sorts of plants and herbs grew in the crevices in abundance, and even shrubs, like the holly, the briar, or the white thorn. You would have said, to look at it, that it was a mass of rock, and not a building; but behind the foliage that covered it were loopholes, through which the archers discharged their arrows at the passersby, as sportsmen shoot down deer or rabbits from an ambush.

'A broad moat, filled by the waters of the lake, surrounded the walls, and on the top were erected four lofty square towers, from which hung, suspended on long iron rods, the unfortunate peasants who had ventured to poach over the domains of the Wild Counts.

'As a matter of course, the crows, the owls, and sparrowhawks were fond of a place where flesh was so abundant. They were to be seen in every nook and corner of the Veierschloss, scratching their necks with their claws, or smoothing their feathers whilst waiting for the dinner hour, or else ranged in single file on the ramparts, their necks sunk in their shoulders, and their bills still dripping with blood, digesting the frightful repast they had just made. In the evening their ominous cries filled the valley, harmonising strangely with the boisterous songs of the *reiters*, as in a well-ordered farmyard the chirping of the sparrows mingles pleasantly with the monotonous beat of the flails in harvest time.

'Such was the manner of life, Mr. Theodore, of these Burck-ars and the pack of scoundrels they had collected together to do their wicked behests, and it seemed as if this state of things would last forever. Happily, when the sufferings of men become greater than they can bear, the Lord of Heaven comes to their aid in ways which these bandits never suspect.

'The last of these Burckars was called Vittikâb. He resembled all the rest of his race in his features, the colour of his beard, the length of his arms, his love of gold and silver, of the chase, of horses, and dogs.

'And since we are on the subject, I should tell you that the Wild Counts had succeeded in producing, by a cross between the shepherd's dog, the mastiff, and the wolf, a race of dogs so hardy and indefatigable in the chase, that none like them had ever been seen before. They were a sort of dog-wolf, thin and muscular, with straight upright ears, yellow eyes, and square mas-sive jaws, which held their prey like a vice. They had the long trailing tail, square sinewy legs, and jet black claws which you often see in beasts of prey. In all the old books on hunting you read of these dogs; and many attempts have been made to restore the breed, for in boar-hunting in particular they have never had their equal; but all in vain, the race is extinct, and never can be revived.

'Vittikâb, as may be supposed, had the same character and tastes as the other Burckars—he was the greatest hunter and the greatest plunderer of his time. I remember when a child to have seen an old almanac in which there was a representation of his pillage of Landau. All the houses were in flames; the inhabitants had taken refuge on the roofs, and were raising their hands to heaven. Mattresses were being flung out of the windows, and in the distance was seen a party of *trabans*, riding to and fro with young children impaled like frogs on the points of their lances. It made one's blood run cold to look at it. When you think that men have been capable of such deeds, you cannot help shudder-ing. At the bottom of the picture you read, "*The Great Pillage of Landau, in the year 1460;*" and on the opposite page you saw the portrait of Vittikâb, a fierce-looking man, with a sort of iron pot on his head, with a projecting visor or beak which reached from his forehead to below the nose. At the first look of him you said to yourself. "That man ought to have been flayed alive; he must have been the greatest villain on earth.'"

At this part of his story Father Frantz, who was quite pale with indignation, gravely lighted his pipe at the candle. His eyelids were cast down, and as he waited till the tobacco was fully ignited, it was evident from the expression of his face that gloomy thoughts were working in his mind. At last he replaced the candle in the middle of the table and proceeded:

'And now I am forced to tell you that, amongst the number of Vittikâb's followers, was my grandfather in the seventh or eighth remove That gives me pain every time I think of it. I would far rather be descended from one of those wretched peasants, who for hundreds of years have suffered barbarities and injustice from such scoundrels, for in that case I could pity the fate of my ancestors; but as it is I am forced to blush for them. However, as I can't mend the past, I look upon it as a punishment for my pride, if I was capable of such a feeling; but you are well aware, Mr. Theodore, that I have none, and that I only stand up for the honour of my post, as every man ought to do when he feels he deserves it.

'This Honeck, then, was the chief huntsman of the Veierschloss. If you pass by the Lake of the Wild Counts tomorrow, you will see the remains of the castle. It is now nothing but a great heap of ruins which covers at least five acres of the heath. Two of the towers, those next the mountain, are still standing. Between these two towers can be seen the arch of the entrance gate, and above the gateway, to the right, near the loophole from which projected one of the beams of the drawbridge, there is a round-shaped window. It was there that Zapheri Honeck lived, in a sort of vaulted cell above the guard-room. You cannot climb up to it now, as the steps are broken away, but in my young days I remember well my grandfather Gottlieb taking me there and telling me this story.

'From his vaulted room Zapheri could see on the one side the face of the mountain opposite, and on the other he looked into the outer court of the Veierschloss; for there were two courts, surrounded by high walls and as gloomy as wells. In the first the grand huntsman had under his eye the kennels of all the Burckar hounds ranged in one long row. To the right a staircase led up to the apartments of the Wild Count; to the left a similar staircase gave access to the gallery of the *reiters*, and at the back were the kitchens, the shambles, and the laundry. In the second court, which was entered through a wide gateway, were the stables and wood-sheds. You can see all that tomorrow, and you will admit that it was solidly and well built.

'Honeck did little else but sleep in this apartment; almost all the rest of his time he was coursing over the mountains. I can't tell you whether he took part in Vittikâb's plundering expeditions or not; but he could not have been much better than the others, more especially as the Wild Count was very fond of him. The Count never set out for the chase without him; they galloped side by side through the woods like the wind, and each understood as well as the other all the ruses and habits of the game. No one in the whole country could sound the horn like this Honeck except Vittikâb himself, whose horn was three times as large, and whose blast seemed as if it would burst the brass asunder. When they sounded the fanfare together you could hear them from the peaks of the Hôwald to those of the Steinberg, and the woods echoed to their inmost recesses.

'Honeck had something cheerful and even jovial in his manners and appearance, but Vittikâb was always as gloomy as the night. His tawny eyes seemed ever searching for something to kill, and he never laughed. Every evening, to while away the time, he sent for Honeck to come up to his apartment—a sort of vaulted cavern hung round with battleaxes, two-handed swords, curious pieces of armour, and implements of the chase—and, pointing to the table, said: "Eat, drink, your master commands you!" and the huntsman, who asked for no better, took his seat before the venison pastry, eating heartily, and washing down the meal with huge goblets of the monks' wine, as the Burckar called it. It was part of the booty got at the pillage of Marmoutier. Then they got drunk together. Honeck bore the usual evidence of his debauches in his mottled cheeks and crimson-tipped nose; but the more Vittikâb drank the paler he grew, the gloomier were his thoughts, and the deeper his scowl, and the more he was haunted with a longing to kill. Sometimes at nightfall, when the owls had congregated in thousands outside, and were chattering and hooting together among the mouldings of the battlements, shaking their wings and clacking their beaks softly, the Wild Count would glare at his friend Honeck by the half hour together without winking an eye, his lips tightly pressed together, and his nose curving with a fierce and terrible air. And when the other expected it the least, he would suddenly cry out:

"'Why do you laugh, you scurvy hound?'

'Honeck, like almost all old sportsmen, had a trick of shutting his left eye. It was a nervous twitch, and he could not help it.

"'I was not laughing, my lord," replied he.

"'And I say you were laughing," thundered the Burckar.

"'Since it is your pleasure to say so, I did laugh," said Honeck, "but I could not help it."

"'And why did you laugh?" repeated the Count, furious.

"'I was thinking of the chase, and—"

"'You lie—you were thinking of—of—something else—"

"'And what, in the fiend's name, do you say I was thinking of?" exclaimed Zapheri. "If you will only tell me what you wish me to think about, I will always say that, and then you will be content."

'This reply calmed Vittikâb as long as he still retained a glimmering of reason, but at other times it only increased his fury. His tawny eyes assumed a deep golden tint, instead of, as usual, being injected with blood, and then Honeck had nothing for it but to fly; for when his countenance assumed this appearance the Burckar always attempted to strangle his huntsman. So, without losing a moment, or stopping to bid goodbye, the latter, at the first lightning flash from his master's eye, made a rush for the door, the Count following like a maddened wolf, and stammering: "Stop there, stop, I tell you, or I will have you hung!" But Zapheri paid no attention, and stumbled down the stairs as if he would break his neck. The dogs began to howl in the courtyard, the *reiters* hastened out of the guard-room to see what was the matter, and the Count, once in the open air, immediately grew calmer; the howling of the dogs seemed to sober him, and he staggered back to his room, muttering some confused words.

"'Honeck climbed up to his den, and hastily shot the two great bolts of the oak door. Then he threw himself on his bear-skin rug to sleep off his debauch.

'It was in this way that the two drunkards passed the days and nights which God had given them. The same scene was repeated regularly every evening, unless, during supper, a great storm was heard rising outside. This was Vittikâb's happiest time. He listened with delight to the thunder growling amongst the gorges of the Hôwald, and when the rain and wind and hail seemed to battle together in the air, when the waters of the lake, lashed to fury, dashed in sheets of foam against the ramparts of the Veierschloss, when the owls and hawks, startled from their nests amongst the battlements, flew off screaming into the darkness, like dead leaves whirled away by the storm, the Wild Count started up from his seat and shouted: "To the road!"

'Then they descended the stairs together, Honeck and he, staggering and supporting themselves against each other, and saddled their horses. The *reiters*, who had seen them come down, hastened to lower the drawbridge, and they galloped off like the wind, and were soon lost to view in the darkness. Then Vittikâb laughed loud amidst the howling of the storm, the crashing of trees, and the beating of the rain, and his laugh sounded like the grinding of teeth. And when they were returning at daybreak through the distant villages, he would say to his huntsman:

"'Honeck, I shall be able to get some sleep this morning; that has not happened to me for many a day.'

'And the poor inhabitants of the villages in the forest, the wood-cutters and charcoal burners—often without food or work, their thatched roofs letting in the rain, their wives and children shivering with cold—standing, with haggard looks, on the threshold of their wretched huts, and seeing the terrible Burckar pass by, with his cheeks hollower and his eyes more deeply sunk than their own, said to each other:

'"How can so great a lord, a man so powerful as Vittikâb, who possesses all the good things of the earth, whose granaries bend under their load of grain, whose cellars are full of gold, how can he look so wretched? Ah! if we were in his place, if we had the hundredth part of his possessions, even the crumbs that fall from his table, how happy we should be! It is we who would bless the Lord!"

'Yes, yes, it is easy to say, "How happy should we be!" but we should first see into the hearts of others, before wishing to be in their place. The sparrows too suffer cold and hunger every winter; they chirp piteously, and ask to be fed; but when spring comes how gay they are, how they chase each other from branch to branch, how they pour forth their songs! Of what use is it to have eternal spring if we can enjoy nothing? Of what use is it to be the owner of the fairest meadow on the mountain side, if the dew of heaven never falls on it, and the grass withers away. Of what use is it to be stronger, richer, more powerful than all the world, if one look of tenderness never comes to pour its balm on the heart; if the memory' of one good action never comes to soothe the conscience? Each feels where his burthen galls, but he cannot know the burthen of others. Before wishing to change, it would be well to try the other side a little.'

The old forester, at this part of the story, gave me a friendly smile, and filled our glasses.

'To your health, Mr. Theodore!'

'To yours, Father Frantz!'

'You imagine, perhaps,' resumed he, 'that it was a feeling of remorse for all his murders, burnings, and robberies that made the Burckar so miserable? Well, on the contrary, he only regretted that he had not committed more! What made this brigand so furious against the human race, you are about to hear, and then you will see if there is not a Providence on earth. You will see if the poor and honest have not more cause for rejoicing than those who are rich and prosperous outwardly, but who have a gnawing worm at their hearts.

'Twenty years before this, when Vittikâb was about thirty, he had married a daughter of the noble family of Lichtenberg, called Ursula. The Wild Count loved this young woman, who was very beautiful and better instructed than himself in matters pertaining to our holy religion, and sometimes listened to her when she implored him to cancel the debt of some wretched serf instead of ordering him to be hung. He acted in this way in the hope of her soon giving birth to an heir to the noble house of Burckar, who would also have a claim to the succession of the Lichtenbergs, since Ursula was an only child. These ideas had a softening effect on his character.

'But when the child came, you may imagine his rage when he saw before him a regular monster, a hideous object, with scarcely any resemblance to man. In place of saying to himself that this came of the cruelty of the Burckars, who, from father to son, for generations, had acted more like wolves than men, and submitting himself to the just chastisement of the Lord, he tore the infant from its mother, in order to strangle it. The young wife, who, notwithstanding all, loved the poor creature—for you are aware, Mr. Theodore, that the hearts of mothers are so made that they love their children the more in proportion to their weakness, their defects, and infirmities: the Eternal has so willed it out of pity for such weak beings as children are; He has provided that the love shall be as great as the need of it, and we should bless His holy name for His infinite goodness, since this mother's love He has drawn from His own Divine love—well, this poor mother threw herself on the arms of the Wild Count, pouring forth lamentations and entreaties, and with such touching words and such floods of tears, that he, although the greatest monster of his race, was almost softened, and even felt a touch of pity for the unfortunate creature.

'Notwithstanding, however, he rudely repulsed his wife, and

70

took refuge in his den, at the opposite end of the gallery. And as he passed along behind the balustrade, and saw all the huntsmen, and prickers and *reiters* below in the courtyard, with their trumpets and horns of chase, waiting for the birth of the young Burckar to salute him with a warlike fanfare like his noble ancestors, he shouted in a terrible voice:

"'The Burckar is dead! Send Goëtz to me. The others may go the devil!"

'Then he entered his den.

'This Goëtz, whom he had sent for, was an old huntsman of about fifty years of age, still strong and hearty, and who had been a sort of valet or attendant of Vittikâb's from his childhood. He was the most devoted servant of his house. Some time previously, this man, when attempting to kill a wild boar at bay— kneeling down and holding the hunting-sword firmly before him, and shouting the Burckar cry of *"Wildsav!"* after the usual custom—had missed the throat, and the furious animal, by a thrust of his tusk under the hip-joint, had rendered him lame for the rest of his days. He was rough in his ways and hard-favoured, but this did not prevent him from having a tolerably kind heart all the same.

'Two minutes afterwards he entered the Wild Count's chamber, and the latter, pointing to the monster stretched on the table, shouted:

"'Behold! look at that—it is a Burckar!"

'The other started back, and the Count laughing as a fox docs when caught by the neck in a trap, said:

"'That's your master's flesh and blood. I thought at first of strangling it; but the blood of the Burckars is not to be shed so. Listen, old man. You are a cripple for life, you can't hunt on foot, and it's with difficulty you can mount a horse; well! you shall take this descendant of Virimar's and shut yourself up with him in the Marten's tower, and live there together. Perhaps he may look better as he grows up." And as Goëtz was about to make some observation:

"'I am ashamed of my own flesh and blood," said Vittikâb; "I must conceal him somewhere, and I have no one but you that I can depend upon. If you refuse me, I will throw the monster into the lake; but woe to you if I repent what I have done afterwards."

"'It is good," replied Groetz; "I will obey." The same day it was reported over the castle that the child was about to be buried. Groetz tod Vittikâb descended into the vault of Virimar, the first of the Burckars, with a little coffin, followed by some twenty *reiters* carrying torches. The coffin was placed in the tomb of Virimar, and then Groetz retired into the Marten's tower with the monster, and Hatvine, Vittikâb's nurse—an old gray-haired pillager who followed his expeditions on a mule, to dress the wounds and look after the booty—Hatvine was charged with the duty of carrying food to these two deserted creatures. Every morning she left the kitchen and climbed up to the top of the castle, carrying a large saucepan in her hand. She took her way by the gallery staircase, and mounted to the Marten's tower, the highest in the Veierschloss.

'The mother, who moaned, and cried, and sobbed, day and night, to see her son, at last died of grief; and the women of Lichtenberg, who had followed her to the Veierschloss as her attendants, disappeared without anyone knowing what had become of them. The midwife Lisbeth, of Pirmasens, who had delivered the countess, was devoured by two gigantic mastiffs one evening that she chanced to go down in the courtyard. These two dogs, which on account of their ferocity were never loosed except for some great wolf-hunt, happened to be wandering about that night; they devoured the midwife, and that was an end of the matter.

'Vittikâb, after these strange events, became almost wild with rage; he vowed vengeance on all the world, and especially against children. It was at this time that he undertook his great wars against Treves, Lutzelstein, Schirmeck, and Landau. All Hundsrück, Alsace, and the Vosges echoed with the details of these terrible engagements, and the memory of them has been handed down from generation to generation for four centuries, to show to what a pitch the cruelty of men without faith, religion, or honour, can go. The wild beasts, if they could write the deeds they have done, would not have so terrible a history to relate. But what can you expect? Take away the fear of God and the love of our neighbour, which are taught us in the Gospel, from our hearts, and we all, no matter who we are, would listen to nothing but our interests, our ambition and our hatreds. We should become worse than the beasts, seeing that we should have more means of injuring or destroying one another than they.

'At the close of these wars, which lasted for eight years, Vittikâb returned to the Veierschloss, looking quite pale, in place of being ruddy and sunburnt as formerly, and constantly plunged in gloom, instead of leading, as he used to do, a jovial life with his captain Jacobus, his lieutenant Kraft, and his old nurse Hatvine. He could now bear no one's society but Honeck's, because they hunted and drank together.

'He was always brooding over some dark design or other: sometimes determining to rush up and massacre the monster; sometimes to take him, notwithstanding his deformity, and proclaim him Burckar, exterminating all who should object to his malformation. For at the thought that the Geroldseks, the Dagsbourgs, the Lutzelsteing, his next of kin, all robber barons like himself, hunting, warring, ever seeking to destroy and injure each other—at the thought that these cousins, whom he wished in hell, would one day inherit his wide possessions; that they would divide amongst them his forests, his dogs, his horses, and the gold which had been heaped up by the Burckars for so many generations in the vaults of the Veierschloss—at the bare idea that this must happen sooner or later, fiery flames seemed to pass before his eyes, he trembled from head to foot, and paced hurriedly backwards and forwards along the galleries of the castle, his eyes staring wildly, his red beard bristling with rage, and his look gloomy and abstracted, like a tiger fretting behind the bars of his cage.

'"How can I prevent this?" he thought; "how can I prevent

this?" The more he thought over it, the less did he see any way of escape. He would gladly have burnt everything, the Veierschloss and the surrounding forests; but the land would still remain, the gold would be unconsumed in the vaults, and his cousins could rebuild the ruined walls. "What am I to do?" he kept repeating. Then he drank deep to brighten his ideas; and at nightfall he might be seen clinging to the balustrades with his long hairy fingers, and climbing the stairs to the Marten's tower. He went to see if the monster, whom old Goëtz had christened by the name of Hasoum, was becoming more like a human being; but he always came down again more horror-stricken than ever.

'Old Hatvine and Goëtz were the only persons in the secret. Suspicions were indeed rife in the Veierschloss that something mysterious was going on in the tower, but no person durst venture to go and see; for if Vittikâb had chanced by any evil fortune to meet you on the stairs, he would have cleft you to the chin.

'Things remained in this state for twelve years, during which time fresh expeditions were undertaken against the castles of Triefels, Haut-Barr, Fenetrange, and many others: for in those savage times all the barons of the Vosges and Mont-Tonnerre were perpetually at war with each other. For one trooper that was killed, twenty presented themselves to fill his place. The peasants were ground down with requisitions of all kinds: but when in this way they had lost everything they possessed, when they had neither house nor home, the idea of turning *reiter*, and abandoning father and mother, wife and children; of thinking henceforth only of themselves; of drinking, singing, gorging, pillaging, burning, sacking, and hanging, in place of being burned, sacked, or hanged themselves—this devilish idea at last got the upper hand, and so the supply of *reiters* never failed. To remain an honest man required the courage of a martyr.

'Vittikâb, then, as I have said, succeeded in all his enterprises; but what good was it to him? When he looked proudly at his old oaks and beeches in returning from the chase, the thought instantly occurred to him—"My cousins will one day possess these noble forests!" When his vassals came in hundreds with

their carts of wheat, barley, oats, and hay, their fowls, and butter, and eggs, at rent-time, in place of being content, he said to
himself—"All these riches will sooner or later be my cousins'."
When he had made a fortunate campaign, and returned with
his mules bending beneath the weight of the gold and silver pillaged from the churches, the convents, and the villages of Alsace
or Lorraine, he did not, as formerly, ride along whistling and
singing with his captain Jacobus and his stout *reiters*, but followed the cavalcade gloomy and alone, grinding his teeth and
muttering: "It is for these Greroldseks and Dagsbourgs that I
have once more risked my neck. I fill the vaults of Virimar, but
they will empty them." And so on, from day to day and year to
year. The older he grew, the more envenomed was the sore.

'And then, from time to time, and especially in the evenings,
after Honeck had left him, a terrible idea used to haunt him.
He remembered all at once that, at the burning of Landau, as
an old bald-headed blacksmith was running down the street of
the Three Lances, dragging his grandson after him on a mattress
to save him from the carnage, he had ordered them both to be
thrown into the flames; and that the old man, standing upright
amidst the blazing mass, and holding the child aloft with both
hands to preserve him as long as possible from destruction, had
shouted:

'"Burckar without compassion! Burckar without heart or
feeling! you will one day have need of compassion and pity, and
you will not find them. Murderer of children! you will one day
ask for children, but you will not have them. Accursed be ye—
accursed as Herod!"

'He saw this all before him in the gloom; he saw the face of
the old man, his eyes sparkling with terror and rage; he heard his
despairing voice, and, in spite of the intoxication of the wine, he
stammered out: "You lie! you lie!—I *shall* have children." And
the old man seemed to reply: "It is you who lie! you will have
no children—you will have nothing but monsters! "

'This vision, however, did not prevent him from always saying to himself: "I am still young. I may marry. I may choose a

wife of noble blood and unblemished race, who will purify the tainted blood of the Burckars. I may have children."

'The twelfth year was drawing to a close when an event took place which turned his thoughts more than ever in this direction. It was in the beginning of autumn. Information had been received on the evening before that a company of merchants from Flanders were to pass through the defiles of the Hôwald with a long train of mules laden with money and silk stuffs; and without losing a moment, the robber, at the head of his *reiters*, commanded by his captain Jacobus and his lieutenant Kraft, had hurried off to plant themselves in ambuscade at the farther end of the Valley of the Bocks, about five or six leagues from the Veierschloss.

'The merchants were a long time in making their appearance, but at last they came in sight, between eleven and twelve o'clock at night. Then Vittikâb and his followers, shouting their war-cry of "*Wildsau!*" dashed forwards. But what was their surprise to hear, instead of cries of alarm and entreaties for mercy, a second war-cry—that of the Geiersteins: "*Haslach!*"—echoing in front of them from another mountain-gorge. It was the terrible hunchback of Geierstein, the famous brigand Bockel, who, forewarned, like Vittikâb, of the passing of the merchants, had come to dispute the prey with him.

'This Bockel, who presented a truly monstrous appearance, from the gigantic breadth of his humped shoulders, and his projecting teeth, or rather tusks, which gave him somewhat the look of a wild boar at bay, did not easily let go what he fancied was in his power. He was quite as resolute as the Wild Count, equally vigorous in frame, and had about the same number of men. The indignation and rage on both sides, when they discovered that, in place of seizing their booty, they had to fight for it, knew no bounds. The moonlight in the open valley was magnificent. Without saying a word or attempting any parley or explanation, the Burckars and Geiersteins swooped down on each other like two flocks of vultures, and for a quarter of an hour nothing was heard but the sound of maces and battle-axes ringing on cuirass and helmet, like the hammer on an anvil, the cries of rage and pain of the wounded, and the panting exclamations and defiant shouts of the chiefs, who each singled out the other for attack. Soon nothing was to be seen in the meadows around but struggling troopers, riderless horses galloping wildly in every direction, their manes floating in the air, and the gleam of spears and battle-axes and armour all huddled confusedly together in the centre of the valley.

'The merchants, during this time, were making the best of their way from the scene of action, in the hope of reaching the plains. Vittikâb and the hunchback, seeing this, fairly foamed with rage. They were just then locked in deadly grip. Vittikâb with his dagger was endeavouring to discover a joint in his opponent's coat of mail, but without success, and, abandoning the attempt, he seized Bockel by the throat to strangle him; but the latter at the same instant dealt him such a blow on the head with his battle-axe, that the iron pot with the projecting beak was smashed through, and, but for the thickness of his skull, Vittikâb would have at last reaped the just recompense of his crimes. He fell from his horse as if dead.

'The hunchback would gladly have put an end to him on the spot, for he had long vowed vengeance on the Wild Count, whom he accused of baulking him of his richest booty; but unfortunately Captain Jacobus had just then gained a marked advantage over the Geiersteins; he had himself killed three, Kraft two: Bockel saw that his band was considerably reduced in numbers, and judged it prudent to beat a retreat. The Burckars remained masters of the field of battle, but the merchants had gained the open country, and were safe. Thus ended this encounter.

'Vittikâb was brought back to the Veierschloss on a mule. Old Hatvine shaved his head to make sure that the skull was not fractured. The blood was issuing from his nose and mouth and ears. In this way he lost a great deal, and this it was doubtless which saved him, not to speak of the ointments and herbs which Hatvine employed. In short, he escaped once more with his life; but for three months he was unable to sit on horseback, as every trot of the horse seemed to tear his brain in pieces. He was terribly enraged against Bockel, who, on his side, regretted bitterly not having, by one good blow, put an end to his most formidable adversary.

'This event rendered the Wild Count more gloomy than ever. "I am getting old," said he to himself. " Once on a time I would have parried that blow of the battle-axe. I would have found the crevice quicker below the *gorget*. I would have finished him in some way—I am growing old!"

'And then he reflected that, if the stroke of the battle-axe had been one atom heavier, it would have split his skull, and there would have been an end of the Burckars present and future. His hair grew again over the wound; but it was remarked that it had become white all over that side of his head. His beard became grizzled, his eyes sunk in their sockets—it was the beginning of the end. He felt this himself, and the monks' wine tasted bitter to him.

'One evening, when he was getting drunk as usual with his huntsman—who never uttered a word, and only raised his elbow and winked with one eye from time to time—Vittikâb, who seemed gloomy and thoughtful beyond his usual wont, sat listening to a screech-owl, in an adjoining loophole, uttering his melancholy cry from time to time. All at once, rousing himself from his reverie, he said:

'"Tomorrow, at daybreak, you will saddle two horses, and we will start together. Do you hear?"

'"For the chase?" inquired Honeck.

'"No; to pay a visit to the Botericks, at Birckenstein, on the other side of the Losser."

'After these words he was silent, and Honeck, bowing low, said,

'"Very good, my lord, very good!"

'But he could not imagine what the Wild Count would be at; for the barons of Roterick had been enemies of the Burckars for centuries, and, until then, Vittikâb, far from going to pay them a visit, treated them with contempt, and even turned them into ridicule on every occasion.

'You must know, Mr. Theodore, that the Botericks belonged to the oldest nobility of Germany. They were both better born and more courageous at bottom than the Burckars, but sunk in poverty and ruin; just as all honest men in this world are ruined sooner or later by rogues, when they show themselves too confiding and generous, and don't keep on their guard. These latter, then, had been cheated and plundered by the Burckars from the earliest times, but without ever having been conquered by them. They had defended our holy religion against the Saracens, and the mother-country against the Turks, Spaniards, and Italians. They had followed the Crusades for the conquest of the Holy Sepulchre, and the Emperor, whenever he took the field to avenge the honour or maintain the rights of old Germany, no matter against what enemy.

'The Burckars, during this time, remained shut up in their mountain-fortresses, from which they issued forth only to plunder and destroy; and the Rotericks, on their return from their distant campaigns, always found that these robbers had seized on some strip of woodland, some valley, or mountain-lake, or perhaps even a village or two. This aroused their indignation; they disputed, they fought; but, on returning from war, people are generally weak, and, as both money and men were wanting, the Rotericks could not support their rights to the end, and the matter always ended by the Burckars keeping possession of the property they had seized. They called that cleverness; and if that be so, thieves and robbers are clever enough; it only requires that you should have neither heart, nor honour, nor justice, and then take advantage of these good qualities in others.

'It was in this way that the Rotericks found themselves gradually stripped of all their possessions, and the Burckars, who always feared them, being unable to conquer them in open fight, at last ended by burning their castle of Birckenstein.

'After all this, everyone may imagine the feelings of the last of the Rotericks towards the last of the Burckars. He called

79

him nothing but bandit and robber. Vittikâb, on his side, spoke of the other as a barefooted beggar, because he was really poor, and his old castle, rendered totally defenceless on the side next the mountain, where its only rampart was a row of wooden palisades, and containing little more than some stables and hay-lofts, with four cows, an aged pony, and two lean dogs, and an old dovecot surrounded by a few fluttering and cooing pigeons, presented rather the appearance of a miserable burnt-out farm-house than the residence of a noble.

'But all this did not prevent Roterick from holding his head up proudly, as if he had still a couple of thousand *reiters* at his back, and, when he bestrode his old pony, with his sword by his side, from looking down on Vittikâb from an imaginary height of grandeur and importance. He lived in the most miserable manner, it is true, with his daughter Vulfhild and his old groom Peters; the revenues of one poor village, and a few head of game from the neighbouring moors, scarcely sufficed to procure them the necessaries of life; but just in proportion as the blood of the Wild Counts was tainted and degraded, so was that of the Rot-ericks rich, noble, and flourishing. Throughout all Germany the saying was: *"Roterick red blood! Burchar bad blood!"* Vittikâb knew this well; he had reflected long on the subject, and had formed the resolution—in order to have children with human faces—to marry Vulfhild, and to grant the old baron all the amends and satisfaction he could require.

'He said nothing of all this in the meantime, and set off the following morning very early with Honeck for Birckenstein. Roterick, in his doublet of reddish-coloured leather, tall, thin, wiry, with d keen grey eye, and hair as white as snow, but still firm and upright in spite of his advanced age, happened to be standing in the gateway of the old tower, the arch of which stood out against the blue sky, the walls beyond having fallen in, and was gazing proudly over his heaths and moors, as the Burckar and his huntsman came in view. At first his indigna-tion knew no bounds. He ordered them not to approach nearer at their peril, and old Peters hastened up with an immensely long halbert; but Vittikâb, having stated that he came to make amends for the injuries committed by his ancestors, and to form a lasting alliance with the Rotericks, the old noble, astonished at language so new to him from such a quarter, permitted them to alight in the courtyard.

'Then Vittikâb and he proceeded into the guard-chamber— almost the only room left intact in the castle of Birckenstein— and conversed together for two long hours.

'God knows what the Wild Count promised the old man, but it may be supposed he promised him all that the latter could have asked if he had been strong, and in a position to claim his rights with weapons in his hands: the rebuilding of his castle, and the restoration of his lands, his stud of horses, and his hounds. Something like this must have been agreed to, for at the end of the conference they were apparently reconciled. Vittikâb, accompanied by the baron, went to pay a visit to Vulfhild, who sat in an old moss-grown tower from morning till night, working tapestry, in company with two aged crones. Notwithstanding the fierce and gloomy look of the Burckar, and his great shock of hair, half red and half grey, Roterick's daughter consented to become the *chatelaine* of the Veierschloss, and permitted the Wild Count to kiss her long white hands.

'One thing is certain, that on his return, Vittikâb, who galloped along at full speed beside his huntsman, looked twenty years younger. His pale cheeks had got back their natural colour, he laughed loud, and shouted in his eagle's voice, turning round in his stirrups:

"'Zapheri, all goes well. We shall have children this time— real children. We will train them to the chase. Ha! ha! ha! They will be stout Burckars; their arms will be long and hairy, but they will be men!"

"'I believe you, my lord," replied the other, without in the least understanding what these words meant. "All that my lord wishes, he can do. No one can say to the contrary."

"'Yes," continued Vittikâb, "the old race of the Burckars is not dead. The Geroldseks and the Dagsbourgs won't now be able to plunge their hands up to the elbows in Virimar's gold. They will never hunt our game, nor mount our horses."

'And rising to his full height in his stirrups, his two arms in the air, and his long tawny face kindling with joy, he uttered shouts of triumph, which echoed through the woods around.

'Honeck had never but once before seen him in so joyous a mood: it was at the storm of Landau, when he had scaled the walls, and was standing on the top, dashing down the levelled lances with his battle-axe, as the mower strikes down the grain in autumn.

'But when he approached the Veierschloss, the Burckar grew calmer, without his joy however lessening in the least. He put his horn to his lips to warn the *reiters* to lower the drawbridge, and the bridge having been lowered, they both crossed it at a walking pace.

'In the courtyard was the captain Jacobus, the lieutenant Kraft, and a good number of troopers. Vittikâb, before putting his foot to the ground, said to the assembled company, in a clear determined voice:

'"I have to inform you that I, Vittikâb, the Wild Count, and lord of the Veierschloss, have this day betrothed myself to the noble lady Vulfhild of Roterick, and that the marriage will take place in three weeks. It is my will that everyone should rejoice, as on a day of victory at the dividing of the spoil. The wine shall not fail you. He who does not enjoy himself deserves to be hanged, and anyone who shall venture to find fault with what has been done, will answer for it to me. Be merry, therefore; it is my will!"

'And, darting a fierce look around the stupified assemblage, he climbed the staircase leading to the galleries, amidst shouts of "Long live our Wild Count! Long live the noble lady Vulfhild!" Just as men have always done for ages on ages, flattering and cringing to those who have the upper hand.'

Here Father Frantz made a fresh pause, to shake out the ashes of his pipe and lay it in the window-seat. Then, after a few moments' silence, looking at me kindly—

'Mr. Theodore,' said he, 'I am sure you never caused mortal man to shed a tear of suffering. I may say as much for myself, although my head is white, and my hour is fast approaching. This is why we can sit here calm and tranquil in the night hours; this is why we have nothing to trouble us. We have put our trust in God. The spirits of darkness may prowl around us, but they cannot enter our hearts, they cannot whisper evil thoughts in our ears; for we see things simply and clearly, as God has made them in his wisdom, and nothing terrifies us. If death at this moment were to knock at the door and say: "Frantz Honeck, it is time!" I would look him calmly in the face, and rise to meet him. "Leave me but one minute," I would say, "to give a last kiss to my little Louise, and then I will follow you with confidence." Yes, although death is a terrible thing, and seldom comes without cruel pain and suffering, I trust I shall be able to say this at my last hour.

'But, Mr. Theodore, it will not be so with everyone in this world. If the Spirit of Darkness has no power over the honest man, he has all power over the heart of the evil-doer. It is a house opened wide to admit him, doors, windows, and skylights. He enters it and leaves it at his pleasure; he sits and lies down, and walks to and fro; he thinks and sleeps there; it is his inn, his chosen retreat, and his dwelling-place. So, when a villain looks at you, you see, behind those two dark windows, the hideous being that comes and goes, that stops, that looks at you, and watches all your doings, in order to try and find some means of injuring and ruining you; that laughs pleasantly or bursts into a fit of rage, according as he hopes to deceive you or finds that he is discovered.

'The faces of great criminals are, so to speak, a mirror in which you can see the abominable monster within. But the worst of all is, that when once he is firmly established in his lurking-place, the evil spirit is never content. The master of the house may straggle as much as he will; he may beg for mercy, and exclaim: "I will not do this thing or that!" From the moment that he has allowed himself to be bound hand and foot like a coward, he must obey.

'Now this was just the case with Vittikâb. After having committed all the crimes against the human race that a man could be guilty of, there was one still remaining, the greatest of all, before which he had hitherto recoiled; but, as it always happens in such circumstances, the devil ended by getting the upper hand.

'That day, from the Wild Count's return up to midnight, the Veierschloss re-echoed with the uproar of the revellers, the shouting of drinking-songs and the clinking of goblets, like an immense tavern. Six great hogsheads of wine had been broached in the middle of the courtyard, and everyone rushed to fill his pitcher as often as he liked, and pour the liquor down his gaping throat as down a tun-dish.

'Very soon in every nook and corner of the castle, along the ramparts, on the steps of the staircases, behind the balustrades, in short everywhere, nothing was to be seen but knights and troopers, huntsmen and prickers, lying like sacks right and left, their legs wide apart, their faces of a deep purple, their lower lip dropped, a fragment of a broken pitcher in their hand—dead drunk. Thus it was that the betrothal of Vittikâb and his bride was celebrated in a manner worthy of him.

'If Bockel had only known that, the terrible hunchback would have had nothing to do but hasten to the spot, dash the chains of the drawbridge to pieces with his battle-axe, and cut the throats of all these drunkards. Not one would have had strength enough to rise and seize a pike to defend himself; no, not even the lieutenant Kraft, the soberest of them all, or the captain Jacobus, who could drink six quarts of *Markobrunner* without being drunk; and least of all Zapheri Honeck, who had far exceeded his usual allowance, which was anything but a small one. Unfortunately, Bockel did not hear of it until four or five days afterwards, when it was too late.

'Now, whilst these things were passing in the lower stories of the Veierschloss, Goëtz, Hasoum's guardian, who had grown old and shrivelled in the Marten's tower, like a snail in its shell, asked himself: "What is this that is going on in the castle? What extraordinary rejoicings are these? Have we won some battle and got a large amount of booty?" And the old man listened and reflected, and did not know what to think. During the twenty years he had spent in the tower he had learned to distinguish every sound that took place in the fortress, from the highest summit of the towers to the lowest depths of the cellars. He knew every trumpet-blast, whether it sounded for the *réveillée*, for meals, or for bedtime; it was his clock.

'Thus alone could he measure the lapse of time. He could distinguish the step of the sentinel on the outworks, the going and coming of the troopers in the courtyards, along the galleries, and on the stairs; the extreme fineness of his ear was such that he knew every family of crows or owls that lived under the projecting cornices of the building, the spots which they preferred as the starting-point for their morning flight, the holes in which they built their nests, and the number of their young. And this wonderful acuteness of hearing had even increased of late as his eyesight grew dimmer, and he had no longer the resource, as formerly, in his loneliness of wandering along the battlements at night and gazing in the distance at the mountains, the glens, the valleys, the peaks, and the woods that he had known so well in happier times, the forest paths through which he had roamed, and the springs at which he had slaked his thirst.

'Goëtz was now almost quite bald, and had only a scanty fringe of snow-white hair behind each ear. His features were deeply furrowed with wrinkles; the blaze of light to which he was constantly exposed in his lofty dwelling-place had forced him to keep his eyes half closed, and he could now scarcely raise his eyelids in the least. His hands, once so muscular, were nerveless and ridged with large projecting veins; his knees trembled beneath him; he spoke slowly, never having occasion to open his lips except in the few words which he exchanged day by day with Hatvine, and now and then, at distant intervals, in a brief conversation with Vittikâb, when the Wild Count paid a visit to the tower.

'But although thus shut out from the rest of mankind, he

had become more and more attached to the monster Hasoum. He loved him as if he had been his own child; he thought him almost handsome, and every evening he climbed up to the topmost story of the tower to gaze at him when asleep. "Poor creature!" thought he, "the descendant of so many illustrious chiefs, and so famous a race, your father is ashamed of you; but I love you, for you are not ill-natured! You cannot speak, it is true, your tongue is dead; but your eyes speak, and they tell me you love me! And, ah! I love you too; but I am growing old, and when Goëtz is no longer here, what will become of you, poor dear child of my masters? What will become of you? What will they do with you?"

'And the poor old man's voice quavered, a tear trickled down his cheek, he descended the stairs again almost heart-broken; and he who formerly was not a whit better than the Burckars his masters, he who had more than once dipped his hands in blood at Treves, at Lutzelstein, at Landau, and had never in his life perhaps given a thought to God in the days of his health and strength, now prayed with his whole heart, and called down the blessings of Heaven on the head of Hasoum.

'So this evening Goëtz said to himself: "Why are they singing in that way? Something strange must have happened, and yet Hatvine said nothing about it when she brought our breakfast this morning." She could not have said anything about it, you see, because Vittikâb and Honeck had not returned at that time; but the circumstance made him uneasy.

'In the meantime night came on. All the sounds in the Veierschloss died away one by one, and the silence grew deeper and deeper in the air around, on the battlements, and in the courtyards of the castle. A few embers still smouldered underneath the ashes in the little arched recess of the chimney, and Goëtz, sitting close beside it, with his back against the wall, and his large bald head drooping on his breast, had sunk into a doze.

'At last, about eleven o'clock, a blast from the horn of the officer of the watch passed over the surface of the lake, dying away in the distance like a sigh; the echoes of the Hôwald took it up one by one, and then all sank again into silence. Goëtz rose from his seat to retire to rest, when, just as he was about lighting his torch, a sound caught his ear; he listened, and could distinguish a feint noise approaching nearer and nearer. " It is Vittikâb," murmured the old man; "he is coming here!" And, in feet, a few moments afterwards steps were heard ascending the staircase of the tower, and rapidly crossing the platform. The door opened; it was the Count, the projecting beak of his helmet turned round behind, his huge frame clad in a doublet of reddish leather, and his *poignard* suspended on his thigh by two little chains in the form of a triangle.

'"Where is Hasoum?" was the first question he asked.

'"He is sleeping, my lord," replied Goëtz, pointing towards the ceiling above.

'"Good."

'And Vittikâb, turning round, threw a searching glance over the adjoining platform and battlements, which he had never done before; then he entered the tower, shot the bolt, and pointing to a bench near the oak table: "Sit down there," said he to the old man, in a peremptory tone.

'Goëtz obeyed, almost speechless from surprise and apprehension; for, for the first time during twenty years, Vittikâb was not drunk. His manner was calm, gloomy, and cold. God only knows what passed between the old huntsman and the Wild Count, what words were exchanged, what orders given, what promises made! But they must have been weighty and serious, for when, about an hour afterwards, they came out together on the battlements again, the Burckar was as pale as death, with his nose curving fiercely over his moustache, and his lips firmly set; Goëtz bareheaded, his scanty fringe of hair bristling with terror, and his eyes swelled with crying.

'In this way they crossed the broad flags of the platform. The moon was shining down brilliantly from the blue vault of heaven, throwing the massive sculptures of the balustrade into strong relief. At the angle of the great staircase, from which the eye could plunge down into the dark courtyard below, Vittikâb turned round, with one foot on the upper step, and his hand resting on the hilt of his *poignard*, and said in a low determined voice:

"'You understand me?"

"'You shall be obeyed, my lord," replied the old man in the same mysterious manner.

'The Wild Count descended the stairs, and Goëtz, leaning on the corner of the lofty balustrade, looked after him for some moments with a dull stupified gaze; then, when he had altogether disappeared, raising his withered hands to heaven with a despairing gesture impossible to describe, he re-entered the tower, uttering low groans and little cries of distress and grief, which he tried to suppress for fear of wakening Hasoum. But he could not keep them back, and trembled like a leaf from head to foot. Fortunately the poor creature entrusted to his care was a sound sleeper. All day long he was constantly in motion, climbing from beam to beam, to the very summit of the Marten's tower, one hundred and twenty feet above the level of the lake, and gazing through the narrow loopholes at the wide stretch of wood and water, mountain peaks, and fertile valleys, which surrounded the castle. This was his whole life. He slept soundly, and Goëtz might sob and groan as much as he pleased.

'You may well imagine, Mr. Theodore, that in the midst of all the grand preparations which were making for Vittikâb's wedding, no person troubled his head about Goëtz, and that all this took place without exciting any notice. But He who sees everything had been a spectator of the interview between the Wild Count and his old retainer; His patience was beginning to weary, the hour of retribution was at hand!

'The following morning, Vittikâb despatched some thirty of his troopers in every direction through the Hundsrück; some to collect together, with the utmost speed, all the carpenters, cabinet-makers, and smiths to be found in the towns and villages for twenty miles round; others, to give notice to the most celebrated furnishers, cooks, and confectioners in the whole country, even as far as Strasbourg, Spires, and Mayence; and others again bearing letters of invitation to the *margraves, burgraves,* counts, and barons on the banks of the Rhine, the Meuse, and the Moselle.

'The famous architect, Jerome of Spires, arrived two days afterwards. He undertook to erect an immense covered arcade over the great courtyard, to serve as the banquet-hall for this feast of Belshazzar; and thenceforward the vaulted roofs, the corridors, and staircases of the Veierschloss, instead of the sound of trumpet-calls, the barking of dogs, and the clash of arms, echoed only with the sound of the saw, the axe, and the hammer.

'The forests around, which were swarming with wood-cutters, resounded night and day with the crash of huge pines and lofty oaks, falling one after another, and the creaking of heavy waggons, each drawn by three pairs of oxen, and almost crushed to the earth beneath the enormous trunks.

'Then numerous scaffoldings were seen rising in all directions about the ramparts; the triangular cranes stood out against the sky on the summits of the towers, furnished with ropes and pulleys for raising the beams to the level of the platforms; swarms of workmen hurried to and fro, hauling at the pulleys, turning the winches, squaring the immense logs, or cutting mortises for the joints.

'The old architect Jerome, standing at the foot of the great staircase, with his long yellow beard trimmed to a point, his bald head, his robe of black velvet with wide hanging sleeves, his rules, his squares, and his compass, was busy from morning till night, drawing red and black lines on sheets of parchment. The troopers stood round him in groups, looking over his shoulder, without in the least comprehending what he was about, and the master workmen came in files to receive his orders, and carry them to every corner of the building.

'The uprights were soon fixed in their places, and it was not long before the roofs of the arcade began to show their rounded outline against the sky.

'But amidst all this bustle of preparation the busiest man perhaps in the whole castle was Zapheri Honeck; for if the Wild

Counts were anxious to display their taste in sumptuous buildings, decorations, and feasts, they piqued themselves much more on the scale of their hunting expeditions, being reckoned the most famous sportsmen in all Germany.

'Now, Master Honeck, as first huntsman to the Burckar, was entrusted with this part of the festivities, and to enable him to perform his task properly, the Count had placed his whole establishment of horses and hounds at his disposal.

'But to employ all these in a way worthy of the great occasion was no slight task, Mr. Theodore, and required all the natural talent and consummate experience of a man like Zapheri, thoroughly acquainted with the country, and well up in organising cavalcades, placing relays, encouraging the dogs, and tracking the game.

'Honeck felt himself quite equal to the occasion, and had no dread of meeting the scrutiny of the great lords, all sportsmen of the first order, who were to be present at the festival, and who were sure to cast a critical eye on all that took place, to blame as much as possible, to praise as little, and to carry back to their chateaux an increased sense of their own merits and importance in proportion as they were able to find fault with others. No, he had no fear on that score, for he was the most skilful huntsman of his time, notwithstanding his habits of drunkenness and his extraordinary gluttony.

'Without losing a moment, he summoned all his prickers and scouts around him, and divided the mountain into districts, giving each a portion, in order that the tracks might be thoroughly followed up, and no part of the forest omitted. He enjoined on them to give all their attention to coveys of game, herds of boars, and packs of wolves, neglecting single animals:"For," said he,"to let slip two hundred horses and three hundred dogs on a solitary track, would be like letting down all the nets in the castle into the lake for a single fish. Every man in the hunt should at least have the chance of a blow at something!" He ordered them to bring him specimens of all the droppings found, and to observe carefully the appearance of the broken branches, and other marks, such as those made by the deer in sharpening their ant-lers against the trunks of the trees. In short, he forgot no detail belonging to his profession, and set out himself every morning to examine the tracks which his scouts had given him notice of the evening before in their reports.

'In this way the time fixed on for the festival drew on.

'Frequently, at night, Honeck, worn out with fatigue and splashed with mud up to the arm-pits, for he visited even the marshes of the Losser, where the game of that district were in the habit of going to quench their thirst,—frequently, I say, when returning this way, in a grave and thoughtful mood, his mind ab-sorbed in his duties, he heard Vittikâb's voice shouting:

'"Hey! Zapheri!—Zapheri! Why, you pass like the wind! Come this way."

'Then turning, and seeing the Count smiling at him from the gallery above, he raised his cap with its plume of hawk's feathers, and drew: looking as agreeable as possible.

'Vittikâb, since his visit to old Goëtz, was no longer like the same being. He even laughed sometimes now, and robbed his hands with an air of inward satisfaction. Those who had seen him formerly scarcely recognised him. In place of the pale, care-worn face, with which everyone was so familiar, his features now wore a calm, satisfied, and even joyous expression. The work-men, whom his manners and appearance had at first terrified, now said to each other: "How apt people are to be mistaken sometimes! Why, he is the best nobleman, and the kindest, we ever met. He considers the poorest workman in the place. We oughtn't to judge people at first sight;" and every evening, after work was over, they sang long ditties in chorus, always begin-ning with love, and ending with plague, famine, or war. Vittikâb, who had completely recovered his good-humour, listened to them with pleasure from his lofty gallery, and sometimes, during working hours, he would send them a few pitchers of wine to encourage them.

'So, as I have said, the Count frequently, seeing his huntsman passing at nightfall, would cry:

'"Honeck!"

'The latter mounted up to the Count's apartments, and the Burckar, pointing to the arcades, would exclaim:

'"See there! We are getting on famously!"

'Then, taking him by the arm, he showed him the rich stuffs of Flanders, and the ornaments of gold and silver of every kind, all huddled together pell-mell in a great room, previous to their final arrangement on the day of the ceremony. Honeck, who was thinking of nothing but his game, replied: "Ah! ah! yes, my lord, they are beautiful—magnificent!" until Vittikâb put him on the chapter of the hunting preparations by suddenly saying:

'"Well! and our hunt? You say nothing about it! Are you getting on well?"

'Honeck's face immediately brightened, and he replied:

'"Yes, my lord, yes—I think we shall do well."

'"Very good," said Vittikâb; "that is all I want to know. I have no time to attend to such matters myself. I leave everything to you."

'Instead of flying into a rage, and ordering right and left in a savage voice, he had grown quite kind and good-humoured; and, in fact, he had good reason to be so, since everything happened just as he wished, and seemed almost to come of its own accord.

'In the meantime the wedding day drew near; all the principal carpenter-work was finished, and the decorations were being put up.

'Never had there been so fine an autumn seen as in that year. The sun shone brilliantly from morning till night. Only a few light fleecy clouds were seen now and then in the blue expanse which stretched over mountain and valley. Women and children, summoned from the villages around, brought quantities of evergreens and moss to the castle, to decorate the arches and windows; for green is the fairest colour of all, being the pleasantest for the eye to rest on, and this is why the Lord has chosen it as the covering of the whole earth.

'Underneath the arched roofs of the banquet-hall the workmen stretched long festoons of silk, entirely concealing the wood-work, and suspended rows of banners along the walls. Others arranged the tables below. The great entrance-gate, the drawbridge, and all the front of the building, was one mass of pine branches, the tops of which reached nearly to the battlements. The gloomy Veierschloss had never before presented such an appearance. Like Vittikâb himself, it had grown suddenly gay and joyous.

'The hawk's nest was carpeted with moss, like the linnet's. But of what use are all the decorations in the world when the Lord is weary of us, and has said to Himself, " I will make an end of this"?

'One morning, two days before the marriage, as Master Zapheri Honeck was passing his game-bag over his shoulder previous to setting out on his daily rounds, the door of his cell over the guard-room opened, and the second huntsman, Kasper Rebock, entered. Rebock had passed the night outside the castle; it was thought that a herd of deer had led him a dance somewhere about the Hôwald or the Gaisenberg. He was a thorough sportsman, and all true sportsmen are like thoroughbred hounds, who will never abandon the scent except in the last extremity. The former often pass two or three nights in succession in the open air, with nothing but a crust of bread in their bag; and as for well-trained hounds, they will sometimes not return home for eight days together, when everyone thinks they have died of hunger or been eaten by wolves, Rebock, as I have said, came in, covered with dried mud up to the shoulders.

'"Oh! you are back?" said Honeck, impatient to be off; "you have followed some new track, and have come to make your report? Very good, very good, we will talk of that in the evening."

'"It is true, Master Honeck; I have come to speak to you of a new track, but a track so extraordinary that I have never seen anything like it."

'He opened his bag, and laid on the table a mossy sod, which bore the distinct impress of a long narrow paw, with four claws in front, and one at the side. At the first glance Honeck saw that it was something strange and unusual; but he said nothing, and, taking the sod, he carried it to the grated opening, to examine it better in the light. Rebock, leaning on his hunting-spear, watched him in silence. For a long time Honeck examined the foot-mark carefully, knitting his brows and compressing his lips. At last he said:

'"Yes, that is probably something new. At first I thought Blac or Spitz had been trying some trick on us, but they are not cleverer enough to mark the toes and claws and joints in this manner. It is no doubt the footprint of some animal. I should say it was a bear of the Alps, if all the claws were in the same line; but, to say the truth, Rebock, I cannot at this moment tell what it is."

'And, looking at the huntsman, whose face was beaming with delight:—

'"Where the devil did you find this?" said he. "Come! sit down here, and tell me the whole story."

'They seated themselves opposite each other at the corner of the table, each resting his head on his hand; and Rebock, quite proud of having discovered a track which Master Honeck was unacquainted with, entered into the most minute details respecting his astonishing discovery. He said that on the morning of the previous day, about nine or ten o'clock, being on the track of a herd of deer, he had discovered this foot-print under a wild apple tree, and that, immediately suspecting that it was some pleasantry of his comrades, he had kneeled down to examine the thing closely, and became at once convinced that some extraordinary animal was in question. That then, abandoning the pursuit of the deer, he had followed this new track, which, from the heights of the Kirschberg, had descended to the marshes of the Losser, and at last became lost to view in the mud.

'That, in his ardour, he could not bring himself to give up the pursuit, and had advanced as far as the great willow on the riverbank; but that then, having lost his boots, and feeling the ground giving way under his feet, he had been obliged to return, and make the circuit of the marsh to endeavour to recover the track at the opposite extremity. Unfortunately, as the marshes of the Losser are three good leagues in circumference, and as a man cannot walk fast who has to follow the track of foot-prints amongst reeds and rushes, it took Rebock five hours to accomplish the distance, and it was only at the extreme farther end, amongst the heaths of Hasenbruck, that he was fortunate enough to recover the trace of the foot-marks ascending to-wards the Rock of the Three Wheat-Ears.

'One circumstance which particularly surprised Honeck was, that the huntsman added that, having chanced to come upon a fire left by the woodcutters, he had remarked that the animal, in place of flying from it, as every other beast of the forest does, had remained in the neighbourhood, that it had gone round it several times, as the marks of the long paws were everywhere to be seen on the sand along with the prints of the heavy hob-nailed shoes and clogs of the woodmen; and that at last it had stopped for some time quite close to the brazier, as was plainly distinguishable from the depth of the footprints there.

'"Are you sure the fire was burning at the time?" enquired Honeck.

'"I put my hand on the ashes," replied Rebock, "and they were still warm, and, as the animal must have been there long before me, the fire was doubtless burning brightly and sending up smoke when it reached the place."

'"It is strange," exclaimed Honeck, "altogether strange!"

' And in fact, he had good reason to be surprised, for the most formidable animals of the woods are afraid of fire, so that this animal must be more terrible than all the rest.

'Lastly, Rebock said that, still following the track, he had reached the level ground on the top of the Rock of the Three Wheat-Ears about seven o'clock in the evening, and that, hav-ing searched long and carefully amongst the brambles, he had discovered the animal's hiding-place, which was neither more nor less than a regular cavern, low-mouthed and deep, and run-ning under the rocks. He had not ventured to enter it, saying to himself that, judging from the claws of the beast, it would have torn him limb from limb if it had unfortunately happened to be inside, which Master Zapheri could understand very well.

'This was Rebock's story, and you may imagine if Master Honeck, on the eve of his great hunting-party, was not delighted to hear such a piece of news.

'"Very good," said he, rising; "I will look into this myself. You must say nothing of it to anyone, Rebock. If it is an animal of high venery, like the bear, the wild boar, or the stag, we will give chase to it. But we must leave the Count the pleasure of the surprise. It will be capital sport to astonish all the assembled company, to see all these *margraves*, *burgraves*, and *landgraves*, with their faces a yard long, biting their lips with vexation, and to have it said, even as far as Switzerland, that we have game in these parts that is to be found nowhere else."

'"Your mind may be easy on that point, Master Honeck," replied Rebock; "you know it is not my custom to talk. So that my masters are pleased, I don't trouble my head about anything else."

'Then he went to take a few hours' rest, and Zapheri set off without further delay. He was out the whole day long; it was only at nightfall, between eight and nine o'clock, that he emerged from the woods, and advanced towards the Veierschloss.

'Not only had he verified the truth of Rebock's report, but he himself had discovered a host of additional proofs that the animal differed entirely from the other denizens of the mountain in its halts, its hiding-places, its ruses, its habits, and instincts. What was this creature? Whence came it? How was it that it had never been seen before in the Hôwald? How could it have followed its predatory habits, and satisfied its voracity on all the other animals of the forest for several years, without leaving behind it the smallest trace of its presence? This was what completely puzzled the huntsman, nor could he form any connected idea on the subject.

'But the main point for him was to get his dogs on the scent of this beast, and to astonish the whole of Vittikâb's guests by something truly extraordinary. "What a hunt we shall have!" said he to himself, "what a hunt!—fifteen herds of deer, twelve droves of wild boars, six packs of wolves, as many foxes and hares as you like, and this beast, this surprising beast, the only one of its kind, a beast that no one has even heard of before. Ah! the Count has indeed good reason to be content; everything comes to him, as it were, in his sleep. He has only to wish for a young, handsome, and noble wife, and she immediately makes her appearance; he has only to wish for a grand hunt, and all the animals of the forest are delighted to give him rendezvous, and only wait the signal of the chase."

'Thus reasoned Honeck, striding along towards the Veierschloss at a rapid pace. He saw in the distance the great entrance-gate thrown open, and the courtyard within blazing with torches. Several great personages, the Counts of Simmeringen, Loetenbach, and Triefels, had already arrived with their numerous retinues, and the retainers of the castle were hurrying about, conducting them to the apartments prepared for them, and offering them suitable refreshments, agreeably to Vittikâb's orders.

'In the midst of all this noise and bustle Zapheri Honeck had no difficulty in entering unperceived through a postern door in the barbican, slipping quietly into the kitchen, making a hasty meal, and washing it down with a good pull or two at the wine-pitcher, before mounting to his cell to get some sleep, as a preparation for the fatigues of the following day.

'Meantime, Mr. Theodore, you may imagine the astonishment of the *margraves*, the *landgraves*, and the *burgraves*, of plain and mountain, on hearing that the Wild Count was about to marry a Boterick. It was not only because he was old, grey-haired, and had been a widower for twenty years, because he loved nothing but plunder and the chase, and got drunk regularly every day, that people wondered so; it was, above all, on account of Vulfhild's family, for the Rotericks had been enemies of the Burckars for hundreds of years, and everyone thought they could never be reconciled.

'But Vittikâb, in his towering pride, treated all these remarks with contempt. He was sure, beforehand, that everyone would come to his wedding; some from curiosity, others from love of good cheer and choice wines, others again to join in the great hunt, and all to have it to say at some future time: "We were present at that great entertainment, at that feast of Belshazzar. Nothing like it will ever be seen again in our days!"

'He was not mistaken.

'When the news came of the immense works that were going on at the Veierschloss—the summoning of architects, jewellers, dealers in silken and velvet stuffs, and the most famous cooks in all Germany—everyone took the road with their wives and children and servants, in great state, with falcon on fist and hound in leash. Every path through the Hundsruck was thronged with these cavalcades, and the poor inhabitants of the mountain followed them in their rags, as if on a pilgrimage, hoping to gather some of the crumbs which fell from the banquet-tables.

'Such was the state of affairs on the last day of the preparations, when Master Zapheri Honeck returned from the Rock of the Three Wheat-Ears. That day Jerome of Spires had promised that all should be completed the following morning, the last blow of the hammer given, the last peg driven into its place.

'You have heard, Mr. Theodore, how the Prince of Darkness, wishing to get possession of the soul of the Prior of Sempach, promised to build him a cathedral, as magnificent as that of Cologne, in a single night, and how all his legions of devils hastened to obey his summons and set to work; some, not bigger than snails or crickets, with their gimlets and augers; others, as high as towers, with their hatchets, their saws, and their trowels; others again, larger still, carrying great rocks and beams on their shoulders; so that on the following morning the spire of the building was seen shooting up into the clouds, and there was only one thing wanting to complete the edifice—the crucifix!—which saved the prior's soul.

'Picture to yourself such a work as that, and the noise it must have made, while such mountains of stone were being heaped on the top of each other, such huge beams squared and fitted, and such thousands of nails driven. The uproar was heard as far as Rotterdam, in Holland.

'Well, it was almost the same thing at the Veierschloss. Honeck, in his little den over the guard-room, couldn't close an eye. It was to no purpose that he turned and twisted on his bearskin, sleep would not come to him; in the first place on account of the frightful noise, but also because a thousand strange ideas were passing through his mind, without his knowing how or why they came there.

'One thing is certain, that whenever in the course of our lives we are threatened with some great danger, we feel restless, uneasy, and anxious, and, as it were, beside ourselves. Many think that at such times the souls of our departed friends or relations hover about us, and seek to warn us. They may not be far wrong in this; but we cannot know for certain, until the day come when we ourselves shall be among the number of these wandering souls.

'The upshot was, that Honeck did not get a wink of sleep. The idea of the strange animal that he had been pursuing haunted him incessantly. In imagination he followed the footprints over again, now in the marshes of the Losser, then on the heathy moors of the Hôwald, and again amongst the brambles of the Rock of the Three Wheat-Ears, within a few paces of the cavern, and from these footprints he endeavoured to form some idea of the strength and size of the animal. Then he asked himself how it was that he had never remarked this footprint before, he who for the last thirty years had seen those of every animal in the forest a thousand times, and could distinguish at a glance even the passage of a squirrel over the dry leaves! "This beast must have started up out of the ground," said he to himself, " or come across the sea, or have been hunted from Poland,, or someplace still farther off."

'When he thought of the Count's surprise, he was uplifted with joy, and yet at the same time he could not shake off a strange feeling of uneasiness. At last he got up, and leaning his two elbows on the sill of the grated opening, which, like all the other windows of the castle, was ornamented with wreaths of evergreens, he looked down into the dark courtyard, snuffing up the sweet scent of the leaves and flowers which covered the walls and pavement, as in the procession of the *Fête-Dieu*. In the deep shadow he caught confused glimpses of groups of workmen mounted on ladders, or clustering on the balustrades and galleries, hanging up banners and garlands. The torches, flitting here and there through the immense building like a swarm of fire-flies, threw a passing gleam on these busy crowds, and then disappeared in the darkness.

'The courtyard, with its covered arcade, one hundred and fifty feet high, seemed like some vast cathedral; the slightest sounds reverberated through it from end to end. Jerome of Spires, standing in the centre, was giving his orders and hurrying on the work. And as Honeck continued to gaze down thoughtfully in the way we have described, he all at once perceived the old architect perched on a tall ladder, which seemed no thicker than a thread, lighted from below by a torch, which threw his long angular shadow to the very summit of the vaulted roof. For a moment he fancied he saw before him the Prince of Darkness himself, with his long goat's beard, in this fantastic outline. But at the same instant he saw, far above, on the highest point of the roof, a black speck, about as large as a fly, letting fall a thread into empty space, and he heard old Jerome with his thin shrill voice shouting:

'"Let go!" The thread descended, and then a voice, distant and faint as a sigh, called from above:

'"Any lower?"

'"No; that will do," answered Jerome, climbing down again from his ladder. Honeck then perceived that they had been hanging the great chandelier from the centre of the roof.

'He was just about to leave the window, when the doorway opposite, leading to Virimar's treasure-vault, was suddenly lighted up with a ruddy glow, and some twenty *reiters* issued forth, two and two, and mounted to the galleries above, carrying great baskets, heaped with gold and silver cups enriched with pearls, the great wassail-bowl, and all sorts of plate and jewellery required for the festivities. Hatvine, with a bunch of keys at her girdle, and holding a torch above her head, led the way. Zapheri, who was worn out with fatigue and loss of sleep, gazed at these things as if. in a dream.

'At last the grey daylight appeared, the noises died away one by one; the workmen had finished their task, and old Jerome had retired to bed. Then the huntsman threw himself on his rug again, in hopes of getting a little repose, and this time he slept like a top.

'He had been sleeping a long time, and the sun's rays were streaming in brightly through the countless banners, and flags, and standards that hung in the great banquet-hall, when all at once the blare of trumpets, bugles, and horns echoed like a peal of thunder through the vaulted roofs, and awoke him with a start. He leaned upon his elbow and listened. All around, along the galleries, in the courtyard, on the drawbridge, the glacis, and the covered way, went up a deep confused hum, like the waves of the sea, and amidst this could be distinguished the clash of arms, the neighing of horses, and the sound of voices. Honeck at once saw that the festivities had commenced.

'He jumped up, quite pale, and leaning out underneath the garlands of evergreens which surrounded his window, a most dazzling spectacle met his eyes. All around, the balustrades of the galleries, the staircases, and windows were filled with a mass of heads, leaning over each other to see more distinctly. Below, on the right, were marshalled the *reiters*, on the left the *trabans*, while in the background, on a sort of platform or dais, approached by a lofty flight of steps, sat Vittikâb on his throne.

'The *cuirasses* of the knights, and their helmets, glittered like mirrors. At their head, in front of the throne, was their captain, Jacobus, his lofty plume almost touching the banners overhead, and his scarlet mantle covering the croup of his horse. You would have said, to look at him, he was ten feet high.

'All the knights had their long straight swords buckled on their thighs. The *trabans* in their coats of mail and their head-gear, in form like a monk's cowl, showing a wolfs head in front, stood with their maces on their shoulders. Kraft, wearing like them merely a coat of mail and a leather *caque*, was stationed opposite the throne, beside Jacobus, and seemed equally grand, haughty, and terrible as his comrade.

'Between the knights and *trabans*, and reaching from the entrance-gate to the very steps of the throne, was laid a carpet composed entirely of the skins of animals, bears, wolves, wild boars, badgers, stags, roe-bucks, foxes—every beast of the forest was there; it was something magnificent to see! The Burckars alone could boast of such a carpet; for, let me tell you, it takes no small sight of furs to cover two hundred yards of flags in length by thirty in breadth. Honeck himself was astonished at it. But what struck him above all with admiration was neither the knights, nor the *trabans*, nor Kraft, nor the thousands of banners, nor the crowds that filled the galleries, nor the garlands, nor this noble carpet, although no one knew its great value better than he—it was Vittikâb himself, seated on his throne.

'Picture to yourself, Mr. Theodore, a sort of savage god, low, thickset, broad-shouldered, and bull-necked, full of strength, confidence, and arrogance, and with an expression of ferocious joy gleaming in his eyes, which seemed to say: "Behold the God of Terror!" Picture to yourself such a being, with his wolfs head, seated at the top of a lofty flight of steps, in a massive iron chair which was forged in the time of our Lord, and clothed like Herod, his great beard spread over his breast, and the coronet of the Wild Counts on his shock of red hair. Such was exactly the appearance of Vittikâb.

'He had put on the robes of state of his great-grandfather Zweitibolt—robes so old that they were as stiff as pasteboard, and so thickly covered with gold embroideries that the red velvet underneath could scarcely be seen. On his shoulders were two things like epaulets, which fell down below the elbow; his silver cuirass bulged out between, his shoulders like a carp's back, and over it were hung a number of massive chains of gold, which tinkled as he moved. A sort of kilt or petticoat of boar's skin covered his thighs, and his sandals were fastened with embroidered thongs which were laced up to the knee, He held in his hand a mace, sparkling with large diamonds, by way of sceptre; his coronet blazed on his forehead like the stars of heaven, and his whole appearance was so rich and imposing that one would have thought Zweitibolt himself had come to life again, and taken his seat in his iron chair, to hear himself saluted as the Wild Count by his subjects.

'Honeck, seeing him thus—towering above all these cuirasses, these helmets, these swords, these daggers, these battle-axes, and surrounded by a forest of waving banners, standards, pennons, and garlands, and by hundreds of noble lords and ladies, who had come from such a distance, and were leaning over the balustrades, gazing down in envy and admiration—Honeck, seeing him thus, said to himself: "Yes, the Burckars are indeed great and mighty! They are as far above all other lords as the oak is above the birch!" And he felt a sort of veneration for his master such as he had never done before—he could almost have fallen down and worshipped him without shame.

'After he had taken a general view of the scene, allowing his dazzled eyes to wander at random over the crowd, by degrees he recognised in the distance several of his confreres, the huntsmen of Triefels, Haut-Barr, Geroldsek, and others, who had come in the retinues of their masters, and were ranged along the upper seats of the rows of benches that lined the walls, some clad in black and red, others in green and yellow, their hunting-horns slung over their shoulders, and their caps of white or blue, with a plume of heron's feathers, over one ear. It was a real pleasure to him to meet a few faces that he knew amongst this innumerable crowd of strangers. He was full of admiration also for the noble ladies of Steinbourg, Rethal, and Reinstein, whose lofty head-gear, trimmed with rich lace, could easily be distinguished far off in the galleries amongst the thousand head-dresses of every form and colour, the waving plumes, and glittering helmets. One could never have felt tired of looking at all these rich costumes.

'The huntsman had been gazing in a sort of ecstasy at this strange and wonderful scene for perhaps half an hour, when all at once the *major-domo*, Erhard, clad in a long jacket of silver-grey plush, a little ivory cane in his hand, and followed by a tall Swiss with a halbert over his shoulder, advanced gravely between the ranks of the knights and *trabans* to the steps of the throne, and then, turning round, he raised his cane with a majestic air. Instantly the trumpets and horns sounded, and from the farther extremity of the hall a *seigneur* advanced, holding his lady by the hand, her long train borne up by a page, to prevent it trailing on the ground. As soon as they had reached the foot of the throne the trumpets ceased, and the *major-domo* cried, in a voice as clear as that of the cranes when winging their flight through the mists of autumn:

'"The high and *puissant* Margrave Von Somelstein and his noble spouse!"

'Then Vittikâb descended three steps whilst the others ascended, and Jacobus and Kraft, on the right and left, lowered, the one his sword, and the other his mace, with a majestic air. Vittikâb, swelling with gratified vanity, smiled; then the trumpets sounded afresh, the noble and his lady, with the page, descended the steps, and passed into the gallery on the right.

'Matters went on in this way for three mortal hours. Every minute the trumpets sounded, a *seigneur* and his lady advanced, the *major-domo* shouted their names and titles, and Vittikâb descended two, three, or four steps, according to the rank and dignity of the person. Then the trumpets began again: it seemed as if it would never have an end.

'In spite of the beauty and magnificence of the ceremony, and the grandeur of the whole scene, the heat was so great, and the trumpet blasts, and the bowings and curtseyings, were repeated so often, that at last it became rather tiresome.

'"If this is to last till evening," thought Honeck, "I had better have a drink of something, to help to pass the time."

'He was repeating this to himself for the hundredth time, when loud shouts were heard outside, which seemed to come from the glacis and the outskirts of the forest, where the poor people had collected in the hope of picking up the fragments of the feast.

"'Long live Roterick! Long live Vulfhild! Long live the fair young lady!"

'The cries came nearer and nearer, and were caught up and prolonged by the echoes of the Hôwald. Very soon the trot of a large cavalcade could be distinguished, and the challenge of the sentinel on the outworks. The noise and tumult grew greater every moment.

'Honeck, who felt impatient to know what was going on, leaned more than half-way out of the window, underneath the garlands of evergreens, and almost at the same instant the heavy trot of the horses thundered over the bridge; then the sound of wheels was heard, followed by the clatter of the iron-shod hoofs on the pavement, and the flourish of trumpets from the great hall.

'A confused murmur ran round the galleries and staircases, spreading by degrees through every corner of the immense building. All the company rose to their feet, and leaned over to see the entrance of the bride.

'But Honeck paid no attention to the spectators. His eyes were riveted on the courtyard below, where the first two trumpeters advanced from beneath the arched gateway, sounding their trumpets, their cheeks puffed out till they were on a level with the point of their nose. Then, after the trumpeters, came a long file of horsemen, mounted on snow-white steeds caparisoned with gold-embroidered housings, and serving as escort to a sort of canopy or dais of purple cloth, which the huntsman recognised as having been taken, twelve years before, by the Burckars at the pillage of Treves. It had belonged to the bishop, Werner. Each of the four corners was ornamented with a plume of white ostrich feathers; the fringes were a foot in depth, and the poles which supported it were of solid silver.

'Underneath, on a magnificent car, sat Vulfhild, throned in state.

'Then came the retainers, headed by old Roterick himself, whose tall figure, clothed in a complete suit of armour, and bright red plume, had a noble and commanding appearance. You may imagine the cries of "Long live Roterick! long live Vulfhild! long live the Burckars!" which echoed through the courtyard. Strong as they were, the roofs of the banqueting-hall shook and trembled, the old fortress hummed like a great drum, and clouds of jackdaws and owls, terrified at the noise, darted out of their lofty niches, whirling and fluttering wildly amidst the silken draperies, the banners, and pennons of the great hall, and filling the air with their screams.

'Vittikâb had risen from his seat. An expression of savage joy gleamed in his eyes and lighted up his features; his beard seemed absolutely to bristle with pride and triumph. He descended from his throne, striding onwards with his long wolf-like step, without looking to the right or left, and without replying to the salutes of his knights and *trabans*, who lowered their flashing swords with a military flourish as he passed. In a second he was beside the car, and pushing aside the draperies with his muscular arms, he lifted Vulfhild, with his long hairy hands, as if she had been some white bird, and placed her lightly on the ground.

'Then all the assembly had a full view of her as she stood, tall, slender, and haughty, dressed in a long robe of dark green velvet, the boar's head of the Burckars embroidered in silver on her *stomacher*, and her magnificent auburn tresses twisted in great folds, and drooping over her snow-white neck behind, where they were fastened by a golden arrow. Everyone could admire the rows of pearls which hung down over her rounded bosom, her broad majestic forehead, her aquiline nose, her large almond-shaped grey eyes, her thin curving lips and square projecting chin. She was truly a wife suitable for the Wild Count.

'Vittikâb, without saying a word, smiled; then, leading Vulfhild across the hall and up the steps of the dais, amidst thunders of applause from the spectators, mingled with the neighing of horses, the distant baying of the hounds, and the screaming of the owls and hawks, he placed her on a seat to the left of his chair of state, and standing beside her and laying his hand on the young girl's shoulder, who seemed proud of being thus, as it were, in the eagle's clutch, he cried in a loud clear voice, which sounded like thunder pealing amidst the storm:

'"Behold the wife of the fortieth Burckar, Vittikâb, the Wild Count, Burgrave of Veierschloss, Margrave of Hôwald, and Hosser! Woe to him who shall dispute her hand with me!"

'Then he seated himself abruptly, with a fierce air, and the whole assembly was agitated like the leaves of the forest after a storm. It seemed to the spectators as if the Count had thrown down a challenge to battle, but no one said anything; and twelve *trabans*, the wolf's head drooping over their helmets in front, and the skin falling down their backs almost to the saddle, their chests protected by *cuirasses* of thick leather, and their arms and legs bare, advanced to the foot of the throne.

'They held straight trumpets in their hands, wide at the mouth and nearly six feet in length, the pennons floating down to their stirrups; and, wheeling round and facing the crowd, they commenced to sound the march of Virimar, an air which went back to the times when the first Burckars had swept down on the marshes of the Losser, an air so wild and terrible that your hair stood on end while listening to it. It was as it were the *Marseillaise* of the Wild Counts, and was never heard except at the coronation or marriage of a Burckar, or during some great battle. At the sound of it the wounded strove frantically to raise themselves and renew the fight: it made your very flesh creep.

'Honeck, at the first notes of this air, turned quite pale; he had never heard it but twice before—at Vittikâb's first marriage, and at the fifth assault of the Felon's Tower at Lutzelstein. It seemed to him as if the scene were once more passing before his eyes! The air reminded him of the olden time, and of the past glories of his masters, and a thousand ideas passed through his mind as he listened, thronging as thick as the swarms of midges that dance in the sunshine in the early days of spring. He trembled to his very finger-ends, without knowing why.

'What he felt, all the other old bandits of the Veierschloss felt also. The rest of the company, on the contrary, the *burgraves* and *margraves*, remembering to have heard this barbarian music, which sounded like the howling of wolves, around their *châteaux* and castles, or on hard-fought battlefields, felt a chill creeping over them, and became thoughtful and uneasy.

'When the air ceased, the silence was almost oppressive. Vittikâb and Vulfhild rose, and, descending from their thrones, they advanced with slow and stately step between the ranks of the *reiters* and *trabans*. At the same moment the doors of the two galleries, to the right and left, were thrown open, and all the nobles with their ladies—barons, *margraves*, and *burgraves*—thronged out and followed the Wild Count in their order of precedence. All this grand procession wound along right beneath Honeck's eyes, mounted the grand staircase, and passed on towards the great banquet-hall.

'Long after the last of the noble personages had disappeared, Master Zapheri sat buried in thought, with his elbows resting on the window-sill, fancying he still heard the march of Virimar, and recalling to mind the scenes of his master's first marriage and the assault of Lutzelstein. All these past events flitted before his mind as if in a panorama. Below, in the courtyard, the silence, after all the noise and tumult, seemed to grow deeper every minute. The retainers withdrew one by one, and the knights and *trabans* led their horses off to the stables.

'Just as Honeck, rousing himself at length from his reverie, was about to leave the window, he cast a last glance upwards towards the vaulted roof of the arcade, and through a trap-door which had been left open to admit the fresh air, he caught a glimpse of a pale, worn face leaning out of a window at the very top of the principal tower. This distant figure, seen thus through the opening in the roof, and standing out against the blue sky, had such a strange fantastic effect, that the huntsman stopped to examine it more closely. He then saw that it was old Goëtz, but so worn and haggard, with such hollow cheeks and deep-sunk eyes, that Honeck fairly started with surprise and fright.

'"Good heavens!" said he, " how old the poor devil is getting.

And yet Hatvine always told us how fresh and hale he looked, in spite of his great age. Well, it's the way with all of us! Such a stout fellow, too, as he was, some twenty years ago, and as good a hunter as ever brought stag to bay! That's the way you will be yourself, Honeck, one of these days—an old battered owl, with scarcely a feather left, and nailed up against a barn-door to frighten the crows."

'Zapheri was right. Goëtz had grown old, very old, since Vittikâb's last visit. There are times when weeks count as years.

'The sight of the old huntsman, however, had suddenly reminded Honeck that the hunt was to take place on the following day; and then, reflecting that all the great personages he had just seen would sit in judgment on him on this solemn occasion, he was filled with overpowering anxiety, resulting from the fears he had entertained, on the one hand, of not justifying the confidence his master placed in him, and on the other from his enthusiastic hopes of surpassing his utmost expectations. "What a rare piece of luck it is," said he to himself, "that we have such an extraordinary animal to pursue! After so many and such grand ceremonies, we wanted something better than boars, roe-bucks, and deer—we wanted some rare, unique animal, such as was never before seen in the range of the Vosges or the Hundsrück. Well, St. Hubert has sent us just such a one!"

'Instead of losing his time carousing with his *confrères* of Triefels, Geroldsek, and Bamberg, as he would not have failed to do on any other occasion, he hastened to collect his huntsmen, and give them all the needful directions about coupling the dogs and placing relays in the direction of the Losser and the Rock of the Three Wheat-Ears. And whilst the banquet-chambers and galleries of the Veierschloss resounded with the clinking of glasses, the clattering of flagons, the noise of drinking-songs, and bursts of laughter, which almost shook the roof, and while all the guests of the Wild Count, as well as the knights and *trabans*, and retainers of the castle, gave themselves up to feasting and enjoyment, he thought of nothing but his responsibility for the success of the hunt, and took his measures accordingly. In this task he spent the rest of the day, and even a portion of the night; but when he had done, everything was in order, and the Burckar's triumph was secured!'

At this portion of his narrative Father Frantz stopped to take breath. I had been listening attentively, with my head resting on my hand and my elbow on the table, gazing absently before me, lost in the memories of another and distant age, and, as he ceased speaking, I turned my head and gave a glance towards the little window, where the vine-leaves were trembling in the night breeze. A pale light was beginning to appear on the horizon above the belt of pines. The forester opened the window, and the pure night air which entered cooled and refreshed us. We listened; the birds were still asleep, and the monotonous plash of the little fountain in the farmyard was the only sound that broke the silence.

'The day is dawning,' said I to Father Frantz, who was gazing out at the hill opposite.

'Yes,' replied he, pointing to the hill-top, 'if we were up yonder, we should see him rising amidst the mists of Switzerland, behind the Black Forest, but it will be an hour yet before he makes his appearance in our valleys.'

Then, coming back to his seat, he resumed:

'It was on the following morning that you should have seen the great courtyard of the Veierschloss, just before the chase set out; you should have seen the long rows of horses, the finest in all Germany—tall, fine-limbed animals, chosen from every country in Europe, and the worst of which had cost the Wild Count their weight in silver—you should have seen them, fastened to rings along the walls, from the farthest end of the courtyard to the entrance-gate, neighing, pawing the flags with their iron-shod hoofs, tossing their heads and champing their bits in their impatience to be off. It was a noble sight.

'And the Burckar hounds, coupled together and straining in the leash, in packs of six, eight, and ten—terrible animals, with tawny hides, large flat heads, orange-coloured eyes, long backs, and trailing tails, yawning like wolves from ear to ear, and stretching themselves from time to time, shooting out their claws, and uttering little fierce whining cries—you should have seen them! Behind them stood the huntsmen and prickers, dressed in leather jerkins, their sinewy legs cased in gaiters fastened with rows of bone buttons, their broad felt hats, with a heron's plume, resting on their necks behind, their horns, with a double circle of brass, slung round their shoulders, the ends of the leashes twisted round their hand and wrist up to the elbow, and the cow-hide whip in the other hand ready to strike.

'Farther on, the prickers of the *margraves*, *burgraves*, and *landgraves*, all strapping fellows, tall and strong-built, and magnificently dressed in the liveries of their masters, held each a thoroughbred horse by the bridle; animals of rare beauty, I need scarcely say, for in those times it was the chief pride of the nobles to surpass each other in the breeding and excellence of their horses. He would have been a good judge who could have said, "This one is better than that;" for all were chosen expressly for their beauty, strength, and speed.

'A few palfreys with large pads of brocaded velvet, and housings to match, were also in attendance for the use of the ladies who meant to follow the chase. Every moment the general impatience increased, the horses pawed the ground more fiercely than ever, the dogs tugged at the leashes and howled piteously. Every now and then the lash of a huntsman's whip whistling through the air, followed by a smart cut, would impose silence for a moment, but immediately afterwards the noises commenced again worse than ever.

'Honeck strode up and down amidst the crowd, his bushy red whiskers bristling with impatience and anxiety, and his eyes directed every moment towards the gallery. The nervous quiver of his eyebrows seemed to say, "What can they be about?—Will they never come? The dew is drying fast, the sun is getting high, the dogs will have no nose at all!" Then, turning to the huntsmen, he vented his anger on them:

'"Yokel! will you shorten those leashes! Must I be always telling you that the longer your leash is, the less hold you have on the dogs? Is that any way, Kasper, to carry your horn—on the right shoulder? If you think to distinguish yourself by such means, I can tell you you are mistaken!"

'And, resuming his march, he muttered some unintelligible words to himself.

'At last, towards seven o'clock, the lofty entrance-door of the great hall was thrown wide open, and all the guests, noble lords and ladies, dressed in hunting costume, advanced along the gallery, Vittikâb leading the way. Vittikâb alone, of all the company, had retained the old costume of the chase, and appeared in a thick leather vest, deerskin kilt, and bare legs. He had also resumed his iron *casque*, the projecting beak being turned round to the back. He seemed in high spirits; the wine-drops stood thick on his heavy moustache. On his right walked the fair Vulfhild, raising her head with a haughty air, like some snow-white falcon, while he, Vittikâb, with his broad shoulders and thick short neck, seemed rather to resemble the vulture of the Alps, the fierce *lämmergeier*, who darts from his eyrie with a joyous scream, as if he already felt his bleeding prey struggling in his clutches. He could not altogether get over his old habits, and had drunk freely, but was not what you would call intoxicated.

'Those who followed were one mass of silk and jewels, in the newest style of the time, for luxury was increasing from day to day, and already more than one petty *seigneur* had sold his little possessions to enable him to appear at court in splendid attire. They would have been ashamed of Vittikâb, if he had not been the Wild Count, lord of the Veierschloss, of Hôwald, and of the Losser.

'As he descended the grand staircase, looking over the balustrade at his dogs and horses in the courtyard below, he cried out:

'"Honeck!"

'"My lord?" replied the huntsman, advancing with uncovered head, and the plume of his hat sweeping the ground.

'"Well, Honeck," said he in a good-humoured tone, "what do you promise us today? You don't forget, I hope, that we are to hunt today in the presence of the most famous sportsmen of the Black Forest, the Ardennes, and the Vosges, our rivals and masters?"

'He said that out of courtesy, looking as he spoke at some of the forest *margraves* and *burgraves*, such as old Hatto of Triefels, Lazarus Schwendi of High Landsberg, and others who piqued themselves on their skill in the chace, and who were highly flattered at such a compliment from the lips of a Burckar. Honeck, still with head bent low, said nothing. Vittikâb continued:

'"Yes, we shall have judges with us today. Speak, then; can you promise us sport worthy of such company, and worthy of our own reputation?"

'Then Honeck, raising his head, replied gravely:

'"My lord, I venture to promise you that the hunt will be a noble one. St. Hubert sends us game worthy of the Burckars and their noble guests."

'He was unwilling to say more, for fear of depriving the company of the pleasure of the surprise; consequently, everyone concluded that some enormous wild boar was in prospect, and Vittikâb, smiling, said:

'"You bring good news! Since it is as you say, you shall yourself sound the depart; it will serve as your reward. Come, my lords, to horse!"

'All the guests dispersed immediately through the courtyard, some assisting their ladies to mount, and others jumping themselves into the saddle. Then everyone took his place: Roterick and Vulfhild in the first line; Vittikâb in front, for the purpose of leading the chase; and Honeck reining in on one side to allow the cavalcade to pass; the huntsmen and prickers with the dogs bringing up the rear.

'When Master Zapheri saw that all was in order, he put his horn to his lips and blew the depart, as no one but he or Vittikâb himself could sound it. The Veierschloss and the surrounding mountains rang with the trumpet's notes like a bell, and the distant echoes took them up and prolonged them far and wide. Then the cavalcade set off amidst the shouting of men, the neighing of horses, and the deep baying of the hounds.

'But at this moment a strange event took place, an event, Mr. Theodore, which ought to have made the spectators reflect, for it was a sign from heaven, and the Lord never sends such signs except on great occasions. He had decreed that the Burckar should that day be punished, and He wished beforehand to give a warning of the wrath to come, in order that all who beheld might call it to mind afterwards, and recognise that everything comes from God, and that nothing happens by chance.

'Now, as Vittikâb, who was the befit horseman of his time, and whose whole life had been passed in subduing the most furious and ungovernable animals, was about to cross the bridge, his horse stopped. At first he felt surprised at this, for the horse was a favourite one, which he had ridden frequently, and which he had chosen expressly for this hunt. He endeavoured, therefore, to manage him quietly, but the horse would not move. Then the Count gave him the spur, but the horse instantly reared and plunged, trying to unseat his rider, and the whole cavalcade scattered right and left, to avoid the heels of the restive animal. Vittikâb grew pale with anger, and, with his iron grasp forcing the horse on his haunches, he reined him in till he rose straight in the air, so that the Count's helmet rang three times against the teeth of the portcullis overhead; then, throwing himself on his neck, like a wolf as he was, the Burckar drove his spurs into the horse's sides with such force that the furious animal, with mane erect, and nostrils quivering with pain and terror, dashed forward like a thunderbolt, and all the others followed at like speed.

'Those who stood in the gateway, under the arched recesses of the guard-room door, saw nothing but a confused mass of tossing manes and tails, croups bounding in the air, iron-shod hoofs striking fire from the pavement, and fluttering robes waving from side to side like banners in the breeze. This lasted only for a second or two between the walls of the advance; but it seemed like some terrible vision, and for long after, amidst the bayings of the hounds and the wailing blast of Honeck's horn, the thundering gallop of the horsemen could be heard in the distance, like the sound of a hundred hammers striking on the anvil.

'At last, Honeck, in his turn, put spurs to his horse, and the rest of the huntsmen followed him on foot, dragged forward by the panting and struggling hounds.

'Once outside the glacis, the cavalcade swept up the face of the Gaisenberg opposite, in order to gain the woods. Rebock, the second huntsman, galloped alongside, having received orders to post the hunters around the animal's retreat, and, when all the arrangements were made, to give three blasts of his horn, as a signal to Honeck to loose the dogs.

'Zapheri led the pack along the bottom of the valley to the left, skirting the shore of the lake, with the object of crossing the glen of the Alders, and thus reaching the marshes of the Losser, from which the foot-prints of the animal could be traced upwards towards the Rock of the Three Wheat-Ears.

'The weather was magnificent. Not a cloud was visible in the blue expanse of heaven; the gigantic oaks, which the autumn was just beginning to touch with brown, and the tall pines, formed a sort of diadem of verdure around the sleeping lake, which reflected every twig and leaf in its glassy surface, as the flowers and mosses and grass are mirrored in some clear mountain spring, which they serve to shelter from the summer breeze. The impatient yelping of the hounds could be heard for miles around. Honeck, without drawing bridle, turned round in his stirrups to get a view of the cavalcade. It was gliding swiftly over the heath and brushwood on the mountainside, rising and felling with the inequalities of the ground, like some immense *banderole* of a thousand variegated colours! It was a glorious sight to see! But in a few minutes it had disappeared from view in the forest. Then the huntsman followed closer on the pack, shouting:

'"All goes well! All goes well! In an hour or two you will see brave sights. Silence! you loud-tongued brawlers; can't you have a little patience? You will have time enough to give tongue by and by. Those who bark the loudest don't always hold the fastest."

'Then the dogs redoubled their cries as they penetrated deeper into the mountain ravine, bordered on each side by an almost perpendicular wall of rock.

'That was a sight for a painter to see, Mr. Theodore, a pack starting for the chase, an immense pack, half dog half wolf, in leashes of six, eight, and ten, their noses in the air, bounding and jumping on each other's backs to get on the faster, and filling the air with their yells and barkings. The first that leaped a mountain stream pulling in the others after them, which turned over and over in the water with their paws in the air, without missing a single bark, so frantic were they for the chase; and the huntsmen, dragged forward by main force, resisting and endeavouring to steady themselves on their legs at every step, for if they had fallen, the dogs would have continued to drag them on over bush and briar without ever looking behind. Then the rocks, the heather, seen by the fitful light that made its way in from above—yes, it would have been a sight worth your seeing, I can answer for it. And the joy of the huntsmen, the excitement caused by the rapid motion, the hope of arriving the first, the idea of distinguishing themselves—all that was worthy of being painted too.

'Never had Honeck felt more confident of success. But when, after advancing in this way for about an hour, the sunlight was seen entering at the opposite end of the gloomy defile, and the dogs, plunging amongst the reedy banks of the Losser, came upon the scent, he began to feel seriously alarmed, for all at once the barking and yelping changed into long furious yells, so savage and melancholy that you could compare it to nothing but the howling of famished wolves, when, crouching in the snow, with their noses between their paws, and their sides drawn in with hunger, they call to each other from one mountain to another, summoning their forces for an attack on the cattle-sheds. Nor is this to be wondered at, for these Burckar dogs had wolves' blood in their veins, like their master, and at times clearly showed their wolfish origin by their manner of squatting on their haunches, or pursuing the game, or stretching themselves to rest, but particularly by their savage howling.

'Honeck, then, on hearing these savage cries, was afraid that the animal, thus warned beforehand, might break through the circle of hunters before the dogs could get up.

'"The devil strangle you!" said he to himself. "Did ever anyone see the like? Hold your tongues, will you, you stupid brutes! Don't you know that the animal will make his escape?"

'But it was in vain he scolded; the Burckar dogs, with their noses in the air, went on howling mournfully as before. In this extremity a brilliant idea struck Zapheri, which showed him to be a true sportsman. As he could not strike the dogs, lest it might only make them redouble their cries, he galloped off before them at full speed, shouting to the huntsman;

'"Hold firm!"

'Then the dogs, thinking that the beast was in view, ceased barking, and tugged at their leashes with incredible fury. At the same moment the three blasts of Rebock's horn echoed from the mountain above, and Honeck, rejoiced at the idea that the pack would now start altogether, immediately ordered them to be uncoupled. In two seconds there was not one of them in the valley. To the right and left, along the rocks, amidst the heather and brambles, for three or four hundred feet up the mountainside, they rushed onward with their noses on the ground, turning, and winding, sometimes bounding on ahead, sometimes doubling back, but never for a moment losing their hold on the scent.

'"Heaven grant that the beast may not have broken away before the circle was made!" exclaimed Honeck.

'All the other huntsmen made the same reflection.

'Zapheri, seeing the hounds thus settled properly to their work, and wishing to assure himself that the circle had been properly formed, spurred straight for the great flat rock that formed the summit of the mountain range, and a quarter of an hour afterwards he was tying his horse to a stunted tree at the foot of the cliff, and climbing up its face on his hands and knees. When he reached the top, from which the eye took in at one sweep the immense horizon on all sides, with all the lower peaks of the range, the wooded valleys between, and, in the far distance on the left, the fertile plains of the Palatinate, he could see at a glance the positions of the hunters and the progress of the chase.

'The first leash of hounds that had been slipped had already passed the cavern of the Three Wheat-Ears—a proof that the animal was no longer there; but, before deciding on his course of action, the huntsman waited for a few minutes longer. About two or three thousand yards to the right he saw the long straggling lines of the Burckar hounds pressing forwards with their noses to the ground, turning, and twisting, and following every winding of the scent, just as you, Mr. Theodore, would follow a line on the paper with your pencil. Not one followed another without himself going round every loop and turn, which proved that they were true hounds, for such trust to nothing but their own noses. In this way they arrived one after another at the beast's cavern, each dog entering, and immediately after leaving it, and then rushing forward with increased speed down the opposite slope of the mountain.

'Honeck, no longer entertaining any doubt of the animal's flight, put his horn to his lips to announce the fact to the hunt. Scarcely had he sounded, when Vittikâb's bugle answered him from the depths below, and instantly he saw the Wild Count start forward from his post at full gallop, following close on the heels of the leading dogs of the pack. Two or three other old hunters—Hatto of Triefels, Lazarus Schwendi, and Elias Rouffacher—followed the Count at full speed; then Vulfhild, in her turn, gave the rein to her palfrey, flying forward like an unhooded falcon, her long robe fluttering behind her; and all the rest of the hunt came after as fast as their horses could carry them.

'Then Honeck, seeing the pack quit the circle which had been formed, sounded the departure for the first relay, and the hunt forthwith swept on with one accord; sixty dogs in front, and fifty horsemen following close behind. It was a marvellous sight to see!

'After watching the chase for a moment, and saying to himself that his master, Vittikâb, was still, as ever, the first hunter in all Germany, that with one glance he could distinguish the false issues, no matter how cunningly contrived, from the true, that no one could drive the game with as steady and sure an eye and hand, Honeck's attention was naturally directed to the animal which the dogs were pursuing, and here he was at once fairly confounded by its strange ruses, its unlooked-for resources, and the complete contrast between its movements and manner of proceeding and those of all the other beasts of the Hôwald.

'In the first place he perceived that this animal never once broke cover, but kept closely within the shelter of the woods, and rather on the outskirts than in the interior, in order apparently to be able to watch his enemies' approach from a distance. That this was so, was plain to be seen, for every minute he saw a file of dogs enter the forest, and immediately leave it again, without ever going far from the margin, and the horsemen following them in like manner. But besides this he was convinced that the animal, when it saw itself hard pressed, endeavoured to elude pursuit by climbing up a tree, for at times the dogs would rush up to some spot in a body, as if sure of the scent, and then all at once would stop short, and begin to circle about with short howls, their noses in the air, and at last would return on their own tracks.

'After two long hours spent in this way, and after many detours, the whole hunt suddenly set off like the wind, Vittikâb leading the way, towards the lower spurs of the mountain range bordering on the plains. The sound of the horns grew fainter and fainter, and at last died away in the distance; only, at long intervals, the blast of the Wild Count's bugle was wafted towards him on the breeze like the hum of some summer insect. The hunt was now more than three leagues on the other side of the Losser, and the two relays of dogs which had been stationed at the Gaisenberg were henceforth useless.

'The day was growing hotter and hotter, and Honeck, who could no longer see anything from his rocky perch, was about to descend, when, in the extreme distance, a faint blast of the Count's bugle, which he would have known amongst a thousand, arrested his steps. He listened eagerly, with his eyes riveted in the direction of the sound. The baying of the dogs was borne upwards confusedly on the mountain echoes, then, suddenly, about half a league from the rock, Vittikâb came in view, alone, sweeping on like lightning towards the edge of the forest. He kept sounding his bugle with a steady furious blast, which made the woods tremble again. A few other horns now began to be heard in the distance; the whole hunt was returning on its steps, after making an immense circuit.

"'I would wager anything," said the huntsman to himself, "that Vittikâb is the only man on the right scent. Although the devil himself could scarcely make anything of it, I would trust him for being in the right."

'But what rejoiced him above all, and made his heart leap, was to hear old Tobie, a tall, broad-chested hound, the best nose and the best voice in the pack, giving tongue at regular intervals, and at each cry to hear the deep blast of the bugle answering, showing evidently that the Count was encouraging on the old hound.

'And in fact, a few minutes afterwards, Zapheri saw them appear in view a full mile below where he stood; only now Tobie was not alone, more than a hundred dogs galloped alongside, and all so close together that it seemed, at that height, as if you could have covered them with your hand. They were then passing through the Heron's Gorge.

'A minute after, old Hatto, then Rouffacher, then several other nobles, and last of all Vulfhild, passed through the gorge. At the head of a second party was old Roterick, who could easily be recognised by his tall figure and the bright red plume in his cap.

"'Ha! ha!" said Honeck to himself, "the chase is coming this way at last."

'And he became more and more attentive. As he was gazing downwards eagerly, no longer thinking of the heat, all at once he

heard Rebock's voice close beside him, calling to him breath-
lessly up a sort of cleft in the rock which was thickly set with
brambles:

"'Master Honeck!'"

"'Hallo! Can that be you, Rebock?" replied he, quite surprised.

"'Yes, it is I. I have just tied my horse here beside yours. What
an animal we have started, Master Zapheri, what an animal! It's
he that can lead a hunt by the nose. Gracious Powers! what a
chase he has given us!"

"'Yes, yes,' replied the chief huntsman, curtly; I saw it all. It
was a fine hunt. I couldn't join in, unfortunately; but even to
see the Wild Count hunt makes a man proud to have such a
master."

"'That's true, Master Honeck; only, look you, I fear we shan't
bring the beast to bay."

"'Well, what then? We'll bring him to bay tomorrow. What
we get without trouble isn't worth the picking up. But hush!
The noise is coming this way. Listen!"

'Vittikâb's bugle was heard echoing through the valley below
like thunder. Honeck leaned forward over the edge of the cliff.
He couldn't see the Count, but the whole pack was rushing like
an arrow towards a deep gorge, some five or six hundred yards to
the left of the plateau where the two men were stationed. This
was the gorge of the Iron Pot, and was so called from its ending
in a perpendicular wall of dark rock, a hundred feet high, and
hollowed out something in the form of a caldron or pot. The
gorge itself, of a horse-shoe shape, was also bounded oil both
sides by perpendicular rocks. Honeck, on seeing the dogs take
this direction, gave a cry:

"'We have him! He has entered the Iron Pot!"

"'Master Honeck," said Rebock, "I would be glad to think
so; but, saving your favour, he's too cunning for that."

"'Remember it's a strange beast, and doesn't know the country," exclaimed Zapheri, clambering down the cleft. Rebock
followed, only half convinced. At the foot of the rock they re-

mounted their horses, and, galloping along the crest of the hill, in five minutes reached a spot right over the head of the gorge. Honeck, who could scarcely contain himself for joy, leaped to the ground, and, throwing the reins to his companion, exclaimed: "Do you hear? Do you hear? The battle is begun already! Was I right, or not?" And, without waiting for a reply, he scrambled forward through the brambles at the top of his speed, whilst Rebock, who had dismounted also, hastily fastened the horses to the trunk of a young beech-tree. That done, he followed Honeck as fast as his legs could carry him.

"'A confused murmur of voices and cries was carried upwards from the Iron Pot. It was easy to conclude from the howling of the dogs, the gnashing of teeth, the snapping of branches, and the various medley of sounds that rose from the abyss below, that the whole pack were engaged in the attack, and that the beast was making a furious resistance.

'The two huntsmen, trembling with eagerness, advanced to the edge of the precipice, end leaned over to see what was going on below. But scarcely had they cast their eyes downwards when they both turned as pale as death. For they saw a sight such as no one had ever seen before them, Mr. Theodore, and one which, please God, no one will ever see again to all eternity!

'And in the first place, picture to yourself this immense funnel or tun-dish, nearly a hundred feet broad and sixty deep, surrounded with its perpendicular wall of rock, glistening like bronze, out of which bubbles a spring of the purest water, as cold as ice, both summer and winter. On the heights above, the sun shines brightly on the heath and brambles, and myriads of insects sport in his beams; light, and warmth, and life are on every side; but in this gloomy moat the sun never shines except at full noonday. On looking down, the first thing that meets your eye are five or six old stunted hollies, that seem as if they required all the heat that enters for themselves, and stretch their branches far and wide to catch it as it falls. Lower down, through their leaves, you can see a confused heap of sharp edged rocks, through which trickles a tiny stream of water over a bed of black pebbles.

'The Creator has put nothing there to please the eye, neither mosses, nor grass, nor anything. It's a regular cut-throat looking den. It serves sometimes as a sort of trap for young wolves or foxes; but never for old ones, for if ever they have the luck to get out of it once you never catch them going there again.

'The only thing at all remarkable in the gorge is a sort of round opening or cave in the perpendicular rock, about ten or twelve feet above the stream, and right in the centre of the wall at the end. How came this cave there? No one knows. It is doubtless the work of nature, like so many others of the like kind, although, from its regular shape, it would almost seem to have been fashioned by man. A few large blocks of rock, lying piled up against the wall, enable one to climb up to it; but it doesn't repay the trouble, as it is only about four feet in depth.

'Well, about fifty or sixty yards to their left, Rebock and Honeck saw, standing in this sort of niche, a creature covered with hair like a bear, about six feet high, and neither man nor beast; for he had two legs like us, very strong and muscular, and a little bowed out at the knees, ending in something like paws furnished with long claws. He had arms too, but his hands were nearly a yard long, and although his face resembled a man's, having the eyes in front, he had the ears of a wolf, a flat nose, and his upper lip was split in the centre, showing a row of enormous teeth.

'In addition to all this, he had such a mass of long yellow hair that it fell about his broad shoulders like a lion's mane. Horrible to look at as this creature must have been at all times, you may imagine its appearance when fighting against the Burckar dogs, whirling round its head with terrific force an enormous branch torn from the trunk of an old oak which had fallen over the precipice, rolling its eyes furiously, grinning so as to show its projecting teeth, and howling in a voice as weird and melancholy as the winds of winter sweeping over the Krapenfeltz. Yes, you may imagine the stupefaction of the two huntsmen at such a sight.

'As for the Burckar hounds, you can also imagine their fury, for you are aware that the greater the astonishment of dogs at seeing any unusual and frightful looking animal, the greater is their rage when they are induced to attack it. Fear seems to render them absolutely savage, and in this way you can account for them not flying before this monster.

'It was a terrific battle, a scene like that of the lions' den which we read of in the Holy Scripture. The dogs were making furious leaps of not less than fifteen feet, sometimes separately, sometimes all together, over the fallen blocks, to endeavour to reach the cave. At times you saw nothing but a mass of gaping jaws encircled with foam, darting upwards; and then the baffled hounds fell back again to earth with broken backs or fractured skulls, or limped off, maimed and crippled, with howls that you could have heard a mile off. Some, who were stretched help-less in the course of the streamlet, turned their heads feebly to lap a few drops of water; others were in full flight, looking behind them from time to time with a furious air, but without the courage to renew the fight; others again, who had come up late, rushed forward, panting, with wide-open jaws, and, without stopping to take breath, entered the howling mass, bounding, snapping, and falling back to earth again with the others.

'At each blow which he dealt with his club, the monster ut-tered a sort of grunt like a wood-cutter swinging his axe. You could see nothing but his two long hairy arms going like the sails of a windmill, his huge head grinning above, his mane fly-ing from side to side at every stroke, and his torn and bleeding legs spread wide apart to enable him the better to keep his bal-ance.

'The barking and howling of the dogs, the sound of blows, and the furious cries of the animal, echoing through the narrow gorge, formed a sort of continuous roar that almost deafened you, whilst the bats and owls, and other birds of night, which had taken refuge at the approach of day in hundreds in the rock-crevices of the Iron Pot, terrified at the uproar, flew wildly up-wards, fluttering and screaming, until, dazzled by the sunlight, they plunged down again into the abyss.

'Amidst all the confusion of the scene, Honeck's observation was attracted to one or two old hounds which crept along close up to the rocky wall, at the one side of the cave, instead of attacking in front, and amongst these he remarked especially old Tobie, whose custom it was always to seize the boar by the ear when turned to bay. He saw him, in this position, crouch low two or three times, as if preparing to spring, and then, judging the distance too great, advancing a little closer, his eyes blazing like two lighted candles. At this sight he felt a thrill of joy, and at the same time a feeling of terror, for to see the monster slaughtering his dogs in this way, and yet not to know whether he was a man or a wild beast, made the big drops of sweat run down his forehead; but still he dared not wish for his death.

'In the midst of this uproar the sound of Vittikâb's horn was heard approaching. He was apparently entering the lower end of the gorge, and was blowing such a furious and prolonged blast, that the brazen notes, echoing from side to side, drowned all the other medley of noises, as a thunder peal drowns the howling of the wind and the roar of the torrent in a storm amongst the mountains. Very soon the clatter of his horse's hoofs over the pebbles could be heard mingling with the roar of the trumpet; but just as the blast was at its loudest, and was already striking the face of the rocky wall in front, a hoarse cry was suddenly heard ascending from the abyss, the bugle notes ceased, and no sound was heard except the furious *mêlée* between the hounds and the strange animal.

'Honeck and Rebock turned their heads in the direction of the sound, and what do you think they saw? At a sharp turn in the gorge Vittikâb had suddenly reined in his horse, throwing the foaming animal on his haunches, and was leaning forward in his saddle as pale as death, his lips wide apart, his eyes staring wildly, and clinging with both hands to the pommel with such an expression of terror in his features that the two huntsmen fancied for a moment that they had some unearthly visitant before their eyes, and a cold shudder ran through every limb.

'At the same moment the animal uttered a terrible cry of distress; you would have said he was calling Vittikâb to his assistance. But it was too late. Tobie had been drawing closer and closer, and now sprang with a terrible bound at his throat. The monster, rolling downward from the mouth of the cave, fell right in the midst of the dogs, and for an instant or two nothing was to be seen but his long sinewy arms raised feebly at intervals above the sea of howling heads; then they sank down, and nothing was to be heard but the deep growling and gnashing of teeth of the dogs at their deadly work.

'Then a terrific cry, like the scream of an eagle defending her young, echoed through the gorge, and Vittikâb, whirling his battle-axe aloft, fell on the writhing heap of dogs like a lion bounding on a pack of wolves, striking and cutting and smashing with indescribable fury. In a few seconds he was covered with the blood and brains of his victims; then, stooping suddenly from his saddle, he seized the animal by his long mane-like hair, and lifted him in his long arms like a loose bundle of rags, shouting at the same time in a hoarse choking voice:

'"Hasoum! Hasoum! it is I!"

'But he spoke to a senseless lump of clay, limp and bleeding, the huge jaws wide open, and the long limbs hanging helplessly down without life or motion. When, after looking closely at him, Vittikâb saw that he was quite dead, with a loud groan of anguish he laid him before him across the saddle, and, dashing the spurs into his horse, rode off at full speed.

'At this moment Honeck and Rebock, as if moved by a common impulse, looked at each other, and both started back, so pale and terror-stricken was the expression of their faces.

'"To the castle!" said Honeck, shivering as if with cold.

'They ran to where their horses were fastened, leaped into the saddle, and, choosing the shortest way, galloped down the mountainside towards the Veierschloss.

'Having reached the foot of the hill, they saw the Count already in the road skirting the lake. He was still holding the body before him on the saddle, and, bending over it with curving nose and teeth hard set, he stared with a stony gaze between his horse's ears, and flew onwards like the wind over the heath, his helmet off and hanging down his back. A long way behind came the rest of the hunt in straggling groups, *seigneurs* and noble *dames*, their robes fluttering and plumes waving in the wind. They had seen the Wild Count pass in front of them as I have described, and the consternation was general.

'Just at this hour Captain Jacobus was pacing backwards and forwards on the battlements of the advance. A great banquet was to be given in the courtyard of the Veierschloss on the return of the hunt, to celebrate the betrothals; and the long tables covered with snow-white damask, which stretched from end to end of the great hall, were loaded with glittering plate which had been pillaged by the Burckars from father to son for hundreds of years. These festivities annoyed the Captain; his mind was running on the thought that a young woman would soon be mistress in the castle, and would look down on the stout-hearted *reiters* from the height of her lofty position. The idea was a most unwelcome one, and he had been thinking ever since the evening before of entering the service of John George the Count Palatine. He was walking up and down, as I have said, with his hands behind his back, musing on all these things, when he perceived in the valley below, where the shadows were now beginning to lengthen, the long cavalcade of knights and ladies sweeping round the lake amidst clouds of dust.

'"Oh, oh!" said he to himself, "here is the hunt returning: the banquet will commence immediately."

'He descended to warn the *wachtmeister*, and the guard had hardly time to lower the bridge, when Vittikâb dashed over it like a thunderbolt, shouting, "Goëtz!—send Goëtz to me!" in so loud and stern a voice that one would have fancied it was the war-cry of the Burckars.

'All the galleries and staircases were' instantly thronged with *reiters* and *trabans*, mustering as if to repel an assault. They saw the Count leap from his horse, and lay the body of the beast on the table of honour, in the middle of the vases of flowers, and the gold and silver cups and vessels. His face was so changed by grief and terror that they would scarcely have recognised it.

'Two or three of the *reiters* climbed up to the Marten's tower to search for Goëtz, and at the same moment, Honeck, Rebock, old Hatto, Lazarus Schwendi, Vulfhild, Boterick, and some fifty others, dashed under the gateway. In an instant the whole courtyard was a scene of noise and tumult; the shouts of the attendants, the clash of arms, and the neighing of horses echoing through every corner of the Veierschloss.

'Vittikâb stood in front of the table, on which he had thrown his helmet beside the body of the beast, and with his mass of red hair, slightly tinged with gray, falling in matted locks over his forehead, his teeth tightly clenched, his eyes starting out of his head, and his thick moustache bristling with rage and agony, he stared at the surrounding crowd, who had gathered round on foot and horseback to gaze at the monster, and, seeing its mouth covered with foam, its cut and bleeding throat, its wolf-like ears, and its great red mane clotted with blood, shuddered inwardly, asking themselves where such a being could have come from.

'The Count, who was deadly pale, seemed to pay no attention to these things. He looked fixedly before him, but without appearing to see anything, and every now and then a sort of convulsive quiver passed over his face. But when the sound of steps was at last heard on the great staircase, he turned round abruptly, and seeing old Goëtz leaning over the balustrade as if petrified, his eyes wide with horror at the sight of the beast, he shouted to him:

'"You did not do what I told you, Goëtz!"

'"My lord, I could not," replied the old man. "I could not bring myself to do it—I let him go. I thought that the Lord would have pity on the poor creature. Do to me according to your good pleasure!"

'"*He* had some bowels of companion," said the Count. "Yes, the servant had pity, the father had none!"

'And, seeing the astonishment of the spectators, he added in a hoarse voice, pointing to the beast:

"'He is my son—he is the last of the Burckars! For the last twenty years I have concealed him in the Marten's tower. I was ashamed of him. At last I determined to kill him. I went up to the tower to tell the old man; he implored me to have pity, he went on his knees to me. I was deaf to his prayers! The old man had more compassion than the father, he let him go."

'In saying this the Burckar's face had such a wild and frantic expression that the spectators grew pale.

"'Listen," said he; "it arose from my shame. I thought to myself, he has the ears of a wolf, people will say the Burckars have ceased to be men, they have become wild beasts—I must hide him! It was the Master above who did that to punish me! For twenty years it has been my dream, night and day, to have children. I massacred those of others from envy of their good fortune. It broke my heart to think of the old race dying out. At last I thought of Roterick. You know, Roterick, how I went to see you. I laughed, but if I could I would have strangled you where you stood, for I am a Burckar, and I hate you and yours. But I laughed, I promised everything, I gave up everything; I wanted your pure blood; I wanted to have children with human faces, real children. Then I ordered the other to be killed!"

'As he went on, he grew more and more excited. His voice, at first low and husky, grew clear and ringing.

"'It is terrible," he continued, as if speaking to himself, "a father ordering his son to be put to death from pride. Oh! I am accursed—accursed to all eternity! Yes, it is terrible. Have you ever read or heard of such a thing?" he exclaimed in a sort of shout. "No, you have never heard of such a thing, there was never anything like it since the creation of the world. It is the old man of Landau who has been the cause of all. Ah, the wretch! If I could only see him burning in the flames once more!"

'Then in a still louder voice he exclaimed:

"'The priest told no lie!"

'No one understood what he meant about the old man at Landau and the priest. Honeck alone remembered the scene. The face of the old blacksmith, dragging his grandson along on a mattress, passed before his eyes like a lightning flash, and also the figure of the bishop, Werner, standing on the steps of the cathedral with outstretched hands, calling down curses on the Burckar, and exclaiming: "Accursed be ye! May the vengeance of the Almighty descend on you all, for you are not men but monsters!" All this flashed on Honeck's memory, and he understood the meaning of Vittikâb's words.

'As the Wild Count went on, his voice was occasionally choked with sobs, and even tears. It was a fearful sight to see such a man weep, and more than one turned their heads in terror; but he now no longer paid any attention to what was going on around him.

'"After all," continued he, "men are a set of cowards—it is they themselves who are to blame. They permit us to work our pleasure on them, they allow us to pillage, to burn and destroy, in place of rising in a body and hunting us like wild beasts. Yes, you are a set of cowards, curses on you too, wretches that you are! For if you had not been a pack of cowards we should not have been what we are. But this poor creature, what had he done that he should be devoured by dogs? What could he do, shut up in a tower? Why did the Master on high not take pity on him?"

'And throwing himself on the monster, and clasping him in his arms, he burst into an agony of tears, exclaiming:

'"Oh, my poor child! you have paid dearly for the sins of your forefathers, you have paid for mine, for Rouch's, for Virimar's, for all our accursed race. Is that just? No, no! It is on us, the real monsters, the monsters of iniquity, that the thunderbolt should have fallen."

'His voice died away, and for a long time nothing was heard but his low sobs. It would have melted the sternest heart to see him. A large number of the *reiters*, beholding their chief, a man noted for his cruel and savage disposition, crying like a child, turned away unable to bear the spectacle. Then, suddenly starting up, and gazing wildly round at the terrified spectators, he exclaimed:

'"I have been crying! Vittikâb crying! Oh, if I could only

purchase another day of life for him by exterminating you all, I would not weep then!"

'His bloodshot eyes glared ferociously. A cold shudder went through the crowd. Then, passing his arm across his eyes, he went on:

"'Ah! if you had seen him fight! He was a Burckar, a true Burckar—one against a host! It was then I knew him—it was then my bowels yearned towards him. I was proud of him—yes, proud of him. If I could only bring him to life again, he should be your master!"

'And, raising both hands to heaven, he shouted in a voice which could be heard across the lake:

"'Rouch, Virimar, Zweitibold, all you my forefathers, will you not come and awaken him? Will you allow the old race to perish?"

'A breathless silence followed. Not a soul moved; every eye and ear were on the stretch. They half expected to see these old brigand nobles, these plunderers and murderers, issue from the vaults of the castle to behold the monster. But in a few moments Vittikab's head sank on his breast, and, looking steadily at Hasoum, he said:

"'It is all over! Thus ends a race of warriors—in monsters! The others, foxes as they are, the Geroldseks and Dagsbourgs, may now divide the spoil—all that we have got by conquest for the last thousand years! They may now enter without fear within the walls of the Veierschloss, they will no longer be met with the wolfs howl of the Burckars that has so often made them tremble. All is indeed over!"

'Then, addressing his retainers:

"'*Trabans* and *reiters*," said he, looking round on them with his yellow gleaming eyes, "take all this gold, this silver, all the treasures that are heaped up in the vaults of Virimar. They are all yours. I give them to you, take them with you. What was got by pillage should go by pillage!"

'Then, raising his long arms wildly above his head, he shouted:

'"And now, let the winds howl, let the night-birds shriek, let the torrents roar, let all the voices of heaven and earth tell this terrible story to future generations, for ages upon ages! And when the poor folks, sitting in the evenings by their firesides, hear these sounds, let them whisper to each other, 'There is the great hunt of the Wild Count crossing the mountain! Do you hear the blast of the horns, and the neighing of the horses, and the baying of the Burckar hounds following on the track of Hasoum?' And, when they hear them, let them remember that One above is the Master of all, and without Him we are nothing!"

'Then he took the monster in his arms, and, hugging him frantically to his breast, he mounted the great staircase amidst profound silence, crossed the gallery, and disappeared from the eyes of the spectators in his vaulted chamber.

'No sooner was he out of sight than the *trabans* and *reiters* threw themselves on the gold and silver plate that covered the tables, broke open the vaults of Virimar, heaped the treasures on their horses, and fled pell-mell. *Margraves, burgraves,* counts, barons, huntsmen and prickers, the old Hatvine herself on her mule, and Goëtz, made their escape as fast as they could from the accursed spot. In an hour's time the Veierschloss was almost as completely deserted as it is at this moment. Honeck alone refused to take any part of the spoil, and remained in the courtyard tying up the dogs, which came in one after the other and took their places in the kennel from habit. He reproached himself terribly for what had happened, attributing the whole misfortune to himself, and cursing himself for ever having entertained the idea of hunting the strange animal. He loved Vittikâb, and sat for a long time watching his door in a very melancholy mood.

'At last, unable to stand it any longer, he mounted the stairs to endeavour to see him and speak to him. He knocked gently at the door, but, there being no answer, he entered, and saw the Wild Count lying stretched on the body of his son. He stood looking at him for a long time without venturing to break the silence. Vittikâb never stirred. It was not until half an hour afterwards, that, hearing Honeck move, he raised his head, showing his face bathed in tears, and said:

"'What have you come here for?"

"'Master, keep me with you."

"'Begone!" replied the Burckar.

"'Master," said Honeck, "all the others are gone; there is no one left to serve you but me."

"'I have no longer need of anyone to serve me!" replied the Count, opening the door and pushing the huntsman outside.

'Honeck heard him shoot the bolts, and descended the stairs. On reaching the courtyard he saw that two more of the hounds had come in, and he tied them up in their places. Then he mounted to his chamber, took his stick, and set off. He reckoned on getting employment without difficulty from some of the neighbouring forest *seigneurs*, as his skill in the chase was well known throughout the entire Hundsrück; but he felt as if his heart would burst on leaving the old castle of the Burckars, where he had spent his youth, and where all his ancestors had lived, from father to son, for hundreds of years.

'He walked on at random, without once turning his head.'

'At last, at nightfall, when passing near the Gaisenberg, he felt a wish to take another look at the old towers, which he had so often saluted with a cheerful flourish of his horn when returning from the chase through the glades of the Hôwald. He climbed the hill to the right, therefore, above the lake, but had not gone far before he saw lying across the path the body of a *reiter*, whom his comrades had murdered for his share of the booty—a thing which happened to many of them that night. The huntsman stepped across the corpse and proceeded on his way. On reaching the top of the hill, he seated himself on a rock amongst the heather, with his stick between his knees, and there he remained till far on in the night, not being able to bring himself to descend on the other side. The moon rose, shedding a melancholy light on the woods and rocks around; the silence grew deeper on the mountain; but still he never moved.

"'Yonder, Honeck," said he to himself, "yonder is your old nest, which you are going to leave, perhaps forever. Who knows if you will ever see it again?"

'He was in despair at the idea of having been the cause, although unintentionally, of such a terrible catastrophe, and the tears ran silently down his great moustache. He was then forty years old, and if it is a difficult thing to tear up a tree at that age to transplant it elsewhere, how much more tender are the fibres of the human heart, and how much deeper do they strike their roots! It seems as if they twined themselves around every stone of the house in which we have spent our early days, and this is the reason, Mr. Theodore, why the poorest peasant clings so closely to his wretched hut. The Lord has arranged that wisely, as He has all the rest.

'Honeck was still sitting there, silently bemoaning himself, when all at once a fire broke out in the Veierschloss, making its appearance first in the hayloft of the cavalry stables and the woodsheds in the inner courtyard. Dense clouds of smoke, mingled with sparks, rose into the sky in huge columns, and, the night being quite calm, formed a sort of funeral canopy over the building. Then the beams and rafters of the old fortress, as dry as tinder with age, took fire and blazed up like straw, and the flames, leaping from storey to storey, climbed up by degrees to the highest towers, and at last completely enveloped them. The waters of the lake below reflected back the appalling catastrophe from its glassy surface, whilst thousands of bats and owls and other birds could be seen against the brilliant background of the flames, winging their flight from the burning castle.

'Honeck at once perceived that Vittikâb had set fire to the building himself, and never moved from his place, knowing that he could be of no use, and could not stay the progress of the flames. He looked on, mute with terror. But what raised his grief to the highest pitch, was to hear the neighing of the horses that had been left in the stables, and the long plaintive howls of the dogs that he himself had fastened in their places. The sounds were carried to him across the lake, like an endless wail, and seemed to burn into his brain, as he thought of the terrible sufferings of the poor animals in that blazing furnace.

'At last his mind gave way. No one knows how long he remained in this state, but some time afterwards a party of poor wood-cutters from Lembach found him wandering in the forest, and brought him to their homes. By degrees his reason returned; but, recognising the hand of the Almighty in what had taken place, he would never again enter the service of a *seigneur*, and became a wood-cutter at Homatt, in the neighbourhood of Pirmasens. Here he led a simple and laborious life, married the daughter of a wood-cutter like himself, and had two children by her.

'I am a descendant of this Honeck.

'As, doubtless, he had grievous faults to expiate, but not so great as to bring on his posterity the lot of the Burckars his masters, our family was afflicted merely with a temporary infirmity. Every autumn one of us falls into a sort of deep sleep, which lasts for two or three days, and which corresponds, in point of time, with the great hunt in which Hasoum perished, and with the burning of the Veierschloss.

'If you wish to know the explanation of all this, Mr. Theodore, I must tell you that the Wild Count then returns to earth, as a punishment for his crimes, and begins over again the hunt of his son Hasoum. This hunt starts from the Veierschloss, descends into the plains of the Palatinate, makes the circuit of , the Hundsrück, including Mount Tonnerre, gains the Vosges by way of Bitche, Lutzelstein, and Lutzelbourg, descends again to the foot of the Jura, and is at last lost to view in the waters of the lake.

'But the most extraordinary thing is, that, all along the route, the Burckar draws after him the souls of the descendants of his former retainers. It comes upon you like a hurricane; your spirit is snatched away at once, leaving your body fast asleep, and away you rush, bounding over rocks, and brambles, and rivers, at the heels of the terrible Burckar dogs, blowing your horn as if you would burst your cheeks, and shouting: "*Hallali! Hallali!*" like one possessed. You are whirled past so many lakes, and mountains, and peaks, and rivers, and are so bewildered with the strange sights you see during these two or three days, that on awaking you fancy it was all a dream!

'This is what used to happen to me in my boyhood, and this is what is now happening to Louise. If I were to take you to her room, you would see her lying there on her bed, with her hands clasped, as colourless as wax, like the figure of a saint in her shrine. But it wouldn't be suitable;—no, you are too young: otherwise I would show her to you, and you would offer up a prayer for her, for this sleep looks just like death. The Burckar came to carry off her spirit last night, just at the moment when the dogs began to howl so loudly. Where are they now? On the peaks of the Jura, in the gorges of the Hôwald, or in the recesses of the Black Forest? Who can tell?'

Father Frantz was silent for a little. And as I looked at him, lost in amazement at this strange story, he went on:

'I thought it right, Mr. Theodore, to tell yon these things, as otherwise you might have formed unjust ideas about us; you might have imagined that I had some bad deeds to conceal, and that I mistrusted you on that account.'

'Ah! Father Honeck,' exclaimed I, ' how could you ever for a moment think'—

'No,' continued he; 'I like openness before everything. Mysteries I look upon as only fit for knaves. When we have nothing to reproach ourselves with, we can tell everything.'

'Well! after all, I suppose you are right, Father Frantz,' replied I, 'and I thank you for the confidence you have placed in me. Your story contains most important instruction for all. It proves that if men, by the proper use of the talents given them, can better their circumstances and improve their moral character; on the other hand, by giving the reins to their appetites and passions, they sink lower and lower in the scale of creation, and at last end by becoming even worse than the brutes. Those who imagine they can outrage the laws of God and man with impunity, on account of their superior strength or cunning, will do well to reflect on this.'

The old forester rose without making any reply.

Meanwhile the day had broken—the first early dawn, spar-

kling with the fresh dewdrops, and perfumed with the sweet
scent of the woods. We walked out into the little garden to enjoy
the pure morning air. The birds were warbling all around, and
the sun was just beginning to peep above the tops of the pine
trees.

'Then you still think of going, Mr. Theodore?' said Father
Honeck.

'Yes; I must leave you, Father Frantz. If I could only remain
here I should be the happiest of men; but I have my living to
earn, and I cannot afford to be idle. I have got a large store
of ideas laid up, and must set to work again. Ah! if I was only
rich!'

'Well, at all events, you will be the better for a few hours'
sleep before you go. I shan't be sorry myself to get a little rest.'

He entered his chamber, and I climbed up to mine. Two or
three hours afterwards the good man pushed open my door, and
seeing me lying with my eyes wide open:

'Well!' said he, with a smile, 'are you rested?'

'Yes, Father Frantz; I even think I have been sleeping, but I
am not quite sure.'

'Well, well,' said he with an air of good humour, 'all the better
if you have.'

And, taking up my knapsack by the strap, he added:

'We must have a crust of bread and a glass of wine together,
and after that I will convey you as far as the Three Fountains.'

In passing along the little gallery with its hanging drapery of
honeysuckle, I felt a sharp pang at the idea of not bidding Louise
farewell. Father Frantz no doubt guessed my thoughts, for, stopping at the door of her room, he said:

'Just wait here for a moment.'

He entered, and returning in a few seconds, made a sign to
me to approach.

'You are now on the point of leaving us,' said he in a low
voice. 'Come! since you are going away, it is quite right you
should see her.'

I approached the bed, and saw Louise lying asleep underneath the little blue curtains, as the old forester had described her to me. She looked more beautiful than I can describe, and I felt then how much I loved her. After a few moments the old man, who stood beside me in an attitude of contemplation, murmured:

'When one thinks that her spirit is elsewhere!—It is strange, is it not?'

And looking at me, with tears in his eyes:

'If her soul was here,' said he, 'Louise would wish you a pleasant journey, and you would kiss her, would you not? Give her a kiss, then; there is no harm in that.'

Trembling with agitation, I pressed my lips lightly on the forehead of the young girl, and then followed the old man slowly out of the room, my heart swelling with mingled feelings of grief and love, and for the last time descended the steps of the old gallery.

After we had breakfasted, Father Frantz accompanied me as far as the Three Fountains, We were deeply moved on parting from each other.

'A pleasant journey, Mr. Theodore,' said the old forester, squeezing my hand warmly in his. 'Won't you think of us sometimes? And if ever you return to the Hundsrück, don't forget Father Frantz's house.'

The only answer I could make was to throw my arms round the old man's neck, and hold him tightly to my breast, as friends do who are bidding each other a long farewell. Then, without saying a word, for my heart felt as if it would burst, I turned into the path of the Three Fountains, and hurried along under the shade of the dark pine trees. But after walking on in this way for a few minutes, feeling my utter loneliness, and thinking of all that I had left behind, of my quiet, peaceful life in the woods, the good old Father Honeck, and Louise, my dear little Louise, I could not help bursting into tears.

Featherston's Story
By Mrs. Henry Wood

I have called this Featherston's story, because it was through him that I heard about it—and, indeed, saw a little of it towards the end.

1

Buttermead, the wide straggling district to which Feathers ton enjoyed the honour of being doctor-in-ordinary, was as rural as any that can be found in Worcestershire. Featherston's house stood at the end of the village. Whitney Hall lay close by; as did our school, Dr. Frost's. In the neighbourhood were scattered a few other substantial residences, some farmers' homesteads and labourers' cottages. Featherston was a slim man, with long thin legs and a face grey and careworn. His patients (like the soldier's steam arm) gave him no rest day or night.

There is no need to go into details here about Featherston's people. His sister, Mary Ann, lived in his house at one time, and for everyday ailments was almost as good a doctor as he. She was not at all like him: a merry, talkative, sociable little woman, with black hair and quick, kindly dark eyes.

Our resident French master in those days at Dr. Frost's was one Monsieur Jules Carimon: a small man with honest blue eyes in his clean-shaven face, and light brown hair cropped close to his head. He was an awful martinet at study, but a genial little gentleman out of it. To the surprise of Buttermead, he and Mary Featherston set up a courtship. It was carried on in sober fash-ion, as befitted a sober couple who had both left thirty years, and the rest, behind them; and after a summer or two of it they laid plans for their marriage and for living in France.

"I'm sure I don't know what on earth I shall do amongst the French, Johnny Ludlow," Mary said to me in her laughing way, when I and Bill Whitney were having tea at Featherston's one half-holiday, the week before the wedding. "Jules protests they are easier to get on with than the English; not so stiff and formal; but I don't pay attention to all he says, you know."

Monsieur Jules Carimon was going to settle down at his native place, Sainteville—a town on the opposite coast, which had a service of English steamers running to it two or three times a-week. He had obtained the post of first classical master at the college there, and meant to eke out his salary (never large in French colleges) by teaching French and mathematics to as many English pupils as he could obtain out of hours. Like other northern French seaport towns, Sainteville had its small colony of British residents.

"We shall get on; I am not afraid," answered Mary Featherston to a doubting remark made to her by old Mrs. Selby of the Court. "Neither I nor Jules have been accustomed to luxury, and we don't care for it. We would as soon make our dinner of bread-and-butter and radishes, as of chicken and apple-tart."

So the wedding took place, and they departed the same day for Sainteville. And of the first two or three years after that there's nothing good or bad to record.

Selby Court lay just outside Buttermead. Its mistress, an ancient lady now, was related to the Preen family, of whom I spoke in that story which told of the tragical death of Oliver. Lavinia Preen, sister to Oliver's father, Gervase Preen, but younger, lived with Mrs. Selby as a sort of adopted daughter; and when the death of the father, old Mr. Preen, left nearly all his large family with scarcely any cheese to their bread, Mrs. Selby told Ann Preen, the youngest of them all, that she might come to her also. So Lavinia and Ann Preen lived at the Court, and had no other home.

These two ladies were intimate with Mary Featherston, all

three being much attached to one another. When Mary married and left her country for France, the Miss Preens openly resented it, saying she ought to have had more consideration. Did some premonitory instinct prompt that unreasonable resentment? I cannot say. No one can say. But it is certain that had Mary Featherston not gone to live abroad, the ominous chain of events fated to engulf the sisters could not have touched them, and this account, which is a perfectly true one, would never have been written.

For a short time after the marriage they and Mary Carimon exchanged a letter now and then; not often, for foreign postage was expensive; and then it dropped altogether,

Mrs. Selby became an invalid, and died. She left each of the two sisters seventy pounds a-year for life; if the one died, the other was to enjoy the whole; when both were dead, it would lapse back to the Selby estate.

"Seventy pounds a-year!" remarked Ann Preen to her sister. "It does not seem very much, does it, Lavinia? Shall we be able to live upon it?"

They were seated in the wainscoted parlour at Selby Court, talking of the future. The funeral was over, and they must soon leave; for the house was waiting to be done up for the reception of its new master, Mr. Paul Selby, an old bachelor full of nervous fancies.

"We must live upon it, Nancy," said Lavinia in answer to her.

She was the stronger-minded of the two, and she looked it. A keen, practical woman, of rather more than middle height, with smooth brown hair, pleasant, dark hazel eyes, and a bright glow in her cheeks. Ann (or Nancy, as she was more often called) was smaller and lighter, with a pretty face, a shower of fair ringlets, and mild, light-blue eyes; altogether not unlike a pink-and-white wax doll.

"We should have been worse off, Nancy, had she not left us anything; and sometimes I have feared she might not," remarked Lavinia cheerfully. "It will be a hundred and forty pounds between us, dear; we can live upon that."

"Of course we can, if you think so, Lavinia," said the other, who deemed her elder sister wiser than anyone in the world, and revered her accordingly.

"But we should live cheaper abroad than here, I expect," continued Lavinia. "It's said money goes twice as far in France as in England. Suppose we were to go over, Nancy, and try? We could come back if we did not like it."

Nancy's eyes sparkled. "I think it would be delightful," she said. "Money go further in France—why, to be sure it does! Aunt Emily is able to live like a princess at Tours, by all accounts. Yes, yes, Lavinia, let us try France!"

★★★★★★

One fine spring morning the Miss Preens packed up their bag and baggage and started for the Continent. They went direct to Tours, intending to make that place their *pied-à-terre*, as the French phrase it; at any rate, for a time. It was not, perhaps, the wisest thing they could have done.

For Mrs. Magnus, formerly Emily Preen, and their late father's sister, did not welcome them warmly. She lived in style herself, one of the leading stars in the society of Tours; and she did not at all like that two middle-aged nieces, of straitened means, should take up their abode in the next street. So Mrs. Magnus met her nieces with the assurance that Tours would not do for them; it was too expensive a place; they would be swamped in it. Mrs. Magnus was drawing near to the close of her life then; had she known it, she might have been kinder, and let them remain; but she was not able to foresee the hour of that great event which must happen to us all any more than other people are. Oliver Preen was with her then, revelling in the sunny days which were flitting away on gossamer wings.

"Lavinia, do you think we can stay at Tours?"

The Miss Preens had descended at a fourth-rate hotel, picked out of the guide-book. When Ann asked this question, they were sitting after dinner in the *table d'hôte* room, their feet on the sanded floor. Sanded floors were quite usual at that time in many parts of France.

"Stay here to put up with Aunt Emily's pride and insolence!" quickly answered Miss Preen. "No. I will tell you what I have done, Ann. I wrote yesterday to Mary Carimon, asking her about Sainteville; whether she thinks it will suit us, and so on. As soon as her answer comes—she's certain to say yes—we will go, dear, and leave Mrs. Magnus to her grandeur. And, once we are safe away, I shall write her a letter," added Lavinia, in decisive tones; "a letter which she won't like."

Madame Carimon's answer came by return of post. It was as cordial as herself Sainteville would be the very place for them, she said, and she should count the hours until they were there.

The Miss Preens turned their backs upon Tours, shaking its dust off their shoes. Lavinia had a little nest of accumulated money, so was at ease in that respect. And when the evening of the following day the railway terminus at Sainteville was reached, the pleasant, smiling face of Mary Carimon was the first they saw outside the *barrière*. She must have been nearly forty now, but she did not look a day older than when she had left Buttermead. Miss Lavinia was a year or two older than Mary; Miss Ann a year or two younger.

"You must put up at the Hôtel des Princes," remarked Madame Carimon. "It is the only really good one in the town. They won't charge you too much; my husband has spoken to the landlady. And you must spend tomorrow with me."

The hotel omnibus was waiting for them and other passengers, the luggage was piled on the roof, and Madame Carimon accompanied them to the hotel. A handsome hotel, the sisters thought; quite another thing from the one at Tours. Mary Carimon introduced them to the landlady, Madame Podevin, saw them seated down to tea and a cold fowl, and then left for the night.

With Sainteville the Miss Preens were simply charmed. It was a fresh, clean town, with wide streets, and good houses and old families, and some bright shops. The harbour was large, and the pier extended out to the open sea.

"I *should* like to live here!" exclaimed Miss Lavinia, sitting down at Madame Carimon's, in a state of rapture. "I never saw such a nice town, or such a lovely market."

They had been about all the morning with Madame Carimon. It was market-day, Wednesday. The market was held on the Grande Place; and the delicious butter, the eggs, the fresh vegetables, the flowers and the poultry, took Miss Lavinia's heart by storm. Nancy was more taken with the picturesque market-women, in their white caps and long gold ear-rings. Other ladies were doing their marketing as well as Madame Carimon. She spoke to most of them, in French or in English, as the case might be. Under the able tuition of her husband, she talked French fluently now.

Madame Carimon's habitation—very nice, small and compact—was in the Rue Pomme Cuite. The streets have queer names in some of these old French towns. It was near the college, which was convenient for Monsieur Carimon. Here they lived, with their elderly servant, Pauline. The same routine went on daily in the steady little domicile from year's end to year's end.

"Jules goes to the college at eight o'clock every week-day, after a cup of coffee and a *petit pain*," said *madame* to her guests, "and he returns at five to dinner. He takes his *déjeûner* in the college at twelve, and I take mine alone at home. On Sundays he has no duty: we attend the French Protestant Church in a morning, dine at one o'clock, and go for a walk in the afternoon."

"You have no children, Mary?"

Mary Carimon's lively face turned sad as she answered: "There was one little one; she stayed with us six months, and then God took her. I wrote to you of it, you know, Lavinia. No, we have not any children. Best not, Jules says; and I agree with him. They might only leave us when we have learnt to love them; and that's a trial hard to bear. Best as it is."

"I'm sure I should never learn to speak French, though we lived here for a century," exclaimed Miss Lavinia. "Only to hear you jabbering to your servant, Mary, quite distracts one's ears."

"Yes, you would. You would soon pick up enough to be understood in the shops and at market."

At five o'clock, home came Monsieur Carimon. He welcomed the Miss Preens with honest, genuine pleasure, interspersed with a little French ceremony; making them about a dozen bows apiece before he met the hands held out to him.

They had quite a gala dinner. Soup to begin with—broth, the English ladies inwardly pronounced it—and then fish. A small cod, bought by Madame Carimon at the fish-market in the morning, with oyster sauce. Ten *sous* she had given for the cod, for she knew how to bargain now, and six *sous* for a dozen oysters, as large as a five-*franc* piece. This was followed by a delicious little *fricandeau* of veal, and that by a *tarte à la crême* from the pastrycook's. She told her guests unreservedly what all the dishes cost, to show them how reasonably people might live at Sainteville.

Over the coffee, after dinner, the question of their settling in the place was fully gone into, for the benefit of Monsieur Carimon's opinions, who gave them in good English.

"Depend upon it, Lavinia, you could not do better," remarked Mary Carimon. "If you cannot make your income do here, you cannot anywhere."

"We want to make it do well; not to betray our poverty, but to be able to maintain a fairly good appearance," said Lavinia. "You understand me, I am sure, *monsieur*."

"But certainly, *mademoiselle*," he answered; "it is what we all like to do at Sainteville, I reckon."

"And *can* do, if we are provident," added *madame*. "French ways are not English ways. Our own income is small, Lavinia, yet we put by out of it."

"A fact that goes without saying," confirmed the pleasant little man. "If we did not put by, where would my wife be when I am no longer able to work?"

"Provisions being so cheap—— What did you say, Nancy?" asked Madame Carimon, interrupting herself.

"I was going to say that I could live upon oysters, and should like to," replied Nancy, shaking back her flaxen curls with a laugh. "Half-a-dozen of those great big oysters would make me a lovely dinner any day—and the cost would be only three half-pence."

"And only fivepence the cost of that beautiful fish," put in her sister. "In Sainteville our income would amply suffice."

"It seems to me that it would, *mesdemoiselles*," observed Monsieur Carimon. "Three thousand five hundred *francs* yearly! We French should think it a sufficient sum. Doubtless much would depend upon the way in which you laid it out."

"What should we have to pay for lodgings, Mary?" inquired Lavinia. "Just a nice sitting-room and two small bedrooms; or a large room with two beds in it; and to be waited on "

"Oh, you won't find that at Sainteville," was the unexpected answer. "Nobody lets lodgings English fashion: it's not the custom over here. You can find a furnished apartment, but the people will not wait upon you. There is always a little kitchen let with the rooms, and you must have your own servant."

It was the first check the ladies had received. They sat thinking. "Dear me!" exclaimed Nancy. "No lodgings!"

"Would the apartments you speak of be very dear?" asked Lavinia.

"That depends upon the number of rooms and the situation," replied Madame Carimon. "I cannot call to mind just now any small apartment that is vacant. If you like, we will go tomorrow and look about."

It was so arranged. And little Monsieur Carimon attended the ladies back to the Hôtel des Princes at the sober hour of nine, and bowed them into the *porte coch*ère with two sweeps of his hat, wishing them the good-evening and the very goodnight.

2

Thursday morning. Nancy Preen awoke with a sick headache, and could not get up. But in the afternoon, when she was better, they went to Mary Carimon's, and all three set out to look for an apartment—not meeting with great success.

All they saw were too large, and priced accordingly. There was one, indeed, in the Rue Lamartine, which suited as to size, but the rooms were inconvenient and stuffy; and there was another small one on the Grande Place, dainty and desirable, but the rent was very high. Madame Carimon at once offered the landlord half-price, French custom: she dealt at his shop for her groceries. No, no, he answered; his apartment was the nicest in the town for its size, as *mesdames* saw, and it was in the best situation—and not a single *sou* would the worthy grocer abate.

They were growing tired, then; and five o'clock, the universal hour at Sainteville for dinner, was approaching.

"Come round to me after dinner, and we will talk it over," said Mary Carimon, when they parted. "I will give you a cup of tea."

They dined at the *table d'hôte*, which both of them thought charming, and then proceeded to the Rue Pomme Cuite. Monsieur Carimon was on the point of going out, to spend an hour at the Café Pillaud, but he put down his hat to wait awhile, out of respect to the ladies. They told him about not having found an apartment to suit them.

"Of course we have not searched all parts of the town, only the most likely ones," said Madame Carimon. "There are large apartments to be had, but no small ones. We can search again tomorrow."

"I suppose there's not a little house to be had cheap, if we cannot find an apartment?" cried Miss Nancy, who was in love with Sainteville, and had set her heart upon remaining there.

"*Tiens,*" quickly spoke Monsieur Carimon in French to his wife, "there's the Petite Maison Rouge belonging to Madame Veuve Sauvage, in the Place Ronde. It is still to let: I saw the *affiche* in the shop window today. What do you think of it, Marie?"

Madame Carimon did not seem to know quite what to think. She looked at her husband, then at the eager faces of her two friends; but she did not speak.

About half-way down the Rue Tessin, a busy street leading to the port, was a wide opening, giving on to the Place Ronde. The Place Ronde agreed with its name, for it was somewhat in form of a horseshoe. Some fifteen or sixteen substantial houses were built round it, each having a shop for its basement; and trees, green and feathery, were scattered about, affording a slight though pleasant shelter from the hot sun in summer weather.

The middle house at the bottom of the Place Ronde, exactly facing the opening from the Rue Tessin, was a very conspicuous house indeed, inasmuch as it was painted red, whilst the other houses were white. All of them had green *persienne* shutters to the upper windows. The shop, a large one, belonging to this red house was that of the late Monsieur Jean Sauvage, "*Marchand de Vin en gros et en détail*," as the announcement over his door used to run in the later years of his life. But when Jean Sauvage commenced business, in that same shop, it was only as a retail vendor. Casting about in his mind one day for some means by which his shop might be distinguished from other wine-shops and attract customers, he hit upon the plan of painting the house red. No sooner thought of than done. A painter was called, who converted the white walls into a fiery vermilion, and stretched a board across the upper part, between the windows of the first and second floors, on which appeared in large letters "*A la Maison Rouge.*"

Whether this sort of advertisement drew the public, or whether it might have been the sterling respectability and devotion to business of Monsieur Sauvage, he got on most successfully. The *Marchand en détail* became also *Marchand en gros*, and in course of time he added liqueurs to his wines. No citizen of Sainteville was more highly esteemed than he, both as a man and a tradesman. Since his death the business had been carried on by his widow, aided by the two sons, Gustave and Emile. Latterly Madame Veuve Sauvage had given up all work to them; she was now in years, and had well earned her rest. They lived in the rooms over the shop, which were large and handsome. In former days, when the energies of herself and her husband were chiefly devoted to acquiring and saving money, they had let these upper rooms for a good sum yearly. Old Madame Sauvage might be seen any day now sitting at a front-window, looking out upon the world between her embroidered white curtains.

The door of this prosperous shop was between the two windows. The one window displayed a few bottles of wine, most of them in straw cases; in the other window were clear flacons of liqueurs: *chartreuse*, green and yellow; *curaçoa*, warm and ruby; *eau de vie de Danzick*, with its fluttering gold leaf; and many other sorts.

However, it is not with the goods of Madame Veuve Sauvage that we have to do, but with her premises. Standing in front of the shop, as if coveting a bottle of that choice wine for today's dinner, or an immediate glass of delicious liqueur, you may see on your right hand, but to the left of the shop, the private door of the house. On the other side the shop is also a door which opens to a narrow entry. The entry looks dark, even in the midday sun, for it is pretty long, extending down a portion of the side of the Maison Rouge, which is a deep house, and terminating in a paved yard surrounded by high buildings. At the end of the yard is a small dwelling, with two modern windows, one above the other. Near the under window is the entrance-door, painted oak colour, with a brass knob, a bell-wire with a curious handle, and a knocker. This little house the late Monsieur Sauvage had also caused to be converted into a red one, the same as the larger.

In earlier days, when Jean Sauvage and his wife were putting their shoulders to the wheel, they had lived in the little house with their children; the two sons and the daughter, Jeanne. Jeanne Sauvage married early and very well, an *avocat*. But since they had left it, the house in the yard seemed to have been, as the Widow Sauvage herself expressed it, unlucky. The first of the tenants had died there; the second had disappeared—decamped in fact, to avoid paying rent and other debts; the third had moved into a better house; and the fourth, an old widow lady, had also died, owing a year's rent to Madame Sauvage, and leaving no money to pay it.

It was of this small dwelling, lying under the shadow of the Maison Rouge, that Monsieur Carimon had thought. Turning to the Miss Preens, he gave them briefly a few particulars, and said he believed the house was to be had on very reasonable terms.

"What do you call it?" exclaimed Lavinia. "The little red house?"

"Yes, we call it so," said Monsieur Carimon. "Emile Sauvage was talking of it to me the other evening at the *café*, saying they would be glad to have it tenanted."

"I fear our good friends here would find it dull," remarked Madame Carimon to him. "It is in so gloomy a situation, you know, Jules."

"*Mon amie,* I do not myself see how that signifies," said he in reply, "If your house is comfortable inside, does it matter what it looks out upon?"

"Very true," assented Miss Lavinia, whose hopes had gone up again. "But this house may not be furnished, Mary."

"It is partly furnished," said Madame Carimon. "When the old lady who was last in it died, they had to take her furniture for the rent. It was not much, I have heard."

"We should not want much, only two of us," cried Miss Ann eagerly. "Do let us go to look at it tomorrow!"

On the following day, Friday, the Miss Preens went to the Place Ronde, piloted by Mary Carimon. They were struck with admiration at the Maison Rouge, all a fiery glow in the morning sun, and a novelty to English eyes. Whilst Madame Carimon went into the shop to explain and ask for the key, the sisters gazed in at the windows. Lying on the wine-bottles was a small black board on which was written in white letters, "*Petite Maison à louer.*"

Monsieur Gustave Sauvage, key in hand, saluted the ladies in English, which he spoke fairly well, and accompanied them to view the house. The sun was very bright that day, and the confined yard did not look so dull as at a less favourable time; and perhaps the brilliant red of the little house, at which Nancy laughed, imparted a cheerfulness to it. Monsieur Gustave opened the door with a latch-key, drew back, and waited for them to enter.

The first to do so, or to attempt to do so, was Miss Preen. But no sooner had she put one foot over the threshold than she drew back with a start, somewhat discomposing the others by the movement.

"What is it, Lavinia?" inquired Ann.

"Something seemed to startle me, and throw me backward!" exclaimed Lavinia Preen, regaining her breath. "Perhaps it was the gloom of the passage: it is very dark."

"*Pardon, mesdames,*" spoke Monsieur Gustave politely. "If the ladies will forgive my entering before them, I will open the *salon* door."

The passage was narrow. The broad shoulders of Monsieur Gustave almost touched the wall on either side as he walked along. Almost at the other end of it, on his left hand, was the *salon* door; he threw it open, and a little light shone forth. The passage terminated in a small square recess. At the back of this was fixed a shallow marble slab for holding things, above which was a cupboard let into the wall. On the right of the recess was the staircase; and opposite the staircase the kitchen-door, the kitchen being behind the *salon*.

The *salon* was nice when they were in it; the paint was fresh, the paper light and handsome. It was of good size, and its large window looked to the front. The kitchen opened upon a small backyard, furnished with a pump and a shed for wood or coal. On the floor above were two very good chambers, one behind the other. Opposite these, on the other side of the passage, was another room, not so large, but of fair size. It was apparently built out over some part of the next-door premises, and was lighted by a skylight. All the rooms were fresh and good, and the passage had a window at the end.

Altogether it was not an inconvenient abode for people who did not go in for show. The furniture was plain, clean and useful, but it would have to be added to. There were no grates, not even a cooking-stove in the kitchen. It was very much the Sainteville custom at that period for tenants to provide grates for themselves, plenty of which could be bought or hired for a small sum. An easy-chair or two would be needed; tea-cups and saucers and wine-glasses; and though there were washing-stands, these contained no jugs or basins; and there were no sheets or tablecloths or towels, no knives or forks, no brooms or brushes, and so on.

"There is only this one sitting-room, you perceive," remarked Madame Carimon, as they turned about, looking at the *salon* again, after coming downstairs.

"Yes, that's a pity, on account of dining," replied Miss Nancy.

"One of our tenants made a pretty *salon* of the room above this, and this the *salle à manger*," replied Monsieur Gustave. "*Mesdames* might like to do the same, possibly?"

He had pointedly addressed Miss Laviaia, near whom he stood. She did not answer. In fact—it was a very curious thing, but a fact—Miss Lavinia had not spoken a word since she entered. She had gone through the house taking in its features in complete silence, just as if that shock at the door had scared away her speech.

The rent asked by Monsieur Gustave, acting for his mother, was very moderate indeed—twenty pounds a-year, including the use of the furniture. There would be no taxes to pay, he said; absolutely none; the taxes of this little house, being upon their premises, were included in their own. But to ensure this low rental, the house must be taken for five years.

"Of course we will take it—won't we, Lavinia?" cried Miss Ann in a loud whisper. "Only twenty pounds a-year! Just think of it!"

"Sir," Miss Lavinia said to Monsieur Gustave, speaking at last, "the house would suit us in some respects, especially as regards rent. But we might find it too lonely: and I should hardly like to be bound for five years."

All that was of course for *mesdames'* consideration, he frankly responded. But he thought that if the ladies were established in it with their *ménage* about them, they would not find it lonely.

"We will give you an answer tomorrow or Monday," decided

Miss Lavinia.

They went about the town all that day with Madame Carimon; but nothing in the shape of an apartment could be found to suit them. *Madame* invited them again to tea in the evening. And by that time they had decided to take the house. Nancy was wild about it. What with the change from the monotony of their country house to the bright and busy streets, the gay outdoor life, the delights of the *table d'hôte*, Ann Preen looked upon Sainteville as an earthly paradise.

"The house is certainly more suited to you than anything else we have seen," observed Madame Carimon. "I have nothing to say against the Petite Maison Rouge, except its dull situation."

"Did it strike you, Mary, apart from its situation, as being gloomy?" asked Lavinia.

"No. Once you are in the rooms they are cheerful enough."

"It did me. Gloomy, with a peculiar gloom, you understand, I'm sure the passage was dark as night. It must have been its darkness that startled me as we were going in."

"By the way, Lavinia, what was the matter with you then?" interrupted her sister.

"I don't know, Nancy; I said at the time I did not know. With my first step into the passage, some horror, seemed to meet me and drive me backward."

"Some horror!" repeated Nancy.

"I seemed to feel it so. I had still the glare of the streets and the fiery red walls in my eyes, which must have caused the house passage to look darker than it ought. That was all, I suppose— but it turned me sick with a sort of fear; sick and shivery."

"That *salon* may be made as pretty a room as any in Sainteville," remarked Madame Carimon. "Many of the English residents here have only one *salon* in their apartments. You see, we don't go in for ceremony; France is not like England."

On the morrow the little house under the wing of the Maison Rouge was secured by the Miss Preens. They took it in their joint names for five years. To complete the transaction they were ushered upstairs to the *salon* and presence of Madame Veuve Sauvage—a rather stately looking old lady, attired in a voluminous black silk robe and a mourning cap of fine muslin. *Madame*, who could not speak a syllable of English, conversed graciously with her future tenants through the interpretation of Mary Carimon, offering to be useful to them in any way she could. Lavinia and Ann Preen both signed the *bail*, or agreement, and Madame Veuve Sauvage likewise signed it; by virtue of which she became their landlady, and they her tenants of the little house for five years. Madame Carimon, and a shopman who came upstairs for the purpose, signed as witnesses.

Wine and the little cakes called *pistolets* were then introduced; and so the bargain was complete.

Oh if some kindly spirit from the all-seeing world above could only have whispered a hint to those ill-fated sisters of what they were doing!—had only whispered a warning in time to prevent it! Might not that horror, which fell upon Lavinia as she was about to pass over the door-sill, have served her as such? But who regards these warnings when they come to us? Who personally applies them? None.

Having purchased or hired the additional things required, the Miss Preens took possession of their house. Nancy had the front bed-chamber, which Lavinia thought rather the best, and so gave it up to her; Lavinia took the back one. The one opposite, with the skylight, remained unoccupied, as their servant did not sleep in the house. Not at all an uncommon custom at Sainteville.

An excellent servant had been found for them in the person of Flore Pamart, a widow, who was honest, cooked well, and could talk away in English; all recommendations that the ladies liked. Flore let herself in with a latch-key before breakfast, and left as soon after five o'clock in the evening as she could get the dinner things removed. Madame Flore Pamart had one little boy named Dion, who went to school by day, but was at home night and morning; for which reason his mother could only take a daily service.

Thus the Miss Preens became part of the small colony of English at Sainteville. They took sittings in the English Protestant Church, which was not much more than a room; and they subscribed to the casino on the port when it opened for the summer season, spending many an evening there, listening to the music, watching the dancing when there was any, and chattering with the acquaintances they met. They were well regarded, these new-comers, and they began to speak French after a fashion. Now and then they went out to a *soirée*; once in a way gave one in return. Very sober *soirées* indeed were those of Sainteville; consisting (as Sam Weller might inform us) of tea at seven o'clock with hot *galette*, conversation, cake at ten (*gâteau Suisse* or *gâteau au rhum*), and a glass of Picardin wine.

They were pleased with the house, once they had settled down in it, and never a shadow of regret crossed either of them for having taken the Petite Maison Rouge.

In this way about a twelvemonth wore on.

3

It was a fine morning at the beginning of April; the sun being particularly welcome, as Sainteville had latterly been favoured with a spell of ill-natured, bitter east winds. About eleven o'clock, Miss Preen and her sister turned out of their house to take a walk on the pier—which they liked to do most days, wind and weather permitting. In going down the Rue des Arbres, they were met by a fresh-looking little elderly gentleman, with rather long white hair, and wearing a white necktie. He stopped to salute the ladies, bowing ceremoniously low to each of them. It was *Monsieur le Docteur* Dupuis, a kindly man of skilful reputation, who had now mostly, though not altogether, given up practice to his son, Monsieur Henri Dupuis. Miss Lavinia had a little acquaintance with the doctor, and took occasion to ask him news of the public welfare; for there was raging in the town the malady called "*la grippe*," which, being interpreted, means influenza.

It was not much better at present. Monsieur Dupuis answered; but this genial sunshine he hoped would begin to drive it away; and, with another bow, he passed onward.

The pier was soon reached, and they enjoyed their walk upon

it. The sunlight glinted on the rather turbulent waves of the sea in the distance, but there was not much breeze to be felt on land. When nearing the end of the pier their attention was attracted to a fishing-boat, which was tumbling about rather unaccountably in its efforts to make the harbour.

"It almost looks from here as though it had lost its rudder, Nancy," remarked Miss Lavinia.

They halted, and stood looking over the side at the object of interest; not particularly noticing that a gentleman stood near them, also looking at the same through an opera-glass. He was spare, of middle height and middle age; his hair was grey, his face pale and impassive; the light over-coat he wore was of fashionable English cut.

"Oh, Lavinia, look, look! It is coming right on to the end of the pier," cried Ann Preen.

"Hush, Nancy, don't excite yourself," said Miss Lavinia, in lowered tones. "It will take care not to do that."

The gentleman gave a wary glance at them. He saw two ladies dressed alike, in handsome black velvet mantles, and bonnets with violet feathers; by which he judged them to be sisters, though there was no resemblance in face. The elder had clear-cut features, a healthy colour, dark brown hair, worn plain, and a keen, sensible expression. The other was fair, with blue eyes and light ringlets.

"Pardon me," he said, turning to them, and his accent was that of a gentleman. "May I offer you the use of my glasses?"

"Oh, thank you!" exclaimed Nancy, in a light tone bordering on a giggle; and she accepted the glasses. She was evidently pleased with the offer and with the stranger.

Lavinia, on the contrary, was not. The moment she saw his full face she shrank from it—shrank from him. The feeling might have been as unaccountable as that which came over her when she had been first entering the Petite Maison Rouge; but it was there. However, she put it from her, and thanked him.

"I don't think I see so well with the glasses as without them; it seems all a mist," remarked Nancy, who was standing next the stranger.

"They are not properly focused for you. Allow me," said he, as he took the glasses from her to alter them. "Young eyes need a less powerful focus than elderly ones like mine."

He spoke in a laughing tone; Nancy, fond of compliments, giggled outright this time. She was approaching forty; he might have been ten years older. They continued standing there, watching the fishing-boat, and exchanging remarks at intervals. When it had made the harbour without accident, the Miss Preens wished him good-morning, and went back down the pier; he took off his hat to them, and walked the other way.

"What a *charming* man!" exclaimed Nancy, when they were at a safe distance.

"I don't like him," dissented Lavinia.

"Not like him! "echoed the other in surprise. "Why, Lavinia, his manners are delightful. I wonder who he is?"

When nearly home, in turning into the Place Ronde, they met an English lady of their acquaintance, the wife of Major Smith. She had been ordering a dozen of *vin* Picardin from the Maison Rouge. As they stood talking together, the gentleman of the pier passed up the Rue de Tessin. He lifted his hat, and they all, including Mrs. Smith, bowed.

"Do you know him?" quickly asked Nancy, in a whisper.

"Hardly that," answered Mrs. Smith. "When we were passing the Hôtel des Princes this morning, a gentleman turned out of the courtyard, and he and my husband spoke to one another. The major said to me afterwards that he had formerly been in the—I forget which—regiment. He called him Mr. Fennel."

Now, as ill-fortune had it, Miss Preen found herself very poorly after she got home. She began to sneeze and cough, and thought she must have taken cold through standing on the pier to watch the vagaries of the fishing-smack.

"I hope you are not going to have the influenza!" cried Nancy, her blue eyes wide with concern.

But the influenza it proved to be. Miss Preen seemed about to have it badly, and lay in bed the next day. Nancy proposed to send Flore for Monsieur Dupuis, but Lavinia said she knew how to treat herself as well as he could treat her.

The next day she was no better. Poor Nancy had to go out alone, or to stay indoors. She did not like doing the latter at all; it was too dull; her own inclination would have led her abroad all day long and every day.

"I saw Captain Fennel on the pier again," said she to her sister that afternoon, when she was making the tea at Lavinia's bedside, Flore having carried up the tray.

"I hope you did not talk to him, Ann," spoke the invalid, as well as she could articulate.

"I talked a little," said Nancy, turning hot, conscious that she had gossiped with him for three-quarters-of-an-hour. "He stopped to speak to me; I could not walk on rudely."

"Anyway, don't talk to him again, my dear. I do not like that man."

"What is there to dislike in him, Lavinia?"

"That I can't say. His countenance is not a good one; it is shifty and deceitful. He is a man you could never trust."

"I'm sure I've heard you say the same of other people."

"Because I can read faces," returned Lavinia.

"Oh—well—I consider Captain Fennel's is a *handsome* face," debated Nancy.

"Why do you call him 'Captain'?"

"He calls himself so," answered Nancy. "I suppose it was his rank in the army when he retired. They retain it afterwards by courtesy, don't they, Lavinia?"

"I am not sure. It depends upon whether they retire in rotation or sell out, I fancy. Mrs. Smith said the major called him Mr. Fennel, and he ought to know. There, I can't talk any more, Nancy, and the man is nothing to us, that we need discuss him."

La grippe had taken rather sharp hold of Lavinia Preen, and she was upstairs for ten days. On the first afternoon she went down to the salon. Captain Fennel called, very much to her surprise; and, also to her surprise, he and Nancy appeared to be pretty intimate.

In point of fact, they had met every day, generally upon the pier. Nancy had said nothing about it at home. She was neither sly nor deceitful in disposition; rather notably simple and unsophisticated; but, after Lavinia's reproof the first time she told about meeting him, she would not tell again.

Miss Preen behaved coolly to him; which he would not appear to see. She sat over the fire, wrapped in a shawl, for it was a cold afternoon. He stayed only a little time, and put his card down on the slab near the stairs when he left. Lavinia had it brought to her.

"Mr. Edwin Fennel."

"Then he is not Captain Fennel," she observed. "But, Nancy, what in the world could have induced the man to call here? And how is it you seem to be familiar with him?"

"I have met him out-of-doors, sometimes, while you were ill," said Nancy. "As to his calling here—he came, I suppose, out of politeness. There's no harm in it, Lavinia."

Miss Lavinia did not say there was. But she disliked the man too much to favour his acquaintanceship. Instinct warned her against him.

How little was she prepared for what was to follow! Before she was well out-of-doors again, before she had been anywhere except to church, Nancy gave her a shock. With no end of simperings and blushings, she confessed that she had been asked to marry Captain Fennel.

Had Miss Lavinia Preen been herself politely asked to marry a certain gentleman popularly supposed to reside underground, she would not have been much more indignantly startled. Perhaps "frightened" would be the better word for it.

"But—you *would* not, Nancy!" she gasped, when she found her voice.

"I don't know," simpered foolish Nancy. "I—I—think him very nice and gentlemanly, Lavinia."

Lavinia came out of her fright sufficiently to reason. She strove to show Nancy how utterly unwise such a step would be. They knew nothing of Captain Fennel or his antecedents; to become his wife might just be courting misery and destruction. Nancy ceased to argue; and Lavinia hoped she had yielded.

Both sisters kept a diary. But for that fact, and also that the diaries were preserved, Featherston could not have arrived at the details of the story so perfectly. About this time, a trifle earlier or later, Ann Preen wrote as follows in hers:

April 16th.—I met Captain Fennel on the pier again this morning. I do think he goes there because he knows he may meet me. Lavinia is not out yet; she has not quite got rid of that Grip, as they stupidly call it here. I'm sure it has gripped *her.* We walked quite to the end of the pier, and then I sat down on the edge for a little while, and he stood talking to me. I do wish I could tell Lavinia of these meetings; but she was so cross the first day I met him, and told her of it, that I don't like to. Captain Fennel lent me his glasses as usual, and I looked at the London steamer, which was coming in. Somehow we fell to talking of the Smiths; he said they were poor, had not much more than the major's half-pay. 'Not like you rich people, Miss Nancy,' he said—he thinks that's my right name. 'Your income is different from theirs.' 'Oh,' I screamed out, 'why, it's only a hundred and forty pounds a-year!' 'Well,' he answered, smiling, 'that's a comfortable sum for a place like this; five *francs* will buy as much at Sainteville as half-a-sovereign will in England.' Which is pretty nearly true.

Skipping a few entries of little importance, we come to another:

May 1st, and such a lovely day!—It reminds me of one May-day at home, when the Jacks-in-the-green were dancing on the grass-plot before the Court windows at Buttermead, and Mrs. Selby sat watching them, as pleased as they were, saying she should like to dance, too, if she could only go first to the mill to be ground young again. Jane and Edith Peckham were spending the day with us. It was just such a day as this, warm and bright; light, fleecy

160

clouds flitting across the blue sky. I wish Lavinia were out to enjoy it! but she is hardly strong enough for long walks yet, and only potters about, when she does get out, in the Rue des Arbres or the Grande Place, or perhaps over to see Mary Carimon.

I don't know what to do. I lay awake all last night, and sat moping yesterday, thinking what I *could* do. Edwin wants me to marry him; I told Lavinia, and she absolutely forbids it, saying I should rush upon misery. *He* says I should be happy as the day's long. I feel like a distracted lunatic, not knowing which of them is right, or which opinion I ought to yield to. I have obeyed Lavinia all my life; we have never had a difference before; her wishes have been mine, and mine have been hers. But I *can't* see why she need have taken up this prejudice against him, for I'm sure he's more like an angel than a man; and, as he whispers to me, Nancy Fennel would be a prettier name than Nancy Preen. I said to him today, 'My name is Ann, not really Nancy.' 'My dear,' he answered, ' I shall always call you Nancy; I love the simple name.'

I no longer talk about him to Lavinia, or let her suspect that we still meet on the pier. It would make her angry, and I can't bear that. I dare not hint to her what Edwin said today—-that he should take matters into his own hands. He means to go over to Dover, *via* Calais; stay at Dover a fortnight, as the marriage law requires, and then come back to fetch me; and after the marriage has taken place we shall return here to live.

Oh dear, what am I to do? It will be a *dreadful* thing to deceive Lavinia; and it will be equally dreadful to lose *him*. He declares that if I do not agree to this he shall set sail for India (where he used to be with his regiment), and never, never see me again. Good gracious! *never* to see me again!

The worst is, he wants to go off to Dover at once, giving one no time for consideration! Must I say Yes, or No? The uncertainty shakes me to pieces. He laughed today when I said something of this, assuring me Lavinia's anger would pass away like a summer cloud when I was his wife; that sisters had no authority over one another, and that Lavinia's opposition arose from selfishness only, because she did not want to lose me. 'Risk it, Nancy,' said he; 'she will receive you with open arms when I bring you back from Dover,' If I could only think so! Now and then I feel inclined to confide my dilemma to Mary Carimon, and ask her opinion, only that I fear she might tell Lavinia.

Mr. Edwin Fennel quitted Sainteville. When he was missed people thought he might have gone for good. But one Saturday morning some time onwards, when the month of May was drawing towards its close, Miss Lavinia, out with Nancy at market, came full upon Captain Fennel in the crowd on the Grande Place. He held out his hand.

"I thought you had left Sainteville, Mr. Fennel," she remarked, meeting his hand and the sinister look in his face unwillingly.

"Got back this morning," he said; "travelled by night. Shall be leaving again today or tomorrow. How are *you*, Miss Nancy?"

Lavinia pushed her way to the nearest poultry stall. "Will you come here, Ann?" she said. "I want to choose a fowl."

She began to bargain, half in French, half in English, with the poultry man, all to get rid of that other man, and she looked round, expecting Nancy had followed her. Nancy had not stirred from the spot near the butter-baskets: she and Captain Fennel had their heads together, he talking hard and fast.

They saw Lavinia looking at them; looking angry, too, "Remember," impressively whispered Captain Fennel to Nancy: and, lifting his hat to Lavinia, over the white caps of the market-women, he disappeared across the Place.

"I wonder what that man has come back for?" cried Miss Preen, as Nancy reached her—not that she had any suspicion. "And I wonder you should stay talking with him, Nancy!" Nancy did not answer.

Sending Flore—who had attended them with her market-basket—home with the fowl and eggs and vegetables, they called at the butcher's and the grocer's, and then went home themselves. Miss Preen then remembered that she had forgotten one or two things, and must go out again. Nancy remained at home. When Lavinia returned, which was not for an hour, for she had met various friends and stayed to gossip, her sister was in her room. Flore thought Mademoiselle Nancy was setting her drawers to rights: she had heard her opening and shutting them.

Time went on until the afternoon. Just before five o'clock, when Flore came in to lay the cloth for dinner, Lavinia, sitting at the window, saw her sister leave the house and cross the yard, a good-sized paper parcel in her hand.

"Why, that is Miss Nancy," she exclaimed, in much surprise. "Where can she be going to now?"

"Miss Nancy came down the stairs as I was coming in here," replied Flore. "She said to me that she had just time to run to Madame Carimon's before dinner."

"Hardly," dissented Miss Lavinia. "What can she be going for?"

As five o'clock struck, Flore (always punctual, from self-interest) came in to ask if she should serve the fish; but was told to wait until Miss Nancy returned. When half-past five was at hand, and Nancy had not appeared, Miss Preen ordered the fish in, remarking that Madame Carimon must be keeping her sister to dinner.

Afterwards Miss Preen set out for the *casino*, expecting she should meet them both there; for Lavinia and Nancy had intended to go. Madame Carimon was not a subscriber, but she sometimes paid her ten *sous* and went in. It would be quite a pretty sight tonight—a children's dance. Lavinia soon joined some friends there, but the others did not come.

At eight o'clock she was in the Rue Pomme Cuite, approaching Madame Carimon's. Pauline, in her short woollen petticoats, and shoeless feet thrust into wooden *sabots*, was splashing buckets of water before the door to scrub the pavement, and keeping up a screaming chatter with the other servants in the street, who were doing the same, Saturday-night fashion.

Madame Carimon was in the *salon*, sitting idle in the fading light; her sewing lay on the table. Lavinia's eyes went round the room, but she saw no one else in it.

"Mary, where is Nancy?" she asked, as Madame Carimon rose to greet her with outstretched hands.

"I'm sure I don't know," answered Madame Carimon lightly. "She has not been here. Did you think she had?"

"She dined here—did she not?"

"What, Nancy? Oh no! I and Jules dined alone. He is out now, giving a French lesson. I have not seen Nancy since—let me see—since Thursday, I think; the day before yesterday."

Lavinia Preen sat down, half-bewildered. She related the history of the evening.

"It is elsewhere that Nancy is gone," remarked Madame Carimon. "Flore must have misunderstood her."

Concluding that to be the case, and that Nancy might already be at home, Lavinia returned at once to the Petite Maison Rouge, Mary Carimon bearing her company in the sweet summer twilight. Lavinia opened the door with her latch-key. Flore had departed long before. There were three latch-keys to the house, Nancy possessing one of them.

They looked into every room, and called out "Nancy! Nancy!" But she was not there.

Nancy Preen had gone off with Captain Fennel by the six-o'clock train, *en route* for Dover, there to be converted into Mrs. Fennel.

And had Nancy foreseen the terrible events and final crime which this most disastrous step would bring about, she might have chosen, rather than take it, to run away to the Protestant cemetery outside the gates of Sainteville, there to lay herself down to die.

4

"Where *can* Nancy be?"

Miss Preen spoke these words to Mary Carimon in a sort of flurry. After letting themselves into the house, the Petite Maison

Rouge, and calling up and down it in vain for Nancy, the question as to where she could be naturally arose.

"She must be spending the evening with the friends she stayed to dine with," said Madame Carimon.

"I don't know where she would be likely to stay. Unless—yes—perhaps at Mrs. Hardy's."

"That must be it, Lavinia," pronounced Madame Carimon.

It was then getting towards nine o'clock. They set out again for Mrs. Hardy's to escort Nancy home. She lived in the Rue Lothaire; a long street, leading to the railway-station.

Mrs. Hardy was an elderly lady. When near her door they saw her grand-nephew, Charles Palliser, turn out of it. Charley was a good-hearted young fellow, the son of a rich merchant in London. He was staying at Sainteville for the purpose of acquiring the art of speaking French as a native.

"Looking for Miss Ann Preen!" cried he, as they explained in a word or two. "No, she is not at our house; has not been there. I saw her going off this evening by the six-o'clock train."

"Going off by the six-o'clock train!" echoed Miss Lavinia, staring at him. "Why, what do you mean, Mr, Charles? My sister has not gone off by any train."

"It was in this way," answered the young man, too polite to flatly contradict a lady. "Mrs. Hardy's cousin, Louise Soubitez, came to town this morning; she spent the day with us, and after dinner I went to see her off by the train. And there, at the station, was Miss Ann Preen."

"But not going away by train," returned Miss Lavinia.

"Why, yes, she was. I watched the train out of the station. She and Louise Soubitez sat in the same compartment."

A smile stole to Charles Palliser's face. In truth, he was amused at Miss Lavinia's consternation. It suddenly struck her that the young man was joking.

"Did you speak to Ann, Mr. Charles?"

"Oh yes; just a few words. There was not time for much conversation; Louise was late."

Miss Preen felt a little shaken.

"Was Ann alone?"

"No; she was with Captain Fennel."

And, with that, a suspicion of the truth, and the full horror of it, dawned upon Lavinia Preen. She grasped Madame Carimon's arm and turned white as death.

"It never can be," she whispered, her lips trembling; "it never can be! She cannot have—have—run away—with that man!"

Unconsciously perhaps to herself, her eyes were fixed on Charles. He thought the question was put to him, and answered it.

"Well—I—I'm afraid it looks like it, as she seems to have said nothing to you," he slowly said. "But I give you my word, Miss Preen, that until this moment that aspect of the matter never suggested itself to me. I supposed they were just going up the line together for some purpose or other; though, in fact, I hardly thought about it at all."

"And perhaps that is all the mystery!" interposed Madame Carimon briskly. "He may have taken Ann to Drecques for a little jaunt, and they will be back again by the last train. It must be almost due, Lavinia."

With one impulse they turned to the station, which was near at hand. Drecques, a village, was the first place the trains stopped at on the up-line. The passengers were already issuing from the gate. Standing aside until all had passed, and not seeing Nancy anywhere, Charley Palliser looked into the omnibuses. But she was not there.

"They may have intended to come back and missed the train. Miss Preen; it's very easy to miss a train," said he in his good nature.

"I think it must be so, Lavinia," spoke up Madame Carimon. "Any way, we will assume it until we hear to the contrary. And, Charley, we had better not talk of this tonight."

"*I* won't," answered Charley earnestly. "You may be sure of me."

Unless Captain Fennel and Miss Ann Preen chartered a balloon, there was little probability of their reaching Sainteville that evening, for this had been the last train. Lavinia Preen passed a night of discomfort, striving to *hope against hope*, as the saying runs. Not a very wise saying; it might run better, striving to hope against despair.

When Sunday did not bring back the truants, or any news of them, the three in the secret—Mary Carimon, Lavinia, and Charley Palliser—had little doubt that the disappearance meant an elopement. Monsieur Jules Carimon, not easily understanding such an escapade, so little in accordance with the customs and manners of his own country, said in his wife's ear he hoped it would turn out that there was a marriage in the case.

Miss Preen received a letter from Dover pretty early in the week, written by Ann. She had been married that day to Captain Fennel.

Altogether, the matter was the most bitter blow ever yet dealt to Lavinia Preen. No living being knew, or ever would know, how cruelly her heart was wrung by it. But, being a kindly woman of good sound sense, she saw that the best must be made of it, not the worst; and this she set herself out to do. She began by hoping that her own instinct, warning her against Captain Fennel, might be a mistaken one, and that he had a good home to offer his wife and would make her happy in it.

She knew no more about him—his family, his fortune, his former life, his antecedents—than she knew of the man in the moon. Major Smith perhaps did; he had been acquainted with him in the past. Nancy's letter, though written the previous day, had been delivered by the afternoon post. As soon as she could get dinner over, Lavinia went to Major Smith's. He lived at the top of the Rue Lambeau, a street turning out of the Grande Place. He and his wife, their own dinner just removed, were sitting together, the major indulging in a steaming glass of *schiedam* and water, flavoured with a slice of lemon. He was a very jolly little man, with rosy cheeks and a bald head. They welcomed Miss Lavinia warmly. She, not quite as composed as usual, opened her business without preamble; her sister Ann had married Captain Fennel, and she had come to ask Major Smith what he knew of him.

"Not very much," answered the major.

There was something behind his tone, and Lavinia burst into tears. Compassionating her distress, the major offered her a comforting glass, similar to his own. Lavinia declined it.

"You will tell me what you know," she said: and he proceeded to do so.

Edwin Fennel, the son of Colonel Fennel, was stationed in India with his regiment for several years. He got on well enough, but was not much liked by his brother officers: they thought him unscrupulous and deceitful. All at once, something very disagreeable occurred, which obliged Captain Fennel to quit Her Majesty's service. The affair was hushed up, out of consideration to his family and his father's long-term of service. "In fact, I believe he was allowed to retire, instead of being cashiered," added the major, "but I am not quite sure which it was."

"What was it that occurred—that Captain Fennel did, to necessitate his dismissal?" questioned Lavinia.

"I don't much like to mention it," said the major, shaking his head. "It might get about, you see. Miss Preen, which would make it awkward for him. I have no wish, or right either, to do the man a gratuitous injury."

"I promise you it shall not get about through me," returned Lavinia; "my sister's being his wife will be the best guarantee for that. You must please tell me. Major Smith."

"Well, Fennel was suspected—detected, in short—of cheating at cards."

Lavinia drew a deep breath. "Do you know," she said presently, in an undertone, "that when I first met the man I shrank from his face."

"Oh my! And it has such nice features!" put in Mrs. Smith, who was but a silly little woman.

"There was something in its shifty look which spoke to me as a warning," continued Lavinia. "It did, indeed. All my life I have been able to read faces, and my first instinct has rarely, if ever, deceived me. Each time I have seen this man since, that instinct against him has become stronger."

Major Smith took a sip at his *schiedam*. "I believe—between ourselves—he is just a *mauvais sujet*," said he. "He has a brother who is one, out and out; as I chance to know."

"What is Edwin Fennel's income, major?"

"I can't tell at all. I should not be surprised to hear that he has none."

"How does he live then?" asked Lavinia, her heart going at a gallop.

"Don't know that either," said the major. "His father is dead now and can't help him. A very respectable man, the old colonel, but always poor."

"He cannot live upon air; he must have some means," debated Lavinia.

"Lives upon his wits, perhaps; some men do. He wanted to borrow ten pounds from me a short time ago," added the major, taking another sip at his tumbler; "but I told him I had no money to lend—which was a fact. I have an idea that he got it out of Charley Palliser."

The more Lavinia Preen heard of this unhappy case, the worse it seemed to be. Declining to stay for tea, as Mrs. Smith wished, she betook her miserable steps home again, rather wishing that the sea would swallow up Captain Fennel.

The next day she saw Charles Palliser. Pouncing upon him as he was airing his long legs in the Grande Place, she put the question to him in so determined a way that Charley had no chance against her. He turned red.

"I don't know who can have set that about," said he. "But it's true. Miss Preen. Fennel pressed me to lend him ten pounds for a month; and I—well, I did it. I happened to have it in my pocket, you see, having just cashed a remittance from my father."

"Has he repaid you, Mr. Charles? "

"Oh, the month's not quite up yet," cried Charley. "Please don't talk of it. Miss Preen; he wouldn't like it, you know. How on earth it has slipped out I can't imagine."

"No, I shall not talk of it," said Lavinia, as she wished him good-day and walked onwards, wondering what sort of a home Captain Fennel meant to provide for Ann.

Lavinia Preens cup of sorrow was not yet full. A morning or two after this she was seated at breakfast with the window open, when she saw the postman come striding across the yard with a letter. It was from the bride; a very short letter, and one that Miss Lavinia did not at once understand. She read it again.

My dear Lavinia,

All being well, we shall be home tomorrow; that is, on the day you receive this letter; reaching Sainteville by the last train in the evening. Please get something nice and substantial for tea, Edwin says, and please see that Flore has the bedroom in good order.

Your affectionate sister,

Ann Fennel.

The thing that Miss Lavinia did, when comprehension came to her, was to fly into a passion.

"Come home here—*he!*—is that what she means?" cried she. "Never. Have that man in my house? Never, never."

"But what has *mademoiselle* received?" exclaimed Flore, appearing just then with a boiled egg. "Is it bad news?"

"It is news that I will not put up with—will not tolerate," cried Miss Lavinia. And, in the moment's dismay, she told the woman what it was.

"*Tiens!*" commented Flore, taking a common-sense view of matters: "they must be coming just to show themselves to *mademoiselle* on their marriage. Likely enough they will not stay more than a night or two, while looking out for an apartment."

Lavinia did not believe it; but the very suggestion somewhat soothed her. To receive that man even for a night or two, as Flore put it, would be to her most repugnant, cruel pain, and she resolved not to do it. Breakfast over, she carried the letter and her trouble to the Rue Pomme Cuite.

"But I am afraid, Lavinia, you cannot refuse to receive them," spoke Madame Carimon, after considering the problem.

"Not refuse to receive them!" echoed Lavinia. "Why do you say that?"

"Well," replied Mary Carimon uneasily, for she disliked to add to trouble, "you see the house is as much Ann's as yours. It was taken in your joint names. Ann has the right to return to it; and also, I suppose"—more dubiously—"to introduce her husband into it."

"Is that French law?"

"I think so. I'll ask Jules when he comes home to dinner. Would it not be English law also, Lavinia?"

Lavinia was feeling wretchedly uncomfortable. With all her plain common-sense, this phase of the matter had not struck her.

"Mary," said she—and there stopped, for she was seized with a violent shivering, which seemed difficult to be accounted for. "Mary, if that man has to take up his abode in the house, I can never remain in it, I would rather die."

"Look here, dear friend," whispered Mary: "life is full of trouble—as Job tells us in the Holy Scriptures—none of us are exempt from it. It attacks us all in turn. The only one thing we can do is to strive to make the best of it, under God; to ask Him to help us. I am afraid there is a severe cross before you, Lavinia; better *bear* it than fight against it."

"I will never bear *that*," retorted Lavinia, turning a deaf ear in her anger. "You ought not to wish me to do so."

"And I would not if I saw anything better for you."

Madame Veuve Sauvage, sitting as usual at her front-window that same morning, was surprised at receiving an early call from her tenant, Miss Preen. *Madame* handed her into her best crimson velvet *fauteuil*, and they began talking.

Not to much purpose, however; for neither very well understood what the other said. Lavinia tried to explain the object of her visit, but found her French was not equal to it. Madame called her maid, Mariette, and sent her into the shop below to ask Monsieur Gustave to be good enough to step up.

Lavinia had gone to beg of them to cancel the agreement for

the little house, so far as her sister was concerned, and to place it in her name only.

Monsieur Gustave, when he had mastered the request, politely answered that such a thing was not practicable; Miss Ann's name could not be struck out of the lease without her consent, or, as he expressed it, breaking the *bail*. His mother and himself had every disposition to oblige Miss Preen in any way, as indeed she must know, but they had no power to act against the law.

So poor Miss Lavinia went into her home wringing her hands in despair. She was perfectly helpless.

5

The summer days went on. Mr. Edwin Fennel, with all the impudence in the world, had taken up his abode in the Petite Maison Rouge, without saying with your leave or by your leave.

"How could you *think* of bringing him here, Ann?" Lavinia demanded of her sister in the first days.

"I did not think of it; it was he thought of it," returned Mrs. Fennel in her simple way. "I feared you would not like it, Lavinia; but what could I do? He seemed to look upon it as a matter of course that he should come."

Yes, there he was; "a matter of course;" making one in the home. Lavinia could not show fight; he was Ann's husband, and the place was as much Ann's as hers. The more Lavinia saw of him the more she disliked him; which was perhaps unreasonable, since he made himself agreeable to her in social intercourse, though he took care to have things his own way. If Lavinia's will went one way in the house and his the other, she found herself smilingly set at naught. Ann was his willing slave; and when opinions differed she sided with her husband.

It was no light charge, having a third person in the house to live upon their small income, especially one who studied his appetite. For a very short time Lavinia, in her indignation at affairs generally, turned the housekeeping over to Mrs. Fennel. But she had to take to it again. Ann was naturally an incautious manager; she ordered in delicacies to please her husband's palate without regard to cost, and nothing could have come of that but debt and disaster.

That the gallant ex-Captain Fennel had married Ann Preen just to have a roof over his head, Lavinia felt as sure of as that the moon occasionally shone in the heavens. She did not suppose he had any other refuge in the wide world. And through something told her by Ann she judged that he had believed he was doing better for himself in marrying than he had done.

The day after the marriage Mr. and Mrs. Fennel were sitting on a bench at Dover, romantically gazing at the sea, honeymoon fashion, and talking of course of hearts and darts. Suddenly the bridegroom turned his thoughts to more practical things.

"Nancy, how do you receive your money—half-yearly or quarterly?" asked he.

"Oh, quarterly," said Nancy. "It is paid punctually to us by the acting-trustee, Colonel Selby."

"Ah, yes. Then you have thirty-five pounds every quarter?"

"Between us, we do," assented Nancy. "Lavinia has seventeen pounds ten, and I have the same; and the colonel makes us each give a receipt for our own share."

Captain Fennel turned his head and gazed at her with a hard stare.

"You told me your income was a hundred and forty pounds a-year."

"Yes, it is that exactly," said she quietly; "mine and Lavinia's together. We do not each have that, Edwin; I never meant to imply—"

Mrs. Fennel broke off, frightened. On the captain's face, cruel enough just then, there sat an expression which she might have thought diabolical had it been anyone else's face. Any way, it scared her.

"What is it?" she gasped.

Rising rapidly, Captain Fennel walked forward, caught up some pebbles, flung them from him and waited, apparently watching to see where they fell. Then he strolled back again.

"Were you angry with me?" faltered Nancy. "Had I done

anything?"

"My dear, what should you have done? Angry?" repeated he, in a light tone, as if intensely amused. "You must not take up fancies, Mrs. Fennel."

"I suppose Mrs. Selby thought it would be sufficient income for us, both living together," remarked Nancy. "If either of us should die it all lapses to the other. We found it quite enough last year, I assure you, Edwin; Sainteville is so cheap a place."

"Oh, delightfully cheap!" agreed the captain.

It was this conversation that Nancy repeated to Lavinia; but she did not speak of the queer look which had frightened her. Lavinia saw that Mr, Edwin Fennel had taken up a wrong idea of their income. Of course the disappointment angered him.

An aspect of semi-courtesy was outwardly maintained in the intercourse of home life. Lavinia was a gentlewoman; she had not spoken unpleasant things to the captain's face, or hinted that he was a weight upon the housekeeping pocket; whilst he, as yet, was quite officiously civil to her. But there was no love lost between them; and Lavinia could not divest her mind of an undercurrent of conviction that he was, in some way or other, a man to be dreaded.

Thus Captain Fennel (as he was mostly called), being dom- iciled with the estimable ladies in the Petite Maison Rouge, grew to be considered one of the English colony of Sainteville, and was received as such. As nobody knew aught against him, nobody thought anything. Major Smith had not spoken of an- tecedents, neither had Miss Preen; the Carimons, who were in the secret, never spoke ill of any one: and as the captain could assume pleasing manners at will, he became fairly well liked by his country-people in a passing sort of way.

Lavinia Preen sat one day upon the low edge of the pier, her back to the sun and the sea. She had called in at the little shoe- shop on the port, just as you turn out of the Rue Tessin, and had left her parasol there. The sun was not then out in the grey sky, and she did not miss it. Now that the sun was shining, and the grey canopy above had become blue, she said to herself that she had been stupid. It was September weather, so the sun was not unbearable.

Lavinia Preen was thinner; the thraldom of the past three months had made her so. Now and then it would cross her mind to leave the Petite Maison Rouge to its married inmates; but for Nancy's sake she hesitated. Nancy had made the one love of her life, and Nancy had loved her in return. Now, the love was chiefly given to the new tie she had formed; Lavinia was second in every respect.

"They go their way now, and I have to go mine," sighed Lavinia, as she sat this morning on the pier. "Even my walks have to be solitary."

A cloud came sailing up and the sun went in again. Lavinia rose; she walked onwards till she came to the end of the pier, where she again sat down. The next moment, chancing to look the way she had come, she saw a lady and gentleman advancing arm-in-arm.

"Oh, *they* are on the pier, are they!" mentally spoke Lavinia. For it was Mr. and Mrs. Edwin Fennel.

Nancy sat down beside her. "It is a long walk!" cried she, drawing a quick breath or two. "Lavinia, what do you think we have just heard?"

"How can I tell?" returned the elder sister.

"You know those queer people, an old English aunt and three nieces, who took Madame Gibon's rooms in the Rue Ménar? They have all disappeared and have paid nobody," continued Nancy. "Charley Palliser told us just how; he was laughing like anything over it."

"I never thought they looked like people to be trusted," remarked Lavinia. "Dear me! here's the sun coming out again."

"Where is your parasol?"

Lavinia recounted her negligence in having left it at the shoe-mart. Captain Fennel had brought out a small silk umbrella; he turned from the end of the pier, where he stood looking out to sea, opened the umbrella, and offered it.

"It is not much larger than a good-sized parasol," remarked

he. "Pray take it, Miss Lavinia."

Lavinia did so after a moment's imperceptible hesitation, and thanked him. She hated to be under the slightest obligation to him, but the sun was now full in her eyes, and might make her head ache.

The pleasant smell of a cigar caused them to look up. A youngish man, rather remarkably tall, with a shepherd's plaid across his broad shoulders, was striding up the pier. He sat down near Miss Preen, and she glanced round at him. Appearing to think that she looked at his cigar, he immediately threw it into the sea behind him.

"Oh, I am sorry you did that," said Lavinia, speaking impulsively. "I like the smell of a cigar."

"Oh, thank you; thank you very much," he answered. "I had nearly smoked it out."

Voice and manner were alike pleasant and easy, and Lavinia spoke again—some trivial remark about the fine expanse of sea; upon which they drifted into conversation. We are reserved enough with strangers at home, we Islanders, as the world knows, but most of us are less ungracious abroad.

"Sainteville seems a clean, healthy place," remarked the newcomer.

"Very," said Miss Lavinia. "Do you know it well?"

"I never saw it before today," he replied. "I have come here from Douai to meet a friend, having two or three days to spare."

"Douai is a fine town," remarked Captain Fennel, turning to speak, for he was still looking out over the sea, and had his opera-glasses in his hand. "I spent a week there not long ago."

"Douai!" exclaimed Nancy. "That's the place where the great Law Courts are, is it not? Don't you remember the man last year, Lavinia, who committed some dreadful crime, and was taken up to Douai to be tried at the Assizes there?"

"We have a great case coming on there as soon as the Courts meet," said the stranger, who seemed a talkative man; "and that's what I am at Douai for. A case of extensive swindling."

"You are a lawyer, I presume?" said Miss Preen.

The stranger nodded; "Being the only one of our London firm who can speak French readily, and we are four of us in it, I had to come over and watch this affair and wait for the trial. For the young fellow is an Englishman, I am sorry to say, and his people, worthy and well-to-do merchants, are nearly mad over it."

"But did he commit it in England?" cried Miss Preen.

"Oh no; in France, within the *arrondissement* of the Douai Courts. He is in prison there. I dare say you get some swindling in a petty way even at Sainteville," added the speaker.

"That we do," put in Nancy. "An English family of ladies ran away only yesterday, owing twenty pounds at least, it is said."

"Ah," said the stranger, with a smile, "I think the ladies are sometimes more clever at that game than the men. By the way," he went on briskly, "do you know a Mr. Dangerfield at Sainteville?"

"No," replied Lavinia.

"He is staying here, I believe, or has been."

"Not that I know of," said Lavinia. "I never heard his name."

"Changed it again, probably," carelessly observed the young man.

"Is Dangerfield not his true name, then?"

"Just as much as it is mine, madam. His real name is Fennel; but he has found it convenient to drop that on occasion."

Now it was a curious fact that Nancy did not hear the name which the stranger had given as the true one. Her attention was diverted by some men who were working at the mud in the harbour, for it was low water, and who were loudly disputing together. Nancy had moved to the side of the pier to look down at them.

"Is he a swindler, that Mr. Dangerfield?" asked she, half-turning her head to speak. But the stranger did not answer.

As to Lavinia, the avowal had struck her speechless. She glanced at Captain Fennel. He had his back to them, and stood immovable, apparently unconcerned, possibly not having heard.

A thought struck her—and frightened her.

"Do you know that Mr. Dangerfield yourself?" she asked the stranger, in a tone of indifference.

"No, I do not," he said; "but there's a man coming over in yonder boat who does."

He pointed over his shoulder at the sea as he spoke. Lavinia glanced quickly in the same direction.

"In yonder boat?" she repeated vaguely.

"I mean the London boat, which is on its way here, and will get in this evening," he explained.

"Oh, of course," said Lavinia, as if her wits had been wool-gathering.

The young man took out his watch and looked at it. Then he rose, lifted his hat, and, with a general good-morning, walked quickly down the pier.

Nancy was still at the side of the pier, looking down at the men. Captain Fennel put up his glasses and sat down beside Lavinia, his impassive face still as usual.

"I wonder who that man is?" he cried, watching the footsteps of the retreating stranger,

"Did you hear what he said?" asked Lavinia, dropping her voice.

"Yes. Had Nancy not been here, I should have given him a taste of my mind; but she hates even the semblance of a quarrel. He had no right to say what he did."

"What could it have meant?" murmured Lavinia.

"It meant my brother, I expect," said Captain Fennel savagely, and, as Lavinia thought, with every appearance of truth. "But he. has never been at Sainteville, so far as I know; the fellow is mistaken in that."

"Does he pass under the name of Dangerfield?"

"Possibly. This is the first I've heard of it. He is an extravagant man, often in embarrassment from debt. There's nothing worse against him."

He did not say more; neither did Lavinia. They sat on in silence. The tall figure in the Scotch plaid disappeared from sight;

the men in the harbour kept on disputing.

"How long are you going to stay here?" asked Nancy, turning towards her husband.

"I'm ready to go now," he answered. And giving his arm to Nancy, they walked down the pier together.

Never a word to Lavinia; never a question put by him or by Nancy, if only to say, "Are you not coming with us?" It was ever so now. Nancy, absorbed in her husband, neglected her sister.

Lavinia sighed. She sat on a little while longer, and then took her departure.

The shoe-shop on the port was opposite the place in the harbour where the London steamers were generally moored. The one now there was taking in cargo. As Lavinia was turning into the shop for her parasol, she heard a stentorian English voice call out to a man who was superintending the work in his shirt-sleeves: "At what hour does this boat leave tonight?"

"At eight o'clock, sir," was the answer. "Eight sharp; we want to get away with the first o' the tide."

From Miss Lavinia Preen's Diary.

September 22nd.—The town clocks have just struck eight, and I could almost fancy that I hear the faint sound of the boat steaming down the harbour in the dark night, carrying Nancy away with it, and carrying him. However, that is fancy and nothing else, for the sound could not penetrate to me here.

Perhaps it surprised me, perhaps it did not, when Nancy came to me this afternoon as I was sitting in my bedroom reading Scott's *Legend of Montrose*, which Mary Carimon had lent me from her little stock of English books, and said she and Captain Fennel were going to London that night by the boat. He had received a letter, he told her, calling him thither. He might tell Nancy that if he liked, but it would not do for me. He is going, I can only believe, in consequence of what that gentleman in the shepherd's plaid said on the pier today. Can it be that the "Mr. Dangerfield" spoken of applies to Edwin Fennel himself and not to his brother? Is he finding himself in some dangerous strait, and is running away from the individual coming over in the approaching boat, who personally knows Mr. Dangerfield? "Can you lend me a five-pound note, Lavinia?" Nancy went on, when she had told me the news; "lend it to myself, I mean. I will repay you when I receive my next quarter's income, which is due, you know, in a few days." I chanced to have a five-pound note by me in my own private store, and I gave it her, reminding her that unless she did let me have it again, it would be so much less in hand to meet expenses with, and that I had found difficulty enough in the past quarter.

"On the other hand," said Nancy, "if I and Edwin stay away a week or two, you will be spared our housekeeping; and when our money comes, Lavinia, you can open my letter and repay yourself if I am not here. I don't at all know where we are going to stay," she said, in answer to my question. "I was beginning to ask Edwin just now in the other room, but he was busy packing his portmanteau, and told me not to bother him."

And so, there it is: they are gone, and I am left here all alone.

I wonder whether any Mr, Dangerfield has been at Sainteville? I think we should have heard the name. Why, that is the door-bell! I must go and answer it.

It was Charley Palliser. He had come with a message from Major and Mrs. Smith. They are going to Drecques to-morrow morning by the eleven-o'clock train with a few friends and a basket of provisions, and had sent Charley to say they would be glad of my company. "Do come. Miss Preen," urged Charley as I hesitated; "you are all alone now, and I'm sure it must be dreadfully dull."

"How do you know I am alone?" I asked.

"Because," said Charley, "I have been watching the London boat out, and I saw Captain Fennel and your sister go by it. Major and Mrs. Smith were with me. It is a lovely night."

"Wait a moment," I said, as Charley was about to depart when I had accepted the invitation. "Do you know whether an Englishman named Dangerfield is living here?"

"Don't think there is; I have not met with him," said Charley "Why, Miss Preen?"

"Oh, only that I was asked today whether I knew any one of that name," I returned carelessly. "Goodnight, Mr. Charles. Thank you for coming."

They have invited me, finding I was left alone, and I think it very kind of them. But the Smiths are both kind-hearted people.

September 23rd.—Half-past nine o'clock, p.m. Have just returned from Drecques by the last train after spending a pleasant day. Quiet, of course, for there is not much to do at Drecques except stroll over the ruins of the old castle, or saunter about the quaint little ancient town, and go into the grand old church. It was so fine and warm that we had dinner on the grass, the people at the cottage bringing our plates and knives and forks. Later in the day we took tea indoors. In the afternoon, when all the rest were scattered about and the major sat smoking his cigar on the bench under the trees, I sat down by him to tell him what happened yesterday, and I begged him to give me his opinion. It was no betrayal of confidence, for Major Smith is better acquainted with the shady side of the Fennels than I am.

"I heard there was an English lawyer staying at the Hotel des Princes, and that he had come here from Douai," observed the major. "His name's Lockett. It must have been he who spoke to you on the pier."

"Yes, of course. Do you know, major, whether anyone has stayed at Sainteville passing as Mr. Dangerfield?"

"I don't think so," replied the major. "Unless he has kept himself remarkably quiet."

"Could it apply to Captain Fennel?"

"I never knew that he had gone under an assumed name.

The accusation is one more likely to apply to his brother than to himself. James Fennel is unscrupulous, very incautious: notwithstanding that, I like him better than I like the other. There's something about Edwin Fennel that repels you; at least, it does me; but one can hardly help liking James, *mauvais sujet* though he is," added the speaker, pausing to flirt off the ashes of his cigar.

"The doubt pointing to Edwin Fennel in the affair is his suddenly decamping," continued Major Smith. "It was quite *impromptu*, you say, Miss Preen?"

"Quite so, I feel sure he had no thought of going away in the morning; and he did not receive any letter from England later, which was the excuse he gave Nancy for departing. Rely upon it that what he heard about the Mr. Dangerfield on the pier drove him away."

"Well, that looks suspicious, you see."

"Oh yes, I do see it," I answered, unable to conceal the pain I felt. "It was a bitter calamity. Major Smith, when Nancy married him."

"I'll make a few cautious inquiries in the town, and try to find out if there's anything against him in secret, or if any man named Dangerfield has been in the place and got into a mess. But, indeed, I don't altogether see that it could apply to him," concluded the major after a pause. "One can't well go under two names in the same town; and everyone knows him as Edwin Fennel.—Here they are, some of them, coming back!" And when the wanderers were close up, they found Major Smith arguing with me about the architecture of the castle.

Ten o'clock. Time for bed. I am in no haste to go, for I don't sleep as well as I used to.

A thought has lately sometimes crossed me that this miserable trouble worries me more than it ought to do. "Accept it as your cross, and *yield* to it, Lavinia," says Mary Carimon to me. But I *cannot* yield to it; that is, I cannot in the least diminish the anxiety which always clings to me, or forget the distress and dread that lie upon me like a shadow. I know that my life has been on the whole an easy life—that during all the years I spent at Selby Court I never had any trouble; I know that crosses do come to us all, earlier or later, and that I ought not to be surprised that "no new thing has happened to me," the world being full of such experiences. I suppose it is because I have been so exempt from care, that I feel this the more.

Half-past ten! just half-an-hour writing these last few lines and *thinking!* Time I put up. I wonder when I shall hear from Nancy?

6

A curious phase, taken in conjunction with what was to follow, now occurred in the history. Miss Preen began to experience a nervous dread at going into the Petite Maison Rouge at night.

She could go into the house ten times a-day when it was empty; she could stay in the house alone in the evening after Flore took her departure; she could be its only inmate all night long; and never at these times have the slightest sense of fear. But if she went out to spend the evening, she felt an unaccountable dread, amounting to horror, at entering it when she arrived home.

It came on suddenly. One evening when Lavinia had been at Mrs. Hardy's, Charley Palliser having run over to London, she returned home a little before ten o'clock. Opening the door with her latch-key, she was stepping into the passage when a sharp horror of entering it seized her. A dread, as it seemed to her, of going into the empty house, up the long, dark, narrow passage. It was the same sort of sensation that had struck her the first time she attempted to enter it under the escort of Monsieur Gustave Sauvage, and it came on now with as little reason as it had come on then. For Lavinia this night had not a thought in her mind of fear or loneliness, or anything else unpleasant. Mrs. Hardy had been relating a laughable adventure that Charley Palliser met with on board the boat when going over, the account of which he had written to her, and Lavinia was thinking brightly of it all the way home. She was smiling to herself as she unlatched the door and opened it. And then, without warning, arose the horrible fear.

How she conquered it sufficiently to enter the passage and reach the slab, where her candle and matches were always placed, she did not know. It had to be done, for Lavinia Preen could not remain in the dark yard all night, or patrol the streets; but her face had turned moist, and her hands trembled.

That was the beginning of it. Never since had she come home in the same way at night but the same terror assailed her; and I must beg the reader to understand that this is no invention. Devoid of reason and unaccountable though the terror was, Lavinia Preen experienced it.

She went out often—two or three times a-week, perhaps—either to dine or to spend the evening. Captain Fennel and Nancy were still away, and friends, remembering Miss Preen's solitary position, invited her.

October had passed, November was passing, and as yet no news came to Lavinia of the return of the travellers. At first they did not write to her at all, leaving her to infer that as the boat reached London safely they had done the same. After the lapse of a fortnight she received a short letter from Nancy telling her really nothing, and not giving any address. The next letter came towards the end of November, and was as follows:

My dear Lavinia,

I have not written to you, for, truly, there is nothing to write about, and almost every day I expect Edwin to tell me we are going home. Will you *kindly* lend me a ten-pound note? Please send it in a letter. We are staying at Camberwell, and I enclose you the address in strict confidence. Do not repeat it to any one—not even to Mary Carimon. It is a relation of Edwin's we are staying with, but he is not well off! I like his wife. Edwin desires his best regards.

Your loving sister,   Nancy.

Miss Preen did not send the ten-pound note. She wrote to tell Nancy that she could not do it, and was uncomfortably pressed for money herself in consequence of Nancy's own action.

The five-pound note borrowed from Lavinia by Nancy on her departure had not been repaid; neither had Nancy's share of the previous quarter's money been remitted. On the usual day of payment at the end of September, Lavinia's quarterly income came to her at Sainteville, as was customary; not Nancy's. For Nancy there came neither money nor letter. The fact was, Nancy, escorted by her husband, had presented herself at Colonel Selby's bank—he was junior partner and manager of a small private bank in the City—the day before the dividends were due, and personally claimed the quarterly payment, which was paid to her.

But now, the summary docking of just half their income was a matter of embarrassment to Miss Preen, as may readily be imagined. The house expenses had to go on, with only half the money to meet them. Lavinia had a little nest-egg of her own, it has been said before, saved in earlier years; and this she drew upon, and so kept debt down. But it was very inconvenient, as well as vexatious. Lavinia told the whole truth now to Mary Carimon and her husband, with Nancy's recent application for a ten-pound note, and her refusal. Little Monsieur Carimon muttered a word between his closed lips which sounded like "Rat," and was no doubt applied to Edwin Fennel.

Pretty close upon this, Lavinia received a blowing-up letter from Colonel Selby. Having known Lavinia when she was in pinafores, the colonel, a peppery man, considered he had a right to take her to task at will. He was brother to Paul Selby, of Selby Court, and heir presumptive to it. The colonel had a wife and children, and much ado at times to keep them, for his income was not large at present, and growing-up sons are expensive.

Dear Lavinia,
What in the name of common sense could have induced you to imagine that I should pay the two quarterly incomes some weeks before they were due, and to send Ann

185

and that man Fennel here with your orders that I should do so? Pretty ideas of trusteeship you must have! If you are over head and ears in debt, as they tell me, and for that reason wish to forestall the time for payment, *I* can't help it. It is no reason with me. Your money will be forwarded to Sainteville, at the proper period, to *yourself*. Do not ask me again to pay it into Ann's hands, and to accept her receipt for it. I can do nothing of the kind. Ann's share will be sent at the same time. She tells me she is returning to you. She must give me her own receipt for it, and you must give me yours.

Your affectionate kinsman,

William Selby.

Just for a few minutes Lavinia Preen did not understand this letter. What could it mean? Why had Colonel Selby written it to her? Then the truth flashed into her mind.

Nancy (induced, of course, by Edwin Fennel) had gone with him to Colonel Selby, purporting to have been sent by Lavinia, to ask him to pay them the quarter's money not due until the end of December, and not only Nancy's share but Lavinia's as well.

"Why, it would have been nothing short of swindling!" cried Lavinia, as she gazed in dismay at the colonel's letter.

In the indignation of the moment, she took pen and ink and wrote an answer to William Selby. Partly enlightening him—not quite—but telling him that her money must never be paid to anyone but herself, and that the present matter had better be hushed up for Ann's sake, who was as a reed in the hands of the man she had married.

Colonel Selby exploded a little when he received this answer. Down he sat in his turn, and wrote a short, sharp note to Edwin Fennel, giving that estimable man a little of his mind, and warning him that he must not be surprised if the police were advised to look after him.

When Edward Fennel received this decisive note through an address he had given to Colonel Selby, but not the one at Camberwell, he called Miss Lavinia Preen all the laudatory names in the thieves' dictionary.

And on the feast of St. Andrew, which as everyone knows is the last day of November, the letters came to an end with the following one from Nancy:

> All being well, my dear Lavinia, we propose to return home by next Sunday's boat, which ought to get in before three o'clock in the afternoon. On Wednesday, Edwin met Charley Palliser in the Strand, and had a chat with him, and heard all the Sainteville news; not that there seemed much to hear. Charley says he runs over to London pretty often now, his mother being ill. Of course you will not mind waiting dinner for us on Sunday.
>
> Ever your loving sister,
>
> Ann.

So at length they were coming! Either that threat of being looked after by the police had been too much for Captain Fennel, or the failure to obtain funds was cutting short his stay in London. Any way, they were coming. Lavinia laid the letter beside her breakfast-plate and fell into thought. She resolved to welcome them graciously, and to say nothing about bygones.

Flore was told the news, and warned that instead of dining at half-past one on the morrow, the usual Sunday hour, it would be delayed until three. Flore did not much like the prospect of her afternoon's holiday being shortened, but there was no help for it. Lavinia provided a couple of ducks for dinner, going into the market after breakfast to buy them; the dish was an especial favourite of the captain's. She invited Mary Carimon to partake of it, for Monsieur Carimon was going to spend Sunday at Lille with an old friend of his, who was now master of the college there.

On this evening, Saturday, Lavinia dined out herself. Some ladies named Bosanquet, three sisters, with whom she had become pretty intimate, called at the Petite Maison Rouge, and carried her off to their home in the Rue Lamar tine, where they had lived for years. After a very pleasant evening with them, Lavinia left at ten o'clock.

And when she reached her own door, and was putting the latch-key into the lock, the old fear came over her. Dropping her hands, she stood there trembling. She looked round at the silent, deserted yard, she looked up at the high encircling walls; she glanced at the frosty sky and the bright stars; and she stood there shivering.

But she must go in. Throwing the door back with an effort of will, she turned sick and faint: to enter that dark, lonely, empty house seemed beyond her strength and courage. What could this strange feeling portend?—why should it thus attack her? It was just as if some fatality were in the house waiting to destroy her, and a subtle power would keep her from entering it.

Her heart beating wildly, her breath laboured, Lavinia went in; she shut the door behind her and sped up the passage. Feeling for the match-box on the slab, put ready to her hand, she struck a match and lighted the candle. At that moment, when turning round, she saw, or thought she saw, Captain Fennel. He was standing just within the front-door, which she had now come in at, staring at her with a fixed gaze, and with the most malignant expression on his usually impassive face. Lavinia's terror partly gave place to astonishment. Was it he himself? How had he come in?

Turning to take the candle from the slab in her bewilderment, when she looked again he was gone. What had become of him? Lavinia called to him by name, but he did not answer. She took the candle into the salon, though feeling sure he could not have come up the passage; but he was not there. Had he slipped out again? Had she left the door open when thinking she closed it, and had he followed her in, and was now gone again? Lavinia carried her lighted candle to the door, and found it was fastened. She had not left it open.

Then, as she undressed in her room, trying all the while to solve the problem, an idea crept into her mind that the appearance might have been supernatural. Yet—supernatural visitants of the living do not appear to us, but of the dead. Was Edwin Fennel dead?

So disturbed was the brain of Lavinia Preen that she could not get to sleep; but tossed and turned about the bed almost until daybreak, At six o'clock she fell into an uneasy slumber, and into a most distressing dream.

It was a confused dream; nothing in it was clear. All she knew when she awoke, was that she had appeared to be in a state of inexplicable terror, of most intense apprehension throughout it, arising from some evil threatened her by Captain Fennel.

7

It was a fine, frosty day, and the first of December. The sun shone on the fair streets of Sainteville and on the small congregation turning out of the English Protestant Church after morning service.

Lavinia Preen went straight home. There she found that Madame Carimon, who was to spend the rest of the day with her— *monsieur* having gone to Lille—had not yet arrived, though the French Church Evangélique was always over before the English. After glancing at Flore in the kitchen, busy over the fine ducks, Lavinia set off for the Rue Pomme Cuite.

She met Mary Carimon turning out of it. "Let us go and sit under the wall in the sun," said Mary. "It is too early yet for the boat."

This was a high wall belonging to the strong north gates of the town, near Madame Carimon's. The sun shone full upon the benches beneath it, which it sheltered from the bleak winds; in front was a patch of green grass, on which the children ran about amidst the straight poplar trees. It was very pleasant sitting there, even on this December day—bright and cheerful; the wall behind them was quite warm, the sunshine rested upon all.

Sitting there, Lavinia Preen told Madame Carimon of the curious dread of entering her house at night, which had pursued her for the past two months that she had been alone in it, and which she had never spoken of to any one before. She went on to speak of the belief that she had seen Captain Fennel the previous night in the passage, and of the dream which had visited her when at length she fell asleep.

Madame Carimon turned her kindly, sensible face and her quiet, dark, surprised eyes upon Lavinia. "I cannot understand you," she said.

"You mean, I suppose, that you cannot understand the facts, Mary. Neither can I. Why this fear of going into the house should lie upon me is most strange. I never was nervous before."

"I don't know that that is so very strange," dissented Mary Carimon, after a pause. "It must seem lonely to let one's self into a dark, empty house in the middle of the night; and your house is in what may be called an isolated situation; I should not much like it myself. That's nothing. What I cannot understand, Lavinia, is the fancy that you saw Captain Fennel."

"He appeared to be standing there, and was quite visible to me. The expression on his face, which seemed to be looking straight into mine, was most malicious. I never saw such an expression upon it in reality."

Mary Carimon laughed a little, saying she had never been troubled with nervous fears herself; she was too practical for anything of the sort.

"And I have been practical hitherto," returned Lavinia. "When the first surprise of seeing him there, or fancying I saw him there, was over, I began to think, Mary, that he might be dead; that it was his apparition which had stood there looking at me.

Mary Carimon shook her head. "Had anything of that sort happened, Nancy would have telegraphed to you. Rely upon it, Lavinia, it was pure fancy. You have been disagreeably exercised in mind lately, you know, about that man; hearing he was coming home, your brain was somewhat thrown off its balance."

"It may be so. The dream followed on it; and I did not like the dream."

"We all have bad dreams now and then. You say you do not remember much of this one."

"I think I did not know much of it when dreaming it,"

quaintly spoke Lavinia. "I was in a sea of trouble, throughout which I seemed to be striving to escape some evil menaced me by Captain Fennel, and could not do so. Whichever way I turned, there he was at a distance, scowling at me with a threatening, evil countenance. Mary," she added in impassioned tones, "I am sure some ill awaits me from that man."

"I am sure, were I you, I would put these foolish notions from me," calmly spoke Madame Carimon. "If Nancy set up a vocation for seeing ghosts and dreaming dreams, one would not so much wonder at it. *You* have always been reasonable, Lavinia; be so now."

Miss Preen took out her watch and looked at it. "We may as well be walking towards the port, Mary," she remarked. "It is past two. The boat ought to be in sight."

Not only in sight was the steamer, but rapidly nearing the port. She had made a calm and quick passage. When at length she was in and about to swing round, and the two ladies were looking down at it, with a small crowd of other assembled spectators, the first passengers they saw on board were Nancy and Captain Fennel, who began to wave their hands in greeting and to nod their heads.

"Anyway, Lavinia, it could not have been his ghost last night," whispered Mary Carimon.

★★★★★★

Far from presenting an evil countenance to Lavinia, as the days passed on. Captain Fennel appeared to wish to please her, and was all suavity. So at present nothing disturbed the peace of the Petite Maison Rouge.

"What people were they that you stayed with in London, Nancy?" Lavinia inquired of her sister on the first favourable opportunity.

Nancy glanced round the *salon* before answering, as if to make sure they were alone; but Captain Fennel had gone out for a stroll,

"We were at James Fennel's, Lavinia."

"What—the brother's! And has he a wife?"

"Yes; a wife, but no children. Mrs. James Fennel has money of her own, which she receives weekly."

"Receives weekly!" echoed Lavinia.

"She owns some little houses which are let out in weekly tenements; an agent collects the rents, and brings her the money every Tuesday morning. She dresses in the shabbiest things sometimes, and does her own housework, and altogether is not what I should call quite a lady, but she is very good-hearted, She did her best to make us comfortable, and never grumbled at our staying so long. I expect Edwin paid her something. James only came home by fits and starts. I think he was in some embarrassment—debt, you know. He used to dash into the house like a whirlwind when he did come, and steal out of it when he left, peering about on all sides."

"Have they a nice house?" asked Lavinia.

"Oh, good gracious, no! It's not a house at all, only small lodgings. And Mrs. James changed them twice over whilst we were there. When we first went they were at a place called Ball's Pond."

"Why did you remain all that time?"

Mrs. Edwin Fennel shook her head helplessly; she could not answer the question. "I should have liked to come back before," she said; "it was very wearisome, knowing nobody and having nothing to do. Did you find it dull here, Lavinia, all by yourself?"

"'Dull' is not the right word for it," answered Lavinia, catching her breath with a sigh. "I felt more lonely, Ann, than I shall ever care to feel again. Especially when I had to come home at night from some *soirée*, or from spending the evening quietly with Mary Carimon or any other friend." And she went on to tell of the feeling of terror which had so tried her.

"I never heard of such a thing!" exclaimed Ann, "How silly you must be, Lavinia! What could there have been in the house to frighten you?"

"I don't know; I wish I did know," sighed Lavinia, just as she had said more than once before,

Nancy, who was attired in a bright ruby cashmere robe, with a gold chain and locket, some blue ribbons adorning her light ringlets, for she had made a point of dressing more youthfully than ever since her marriage, leaned back in her chair, as she sat staring at her sister and thinking.

"Lavinia," she said huskily, "you remember the feeling you had the day we were about to look at the house with Mary Carimon, and which you thought was through the darkness of the passage striking you unpleasantly? Well, my opinion is that it must have given you a scare."

"Why, of course it did."

"Ah, but I mean a scare which lasts," said Ann; "one of those scares which affect the mind and take very long to get rid of You recollect poor Mrs, Hunt, at Buttermead? She was frightened at a violent thunderstorm, though she never had been before; and for years afterwards, whenever it thundered, she became so alarmingly ill and agitated that Mr. Featherston had to be run for. He called it a scare. I think the fear you felt that past day must have left that sort of scare upon you. How else can you account for what you tell me?"

Truth to say, the same idea had more than once struck Lavinia. She knew how devoid of reason some of these "scares" are, and yet how terribly they disturb the mind on which they fasten.

"But I had quite forgotten that fear, Ann," she urged in reply. "We had lived in the house eighteen months when you went away, and I had never recalled it."

"All the same, I think you received the scare; it had only lain dormant," persisted Ann.

"Well, well; you are back again now, and it is over," said Lavinia. "Let us forget it. Do not speak of it again at all to any one, Nancy love."

8

Winter that year had quite set in when Sainteville found itself honoured with rather a remarkable visitor; one Signor Talcke, who descended, one morning at the beginning of December, at the Hôtel des Princes. Though he called himself "*Signor*," it seemed uncertain to what country he owed his birth. He spoke five or six languages as a native, including Hindustani. Signor Talcke was a professor of occult sciences; he was a great astronomer; astrology he had at his fingers' ends. He was a powerful mesmerist; he would foretell the events of your life by your hands, or your fortune by the cards.

For a fee of twenty-five *francs*, he would attend an evening party, and exhibit some of his powers. Amidst others who engaged him were the Miss Bosanquets, in the Rue Lamartine. A relative of theirs, Sir George Bosanquet, K.C.B., had come over with his wife to spend Christmas with them. Sir George laughed at what he heard of Signor Talcke's powers of reading the future, and said he should much like to witness a specimen of it. So Miss Bosanquet and her sisters hastily arranged an evening entertainment, engaged the mystical man, and invited their friends and acquaintances, those of the Petite Maison Rouge included.

It took place on the Friday after Christmas-Day. Something that occurred during the evening was rather remarkable. Miss Preen's diary gives a full account of it, and that shall be transcribed here. And I, Johnny Ludlow, take this opportunity of assuring the reader that what she wrote was in faithful accordance with the facts of the case.

From Miss Preen's Diary.

Saturday morning.—I feel very tired; fit for nothing. Nancy has undertaken to do the marketing, and is gone out for that purpose with her husband. It is to be hoped she will be moderate, and not attempt to buy up half the market. I lay awake all night, after the evening at Miss Bosanquet's, thinking how foolish Ann was to have had her "future cast," as that Italian (if he is Italian) called it, and how worse than foolish I was to let what he said worry me. "As if there could be anything in it!" laughed Ann, as we were coming home; fortunately she is not as I am in temperament—nervously anxious. "It is only nonsense," said

Miss Anna Bosanquet to me when the *signor's* predictions were at an end; "he will tell someone else just the same next time." But *I* did not think so. Of course, one is at a loss how to trust this kind of man. Take him for all in all, I rather like him; and he appears to believe implicitly in what he says: or, rather, in what he tell us the cards say.

They are charming women, these three sisters—Grace, Rose, and Anna Bosanquet; good, considerate, high-bred ladies, I wonder how it is they have lived to middle life without any one of them marrying? And I often wonder how they came to take up their residence at Sainteville, for they are very well off, and have great connections. I remember, though, Anna once said to me that the dry, pure air of the place suited her sister Rose, who has bad health, better than any other they had tried.

When seven o'clock struck, the hour named, Nancy and I appeared together in the sitting-room, ready to start, for we observe punctuality at Sainteville. I wore my black satin, handsome yet, trimmed with the rich white lace that Mrs. Selby gave me. Nancy looked very nice and young in her lilac silk. She wore a white rose in her hair, and her gold chain and locket round her neck. Captain Fennel surprised us by saying he was not going—his neuralgia had come on. I fancied it was an excuse—that he did not wish to meet Sir George Bosanquet. He had complained of the same thing on Christmas-Day, so it might be true. Ann and I set off together, leaving him nursing his cheek at the table.

It was a large gathering for Sainteville—forty guests, I should think; but the rooms are large. Professor Talcke exhibited some wonderful feats in—what shall I call it?—necromancy?—as good a word, perhaps, as any other. He mesmerized some people, and put one of them into a state of clairvoyance, and her revelations took my breath away. Signer Talcke assured us that what she said would be found minutely true. I think he has the strangest eyes

I ever saw: grey eyes, with a sort of light in their depths. His features are fair and delicate, his voice is gentle as a woman's, his manner retiring; Sir George seemed much taken with him.

Later, when the evening was passing, he asked if any one present would like to have their future cast, for he had cards which would do it. Three of his listeners pressed forward at once; two of them with gay laughter, the other pale and awestruck. The *signor* went into the recess in the small room, and sat down behind the little table there, and as many as could crowd round to look on, did so. I don't know what passed; there was no room for me; or whether the "Futures" he disclosed were good or bad. I had sat on the sofa at a distance, talking with Anna Bosanquet and Madame Carimon.

Suddenly, as we were for a moment silent, Ann's voice was heard, eager and laughing:

"Will you tell my fortune, Signor Talcke? I should like to have mine revealed."

"With pleasure, *madame*," he answered. We got up and drew near. I felt vexed that Ann should put herself forward in any such matter, and whispered to her; but she only shook her curls, laughed at me, and persisted. Signor Talcke put the cards in her hands, telling her to shuffle them.

"It is all fun, Lavinia," she whispered to me. "Did you hear him tell Miss Peet she was going to have money left her?"

After Ann had shuffled the cards, he made her cut them into three divisions, and he then turned them up on the table himself, faces upwards, and laid them out in three rows. They were not like the cards we play with; quite different from those; nearly all were picture-cards, and the plain ones bore cabalistic characters. We stood looking on with two or three other people; the rest had dispersed, and had gone into the next room to listen to the singing.

At first Signor Talcke never spoke a word. He looked at

the cards, and looked at Nancy; looked, and looked again. "They are not propitious," he said in low tones, and picked them up, and asked Nancy to shuffle and cut them again. Then he laid them as before, and we stood waiting in silence.

Chancing at that moment to look at Signor Talcke, his face startled me. He was frowning at the cards in so painful a manner as to quite alter its expression. But he did not speak. He still only gazed at the cards with bent eyes, and glanced up at Ann occasionally. Then, with an impatient sweep of the hand, he pushed the cards together.

"I must trouble you to shuffle and cut them once more, *madame*," he said. "Shuffle them well."

"Are they still unpropitious?" sked a jesting voice at my elbow. Turning, I saw Charley Palliser's smiling face. He must have been standing there, and heard Signor Talcke's previous remark.

"Yes, sir, they are," replied the *signor*, with marked emphasis. "I never saw the cards so unpropitious in my life."

Nancy took up the cards, shuffled them well, and cut them three times. Signor Talcke laid them out as before, bent his head, and looked attentively at them. He did not speak, but there was no mistaking the vexed, pained, and puzzled look on his face.

I do not think he knew Nancy, even by name. I do not think he knew me, or had the least notion that we were related. Neither of us had ever met him before. He put his hand to his brow, still gazing at the cards.

"But when are you going to begin my fortune, sir?" broke in Nancy.

"I would rather not tell it at all, *madame*," he answered.

"*Cannot* you tell it?—have your powers of forecasting inconveniently run away?" said she incautiously, her tone mocking in her disappointment.

"I could tell it, all too surely; but you might not like to hear it," returned he.

"Our magician has lost his divining-rod just when he needed it," observed a gentleman with a grey beard, a stranger to me, who was standing opposite, speaking in a tone of ill-natured satire; and a laugh went round.

"It is not that," said the *signor*, keeping his temper perfectly. "I could tell what the cards say, all too certainly; but it would not give satisfaction."

"Oh yes, it would," returned Nancy. "I should like to hear it, every bit of it. Please do begin."

"The cards are dark, very dark indeed," he said; "I don't remember ever to have seen them like it. Each time they have been turned the darkness has increased. *Nothing* can show worse than they do now."

"Never mind that," gaily returned Ann. "You undertook to tell my fortune, sir; and you ought not to make excuses in the middle of it. Let the cards be as dark as night, we must hear what they say."

He drew in his thin lips for a moment, and then spoke, his tone quiet, calm, unemotional.

"Some great evil threatens you," he began; "you seem to be living in the midst of it. It is not only you that it threatens; there is another also—"

"Oh, my goodness!" interrupted Nancy, in her childish way. "I hope it does not threaten Edwin. What *is* the evil?—sickness?"

"Worse than that. It—is—" Signor Talcke's attention was so absorbed by the aspect of the cards that, as it struck me, he appeared hardly to heed what he was saying. He had a long, thin black pencil in his long, thin fingers, and kept pointing to different cards as if in accordance with his thoughts, but not touching them. "There is some peculiar form of terror here," he went on. "I cannot make it out; it is very unusual. It does not come close to you; not yet, at any rate; and it seems to surround you. It seems to be in the house. May I ask"—quickly lifting his eyes to Ann—"whether you are given to superstitious fears?"

198

"Do you mean ghosts?" cried Ann, and Charley Palliser burst out laughing. "Not at all, sir; I don't believe in ghosts. I'm sure there are none in our house."

Remembering my own terror in regard to the house, and the nervous fancy of having seen Captain Fennel in it when he was miles away, a curious impression came over me that he must surely be reading my fortune as well as Nancy's. But I was not prepared for her next words. Truly she has no more reticence than a child.

"My sister has a feeling that the house is lonely. She shivers when she has to go into it after nightfall."

Signor Talcke let his hands fall on the table, and lifted his face. Apparently, he was digesting this revelation. I do not think he knew the "sister" was present. For my part, disliking publicity, I slipped behind Anna Bosanquet, and stood by Charley Palliser.

"Shivers?" repeated the Italian.

"Shivers and trembles, and turns sick at having to go in," affirmed Nancy. "So she told me when I arrived home from England."

"If a feeling of that sort assailed me, I should never go into the house again," said the *signor*.

"But how could you help it, if it were your home?" she argued.

"All the same. I should regard that feeling as a warning against the house, and never enter it. Then you are not yourself troubled with superstitious fears?" he broke off, returning to the business in hand, and looking at the cards. "Well—at present—it does not seem to touch you, this curious terror which is assuredly in the house—"

"I beg your pardon," interrupted Ann. "Why do you say 'at present'? Is it to touch me later?"

"I cannot say. Each time that the cards have been spread it has shown itself nearer to you. It is not yet very near. Apart from that terror—or perhaps remotely connected with it—I see evil threatening you—great evil."

"Is it in the house?"

"Yes; hovering about it. It is not only yourself it seems to threaten. There is someone else. And it is nearer to that person than it is to you."

"But who is that person?—man or woman?"

"It is a woman. See this ugly card," continued he, pointing with his pencil; "it will not be got rid of, shuffle as you will; it has come nearer to that woman each time."

The card he pointed to was more curious-looking than any other in the pack. It was not unlike the nine of spades, but crowded with devices. The gentleman opposite, whom I did not know, leaned forward and touched the card with the tip of his forefinger.

"*Le cercueil, n'est-ce-pas?*" said he.

"My" whispered an English lad's voice behind me. "*Cercueil?* that means coffin."

"How did you know?" asked Signer Talcke of the grey-bearded man.

"I was at the *Sous-Préfect's soirée* on Sunday evening when you were exhibiting. I heard you tell him in French that that was the ugliest card in the pack: indicating death."

"Well, it is not this lady the card is pursuing," said the *signor*, smiling at Ann to reassure her. "Not yet awhile, at least. And we must all be pursued by it in our turn, whenever that shall come," he added, bending over the cards again. "Pardon me, *madame*—may I ask whether there has not been some unpleasantness in the house concerning money?"

Nancy's face turned red. "Not—exactly," she answered with hesitation. "We are like a great many more people—not as rich as we should wish to be."

"It does not appear to lie precisely in the want of money: but certainly money is in some way connected with the evil," he was beginning to say, his eyes fixed dreamily on the cards, when Ann interrupted him.

"That is too strong a word—evil. Why do you use it?"

"I use it because the evil is there. No lighter word would be appropriate. There is some evil element pervading your house, very grave and formidable; it is most threatening; likely to go on to—to—darkness. I mean that it looks as if there would be some great break-up," he corrected swiftly, as if to soften the other word.

"That the house would be broken up?" questioned Ann.

He stole a glance at her. "Something of that sort," he said carelessly.

"Do you mean that the evil comes from an enemy?" she went on.

"Assuredly."

"But we have no enemy. I'm sure we have not one in all the world."

He slightly shook his head. "You may not suspect it yet, though I should have said"—waving the pencil thoughtfully over some of the cards—"that he was already suspected—doubted."

Nancy took up the personal pronoun briskly. "He!—then the evil enemy must be a man? I assure you we do not know any man likely to be our enemy or to wish us harm. No, nor woman either. Perhaps your cards don't tell true tonight, Signor Talcke?"

"Perhaps not, *madame*; we will let it be so if you will," he quietly said, and shuffled all the cards together.

That ended the *séance*. As if determined not to tell any more fortunes, the *signor* hurriedly put up the cards and disappeared from the recess. Nancy did not appear to be in the least impressed.

"What a curious 'future' it was!" she exclaimed lightly to Mary Carimon. "I might as well not have had it cast. He told me nothing."

They walked away together. I went back to the sofa and Anna Bosanquet followed me.

"Mrs. Fennel calls it 'curious,'" I said to her. "I call it more than that—strange; ominous. I wish I had not heard it."

"Dear Miss Preen, it is only nonsense," she answered. "He will tell someone else the same next time." But she only so spoke to console me.

A wild wish flashed into my mind—that I should ask the man to tell *my* future. But had I not heard enough? Mine was blended with this of Ann's. I was the other woman whom the dark fate was more relentlessly pursuing. There could be no doubt of that. There could be as little doubt that it was I who already suspected the author of the "evil." What can the "dark fate" be that we are threatened with? Debt? Will his debts spring upon us and break up our home, and turn us out of it? Or will it be something worse? That card which followed me meant a coffin, they said. Ah me! Perhaps I am foolish to dwell upon such ideas. Certainly they are more fitting for the world's dark ages than for this enlightened nineteenth century of it.

Charley Palliser gallantly offered to see us home. I said no; as if we were not old enough to go by ourselves; but he would come with us. As we went along Ann began talking of the party, criticizing the dresses, and so on. Charley seemed to be unusually silent.

"Was not mine a grand fortune?" she presently said with a laugh, as we crossed the Place Ronde.

"Stunning," said he.

"As if there could be anything in it, you know! Does the man think we believe him, I wonder?"

"Oh, these conjurers like to fancy they impose on us," remarked Charley, shaking hands as we halted before the house of Madame Sauvage.

And I have had a wretched night, for somehow the thing has frightened me. I never was superstitious; never; and I'm sure I never believed in conjurers, as Charles had it. If I should come across Signor Talcke again while he stays here, I would ask him——Here comes Nancy! and Flore behind her with the marketings. I'll put up my diary.

"I've bought such a lovely capon," began Nancy, as Lavinia

went into the kitchen. "Show it to *madame*, Flore."

It was one that even Lavinia could praise; they both understood poultry. "It really is a beauty," said Lavinia. "And did you remember the *salsifis*? And, Ann, where have you left your husband?"

"Oh, we met old Mr. Griffin, and Edwin has gone up to Drecques with him. My opinion is, Lavinia, that that poor old Giiffin dare not go about far by himself since his attack. He had to see his landlord at Drecques today, and he asked Edwin to accompany him. They went by the eleven-o'clock train."

Lavinia felt it a relief. Even that little absence, part of a day, she felt thankful for, so much had she grown to dislike the presence in the house of Edwin Fennel.

"Did you tell your husband about your 'fortune,' Nancy?"

"No; I was too sleepy last night to talk, and I was late in getting up this morning. I'm not sure that I shall tell him," added Mrs. Fennel thoughtfully; "he might be angry with me for having had it done."

"That is more than likely," replied Lavinia.

Late in the afternoon, as they were sitting together in the *salon*, they saw the postman come marching up the yard. He brought two letters—one for Miss Preen, the other for her sister.

"It is the remittance from William Selby," said Lavinia as she opened hers. "He has sent it a day or two earlier than usual; it is not really due until Monday or Tuesday."

Seventeen pounds ten shillings each. Nancy, in a hasty sort of manner, put her cheque into the hands of Lavinia, almost as if she feared it would burn her own fingers. "You had better take it from me whilst you can," she said in low tones.

"Yes; for I must have it, Ann," was the answer. "We are in debt—as you may readily conceive—with only half the usual amount to spend last quarter."

"It was not my fault; I was very sorry," said Ann humbly; and she rose hastily to go to the kitchen, saying she was thirsty, and wanted a glass of water. But Lavinia thought she went to avoid being questioned.

Lavinia carried the two cheques to her room and locked them up. After their five-o'clock dinner, each sister wrote a note to Colonel Selby, enclosing her receipt. Flore took them out to post when she left. The evening passed on. Lavinia worked; Nancy nodded over the fire: she was very sleepy, and went to bed early.

It was past eleven o'clock when Captain Fennel came in, a little the worse for something or other. After returning from Drecques by the last train, he had gone home with Mr. Griffin to supper. He told Lavinia, in words running into one another, that the jolting train had made him giddy. Of course she believed as much of that as she liked, but did not contradict it. He went to the cupboard in the recess, unlocked it to get out the cognac, and then sat down with his pipe by the embers of the dying fire. Lavinia, unasked, brought in a decanter of water, put it on the table with a glass, and wished him goodnight.

All next day Captain Fennel lay in bed with a racking headache. His wife carried up a choice bit of the capon when they were dining after morning service, but he could not so much as look at it. Being a fairly cautious man as a rule, he had to pay for—for the jolting of the train.

He was better on Monday morning, but not well, still shaky, and did not come down to breakfast. It was bitterly cold—a sort of black frost; but Lavinia, wrapping herself up warmly, went out as soon as breakfast was over.

Her first errand was to the bank, where she paid in the cheques and received French money for them. Then she visited sundry shops; the butcher's, the grocer's, and others, settling the accounts due. Last of all, she made a call upon Madame Veuve Sauvage, and paid the rent for the past quarter. All this left her with exactly nineteen pounds, which was all the money she had to go on with for every purpose until the end of March—three whole months.

Lunch was ready when she returned. Taking off her things upstairs and locking up her cash, she went down to it. Flore had made some delicious *soupe maigre*. Only those who have tried it know how good it is on a sharp winter's day. Captain Fennel seemed to relish it much, though his appetite had not quite come back to him, and he turned from the dish of scrambled eggs which supplemented the soup. In the evening they went, by appointment, to dine at Madame Carimon's, the other guests being Monsieur Henri Dupuis with his recently married wife, and Charles Palliser.

After dinner, over the coffee, Monsieur Henri Dupuis suddenly spoke of the *soirée* at Miss Bosanquet's the previous Friday, regretting that he and his wife had been unable to attend it. He was engaged the whole evening with a patient dangerously ill, and his wife did not like to appear at it without him. Nancy—Nancy!—then began to tell about the "fortune" which had been forecast for her by Signor Talcke, thinking possibly that her husband could not reproach her for it before company. She was very gay over it; a proof that it had left no bad impression on her mind.

"What's that, Nancy?" cried Captain Fennel, who had listened as if he disbelieved his ears. "The fellow told you we had something evil in our house?"

"Yes, he did," assented Nancy. "An evil influence, he said, which was destined to bring forth something dark and dreadful."

"I am sorry you did not tell this before," returned the captain stiffly. "I should have requested you not again to allude to such folly. It was downright insolence."

"I—you—you were out on Saturday, you know, Edwin, and in bed with your headache all Sunday; and today I forgot it," said Nancy in less brave tones.

"Suppose we have a game at wholesome card-playing," interposed Mary Carimon, bringing forth a new pack. "Open them, will you, Jules? Do you remember, *mon ami*, having your fortune told once by a gipsy woman when we were in Sir John Whitney's coppice with the two Peckham girls? She told you you would fall into a rich inheritance and marry a Frenchwoman."

"Neither of which agreeable promises is yet fulfilled," said little Monsieur Carimon with his happy smile. Monsieur Carimon had heard the account of Nancy's "forecast" from his wife; he was not himself present, but taking a hand at whist in the card-room.

They sat down to a round game—spin. Monsieur Henri Dupuis and his pretty young wife had never played it before, but they soon learned it and liked it much. Both of them spoke English well; she with the prettiest accent imaginable. Thus the evening passed, and no more allusion was made to the fortune-telling at Miss Bosanquet's.

That was Monday. On Tuesday, Miss Preen was dispensing the coffee at breakfast in the Petite Maison Rouge to her sister and Mr. Fennel, when Flore came bustling in with a letter in her hand.

"*Tenez, madame,*" she said, putting it beside Mrs. Fennel. "I laid it down in the kitchen when the *facteur* brought it, whilst I was preparing the *déjeûner*, and forgot it afterwards."

Before Nancy could touch the letter, her husband caught it up. He gazed at the address, at the postmark, and turned it about to look at the seal. The letters of gentlefolk were generally fastened with a seal in those days: this had one in transparent bronze wax.

Mr. Fennel put the letter down with a remark peevishly uttered. "It is not from London; it is from Buttermead."

"And from your old friend, Jane Peckham, Nancy," struck in Lavinia. "I recognize her handwriting."

"I *am* glad," exclaimed Nancy. "I have not heard from them for ages. Why now—is it not odd?—that Madame Carimon should mention the Peckhams last night, and I receive a letter from them this morning?"

"I supposed it might be from London, with your remittance," said Mr. Fennel to his wife. "It is due, is it not?"

"Oh, that came on Saturday, Edwin," she said, as she opened her letter.

"Came on Saturday!" echoed Captain Fennel ungraciously, as

206

if disputing the assertion.

"By the afternoon post; you were at Drecques, you know."

"The *money* came? *Your* money?"

"Yes," said Nancy, who had stepped to the window to read her letter, for it was a dark day, and stood there with her back to the room.

"And where is it?" demanded he.

"I gave it to Lavinia. I always give it to her."

Captain Fennel glared at his wife for a moment, then smoothed his face to its ordinary placidity, and turned to Lavinia.

"Will you be good enough to hand over to me my wife's money. Miss Preen?"

"No," she answered quietly.

"I must trouble you to do so, when breakfast shall be finished."

"I cannot," pursued Lavinia. "I have paid it away."

"That I do not believe. I claim it from you in right of my wife; and I shall enforce the claim."

"The money is Nancy's, not yours," said Lavinia. "In consequence of your having stopped her share last quarter in London, I was plunged here into debt and great inconvenience. Yesterday morning I went out to settle the debts—and it has taken the whole of her money to do it. That is the state of things, Captain Fennel."

"I am in debt here myself," retorted he, but not angrily. "I owe money to my tailor and bootmaker; I owe an account at the chemist's; I want money in my pockets—and I must indeed have it."

"Not from me," returned Lavinia,

Edwin Fennel broke into a little access of temper. He dashed his serviette on the table, strode to the window, and roughly caught his wife by the arm. She cried out.

"How dared you hand your money to anyone but me?" he asked in a low voice of passion.

"But how are we to live if I don't give it to Lavinia for the housekeeping? "returned Nancy, bursting into tears. "It takes all we have; her share and mine; every farthing of it."

"Let my sister alone, Mr. Fennel," spoke up Lavinia with authority. "She is responsible for the debts we contract in this house, just as much as I am, and she must contribute her part to pay them. You ought to be aware that the expenses are now increased by nearly a third; I assure you I hardly like to face the difficulties I see before me."

"Do you suppose I can stop in the place without some loose cash to keep me going?" he asked calmly. "Is that reasonable, Miss Lavinia?"

"And do you suppose I can keep you and Ann here without her money to help me to do it?" she rejoined. "Perhaps the better plan will be for me to take up my abode elsewhere, and leave the house to you and Ann to do as you please in it."

Captain Fennel dropped his argument, returned to the table, and went on with his breakfast. The last words had startled him. Without Lavinia, which meant without her money, they could not live in the house at all.

Matters were partly patched up in the course of the day. Nancy came upstairs to Lavinia, begging and praying, as if she were praying for her life, for a little ready money for her husband—just a hundred *francs*. Trembling and sobbing, she confessed that she dared not return to him without it; she should be too frightened at his anger.

And Lavinia gave it to her.

9

Matters went on to the spring. There were no outward differences in the Petite Maison Rouge, but it was full of an undercurrent of discomfort. At least for Lavinia. Captain Fennel was simply to her an incubus; and now and again petty accounts of his would be brought to the door by tradespeople who wanted them settled. As to keeping up the legitimate payments, she could not do it.

March was drawing to an end, when a surprise came to them. Lavinia received a letter from Paris, written by Colonel Selby. He had been there for two days on business, he said, and purposed returning via Sainteville, to take a passing glimpse at herself and her sister. He hoped to be down that afternoon by the three-o'clock train, and he asked them to meet him at the Hôtel des Princes afterwards, and to stay and dine with him. He proposed crossing to London by the night boat.

Lavinia read the letter aloud. Nancy went into ecstasies, for a wonder; she had been curiously subdued in manner lately. Edwin Fennel made no remark, but his pale face wore a look of thought.

During the morning he betook himself to the Rue Lothaire to call upon Mr. Griffin; and he persuaded that easy-natured old gentleman to take advantage of the sunny day and make an excursion *en voiture* to the nearest town, a place called Pontipette. Of course the captain went also, as his companion.

Colonel Selby arrived at three. Lavinia and Nancy met him at the station, and went with him in the omnibus to the hotel. They then showed him about Sainteville, to which he was a stranger, took him to see their *domicile*, the little red house (which he did not seem to admire), and thence to Madame Carimon's. In the Buttermead days, the colonel and Mary Featherston had been great friends. He invited her and her husband to join them at the *table d'hôte* dinner at five o'clock.

Lavinia and Nancy went home again to change their dresses for it. Nancy put on a pretty light green silk, which had been recently modernized. Mrs. Selby had kept up an extensive wardrobe, and had left it between the two sisters.

"You should wear your gold chain and locket," remarked Lavinia, who always took pride in her sister's appearance. "It will look very nice upon that dress."

She alluded to a short, thick chain of gold, the gold locket attached to it being set round with pearls, Nancy's best ornament; nay, the only one she had of any value; it was the one she had worn at Miss Bosanquet's celebrated party. Nancy made no answer. She was turning red and white.

"What's the matter?" cried Lavinia,

The matter was, that Mr. Edwin Fennel had obtained possession of the chain and locket more than a month ago. Silly Nancy confessed with trembling lips that she feared he had pledged it.

Or sold it, thought Lavinia. She felt terribly vexed and indignant. "I suppose, Ann, it will end in his grasping everything," she said, "and starving us out of house and home: *myself*, at any rate."

"He expects money from his brother James, and then he will get it back for me," twittered Nancy.

Monsieur Jules Carimon was not able to come to the *table d'hôte*; his duties that night would detain him at the college until seven o'clock. It happened so on occasion. Colonel Selby sat at one end of their party, Lavinia at the other; Mary Carimon and Nancy between them, A gentleman was on the other side of Lavinia whom she did not particularly notice; and, upon his asking the waiter for something, his voice seemed to strike upon her memory. Turning, she saw that it was the tall Englishman they had seen on the pier some months before in the shepherd's plaid, the lawyer named Lockett. He recognized her face at the same moment, and they entered into conversation.

"Are you making any stay at Sainteville?" she inquired.

"For a few days. I must be back in London on Monday morning."

Colonel Selby's attention was attracted to the speakers. "What, is it you, Lockett?" he exclaimed.

Mr. Lockett bent forward to look beyond Lavinia and Madame Carimon. "Why, colonel, are you here?" he cried. So it was evident that they knew one another.

But you can't talk very much across people at a *table d'hôte*; and Lavinia and Mr. Lockett were, so to say, left together again. She put a question to him, dropping her voice to a whisper.

"Did you ever find that person you were looking for?"

"The person I was looking for?" repeated the lawyer, not remembering. "What person was that?"

"The one you spoke of on the pier that day—a Mr. Dangerfield."

"Oh, ay; but I was not looking for him myself. No; I believe he is not dropped upon yet. He is keeping quiet, I expect."

"Is he still being looked for?"

"Little doubt of that. My friend here, on my left, could tell you more about him than I can, if you want to know."

"No, thank you," said Lavinia hastily, in a sort of fear. And she then observed that next to Mr. Lockett another Englishman was sitting, who looked very much like a lawyer also.

After dinner Colonel Selby took his guests, the three ladies, into the little *salon*, which opened to Madame Podevin's *bureau*; for it was she who, French fashion, kept the *bureau* and all its accounts, not her husband. Whilst the coffee which the colonel ordered was preparing, he took from his pocket-book two cheques, and gave one each to Lavinia and Mrs. Fennel. It was their quarterly income, due about a week hence.

"I thought I might as well give it you now, as I am here, and save the trouble of sending," he remarked. "You can write me a receipt for it; here's pen, ink and paper."

Each wrote her receipt, and gave it him. Nancy held the cheque in her hand, looking at her sister in a vacillating manner. "I suppose I ought to give it you, Lavinia," she said. "Must I do so?"

"What do you think about it yourself?" coldly rejoined Lavinia.

"He was so very angry with me the last time," sighed Nancy, still withholding the cheque. "He said I ought to keep possession of my own, and he ordered me to do so in future."

"That he may have the pleasure of spending it," said Mary Carimon in a sharp tone, though she laughed at the same time. "Lavinia has to pay for the bread-and-cheese that you and he eat, Nancy; how can she do that unless she receives your money?"

"Yes, I know; it is very difficult," said poor Nancy,

"Take the cheque, Lavinia; I shall tell him that you and Mary Carimon both said I must give it up."

"Oh, tell him I said so, and welcome," spoke Madame Carimon. "I will tell him so myself, if you like."

As Colonel Selby returned to the room—he had been seeing to his luggage—the coffee was brought in, and close upon it came Monsieur Carimon.

The boat for London was leaving early that night—eight o'clock; they all went down to it to see William Selby off. It was a calm night, warm for the time of year, the moon beautifully bright. After the boat's departure, Lavinia and Ann went home, and found Captain Fennel there. He had just got in, he said, and wanted some supper.

Whilst he was taking it, his wife told him of Mr. Lockett's having sat by them at the *table d'hôte*, and that he and Colonel Selby were acquainted with one another. Captain Fennel drew a grim face at the information, and asked whether the lawyer had also "cleared out" for London.

"I don't think so; I did not see him go on board," said Nancy. "Lavinia knows; she was talking with Mr. Lockett all dinner-time."

Captain Fennel turned his impassive face to Lavinia, as if demanding an answer to his question.

"Mr. Lockett intends to remain here until Sunday, I fancy; he said he had to be in London on Monday morning. He has some friend with him here. I inquired whether they had found the Mr. Dangerfield he spoke of last autumn," added Lavinia slowly and distinctly. "'Not yet,' he answered, 'but he is still being looked for.'"

Whether Lavinia said this with a little spice of malice, or whether she really meant to warn him, she best knew. Captain Fennel finished his supper in silence.

"I presume the colonel did not hand you over your quarter's money?" he next said to his wife in a mocking sort of way. "It is not due for a week yet; he is not one to pay beforehand."

Upon which Nancy began to tremble and looked imploringly at her sister, who was putting the plates together upon the tray. After Flore went home they had to wait upon themselves.

"Colonel Selby did hand us the money," said Lavinia. "I hold both cheques for it."

Well, there ensued a mild disturbance; what schoolboys might

212

call a genteel row. Mr. Edwin Fennel insisted upon his wife's cheque being given to him. Lavinia decisively refused. She went into a bit of a temper, and told him some home truths. He said he had a right to hold his wife's money, and should appeal to the law on the morrow to enforce it. He might do that, Lavinia retorted; no French law would make her give it up. Nancy began to cry.

Probably he knew his threats were futile. Instead of appealing to the law on the morrow, he went off by an early train, carrying Nancy with him. Lavinia's private opinion was that he thought it safer to take her, though it did increase the expense, than to leave her; she might get talking with Mr. Lockett. Ann's eyes were red, as if she had spent the night in crying.

"Has he beaten you?" Lavinia inquired, snatching the opportunity of a private moment.

"Oh, Lavinia, don't, don't! I shall *never* dare to let you have the cheque again," she wailed.

"Where is it that you are going?"

"He has not told me," Nancy whispered back again. "To Calais, I think, or else up to Lille. We are to be away all the week."

"Until Mr. Lockett and his friend are gone," thought Lavinia. "Nancy, how can he find money for it?"

"He has some *napoleons* in his pocket—borrowed yesterday, I think, from old Griffin."

Lavinia understood. Old Griffin, as Nancy styled him, had been careless of his money since his very slight attack of paralysis; he would freely lend to anyone who asked him. She had not the slightest doubt that Captain Fennel had borrowed of him—and not for the first time.

It was on Wednesday morning that they went away, and for the rest of the week Lavinia was at peace. She changed the cheques at the bank as before, and paid the outstanding debts. But it left her so little to go on with, that she really knew not how she should get through the months until midsummer.

On Friday two of the Miss Bosanquets called. Hearing she was alone, they came to ask her to dine with them in the evening.

Lavinia did so. But upon returning home at night, the old horror of going into the house came on again. Lavinia was in despair; she had hoped it had passed away for good.

On Saturday morning at market she met Madame Carimon, who invited her for the following day, Sunday. Lavinia hesitated. Glad enough indeed she was at the prospect of being taken out of her solitary home for a happy day at Mary Carimon's; but she shrank from again risking the dreadful feeling which would be sure to attack her when going into the house at night.

"You must come, Lavinia," cheerily urged Madame Carimon. "I have invited the English teacher at Madame Deauville's school; she has no friends here, poor thing."

"Well, I will come, Mary; thank you," said Lavinia slowly.

"To be sure you will. Why do you hesitate at all? "

Lavinia could not say why in the midst of the jostling market-place; perhaps would not had they been alone. "For one thing, they may be coming home before tomorrow," observed Lavinia, alluding to Mr. and Mrs. Fennel.

"Let them come. You are not obliged to stay at home with them," laughed Mary.

From the Diary of Miss Preen.

Monday morning.—Well, it is over. The horror of last night is over, and I have not died of it. That will be considered a strong expression, should any eye save my own see this diary: but I truly believe the horror would kill me if I were subjected many more times to it.

I went to Mary Carimon's after our service was over in the morning, and we had a pleasant day there. The more I see of Monsieur Jules the more I esteem and respect him. He is so genuine, so good at heart, so simple in manner. Miss Perry is very agreeable; not so young as I had thought—thirty last birthday, she says. Her English is good and refined, and that is not always the ease with the English teachers who come over to France—the French ladies who engage them cannot judge of our accent.

Miss Perry and I left together a little before ten. She wished me goodnight in the Rue Tessin, Madame Deauville's house lying one way, mine another. The horror began to come over me as I crossed the Place Ronde, which had never happened before. Stay; not the horror itself, but the dread of it. An impulse actually crossed me to ring at Madame Sauvage's, and ask Mariette to accompany me up the entry, and stand at my open door whilst I went in to light the candle. But I could see no light in the house, not even in *madame's salon*, and supposed she and Mariette might be gone to bed. They are early people on Sundays, and the two young men have their latch-keys.

I will try to overcome it this time, I bravely said to myself, and not allow the fear to keep me halting outside the door as it has done before. So I took out my latch-key, put it straight into the door, opened it, went in, and closed it again. Before I had well reached the top of the passage and felt for the matchbox on the slab, I was in a paroxysm of horror. Something, like an icy wind coming up the passage, seemed to flutter the candle as I lighted it. Can I have left the door open? I thought, and turned to look. There stood Edwin Fennel. He stood just inside the door, which appeared to be shut, and he was looking straight at me with a threatening, malignant expression on his pale face. "Oh! have you come home tonight?" I exclaimed aloud. For I really thought it was so.

The candle continued to flicker quickly as if it meant to go out, causing me to glance at it. When I looked up again Mr. Fennel was gone. *It was not himself who had been there; it was only an illusion.*

Exactly as he had seemed to appear to me the night before he and Nancy returned from London in December, so he had appeared again, his back to the door, and the evil menace on his countenance. Did the appearance come to me as a warning? or was the thing nothing but a delusion of my own optic nerves?

I dragged my shaking limbs upstairs, on the verge of screaming at each step with the fear of what might be behind me, and undressed and went to bed. For nearly the whole night I could not sleep, and when I did get to sleep in the morning I was tormented by a distressing dream. All, all as it had been that other night from three to four months ago.

A confused dream, no method in it. Several people were about—Nancy for one; I saw her fair curls. We all seemed to be in grievous discomfort and distress; whilst I, in worse fear than this world can know, was ever striving to hide myself from Edwin Fennel, to escape some dreadful fate which he held in store for me. And I knew I should not escape it.

10

Like many another active housewife, Madame Carimon was always busy on Monday mornings. On the one about to be referred to, she had finished her household duties by eleven o'clock, and then sat down in her little *salle-à-manger*, which she also made her workroom, to mend some of Monsieur Carimon's cotton socks. By her side, on the small work-table, lay a silver brooch which Miss Perry had inadvertently left behind her the previous evening. Mary Carimon was considering at what hour she could most conveniently go out to leave it at Madame Deauville's when she heard Pauline answer a ring at the door-bell, and Miss Preen came in.

"Oh, Lavinia, I am glad to see you. You are an early visitor. Are you not well?" continued Madame Carimon, noticing the pale, sad face. "Is anything the matter?"

"I am in great trouble, Mary; I cannot rest; and I have come to talk to you about it," said Lavinia, taking the sable boa from her neck and untying her bonnet-strings. "If things were to continue as they are now, I should die of it."

Drawing a chair near to Mary Carimon, Lavinia entered upon her narrative. She spoke first of general matters. The home discomfort, the trouble with Captain Fennel regarding Nancy's money, and the difficulty she had to keep up the indispensable payments to the tradespeople, expressing her firm belief that in future he would inevitably seize upon Nancy's portion when it came and confiscate it. Next, she went on to tell the story of the past night—Sunday: how the old terrible horror had come upon her of entering the house, of a fancied appearance of Edwin Fennel in the passage, and of the dream that followed. All this latter part was but a repetition of what she had told Madame Carimon three or four months ago. Hearing it for the second time, it impressed Mary Carimon's imagination. But she did not speak at once.

"I never in my life saw anything plainer or that looked more life-like than Captain Fennel, as he stood and gazed at me from the end of the passage with the evil look on his countenance," resumed Lavinia. "And I hardly know why I tell you about it again, Mary, except that I have no one else to speak to. You rather laughed at me the first time, if you remember; perhaps you will laugh again now."

"No, no," dissented Mary Carimon. "I did not put faith in it before, believing you were deceived by the uncertain light in the passage, and were, perhaps, thinking of him, and that the dream afterwards was merely the result of your fright; nothing else. But now that you have had a second experience of it, I don't doubt that you do see this spectre, and that the dream follows as a sequence to it. And I think," she added, slowly and emphatically, "that it has come to warn you of some threatened harm."

"I seem to see that it has," murmured Lavinia. "Why else should it come at all? I wish I could picture it to you half vividly enough: the reality of it and the horror. Mary, I am growing seriously afraid."

"Were I you, I should get away from the house," said Madame Carimon. "Leave them to themselves."

"It is what I mean to do, Mary. I cannot remain in it, apart from this undefined fear—which of course *may* be only superstitious fancy," hastily acknowledged Lavinia. "If things continue in the present state—and there is no prospect of their changing—"

"I should leave at once—as soon as they arrive home," rather sharply interrupted Mary Carimon, who seemed to like the aspect of what she had heard less and less.

"As soon as I can make arrangements. They come home tonight; I received a letter from Nancy this morning. They have been only at Pontipette all the time."

"Only at Pontipette!"

"Nancy says so. It did as well as any other place. Captain Fennel's motive was to hide away from the lawyers we met at the *table d'hôte.*"

"Have they left Sainteville, I wonder, those lawyers?"

"Yes," said Lavinia. "On Friday I met Mr, Lockett when I was going to the Rue Lamartine, and he told me he was leaving for Calais with his friend on Saturday morning. It is rather remarkable," she added, after a pause, "that the first time I saw that appearance in the passage and dreamed the dream, should have been the eve of Mr. Fennel's return here, and that it is the same again now."

"You must leave the house, Lavinia," reiterated Madame Carimon.

"Let me see," considered Lavinia. "April comes in this week. Next week will be Passion Week, preceding Easter. I will stay with them over Easter, and then leave."

Monsieur Jules Carimon's sock, in process of renovation, had been allowed to fall upon the mender's lap. She slowly took it up again, speaking thoughtfully.

"I should leave at once; before Easter. But you will see how he behaves, Lavinia. If not well; if he gives you any cause of annoyance, come away there and then. We will take you in, mind, if you have not found a place to go to."

Lavinia thanked her, and rearranged her bonnet preparatory to returning home. She went out with a heavy heart. Only one poor twelvemonth to have brought about all this change!

At the door of the Petite Maison Rouge, when she reached it, stood Flore, parleying with a slim youth, who held an open paper in his outstretched hand. Flore was refusing to touch the paper, which was both printed and written on, and looked official.

"I tell him that *Monsieur le Capitaine* is not at home; he can bring it when he is," explained Flore to her mistress in English.

Lavinia turned to the young man. "Captain Fennel has been away from Sainteville for a few days; he probably will be here tomorow," she said. "Do you wish to leave this paper for him?"

"Yes," said the messenger, evidently understanding English but speaking in French, as he contrived to slip the paper into Miss Preen's unconscious hand. "You will have the politeness to give it to him, *madame*."

And, with that, he went off down the entry, whistling.

"Do you know what the paper is, Flore?" asked Lavinia.

"I think so," said Flore. "I've seen these papers before today. It's just a sort of order from the law court on Captain Fennel, to pay up some debt that he owes; and, if he does not pay, the court will issue a *procès* against him. That's what it is, *madame*."

Lavinia carried the paper into the *salon*, and sat studying it. As far as she could make it out, Mr. Edwin Fennel was called upon to pay to some creditor the sum of one hundred and eighty-three *francs*, without delay.

"Over seven pounds! And if he does not pay, the law expenses, to enforce it, will increase the debt perhaps by one-half," sighed Lavinia. "There may be, and no doubt *are*, other things at the back of this. Will he turn us out of house and home? "

Propping the paper against the wall over the mantelpiece, she left it there, that it might meet the captain's eye on his return.

Not until quite late that evening did Madame Carimon get her husband to herself, for he brought in one of the young under-masters at the college to dine with them. But as soon as they were sitting cosily alone, he smoking his pipe before bedtime, she told him all she had heard from Lavinia Preen.

"I don't like it, Jules; I don't indeed," she said. "It has made a strangely disagreeable impression on me. What is your opinion?"

Placid Monsieur Jules did not seem to have much opinion one way or the other. Upon the superstitious portion of the tale he, being a practical Frenchman, totally declined to have any at all. He was very sorry for the uncomfortable position Miss Preen found herself in, and he certainly was not surprised she should wish to quit the Petite Maison Rouge if affairs could not be made more agreeable there. As to the Capitaine Fennel, he felt free to confess there was something about him which he did not like: and he was sure no man of honour ought to have run away clandestinely, as he did, with Miss Nancy.

"You see, Jules, what the man aims at is to get hold of Nancy's income and apply it to his own uses—and for Lavinia to keep them upon hers."

"I see," said Jules.

"And Lavinia *cannot* do it; she has not half enough. It troubles me very much," flashed Madame Carimon. "She says she shall stay with them until Easter is over. *I* should not; I should leave them to it tomorrow."

"Yes, my dear, that's all very well," nodded Monsieur Jules; "but we cannot always do precisely what we would. Miss Preen is responsible for the rent of that house, and if Fennel and his wife do not pay it, she would have to. She must have a thorough understanding upon that point before she leaves it."

By the nine-o'clock train that night they came home, Lavinia, pleading a bad headache and feeling altogether out of sorts, got Flore to remain for once, and went herself to bed. She dreaded the very sight of Captain Fennel,

In the morning she saw that the paper had disappeared from the mantelpiece. He was quite jaunty at breakfast, talking to her and Nancy about Pontipette; and things passed pleasantly. About eleven o'clock he began brushing his hat to go out.

"I'm going to have a look at Griffin, and see how he's getting on," he remarked. "Perhaps the old man would enjoy a drive this fine day; if so, you may not see me back till dinner-time."

But just as Captain Fennel turned out of the Place Ronde to the Rue Tessin, he came upon Charles Palliser, strolling along.

"Fine day, Mr. Charles," he remarked graciously.

"Capital," assented Charles, "and I'm glad of it; the old gentleman will have a good passage. I've just seen him off by the eleven train."

"Seems to me you spend your time in seeing people off by trains. Which old gentleman is it now?—him from below? "

Charley laughed. "It's Griffin this time," said he. "Being feeble, I thought I might be of use in starting him, and went up."

"Griffin!" exclaimed Captain Fennel. "Why, where's he gone to?"

"To Calais. *En route* for Dover and—"

"What's he gone for? When's he coming back?" interrupted the captain, speaking like a man in great amazement.

"He is not coming back at all; he has gone for good," said Charley. "His daughter came to fetch him."

"Why on earth should she do that?"

"It seems that her husband, a clergyman at Kensington, fell across Major Smith last week in London, and put some pretty close questions to him about the old man, for they had been made uneasy by his letters of late. The major—"

"What business had the major in London?" questioned Captain Fennel impatiently.

"You can ask him," said Charles equably, "I didn't. He is back again. Well, Major Smith, being questioned, made no bones about it at all; said Griffin and Griffin's money both wanted looking after. Upon that, the daughter came straight off, arriving here on Sunday morning; she settled things yesterday, and has carried her father away today. He was as pleased as Punch, poor childish old fellow, at the prospect of a voyage in the boat."

Whether this information put a check upon any little plan Captain Fennel may have been entertaining, Charles Palliser could not positively know; but he thought he had never seen so evil an eye as the one glaring upon him. Only for a moment; just a flash; and then the face was smoothed again. Charley had his ideas—and all his wits about him; and old Griffin had babbled publicly.

Captain Fennel strolled by his side towards the port, talking of Pontipette and other matters of indifference. When in sight of the harbour, he halted.

"I must wish you good-day now, Palliser; I have letters to write," said he; and walked briskly back again.

Lavinia and Nancy were sitting together in the *salon* when he reached home. Nancy was looking scared.

"Edwin," she said, leaving her chair to meet him—"Edwin, what do you think Lavinia has been saying? That she is going to leave us."

"Oh, indeed," he carelessly answered.

"But it is true, Edwin; she means it."

"Yes, I mean it," interposed Lavinia very quietly. "You and Nancy will be better without me; perhaps happier."

He looked at her for a full minute in silence, then laughed a little. "Like Darby and Joan," he remarked, as he put his writing-case on the table and sat down to it.

Mrs. Fennel returned to her chair by Lavinia, who was sitting close to the window mending a lace collar which had been torn in the ironing. As usual Nancy was doing nothing.

"You *couldn't* leave me, Lavinia, you know," she said in coaxing tones.

"I know that I never thought to do so, Ann, but circumstances alter cases," answered the elder sister. Both of them had dropped their voices to a low key, not to disturb the letter-writer. But he could hear if he chose to listen. "I began putting my things together yesterday, and shall finish doing it at leisure. I will stay over Easter with you; but go then I shall."

"You must be cruel to think of such a thing, Lavinia."

"Not cruel," corrected Lavinia. "I am sorry, Ann, but the step is forced upon me. The anxieties in regard to money matters are wearing me out; they would wear me out altogether if I did not end them. And there are other things which urge upon me the expediency of departure from this house."

"What things?"

"I cannot speak of them. Never mind what they are, Ann.

They concern myself; not you."

Ann Fennel sat twirling one of her fair silken ringlets be-tween her thumb and finger; a habit of hers when thinking:.

"Where shall you live, Lavinia, if you do leave? Take another apartment at Sainteville?"

"I think not. It is a puzzling question. Possibly I may go back to Buttermead, and get some family to take me in as a board-er," dreamily answered Lavinia. "Seventy pounds a-year will not keep me luxuriously."

Captain Fennel lifted his face. "If it will not keep one, how is it to keep two?" he demanded, in rather defiant tones.

"I don't know anything about that," said Lavinia civilly. "I have not two to keep; only one."

Nancy chanced to catch a glimpse of his face just then, and its look frightened her. Lavinia had her back to him, and did not see it. Nancy began to cry quietly.

"Oh, Lavinia, you will think better of this; you will not leave us!" she implored. "We could not do at all without you and your half of the money."

Lavinia had finished her collar, and rose to take it upstairs. "Don't be distressed, Nancy," she paused to say; "it is a thing that *must be*. I am very sorry; but it is not my fault. As you—"

"You can stay in the house if you choose!" flashed Nancy, growing feebly angry.

"No, I cannot. I *cannot*," repeated Lavinia. "I begin to foresee that I might—might die of it."

11

Sainteville felt surprised and sorry to hear that Miss Preen was going to leave it to its own devices, for the town had grown to like her. Lavinia did not herself talk about going, but the news somehow got wind. People wondered why she went. Matters, as connected with the financial department of the Petite Mai-son Rouge, were known but imperfectly—to most people not known at all; so that reason was not thought of. It was quite understood that Ann Preen's stolen marriage, capped by the bringing home of her husband to the Petite Maison Rouge, had been a sharp blow to Miss Preen: perhaps, said Sainteville now, she had tried living with them and found it did not answer. Or perhaps she was only going away for a change, and would return after a while.

Passion week passed, and Easter week came in, and Lavinia made her arrangements for the succeeding one. On the Tuesday in that next week, all being well, she would quit Sainteville. Her preparations were made; her larger box was already packed and corded. Nancy, of shallow temperament and elastic spirits, seemed quite to have recovered from the sting of the proposed parting; she helped Lavinia to put up her laces and other little fine things, prattling all the time. Captain Fennel maintained his suavity. Beyond the words he had spoken—as to how she expected the income to keep two if it would not keep one—he had said nothing. It might be that he hardly yet believed Lavinia would positively go.

But she was going. At first only to Boulogne-sur-Mer. Monsieur Jules Carimon had a cousin, Madame Degravier, who kept a superior boarding-house there, much patronized by the English; he had written to her to introduce Miss Preen, and to intimate that it would oblige him if the terms were made *très facile*. *Madame* had written back to Lavinia most satisfactorily, and, so far, that was arranged.

Once at Boulogne in peace and quietness, Lavinia would have leisure to decide upon her future plans. She hoped to pay a visit to Buttermead in the summer-time, for she had begun to yearn for a sight of the old place and its people. After that—well, she should see. If things went on pleasantly at Sainteville—that is, if Captain Fennel and Nancy were still in the Petite Maison Rouge, and he was enabled to find means to continue in it— then, perhaps, she might return to the town. Not to make one of the household—never again that; but she might find a little *pied-à-terre* in some other home.

Meanwhile, Lavinia heard no more of the *procès*, and she wondered how the captain was meeting it. During the Easter week she made her farewell calls. That week she was not very much at home; one or other of her old acquaintances wanted her. Major and Mrs. Smith had her to spend a day with them; the Miss Bosanquets invited her also; and so on.

One call, involving also private business, she made upon old Madame Sauvage, Mary Carimon accompanying her. Monsieur Gustave was called up to the *salon* to assist at the conference. Lavinia partly explained her position to them in strict confidence, and the motive, as touching pecuniary affairs, which was taking her away: she said nothing of that other and greater motive, her superstitious fear.

"I have come to speak of the rent," she said to Monsieur Gustave, and Mary Carimon repeated the words in French to old Madame Sauvage. "You must in future look to Captain Fennel for it; you must make him pay it if possible. At the same time, I admit my own responsibility," added Lavinia, "and if it be found totally impracticable to get it from Captain Fennel or my sister, I shall pay it to you. This must, of course, be kept strictly between ourselves, Monsieur Gustave; you and *madame* understand that. If Captain Fennel gained any intimation of it, he would take care not to pay it."

Monsieur Gustave and *madame* his mother assured her that they fully understood, and that she might rely upon their honour. They were grieved to lose so excellent a tenant and neighbour as Miss Preen, and wished circumstances had been more kindly. One thing she might rest assured of—that they should feel at least as mortified at having to apply to her for the rent as she herself would be, and they would not leave a stone unturned to extract it from the hands of Captain Fennel.

"It has altogether been a most bitter trial to me," sighed Lavinia, as she stood up to say farewell to *madame*.

The old lady understood, and the tears came into her compassionate eyes as she held Lavinia's hands between her own. "Ay, for certain," she replied in French. "She and her sons had said so privately to one another ever since the abrupt coming home of the strange captain to the petite *maison à côté*."

On Sunday, Lavinia, accompanied by Nancy and Captain

Fennel, attended morning service for the last time. She spoke to several acquaintances coming out, wishing them goodbye, and was hastening to overtake her sister, when she heard rapid steps behind her, and a voice speaking. Turning, she saw Charley Palliser.

"Miss Preen," cried he, "my aunt wants you to come home and dine with us. See, she is waiting for you. You could not come any one day last week, you know."

"I was not able to come to you last week, Mr, Charles; I had so much to do, and so many engagements," said Lavinia, as she walked back to Mrs. Hardy, who stood smiling.

"But you will come today, dear Miss Preen," said old Mrs. Hardy, who had caught the words. "We have a lovely *fricandeau* of veal, and—"

"Why, that is just our own dinner," interrupted Lavinia gaily. "I should like to come to you, Mrs. Hardy, but I cannot. It is my last Sunday at home, and I could not well go out and leave them."

They saw the force of the objection. Mrs. Hardy asked whether she should be at church in the evening. Lavinia replied that she intended to be, and they agreed to bid each other farewell then.

"You don't know what you've lost. Miss Preen," said Charley comically. "There's a huge cream tart—lovely."

Captain Fennel was quite lively at the dinner-table. He related a rather laughable story which had been told him by Major Smith, with whom he had walked for ten minutes after church, and was otherwise gracious.

After dinner, while Flore was taking away the things, he left the room, and came back with three glasses of liqueur, on a small waiter, handing one to Lavinia, another to his wife, and keeping the third himself. It was the yellow *chartreuse*; Captain Fennel kept a bottle of it and of one or two other choice liqueurs in the little cupboard at the end of the passage, and treated them to a glass sometimes.

"How delightful!" cried Nancy, who liked *chartreuse* and anything else that was good.

They sat and sipped it, talking pleasantly together. The captain soon finished his, and said he should take a stroll on the pier. It was a bright day with a brisk wind, which seemed to be getting higher.

"The London boat ought to be in about four o'clock," he remarked. "It's catching it sweetly, I know; passengers will look like ghosts. *Au revoir*; don't get quarrelling." And thus, nodding to the two ladies, he went out gaily.

Not much danger of their quarrelling. They turned their chairs to the fire, and plunged into conversation, which chanced to turn upon Buttermead. In calling up one reminiscence of the old place after another, now Lavinia, now Nancy, the time passed on. Lavinia wore her silver-grey silk dress that day, with some yellowish-looking lace falling at the throat and wrists.

Flore came in to bring the tea-tray; she always put it on the table in readiness on a Sunday afternoon. The water, she said, would be on the boil in the kitchen by the time they wanted it. And then she went away as usual for the rest of the day.

Not long afterwards, Lavinia, who was speaking, suddenly stopped in the middle of a sentence. She started up in her chair, fell back again, and clasped her hands below her chest with a great cry.

"Oh, Nancy!— Nancy!"

Nancy dashed across the hearthrug. "What is it?" she exclaimed. "What is it, Lavinia?"

Lavinia apparently could not say what it was. She seemed to be in the greatest agony; her face had turned livd. Nancy was next door to an imbecile in any emergency, and fairly wrung her hands in her distress.

"Oh, what can be the matter with me?" gasped Lavinia, "Nancy, I think I am dying."

The next moment she had glided from the chair to the floor, and lay there shrieking and writhing. Bursting away, Nancy ran round to the next house, all closed today, rang wildly at the private door, and when it was opened by Mariette, rushed upstairs to *madame's salon.*

Madame Veuve Sauvage, comprehending that something was amiss, without understanding Nancy's frantic words, put a shawl on her shoulders to hasten to the other house, ordering Mariette to follow her. Her sons were out.

There lay Lavinia, in the greatest agony. Madame Sauvage sent Mariette off for Monsieur Dupuis, and told her to fly. "Better bring Monsieur Henri Dupuis, Mariette," she called after her: "he will get quicker over the ground than his old father."

But Monsieur Henri Dupuis, as it turned out, was absent. He had left that morning for Calais with his wife, to spend two days with her friends who lived there, purposing to be back early on Tuesday morning. Old Monsieur Dupuis came very quickly. He thought Mademoiselle Preen must have inward inflammation, he said to Madame Sauvage, and inquired what she had eaten for dinner. Nancy told him as well as she could between her sobs and her broken speech.

A *fricandeau* of veal, potatoes, a cauliflower *au gratin*, and a *frangipane* tart from the pastrycook's. No fruit or any other dessert. They took a little Bordeaux wine with dinner, and a liqueur glass of *chartreuse* afterwards.

All very wholesome, pronounced Monsieur Dupuis, with satisfaction; not at all likely to disagree with *mademoiselle.* Possibly she had caught a chill.

Mariette had run for Flore, who came in great consternation. Between them all they got Lavinia upstairs, undressed her and laid her in bed, applying hot flannels to the pain—and Monsieur Dupuis administered in a wine-glass of water every quarter-of-an-hour some drops from a glass phial which he had brought in his pocket.

It was close upon half-past five when Captain Fennel came in. He expressed much surprise and concern, saying, like the doctor, that she must have eaten something which had disagreed with her. The doctor avowed that he could not otherwise account for the seizure; he did not altogether think it was produced by a chill; and he spoke again of the dinner. Captain

Fennel observed that as to the dinner they had all three partaken of it, one the same as another; he did not see why it should affect his sister-in-law and not himself or his wife. This reasoning was evident, admitted Monsieur Dupuis; but Miss Preen had touched nothing since her breakfast, except at dinner. In point of fact, he felt very much at a loss, he did not scruple to add; but the more acute symptoms were showing a slight improvement, he was thankful to perceive, and he trusted to bring her round.

As he did. In a few hours the pain had so far abated, or yielded to remedies, that poor Lavinia, worn out, dropped into a comfortable sleep. Monsieur Dupuis was round again early in the morning, and found her recovered, though still feeling tired and very weak. He advised her to lie in bed until the afternoon; not to get up then unless she felt inclined; and he charged her to take chiefly milk food all the day—no solids whatever.

Lavinia slept again all the morning, and awoke very much refreshed. In the afternoon she felt quite equal to getting up, and did so, dressing herself in the grey silk she had worn the previous day, because it was nearest at hand. She then penned a line to Madame Degravier, saying she was unable to travel to Boulogne on the morrow, as had been fixed, but hoped to be there on Wednesday, or, at the latest, Thursday.

Captain Fennel, who generally took possession of the easiest chair in the salon, and the warmest place, resigned it to Lavinia the instant she appeared downstairs. He shook her by the hand, said how glad he was that she had recovered from her indisposition, and installed her in the chair with a cushion at her back and a rug over her knees. All she had to dread now, he thought, was cold; she must guard against that. Lavinia replied that she could not in the least imagine what had been the matter with her; she had never had a similar attack before, and had never been in such dreadful pain.

Presently Mary Carimon came in, having heard of the affair from Mariette, whom she had met in the fish-market during the morning. All danger was over, Mariette said, and *mademoiselle* was then sleeping quietly: so Madame Carimon, not to disturb her, put off calling until the afternoon. Captain Fennel sat talking with her a few minutes, and then went out. For some cause or other he never seemed to be quite at ease in the presence of Madame Carimon.

"I know what it must have been," cried Mary Carimon, coming to one of her rapid conclusions after listening to the description of the illness. "Misled by the sunny spring days last week, you went and left off some of your warm underclothing, Lavinia, and so caught cold."

"Good gracious!" exclaimed Nancy, who had curled herself up on the sofa like a ball, not having yet recovered from her fatigue and fright. "Leave off one's warm things the beginning of April! I never heard of such imprudence! How came you to do it, Lavinia?"

"I did not do it," said Lavinia quietly. "I have not left off" anything. Should I be so silly as to do that with a journey before me?"

"Then what caused the attack?" debated Madame Carimon. "Something you had eaten?"

Lavinia shook her head helplessly. "It could hardly have been that, Mary. I took nothing whatever that Nancy and Captain Fennel did not take. I wish I did know—that I might guard, if possible, against a similar attack in future. The pain seized me all in a moment. I thought I was dying."

"It sounds odd," said Madame Carimon. "Monsieur Dupuis does not know either, it seems. That's why I thought you might have been leaving off your things, and did not like to tell him."

"I conclude that it must have been one of those mysterious attacks of sudden illness to which we are all liable, but for which no one can account," sighed Lavinia. "I hope I shall never have it again. This experience has been enough for a lifetime."

Mary Carimon warmly echoed the hope as she rose to take her departure. She advised Lavinia to go to bed early, and promised to come again in the morning.

While Captain Fennel and Nancy dined, Flore made her mistress some tea, and brought in with it some thin bread-and-butter. Lavinia felt all the better for the refreshment, laughingly remarking that by the morning she was sure she should be as hungry as a hunter. She sat chatting, and sometimes dozing between whiles, until about a quarter to nine o'clock, when she said she would go to bed.

Nancy went to the kitchen to make her a cup of arrowroot. Lavinia then wished Captain Fennel goodnight, and went upstairs. Flore had left as usual, after washing up the dinner-things.

"Lavinia, shall I—— Oh, she has gone on," broke off Nancy, who had come in with the breakfast-cup of arrowroot in her hand. "Edwin, do you think I may venture to put a little brandy into this?"

Captain Fennel sat reading with his face to the fire and the lamp at his elbow. He turned round.

"Brandy?" said he. "I'm sure I don't know. If that pain meant inflammation, brandy might do harm. Ask Lavinia; she had better decide for herself. No, no; leave the arrowroot on the table here," he hastily cried, as Nancy was going out of the room with the cup. "Tell Lavinia to come down, and we'll discuss the matter with her. Of course a little brandy would do her an immense deal of good, if she might take it with safety."

Nancy did as she was told. Leaving the cup and saucer on the table, she went up to her sister. In a minute or two she was back again.

"Lavinia won't come down again, Edwin; she is already half-undressed. She thinks she had better be on the safe side, and not have the brandy."

"All right," replied the captain, who was sitting as before, intent on his book. Nancy took the cup upstairs.

She helped her sister into bed, and then gave her the arrowroot, inquiring whether she had made it well.

"Quite well, only it was rather sweet," answered Lavinia.

"Sweet!" echoed Nancy, in reply. "Why, I hardly put any sugar at all into it; I remembered that you don't like it."

Lavinia finished the cupful. Nancy tucked her up, and gave

her a goodnight kiss. "Pleasant dreams, Lavinia dear," she called back, as she was shutting the door.

"Thank you, Nancy; but I hope I shall sleep tonight without dreaming," answered Lavinia.

As Nancy went downstairs she turned into the kitchen for her own arrowroot, which she had left all that time in the saucepan. Being fond of it, she had made enough for herself as well as for Lavinia.

12

It was between half-past ten and eleven, and Captain and Mrs. Fennel were in their bedroom preparing to retire to rest. She stood before the glass doing her hair, having thrown a thin print cotton cape upon her shoulders as usual, to protect her dress; he had taken off his coat.

"What was that?" cried she, in startled tones.

Some sound had penetrated to their room. The captain put his coat on a chair and bent his ear. "I did not hear anything, Nancy," he answered.

"There it is again!" exclaimed Nancy. "Oh, it is Lavinia! I do believe it is Lavinia!"

Flinging the comb from her hand, Nancy dashed out at the room-door, which was near the head of the stairs; Lavinia's door being nearly at the end of the passage. Unmistakable sounds, now a shriek, now a wail, came from Lavinia's chamber. Nancy flew into it, her fair hair falling on her shoulders.

"What is it, Lavinia? Oh, Edwin, Edwin, come here!" called Mrs. Fennel, beside herself with terror. Lavinia was rolling about the bed, as she had the previous day rolled on the *salon* floor; her face was distorted with pain, her moans and cries agonizing.

Captain Fennel stayed to put on his coat, came to Lavinia's door, and put his head inside it. "Is it the pain again?" he asked.

"Yes, it is the pain again," gasped Lavinia, in answer. "I am dying, I am surely dying!"

That put the finishing-touch to timorous Nancy.

"Edwin, run, run for Monsieur Dupuis!" she implored. "Oh, what shall we do? What shall we do?"

Captain Fennel descended the stairs. When Nancy thought he must have been gone out at least a minute or two, he appeared again with a wine-glass of hot brandy-and-water, which he had stayed to mix.

"Try and get her to take this," he said. "It can't do harm; it may do good. And if you could put hot flannels to her, Nancy, it might be well; they eased the pain yesterday. I'll bring Dupuis here as soon as I can."

Lavinia could not take the brandy-and-water, and it was left upon the grey marble top of the chest of drawers. Her paroxysms increased; Nancy had never seen or imagined such pain, for this attack was worse than the other, and she almost lost her wits with terror. Could she see Lavinia die before her eyes?—no helping hand near to strive to save her? Just as Nancy had done before, she did again now.

Flying down the stairs and out of the house, across the yard and through the dark entry, she seized the bell-handle of Madame Veuve Sauvage's door and pulled it frantically. The household had all retired for the night.

Presently a window above opened, and Monsieur Gustave—Nancy knew his voice—looked out.

"Who's there?" he asked in French. "What's the matter?"

"Oh, Monsieur Gustave, come in for the love of Heaven!" responded poor Nancy, looking up, "She has another attack, worse than the first; she's dying, and there's no one in the house but me."

"Directly, *madame*; I am with you on the instant," he kindly answered. "I but wait to put on my effects."

He was at the Petite Maison Rouge almost as soon as she; his brother Emile followed him in, and Mariette, whom they had called, came shortly. Miss Preen lay in dreadful paroxysms; it did appear to them that she must die. Nancy and Mariette busied themselves in the kitchen, heating flannels.

The doctor did not seem to come very quickly. Captain Fennel at length made his appearance and said Monsieur Dupuis would be there in a minute or two.

"I am content to hear that," remarked Monsieur Gustave in reply. "I was just about to despatch my brother for the first doctor he could find."

"Never had such trouble in ringing up a doctor before," returned Captain Fennel. "I suppose the old man sleeps too soundly to be easily aroused; many elderly people do."

"I fear she is dying," whispered Monsieur Gustave.

"No, no, surely not!" cried Captain Fennel, recoiling a step at the words. "What can it possibly be? What causes the attacks?"

Whilst Monsieur Gustave was shaking his head at this difficult question. Monsieur Dupuis arrived. Monsieur Emile, anxious to make himself useful, was requested by Mariette to go to Flore's *domicile* and ring her up. Flore seemed to have been sleeping with her clothes on, for they came back together.

Monsieur Dupuis could do nothing for his patient. He strove to administer drops of medicinal remedies; he caused her to be nearly smothered in scalding-hot flannels—all in vain. He despatched Monsieur Emile Sauvage to bring in another doctor, Monsieur Podevin, who lived near. All in vain. Lavinia died. Just at one o'clock in the morning, before the cocks had begun to crow, Lavinia Preen died.

The shock to those in the house was great. It seemed to stun them, one and all. The brothers Sauvage, leaving a few words of heartfelt sympathy with Captain Fennel, withdrew silently to their own home. Mariette stayed. The two doctors, shut up in the salon, talked with one another, endeavouring to account for the death.

"Inflammation, no doubt," observed Monsieur Dupuis; "but even so, the death has been too speedy."

"More like poison," rejoined the younger man, Monsieur Podevin. He was brother to the proprietor of the Hôtel des Princes, and was much respected by his fellow-citizens as a safe and skilful practitioner.

"The thought of poison naturally occurred to me on Sunday, when I was first called to her," returned Monsieur Dupuis, "but it could not be borne out. You see, she had partaken of nothing, either in food or drink, but what the other inmates had taken; absolutely nothing. This was assured me by them all, herself included."

"She seems to have taken nothing today, either, that could in any way harm her," said Monsieur Podevin.

"Nothing. She took a cup of tea at five o'clock, which the servant, Flore, prepared and also partook of herself—a cup out of the same teapot. Later, when the poor lady went to bed, her sister made her a basin of arrowroot, and made herself one at the same time."

"Well, it appears strange."

"It could not have been a chill. The symptoms—"

"A chill?—bah!" interrupted Monsieur Podevin. "We shall know more after the post-mortem," he added, taking up his hat. "Of course there must be one."

Wishing his brother practitioner goodnight, he left. Monsieur Dupuis went looking about for Captain Fennel, and found him in the kitchen, standing by the hot stove, and drinking a glass of hot brandy-and-water. The rest were upstairs.

"This event has shaken my nerves, doctor," apologized the captain, in reference to the glass. "I never was so upset. Shall I mix you one?"

Monsieur Dupuis shook his head. He never took anything so strong. The most calming thing, in his opinion, was a glass of *eau sucrée*, with a teaspoonful of orange-flower water in it.

"Sir," he went on, "I have been conversing with my esteemed *confrère*. We cannot, either of us, decide what *mademoiselle* has died of, being unable to see any adequate cause for it; and we wish to hold a post-mortem examination. I presume you will not object to it?"

"Certainly not; I think there should be one," briskly spoke Captain Fennel after a moment's pause, "For our satisfaction, if for nothing else, doctor."

"Very well. Will nine o'clock in the morning suit you, as to time? It should be made early."

"I—expect it will," answered the captain, reflecting, "Do you hold it here?"

"Undoubtedly. In her own room."

"Then wait just one minute, will you, doctor, whilst I speak to my wife. Nine o'clock seems a little early, but I dare say it will suit."

Monsieur Dupuis went back into the *salon*. He had waited there a short interval, when Mrs. Fennel burst in, wild with excitement. Her hair still hung down her back, her eyes were swollen with weeping, her face was one of piteous distress. She advanced to Monsieur Dupuis, and held up her trembling hands.

The old doctor understood English fairly well when it was quietly spoken; but he did not in the least understand it in a storm. Sobbing, trembling, Mrs. Fennel was beseeching him not to hold a post-mortem on her poor dead sister, for the love of mercy.

Surprised and distressed, he placed her on the sofa, soothed her into calmness, and then bade her tell him quietly what her petition was. She repeated it—begging, praying, imploring him not to disturb her sister now she was at rest; but to let her be put into her grave in peace. Well, well, said the compassionate old man; if it would pain the relatives so greatly to have it done, he and Monsieur Podevin would, of course, abandon the idea. It would be a satisfaction to them both to be able to decide upon the cause of death, but they did not wish to proceed in it against the feelings of the family.

Sainteville woke up in the morning to a shock. Half the townspeople still believed that Miss Preen was leaving that day, Tuesday, for Boulogne; and to hear that she would not go on that journey, that she would never go on any earthly journey again, that she was *dead*, shook them to the centre.

What had been the matter with her?—what had killed her so quickly in the midst of life and health? Groups asked this; one group meeting another. "Inflammation," was the answer—for that report had somehow started itself. She caught a chill on the Sunday, probably when leaving the church after morning service; it induced speedy and instant inflammation, and she had died of it.

With softened steps and mournful faces, hosts of people made their way to the Place Ronde. Only to take a glimpse at the outside of the Maison Rouge brought satisfaction to excited feelings. Monsieur Gustave Sauvage had caused his white shop window-blinds to be drawn half-way down, out of respect to the dead; all the windows above had the green *persiennes* closed before them. The calamity had so greatly affected old Madame Sauvage that she lay in bed.

When her sons returned indoors after the death had taken place, their mother called them to her room. Nancy's violent ringing had disturbed her, and she had lain since then in anxiety, waiting for news.

"Better not tell the mother tonight," whispered Emile to his brother outside her door.

But the mother's ears were quick; she was sitting up in bed, and the door was ajar. "Yes, you will tell me, my sons," she said. "I am fearing the worst."

"Well, mother, it is all over," avowed Gustave. "The attack was more violent than the one last night, and the poor lady is gone."

"May the good God have taken her to His rest!" fervently aspirated *madame*. But she lay down in the bed in her distress and covered her face with the white-frilled pillow and sobbed a little. Gustave and Emile related a few particulars.

"And what was really the malady? What is it that she has died of?" questioned the mother, wiping her eyes.

"That is not settled; nobody seems to know," replied Gustave.

Madame Veuve Sauvage lay still, thinking. "I—hope—that—man—has—not—done—her—any—injury!" she slowly said.

"I hope not either; there is no appearance of it," said Monsieur Gustave. "Any way, mother, she had two skilful doctors with her, honest men and upright. Better not admit such thoughts."

"True, true," murmured *madame*, appeased. "I fear the poor dear lady must have taken a chill, which struck inwardly. That handsome *demoiselle*, the cousin of *Monsieur le Procureur*, died of the same thing, you may remember. Goodnight, my sons; you leave me very unhappy."

About eight o'clock in the morning, Monsieur Jules Carimon heard of it. In going through the large iron entrance-gates of the college to his day's work, he found himself accosted by one of two or three young *gamins* of pupils, who were also entering. It was Dion Pamart. The well-informed reader is of course aware that the French educational colleges are attended by all classes, high and low, indiscriminately.

"*Monsieur*, have you heard?" said the lad, with timid deprecation. "*Mademoiselle* is dead."

Monsieur Jules Carimon turned his eyes on the speaker. At first he did not recognize him: his own work lay with the advanced desks.

"Ah, *c'est Pamart, n'est-ce-pas?*" said he, "What did you say, my boy? Someone is dead?"

Dion Pamart repeated his information. The master, inwardly shocked, took refuge in disbelief.

"I think you must be mistaken, Pamart," said he.

"Oh no, I'm not, sir. *Mademoiselle* was taken frightfully ill again last night, and they fetched my mother. They had two doctors to her and all; but they couldn't do anything for her, and she died. Grandmother gave me my breakfast just now; she said my mother was crying too much to come home. The other lady, the captain's wife, has been in hysterics all night."

"Go on to your desks," commanded Monsieur Carimon to the small fry now gathered round him.

He turned back home himself. When he entered *the salle-à-manger*, Pauline was carrying away the last of the breakfast-things. Her mistress stood putting a little water on a musk plant in the window.

"Is it you, Jules?" she exclaimed. "Have you forgotten something?"

Monsieur Jules shut the door. "I have not forgotten anything," he answered. "But I have heard of a sad calamity, and I have come back to prepare you, Marie, before you hear it from others."

He spoke solemnly; he was looking solemn. His wife put down the jug of water on the table. "A calamity?" she repeated.

"Yes.You will grieve to hear it.Your friend. Miss Preen, was—was taken ill last night with the same sort of attack, but more violent; and she—"

"Oh, Jules, don't tell me, don't tell me!" cried Mary Carimon, lifting her hands to ward off the words with a too sure prevision of what they were going to be.

"But, my dear, you must be told sooner or later," remonstrated he; "you cannot go through even this morning without hearing it from one person or another. Flore's boy was my informant. In spite of all that could be done by those about her, poor lady—in spite of the two doctors who were called to her aid—she died."

Madame Carimon was a great deal too much stunned for tears. She sank back in a chair with a face of stone, feeling that the room was turning upside down about her.

An hour later, when she had somewhat gathered her scattered senses together, she set off for the Petite Maison Rouge. Her way lay past the house of Monsieur Podevin; old Monsieur Dupuis was turning out of it as she went by. Madame Carimon stopped.

"Yes," the doctor said, when a few words had passed, "it is a most desolating affair. But, as *madame* knows, when Death has laid his grasp upon a patient, medical craft loses its power to resist him."

"Too true," murmured Mary Carimon. "And what is it that she has died of?"

Monsieur Dupuis shook his head to indicate that he did not know.

"I could have wished for an examination, to ascertain the true cause of the seizure," continued the doctor, "and I come now from expressing my regrets to my *confrère*, Monsieur Podevin. He agrees with me in deciding that we cannot press it in opposition to the family. Captain Fennel was quite willing it should take place, but his wife, poor distressed woman, altogether objects to it."

Mary Carimon went on to the house of death. She saw Lavinia, looking so peaceful in her stillness. A happy smile sat on her countenance. On her white attire lay some sweet fresh primroses, which Flore had placed there. Lavinia loved primroses. She used to say that when she looked at them they brought to her mind the woods and dales of Buttermead, always carpeted with the pale, fair blossoms in the spring of the year. Mrs. Fennel lay in a heavy sleep, exhausted by her night of distress, Flore informed Madame Carimon; and the captain, anxious about her, was sitting in her room, to guard against her being disturbed.

On the next day, Wednesday, in obedience to the laws of France relating to the dead, Lavinia Preen was buried. All the English gentlemen in the town, and some Frenchmen, including Monsieur Carimon and the sons of Madame Veuve Sauvage, assembled in the Place Ronde, and fell in behind the coffin when it was brought forth. They walked after it to the portion of the cemetery consecrated to Protestants, and there witnessed the interment. The tears trickled down Charley Palliser's face as he took his last look into the grave, and he was honest enough not to mind who saw them.

13

In their new mourning, at the English Church, the Sunday after the interment of Lavinia Preen, appeared Captain and Mrs. Fennel. The congregation looked at them more than at the parson. Poor Nancy's eyes were so blinded with tears that she could not see the letters in her Prayer-book. Only one little week ago when she had sat there, Lavinia was on the bench at her side, alive and well; and now—It was with difficulty Nancy kept herself from breaking down.

Two or three acquaintances caught her hand on leaving the church, whispering a few words of sympathy in her ear. Not one but felt truly sorry for her. The captain's hat, which had a wide band round it, was perpetually raised in acknowledgment of silent greetings, as he piloted his wife back to their house, the Petite Maison Rouge.

A very different dinner-table, this which the two sat down to, from last Sunday's, in the matter of cheerfulness. Nancy was about half-way through the wing of the fowl her husband had helped her to, when a choking sob caught her throat. She dropped her knife and fork.

"Oh, Edwin, I cannot! I cannot eat for my unhappy thoughts! This time last Sunday Lavinia was seated at the table with us. Now—" Nancy's speech collapsed altogether.

"Come, come," said Captain Fennel. "I hope you are not going to be hysterical again, Nancy. It is frightfully sad; I know that; but this prolonged grief will do no good. Go on with your dinner; it is a very nice chicken."

Nancy gave a great sob, and spoke impulsively, "I don't believe you regret her one bit, Edwin!"

Edwin Fennel in turn laid down his knife and fork and stared at his wife. A curious expression sat on his face.

"Not regret her," he repeated with emphasis. "Why, Nancy, I regret her every hour of the day. But I do not make a parade of my regrets. Why should I?—to what end? Come, come, my dear; you will be all the better for eating your dinner."

He went on with his own as he spoke. Nancy took up her knife and fork with a hopeless sigh.

Dinner over, Captain Fennel went to his cupboard and brought in some of the *chartreuse*. Two glasses, this time, instead of three. He might regret Lavinia, as he said, every hour of the day; possibly he did so; but it did not seem to affect his appetite, or his relish for good things.

Most events have their dark and their light sides. It could hardly escape the mind of Edwin Fennel that by the death of Lavinia the whole income became Nancy's. To him that must have been a satisfactory consolation.

In the afternoon he went with Nancy for a walk on the pier. She did not want to go; said she had no spirits for it; it was miserable at home; miserable out; miserable everywhere. Captain

Fennel took her off, as he might have taken a child, telling her she should come and see the fishing-boats. After tea they went to church—an unusual thing for Captain Fennel. Lavinia and Nancy formerly went to evening service; he, never.

That night something curious occurred. Nancy went up to bed leaving the captain to follow, after finishing his glass of grog. He generally took one the last thing. Nancy had taken off her gown, and was standing before the glass about to undo her hair, when she heard him leave the parlour. Her bedroom door, almost close to the head of the stairs, was not closed, and her ears were on the alert. Since Lavinia died, Nancy had felt timid in the house when alone, and she was listening for her husband to come up. She heard him lock up the spirit bottle in the little cupboard below, and begin to ascend the stairs, and she opened her door wider, that the light might guide him, for the staircase was in darkness.

Captain Fennel had nearly gained the top, when something— he never knew what—induced him to look round sharply, as though he fancied someone was close behind him. In fact, he did fancy it. In a moment, he gave a shout, dashed onwards into the bedroom, shut the door with a bang, and bolted it. Nancy, in great astonishment, turned to look at him. He seemed to have shrunk within himself in a fit of trembling, his face was ghastly, and the perspiration stood upon his brow.

"Edwin!" she exclaimed in a scared whisper, "what is the matter?"

Captain Fennel did not answer at first. He was getting up his breath.

"Has Flore not gone?" he then said.

"*Flore!*" exclaimed Nancy in surprise. "Why, Edwin, you know Flore goes away on Sundays in the middle of the afternoon! She left before we went on the pier. Why do you ask?"

"I—I thought—some person—followed me upstairs," he replied, in uneasy pauses.

"Oh, my goodness." cried timid Nancy. "Perhaps a thief has got into the house!"

She went to the door, and was about to draw it an inch open, intending to peep out gingerly and listen, when her husband pulled her back with a motion of terror, and put his back against it. This meant, she thought, that he *knew* a thief was there. Perhaps two of them!

"Is there more than one?" she whispered. "Lavinia's silver—my silver, now—is in the basket on the console in the *salon*."

He did not answer. He appeared to be listening. Nancy listened also. The house seemed still as death.

"Perhaps I was mistaken," said Captain Fennel; beginning to recover himself after a bit. "I dare say I was."

"Well, I think you must have been, Edwin; I can't hear anything. We had better open the door."

She undid the bolt as she spoke, and he moved away from it. Nancy cautiously took a step outside, and kept still. Not a sound met her ear. Then she brought forth the candle and looked down the staircase. Not a sign of anything or anyone met her eye.

"Edwin, there's nothing, there's nobody; come and see. You must have fancied it."

"No doubt," answered Captain Fennel. But he did not go to see, for all that.

Nancy went back to the room. "Won't you just look downstairs?" she said. "I—I don't much mind going with you."

"Not any necessity," replied he, and began to undress—and slipped the bolt again.

"Why do you bolt the door tonight?" asked Nancy.

"To keep the thief out," said he, in grim tones, which Nancy took for jesting. But she could not at all understand him.

His restlessness kept her awake. "It *must* have been all fancy," she more than once heard him mutter to himself.

When he rose in the morning, his restlessness seemed still to hang upon him. Remarking to Nancy, who was only half-awake, that his nerves were out of order, and he should be all the better for a sea-bath, he dressed and left the room. Nancy got down at the usual hour, half-past eight; and was told by Flore that *monsieur* had left word *madame* was not to wait breakfast for him: he was gone to have a dip in the sea, and should probably take a long country walk after it.

Flore was making the coffee at the kitchen stove; her mistress stood by, as if wanting to watch the process. These last few days, since Lavinia had been carried from the house, Nancy had felt easier in Flore's company than when alone with her own.

"That's to steady his nerves; they are out of order," replied Nancy, who had as much idea of reticence as a child. "*Monsieur* had a great fright last night, Flore."

"Truly!" said Flore, much occupied just then with her coffee-pot.

"He was coming up to bed between ten and eleven; I had gone on. When nearly at the top of the stairs he thought he heard someone behind him. It startled him frightfully. Not being prepared for it, supposing that the house was empty, you see, Flore, of course it would startle him."

"Naturally, *madame*."

"He cried out, and dashed into the bedroom and bolted the door. I never saw any one in such a state of terror, Flore; he was trembling all over; his face was whiter than your apron."

"*Vraiment!*" returned Flore, turning to look at her mistress in a little surprise. "But, *madame*, what had terrified him? What was it that he had seen?"

"Why, he could have seen nothing," corrected Mrs. Fennel. "There was nothing to see."

"*Madame* has reason; there could have been nothing, the house being empty. But then, what could have frightened him?" repeated Flore.

"Why, he must have fancied it, I suppose. Anyway, he fancied someone was there. The first question he asked me was, whether you were in the house."

"*Moi! Monsieur* might have known I should not be in the house at that hour, *madame*. And why should he show terror if he thought it was me?"

Mrs. Fennel shrugged her shoulders. "It was a moment's scare; just that, I conclude; and it upset his nerves. A sea-bath will put him all right again."

Flore carried the coffee into the *salon*, and her mistress sat down to breakfast.

Now it chanced that this same week a guest came to stay with Madame Carimon. Stella Featherston, from Buttermead, was about to make a sojourn in Paris, and she took Sainteville on her route that she might stay a few days with her cousin, Mary Carimon, whom she had not seen for several years.

Lavinia and Ann Preen had once been very intimate with Miss Featherston, who reached Madame Carimon's on the Thursday. On the Friday morning Mrs. Fennel called to see her—and, in Nancy's *impromptu* way, she invited her and Mary Carimon to take tea at seven o'clock that same evening at the Petite Maison Rouge.

Nancy went home delighted. It was a little *divertissement* to her present saddened life. Captain Fennel knitted his brow when he heard of the arrangement, but made no objection in words. His wife shrank at the frown.

"Don't you like my having invited Miss Featherston to tea, Edwin?"

"Oh! I've no objection to it," he carelessly replied. "I am not in love with either Carimon or his wife, and don't care how little I see of them."

"He cannot come, having a private class on tonight. And I could not invite Miss Featherston without Mary Carimon," pleaded Nancy.

"Just so. I am not objecting."

With this somewhat ungracious assent, Nancy had to content herself. She ordered a *gâteau Suisse*, the nicest sort of *gâteau* to be had at Sainteville; and told Flore that she must for once remain for the evening.

The guests appeared punctually at seven o'clock. Such a thing as being invited for one hour, and strolling in an hour or two after it, was a mark of English breeding never yet heard of in the simple-mannered French town. Miss Featherston, a smart, lively young woman, wore a cherry-coloured silk; Mary Carimon was in black; she had gone into slight mourning for Lavinia. Good little Monsieur Jules had put a small band on his hat.

Captain Fennel was not at home to tea, and the ladies had it all their own way in the matter of talking. What with items of news from the old home, Buttermead, and Stella's telling about her own plans, the conversation never flagged a moment.

"Yes, that's what I am going to Paris for," said Stella, explaining her plans. "I don't seem likely to marry, for nobody comes to ask me, and I mean to go out in the world and make a little money. It is a sin and a shame that a healthy girl, the eldest of three sisters, should be living upon her poor mother in idleness. Not much of a girl, you may say, for I was three-and-thirty last week! but we all like to pay ourselves compliments when age is in question."

Nancy laughed. Almost the first time she had laughed since Lavinia's death.

"So you are going to Paris to learn French, Stella!"

"I am going to Paris to learn French, Nancy," assented Miss Featherston. "I know it pretty well, but when I come to speak it I am all at sea; and you can't get out as a governess now unless you speak it fluently. At each of the two situations I applied for in Worcestershire, it was the one fatal objection: 'We should have liked you, Miss Featherston, but we can only engage a lady who will speak French with the children.' So I made my mind up to *speak* French; and I wrote to good Monsieur Jules Carimon, and he has found me a place to go to in Paris, where not a soul in the household speaks English. He says, and I say, that in six months I shall chatter away like a native," she concluded, laughing.

14

About nine o'clock Captain Fennel came home. He was gracious to the visitors, Stella Featherston thought his manners were pleasing. Shortly afterwards Charley Palliser called. He apologized for the lateness of the hour, but his errand was a good-natured one. His aunt, Mrs. Hardy, had received a box of delicious candied fruits from Marseilles; she had sent him with a few to Mrs. Fennel, if that lady would kindly accept them. The truth was, everyone in Sainteville felt sorry just now for poor Nancy Fennel.

Nancy looked as delighted as a child. She called to Flore to bring plates, turned out the fruits and handed them round. Flore also brought in the *gateau Suisse* and glasses, and a bottle of Picardin wine, that the company might regale themselves. Charley Palliser suddenly spoke; he had just thought of something.

"Would it be too much trouble to give me back that book which I lent you a week or two ago—about the plans of the fortifications?" he asked, turning to Captain Fennel. "I want it sometimes for reference in my studies."

"Not at all; I ought to have returned it to you before this—but the trouble here has driven other things out of my head," replied Captain Fennel. "Let me see—where did I put it? Nancy, do you remember where that book is?—the heavy one, you know, with red edges and a mottled cover."

"That book? Why, it is on the drawers in our bedroom," replied Nancy.

"To be sure; I'll get it," said Captain Fennel.

His wife called after him to bring down the dominoes also; someone might like a game. The captain did not intend to take the trouble of going himself; he meant to send Flore. But Flore was not in the kitchen, and he took it for granted she was upstairs. In fact, Flore was in the yard at the pump; but he never thought of the yard or the pump. Lighting a candle, he strode upstairs.

He was coming down again, the open box of dominoes and Charley Palliser's book in one hand, the candlestick in the other, when the same sort of thing seemed to occur which had occurred on Sunday night. Hearing, as he thought, someone close behind him, almost treading, as it were, upon his heels, and thinking it was Flore, he turned his head round, intending to tell her to keep her distance.

Then, with a frightful yell, down dashed Captain Fennel the few remaining stairs, the book, the candlestick, and the box of dominoes all falling in the passage from his nerveless hands. The dominoes were hard and strong, and made a great crash. But it was the yell which had frightened the company in the *salon*.

They flocked out in doubt and wonder. The candle had gone out; and Charley Palliser was bringing forth the lamp to light up the darkness, when he was nearly knocked down by Captain Fennel, Flore, returning from the pump with her own candle, much damaged by the air of the yard, held it up to survey the scene.

Captain Fennel swept past Charley into the *salon*, and threw himself into a chair behind the door, after trying to dash it to; but they were trooping in behind him. His breath was short, his terrified face looked livid as one meet for the grave.

"Why, what has happened to you, sir?" asked Charles, intensely surprised.

"Oh! he must have seen the thief again!" shrieked Nancy.

"Shut the door; bolt it!" called out the stricken man.

They did as they were bid. This order, as it struck them all, could only have reference to keeping out some nefarious intruder, such as a thief Flore had followed them in, after picking up the debris. She put the book and the dominoes on the table, and stood staring over her mistress's shoulder.

"Has the thief got in again, Edwin?" repeated Mrs. Fennel, who was beginning to tremble. "Did you see him?—or hear him?"

"My foot slipped; it sent me headforemost down the stairs," spoke the captain at last, conscious, perhaps, that something must be said to satisfy the inquisitive faces around him. "I heard Flore behind me, and—"

"Not me, sir," put in Flore in her best English. "I was not upstairs at all; I was out at the pump. There is nobody upstairs, sir; there can't be." But Captain Fennel only glared at her in answer.

"What did you cry out at?" asked Charles Palliser, speaking soothingly, for he saw that the man was pitiably unstrung. "Have you had a thief in the house? Did you think you saw one?"

"I saw no thief; there has been no thief in the house that I know of; I tell you I slipped—and it startled me," retorted the captain, his tones becoming savage.

"Then—why did you have the door bolted, captain?" struck in Miss Stella Featherston, who was extremely practical and matter-of-fact, and who could not understand the scene at all.

This time the captain glared at *her*. Only for a moment; a sickly smile then stole over his countenance.

"Somebody here talked about a thief: I said bolt him out," answered he.

With this general explanation they had to be contented; but to none of them did it sound natural or straightforward.

Order was restored. The ladies took a glass of wine each and some of the *gâteau*, which Flore handed round. Charles Palliser said goodnight and departed with his book. Captain Fennel went out at the same time. He turned into the *café* on the Place Ronde, and drank three small glasses of cognac in succession.

"Nancy, what did you mean by talking about a thief?" began Madame Carimon, the whole thing much exercising her mind.

Upon which, Mrs. Fennel treated them all, including Flore, to an elaborate account of her husband's fright on the Sunday night.

"It was on the stairs; just as it was again now," she said. "He thought he heard someone following behind him as he came up to bed. He fancied it was Flore; but Flore had left hours before. I never saw any one show such terror in all my life. He said it was Flore behind him tonight, and you saw how terrified he was."

"But if he took it to be Flore, why should he be frightened?" returned Mary Carimon.

"Pardon, *mesdames*, but it is the same argument I made bold to use to *madame*," interposed Flore from the background, where she stood. "There is not anything in me to give people fright."

"I—think—it must have been," said Mrs. Fennel, speaking slowly, "that he grew alarmed when he found it was not Flore he saw. Both times."

"Then who was it that he did see—to startle him like that?" asked Mary Carimon.

"Why, he must have thought it was a thief," replied Nancy. "There's nothing else for it."

At this juncture the argument was brought to a close by the entrance of Monsieur Jules Carimon, who had come to escort his wife and Stella Featherston home.

These curious attacks of terror were repeated; not often, but at a few days' interval; so that at length Captain Fennel took care not to go about the house alone in the dark. He went up to bed when his wife did; he would not go to the door, if a ring came after Flore's departure, without a light in his hand. By-and-by he improvised a lamp, which he kept on the slab.

What was it that he was scared at? An impression arose in the minds of the two or three people who were privy to this, that he saw, or fancied he saw, in the house the spectre of one who had just been carried out of it, Lavinia Preen. Nancy had no such suspicion as yet; she only thought her husband could not be well. She was much occupied about that time, having at length nerved herself to the task of looking over her poor sister's effects.

One afternoon, when sitting in Lavinia's room (Flore—who stayed with her for company—had run down to the kitchen to see that the dinner did not burn), Nancy came upon a small, thin green case. Between its leaves she found three one-hundred-*franc* notes—twelve pounds in English value. She rightly judged that it was all that remained of her sister's nest-egg, and that she had intended to take it with her to Boulogne.

"Poor Lavinia!" she aspirated, the tears dropping from her eyes. "Every farthing remaining of the quarter's money she left with me for housekeeping."

But now a thought came to Nancy. Placing the case on the floor near her, intending to show it to her husband—she was sitting on a stool before one of Lavinia's boxes—it suddenly occurred to her that it might be as well to say nothing to him about it. He would be sure to appropriate the money to his own private uses: and Nancy knew that she should need some for hers. There would be her mourning to pay for; and—

The room-door was wide open, and at this point in her reflections Nancy heard the captain enter the house with his latch-key, and march straight upstairs. In hasty confusion, she thrust the little case into the nearest hiding-place, which happened to be the front of her black dress bodice.

"Nancy, I have to go to England," cried the captain. "How hot you look! Can't you manage to do that without stooping?"

"To go to England!" repeated Nancy, lifting her flushed face.

"Here's a letter from my brother; the postman gave it me as I was crossing the Place Ronde. It's only a line or two," he added, tossing it to her. "I must take this evening's boat."

Nancy read the letter. Only a line or two, as he said, just telling the captain to go over with all speed upon a pressing matter of business, and that he could return before the week was ended.

"Oh, but, Edwin, you can't go," began Nancy, in alarm. "I cannot stay here by myself."

"Not go! Why, I must go," he said very decisively. "How do I know what it is that I am wanted for? Perhaps that property which we are always expecting to fall in."

"But I should be so lonely. I could not stay here alone."

"Nonsense!" he sharply answered. "I shall not be away above one clear day; two days at the furthest. This is Thursday, and I shall return by Sunday's boat. You will only be alone tomorrow and Saturday."

He turned away, thus putting an end to the discussion, and entered their own room. As Nancy looked after him in despair, it suddenly struck her how very thin and ill he had become; his face worn and grey.

"He wants a change," she said to herself; "our trouble here has upset him as much as it did me. I'll say no more; I must not be selfish. Poor Lavinia used to warn me against selfishness."

So Captain Fennel went off without further opposition, his wife enjoining him to be sure to return on Sunday. The steamer was starting that night at eight o'clock; it was a fine evening, and Nancy walked down to the port with her husband and saw him

251

on board. Nancy met an acquaintance down there; no other than Charley Palliser. They strolled a little in the wake of the departing steamer; Charley then saw her as far as the Place Ronde, and there wished her goodnight.

And now an extraordinary thing happened. As Mrs. Fennel opened the door with her latch-key, Flore having left, and was about to enter the dark passage, the same curious and unaccountable terror seized her which had been wont to attack Lavinia. Leaving the door wide open, she dashed up the passage, felt for the matchbox, and struck a light. Then, candle in hand, she returned to shut the door; but her whole frame trembled with fear.

"Why, it's just what poor Lavinia felt!" she gasped. "What on earth can it be? Why should it come to me? I will take care not to go out tomorrow night or Saturday."

And she held to her decision. Mrs. Hardy sent Charley Palliser to invite her for either day, or both days; Mary Carimon sent Pauline with a note to the same effect; but Nancy returned a refusal in both cases, with her best thanks.

The boat came in on Sunday night, but it did not bring Captain Fennel. On the Sunday morning the post had brought Nancy a few lines from him, saying he found the business on which he had been called to London was of great importance, and he was obliged to remain another day or two.

Nancy was frightfully put out: not only vexed, but angry. Edwin had no business to leave her alone like that so soon after Lavinia's death. She bemoaned her hard fate to several friends on coming out of church, and Mrs. Smith carried her off to dinner. The major was not out that morning—a twinge of gout in the right foot had kept him indoors.

This involved Nancy's going home alone in the evening, for the major could not walk with her. She did not like it. The same horror came over her before opening the door. She entered somehow, and dashed into the kitchen, hoping the stove was alight: a very silly hope, for Flore had been gone since the afternoon.

Nancy lighted the candle in the kitchen, and then fancied she saw someone looking at her from the open kitchen-door. It looked like Lavinia. It certainly was Lavinia. Nancy stood spellbound; then she gave a cry of desperate horror and dropped the candlestick.

How she picked it up she never knew; the light had not gone out. Nothing was to be seen then. The apparition, if it had been one, had vanished. She got up to bed somehow, and lay shivering under the bedclothes until morning.

Quite early, when Nancy was at breakfast, Madame Carimon came in. She had already been to the fish-market, and came on to invite Nancy to her house for the day, having heard that Mr. Fennel was still absent. With a scared face and trembling lips, Nancy told her about the previous night—the strange horror of entering which had begun to attack her, the figure of Lavinia at the kitchen-door.

Madame Carimon, listening gravely, took, or appeared to take, a sensible view of it. "You have caught up this fear of entering the house, Nancy, through remembering that it attacked poor Lavinia," she said. "Impressionable minds—and yours is one of them—take fright just as children catch measles. As to thinking you saw Lavinia—"

"She had on the gown she wore the Sunday she was taken ill: her silver-grey silk, you know," interrupted Nancy. "She looked at me with a mournful, appealing gaze, just as if she wanted something."

"Ay, you were just in the mood to fancy something of the kind," lightly spoke Madame Carimon. "The fright of coming in had done that for you. I dare say you had been talking of Lavinia at Major Smith's."

"Well, so we had," confessed Nancy.

"Just so; she was already on your mind, and therefore that and the fright you were in caused you to fancy you saw her. Nancy, my dear, you cannot imagine the foolish illusions our fancies play us,"

Easily persuaded, Mrs. Fennel agreed that it might have been so. She strove to forget the matter, and. went out there and then with Mary Carimon.

But this state of things was to continue. Captain Fennel did not return, and Nancy grew frightened to death at being alone in the house after dark. Flore was unable to stay longer than the time originally agreed for, her old mother being dangerously ill. As dusk approached, Nancy began to hate her destiny. Apart from nervousness, she was sociably inclined, and yearned, for company. Now and again the inclination to accept an invitation was too strong to be resisted, or she went out after dinner, uninvited, to this friend or that. But the pleasure was counterbalanced by having to go in again at night; the horror clung to her.

If a servant attended her home, or any gentleman from the house where she had been, she made them go indoors with her whilst she lighted her candle; once she got Monsieur Gustave's errand-boy to do so. But it was almost as bad with the lighted candle—the first feeling of being in the lonely house after they had gone. She wrote letter after letter, imploring her husband to return. Captain Fennel's replies were rich in promises: he would be back the very instant business permitted; probably "tomorrow, or the next day." But he did not come.

One Sunday, when he had been gone about three weeks, and Nancy had been spending the day in the Rue Pomme Cuite, Mary Carimon walked home with her in the evening. Monsieur Jules had gone to see his cousin off by the nine-o'clock train—Mademoiselle Priscille Carimon, who had come in to spend the day with them. She lived at Drecques.

"You will come in with me, Mary?" said Ann Fennel, as they gained the door.

"To be sure I will," replied Madame Carimon, laughing lightly, for none knew about the fears better than she.

Nancy took her hand as they went up the passage. She lighted the candle at the slab, and they went into the *salon*, Madame Carimon sat down for a few minutes, by way of reassuring her. Nancy took off her bonnet and mantle. On the table was a small tray with the tea-things upon it. Flore had left it there in readiness, not quite certain whether her mistress would come in to tea or not.

"I had such a curious dream last night," began Nancy; "those tea-things put me in mind of it. Lavinia—"

"For goodness' sake don't begin upon dreams tonight!" interposed Madame Carimon. "You know they always frighten you."

"Oh, but this was a pleasant dream, Mary. I thought that I and Lavinia were seated at a little table, with two teacups between us full of tea. The cups were very pretty; pale amber with gilt scrolls, and the china so thin as to be transparent. I can see them now. And Lavinia said something which made me smile; but I don't remember what it was. Ah, Mary! if she were only back again with us!"

"She is better off, you know," said Mary Carimon in tender tones.

"All the same, it was a cruel fate that took her; I shall never think otherwise. I wish I knew what it was she died of! Flore told me one day that Monsieur Podevin quite laughed at the idea of its being a chill."

"Well, Nancy, it was you who stopped it, you know."

"Stopped what?" asked Nancy.

"The investigation the doctors would have made after death. Both of them were much put out at your forbidding it: for their own satisfaction they wished to ascertain particulars. I may tell you now that I thought you were wrong to interfere."

"It was Captain Fennel," said Nancy calmly.

"Captain Fennel!" echoed Mary Carimon. "Monsieur Dupuis told me that Captain Fennel wished for it as much as he and Monsieur Podevin."

Captain Fennel's wife shook her head. "They asked him about it before they left, after she died. He came to me, and I said, Oh, let them do what they would; it could not hurt her now she was dead. I was in such terrible distress, Mary, that I hardly knew or cared what I said. Then Edwin drew so dreadful a picture of what post-mortems are, and how barbarously her poor neck and arms would be cut and slashed, that I grew sick and frightened."

"And so you stopped it—by reason of the picture he drew?"

"Yes. I came running down here to Monsieur Dupuis—Monsieur Podevin had gone—for Edwin said it must be my decision, not his, and his name had better not be mentioned; and I begged and prayed Monsieur Dupuis not to hold it. I think I startled him, good old man. I was almost out of my mind; quite wild with agitation; and he promised me it should be as I wished. That's how it all was, Mary."

Mary Carimon's face wore a curious look. Then she rallied, speaking even lightly.

"Well, well; it could not have brought her back to life; and I repeat that we must remember she is better off. And now, Nancy, I want you to show me the pretty purse that Miss Perry has knitted for you, if you have it at hand."

Nancy rose, opened her workbox, which stood on the side-table, and brought forth the purse. Of course Madame Carimon's motive had been to change her thoughts. After admiring the purse, and talking of other pleasant matters, Mary took her departure.

And the moment the outer door had closed upon her that feeling of terror seized upon Nancy. Catching up her mantle with one hand and the candle with the other, she made for the staircase, leaving her bonnet and gloves in the salon. The staircase struck cold to her, and she could hear the wind whistling, for it was a windy night. As to the candle, it seemed to burn with a pale flame and not to give half its usual light.

In her nervous agitation, just as she gained the uppermost stair, she dropped her mantle. Raising her head from stooping to pick it up, she suddenly saw some figure before her at the end of the passage. It stood beyond the door of her own room, close to that which had been her sister's.

It was Lavinia. She appeared to be habited in the silver-grey silk already spoken of. Her gaze was fixed upon Nancy, with the same imploring aspect of appeal, as if she wanted something; her pale face was inexpressibly mournful. With a terrible cry, Nancy tore into her own room, the mantle trailing after her. She shut the door and bolted it, and buried her face in the counterpane in wild agony.

And in that moment a revelation came to Ann Fennel. It was this apparition which had been wont to haunt her husband in the house and terrify him beyond control. Not a thief; not Flore—but Lavinia!

15

On the Monday morning Flore found her mistress in so sick and suffering and strange a state, that she sent for Madame Carimon. In vain Mary Carimon, after hearing Nancy's tale, strove to convince her that what she saw was fancy, the effect of diseased nerves. Nancy was more obstinate than a mule.

"What I saw was Lavinia," she shivered. "Lavinia's apparition. No good to tell me it was not; I have seen it now twice. It was as clear and evident to me, both times, as ever she herself was in life. That's what Edwin used to see; I know it now; and he became unable to bear the house. I seem to read it all as in a book, Mary. He got his brother to send for him, and he is staying away because he dreads to come back again. But you know I cannot stay here alone now."

Madame Carimon wrote off at once to Captain Fennel, Nancy supplying the address. She told him that his wife was ill; in a nervous state; fancying she saw Lavinia in the house. Such a report, she added, should if possible be kept from spreading to the town, and therefore she must advise him to return without delay.

The letter brought back Captain Fennel, Flore having meanwhile remained entirely at the Petite Maison Rouge. Perhaps the captain did not in secret like that little remark of its being well to keep it from the public; he may have considered it suggestive, coming from Mary Carimon. He believed she read him pretty correctly, and he hated her accordingly. Anyway, he deemed it well to be on the spot. Left to herself, there was no telling what ridiculous things Nancy might be saying or fancying.

Edwin Fennel did not return alone. His brother's wife was with him. Mrs. James, they called her, James being the brother's Christian name. Mrs. James was not a lady in herself or in manner; but she was lively and very good-natured, and these qualities were what the Petite Maison Rouge wanted in it just now; and perhaps that was Captain Fennel's motive in bringing her. Nancy was delighted. She almost forgot her fears and fancies. Flore was agreeable also, for she was now at liberty to return to ordinary arrangements. Thus there was a lull in the storm. They walked out with Mrs. James on the pier, and took her to see the different points of interest in the town; they even gave a little *soirée* for her, and in return were invited to other houses.

One day, when the two ladies were gossiping together, Nancy, in the openness of her heart, related to Mrs. James the particulars of Lavinia's unexpected and rather mysterious death, and of her appearing in the house again after it. Captain Fennel disturbed them in the midst of the story. His wife was taking his name in vain at the moment of his entrance, saying how scared *he* had been at the apparition.

"Hold your peace, you foolish woman!" he thundered, looking as if he meant to strike her. "Don't trouble Mrs. James's head with such miserable rubbish as that."

Mrs. James did not appear to mind it. She burst into a hearty laugh. She never had seen a ghost, she said, and was sure she never should; there were no such things. But she should like to hear all about poor Miss Preen's death.

"There was nothing else to hear," the captain growled. "She caught a chill on the Sunday, coming out of the hot church after morning service. It struck inwardly, bringing on inflammation, which the medical men could not subdue."

"But you know, Edwin, the church never is hot, and you know the doctors decided it was not a chill. Monsieur Podevin especially denied it," dissented Nancy, who possessed about as much insight as a goose, and a little less tact.

"Then what did she die of?" questioned Mrs. James. "Was she

poisoned?"

"Oh, how can you suggest so dreadful a thing!" shrieked Nancy. "Poisoned! Who would be so wicked as to poison Lavinia? Everyone loved her."

Which again amused the listening lady. "You have a quick imagination, Mrs. Edwin," she laughed. "I was thinking of mushrooms."

"And I of tinned meats and copper saucepans," supplemented Captain Fennel. "However, there could be no suspicion even of that sort in Lavinia's case, since she had touched nothing but what we all partook of. She died of inflammation, Mrs. James."

"Little doubt of it," acquiesced Mrs. James. "A friend of mine went, not twelve months ago, to a funeral at Brompton Cemetery; the ground was damp, and she caught a chill. In four days she was dead."

"Women have no business at funerals," growled Edwin Fennel. "Why should they parade their grief abroad? You see nothing of the kind in France."

"In truth I think you are not far wrong," said Mrs. James. "It is a fashion which has sprung up of late. A few years ago it was as much unknown with us as it is with the French."

"*They* will be catching it up next, I suppose," retorted the captain, as if the thing were a personal grievance to him.

"Little doubt of it," laughed Mrs. James.

After staying at Sainteville for a month, Mrs. James Fennel took her departure for London. Captain Fennel proposed to escort her over; but his wife went into so wild a state at the mere mention of it, that he had to give it up.

"I dare not stay in the house by myself, Edwin," she shuddered. "I should go to the Vice-Consul and to other influential people here, and tell them of my misery—that I am afraid of seeing Lavinia."

And Captain Fennel believed she would be capable of doing it. So he remained with her.

That the spectre of the dead-and-gone Lavinia did at times appear to them, or else their fancies conjured up the vision, was all too certain. Three times during the visit of Mrs. James the captain had been betrayed into one of his fits of terror: no need to ask what had caused it. After her departure the same thing took place. Nancy had not again seen anything, but she knew he had.

"We shall not be able to stay in the house, Edwin," his wife said to him one evening when they were sitting in the *salon* at dusk after Flore's departure; nothing having led up to the remark.

"I fancy we should be as well out of it," replied he.

"Oh, Edwin, let us go! If we can! There will be all the rent to pay up first."

"All the what?" said he.

"The rent," repeated Nancy; "up to the end of the term we took it for. About three years longer, I think, Edwin. That would be sixty pounds."

"And where do you suppose the sixty pounds would come from?"

"I don't know. There's the impediment, you see," remarked Nancy blankly. "We cannot leave without paying up."

"Unless we made a moonlight flitting of it, my dear."

"That I never will," she rejoined, with a firmness he could not mistake. "You are only jesting, Edwin."

"It would be no jesting matter to pay up that claim, and others; for there are others. Our better plan, Nancy, will be to go off by the London boat some night, and not let anyone know where we are until I can come back to pay. You may see it is the only thing to be done, and you must bring your mind to it."

"Never by me," said Nancy, strong in her innate rectitude. "As to hiding ourselves anywhere, that can never be; I should not conceal my address from Mary Carimon—I *could* not conceal it from Colonel Selby."

Captain Fennel ground his teeth. "Suppose I say that this shall be, that we will go, and order you to obey me? What then?"

"No, Edwin, I could not. I should go in to Monsieur Gustave Sauvage, and say to him, 'We were thinking of running away, but

I cannot do it; please put me in prison until I can pay the debt.' And then—"

"Are you an idiot?" asked Captain Fennel, staring at her.

"And then, when I was in prison," went on Nancy, "I should write to tell William Selby; and perhaps he would come over and release me. Please don't talk in this kind of way again, Edwin. I should keep my word."

Mr. Edwin Fennel could not have felt more astounded had his wife then and there turned into a dromedary before his eyes. She had hitherto been tractable as a child. But he had never tried her in a thing that touched her honour, and he saw that the card which he had intended to play was lost.

Captain Fennel played another. He went away himself.

Making the best he could of the house and its haunted state (though day by day saw him looking more and more like a walking skeleton) throughout the greater part of June, for the summer had come in, he despatched his wife to Pontipette one market day—Saturday—to remain there until the following Wednesday. Old Mrs. Hardy had gone to the homely but comfortable hotel at Pontipette for a change, and she wrote to invite Nancy to stay a short time with her. Charles Palliser was in England. Captain Fennel proceeded to London by that same Saturday night's boat, armed with a letter from his wife to Colonel Selby, requesting the colonel to pay over to her husband her quarterly instalment instead of sending it to herself. Captain Fennel had bidden her do this; and Nancy, of strict probity in regard to other people's money, could not resist signing over her own,

"But you will be sure to bring it all back, won't you, Edwin? and to be here by Wednesday, the day I return?" she said to him.

"Why, of course I shall, my dear,"

"It will be a double portion now—thirty-five pounds."

"And a good thing, too; we shall want it," he returned.

"Indeed, yes; there's such a heap of things owing for," concluded Nancy.

Thus the captain went over to England in great glee, carrying with him the order for the money. But he was reckoning without his host.

Upon presenting himself at the bank in the City on Monday morning, he found Colonel Selby absent; not expected to return before the end of that week, or the beginning of the next. This was a check for Captain Fennel. He quite glared at the gentleman who thus informed him—Mr, West, who sat in the colonel's room, and was his *locum tenens* for the time being.

"Business is transacted all the same, I conclude?" said he snappishly.

"Why, certainly," replied Mr. West, marvelling at the absurdity of the question. "What can I do for you?"

Captain Fennel produced his wife's letter, requesting that her quarter's money should be paid over to him, and handed in her receipt for the same. Mr. West read them both, the letter twice, and then looked direct through his silver-rimmed spectacles at the applicant.

"I cannot do this," said he; "it is a private matter of Colonel Selby's."

"It is not more private than any other payment you may have to make," retorted Captain Fennel.

"Pardon me, it is. This really does not concern the bank at all. I cannot pay it without Colonel Selby's authority: he has neither given it nor mentioned it to me. Another thing: the payment, as I gather from the wording of Mrs. Ann Fennel's letter, is not yet due. Upon that score, apart from any other, I should decline to pay it."

"It will be due in two or three days. Colonel Selby would not object to forestall the time by that short period."

"That would, of course, be for the colonel's own consideration."

"I particularly wish to receive the money this morning."

Mr. West shook his head in answer. "If you will leave Mrs. Fennel's letter and receipt in my charge, sir, I will place them before the colonel as soon as he returns. That is all I can do. Or perhaps you would prefer to retain the latter," he added, handing back the receipt over the desk.

"Business men are the very devil to stick at straws," muttered Captain Fennel under his breath. He saw it was no use trying to move the one before him, and went out, saying he would call in a day or two.

Now it happened that Colonel Selby, who was only staying at Brighton for a rest (for he had been very unwell of late), took a run up to town that same Monday morning to see his medical attendant. His visit paid, he went on to the bank, surprising Mr. West there about one o'clock. After some conference upon business matters, Mr. West spoke of Captain Fennel's visit, and handed over the letter he had left.

Colonel Selby drew in his lips as he read it. He did not like Mr. Edwin Fennel; and he would most assuredly not pay Ann Fennel's money to him. He returned the letter to Mr. West.

"Should the man come here again, West, tell him, as you did this morning, that he can see me on my return—which will probably be on this day week," said the colonel. "No need to say I have been up here today."

And on the following day, Tuesday, Colonel Selby, being then at Brighton, drew out a cheque for the quarter almost due and sent it by post to Nancy at Sainteville.

Thus checkmated in regard to the money, Captain Fennel did not return home at the time he promised, even if he had had any intention of doing so. When Nancy returned to Sainteville on the Wednesday from Pontipette, he was not there. The first thing she saw waiting for her on the table was Colonel Selby's letter containing the cheque for five-and-thirty pounds.

"How glad I am it has come to me so soon!" cried Nancy; "I can pay the bills now. I suppose William Selby thinks it would not be legal to pay it to Edwin."

The week went on. Each time a boat came in, Nancy was promenading the port, expecting to see her husband land from it. On the Sunday morning Nancy received a letter from him, in which he told her he was waiting to see Colonel Selby, to get the money paid to him. Nancy wrote back hastily, saying it had been received by herself, and that she had paid it nearly all away in settling the bills. She begged him to come back by the next boat. Flore was staying in the house altogether, but at an inconvenience.

On the Monday evening Mrs. Fennel had another desperate fright. She went to take tea with an elderly lady and her daughter, Mrs. and Miss Lambert, bidding Flore to come for her at half-past nine o'clock. Half-past nine came, but no Flore; ten o'clock came, and then Mrs. Fennel set off alone, supposing Flore had misunderstood her and would be found waiting for her at home. The moonlit streets were crowded with promenaders returning from their summer evening-walk upon the pier.

Nancy rang the bell; but it was not answered. She had her latch-key in her pocket, but preferred to be admitted, and she rang again. No one came. "Flore must have dropped asleep in the kitchen," she petulantly thought, and drew out her key.

"Flore!" she called out, pushing the door back. "Flore, where are you?"

Flore apparently was nowhere, very much to the dismay of Mrs. Fennel. She would have to go in alone, all down the dark passage, and wake her up. Leaving the door wide open, she advanced in the dark with cautious steps, the old terror full upon her.

The kitchen was dark also, so far as fire or candlelight went, but a glimmer of moonlight shone in at the window. "Are you not here, Flore?" shivered Nancy. But there was no response.

Groping for the matchbox on the mantelshelf over the stove, and not at once finding it, Nancy suddenly took up an impression that someone was standing in the misty rays of the moon. Gazing attentively, it seemed to assume the shadowy form of Lavinia. And with a shuddering cry Nancy Fennel fell down upon the brick floor of the kitchen.

16

It was a lovely summer's day, and Madame Carimon's neat little slip of a kitchen was bright and hot with the morning sun. Madame, herself, stood before the paste-board, making a green-apricot tart. Of pies and tarts *à la mode Anglaise*, Monsieur Jules was more fond than a schoolboy; and of all tarts known to the civilized world, none can equal that of a green apricot.

Madame had put down the rolling-pin, and stood for the moment idle, looking at Flore Pamart, and listening to something that Flore was saying. Flore, whisking out of the Petite Maison Rouge a few minutes before, ostensibly to do her morning's marketings, had whisked straight off to the Rue Pomme Cuite, and was now seated at the corner of the pastry-table, telling a story to Madame Carimon.

"It was *madame's* own fault," she broke off in her tale to remark. "*Madame will* give me her orders in French, and half the time I can't understand them. She had an engagement to take tea at Madame Smith's in the Rue Lambeau, was what I thought she said to me, and that I must present myself there at half-past nine to walk home with her. Well, *madame*, I went accordingly, and found nobody at home there but the *bonne,* Thomasine. Her master was dining out at the *Sous-préfet's,* and her mistress had gone out with some more ladies to walk on the pier, as it was so fine an evening. Naturally I thought my mistress was one of the ladies, and sat there waiting for her and chatting with Thomasine. Madame Smith came in at ten o'clock, and then she said that my lady had not been there and that she had not expected her."

"She must have gone to tea elsewhere," observed Madame Carimon.

"Clearly, *madame*; as I afterwards found. It was to Madame Lambert's, in the Rue Lothaire, that I ought to have gone. I could only go home, as *madame* sees; and when I arrived there I found the house-door wide open. Just as I entered, a frightful cry came from the kitchen, and there I found her dropped down on the floor, half senseless with terror. *Madame*, she avowed to me that she had seen Mademoiselle Lavinia standing near her in the moonlight."

Madame Carimon took up her rolling-pin slowly before she spoke. "I know she has a fancy that she appears in the house."

"Madame Carimon, I think she is in the house," said Flore solemnly. And for a minute or two Madame Carimon rolled her paste in silence.

"Monsieur Fennel used to see her—I am sure he did—and now his wife sees her," went on the woman. "I think that is the secret of his running away so much: he can't bear the house and what is haunting it.

"It is altogether a dreadful thing; I lie awake thinking of it," bewailed Mary Carimon.

"But it cannot be let go on like this," said Flore; "and that's what has brought me running here this morning—to ask you, *madame*, whether anything can be done. If she is left alone to see these sights, she'll die of it. When she got up this morning she was shivering like a leaf in the wind. Has *madame* noticed that she is wasting away? For the matter of that, so was Monsieur Fennel."

Madame Carimon, beginning to line her shallow dish with paste, nodded in assent. "He ought to be here with her," she remarked.

"Catch him," returned Flore, in a heat. "Pardon, *madame*, but I must avow I trust not that gentleman. He is no good. He will never come back to stay at the house so long as there is in it—what is there. He dare not; and I would like to ask him why not. A man with the conscience at ease could not be that sort of coward. Honest men do not fly away, all scared, when they fancy they see a revenant."

Deeming it might be unwise to pursue the topic from this point, Madame Carimon said she would go and see Mrs. Fennel in the course of the day, and Flore clattered off, her wooden shoes echoing on the narrow pavement of the Rue Pomme Cuite.

But, as Madame Carimon was crossing the Place Ronde in the afternoon to pay her visit, she met Mrs. Fennel, Of course, Flore's communication was not to be mentioned.

"Ah," said Madame Carimon readily, "is it you? I was coming to ask if you would like to take a walk on the pier with me. It is

266

a lovely afternoon, and not too hot."

"Oh, I'll go," said Nancy. "I came out because it is so miserable at home. When Flore went off to the fish-market after breakfast, I felt more lonely than you would believe. Mary," dropping her voice, "I saw Lavinia last night."

"Now I won't listen to that," retorted Mary Carimon, as if she were reprimanding a child. "Once give in to our nerves and fancies, there's no end to the tricks they play us. I wish, Ann, your house were in a more lively situation, where you might sit at the window and watch the passers-by."

"But it isn't," said Nancy sensibly. "It looks upon nothing but the walls."

Walking on, they sat down upon a bench that stood back from the port, facing the harbour. Nearly opposite lay the English boat, busily loading for London. The sight made Nancy sigh.

"I wish it would bring Edwin the next time it comes in," she said in low tones.

"When do you expect him?"

"I don't know *when*," said poor Nancy with emphasis. "Mary, I am beginning to think he stays away because he is afraid of seeing Lavinia."

"Men are not afraid of those foolish things, Ann."

"He is. Recollect those fits of terror he had. He used to hear her following him up and downstairs; used to see her on the landings."

Madame Carimon found no ready answer. She had witnessed one of those fits of terror herself.

"Last night," went on Mrs. Fennel, after a pause, "when Flore had left me and I could only shiver in my bed, and not expect to sleep, I became calm enough to ask myself *why* Lavinia should come back again, and what it is she wants. Can you think why, Mary?"

"Not I," said Madame Carimon lightly. "I shall only believe she does come when she shows herself to me."

"And I happened on the thought that, possibly, she may be wanting us to inquire into the true cause of her death. It might have been ascertained at the time, but for my stopping the action of the doctors, you know."

"Ann, my dear, you should exercise a little common sense. I would ask you what end ascertaining it now would answer, to her, dead, or to you, living?"

"It might be seen that she could have been cured, had we only known what the malady was."

"But you did not know; the doctors did not know. It could only have been discovered, even at your showing, after her death, not in time to save her."

"I wish Monsieur Dupuis had come more quickly on the Monday night!" sighed Nancy. "I am always wishing it. You can picture what it was, Mary—Lavinia lying in that dreadful agony and no doctor coming near her. Edwin was gone so long—so long! He could not wake up Monsieur Dupuis. I think now that the bell was out of order."

"Why do you think that now? Captain Fennel must have known whether the bell answered to his summons, or not."

"Well," returned Nancy, "this morning when Flore returned with the fish, she said I looked very ill. She had just seen Monsieur Dupuis in the Place Ronde, and she ran out again and brought him in—"

"Did you mention to him this fancy of seeing Lavinia?" hastily interrupted Madame Carimon.

"No, no; I don't talk of that to people. Only to you and Flore; and—yes—I did tell Mrs. Smith. I let Monsieur Dupuis think I was ill with grieving after Lavinia, and we talked a little about her. I said how I wished he could have been here sooner on the Monday night, and that my husband had rung several times before he could arouse him. Monsieur Dupuis said that was a mistake; he had got up and come as soon as he was called; he was not asleep at the time, and the bell had rung only once."

"What an extraordinary thing!" exclaimed Mary Carimon. "I know your husband said he rang many times."

"That's why I now think the bell must have been out of order; but I did not say so to Monsieur Dupuis," returned Nancy.

"He is a kind old man, and it would grieve him: for of course we know doctors *ought* to keep their door-bells in order."

Madame Carimon rose in silence, but full of thought, and they continued their walk. It was low water in the harbour, but the sun was sparkling and playing on the waves out at sea. On the pier they found Rose and Anna Bosanquet; and in chatting with them Nancy's mood became more cheerful.

That same evening, on that same pier, Mary Carimon spoke a few confidential words to her husband. They sat at the end of it, and the beauty of the night, so warm and still, induced them to linger. The bright moon sailed grandly in the heavens and glittered upon the water that now filled the harbour, for the tide was in. Most of the promenaders had turned down the pier again, after watching out the steamer. What a fine passage she would make, and was making, cutting there so smoothly through the crystal sea!

Mary Carimon began in a low voice, though no one was near to listen and the waves could not hear her. She spoke pretty fully of a haunting doubt that lay upon her mind, as to whether Lavinia had died a natural death.

"If we make the best of it," she concluded, "her dying in that strangely sudden way was unusual; you know that, Jules; quite unaccountable. It never *has* been accounted for."

Monsieur Jules, gazing on the gentle waves as they rose and fell in the moonlight at the mouth of the harbour, answered nothing.

"He had so much to wish her away for, that man: all the money would become Nancy's. And I'm sure there was secret enmity between them—on both sides. Don't you see, Jules, how suspicious it all looks?"

The moonbeams, illumining Monsieur Jules Carimon's face, showed it to be very impassive, betraying no indication that he as much as heard what his wife was talking about.

"I have not forgotten, I can never forget, Jules, the very singular Fate-reading, or whatever you may please to call it, spoken by the Astrologer Talcke last winter at Miss Bosanquet's *soirée*.

You were not in the room, you know, but I related it to you when we arrived home. He certainly foretold Lavinia's death, as I, recalling the words, look upon it now. He said there was some element of evil in their house, threatening and terrible; he repeated it more than once. *In their house*, Jules, and that it would end in darkness; which, as everyone understood, meant death: not for Mrs. Fennel; he took care to tell her that; but for another. He said the cards were more fateful than he had ever seen them. That evil in the house was Fennel."

Still Monsieur Jules offered no comment.

"And what could be the meaning of those dreams Lavinia had about him, in which he always seemed to be preparing to inflict upon her some fearful ill, and she knew she never could and never would escape from it?" ran on Mary Carimon, her eager, suppressed tones bearing a gruesome sound in the stillness of the night. "And what is the explanation of the fits of terror which have shaken Fennel since the death, fancying he sees Lavinia? Flore said to me this morning that she is sure Lavinia is in the house."

Glancing at her husband to see that he was at least listening, but receiving no confirmation of it by word or motion, Mary Carimon continued:

"Those dreams came to warn her, Jules. To warn her to get out of the house while she could. And she made arrangements to go, and in another day or two would have been away in safety. But he was too quick for her."

Monsieur Jules Carimon turned now to face his wife. "*Mon amie, tais toi*," said he with authority. "Such a topic is not convenable," he added, still in French, though she had spoken in English. "It is dangerous."

"But, Jules, I believe it *to have been so*."

"All the same, and whether or no, it is not your affair, Marie. Neither must you make it so. Believe me, my wife, the only way to live peaceably ourselves in the world is to let our neighbours' sins alone."

17

Captain Edwin Fennel was certainly in no hurry to return to Sainteville, for he did not come. Nancy, ailing, weak, wretchedly uncomfortable, wrote letter after letter to him, generally sending them over by some friend or other who might be crossing, to be put in a London letter-box, and so evade the foreign postage. Once or twice she had written to Mrs. James, telling of her lonely life and that she wanted Edwin either to take her out of the dark and desolate house, or else to come back to it himself Captain Fennel would answer now and again, promising to come—she would be quite sure to see him on one of the first boats if she looked out for their arrival. Nancy did look, but she had not yet seen him. She was growing visibly thinner and weaker. Sainteville said how ill Mrs. Fennel was looking.

One evening at the end of July, when the London steamer was due about ten o'clock, Nancy went to watch it in, as usual, Flore attending her. The port was gay, crowded with promenaders. There had been a concert at the Rooms, and the company was coming home from it. Mrs. Fennel had not made one: latterly she had felt no spirit for amusement. Several friends met her; she did not tell them she had come down to meet her husband, if haply he should be on the expected boat; she had grown tired and half ashamed of saying that; she let them think she was only out for a walk that fine evening. There was a yellow glow still in the sky where the sun had set; the north-west was clear and bright with its opal light.

The time went on; the port became deserted, excepting a few passing stragglers. Ten o'clock had struck, eleven would soon strike, Flore and her mistress, tired of pacing about, sat down on one of the benches facing the harbour. One of two young men, passing swiftly homewards from the pier, found himself called to.

"Charley! Charley Palliser!"

Charles turned, and recognized Mrs. Fennel. Stepping across to her, he shook hands.

"What do you think can have become of the boat?" she asked. "It ought to have been in nearly an hour ago."

"Oh, it will be here shortly," he replied. "The boat often makes a slow passage when there's no wind. What little wind we have had today has been dead against it."

"As I've just said to *madame*," put in Flore, always ready to take up the conversation. "Mr. Charles knows there's no fear it has gone down, though it may be a bit late."

"Why, certainly not," laughed Charley. "Are you waiting here for it, Mrs. Fennel?"

"Ye—s," she answered, but with hesitation.

"And as it's not even in sight yet, *madame* had much better go home and not wait, for the air is getting chilly," again spoke Flore,

"We can't see whether it's in sight or not," said her mistress. "It is dark out at sea."

"Shall I wait here with you, Mrs. Fennel?" asked Charley in his good nature.

"Oh no, no; no, thank you," she answered quickly. "If it does not come in soon, we shall go home."

He wished them goodnight, and went onwards.

"She is hoping the boat may bring that mysterious brute, Fennel," remarked Charles to his companion.

"Brute, you call him?"

"He is no better than one, to leave his sick wife alone so long," responded Charles in hearty tones. "She has picked up an idea, I hear, that the house is haunted, and shakes in her shoes in it from morning till night."

The two watchers sat on, Flore grumbling. Not for herself, but for her mistress. A sea-fog was rising, and Flore thought *madame* might take cold. Mrs. Fennel wrapped her light fleecy shawl closer about her chest, and protested she was quite hot. The shawl was well enough for a warm summer's night, but not for a cold sea-fog. About half-past eleven there suddenly loomed into view through the mist the lights of the steamer, about to enter the harbour.

"There she is!" exultingly cried Nancy, who had been shivering inwardly for some time past, and doing her best not to shiver outwardly for fear of Flore. "And now, Flore, you go home as quickly as you can and make a fire in the *salon* to warm us. I'm sure he will need one—at sea in this cold fog."

"If he is come," mentally returned Flore in her derisive heart. She had no faith in the return of Monsieur Fennel by any boat, a day or a night one. But she needed no second prompting to hasten away; was too glad to do it.

Poor Nancy waited on. The steamer came very slowly up the port, or she fancied so; one must be cautious in a fog; and it seemed to her a long time swinging round and settling itself into its place. Then the passengers came on shore one by one, Nancy standing close to look at them. There were only about twenty in all, and Captain Fennel was not one of them. With misty eyes and a rising in her throat and spiritless footsteps, Nancy arrived at her home, the Petite Maison Rouge. Flore had the fire burning in the *salon*; but Nancy was too thoroughly chilled for any salon fire to warm her.

The cold she caught that night stuck to her chest. For some days afterwards she was very ill indeed. Monsieur Dupuis attended her, and brought his son once or twice, Monsieur Henri. Nancy got up again, and was, so to say, herself once more; but she did not get up her strength.

She would lie on the sofa in the *salon* those August days, which were very hot ones, too languid to get off it. Friends would call in to see her; Major and Mrs. Smith, the Miss Bosanquets, the Lamberts, and so on. Madame Carimon was often there. They would ask her why she did not "make an effort" and sit up and occupy herself with a book or a bit of work, or go out a little; and Nancy's answer was nearly always the same—she would do all that when the weather was somewhat cooler. Charley Palliser was quite a constant visitor. An English damsel, who was casting a covetous eye to Charles, though she might have spared herself the pains, took a fit of jealousy and said one might think sick Nancy Fennel was his sweetheart, going there so often. Charley rarely went empty-handed either. Now it would be half-a-dozen nectarines in their red-ripe loveliness, now some choice peaches, then a bunch of hot-house grapes, "purple and gushing," and again an amusing novel just out in England.

******

"Mary, she is surely dying!"

The sad exclamation came from Stella Featherston. She and Madame Carimon, going in to take tea at the Petite Maison Rouge, had been sent by its mistress to her chamber above to take off their bonnets. The words had broken from Stella the moment they were alone.

"Sometimes I fear it myself," replied Madame Carimon. "She certainly grows weaker instead of stronger."

"Does any doctor attend her?"

"Monsieur Dupuis; a man of long experience, kind and clever, I was talking to him the other day, and he as good as said his skill and care seemed to avail nothing: were wasted on her."

"Is it consumption?"

"I think not. She caught a dreadful cold about a month ago through being out in a night fog, thinly clad; and there's no doubt it left mischief behind; but it seems to me that she is wasting away with inward fever."

"I should get George to run over to see her, if I were you, Mary," remarked Stella. "French doctors are very clever, I believe, especially as surgeons; "but for an uncertain case like this they don't come up to the English. And George knows her constitution."

They went down to the *salon*, Mary Carimon laughing a little at the remark. Stella Featherston had not been long enough in France to part with her native prejudices. The family with whom she lived in Paris had journeyed to Sainteville for a month for what they called "*les eaux*," and Stella accompanied them. They were in lodgings on the port.

Mrs. Fennel seemed more like her old self that evening than she had been for some time past. The unexpected presence of her companion of early days changed the tone of her mind and raised her spirits. Stella exerted all her mirth, talked of their doings in the past, told of Buttermead's doings in the present. Nancy was quite gay.

"Do you ever sing now, Stella?" she suddenly asked.

"Why, no," laughed Stella, "unless I am quite alone. Who would care to hear old ditties sung without music?"

"I should. Oh, Stella, sing me a few!" urged the invalid, her tone quite imploring. "It would bring the dear old days back to me."

Stella Featherston had a most melodious voice, but she did not play. It was not unusual in those days for girls to sing without any accompaniment, as Stella had for the most part done.

"Have you forgotten your Scotch songs, Stella?" asked Mary Carimon.

"Not I; I like them best of all," replied Miss Featherston. And without more ado she broke into "*Ye banks and braes.*"

It was followed by "*The Banks of Allan Water,*" and others. Flore stole to the parlour-door, and thought she had never heard so sweet a singer. Last of all, Stella began a quaint song that was more of a chant than anything else, low and subdued:

Woe's me, for my heart is breakin',
I think en my brither sma',
And on my sister greetin',
When I cam' from home awa'.
And O, how my mither sobbit,
As she took from me her hand,
When I left the door of our old house
To come to this stranger land.

There's nae place like our ain home,
O, I would that I were there!
There's nae home like our ain home
To be met wi' onywhere.
And O, that I were back again
To our farm and fields sae green,
And heard the tongues of our ain folk,
And was what I hae been!

A feeling of despair ran through the whole words; and the

tears were running down Ann Fennel's hectic cheeks as the melody died away in a plaintive silence.

"It is what I shall never see again, Stella," she murmured—"the green fields of *our* home; or hear the tongues of all the dear ones there. In my dreams, sometimes, I am at Selby Court, light-hearted and happy, as I was before I left it for this ' stranger land.' Woe's *me*, also, Stella!"

And now I come into the story—I, Johnny Ludlow. For what I have told of it hitherto has not been from any personal knowledge of mine, but from diaries, and from what Mary Carimon related to me, and from Featherston. It may be regarded as singular that I should have been, so to say, present at its ending, but that I *was* there is as true as anything I ever wrote. The story itself is true in all its chief facts; I have already said that; and it is true that I saw the close of it.

18

To say that George Featherston, Doctor-in-ordinary at Buttermead, felt as if he were standing on his head instead of his heels, would not in the least express his mental condition as he stood in his surgery that September afternoon and read a letter, just delivered, from his sister, Madame Carimon.

"Wants me to go to Sainteville to see Ann Preen; thinks she will die if I refuse, for the French doctors can do nothing for her!" commented Featherston, staring at the letter in intense perplexity, and then looking off it to stare at me.

I wonder whether anything in this world happens by chance? In the days and years that have gone by since, I sometimes ask myself whether *that* did: that I should be at that particular moment in Featherston's surgery. Squire Todhetley was staying with Sir John Whitney for partridge shooting. He had taken me with him, Tod being in Gloucestershire; and on this Friday afternoon I had run in to say "How-d'ye-do" to Featherston.

"*Sainteville!*" repeated he, quite unable to collect his senses. "Why, I must cross the water to get *there!*"

I laughed. "Did you think Sainteville would cross to you, sir?"

"Bless me! just listen to this," he went on, reading parts of the letter aloud for my benefit. "'It is a dreadful story, George; I dare not enter into details here. But I may tell you this much: that she is dying of fright as much as of fever—or whatever it may be that ails her physically. I am sure it is not consumption, though some of the people here think it is. It is fright and superstition. She lives in the belief that the house is haunted: that Lavinia's ghost walks in it.'"

"Now what on earth can Mary mean by that?" demanded the doctor, looking off to ask me. "Ann Preen's wits must have left her. And Mary's too, to repeat so nonsensical a thing."

Turning to the next page of the letter, Featherston read on.

"'To see her dying by inches before my eyes, and not make any attempt to. save her, is what I cannot reconcile myself to, George. I should have it on my conscience afterwards. I think there is this one chance for her: that you, who have attended her before and must know her constitution, would see her now. You might be able to suggest some remedy or mode of treatment which would restore her. It might even be that the sight of a home face, of her old home doctor, would do for her what the strange doctors here cannot do. No one knows better than you how marvellously in illness the mind influences the body.'"

"True enough," broke off Featherston. "But it seems to me there must be something mysterious about the sickness," He read on again.

"'Stella, who is here, was the first to suggest your seeing her, but it was already exercising my thoughts. Do come, George! the sooner the better. I and Jules will be delighted to have you with us.'"

Featherston slowly folded up the letter. "What do you think of all this, Johnny Ludlow? Curious, is it not?"

"Very. Especially that hint about the house being haunted by the dead-and-gone Miss Preen."

"I have never heard clearly what it was Lavinia Preen died of," observed Featherston, leaving, doctor-like, the supernatural for the practical. "Except that she was seized with some sort of illness one day and died the next."

"But that's no reason why her ghost should walk. Is it?"

"Nancy's imagination," spoke Featherston slightingly. "She was always foolish and fanciful."

"Shall you go to Sainteville, Mr. Featherston?"

He gave his head a slow, dubious shake, but did not speak.

"Don't I wish such a chance were offered to me!"

Featherston sat down on a high stool, which stood before the physic shelves, to revolve the momentous question. And by the time he took over it, he seemed to find it a difficult task.

"One hardly likes to refuse the request, put as Mary writes it," remarked he presently. "Yet I don't see how I can go all the way over there; or how I could leave my patients here. What a temper some of them would be in!"

"They wouldn't die of it. It would be a rare holiday for you. Set you up in health for a year to come."

"I've not had a holiday since that time at Pumpwater," he rejoined dreamily; "when I went over for a day or two to see poor John Whitney. You remember it, Johnny; you were there."

"Ay, I remember it."

"Not that this is a question of a holiday for me or no holiday, and I wonder you should put it so, Johnny Ludlow; it turns upon Ann Preen. Ann Fennel, that's to say. If I thought I *could* do her any good, and those French doctors can't, why, I suppose I ought to make an effort to go."

"To be sure. Make one also to take me with you!"

"I dare say!" laughed Featherston. "What would the Squire say to that?"

"Bluster a bit, and then see it was the very thing for me, and ask what the cost would be. Mr. Featherston, I shall be ready to start when you are. Please let me go!"

Of course I said this half in jest. But it turned out to be earnest. Whether Featherston feared he might get lost if he crossed the sea alone, I can't say; but he said I might put the question to the Squire if I liked, and he would see him later and second it.

Featherston did another thing. He carried Mary Carimon's

letter that evening to Selby Court. Colonel Selby was staying with his brother for a week's shooting. Mr. Selby, a nervous valetudinarian, would not have gone out with a gun if bribed to it, but he invited his friends to do so. They had just finished dinner when Featherston arrived; the two brothers, and a short, dark, younger man with a rather keen but good-natured face and kindly dark eyes. He was introduced as Mr. David Preen, and turned out to be a cousin, more or less removed, of all the Preens and all the Selbys you have ever heard of, dead or living.

Featherston imparted his news to them, and showed his sister's letter. It was pronounced to be a very curious letter, and was read over more than once. Colonel Selby next told them what he knew and what he thought of Edwin Fennel: how he had persistently schemed to get the quarterly money of the two ladies into his own covetous hands, and what a shady sort of individual he was believed to be. Mr. Selby, nervous at the best of times, let alone the worst, became painfully impressed: he seemed to fear poor Nancy was altogether in a hornet's nest, and gave an impulsive opinion that some one of the family ought to go over with Featherston to look into things.

"Lavinia can't have been murdered, can she?" cried he, his thoughts altogether confused; "murdered by that man for her share of the money? Why else should her ghost come back?"

"Don't make us laugh, Paul," said the colonel to his brother. "Ghosts are all moonshine. There are no such things."

"I can tell you that there *are*, William," returned the elder. "Though mercifully the power to see them is accorded to very few mortals on earth. Can you go with Mr. Featherston to look into this strange business, William?"

"No," replied the colonel, "I could not possibly spare the time. Neither should I care to do it. Any inquiry of that kind would be quite out of my line."

"I will go," quietly spoke David Preen.

"Do so, David," said Mr. Selby eagerly. "It shall cost you nothing, you know." By which little speech, Featherston gathered that Mr. David Preen was not more overdone with riches than

279

were many of the other Preens.

"Look into it well, David. See the doctor who attended Lavinia; see all and every one able to throw any light upon her death," urged Mr. Selby. "As to Ann, she was lamentably, foolishly blameable to marry as she did, but she must not be left at the villain's mercy now things have come to this pass."

To which Mr. David Preen nodded an emphatic assent.

The Squire gave in at last. Not to my pleading—he accused me of having lost my head only to think of it—but to Featherston. And when the following week was wearing away, the exigencies of Featherston's patients not releasing him sooner, we started for Sainteville; he, I, and David Preen. Getting in at ten at night after a boisterous passage, Featherston took up his quarters at Monsieur Garimon's, we ours at the Hôtel des Princes.

She looked very ill. Ill and changed. I had seen Ann Preen at Buttermead when she lived there, but the Ann Preen (or Fennel) I saw now was not much like her. The once bright face was drawn and fallen in, and very nearly as long and grey as Featherston's. Apart from that, a timid, shrinking look sat upon it, as though she feared some terror lay very near to her.

The sick have to be studied, especially when suffering from whims and fancies. So they invented a little fable to Mrs. Fennel—that Featherston and David Preen were taking an excursion together for their recreation, and the doctor had extended it as far as Sainteville to see his sister Mary; never allowing her to think that it was to see *her*. I was with them, but I went for nobody—and in truth that's all I was in the matter.

It was the forenoon of the day after we arrived. David Preen had gone in first, her kinsman and distant cousin, to the Petite Maison Rouge, paving the way, as it were, for Featherston. We went in presently. Mrs. Fennel sat in a large armchair by the salon fire, wrapped in a grey shawl; she was always cold now, she told us; David Preen sat on the sofa opposite, talking pleasantly of home news. Featherston joined him on the sofa, and I sat down near the table.

Oh, she was glad to see us! Glad to see us all. Ours were

home faces, you see. She held my hands in hers, and the tears ran down her face, betraying her state of weakness.

"You have not been very well of late, Mary tells me," Featherston said to her in a break of the conversation. "What has been the matter?"

"I—it came on from a bad cold I caught," she answered with some hesitation. "And there was all the trouble about Lavinia's death. I could not get over the grief."

"Well, I must say you don't look very robust," returned Featherston, in a half-joking tone. "I think I had better take you in hand whilst I am here, and set you up."

"I do not think you can set me up; I do not suppose anyone can," she replied, shaking back her curls, which fell on each side of her face in ringlets, as of old.

Featherston smiled cheerily. "I'll try," said he. "Some of my patients say the same when I am first called in to them; but they change their tone after I have brought back their roses. So will you; never fear. I'll come in this afternoon and have a professional chat with you."

That settled, they went on with Buttermead again; David Preen giving scraps and revelations of the Preen and Selby families; Featherston telling choice items of the rural public in general. Mrs. Fennel's spirits went up to animation.

"Shall you be able to do anything for her, sir?" I asked the doctor as we came away and went through the entry to the Place Ronde.

"I cannot tell," he answered gravely. "She has a look on her face that I do not like to see there."

Betrayed into confidence, I suppose, by the presence of the old friend of her girlhood, Ann Fennel related everything to Mr. Featherston that afternoon, as they sat on the sofa side by side, her hand occasionally held soothingly in his own. He assured her plainly that what she was chiefly suffering from was a disorder of the nerves, and that she must state to him explicitly the circumstances which brought it on before he could decide how to treat her for it.

Nancy obeyed him. She yearned to get well, though a latent impression lay within her that she should not do so. She told him the particulars of Lavinia's unexpected death just when on the point of leaving Sainteville; and she went on to declare, glancing over her shoulders with frightened eyes, that she (Lavinia) had several times since then appeared in the house.

"What did Lavinia die of?" inquired the doctor at this juncture.

"We could not tell," answered Mrs. Fennel. "It puzzled us. At first Monsieur Dupuis thought it must be inflammation brought on by a chill; but Monsieur Podevin quite put that opinion aside, saying it was nothing of the sort. He is a younger and more energetic practitioner than Monsieur Dupuis."

"Was it never suggested that she might, in one way or another, have taken something which poisoned her?"

"Why, yes, it was; I believe Monsieur Dupuis did think so—I am sure Monsieur Podevin did. But it was impossible it could have been the case, you see, because Lavinia touched nothing either of the days that we did not also partake of."

"There ought to have been an examination after death. You objected to that, I fancy," continued Featherston, who had talked a little with Madame Carimon.

"True—I did; and I have been sorry for it since," sighed Ann Fennel. "It was through what my husband said to me that I objected. Edwin thought it would be distasteful to me. He did not like the idea of it either. Being dead, he held that she should be left in reverence."

Featherston coughed. She was evidently innocent as any lamb of suspicion against *him*.

"And now," went on Mr. Featherston, "just tell me what you mean by saying you see your sister about the house."

"We do see her," said Nancy.

"Nonsense! You don't. It is all fancy. When the nerves are unstrung, as yours are, they play us all sorts of tricks. Why, I knew a man once who took up a notion that he walked upon his head, and he came to me to be cured!"

"But it is seeing Lavinia's apparition, and the constant fear of seeing it which lies upon me, that has brought on this nervousness," pleaded Nancy. "It is to my husband, when he is here, that she chiefly appears; nothing but that is keeping him away. I have seen her only three or four times."

She spoke quietly and simply, evidently grounded in the belief. Mr. Featherston wondered how he was to deal with this: and perhaps he was not himself so much of a sceptic in the supernatural as he thought fit to pretend. Nancy continued:

"It was to my husband she appeared first. Exactly a week after her death. No; a week after the evening she was first taken ill. He was coming upstairs to bed—I had gone on—when he suddenly fancied that someone was following him, though only he and I were in the house. Turning quickly round, he saw Lavinia. That was the first time; and I assure you I thought he would have died of it. Never before had I witnessed such mortal terror in man."

"Did he tell you he had seen her?"

"No; never. I could not imagine what brought on these curious attacks of fright, for he had others. He put it upon his health. It was only when I saw Lavinia myself after he went to England that I knew. I knew then what it must have been."

Mr. Featherston was silent.

"She always appears in the same dress," continued Nancy; "a silver-grey silk that she wore at church that Sunday. It was the last gown she ever put on: we took it off her when she was first seized with the pain. And in her face there is always a sad, beseeching aspect, as if she wanted something and were imploring us to get it for her. *Indeed* we see her, Mr. Featherston."

"Ah, well," he said, perceiving it was not from this quarter that light could be thrown on the suspicious darkness of the past, "let us talk of yourself. You are to obey my orders in all respects, Mistress Nancy. We will soon have you flourishing again."

Brave words. Perhaps the doctor half believed in them himself. But he and they received a check all too soon.

That same evening, after David Preen had left—for he went

in to spend an hour at the little red house to gossip about the folks at home—Nancy was taken with a fit of shivering. Flore hastily mixed her a glass of hot wine-and-water, and then went upstairs to light a fire in the bedroom, thinking her mistress would be the better for it. Nancy, who could hear Flore moving about overhead, suddenly remembered something that she wanted brought down. Rising from her chair, she went to the door of the *salon*, intending to call out. A sort of side light, dim and indistinct, fell upon her as she stood in the recess at the foot of the stairs from the lamp in the salon and from the stove in the kitchen, for both doors were open.

"Flore," she was beginning, "will you bring down my—"

And there Ann Fennel's words ended. With a wild cry, which reached the ears of Flore and nearly startled her into fits, Mrs. Fennel collapsed. The servant came dashing downstairs, expecting to hear that the ghost had appeared again.

It was not that. Her mistress was looking wild and puzzled; and when she recovered herself sufficiently to speak, declared that she had been startled by some animal. Either a cat or a rabbit, she could not tell which, the glimpse she caught of it was so brief and slight; it had run against her legs as she was calling out,

Flore did not know what to make of this. She looked about, but neither cat nor rabbit was to be seen; and she told her mistress it could have been nothing but fancy. Mrs. Fennel thought she knew better.

"Why, I felt it and saw it," she said. "It came right against me and ran over my feet. It seemed to be making for the passage, as if it wanted to get out by the front-door."

★★★★★★

We were gathered together in the *salon* of the Petite Maison Rouge the following morning, partly by accident. Ann Fennel, exceedingly weak and nervous, lay in bed. Featherston and Monsieur Dupuis were both upstairs. She put down her illness to the fright, which she talked of to them freely. They did not assure her it was only "nerves"—to what purpose? I waited in the *salon* with David Preen, and just as the doctors came down Madame Carimon came in.

David Preen seized upon the opportunity. Fearing that one so favourable might not again occur, unless formally planned, he opened the ball. Drawing his chair to the table, next to that of Madame Carimon, the two doctors sitting opposite, David Preen avowed, with straightforward candour, that he, with some other relatives, held a sort of doubt as to whether it might not have been something Miss Lavinia Preen took which caused her death; and he begged Monsieur Dupuis to say if any such doubt had crossed his own mind at the time.

The fair-faced little *médecin* shook his head at this appeal, as much as to say he thought that the subject was a puzzling one. Naturally the doubt had crossed him, and very strongly, he answered; but the difficulty in assuming that view of the matter lay in her having partaken solely of the food which the rest of the household had partaken of; that and nothing else. His *confrère*, Monsieur Podevin, held a very conclusive opinion—that she had died of poison.

David Preen drew towards him a writing-case which lay on the table, took a sheet of paper from it, and a pencil from his pocket. "Let us go over the facts quietly," said he; "it may be we shall arrive at some decision."

So they went over the facts, the chief speakers being. Madame Carimon and Flore, who was called in. David Preen dotted down from time to time something which I suppose particularly impressed him.

Miss Preen was in perfectly good health up to that Sunday— the first after Easter. On the following Tuesday she was about to quit Sainteville for Boulogne, her home at the Petite Maison Rouge having become intolerable to her through the residence in it of Captain Fennel.

"Pardon me if I state here something which is not positively in the line of facts; rather, perhaps, in that of imagination," said Madame Carimon, looking up. "Lavinia had gradually acquired a most painful dread of Captain Fennel. She had dreams which she could only believe came to warn her against him, in which he appeared to be threatening her with some evil that she could not escape from. Once or twice—and this I cannot in any way account for—she saw him in the house when he was not in it, not even at Sainteville—"

"What! saw his apparition?" cried Featherston. "When the man was living! Come, come, Mary, that is going too far!"

"*Quelle drole d'idée!*" exclaimed the little doctor.

"He appeared to her twice, she told me," continued Mary Carimon. "She had been spending the evening out each time; had come into the house, this house, closing the street-door behind her. When she lighted a candle at the slab, she saw him standing just inside the door, gazing at her with the same dreadful aspect that she saw afterwards in her dreams. You may laugh, George; Monsieur Dupuis, I think you are already laughing; but I fully believe that she saw what she said she did, and dreamt what she did dream."

"But it could not have been the man's apparition when he was not dead; and it could not have been the man himself when he was not at Sainteville," contended Featherston.

"And I believe that it all meant one of those mysterious warnings which are vouchsafed us from our spiritual guardians in the unseen world," added Madame Carimon, independently pursuing her argument. "And that it came to Lavinia to warn her to escape from this evil house."

"And she did not do it," remarked David Preen. "She was not quick enough. Well, let us go on."

"As Lavinia came out of church, Charles Palliser ran after her to ask her to go home to dine with him and his aunt," resumed Madame Carimon. "If she had only accepted it! The dinner here was a very simple one, and they all partook of it, including Flore—"

"And it was Flore who cooked and served it?" interrupted David Preen, looking at her.

"*Mais oui, monsieur.* The tart excepted; that was *frangipane*, and did come from the pastrycook," added Flore, plunging into

English. "Then I had my own dinner, and I had of every dish; and I drank of the wine. Miss Lavinia would give me a glass of wine on the Sunday, and she poured it out for me herself that day from the bottle of Bordeaux on their own table. Nothing was the matter with any of all that. The one thing I did not have of was the liqueur."

"What liqueur was that?"

"It was *chartreuse*, I believe," said Flore. "While I was busy removing the dinner articles from the *salon, monsieur* was busy at his cupboard outside there, where he kept his bottles. He came into the kitchen just as I had sat down to eat, and asked me for three liqueur glasses, which I gave to him on a plate. I heard him pour the liqueur into them, and he carried them to the ladies."

Mr. David Preen wrote something down here.

"After that the captain went out to walk, saying he would see the English boat enter; and when I had finished washing up I carried the tea-tray to the *salon*-table and went home. Miss Lavinia was quite well then; she sat in her *belle* robe of grey silk talking with her sister. Then, when I was giving my boy Dion his *collation*, a *tartine* and a cooked apple, I was fetched back here, and found the poor lady fighting with pain for her life."

"Did you wash those liqueur glasses?" asked Mr. Feather-ston,

"But yes, sir. I had taken them away when I carried in the tea-things, and washed them at once, and put them on the shelf in their places."

"You see," observed Monsieur Dupuis, "the ill-fated lady appears to have taken nothing that the others did not take also. I applied my remedies when I was called to her, and the following day she had, as I believed, recovered from the attack; nothing but the exhaustion left by the agony was remaining. But that night she was again seized, and I was again fetched to her. The attack was even more violent than the first one. I made a request for another doctor, and Monsieur Podevin was brought. He at once set aside my suggestion of inflammation from a chill, and said it looked to him more like a case of poison."

"She had had nothing but slops all day, *messieurs*, which I made and carried to her," put in Flore; "and when I left, at night, she was, as *Monsieur le Medecin* put it, 'all well to look at.'"

"Flore did not make the arrowroot which she took later," said Mary Carimon, taking up the narrative. "When Lavinia went up to bed, towards nine o'clock, Mrs. Fennel made her a cup of arrowroot in the kitchen—"

"And a cup for herself at the same time, as I was informed, *madame*," spoke the little doctor.

"Oh yes, I know that. Monsieur Dupuis. Mrs. Fennel brought her sister's arrowroot, when it was ready, into this room, asking her husband whether she might venture to put a little brandy into it. He sent her to ask the question of Lavinia, bidding her leave the arrowroot on the table here. She came down for it, saying Lavinia declined the brandy, carried it up to her and saw her take it. Mrs, Fennel wished her goodnight and came down for her own portion, which she had left in the kitchen. Before eleven o'clock, when they were going to bed, cries were heard in Lavinia's room; she was seized with the second attack, and—and died in it."

"This second attack was so violent, so unmanageable," said Monsieur Dupuis, as Mary Carimon's voice faltered into silence, "that I feel convinced I could not have saved her had I been present when it came on. I hear that Captain Fennel says he rang several times at my door before he could arouse me. Such was not the case. I am a very light sleeper, waking, from habit, at the slightest sound. But in this case I had not had time to fall asleep when I fancied I heard the bell sound very faintly. I thought I must be mistaken, as the bell is a loud bell, and rings easily; and people who ring me up at night generally ring pretty sharply. I lay listening, and sometime afterwards, not immediately, it did ring. I opened my window, saw Captain Fennel outside, and was dressed and with him in two minutes."

"That sounds as if he did not want you to go to her too quickly, *monsieur*," observed Mr. Featherston, which went, as the French have it, without saying. "And I have heard of another suspicious fact: that he put his wife up to stop the medical examination after death."

"It amounts to this," spoke David Preen, "according to our judgement, if anything wrong was administered to her, it was given in the glass of liqueur on the Sunday afternoon, and in the cup of arrowroot on the Monday evening. They were the only things affording an opportunity of being tampered with; and in each case the pain came on about two hours afterwards."

Grave suspicion, as I am sure they all felt it to be. But not enough, as Featherston remarked, to accuse a man of murder. There was no proof to be brought forward, especially now that months had elapsed.

"What became of the cup which had contained the arrowroot?" inquired David Preen, looking at Flore. "Was it left in the bedroom?"

"That cup, sir, I found in a bowl of water in the kitchen, and also the other one which had been used. The two were together in the wooden bowl. I supposed Madame Fennel had put them there; but she said she had not."

"Ah!" exclaimed David Preen, drawing a deep breath.

He had come over to look into this suspicious matter; but, as it seemed, nothing could be done. To stir in it, and fail, would be worse than letting it alone.

"Look you," said David Preen, as he put up his note-book. "If it be true that Lavinia cannot rest now she's dead, but shows herself here in the house, I regard it as a pretty sure proof that she was sent out of the world unjustly. But—"

"Then you hold the belief that spirits revisit the earth, *monsieur*," interrupted Monsieur Dupuis, "and that revenants are to be seen?"

"I do, sir," replied David. "We Preens see them. But I cannot stir in this matter, I was about to say, and the man must be left to his conscience."

And so the conference broke up.

The thing which lay chiefly on hand now was to try to bring health back to Ann Fennel. It was thought well to take her out of the house for a short time, as she had such fancies about it; so Featherston gave up his room at Madame Carimon's, and Ann was invited to move into it, whilst he joined us at the hotel. I thought her very ill, as we all did. But after her removal there, she recovered her spirits wonderfully, and went out for short walks and laughed and chatted: and when Featherston and David Preen took the boat back to return home, she went to the port to see them steam off.

"Will it be all right with her?" was the last question Mary Carimon whispered to her brother.

"I'm afraid *not*," he answered. "A little time will show one way or the other. Depends somewhat, perhaps, upon how that husband of hers allows things to go on. I have done what I can, Mary; I could not do more."

Does the reader notice that I did not include myself in those who steamed off? For I did not go. Good, genial little Jules Carimon, who was pleased to say he had always liked me much at school, invited me to make a stay at his house, if I did not mind putting up with a small bedroom in the *mansarde*. I did not mind it at all; it was large enough for me. Nancy was delighted. We had quite a gay time of it; and I made the acquaintance of Major and Mrs. Smith, the Misses Bosanquet and Charley Palliser, who was shortly to quit Sainteville. Charley's impression of Mrs. Fennel was that she would quit it before he did, but in a different manner.

One fine afternoon, when we were coming off the pier, Nancy was walking between me and Mary Carimon, for she needed the support of two arms if she went far—yes, she was as weak as that—someone called out that the London boat was coming in. Turning round, we saw her gliding smoothly up the harbour. No one in these Anglo-French towns willingly misses *that* sight, and we drew up on the quay to watch the passengers land. There were only eight or ten of them.

Suddenly Nancy gave a great cry, which bore a sound both of fear and of gladness—"Oh, there's Edwin!"—and the next moment began to shake her pocket-handkerchief frantically.

A thin, grey, weasel of a man, whose face I did not like, came stalking up the ladder. Yes, it was the ex-captain, Edwin Fennel.

"He has not come for her sake; he has come to grab the quarter's money," spoke Mary, quite savagely, in my ear. No doubt. It would be due the end of September, which was at hand.

The captain was elaborately polite; quite effusive in his greeting to us. Nancy left us and took his arm. At the turning where we had to branch off to the Rue Pomme Cuite, she halted to say goodbye.

"But you are coming back to us, are you not?" cried Madame Carimon to her.

"Oh, I could not let Edwin go home alone," said she, "Nobody's there but Flore, you know."

So she went back there and then to the Petite Maison Rouge, and never came out of it again. I think he was kind to her, that man. He had sometimes a scared look upon his face, and I guessed he had been seeing sights. The man would have given his head to be off again; to remain in that haunted house must have been to him a most intolerable penance; but he had some regard (policy dictating it) for public opinion, and could not well run away from his wife in her failing health.

It was curious how quickly Nancy declined. From the very afternoon she entered the house it seemed to begin. He had grabbed the money, as Mary Carimon called it, and brought her nice and nourishing things; but nothing availed. And a fine way he must have been in, to see that; for with his wife's death the money would go away from him for evermore.

Monsieur Dupuis, sometimes Monsieur Henry Dupuis, saw her daily; and Captain Fennel hastily called in another doctor who had the reputation of being the best in the town, next to Monsieur Podevin; one Monsieur Lamirand. Mary Carimon spent half her time there; I went in most days. It could not be said that she had any special complaint, but she was too weak to live.

In less than three weeks it was all over. The end, when it came, was quite sudden. For a day or two she had seemed so much better that we told her she had taken a turn at last. On the Thursday evening, quite late—it was between eight and nine o'clock—Madame Carimon asked me to run there with some jelly which she had made, and which was only then ready. When I arrived, Flore said she was sure her mistress would like me to go up to her room; she was alone, *monsieur* having stepped out.

Nancy, wrapped in a warm dressing-gown, sat by the fire in an easy-chair and a great shawl. Her fair curls were all put back under a small lace cap, which was tied at the chin with grey ribbon; her pretty blue eyes were bright. I told her what I had come for, and took the chair in front of her.

"You look so well this evening, Nancy," I said heartily—for I had learnt to call her so at Madame Carimon's, as they did. "We shall have you getting well now all one way."

"It is the spurt of the candle before going out," she quietly answered. "I have not the least pain left anywhere—but it is only that."

"You should not say or think so."

"But I know it; I cannot mistake my own feelings. Fancy any one, reduced as I am, getting well again!"

I am a bad one to keep up "make-believes." Truth to say, I felt as sure of it as she did.

"And it will not be very long first. Johnny," she went on, in a half-whisper, "I saw Lavinia today." I looked at her, but made no reply. "I have never seen her since I came back here. Edwin has, though; I am sure of it. This afternoon at dusk I woke up out of a doze, for getting up to sit here quite exhausts me, and I was moving forward to touch the hand-bell on the table there, to let Flore know I was ready for my tea, when I saw Lavinia. She was standing over there, just in the firelight. I thought she seemed to be holding out her hand to me, as if inviting me to go to her, and on her face there was the sweetest smile of welcome; sweeter than could be seen on any face in life. All the sad, mournful, beseeching look had left it. She stood there for about a minute, and then vanished."

"Were you very much frightened?"

"I had not a thought of fear, Johnny. It was the contrary. She looked radiantly happy; and it somehow imparted happiness to me. I think—I think," added Nancy impressively, though with some hesitation, "that she came to let me know I am going to her. I believe I have seen her for the last time. The house has, also, I fancy; she and I will shortly go out of it together."

What could I answer to that?

"And so it is over at last," she murmured, more to herself than to me. "Very nearly over. The distress and the doubt, the terror and the pain. *I* brought it all on; you know that, Johnny Ludlow. I feel sure now that she has pardoned me. I humbly hope that God has."

She caught up her breath with a long-drawn sigh.

"And you will give my dear love to all the old friends in England, Johnny, beginning with Mr. Featherston; he has been very kind to me; you will see them again, but I shall not. Not in this life. But we shall be together in the Life which has no ending."

★★★★★★

At twelve o'clock that night Nancy Fennel died. At least, it was as near twelve as could be told. Just after that hour Flore went into the room, preparatory to sitting up with her, and found her dead—just expired, apparently—with a sweet smile on her face, and one hand stretched out as if in greeting. Perhaps Lavinia had come to greet her.

We followed her to the grave on Saturday. Captain Fennel walked next the coffin—and I wondered how he liked it. I was close behind him with Monsieur Carimon. Charley Palliser came next with little *Monsieur le Docteur* Dupuis and Monsieur Gustave Sauvage. And we left Nancy in the cemetery, side by side with her sister.

Captain Edwin Fennel disappeared. On the Sunday, when we English were looking for him in church, he did not come—his grief not allowing him, said some of the ladies. But an English clerk in the broker's office, hearing this, told another tale. Fennel had gone off by the boat which left the port for London the previous night at midnight.

And he did not come back again. He had left sundry debts behind him, including that owing to Madame Veuve Sauvage. Monsieur Carimon, later, undertook the payment of these at the request of Colonel Selby. It was understood that Captain Edwin Fennel had emigrated to South America. If he had any conscience at all, it was to be hoped he carried it with him. He did not carry the money. The poor little income which he had schemed for, and perhaps worse, went back to the Selby's.

And that is the story. It is a curious history, and painful in more ways than one. But I repeat that it is true.

The Room in the Tower
By E. F. Benson

It is probable that everybody who is at all a constant dreamer has had at least one experience of an event or a sequence of circumstances which have come to his mind in sleep being subsequently realized in the material world. But, in my opinion, so far from this being a strange thing, it would be far odder if this fulfilment did not occasionally happen, since our dreams are, as a rule, concerned with people whom we know and places with which we are familiar, such as might very naturally occur in the awake and daylit world. True, these dreams are often broken into by some absurd and fantastic incident, which puts them out of court in regard to their subsequent fulfilment, but on the mere calculation of chances, it does not appear in the least unlikely that a dream imagined by anyone who dreams constantly should occasionally come true. Not long ago, for instance, I experienced such a fulfilment of a dream which seems to me in no way remarkable and to have no kind of psychical significance. The manner of it was as follows.

A certain friend of mine, living abroad, is amiable enough to write to me about once in a fortnight. Thus, when fourteen days or thereabouts have elapsed since I last heard from him, my mind, probably, either consciously or subconsciously, is expectant of a letter from him. One night last week I dreamed that as I was going upstairs to dress for dinner I heard, as I often heard, the sound of the postman's knock on my front door, and diverted my direction downstairs instead. There, among other correspondence, was a letter from him. Thereafter the fantastic entered, for on opening it I found inside the ace of diamonds, and scribbled across it in his well-known handwriting, "I am sending you this for safe custody, as you know it is running an unreasonable risk to keep aces in Italy." The next evening I was just preparing to go upstairs to dress when I heard the postman's knock, and did precisely as I had done in my dream.

There, among other letters, was one from my friend. Only it did not contain the ace of diamonds. Had it done so, I should have attached more weight to the matter, which, as it stands, seems to me a perfectly ordinary coincidence. No doubt I consciously or subconsciously expected a letter from him, and this suggested to me my dream. Similarly, the fact that my friend had not written to me for a fortnight suggested to him that he should do so. But occasionally it is not so easy to find such an explanation, and for the following story I can find no explanation at all. It came out of the dark, and into the dark it has gone again.

All my life I have been a habitual dreamer: the nights are few, that is to say, when I do not find on awaking in the morning that some mental experience has been mine, and sometimes, all night long, apparently, a series of the most dazzling adventures befall me. Almost without exception these adventures are pleasant, though often merely trivial. It is of an exception that I am going to speak.

It was when I was about sixteen that a certain dream first came to me, and this is how it befell. It opened with my being set down at the door of a big red-brick house, where, I understood, I was going to stay. The servant who opened the door told me that tea was being served in the garden, and led me through a low dark-panelled hall, with a large open fireplace, on to a cheerful green lawn set round with flower beds. There were grouped about the tea-table a small party of people, but they were all strangers to me except one, who was a schoolfellow called Jack Stone, clearly the son of the house, and he introduced me to his mother and father and a couple of sisters. I was, I remember, somewhat astonished to find myself here, for the boy in question was scarcely known to me, and I rather disliked what I knew of him; moreover, he had left school nearly a year before.

The afternoon was very hot, and an intolerable oppression reigned. On the far side of the lawn ran a red-brick wall, with an iron gate in its centre, outside which stood a walnut tree. We sat in the shadow of the house opposite a row of long windows, inside which I could see a table with cloth laid, glimmering with glass and silver. This garden front of the house was very long, and at one end of it stood a tower of three stories, which looked to me much older than the rest of the building.

Before long, Mrs. Stone, who, like the rest of the party, had sat in absolute silence, said to me, "Jack will show you your room: I have given you the room in the tower."

Quite inexplicably my heart sank at her words. I felt as if I had known that I should have the room in the tower, and that it contained something dreadful and significant. Jack instantly got up, and I understood that I had to follow him. In silence we passed through the hall, and mounted a great oak staircase with many corners, and arrived at a small landing with two doors set in it. He pushed one of these open for me to enter, and without coming in himself, closed it after me. Then I knew that my conjecture had been right: there was something awful in the room, and with the terror of nightmare growing swiftly and enveloping me, I awoke in a spasm of terror.

Now that dream or variations on it occurred to me intermittently for fifteen years. Most often it came in exactly this form, the arrival, the tea laid out on the lawn, the deadly silence succeeded by that one deadly sentence, the mounting with Jack Stone up to the room in the tower where horror dwelt, and it always came to a close in the nightmare of terror at that which was in the room, though I never saw what it was. At other times I experienced variations on this same theme. Occasionally, for instance, we would be sitting at dinner in the dining-room, into the windows of which I had looked on the first night when the dream of this house visited me, but wherever we were, there was the same silence, the same sense of dreadful oppression and foreboding. And the silence I knew would always be broken by Mrs. Stone saying to me, "Jack will show you your room: I have given you the room in the tower."

Upon which (this was invariable) I had to follow him up the oak staircase with many corners, and enter the place that I dreaded more and more each time that I visited it in sleep. Or, again, I would find myself playing cards still in silence in a drawing-room lit with immense chandeliers, that gave a blinding illumination. What the game was I have no idea; what I remember, with a sense of miserable anticipation, was that soon Mrs. Stone would get up and say to me, "Jack will show you your room: I have given you the room in the tower." This drawing-room where we played cards was next to the dining-room, and, as I have said, was always brilliantly illuminated, whereas the rest of the house was full of dusk and shadows. And yet, how often, in spite of those bouquets of lights, have I not pored over the cards that were dealt me, scarcely able for some reason to see them. Their designs, too, were strange: there were no red suits, but all were black, and among them there were certain cards which were black all over. I hated and dreaded those.

As this dream continued to recur, I got to know the greater part of the house. There was a smoking-room beyond the drawing-room, at the end of a passage with a green baize door. It was always very dark there, and as often as I went there I passed somebody whom I could not see in the doorway coming out. Curious developments, too, took place in the characters that peopled the dream as might happen to living persons. Mrs. Stone, for instance, who, when I first saw her, had been black-haired, became gray, and instead of rising briskly, as she had done at first when she said, "Jack will show you your room: I have given you the room in the tower," got up very feebly, as if the strength was leaving her limbs. Jack also grew up, and became a rather ill-looking young man, with a brown moustache, while one of the sisters ceased to appear, and I understood she was married.

Then it so happened that I was not visited by this dream for six months or more, and I began to hope, in such inexplicable dread did I hold it, that it had passed away for good. But one night after this interval I again found myself being shown out onto the lawn for tea, and Mrs. Stone was not there, while the others were all dressed in black. At once I guessed the reason, and my heart leaped at the thought that perhaps this time I should not have to sleep in the room in the tower, and though we usually all sat in silence, on this occasion the sense of relief made me talk and laugh as I had never yet done. But even then matters were not altogether comfortable, for no one else spoke, but they all looked secretly at each other. And soon the foolish stream of my talk ran dry, and gradually an apprehension worse than anything I had previously known gained on me as the light slowly faded.

Suddenly a voice which I knew well broke the stillness, the voice of Mrs. Stone, saying, "Jack will show you your room: I have given you the room in the tower." It seemed to come from near the gate in the red-brick wall that bounded the lawn, and looking up, I saw that the grass outside was sown thick with gravestones. A curious greyish light shone from them, and I could read the lettering on the grave nearest me, and it was, "*In evil memory of Julia Stone.*" And as usual Jack got up, and again I followed him through the hall and up the staircase with many corners. On this occasion it was darker than usual, and when I passed into the room in the tower I could only just see the furniture, the position of which was already familiar to me. Also there was a dreadful odour of decay in the room, and I woke screaming.

The dream, with such variations and developments as I have mentioned, went on at intervals for fifteen years. Sometimes I would dream it two or three nights in succession; once, as I have said, there was an intermission of six months, but taking a reasonable average, I should say that I dreamed it quite as often as once in a month. It had, as is plain, something of nightmare about it, since it always ended in the same appalling terror, which so far from getting less, seemed to me to gather fresh fear every time that I experienced it. There was, too, a strange and dreadful consistency about it. The characters in it, as I have mentioned, got regularly older, death and marriage visited this silent family, and I never in the dream, after Mrs. Stone had died, set eyes on her again.

But it was always her voice that told me that the room in the tower was prepared for me, and whether we had tea out on the lawn, or the scene was laid in one of the rooms overlooking it, I could always see her gravestone standing just outside the iron gate. It was the same, too, with the married daughter; usually she was not present, but once or twice she returned again, in company with a man, whom I took to be her husband. He, too, like the rest of them, was always silent. But, owing to the constant repetition of the dream, I had ceased to attach, in my waking hours, any significance to it. I never met Jack Stone again during all those years, nor did I ever see a house that resembled this dark house of my dream. And then something happened.

I had been in London in this year, up till the end of the July, and during the first week in August went down to stay with a friend in a house he had taken for the summer months, in the Ashdown Forest district of Sussex. I left London early, for John Clinton was to meet me at Forest Row Station, and we were going to spend the day golfing, and go to his house in the evening. He had his motor with him, and we set off, about five of the afternoon, after a thoroughly delightful day, for the drive, the distance being some ten miles. As it was still so early we did not have tea at the club house, but waited till we should get home.

As we drove, the weather, which up till then had been, though hot, deliciously fresh, seemed to me to alter in quality, and become very stagnant and oppressive, and I felt that indefinable sense of ominous apprehension that I am accustomed to before thunder. John, however, did not share my views, attributing my loss of lightness to the fact that I had lost both my matches. Events proved, however, that I was right, though I do not think that the thunderstorm that broke that night was the sole cause of my depression.

Our way lay through deep high-banked lanes, and before we had gone very far I fell asleep, and was only awakened by the stopping of the motor. And with a sudden thrill, partly of fear but chiefly of curiosity, I found myself standing in the doorway of my house of dream. We went, I half wondering whether or not I was dreaming still, through a low oak-panelled hall, and out onto the lawn, where tea was laid in the shadow of the house. It was set in flower beds, a red-brick wall, with a gate in it, bounded one side, and out beyond that was a space of rough grass with a walnut tree. The facade of the house was very long, and at one end stood a three-storied tower, markedly older than the rest.

Here for the moment all resemblance to the repeated dream ceased. There was no silent and somehow terrible family, but a large assembly of exceedingly cheerful persons, all of whom were known to me. And in spite of the horror with which the dream itself had always filled me, I felt nothing of it now that the scene of it was thus reproduced before me. But I felt intensest curiosity as to what was going to happen.

Tea pursued its cheerful course, and before long Mrs. Clinton got up. And at that moment I think I knew what she was going to say. She spoke to me, and what she said was:

"Jack will show you your room: I have given you the room in the tower."

At that, for half a second, the horror of the dream took hold of me again. But it quickly passed, and again I felt nothing more than the most intense curiosity. It was not very long before it was amply satisfied.

John turned to me.

"Right up at the top of the house," he said, "but I think you'll be comfortable. We're absolutely full up. Would you like to go and see it now? By Jove, I believe that you are right, and that we are going to have a thunderstorm. How dark it has become."

I got up and followed him. We passed through the hall, and

up the perfectly familiar staircase. Then he opened the door, and I went in. And at that moment sheer unreasoning terror again possessed me. I did not know what I feared: I simply feared. Then like a sudden recollection, when one remembers a name which has long escaped the memory, I knew what I feared. I feared Mrs. Stone, whose grave with the sinister inscription, "*In evil memory,*" I had so often seen in my dream, just beyond the lawn which lay below my window. And then once more the fear passed so completely that I wondered what there was to fear, and I found myself, sober and quiet and sane, in the room in the tower, the name of which I had so often heard in my dream, and the scene of which was so familiar.

I looked around it with a certain sense of proprietorship, and found that nothing had been changed from the dreaming nights in which I knew it so well. Just to the left of the door was the bed, lengthways along the wall, with the head of it in the angle. In a line with it was the fireplace and a small bookcase; opposite the door the outer wall was pierced by two lattice-paned windows, between which stood the dressing-table, while ranged along the fourth wall was the washing-stand and a big cupboard. My luggage had already been unpacked, for the furniture of dressing and undressing lay orderly on the wash-stand and toilet-table, while my dinner clothes were spread out on the coverlet of the bed.

And then, with a sudden start of unexplained dismay, I saw that there were two rather conspicuous objects which I had not seen before in my dreams: one a life-sized oil painting of Mrs. Stone, the other a black-and-white sketch of Jack Stone, representing him as he had appeared to me only a week before in the last of the series of these repeated dreams, a rather secret and evil-looking man of about thirty. His picture hung between the windows, looking straight across the room to the other portrait, which hung at the side of the bed. At that I looked next, and as I looked I felt once more the horror of nightmare seize me.

It represented Mrs. Stone as I had seen her last in my dreams: old and withered and white-haired. But in spite of the evident feebleness of body, a dreadful exuberance and vitality shone through the envelope of flesh, an exuberance wholly malign, a vitality that foamed and frothed with unimaginable evil. Evil beamed from the narrow, leering eyes; it laughed in the demon-like mouth. The whole face was instinct with some secret and appalling mirth; the hands, clasped together on the knee, seemed shaking with suppressed and nameless glee. Then I saw also that it was signed in the left-hand bottom corner, and wondering who the artist could be, I looked more closely, and read the inscription, "Julia Stone by Julia Stone."

There came a tap at the door, and John Clinton entered.

"Got everything you want?" he asked.

"Rather more than I want," said I, pointing to the picture.

He laughed.

"Hard-featured old lady," he said. "By herself, too, I remember. Anyhow she can't have flattered herself much."

"But don't you see?" said I. "It's scarcely a human face at all. It's the face of some witch, of some devil."

He looked at it more closely.

"Yes; it isn't very pleasant," he said. "Scarcely a bedside manner, eh? Yes; I can imagine getting the nightmare if I went to sleep with that close by my bed. I'll have it taken down if you like."

"I really wish you would," I said. He rang the bell, and with the help of a servant we detached the picture and carried it out onto the landing, and put it with its face to the wall.

"By Jove, the old lady is a weight," said John, mopping his forehead. "I wonder if she had something on her mind."

The extraordinary weight of the picture had struck me too. I was about to reply, when I caught sight of my own hand. There was blood on it, in considerable quantities, covering the whole palm.

"I've cut myself somehow," said I.

John gave a little startled exclamation.

"Why, I have too," he said.

Simultaneously the footman took out his handkerchief and

wiped his hand with it. I saw that there was blood also on his handkerchief.

John and I went back into the tower room and washed the blood off; but neither on his hand nor on mine was there the slightest trace of a scratch or cut. It seemed to me that, having ascertained this, we both, by a sort of tacit consent, did not allude to it again. Something in my case had dimly occurred to me that I did not wish to think about. It was but a conjecture, but I fancied that I knew the same thing had occurred to him.

The heat and oppression of the air, for the storm we had expected was still undischarged, increased very much after dinner, and for some time most of the party, among whom were John Clinton and myself, sat outside on the path bounding the lawn, where we had had tea. The night was absolutely dark, and no twinkle of star or moon ray could penetrate the pall of cloud that overset the sky. By degrees our assembly thinned, the women went up to bed, men dispersed to the smoking or billiard room, and by eleven o'clock my host and I were the only two left. All the evening I thought that he had something on his mind, and as soon as we were alone he spoke.

"The man who helped us with the picture had blood on his hand, too, did you notice?" he said.

"I asked him just now if he had cut himself, and he said he supposed he had, but that he could find no mark of it. Now where did that blood come from?"

By dint of telling myself that I was not going to think about it, I had succeeded in not doing so, and I did not want, especially just at bedtime, to be reminded of it.

"I don't know," said I, "and I don't really care so long as the picture of Mrs. Stone is not by my bed."

He got up.

"But it's odd," he said. "Ha! Now you'll see another odd thing."

A dog of his, an Irish terrier by breed, had come out of the house as we talked. The door behind us into the hall was open, and a bright oblong of light shone across the lawn to the iron gate which led on to the rough grass outside, where the walnut tree stood. I saw that the dog had all his hackles up, bristling with rage and fright; his lips were curled back from his teeth, as if he was ready to spring at something, and he was growling to himself. He took not the slightest notice of his master or me, but stiffly and tensely walked across the grass to the iron gate. There he stood for a moment, looking through the bars and still growling. Then of a sudden his courage seemed to desert him: he gave one long howl, and scuttled back to the house with a curious crouching sort of movement.

"He does that half-a-dozen times a day." said John. "He sees something which he both hates and fears."

I walked to the gate and looked over it. Something was moving on the grass outside, and soon a sound which I could not instantly identify came to my ears. Then I remembered what it was: it was the purring of a cat. I lit a match, and saw the purrer, a big blue Persian, walking round and round in a little circle just outside the gate, stepping high and ecstatically, with tail carried aloft like a banner. Its eyes were bright and shining, and every now and then it put its head down and sniffed at the grass.

I laughed.

"The end of that mystery, I am afraid." I said. "Here's a large cat having *Walpurgis* night all alone."

"Yes, that's Darius," said John. "He spends half the day and all night there. But that's not the end of the dog mystery, for Toby and he are the best of friends, but the beginning of the cat mystery. What's the cat doing there? And why is Darius pleased, while Toby is terror-stricken?"

At that moment I remembered the rather horrible detail of my dreams when I saw through the gate, just where the cat was now, the white tombstone with the sinister inscription. But before I could answer the rain began, as suddenly and heavily as if a tap had been turned on, and simultaneously the big cat squeezed through the bars of the gate, and came leaping across the lawn to the house for shelter. Then it sat in the doorway, looking out eagerly into the dark. It spat and struck at John with its paw, as he pushed it in, in order to close the door.

Somehow, with the portrait of Julia Stone in the passage outside, the room in the tower had absolutely no alarm for me, and as I went to bed, feeling very sleepy and heavy, I had nothing more than interest for the curious incident about our bleeding hands, and the conduct of the cat and dog. The last thing I looked at before I put out my light was the square empty space by my bed where the portrait had been. Here the paper was of its original full tint of dark red: over the rest of the walls it had faded. Then I blew out my candle and instantly fell asleep.

My awaking was equally instantaneous, and I sat bolt upright in bed under the impression that some bright light had been flashed in my face, though it was now absolutely pitch dark. I knew exactly where I was, in the room which I had dreaded in dreams, but no horror that I ever felt when asleep approached the fear that now invaded and froze my brain. Immediately after a peal of thunder crackled just above the house, but the probability that it was only a flash of lightning which awoke me gave no reassurance to my galloping heart. Something I knew was in the room with me, and instinctively I put out my right hand, which was nearest the wall, to keep it away. And my hand touched the edge of a picture-frame hanging close to me.

I sprang out of bed, upsetting the small table that stood by it, and I heard my watch, candle, and matches clatter onto the floor. But for the moment there was no need of light, for a blinding flash leaped out of the clouds, and showed me that by my bed again hung the picture of Mrs. Stone. And instantly the room went into blackness again. But in that flash I saw another thing also, namely a figure that leaned over the end of my bed, watching me. It was dressed in some close-clinging white garment, spotted and stained with mould, and the face was that of the portrait.

Overhead the thunder cracked and roared, and when it ceased and the deathly stillness succeeded, I heard the rustle of movement coming nearer me, and, more horrible yet, perceived an odour of corruption and decay. And then a hand was laid on the side of my neck, and close beside my ear I heard quick-taken, eager breathing. Yet I knew that this thing, though it could be perceived by touch, by smell, by eye and by ear, was still not of this earth, but something that had passed out of the body and had power to make itself manifest. Then a voice, already familiar to me, spoke.

"I knew you would come to the room in the tower," it said. "I have been long waiting for you. At last you have come. To-night I shall feast; before long we will feast together."

And the quick breathing came closer to me; I could feel it on my neck.

At that the terror, which I think had paralyzed me for the moment, gave way to the wild instinct of self-preservation. I hit wildly with both arms, kicking out at the same moment, and heard a little animal-squeal, and something soft dropped with a thud beside me. I took a couple of steps forward, nearly tripping up over whatever it was that lay there, and by the merest good-luck found the handle of the door. In another second I ran out on the landing, and had banged the door behind me. Almost at the same moment I heard a door open somewhere below, and John Clinton, candle in hand, came running upstairs.

"What is it?" he said. "I sleep just below you, and heard a noise as if—Good heavens, there's blood on your shoulder."

I stood there, so he told me afterwards, swaying from side to side, white as a sheet, with the mark on my shoulder as if a hand covered with blood had been laid there.

"It's in there," I said, pointing. "She, you know. The portrait is in there, too, hanging up on the place we took it from."

At that he laughed.

"My dear fellow, this is mere nightmare," he said.

He pushed by me, and opened the door, I standing there simply inert with terror, unable to stop him, unable to move.

"Phew! What an awful smell," he said.

Then there was silence; he had passed out of my sight behind the open door. Next moment he came out again, as white as myself, and instantly shut it.

"Yes, the portrait's there," he said, "and on the floor is a thing—a thing spotted with earth, like what they bury people in. Come away, quick, come away."

How I got downstairs I hardly know. An awful shuddering and nausea of the spirit rather than of the flesh had seized me, and more than once he had to place my feet upon the steps, while every now and then he cast glances of terror and apprehension up the stairs. But in time we came to his dressing-room on the floor below, and there I told him what I have here described.

The sequel can be made short; indeed, some of my readers have perhaps already guessed what it was, if they remember that inexplicable affair of the churchyard at West Fawley, some eight years ago, where an attempt was made three times to bury the body of a certain woman who had committed suicide. On each occasion the coffin was found in the course of a few days again protruding from the ground. After the third attempt, in order that the thing should not be talked about, the body was buried elsewhere in unconsecrated ground. Where it was buried was just outside the iron gate of the garden belonging to the house where this woman had lived. She had committed suicide in a room at the top of the tower in that house. Her name was Julia Stone.

Subsequently the body was again secretly dug up, and the coffin was found to be full of blood.

The Crab Spider

A.K.A THE SPIDER OF GUYANA

By Erckmann-Chatrian

The hot springs at Spinbronn, situated in Hundsruck, some leagues from Pirmesans, at one time enjoyed a magnificent reputation. All those who suffered from gout or kidney troubles in Germany used to congregate there. The wild aspect of the country did not deter them. They stayed in pretty cottages at the bottom of the pass and bathed in the waterfall, which fell in thick sheets of foam from a cave at the top of a cliff. They drank a decanter of mineral water or two a day, and the resident doctor, Daniel Hâselnoss, who gave out his prescriptions wearing a large wig and a chestnut-coloured suit, did excellent business.

Today the waters at Spinbronn feature no longer in the 'Codex'; in this poor village, you can see only wretched woodcutters and, sad to relate, Dr. Hâselnoss has long gone. All of which is the result of a series of very strange occurrences which Councillor Bremen, of Pirmesans, related to me one summer evening.

★★★★★★

'You of course know, Maître Frantz,' he said to me, 'that the spring at Spinbronn comes out of a sort of cave, approximately fifteen feet high, and twelve to fifteen feet wide; the water has a temperature of 67° c and is briny. As for the cave, it is entirely covered on the outside with moss, ivy, and brushwood and no one knows its depth, since hot vapours prevent anyone from entering.

'However, a peculiar thing had been remarked since the last

century, that some of the birds of the neighbourhood, thrushes, turtledoves and hawks, were often seen to fly in but never come out. No one knew to what mysterious influence they should attribute this peculiarity.

'In 1801, during the watering season, perhaps owing to the unusually heavy rain that year, the spring became more abundant, and one day the bathers who were walking at the bottom on the lawn saw a human body, dead white, falling from the waterfall.

"You may judge for yourself, Maître Frantz, the general panic. Naturally it was thought that in years gone by a murder had been committed at Spinbronn, and that the body of the victim had been thrown into the spring. But the body weighed no more than twelve pounds, and Dr. Hâselnoss, deduced from this that it must have lain in the sands for more than three centuries to have been reduced to this state of desiccation.

'This line of reasoning, though very plausible, did not prevent a crowd of bathers, who were naturally upset at having drunk from the salty water, from leaving at the end of that day. Those who were genuine sufferers with gout and their kidneys consoled themselves. . . .but more breaking up inside the cavern occurred for all the debris, mud and rubbish which was inside the cave was disgorged over the ensuing days; a real charnel house came down from the mountain, skeletons of animals of every sort—quadrupeds, birds, reptiles—in short all the worst horrors imaginable.

'Hâselnoss immediately published a pamphlet pointing out that all these bones came from an antediluvian world, that they were fossil bones which had accumulated there in a sort of hollow during the deluge that is four thousand years before Christ, that as a consequence they could be considered genuine stones, that people should not be disgusted by them. . . But his work had scarcely reassured the gout sufferers, when one fine morning, the corpse of a fox, then that of a hawk with all its feathers, fell from the waterfall.

"It was impossible to maintain any longer that these remains were previous to the flood. Consequently the feeling of disgust was so great that everyone hastened to pack his belongings and go off to take the waters elsewhere.

'"What a disgrace!" exclaimed the beautiful ladies. . . . ."what a horror!". . . . "That's where the virtue of these mineral waters comes from. We would rather die from kidney stones than continue such treatment."

'After eight days only a huge Englishman remained at Spinbronn, who had at the same time gout in both hands and the feet and who was known as Sir Thomas Haverburch, Commodore. He lived in great style, as was the custom of British people in a foreign country.

'This character, big and fat, with a florid complexion, but whose hands were literally knotted with gout, would have swallowed broth made with dead bodies if he thought it would cure his infirmity. He laughed a great deal at the departure of the other invalids and took up residence in the prettiest cottage, halfway up the hill, declaring his intention of spending the winter at Spinbronn."

At this point Councillor Bremer leisurely slowly inhaled a generous pinch of snuff, as if to rekindle his memories; he shook the delicate lace of his shirt frill with the tips of his fingers and continued.

'Five or six years before the revolution of 1789, a young doctor of Pirmesans, called Christian Weber, had set off for San Domingo in the hope of there making his fortune. He had effectively amassed some one hundred thousand pounds in the exercise of his profession, when the revolt of the negroes broke out.

'There is no need for me to remind you of the barbaric treatment which our unfortunate compatriots suffered in Haiti. Dr. Weber had the good fortune to escape the massacre and was to save a part of his fortune. He then travelled to South America, and spent several years in French Guiana. In 1801 he returned to Pirmesans and established himself at Spinbronn, where Dr. Hâselnoss handed over his house and his dead practice.

'Dr. Christian Weber brought with him an old negress called

311

Agatha—an awesome creature, with a short squat nose, lips as big as your fist, her head covered in a triple row of scarves in garish colours. This poor old woman loved red; she had hooped earrings which dangled as far her shoulders, and the mountain people of Hundsrück would come from twenty miles around to stare at her.

'As for Dr. Weber, he was a tall, gaunt man, invariably dressed in a sky-blue coat with swallow tails and in buckskin breeches. He wore a pliable straw hat and boots with bright yellow tops, on the front of which dangled two silver tassels.

'He wasn't very talkative; his laugh had something of a nervous twitching in it, and his grey eyes, usually calm and meditative, shone with an unnatural glow at the slightest sign of contradiction. Each morning he would go for a walk on the mountain, letting his horse roam and whistling, always in the same monotone, the same melody from a negro song. This eccentric had brought from his travels a number of boxes full of weird insects, some of them bronzy-black and as big as eggs, others small and scintillating like sparks. He seemed to be much more fond of these than of his patients and from time to time, on his way back from his strolls he brought back butterflies pinned to the band of his hat.

'He had hardly settled into Hâselnoss's huge house than he filled its farmyard with foreign birds, Barbary geese with scarlet cheeks, guinea-fowl and a white peacock which usually perched on the garden wall and which shared with the negress the admiration of the mountain folk.

'If I am going into details, Maître Frantz, it's because they remind me of my early youth. Dr. Weber turned out to be at the same time both my cousin and my tutor, and on his return to Germany, he had come to get me and install me in his home at Spinbronn. Black Agatha at first inspired in me some fear, and it was only with some difficulty that I could get used to her unusual features. She was a good woman, she could make spicy dishes well, she hummed strange songs in a guttural voice at the same time snapping her fingers and rhythmically raising her fat legs in turn, so that I ended up liking her very much.

'Dr. Weber had, quite naturally, made friends with Sir Thomas Haverburch, who was in his eyes his most prominent patient, and I wasn't long in realizing that these two eccentrics had long sessions together. They chatted about various mysteries, like the transmission of energy, and they indulged in certain bizarre gestures which they had both observed in the course of their travels, Sir Thomas in the East and my tutor in the Americas. I found it very intriguing.

'As happens with children, I was always on the look-out for what they seemed to want to hide from me. But despairing in the end of discovering anything I resolved to ask Agatha. The poor old woman, after making me promise to say nothing about it, confessed to me that my tutor was a sorcerer. Moreover, Dr. Weber exercised a peculiar influence over the negress's mind and this lady, normally so cheerful and always ready to amuse herself at the slightest thing, trembled like a leaf, when, by chance, her master's grey eyes fell on her.

'All this, Maître Frantz, seems to have no connection with the springs of Spinbronn . . . But, wait, just wait . . . You will see by what a strange string of circumstances my story is related to this.

'I told you that birds would go into the cave and not come out, and even other bigger animals. After the final departure of the bathers, some inhabitants of the village remembered that a young girl, called Loïsa Müller, who lived with her old invalid grandmother in a cottage on the slope of the hill, had suddenly disappeared about five years ago. She had set off one morning to look for grass in the forest, and since then no one had ever heard of her again, except that a few days later, some woodcutters who were coming down from the mountain had found her apron and her sickle a few paces from the cave.

'Since then it was obvious to everyone that the body that had fallen from the waterfall, and about which Hâselnoss had said such very nice things, was none other than that of Loïsa Müller. The poor young girl had undoubtedly been drawn into the cavern by the mysterious influence to which even weaker things were subjected almost daily.

'This influence, what was it? No one knew. But the inhabitants of Spinbronn, superstitious like all mountain folk, claimed that the devil lived in the cave, and the terror spread in the surrounding districts.

'Now, one July afternoon in 1802, my cousin was working on a new classification of the insects in his boxes. He had taken several quite curious ones from them the evening before. I was beside him, holding a lighted candle in my hand and in the other a needle that I heated.

'Sir Thomas, sitting down, his chair leaning against the edge of a window and his feet on a stool, watched us working and smoked a cigar.

'I was on very good terms with Sir Thomas Haverburch, and I used to accompany him every day to the woods in his *barouche*. He enjoyed listening to me chattering in English and wanted to make of me, he would say, a real gentleman.

'When he had labelled all his butterflies, Dr. Weber at last opened the box of his biggest insects and said: "Yesterday I caught a magnificent stag-beetle, the great *Lucanus Cervus* of the oaks of Hartz. It has this peculiarity that its right claw forks into five branches. It's a rare species."

'At the same time I gave him the needle, and as he pierced the insect before fixing it on to the cork strip, Sir Thomas, who up to then was impassive, got up, and drawing near a box, began to consider the crab spider from Guiana that it contained with a feeling of horror that strikingly portrayed itself on his fat red face.

'"There," he exclaimed, "is the most hideous work of creation! I only have to see it and I feel myself shaking all over." In fact a sudden pallor spread all over his face.

'"Bah!" Said my tutor, "all that's just a childish phobia. You heard your nurse cry out when she saw a spider, you were afraid and you have retained the impression. But if you looked at the spider through a powerful microscope, you would be amazed at the perfection of its organs, at their admirable arrangement, and at their very elegance."

"'It disgusts me,' cut in the Commodore abruptly. "Ugh!" He turned on his heel.

"'Oh! I don't know why," he said, "the spider has always made my blood run cold."

'Dr. Weber started to laugh, and I, who shared Sir Thomas's feelings, exclaimed: "Yes, cousin, you should take this nasty creature out of the box. It is disgusting. It mars all the others."

"'You little animal," he said to me, his eyes sparkling, "who is forcing you to look at it? If it doesn't please you, off you go elsewhere!"

'Evidently he was angry. Sir Thomas, who was then in front of the window looking at the mountain, turned round suddenly, came and took me by the hand, and said to me in a kindly way: "Your tutor, Hans, loves his spider. We prefer the trees and the grass. Let's go for a walk."

"'Yes! Go!" shouted the doctor, "and return for supper at six." Then raising his voice, "No hard feelings, Sir Haverburch!"

'Sir Thomas wanted to drive himself and dismissed his servant. He made me sit beside him on the same seat and we set off for the Rothalps.

'While the carriage slowly climbed the sandy path, a sadness that I could not control took hold of my soul. Sir Thomas, for his part, was serious. He was aware of my sadness and said to me: "You don't like spiders, Hans, no more do I. But, thank Heaven, there are no dangerous ones in this country. The crab spider which your tutor has in his box comes from French Guiana. It lives for years, in the huge swampy forests constantly filled with humid vapours and burning gases; it needs this temperature to live. Its web, or to be more precise, its huge net, envelops an entire thicket. It captures birds in it, just like our spiders catch flies. I have seen others in the collections of those people who study such things but it could not live long in this cold climate. All those that ever escaped no doubt perished very quickly. But chase from your mind these revolting images and have a pull at my old Burgundy!"

'Then, turning round, he lifted up the lid of the second seat and took out of the straw a sort of a gourd, from which he filled to the brim a leather cup and handed it to me.

'The carriage, harnessed to a small horse from the Ardennes, thin and nervous as a goat, climbed up the precipitous path. Myriads of insects buzzed in the heather. On the right, a hundred paces at the most, stretched above us the dark edge of the forests of Rothalps, whose sinister depths, full of brambles and rank weeds, revealed now and then some clearings, flooded with light. On our left, tumbled the stream of Spinbronn. The higher we climbed the more the silvery sheets of water floating in the abyss took on an azure hue, and redoubled their thundering roar.

'I was enthralled by the spectacle. Sir Thomas, leaning back on his seat, his knees up to his chin, gave way to his customary dreaming, while the horse, straining with its legs and leaning its head on the harness, so as to balance the carriage, suspended us as it were from the edge of the rock. Soon, however, we reached a shallower slope, surrounded with shadows. I had still got my head turned and my eyes lost in the boundless view. At the sight of the shadows I turned around and saw, within a hundred paces, the cave of Spinbronn. The surrounding underwood was magnificently green, and the spring, which before falling from the *plateau* stretched over a bed of sand and black pebbles, was so limpid that one would have thought it frozen over, had not light wisps of steam covered its surface.

'The horse had just stopped of its own accord to breathe. Sir Thomas, standing up, gazed for a few seconds at the scenery.

'"How calm everything is," he said; then after a moment's silence, "If you weren't here, Hans, I would willingly take a bathe in the pool."

'"But, Commodore," I said to him, "why not go for a bathe? I can very easily go for a short stroll roundabouts. There is on the mountain nearby a huge pasture all covered with strawberries. I shall go and pick some of them. I shall be back in an hour."

'"I'd really like to, Hans, it's a good idea. Dr. Weber claims that I drink too much burgundy. You have to fight wine with mineral water. This sandy bed pleases me."

'Then both of us having climbed down, he tied the horse to the trunk of a small birch tree and shook my hand as if to say to me, "You can go."

'I saw him sit down on the moss and take off his boots. As I moved away he turned round and shouted: "In an hour, Hans!" These were his last words.

★★★★★★

'An hour later I returned to the spring. The horse, the carriage and Sir Thomas's clothes were the only things to be seen. The sun was setting. The shadows lengthened. There was no bird song under the foliage, not an insect buzzed in the tall grasses; a deathly silence hovered over the solitude.

'This silence terrified me. I climbed on to the rock which towers over the cave. I looked right and left. No one! I called out. No reply! The sound of my voice, repeated by the echoes, made me afraid. Night was coming down slowly. An indescribable anguish oppressed me. Suddenly the story of the young girl who had disappeared came to my mind; and I started to run down. But, having arrived in front of the cave, I stopped, overcome by an inexpressible terror. Glancing into the black shadow of the spring, I could see two motionless red blobs . . . then huge lines splashing about in a peculiar way in the midst of the darkness, and this at a depth where perhaps no human eyes had yet penetrated. Fear gave to my sight, to all my senses a subtlety of perception unheard of. For some seconds I heard, quite clearly, a cicada singing its evening lament on the edge of the wood. Then my heart, for a moment stilled by emotion, started to beat furiously and I heard nothing else!

'Then, uttering a terrified cry, I ran off, leaving behind the horse, the carriage. In less than twenty minutes, leaping over locks, brushwood, I had reached the threshold of our house, burst through the front door and shouted in a choked voice: Run! Run! Sir Haverburch is dead! Sir Haverburch is in the cave!"

'After these words, uttered in the presence of my tutor, old Agatha and two or three people invited that evening by the doctor, I fainted. I have learned since that I was delirious for an hour

'The entire village went off to look for the Commodore. Christian Weber had dragged them off. At ten o'clock in the evening, the entire crowd came back, bringing with them the coach and, in the coach Sir Haverburch's clothes. They had discovered nothing. It was impossible to go ten steps into the cave without being suffocated by the hot vapours from the spring.

'During their absence Agatha and I had remained seated in the corner of the chimney. I, muttering in terror incoherent words, she, her hands crossed on her knees, her eyes wide open, going from time to time to the window to see what was going on, because one could see from the foot of the mountain torches running through the woods. One could hear voices, far away, hailing one another in the night

'When her master approached, Agatha started to tremble. The doctor came in suddenly, pale, his lips tight, despair imprinted on his face. About twenty woodcutters followed him in confusion, with their large wide-rimmed felt hats, their weather-beaten faces, waving the remnants of their torches. Hardly were they in the room than the sparkling eyes of my tutor seemed to look for something. He saw the negress, and without a single word being exchanged between them, the poor woman started to cry out.

'"No! No! I don't want to!"

'"And I want to!" replied the doctor harshly.

'You might have said that the negress had been seized by an invincible power. She shuddered from head to toe and, Christian Weber pointing out a seat for her, she sat on it with a corpse-like rigidity.

'All those present, witnesses of this frightening spectacle, good-living people of coarse primitive manners, but full of pious sentiments, crossed themselves, and I, who didn't know then, even by name, the terrible magnetic power of the will, I started to

318

tremble, thinking that Agatha was dead.

'Christian Weber had gone up to the negress and passed his hand over her brow in a rapid movement.

'"Are you there?" he said.

'"Yes, master."

'"Sir Thomas Haverburch?"

'At these words she had a renewed trembling fit.

'"Can you see him?"

'"Yes! Yes!" she said in a choking voice. "I see him."

'"Where is he?"

'"Up there! At the bottom of the cave! Dead!"

'"Dead!" said the doctor. "How?"

'"The spider! Oh, the dreadful crab spider! Oh!"

'"Calm yourself," said the doctor, quite pale. "Tell us clearly."

'"The crab spider has him by the throat. . . he is there . . . at the bottom . . . under the rock . . . swathed in cobwebs . . . Ah!"

'Christian Weber turned a cold look to those present, who, stooping in a circle, their eyes popping out of their heads, listened. I heard him murmur: "Horrible! Horrible!" Then he resumed.

'"Can you see him?"

'"I can see him."

'"And the spider. Is it big?"

'"Oh! Master, never . . . never have I seen one so huge, neither on the banks of the Mocaris nor in the lowlands of Konanama . . . It is as big as my head!"

'There was a lengthy silence. All those present looked at each other, their faces livid, their hair standing on end. Christian Weber alone appeared calm. Having passed his hands several times over the brow of the negress, he began.

'"Agatha, tell us how death struck Sir Haverburch."

'"He was bathing in the pool of the stream . . . The spider saw him from behind, his back naked. It was hungry, it had been fasting for a long time. It saw him, his arms on the water. Suddenly, it dashed out, as quick as lightning, and placed its claws around the Commodore's neck, and he shouted 'My God! My God!' It bit him and ran off. Sir Haverburch collapsed into the water and died. Then the spider came back and surrounded him with its web, and it swam gently, gently as far as the bottom of the cave. It pulled the thread. Now it's completely black."

'The doctor turned towards me, no longer afraid. He said: "Is it true, Hans, that the Commodore went for a bathe?"

'"Yes, cousin."

'"At what time?"

'"At four o'clock."

'"At four o'clock. It was very hot, wasn't it?"

'"Ah yes!"

'"That's it!" he said, beating his brow. "The monster could come out without fear!"

He uttered some unintelligible words, then, looking at the mountain folk.

'"My friends!" he exclaimed. "That's where this mass of debris comes from . . . the body, the skeletons which frightened the bathers . . . that's what has ruined you all . . . It's a crab spider—God knows where it came from—but it's there . . . hiding in its web. . . and on the lookout for its prey from the bottom of the cave! Who can tell the number of its victims?"

'Then filled with a sort of rage he left, shouting: "Faggots! Faggots!"

'All the woodcutters followed him in the utmost confusion. Ten minutes later, two big coaches laden with faggots slowly climbed the hill. A long procession of woodcutters, backs bent, axes over their shoulders, followed them into the middle of the dark night. My tutor and I walked in front, holding the horses by the bridle. The melancholy moon dimly lit up this funereal procession. From time to time the wheels creaked, then the carriages, raised up by the stony ruggedness of the path, fell back into the ruts with a heavy jolt.

'Drawing near the cave, our procession halted. The torches were lit and the crowd moved forward towards the abyss. The limpid water, flowing over the sand, reflected the bluish flames of the resinous torches, whose beams lit up the tops of the black pines leaning over the rock.

'"We must unload here," said the doctor. "Then we must block the entrance to the cave."

'And it was with a feeling of terror, that each one set to his task of carrying out their orders. The faggots fell from the top of the carts. Some stakes, placed below the opening of the spring, prevented the water from dragging them off.

'At about midnight the entrance to the cave was literally shut. The water whistling beneath, poured out right and left over the moss. The upper faggots were perfectly dry. Then Doctor Weber, seizing hold of a torch, set fire to them himself. The flames, rushing up from twig to twig, crackling angrily, soon leapt up to the sky, chasing before them clouds of smoke.

'It was a strange and wild spectacle, to see these huge woods with their quivering shadows lit up in this way.

'The cave disgorged a black smoke, which gradually increased until it was pouring out. All around waited the woodcutters, sombre and motionless, their eyes fixed on the entrance. And I myself, though fear made me tremble from head to toe, was unable to take my eyes away from it.

'We had already been waiting a quarter of an hour, and the doctor was beginning to get impatient, when a black object, with long hooked legs, suddenly appeared in the shadow and scuttled towards the opening.

'A general uproar resounded around the pile of faggots. The spider, chased by the fire, went back into its cave. Then, choked by the smoke, it returned to the charge and rushed to the middle of the flames. Its long hairy legs caught the flames and shrivelled up. It was as big as my head and a violet crimson; I can only describe it as a bladder full of blood—the blood of Sir Thomas Haverburch!

'One of the woodcutters, afraid of seeing it cross the fire, threw his axe at it, and hit it so well that its blood for a moment covered all the fire around it. But then the flames burned up more fiercely above and consumed the horrible insect.'

★★★★★★

'Such, Maître Frantz, is the strange event that destroyed the fine reputation that the waters of Spinbronn previously enjoyed. I can assure you of the scrupulous accuracy of my account. But as far as explaining it to you, that would be impossible. However, it is not absurd to imagine that insects, subjected to the raised temperature of certain spring waters, which provide for them the same conditions of existence and development as the scorching climates of Africa and South America, can reach incredible sizes. Dr. Weber was of the opinion that the spider must have escaped from someone's collection and found the hot cave before it was killed by the cold climate.

'Be that as it may, my tutor, thinking that it would be impossible after this event to revive the waters of Spinbronn, resold Hâselnoss's house, and returned to South America with his negress and his insect collections. I was sent to boarding school in Strasbourg, where I stayed till 1809.

'The chief political events of the era at this time absorbed the attention of Germany and France and the facts that I have just related to you went completely unnoticed.

'But nobody drinks the waters of Spinbronn even to this day.'

The Mysterious Stranger

Anonymous

To die?—to sleep!
Perchance to dream? Ay, there's the rub.—Hamlet

Boreas, that fearful north-west wind, which in the spring and autumn stirs up the lowest depths of the wild Adriatic, and is so dangerous to vessels, was howling through the woods, and tossing the branches of the old knotty oaks in the Carpathian Mountains, when a party of five riders, who surrounded a litter drawn by a pair of mules, turned into a forest-path, which offered some protection from the April weather, and allowed the travellers in some degree to recover their breath. It was already evening and bitterly cold; the snow fell every now and then in large flakes. A tall old gentleman, of aristocratic appearance, rode at the head of the troop.

This was the Knight of Fahnenberg, in Austria. He had inherited from a childless brother a considerable property, situated in the Carpathian Mountains; and he had set out to take possession of it, accompanied by his daughter Franziska, and a niece about twenty years of age, who had been brought up with her. Next to the knight rode a fine young man of some twenty and odd years—the Baron Franz von Kronstein; he wore, like the former, the broad-brimmed hat with hanging feathers, the leather collar, the wide riding-boots—in short, the travelling dress which was in fashion at the commencement of the seventeenth century.

The features of the young man had much about them that was open and friendly, as well as some mind; but he expression was more of a dreamy and sensitive softness than of youthful daring, although no one could deny that he possessed much of youthful beauty. As the cavalcade turned into the oak wood, the young men rode up to the litter, and chatted with the ladies who were seated therein. One of these—and to her his conversation was principally addressed—was of dazzling beauty. Her hair flowed in natural curls round the fine oval of her face, out of which beamed a pair of star-like eyes, full of genius, lively fancy, and a certain degree of archness.

Franziska von Fahnenberg seemed to attend but carelessly to the speeches of her admirer, who made many kind inquiries as to how she felt herself during the journey, which had been attended with many difficulties: she always answered him very shortly, almost contemptuously; and at length remarked, that if it had not been for her father's objections, she would long ago have requested the baron to take her place in their horrid cage of litter, for, to judge by his remarks, he seemed incommoded by the weather; and she would so much rather be mounted on a spirited horse, and face wind and storm, then be mewed up there, dragged up the hills by those long-eared animals, and mope herself to death with *ennui*.

The young lady's words, and, still more, the contemptuous tone in which they were uttered, appeared to make the most painful impression on the young man: he made her no reply at the moment, but the absent air with which he attended to the kindly-intended remarks of the other young lady, shewed how much he was disconcerted.

'It appears, dear Franziska,' said he at length in a kindly tone, 'that the hardships of the road have affected you more than you will acknowledge. Generally so kind to others, you have been very often out of humour during the journey, and particularly with regard to your humble servant and cousin, who would gladly bear a double or treble share of the discomforts, if he could thereby save you from the smallest of them.'

Franziska shewed her look that she was about to reply with some bitter jibe, when the voice of the knight was heard calling for his nephew, who galloped off at the sound.

'I should like to scold you well, Franziska,' said her companion somewhat sharply, 'for always plaguing your poor Cousin Franz in this shameful way; he who loves you so truly, and who, whatever you may say, will one day be your husband.'

'My husband!' replied the other angrily. 'I must either completely alter my ideas, or he his whole self, before that takes place. No, Bertha! I know that this is my father's darling wish, and I do not deny the good qualities Cousin Franz may have, or has, since I see you are making a face; but to marry an effeminate man—never!'

'Effeminate! You do him great injustice,' replied her friend quickly. 'Just because instead of going off to the Turkish war, where little honour was to be gained, he attended to your father's advice and stayed at home, to bring his neglected estate into order, which he accomplished with care and prudence; and because he does not represent this howling wind as a mild zephyr—for reasons such as these you are pleased to call him effeminate.'

'Say what you will, it is so,' cried Franziska obstinately. 'Bold, aspiring, even despotic, must be the man who is to gain my heart; these soft, patient, and thoughtful natures are utterly distasteful to me. Is Franz capable of deep sympathy, either in joy or sorrow? He is always the same—always quiet, soft, and tiresome.'

'He has a warm heart, and is not without genius,' said Bertha.

'A warm heart! That may be,' replied the other; 'but I would rather be tyrannised over, and kept under a little by my future husband, than be loved in such a wearisome manner. You may say he has genius, too. I will not exactly contradict you, since that would be unpolite, but it is not easily discovered. But even allowing you are right in both statements, still the man who does not bring these qualities into action is a despicable creature. A man may do many foolish things, he may even be a little wicked now and then, provided it is in nothing dishonourable; and one can forgive him, if he is only acting on some fixed theory for some special object. There is for instance, your faithful admirer, the Castellan of Glogau, Knight of Woislaw; he loves you most truly, and is now quite in a position to enable you to marry comfortably. The brave man has lost his right hand—reason enough for remaining seated behind the stove, or near the spinning-wheel of his Bertha; but what does he do?—He goes off to the war in Turkey; he fights for a noble thought'—

'And runs the chance of getting his other hand chopped off, and another great scar across his face,' put in her friend.

'Leaves his lady-love to weep and pine a little,' pursued Franziska, 'but returns with fame and marries, and is all the more honoured and admired! This is done by a man of forty, a rough warrior, not bred at court, a soldier who has nothing but his cloak and sword. And Franz—rich, noble—but I will not go on. Not a word more on this detested point, if you love me, Bertha.'

Franziska leaned back in the corner of the litter with a dissatisfied air, and shut her eyes, as though overcome by fatigue, she wished to sleep.

'This awful wind is so powerful, you say, that we must make a detour to avoid its full force,' said the knight to an old man, dressed in a fur-cap and a cloak of rough skin, who seemed to be the guide of the party.

'Those who have never personally felt the *Boreas* storming over the country between Sessano and Trieste, can have no conception of the reality,' replied the other. 'As soon as it commences, the snow is blown in thick long columns along the ground. That is nothing to what follows. These columns become higher and higher, as the wind rises, and continue to do so until you see nothing but snow above, below, and on every side—unless, indeed, sometimes, when sand and gravel are mixed with the snow, and at length it is impossible to open your eyes at all. Your only plan for safety is to wrap your cloak around you, and lie down flat on the ground. If your home were but a few hundred yards off, you might lose your life in the attempt to reach it.'

'Well, then, we owe you thanks, old Kumpan,' said the knight, though it was with difficulty he made his words heard above the roaring of the storm; 'we owe you thanks for taking us this round, as we shall thus be enabled to reach our destination without danger.'

'You may feel sure of that, noble sir,' said the old man. 'by midnight we shall have arrived, and that without any danger by the way if'— Suddenly the old man stopped, he drew his horse sharply up, abd remained in an attitude of attentive listening.

'It appears to me we must be in the neighbourhood of some village,' said Franz von Kronstein; 'for between the gusts of the storm, I hear a dog howling.'

'It is no dog, it is no dog!' said the old man uneasily, and urging his horse to a rapid pace. 'for miles around there is no human dwelling; and except in the castle of Klatka, which indeed lies in the neighbourhood, but has been deserted for more than a century, probably no one has lived here since the creation.— But there again,' he continued; 'well if I wasn't sure of it from the first.'

'That howling seems to fidget you, old Kumpan,' said the knight, listening to a long-drawn fierce sound, which appeared nearer than before, and seemed to be answered from a distance.

'That howling comes from no dogs,' replied the old guide uneasily. 'Those are reed-wolves; they may be on our track; and it would be as well if the gentlemen looked to their firearms.'

'Reed-wolves? What do you mean?' inquired Franz in surprise.

'At the edge of this wood,' said Kumpan, 'there lies a lake about a mile long, whose banks are covered with reeds. In these a number of wolves have taken up their quarters, and feed on wild birds, fish, and such like. They are shy in the summer-time, and a boy of twelve might scare them; but when the birds migrate, and the fish are frozen up, they prowl about at night, and then they are dangerous. They are worst, however, when *Boreas* rages, for then it is just as if the fiend himself possessed them: they are so mad and fierce, that man and beast become alike their victims' and a party of them have been known even to attack the ferocious bears of these mountains, and, what is more, to come off victorious.' The howl was now again repeated more distinctly, and from two opposite directions. The riders in alarm felt for their pistols, and the old man grasped the spear which hung at his saddle.

'We must keep close to the litter; the wolves are very near us,' whispered the guide. The riders turned their horses, surrounded the litter, and the knight informed the ladies, in a few quieting words, of the cause of this movement.

'Then we *shall* have an adventure—some little variety!' cried Franzisca with sparkling eyes.

'How can you talk so foolishly?' said Bertha in alarm.

'Are we not under manly protection? Is not Cousin Franz on our side?' said the other mockingly.

'See, there is a light gleaming among the twigs; and there is another,' cried Bertha. 'There must be people close to us.'

'No, no,' cried the guide quickly. 'Shut up the door, ladies. Keep close together, gentlemen. It is the eyes of the wolves you see sparkling there.' The gentlemen looked towards the thick underwood, in which every now and then little bright spots appeared, such as in summer would have been taken for glow-worms; it was just the same greenish-yellow light, but less un-steady, and there were always two flames together. The horses began to be very restive, they kicked and dragged at the rein; but the mules behaved tolerably well.

'I will fire on the beasts, and teach them to keep their dis-tance,' said Franz, pointing to the spot where the lights were thickest.

'Hold, hold, Sir Baron!' cried Kumpan quickly, and seizing the young man's arm. 'You would bring such a host together by the report, that, encouraged by numbers, they would be sure to make the first assault. However, keep your arms in readiness, and if an old she-wolf springs out—for these always lead the attack—take good aim and kill her, for then there must be no further hesitation.' By this time, the horses were almost unman-ageable, and terror had also infected the mules. Just as Franz was turning towards the litter to say a word to his cousin, an animal, about the size of a large hound, sprang from the thicket and seized the foremost mule.

'Fire, baron! A wolf!' shouted the guide.

The young man fired, and the wolf fell to the ground. A fearful howl rang through the wood.

'Now. Forward! Forward without a moment's delay!' cried Kumpan. 'We have not above five minutes' time. The beasts will tear their wounded comrade to pieces, and, if they are very hungry, partially devour her. We shall, in the meantime, gain a little start, and it is not more than an hour's ride to the end of the forest. There—do you see—these are the towers of Klatka between the trees—out there where the moon is rising, and from that point the wood becomes less dense.

The travellers endeavoured to increase their pace to the utmost, but the litter retarded their progress. Bertha was weeping with fear, and even Franzisca's courage had diminished, for she sat very still. Franz endeavoured to reassure them. They had not proceeded many moments when the howling recommenced, and approached nearer and nearer.

'There they are again, and fiercer and more numerous than before,' cried the guide in alarm.

The lights were soon visible again, and certainly in greater numbers. The wood had already become less thick, and the snowstorm having ceased, the moonbeams discovered many a dusky form amongst the trees, keeping together like a pack of hounds, and advancing nearer and nearer till they were within twenty paces, and on the very path of the travellers. From time to time a fierce howl arose from their centre, which was answered by the whole pack, and was at length taken up by single voices in the distance.

The party now found themselves some few hundred yards from the ruined castle of which Kumpan had spoken. It was, or seemed by moonlight to be, of some magnitude. Near the tolerably preserved principal building lay the ruins of a church, which must once have been beautiful, placed on a little hillock, dotted with single oak-trees and bramble-bushes. Both castle and church were still partially roofed in; and a path led from the castle gate to an old oak-tree, where it joined at right angles the one along which the travellers were advancing.

The old guide seemed in much perplexity.

'We are in great danger, noble sir,' said he. 'The wolves will very soon make a general attack. There will then be only one way of escape: leaving the mules to their fate, and taking the young ladies on your horses.'

'That would be all very well, if I had not thought of a better plan,' replied the knight. 'Here is the ruined castle; we can surely reach that, and then, blocking up the gates, we must just await the morning.'

'Here? In the ruins of Klatka?—Not for all the wolves in the world!' cried the old man. 'Even by daylight no one likes to approach the place, and now, by night!—The castle, Sir Knight, has a bad name.'

'On account of robbers?' asked Franz.

'No; it is haunted,' replied the other.

'Stuff and nonsense!' said the baron. 'Forward to the ruins; there is not a moment to be lost.'

And this was indeed the case. The ferocious beasts were but a few steps behind the travellers. Every now and then they retired, and set up a ferocious howl. The party had just arrived at the old oak before mentioned, and were about to turn into the path to the ruins, when the animals, as though perceiving the risk they ran of losing their prey, came so near that a lance could easily have struck them. The knight and Franz faced sharply about, spurring their horses amidst the advancing crowds, when suddenly, from the shadow of the oak stepped forth a man, who in a few strides placed himself between the travellers and their pursuers. As far as one could see in the dusky light, the stranger was a man of a tall and well-built frame; he wore a sword by his side, and a broad-brimmed hat was on his head. If the party were astonished at his sudden appearance, they were still more so at what followed. As soon as the stranger appeared, the wolves gave over their pursuit, tumbled over each other, and set up a fearful howl. The stranger now raised his hand, appeared to wave it, and the wild animals crawled back into the thickets like a pack of beaten hounds.

Without casting a glance at the travellers, who were too much overcome by astonishment to speak, the stranger went up the path which led to the castle, and soon disappeared beneath the gateway.

'Heaven have mercy on us!' murmured old Kumpan in his beard, as he made the sign of the cross.

'Who was that strange man?' asked the knight with surprise, when he had watched the stranger as long as he was visible, and the party had resumed their way.

The old guide pretended not to understand, and riding up to the mules, busied himself with arranging the harness, which had become disordered in their haste : more than a quarter of an hour elapsed before he rejoined them.

'Did you know the man who met us near the ruins, and who freed us from our four-footed pursuers in such a miraculous way?' asked Franz of the guide.

'Do I know him? No, noble sir; I never saw him before,' replied the guide hesitatingly.

'He looked like a soldier, and was armed,' said the baron. 'Is the castle, then, inhabited?'

'Not for the last hundred years,' replied the other. 'It was dismantled because the possessor in those days had iniquitous dealings with some Turkish-Sclavonian hordes, who had advanced as far as this; or rather'—he corrected himself hastily—'he is *said* to have had such, for he might have been as upright and food a man as ever ate cheese fried in butter.'[1]

'And who is now the possessor of the ruins and of these woods?' inquired the knight.

'Who but yourself, noble sir!' replied Kumpan. 'For more than two hours we have been on your estate, and we shall soon reach the end of the wood,'

---

1. A favourite dish in those parts.

'We hear and see nothing more of the wolves,' said the baron after a long pause. 'Even their howling has ceased. The adventure with the stranger still remains to me inexplicable, even if one were to suppose him a huntsman'

'Yes, yes; that is most likely what he is,' interrupted the guide hastily, whilst he looked uneasily round him. 'The brave good man, who came so opportunely to our assistance, must have been a huntsman. Oh, there are many powerful woodsmen in this neighbourhood! Heaven be praised!' he continued, taking a deep breath,' there is the end of the wood, and in a short hour we shall be safely housed.'

And so it happened. Before an hour had elapsed, the party passed through a well-built village, the principal spot on the estate, towards the venerable castle, the windows of which were brightly illuminated, and at the door stood the steward and other dependents, who, having received their new lord with every expression of respect, conducted the party to the splendidly furnished apartments.

Nearly four weeks passed before the travelling adventures again came on the *tapis*. The knight and Franz found such constant employment in looking over all the particulars of the large estate, and endeavouring to introduce various German improvements, that they were very little at home. At first, Franziska was charmed with everything in a neighbourhood so entirely new and unknown. It appeared to her so romantic, so very different from her German Fatherland, that she took the greatest interest in everything, and often drew comparisons between the countries, which generally ended unfavourably for Germany.

Bertha was of exactly the contrary opinion : she laughed at her cousin, and said that her liking for novelty and strange sights must indeed have come to a pass, when she preferred hovels in which the smoke went out of the doors and windows instead of the chimney, walls covered with soot, and inhabitants not much cleaner, and of unmannerly habits, to the comfortable dwellings and polite people of Germany. However, Franziska persisted in her notions, and replied that everything in Austria was flat, *en-*

332

nuyant, and common ; and that a wild peasant here, with his rough coat of skin, had ten times more interest for her than a quiet Austrian in his holiday suit, the mere sight of whom was enough to make one yawn.

As soon as the knight had got the first arrangements into some degree of order, the party found themselves more together again Franz continued to shew great attention to his cousin, which however, she received with little gratitude, for she made him the butt of all her fanciful humours, that soon returned when after a longer sojourn she had become more accustomed to her new life. Many excursions into the neighbourhood were undertaken, but there was little variety in the scenery, and these soon ceased to amuse.

The party were one day assembled in the old-fashioned hall, dinner had just been removed, and they were arranging in which direction they should ride. 'I have it!' cried Franziska suddenly. 'I wonder we never thought before of going to view by day the spot where we fell in with our night-adventure with wolves and the Mysterious Stranger.'

'You mean a visit to the ruins—what were they called?' said the knight.

'Castle Klatka,' cried Franziska gaily. 'Oh, we really must ride there! It will be so charming to go over again by daylight, and in safety, the ground where we had such a dreadful fright.'

'Bring round the horses,' said the knight to a servant; 'and tell the steward to come to me immediately.' The latter, an old man, soon after entered the room.

'We intend taking a ride to Klatka,' said the knight: 'we had an adventure there on our road.'

'So old Kumpan told me,' interrupted the steward.

'And what do you say about it?' asked the knight.

'I really don't know what to say,' replied the old man, shaking his head. 'I was a youth of twenty when I first came to this castle, and now my hair is gray; half a century has elapsed during that time. Hundreds of times my duty has called me into the neighbourhood of those ruins, but never have I seen the Fiend of Klatka.'

'What do you say? Who do you call by that name?' inquired Franziska, whose love of adventure and romance was strongly awakened.

'Why, people call by that name the ghost or spirit who is supposed to haunt the ruins,' replied the steward. 'They say he only shews himself on moonlight nights'—

'That is quite natural,' interrupted Franz smiling. 'Ghosts can never bear the light of day; and if the moon did not shine how could the ghost be seen? for it is not to be supposed that anyone for a mere freak would visit the ruins by torchlight.'

'There are some credulous people, who pretend to have seen this ghost,' continued the steward. 'Huntsmen and wood-cutters say they have met him by the large oak on the cross-path. That noble sir, is supposed to be the spot he inclines most to haunt, for the tree was planted in remembrance of the man who fell there.'

'And who was he?' asked Franziska with increasing curiosity

'The last owner of the castle, which was at that time a sort of robber's den, and the headquarters of all depredators in the neighbourhood,' answered the old man. 'They say this man was of superhuman strength, and was feared not only on account of his passionate temper, but of his treaties with the Turkish hordes Any young woman, too, in the neighbourhood to whom he took a fancy, was carried off to his tower, and never heard of more When the measure of his iniquity was full, the whole neighbourhood rose in a mass, besieged his stronghold, and at length he was slain on the spot where the huge oak-tree now stands.'

'I wonder they did not burn the whole castle, so as to erase the very memory of it,' said the knight.

'It was a dependency of the church, and that saved it,' replied the other. 'Your great-grandfather afterwards took possession of it, for it had fine lands attached. As the Knight of Klatka was of good family, a monument was erected to him m the church, which now lies as much in ruin as the castle itself.'

'Oh, let us set off at once! Nothing shall prevent my visiting so interesting a spot,' said Franziska eagerly. 'The imprisoned damsels who never reappeared, the storming of the tower, the death of the knight, the nightly wanderings of his spirit round the old oak, and, lastly, our own adventure, all draw me thither with an indescribable curiosity.'

When a servant announced that the horses were at the door, the young girls tripped laughingly down the steps which led to the coach-yard. Franz, the knight, and a servant well acquainted with the country, followed; and in a few minutes the party were on their road to the forest.

The sun was still high in the heavens, when they saw the towers of Klatka rising above the trees. Everything in the wood was still, except the cheerful twitterings of the birds as they hopped about amongst the bursting buds and leaves, and announced that spring had arrived.

The party soon found themselves near the old oak at the bottom of the hill on which stood the towers, still imposing in their ruin. Ivy and bramble bushes had wound themselves over the walls, and forced their deep roots so firmly between the stones, that they in a great measure held these together. On the top of the highest point, a small bush in its young fresh verdure swayed lightly in the breeze.

The gentlemen assisted their companions to alight, and leaving the horses to the care of the servant, ascended the hill to the castle. After having explored this in every nook and cranny, and spent much time in a vain search for some trace of the extraordinary stranger, whom Franziska declared she was determined to discover, they proceeded to an inspection of the adjoining church. This they found to have better withstood the ravages of time and weather in the nave, indeed, was in complete dilapidation, but the chancel and altar were still under roof, as well as a sort of chapel which appeared to have been a place of honour for the families of the old knights of the castle. Few traces remained, however, of the magnificent painted glass which must once have adorned the windows, and the wind entered at pleasure through the open spaces.

The party were occupied for some time in deciphering the inscriptions on a number of tombstones, and on the walls, principally within the chancel. They were generally memorials of the ancient lords, with figures of men in armour, and women and children of all ages. A flying raven and various other devices were placed at the corners. One gravestone, which stood close to the entrance of the chancel, differed widely from the others; there was no figure sculptured on it, and the inscription, which, on all besides, was a mere mass of flattering eulogies, was here simple and unadorned; it contained only these words: '*Ezzelin von Klatka fell like a knight at the storming of the castle*'—on such a day and year.

'That must be the monument of the knight whose ghost is said to haunt these ruins,' cried Franziska eagerly. 'What a pity he is not represented in the same way as the others—I should so like to have known what he was like!'

'Oh, there is the family-vault, with steps leading down to it and the sun is lighting it up through a crevice,' said Franz, stepping from the adjoining vestry.

The whole party followed him down the eight or nine steps which led to a tolerably airy chamber, where were placed a number of coffins of all sizes, some of them crumbling into dust. Here again, one close to the door was distinguished from the others by the simplicity of its design, the freshness of its appearance, and the brief inscription: '*Ezzelinus de Klatka, Eques.*'

As not the slightest effluvium was perceptible, they lingered sometime in the vault; and when they reascended to the church, they had a long talk over the old possessors, of whom the knight now remembered he had heard his parents speak. The sun had disappeared, and the moon was just rising as the explorer turned to leave the ruins. Bertha had made a step into the nave, when she uttered a slight exclamation of fear and surprise Her eyes fell on a man who wore a hat with drooping feathers, a sword at his side, and a short cloak of somewhat old-fashioned cut over his shoulders. The stranger leaned carelessly on a broken column at the entrance; he did not appear to take any notice of the party; and the moon shone full on his pale face.

The party advanced towards the stranger.

'If I am not mistaken,' commenced the knight; 'we have met before.'

Not a word from the unknown.

'You released us in an almost miraculous manner,' said Franziska 'from the power of those dreadful wolves. Am I wrong in supposing it is to you we are indebted for that great service?'

'The beasts are afraid of me,' replied the stranger in a deep, fierce tone, while he fastened his sunken eyes on the girl, without taking any notice of the others.

'Then you are probably a huntsman,' said Franz, 'and wage war against the fierce brutes.'

'Who is not either the pursuer or the pursued? All persecute or are persecuted, and Fate persecutes all,' replied the stranger without looking at him.

'Do you live in these ruins?' asked the knight hesitatingly.

'Yes; but not to the destruction of your game, as you may fear, Knight of Fahnenberg,' said the unknown contemptuously. 'Be quite assured of this; your property shall remain untouched'

'Oh! my father did not mean that,' interrupted Franziska, who appeared to take the liveliest interest in the stranger. 'Unfortunate events and sad experiences have, no doubt, induced you to take up your abode in these ruins, of which my father would by no means dispossess you.'

'Your father is very good, if that is what he meant,' said the stranger in his former tone; and it seemed as though his dark features were drawn into a slight smile; but people of my sort are rather difficult to turn out.'

'You must live very uncomfortably here,' said Franziska, half vexed, for she thought her polite speech had deserved a better reply.

'My dwelling is not exactly uncomfortable, only somewhat small, still quite suitable for quiet people,' said the unknown with a kind of sneer. 'I am not, however, always quiet; I sometimes pine to quit the narrow space, and then I dash away through forest and field, over hill and dale; and the time when I must return to my little dwelling always comes too soon for me.'

'As you now and then leave your dwelling,' said the knight, 'I would invite you to visit us, if I knew'

'That I was in a station to admit of your doing so,' interrupted the other; and the knight started slightly, for the stranger had exactly expressed the half-formed thought. 'I lament,' he continued coldly, 'that I am not able to give you particulars on this point—some difficulties stand in the way: be assured, however, that I am a knight, and of at least as ancient a family as yourself.'

'Then you must not refuse our request,' cried Franziska, highly interested in the strange manners of the unknown. 'You must come and visit us.'

'I am no boon-companion, and on that account few have invited me of late,' replied the other with his peculiar smile; 'besides, I generally remain at home during the day; that is my time for rest. I belong, you must know, to that class of persons who turn day into night, and night into day, and who love everything uncommon and peculiar.'

'Really? So do I! And for that very reason, you must visit us,' cried Franziska. 'Now,' she continued smiling,' I suppose you have just risen, and you are taking your morning airing. Well, since the moon is your sun, pray pay a frequent visit to our castle by the light of its rays. I think we shall agree very well, and that it will be very nice for us to be acquainted.'

'You wish it?—You press the invitation?' asked the stranger earnestly and decidedly.

'To be sure, for otherwise you will not come,' replied the young lady shortly.

'Well, then, come I will!' said the other, again fixing his gaze on her. 'If my company does not please you at any time, you will have yourself to blame for an acquaintance with one who seldom forces himself, but is difficult to shake off.'

When the unknown had concluded these words, he made a slight motion with his hand, as though to take leave of them, and passing under the doorway, disappeared among the ruins. The party soon after mounted their horses, and took the road home.

It was the evening of the following day, and all were again seated in the hall of the castle. Bertha had that day received good news. The knight Woislaw had written from Hungary, that the war with the Turks would be brought to a conclusion during the year, and that although he had intended returning to Silesia, hearing of the knight of Fahnenberg having gone to take possession of his new estates, he should follow the family there, not doubting that Bertha had accompanied her friend. He hinted, that he stood so high in the opinion of his duke on account of his valuable services, that in future his duties would be even more important and extensive; but before settling down to them, he should come and claim Bertha's promise to become his wife.

He had been much enriched by his master, as well as by booty taken from the Turks. Having formerly lost his right hand in the duke's service, he had essayed to fight with his left; but this did not succeed very admirably, and so he had an iron one made by a very clever artist. This hand performed many of the functions of a natural one, but there had been still much wanting; now, however, his master had presented him with one of gold, an extraordinary work of art, produced by a celebrated Italian mechanic. The knight described it as something marvellous, especially as to the superhuman strength with which it enabled him to use the sword and lance.

Franziska naturally rejoiced in the happiness of her friend, who had had no news of her betrothed for a long time before. She launched out every now and then, partly to plague Franz, and partly to express her own feelings, in the highest praise and admiration of the bravery and enterprise of the knight, whose adventurous qualities she lauded to the skies. Even the scar on his face, and his want of a right hand, were reckoned as virtues and Franziska at last saucily declared, that a rather ugly man was infinitely more attractive to her than a handsome one, for as a general rule, handsome men were conceited and effeminate.

Thus, she added, no one could term their acquaintance of the night before handsome, but attractive and interesting he certainly was Franz and Bertha simultaneously denied this. His gloomy appearance, the deadly hue of his complexion, the tone of his voice, were each in turn depreciated by Bertha, while Franz found fault with the contempt and arrogance obvious in his speech. The knight stood between the two parties. He thought there was something in his bearing that spoke of good family, though much could not be said for his politeness; however, the man might have had trial: enough in his life to make him misanthropical. Whilst they were conversing in this way, the door suddenly opened, and the subject of their remarks himself walked in.

'Pardon me, Sir Knight,' he said coldly, 'that I come, if not uninvited, at least unannounced; there was no one in the ante-chamber to do me that service.'

The brilliantly lighted chamber gave a full view of the stranger, He was a man about forty, tall, and extremely thin. His feature! could not be termed uninteresting—there lay in them some-thing bold and daring; but the expression was on the whole anything but benevolent. There was contempt and sarcasm in the cold gray eyes, whose glance, however, was at times so pierc-ing, that no one could endure it long. His complexion was even more peculiar than the features: it could neither be called pale nor yellow; it was a sort of gray, or, so to speak, dirty white, like that of an Indian who has been suffering long from fever; and was rendered still more remarkable by the intense blackness of his beard and short cropped hair.

The dress of the unknown was knightly, but old-fashioned and neglected: there were great spots of rust on the collar and breastplate of his armour; and his dagger and the hilt of his fine-ly-worked sword were marked in some places with mildew. As the party were just going to supper, it was only natural to invite the stranger to partake of it; he complied, however, only in so far that he seated himself at the table, for he ate no morsel. The knight, with some surprise, inquired the reason.

'For a long time past, I have accustomed myself never to eat at night,' he replied with a strange smile. 'My digestion is quite unused to solids, and indeed would scarcely confront them. I live entirely on liquids.'

'Oh then, we can empty a bumper of Rhine-wine together,' cried the host.

'Thanks; but I neither drink wine nor any cold beverage,' replied the other; and his tone was full of mockery. It appeared is if there was some amusing association connected with the idea.

'Then I will order you a cup of *hippocras*'—a warm drink composed of herbs—'it shall be ready immediately,' said Franziska.

'Many thanks, fair lady; not at present,' replied the other. 'But if I refuse the beverage you offer me now, you may be assured that as soon as I require it—perhaps very soon—I will request that, or some other of you.'

Bertha and Franz thought the man had something inexpressibly repulsive in his whole manner, and they had no inclination to engage him in conversation; but the baron, thinking that perhaps politeness required him to say something, turned towards the guest, and commenced in a friendly tone: 'It is now many weeks since we first became acquainted with you; we then had to thank you for a signal service'

'And I have not yet told you my name, although you would gladly know it,' interrupted the other drily. 'I am called Azzo and as'—this he said again with his ironical smile—'with the permission of the Knight of Fahnenberg, I live at the castle of Klatka, you can in future call me Azzo von Klatka.'

'I only wonder you do not feel lonely and uncomfortable amongst those old walls,' began Bertha. 'I cannot understand'

'What my business is there? Oh, about that I will willingly give you some information, since you and the young gentleman there take such a kindly interest in my person,' replied the unknown in his tone of sarcasm.

Franz and Bertha both started, for he had revealed their thoughts as though he could read their souls. 'You see, lady,' he continued, 'there are a variety of strange whims in the world As I have already said, I love what is peculiar and uncommon, at least what would appear so to you. It is wrong in the main to be astonished at anything, for, viewed in one light, all things are alike; even life and death, this side of the grave and the other have more resemblance than you would imagine; You perhaps consider me rather touched a little in my mind, for taking up my abode with the bat and the owl; but if so, why not consider ever hermit and recluse insane? You will tell me that those are holy men. I certainly have no pretension that way; but as they find pleasure in praying and singing psalms, so I amuse myself with hunting. Oh, you can have no idea of the intense pleasure of dashing away in the pale moonlight, on a horse that never tires over hill and dale, through forest and woodland! I rush among the wolves, which fly at my approach, as you yourself perceived as though they were puppies fearful of the lash.'

'But still it must be lonely, very lonely for you,' remarked Bertha.

'So it would by day; but I am then asleep,' replied the strange drily; 'at night I am merry enough.'

'You hunt in an extraordinary way,' remarked Franz hesitatingly.

'Yes; but, nevertheless, I have no communication with robbers as you seem to imagine,' replied Azzo coldly.

Franz again started—that very thought had just crossed his mind. 'Oh, I beg your pardon; I do not know' he stammered.

'What to make of me,' interrupted the other. 'You would therefore, do well to believe just what I tell you, or at least to avoid making conjectures of your own, which will lead to nothing.'

'I understand you: I know how to value your ideas, if no one else does.' cried Franziska eagerly. 'The humdrum, everyday life of the generality of men is repulsive to you; you have tasted the joys and pleasures of life, at least what are so called, and you have found them tame and hollow. How soon one tires of the things one sees all around! Life consists in change. Only in what is new, uncommon, and peculiar, do the flowers of the spirit bloom and give forth scent. Even pain may become a pleasure if it saves one

342

from the shallow monotony of everyday life—a thing I shall hate till the hour of my death.'

'Right, fair lady—quite right! Remain in this mind: this was always my opinion, and the one from which I have derived the highest reward,' cried Azzo; and his fierce eyes sparkled more intensely than ever. 'I am doubly pleased to have found in you a person who shares my ideas. Oh, if you were a man, you would make me a splendid companion; but even a woman may have fine experiences when once these opinions take root in her, and bring forth action!"

As Azzo spoke these words in a cold tone of politeness, he turned from the subject, and for the rest of his visit only gave the knight monosyllabic replies to his inquiries, taking leave before the table was cleared. To an invitation from the knight, backed by a still more pressing one from Franziska to repeat his visit, he replied that he would take advantage of their kindness, and come sometimes.

When the stranger had departed, many were the remarks made on his appearance and general deportment. Franz declared his most decided dislike to him. Whether it was as usual to vex her cousin, or whether Azzo had really made an impression on her, Franziska took his part vehemently. As Franz contradicted her more eagerly than usual, the young lady launched out into still stronger expressions; and there is no knowing what hard words her cousin might have received, had not a servant entered the room.

The following morning, Franziska lay longer than usual in bed. When her friend went to her room, fearful lest she should be ill, she found her pale and exhausted. Franziska complained she had passed a very bad night; she thought the dispute with Franz about the stranger must have excited her greatly, for she felt quite feverish and exhausted, and a strange dream, too, had worried her, which was evidently a consequence of the evening's conversation. Bertha, as usual, took the young man's part, and added, that a common dispute about a man whom no one knew, and about whom any one might form his own opinion, could not possibly have thrown her into her present state. 'At least,' she continued, 'you can let me hear this wonderful dream.'

To her surprise, Franziska for a length of time refused to do so.

'Come tell me,' inquired Bertha, 'what can possibly prevent you from relating a dream—a mere dream? I might almost think it credible, if the idea were not too horrid, that poor Franz is not very far wrong when he says that the thin, corpse-like, dried-up, old-fashioned stranger has made a greater impression on you than you will allow.'

'Did Franz say so?' asked Franziska. 'Then you can tell him he is not mistaken. Yes, the thin, corpse-like, dried-up whimsical stranger is far more interesting to me than the rosy cheeked, well-dressed, polite, and prosy cousin.'

'Strange!' cried Bertha. 'I cannot at all comprehend this almost magic influence which this man, to me so repulsive exercises over you.'

'Perhaps the very reason I take his part, may be that you are all so prejudiced against him,' remarked Franziska pettishly 'Yes, it must be so; for that his appearance should please my eyes, is what no one in his senses could imagine. But,' she continued, smiling and holding out her hand to Bertha, 'is it not laughable that I should get out of temper even with you about this stranger?—I can more easily understand it with Franz—and that this unknown should spoil my morning, as he has already spoiled my evening and my night's rest?'

'By that dream, you mean?' said Bertha, easily appeased, a she put her arm round her cousin's neck and kissed her. 'Now do tell it to me. You know how I delight in hearing anything of the kind.'

'Well, I will, as a sort of compensation for my peevishness towards you,' said the other, clasping her friend's hands. 'Now listen! I had walked up and down my room for a long time; I was excited—out of spirits—I do not know exactly what. It was almost midnight ere I lay down, but I could not sleep. I tossed about, and at length it was only from sheer exhaustion that I dropped off. But what a sleep it was! An inward fear ran through me perpetually. I saw a number of pictures before me as I used to do in childish sicknesses. I do not know whether I was asleep or half awake. Then I dreamed, but as clearly as if I had been wide awake, that a sort of mist filled the room, and out of it stepped the knight Azzo. He gazed at me for a time, and then letting himself slowly down on one knee, imprinted a kiss on my throat. Long did his lips rest there; and I felt a slight pain which always went on increasing, until I could hear it no more.

'With all my strength I tried to force the vision from me, but succeeded only after a long struggle. No doubt I uttered a scream, for that awoke me from my trance. When I came a little to my senses, I felt a sort of superstitious fear creeping over me— how great you may imagine, when I tell you that, with my eyes open and awake, it appeared to me as if Azzo's figure were still by my bed, and then disappearing gradually into the mist vanished at the door!'

'You must have dreamed very heavily, my poor friend,' began Bertha, but suddenly paused. She gazed with surprise at Franziska's throat. 'Why, what is that?' she cried. 'Just look how extraordinary—a red streak on your throat!'

Franziska raised herself, and went to a little glass that stood in the window. She really saw a small red line about an inch long on her neck, which began to smart when she touched it with her finger.

'I must have hurt myself by some means in my sleep,' she said after a pause; 'and that in some measure will account for my dream.'

The friends continued chatting for some time about this singular coincidence—the dream and the stranger; and at length it was all turned into a joke by Bertha.

Several weeks passed. The knight had found the estate and affairs in greater disorder than he at first imagined; and instead of remaining three or four weeks, as was originally intended, their departure was deferred to on indefinite period. This postponement was likewise in some measure occasioned by Franziska's continued indisposition. She who had formerly bloomed like a rose in its young fresh beauty, was becoming daily thinner, more sickly and exhausted, and at the same time so pale, that in the space of a month not a tinge of red was perceptible on the once glowing cheek. The knight's anxiety about her was extreme, and the best advice was procured which the age and country afforded; but all to no purpose. Franziska complained from time to time that the horrible dream with which her illness commenced was repeated, and that always on the day following she felt an increased and indescribable weakness. Bertha naturally set this down to the effects of fever, but the ravages of that fever on the usually clear reason of her friend filled her with alarm.

The knight Azzo repeated his visits every now and then. He always came in the evening, and when the moon shone brightly. His manner was always the same. He spoke in monosyllables, and was coldly polite to the knight; to Franz and Bertha, particularly to the former, contemptuous and haughty; but to Franziska, friendliness itself. Often when, after a short visit, he again left the house, his peculiarities became the subject of conversation. Besides his old way of speaking, in which Bertha said there lay a deep hatred, a cold detestation of all mankind with the exception of Franziska, two other singularities were observable. During none of his visits, which often took place at supper-time, had he been prevailed upon to eat or drink anything, and that without giving any good reason for his abstinence.

A remarkable alteration, too, had taken place in his appearance; he seemed an entirely different creature. The skin, before so shrivelled and stretched, seemed smooth and soft, while a slight tinge of red appeared in his cheeks, which began to look round and plump. Bertha, who could not at all conceal her ill-will towards him, said often, that much as she hated his face before, when it was more like a death's-head than a human being's, it was now more than ever repulsive; she always felt a shudder run through her veins whenever his sharp piercing eyes rested on her. Perhaps it was owing to Franziska's partiality, or to the knight Azzo' own contemptuous way of replying to Franz, or to his haughty way of treating him in general, that made the young man dislike him more and more.

It was quite observable, that whenever Franz made a remark to his cousin in the presence of Azzo, the latter would immediately throw some ill-natured light on it, or distort it to a totally different meaning. This increased from day to day, and at last Franz declared to Bertha, that he would stand such conduct no longer, and that it was only out of consideration for Franziska that he had not already called him to account.

At this time, the party at the castle was increased by the arrival of Bertha's long-expected guest. He came just as they were sitting down to supper one evening, and all jumped up to greet their old friend. The knight Woislaw was a true model of the soldier, hardened and strengthened by war with men and elements. His face would not have been termed ugly, if a Turkish sabre had not left a mark running from the right eye to the left cheek and standing out bright red from the sunburned skin.

The frame of the Castellan of Glogau might almost be termed colossal. Few would have been able to carry his armour, and still fewer move with his lightness and ease under its weight. He did not think little of this same armour, for it had been a present from the *palatine* of Hungary on his leaving the camp. The blue wrought-steel was ornamented all over with patterns in gold; and he had put it on to do honour to his bride-elect, together with the wonderful gold hand, the gift of the duke.

Woislaw was questioned by the knight and Franz on all the concerns of the campaign; and he entered into the most minute particulars relating to the battles, which, with regard to plunder, had been more successful than ever. He spoke much of the strength of the Turks in a hand-to-hand fight, and remarked that he owed the duke many thanks for his splendid gift, for in consequence of its strength, many of the enemy regarded him a something superhuman. The sickliness and deathlike paleness of Franziska was too perceptible not to be immediately noticed by Woislaw; accustomed to see her so fresh and cheerful, he hastened to inquire into the cause of the change.

Bertha related all that had happened, and Woislaw listened with the greatest interest. This increased to the utmost at the account of the often-repeated dream, and Franziska had to give him the most minute particulars of it; it appeared as though he had met with a similar case before, or at least had heard of one. When the young lady added, that it was very remarkable that the wound on her throat which she had at first felt had never healed, and still pained her, the knight Woislaw looked at Bertha as much as to say, that this last fact had greatly strengthened his idea as to the cause of Franziska's illness.

It was only natural that the discourse should next turn to the knight Azzo, about whom every one began to talk eagerly.

Woislaw inquired as minutely as he had done with regard to Franziska's illness, about what concerned this stranger, from the first evening of their acquaintance down to his last visit, without however, giving any opinion on the subject. The party were still in earnest conversation, when the door opened, and Azzo entered. Woislaw's eyes remained fixed on him, as he, without taking any particular notice of the new arrival, walked up to the table, and seating himself, directed most of his conversation to Franziska and her father, and now and then made some sarcastic remark when Franz began to speak. The Turkish war again came on the *tapis*, and though Azzo only put in an occasional remark, Woislaw had much to say on the subject. Thus they had advanced late into the night, and Franz said smiling to Woislaw: 'I should not wonder if day had surprised us, whilst listening to your entertaining adventures.'

'I admire the young gentleman's taste,' said Azzo, with an ironical curl of the lip. 'Stories of storm and shipwreck are, indeed, best heard on *terra firma,* and those of battle and death at a hospitable table or in the chimney-corner. One has then the comfortable feeling of keeping a whole skin, and being in no danger, not even of taking cold.' With the last words, he gave a hoarse laugh, and turning his back on Franz, rose, bowed to the rest of the company, and left the room. The knight, who always accompanied Azzo to the door, now expressed himself fatigued, and bade his friends goodnight.

'That Azzo's impertinence is unbearable,' cried Bertha when he was gone. 'He becomes daily more rough, unpolite, and presuming. If only on account of Franziska's dream, though of course he cannot help that, I detest him. Now, tonight, not one civil word has he spoken to anyone but Franziska, except, perhaps, some casual remark to my uncle.'

'I cannot deny that you are right, Bertha,' said her cousin. 'One may forgive much to a man whom fate has probably made somewhat misanthropical; but he should not overstep the bounds of common politeness. But where on earth is Franz?' added Franziska, as she looked uneasily round.—The young man had quietly left the room whilst Bertha was speaking.

'He cannot have followed the knight Azzo to challenge him?' cried Bertha in alarm.

'It were better he entered a lion's den to pull his mane!' said Woislaw vehemently. 'I must follow him instantly,' he added, as he rushed from the room.

He hastened over the threshold, out of the castle, and through the court, before he came up to them. Here a narrow bridge with a slight balustrade passed over the moat by which the castle was unrounded. It appeared that Franz had only just addressed Azzo in a few hot words, for as Woislaw, unperceived by either, advanced under the shadow of the wall, Azzo said gloomily: 'Leave me, foolish boy—leave me; for by that sun'—and he pointed to the full moon above them—'you will see those rays no more if you linger another moment on my path.'

'And I tell you, wretch, that you either give me satisfaction for your repeated insolence, or you die,' cried Franz, drawing his sword.

Azzo stretched forth his hand, and grasping the sword in the middle, it snapped like a broken reed. 'I warn you for the last time,' he said in a voice of thunder, as he threw the pieces into the moat. 'Now, away—away, boy, from my path, or, by those below us, you are lost!'

'You or I! you or I!' cried Franz madly, as he made a rush at

349

the sword of his antagonist, and strove to draw it from his side Azzo replied not; only a bitter laugh half escaped his lips; then seizing Franz by the chest, he lifted him up like an infant, and was in the act of throwing him over the bridge, when Woislaw stepped to his side. With a grasp of his wonderful hand, into the springs of which he threw all his strength, he seized Azzo's arm, pulled it down, and obliged him to drop his victim. Azzo seemed in the highest degree astonished. Without concerning himself further about Franz, he gazed in amazement or Woislaw.

'Who art thou who darest to rob me of my prey?' he asked hesitatingly. 'Is it possible? Can you be'——

'Ask not, thou bloody one! Go, seek thy nourishment! Soon comes thy hour!' replied Woislaw in a calm but firm tone.

'Ha! now I know!' cried Azzo eagerly. 'Welcome, blood-brother! I give up to you this worm, and for your sake will not crush him. Farewell; our paths will soon meet again.'

'Soon, very soon; farewell!' cried Woislaw, drawing Franz towards him. Azzo rushed away, and disappeared.

Franz had remained for some moments in a state of semi stupefaction, but suddenly started as from a dream. 'I am dishonoured, dishonoured forever!' he cried, as he pressed his clenched hands to his forehead.

'Calm yourself; you could not have conquered,' said Woislaw.

'But I will conquer, or perish!' cried Franz incensed. 'I will seek this adventurer in his den, and he or I must fall.'

'You could not hurt him,' said Woislaw. 'You would infallibly be the victim.'

'Then shew me a way to bring the wretch to judgement,' cried Franz, seizing Woislaw's hands, while tears of anger sprang to his eyes. 'Disgraced as I am, I cannot live.'

'You shall be revenged, and that within twenty-four hours, I hope; but only on two conditions'

'I agree to them! I will do anything'—began the young man eagerly.

'The first is, that you do nothing, but leave everything in my hands,' interrupted Woislaw. 'The second, that you will assist me in persuading Franziska to do what I shall represent to her as absolutely necessary. That young lady's life is in more danger from Azzo than your own.'

'How? What?' cried Franz fiercely. 'Franziska's life in danger! and from that man? Tell me, Woislaw, who is this fiend?'

'Not a word will I tell either the young lady or you, until the danger is passed,' said Woislaw firmly. 'The smallest indiscretion would ruin everything. No one can act here but Franziska herself, and if she refuses to do so, she is irretrievably lost.'

'Speak, and I will help you. I will do all you wish, but I must know'

'Nothing, absolutely nothing,' replied Woislaw. 'I must have both you and Franziska yield to me unconditionally. Come now, come to her. You are to be mute on what has passed, and use every effort to induce her to accede to my proposal.'

Woislaw spoke firmly, and it was impossible for Franz to make any further objection; in a few moments they both entered the hall, where they found the young girls still anxiously awaiting them.

'Oh, I have been so frightened,' said Franziska, even paler than usual, as she held out her hand to Franz. 'I trust all has ended peaceably.'

'Everything is arranged; a couple of words were sufficient to settle the whole affair,' said Woislaw cheerfully. 'But Master Franz was less concerned in it than yourself, fair lady.'

'I! How do you mean?' said Franziska in surprise.

'I allude to your illness,' replied the other.

'And you spoke of that to Azzo? Does he, then, know a remedy which he could not tell me himself?' she inquired, smiling painfully.

'The knight Azzo must take part in your cure; but speak to you about it he cannot, unless the remedy is to lose all its efficacy,' replied Woislaw quietly.

'So it is some secret elixir, as the learned doctors say, who have so long attended me, and through whose means I only grow worse,' said Franziska mournfully.

'It is certainly a secret, but is as certainly a cure,' replied Wois-law.

'So said all, but none has succeeded,' said the young lady peevishly.

'You might at least try it,' began Bertha.

'Because your friend proposes it,' said the other smiling. 'I have no doubt that you, with nothing ailing you, would take all manner of drugs to please your knight; but with me the induce-ment is wanting, and therefore also the faith.'

'I did not speak of any medicine,' said Woislaw.

'Oh! a magical remedy! I am to be cured—what was it the quack who was here the other day called it!—"by sympathy." Yes, that was it.'

'I do not object to your calling it so, if you like,' said Woislaw smiling; 'but you must know, dear lady, that the measures I shall propose must be attended to literally, and according to the strictest directions.'

'And you trust this to me?' asked Franziska,

'Certainly,' said Woislaw hesitating; 'but'—

'Well, why do you not proceed? Can you think that I shall fail in courage?' she asked.

'Courage is certainly necessary for the success of my plan,' said Woislaw gravely; 'and it is because I give you credit for a large share of that virtue, I venture to propose it at all, although for the real harmlessness of the remedy I will answer with my life, provided you follow my directions exactly.'

'Well, tell me the plan, and then I can decide,' said the young lady.

'I can only tell you that when we commence our operations,' replied Woislaw.

'Do you think I am a child to be sent here, there, and every-where, without a reason?' asked Franziska, with something of her old pettishness.

'You did me great injustice, dear lady, if you thought for a moment I would propose anything disagreeable to you, unless demanded by the sternest necessity,' said Woislaw; 'and yet I can only repeat my former words.'

'Then I will not do it,' cried Franziska. 'I have already tried so much, and all ineffectually.'

'I give you my honour as a knight, that your cure is certain, but—you must pledge yourself solemnly and unconditionally to do implicitly what I shall direct,' said Woislaw earnestly.

'Oh, I implore you to consent, Franziska. Our friend would not propose anything unnecessary,' said Bertha, taking both her cousin's hands.

'And let me join my entreaties to Bertha's,' said Franz.

'How strange you all are!' exclaimed Franziska, shaking her head; 'you make such a secret of that which I must know if I am to accomplish it, and then you declare so positively that I shall recover, when my own feelings tell me it is quite hopeless.'

'I repeat, that I will answer for the result,' said Woislaw,' on the condition I mentioned before, and that you have courage to carry out what you commence.'

'Ha! now I understand ; this, after all, is the only thing which appears doubtful to you,' cried Franziska. 'Well, to shew you that our sex are neither wanting in the will nor in the power to accomplish deeds of daring, I give my consent.'

With the last words, she offered Woislaw her hand.

'Our compact is thus sealed,' she pursued smiling. 'Now say, Sir Knight, how am I to commence this mysterious cure?'

'It commenced when you gave your consent,' said Woislaw gravely. 'Now, I have only to request that you will ask no more questions, but hold yourself in readiness to take a ride with, me tomorrow an hour before sunset. I also request that you will not mention to your father a word of what has passed.'

'Strange!' said Franziska.

'You have made the compact; you are not wanting in resolution; and I will answer for everything else,' said Woislaw encouragingly.

'Well, so let it be. I will follow your directions,' said the lady, although she still looked incredulous.

'On our return you shall know everything; before that, it is quite impossible,' said Woislaw in conclusion. 'Now go, dear lady, and take some rest; you will need strength for tomorrow.'

It was on the morning of the following day, the sun had not risen above an hour, and the dew still lay like a veil of pearls on the grass, or dripped from the petals of the flowers, swaying in the early breeze, when the knight Woislaw hastened over the fields towards the forest, and turned into a gloomy path, which by the direction, one could perceive, led towards the towers of Klatka. When he arrived at the old oak-tree we have before had occasion to mention, he sought carefully along the road for traces of human footsteps, but only a deer had passed that way; and seemingly satisfied with his search, he proceeded on his way, though not before he had half drawn his dagger from its sheath, as though to assure himself that it was ready for service in time of need.

Slowly he ascended the path; it was evident he carried something beneath his cloak. Arrived in the court, he left the ruins of the castle to the left, and entered the old chapel. In the chancel, he looked eagerly and earnestly round. A deathlike stillness reigned in the deserted sanctuary, only broken by the whispering of the wind in an old thorn-tree which grew outside. Woislaw had looked long around him ere he perceived the door leading down to the vault; he hurried towards it, and descended. The sun's position enabled its rays to penetrate the crevices, and made the subterranean chamber so light, that one could read easily the inscriptions at the head and feet of the coffins.

The knight first laid on the ground the packet he had hitherto earned under his cloak, and then going from coffin to coffin, at last remained stationary before the oldest of them. He read the inscription carefully, drew his dagger thoughtfully from its case, and endeavoured to raise the lid with its point. This was no difficult matter, for the rusty iron nails kept but a slight hold of the rotten wood. On looking in, only a heap of ashes, some remnants of dress, and a skull were the contents. He quickly closed it again, and went on to the next, passing over those of a woman and two children. Here things had much the same appearance, except that the corpse held together till the lid was raised, and then fell into dust, a few linen rags and bones being alone perceptible. In the third, fourth, and nearly the next half-dozen, the bodies were in better preservation: in some, they looked a sort of yellow brown mummy; whilst in others, a skinless skull covered with hair grinned from the coverings of velvet, silk, or mildewed embroideries; all, however, were touched with the loathsome marks of decay.

Only one more coffin now remained to be inspected; Woislaw approached it, and read the inscription. It was the same that had before attracted the Knight of Fahnenberg Ezzelin von Klatka, the last possessor of the tower, was described as lying therein. Woislaw found it more difficult to raise the lid here; and it was only by the exertion of much strength he a length succeeded in extracting the nails. He did all, however as quietly as if afraid of rousing some sleeper within; he then raised the cover, and cast a glance on the corpse. An involuntary 'Ha!' burst from his lips as he stepped back a pace. If he had less expected the sight that met his eyes, he would have been far more overcome.

In the coffin lay Azzo as he lived and breathed, and as Woislaw had seen him at the supper-table only the evening before. His appearance, dress, and all were the same; besides, he had more the semblance of sleep than of death—no trace of decay was visible—there was even a rosy tint on his cheeks. Only the circumstance that the breast did not heave, distinguished him from one who slept. For a few moments Woislaw did not move; he could only stare into the coffin. With a hastiness in his movements not usual with him, he suddenly seized the lid, which had fallen from his hands, and laying it on the coffin, knocked the nails into their places. As soon as he had completed this work, he fetched the packet he had left at the entrance, and laying it on the top of the coffin, hastily ascended the steps, and quitted the church and the ruins.

The day passed. Before evening, Franziska requested her father to allow her to take a ride with Woislaw, under pretence of shewing him the country. He, only too happy to think this a sign of amendment in his daughter, readily gave his consent; so, followed by a single servant, they mounted and left the castle. Woislaw was unusually silent and serious. When Franziska began to rally him about his gravity, and the approaching sympathetic cure, he replied, that what was before her was no laughing matter; and that although the result would be certainly a cure, still it would leave an impression on her whole future life.

In such discourse they reached the wood, and at length the oak, where they left their horses. Woislaw gave Franziska his arm, and they ascended the hill slowly and silently. They had just reached one of the half-dilapidated outworks where they could catch a glimpse of the open country, when Woislaw, speaking more to himself than to his companion, said: 'In a quarter of an hour, the sun will set, and in another hour the moon will have risen; then all must be accomplished. It will soon be time to commence the work.'

'Then, I should think it was time to intrust me with some idea of what it is,' said Franziska, looking at him.

'Well, lady,' he replied, turning towards her, and his voice was very solemn, 'I entreat you, Franziska von Fahnenberg, for your own good, and as you love the father who clings to you with his whole soul, that you will weigh well my words, and that you will not interrupt me with questions which I cannot answer until the work is completed. Your life is in the greatest danger from the illness under which you are labouring; indeed, you are irrecoverably lost if you do not fully carry out what I shall now impart to you. Now, promise me to do implicitly as I shall tell you; I pledge you my knightly word it is nothing against Heaven, or the honour of your house; and, besides, it is the sole means for saving you.' With these words, he held out his light hand to his companion, while he raised the other to heaven in confirmation of his oath.

'I promise you,' said Franziska, visibly moved by Woislaw's solemn tone, as she laid her little white and wasted hand in his.

'Then come; it is time,' was his reply, as he led her towards the church. The last rays of the sun were just pouring through the broken windows. They entered the chancel, the best preserved part of the whole building; here there were still some old kneeling-stools, placed before the high-altar, although nothing remained of that but the stonework and a few steps; the pictures and decorations had all vanished.

'Say an *Ave*; you will have need of it,' said Woislaw, as he himself fell on his knees.

Franziska knelt beside him, and repeated a short prayer. After a few moments, both rose.

'The moment has arrived! The sun sinks, and before the moon rises, all must be over,' said Woislaw quickly.

'What am I to do?' asked Franziska cheerfully.

'You see there that open vault!' replied the knight Woislaw, pointing to the door and flight of steps: 'you must descend. You must go alone; I may not accompany you. When you have reached the vault you will find, close to the entrance, a coffin, on which is placed a small packet. Open this packet, and you will find three long iron nails and a hammer. Then pause for a moment; but when I begin to repeat the *Credo* in a loud voice, knock with all your might, first one nail, then a second, and then a third, into the lid of the coffin, right up to their heads.'

Franziska stood thunderstruck; her whole body trembled, and she could not utter a word. Woislaw perceived it.

'Take courage, dear lady!' said he. 'Think that you are in the hands of Heaven, and that, without the will of your Creator, not a hair can fall from your head. Besides, I repeat, there is no danger.'

'Well, then, I will do it,' cried Franziska, in some measure regaining courage.

'Whatever you may hear, whatever takes place inside the coffin,' continued Woislaw, 'must have no effect upon you. Drive the nails well in, without flinching: your work must be finished before my prayer comes to an end.'

Franziska shuddered, but again recovered herself. 'I will do it; Heaven will send me strength,' she murmured softly.

'There is one thing more,' said Woislaw hesitatingly; 'perhaps it is the hardest of all I have proposed, but without it your cure will not be complete. When you have done as I have told you, sort of'—he hesitated—'a sort of liquid will flow from the coffin in this dip your finger, and besmear the scratch on your throat.'

'Horrible!' cried Franziska. 'This liquid is blood. A human being lies in the coffin.'

'An *unearthly one* lies therein! That blood is your own, but it flows in other veins,' said Woislaw gloomily. 'Ask no more; the sand is running out.'

Franziska summoned up all her powers of mind and body, went towards the steps which led to the vault, and Woislaw sank on his knees before the altar in quiet prayer. When the lady had descended, she found herself before the coffin on which lay the packet before mentioned. A sort of twilight reigned in the vault and everything around was so still and peaceful, that she felt more calm, and going up to the coffin, opened the packet. She had hardly seen that a hammer and three long nails were its contents when suddenly Woislaw's voice rang through the church, and broke the stillness of the aisles. Franziska started, but recognised the appointed prayer. She seized one of the nails, and with one stroke of the hammer drove it at least an inch into the cover.

All was still; nothing was heard but the echo of the stroke, Taking heart, the maiden grasped the hammer with both hands, and struck the nail twice with all her might, right up to the head into the wood. At this moment commenced a rustling noise; it seemed as though something in the interior began to move and to struggle. Franziska drew back in alarm. She was already on the point of throwing away the hammer, and flying up the steps, when Woislaw raised his voice so powerfully, and it sounded so entreatingly, that in a sort of excitement, such as would induce one to rush into a lion's den, she returned to the coffin, determined to bring things to a conclusion.

Hardly knowing what she did, she placed a second nail in the centre of the lid, and after some strokes, this was likewise buried to its head. The struggle now increased fearfully, as if some living creature were striving to burst the coffin. This was so shaken by it, that it cracked and split on all sides. Half distracted, Franziska seized the third nail; she thought no more of her ailments, she only knew herself to be in terrible danger, of what kind she could not guess: in an agony that threatened to rob her of her senses, and in the midst of the turning and cracking of the coffin, in which low groans were now beard, she struck the third nail in equally tight.

At this moment, she began to lose consciousness. She wished to hasten away, but staggered; and mechanically grasping at something to save herself by, she seized the corner of the coffin, and sank fainting beside it on the ground.

A quarter of an hour might have elapsed, when she again opened her eyes. She looked around her. Above was the starry sky, and the moon, which shed her cold light on the ruins and on the tops of the old oak-trees. Franziska was lying outside the church walls, Woislaw on his knees beside her, holding her hand in his.

'Heaven be praised that you live!' he cried, with a sigh of relief. 'I was beginning to doubt whether the remedy had not been too severe, and yet it was the only thing to save you.'

Franziska recovered her full consciousness very gradually. The past seemed to her like a dreadful dream. Only a few moments before, that fearful scene; and now this quiet all around her. She hardly dared at first to raise her eyes, and shuddered when she found herself only a few paces removed from the spot where she had undergone such terrible agony. She listened half unconsciously, now to the pacifying words Woislaw addressed to her, now to the whistling of the servant, who stood by the horses, and who, to wile away his time, was imitating the evening-song of a belated cow-herd.

'Let us go,' whispered Franziska, as she strove to raise herself. 'But what is this? My shoulder is wet, my throat, my hand'—

'It is probably the evening dew on the grass,' said Woislaw gently.

'No; it is blood!' she cried, springing up with horror in her tone. 'See, my hand is full of blood!'

'Oh, you are mistaken—surely mistaken,' said Woislaw stammering. 'Or perhaps the wound on your neck may have opened? Pray, feel whether this is the case.' He seized her hand, and directed it to the spot.

'I do not perceive anything; I feel no pain,' she said at length, somewhat angrily.

'Then, perhaps, when you fainted, you may have struck a corner of the coffin, or have torn yourself with the point of one of the nails,' suggested Woislaw.

'Oh, of what do you remind me!' cried Franziska shuddering. 'Let us away—away! I entreat you, come! I will not remain a moment longer near this dreadful, dreadful place.'

They descended the path much quicker than they came. Woislaw placed his companion on her horse, and they were soon on their way-home.

When they approached the castle, Franziska began to inundate her protector with questions about the preceding adventure; but he declared that her present state of excitement must make him defer all explanations till the morning, when her curiosity should be satisfied. On their arrival, he conducted her at once to her room, and told the knight his daughter was too much fatigued with her ride to appear at the supper-table. On the following morning, Franziska rose earlier than she had done for a long time. She assured her friend it was the first time since her illness commenced that she had been really refreshed by her sleep, and, what was still more remarkable, she had not been troubled by her old horrible dream. Her improved looks were not only remarked by Bertha, but by Franz and the knight; and with Woislaw's permission, she related the adventures of the previous evening. No sooner had she concluded, than Woislaw was completely stormed with questions about such a strange occurrence.

'Have you,' said the latter, turning towards his host, 'ever heard of Vampires?'

'Often,' replied he; 'but I have never believed in them.'

'Nor did I,' said Woislaw; 'but I have been assured of the existence by experience.'

'Oh, tell us what occurred,' cried Bertha eagerly, as a light seemed to dawn on her.

'It was during my first campaign in Hungary,' began Woislaw 'when I was rendered helpless for some time by this sword-cut of a *janizary* across my face, and another on my shoulder. I had been taken into the house of a respectable family in a small town. It consisted of the father and mother, and a daughter about twenty years of age. They obtained their living by selling the very good wine of the country, and the taproom was always full of visitors. Although the family were well to do in the world, there seemed to brood over them a continual melancholy, caused by the constant illness of the only daughter, a very pretty and excellent girl. She had always before bloomed like a rose, but for some months she had been getting so thin and wasted, and that without an satisfactory reason: they tried every means to restore her, but in vain.

'As the army had encamped quite in the neighbourhood of course a number of people of all countries assembled in the tavern. Amongst these there was one man who came every evening, when the moon shone, who struck everybody by the peculiarity of his manners and appearance; he looked dried up and death-like, and hardly spoke at all; but what he did say was bitter and sarcastic. Most attention was excited towards him by the circumstance, that although he always ordered a cup of the best wine, and now and then raised it to his lips, the cup was always as full after his departure as at first.'

'This all agrees wonderfully with the appearance of Azzo,' said Bertha, deeply interested.

'The daughter of the house,' continued Woislaw,' became daily worse, despite the aid not only of Christian doctors, but of many amongst the heathen prisoners, who were consulted in the hope that they might have some magical remedy to propose. It was singular that the girl always complained of a dream, in which the unknown guest worried and plagued her.'

'Just the same as your dream, Franziska,' cried Bertha.

'One evening,' resumed Woislaw. 'an old Sclavonian—who had made many voyages to Turkey and Greece, and had even seen the New World—and I were sitting over our wine, when the unknown walked silently, as usual, into the room, and sat down at the table. The bottle passed quickly between my friend and me, whilst we talked of all manner of things, of our adventures, and of passages in our lives, both horrible and amusing. We went on chatting thus for about an hour, and drank a tolerable quantity of wine.

'The unknown had remained perfectly silent the whole time, only smiling contemptuously every now and then. He now paid his money, and was going away. All this had quietly worried me—perhaps the wine had got a little into my head—so I said to the stranger: "Hold, you stony stranger; you have hitherto done nothing but listen, and have not even emptied your cup. Now you shall take your turn in telling us something amusing, and if you do not drink up your wine, it shall produce a quarrel between us."

'"Yes," said the Sclavonian, " you must remain; you shall chat and drink, too;" and he grasped—for although no longer young, he was big and very strong—the stranger by the shoulder, to pull him down to his seat again: the latter, however, although as thin as a skeleton, with one movement of his hand flung the Sclavonian to the middle of the room, and half stunned him for a moment. I now approached to hold the stranger back. I caught him by the arm; and although the springs of my iron hand were less powerful than those I have at present, I must have griped him rather hard in my anger, for after looking grimly at me for a moment, he bent towards me and whispered in my ear: "Let me go: from the gripe of your fist, I see you are my brother, therefore do not hinder me from seeking my bloody nourishment. I am hungry!" Surprised by such words, I let him loose, and almost before I was aware, he had left the room.

'As soon as I had in some degree recovered from my astonishment, I told the Sclavonian what I had heard. He started, evidently alarmed. I asked him to tell me the cause of his fears, and pressed him for an explanation of those extraordinary words. On our way to his lodging, he complied with my request. "The stranger," said he, "is a Vampire!"'

'How?' cried the knight, Franziska, and Bertha simultaneously, in a voice of horror. 'So this Azzo was'—

'Nothing less. He also was a Vampire!' replied Woislaw. 'But at all events *his* hellish thirst is quenched for ever; he will never return.—But I have not finished. As in my country, vampires had never been heard of, I questioned the Sclavonian minutely. He said that in Hungary, Croatia, Dalmatia, and Bosnia, these hellish guests were not uncommon. They were deceased persons, who had either once served as nourishment to vampires, or who had died in deadly sin, or under excommunication; and that whenever the moon shone, they rose from their graves, and sucked the blood of the living.'

'Horrible !' cried Franziska. 'If you had told me all this beforehand, I should never have accomplished the work.'

'So I thought; and yet it must be executed by the suffers themselves, while someone else performs the devotions,' replied Woislaw. 'The Sclavonian,' he continued after a short pause, 'added many other facts with regard to these unearthly visitant. He said that whilst their victim wasted, they themselves improve in appearance, and that a vampire possessed enormous strength'—

'Now I can understand the change your false hand produced on Azzo,' interrupted Franz.

'Yes, that was it,' replied Woislaw. 'Azzo, as well as the other vampire, mistook its great power for that of a natural one, and concluded I was one of his own species.—You may now imagine, dear lady,' he continued, turning to Franziska, 'how alarmed I was at your appearance when I arrived: all you and Bertha told me increased my anxiety; and when I saw Azzo I could doubt no longer that he was a vampire. As I learned from your account that a grave with the name Ezzelin von Klatka lay in the neighbourhood, I had no doubt that you might be saved: I could only induce you to assist me. It did not appear to me advisable to impart the whole facts of the case, for your bodily powers were so impaired, that an idea of the horrors before you might have quite unfitted you for the exertion; for this reason, I arranged everything in the manner in which it has taken place.'

'You did wisely,' replied Franziska shuddering. 'I can never be grateful enough to you. Had I known what was required of me, I never could have undertaken the deed.'

'That was what I feared,' said Woislaw; 'but fortune has favoured us all through.'

'And what became of the unfortunate girl in Hungary? inquired Bertha.

'I know not,' replied Woislaw. 'That very evening there was an alarm of the Turks, and we were ordered off. I never heard anything more of her.'

The conversation upon these strange occurrences continued for some time longer. The knight determined to have the vault at Klatka walled up forever. This took place on the following day the knight alleging as a reason, that he did not wish the dead to be disturbed by irreverent hands.

Franziska recovered gradually. Her health had been so severely shaken, that it was long ere her strength was so much restored as to allow of her being considered out of danger. The young lady's character underwent a great change in the interval. Its former strength was, perhaps, in some degree diminished, but in place of that, she had acquired a benevolent softness, which brought out all her best qualities. Franz continued his attentions to his cousin; but, perhaps, owing to a hint from Bertha, he was less assiduous in his exhibition of them.

His inclinations did not lead him to the battle, the camp, or the attainment of honours: his great aim was to increase the good condition and happiness of his tenants, and to this he contributed the whole energy of his mind. Franziska could not withstand the unobtrusive signs of the young man's continued attachment; and it was not long ere the credit she was obliged to yield to his noble efforts for the welfare of his fellow-creatures, changed into a liking, which went on increasing, until at length it assumed the character of love. As Woislaw insisted on making Bertha his wife before he returned to Silesia, it was arranged that the marriage should take place at their present abode. How joyful was the surprise of the knight of Fahnenberg, when his daughter and Franz likewise entreated his blessing, and expressed their desire of being united on the same day! This day soon came round, and it saw the bright looks of two happy couples.

The Upper Berth

By F. Marion Crawford

1

Somebody asked for the cigars. We had talked long, and the conversation was beginning to languish; the tobacco smoke had got into the heavy curtains, the wine had got into those brains which were liable to become heavy, and it was already perfectly evident that, unless somebody did something to rouse our oppressed spirits, the meeting would soon come to its natural conclusion, and we, the guests, would speedily go home to bed, and most certainly to sleep. No one had said anything very remarkable; it may be that no one had anything very remarkable to say. Jones had given us every particular of his last hunting adventure in Yorkshire. Mr. Tompkins, of Boston, had explained at elaborate length those working principles, by the due and careful maintenance of which the Atchison, Topeka, and Santa Fé Railroad not only extended its territory, increased its departmental influence, and transported live stock without starving them to death before the day of actual delivery, but, also, had for years succeeded in deceiving those passengers who bought its tickets into the fallacious belief that the corporation aforesaid was really able to transport human life without destroying it.

Signor Tombola had endeavoured to persuade us, by arguments which we took no trouble to oppose, that the unity of his country in no way resembled the average modern torpedo, carefully planned, constructed with all the skill of the greatest European arsenals, but, when constructed, destined to be di-

rected by feeble hands into a region where it must undoubtedly explode, unseen, unfeared, and unheard, into the illimitable
wastes of political chaos.

It is unnecessary to go into further details. The conversation
had assumed proportions which would have bored Prometheus
on his rock, which would have driven Tantalus to distraction,
and which would have impelled Ixion to seek relaxation in the
simple but instructive dialogues of Herr Ollendorff, rather than
submit to the greater evil of listening to our talk. We had sat
at table for hours; we were bored, we were tired, and nobody
showed signs of moving.

Somebody called for cigars. We all instinctively looked towards the speaker. Brisbane was a man of five-and-thirty years of
age, and remarkable for those gifts which chiefly attract the attention of men. He was a strong man. The external proportions
of his figure presented nothing extraordinary to the common
eye, though his size was above the average. He was a little over
six feet in height, and moderately broad in the shoulder; he did
not appear to be stout, but, on the other hand, he was certainly
not thin; his small head was supported by a strong and sinewy
neck; his broad, muscular hands appeared to possess a peculiar
skill in breaking walnuts without the assistance of the ordinary
cracker, and, seeing him in profile, one could not help remarking
the extraordinary breadth of his sleeves, and the unusual thickness of his chest. He was one of those men who are commonly
spoken of among men as deceptive; that is to say, that though he
looked exceedingly strong he was in reality very much stronger
than he looked. Of his features I need say little. His head was
small, his hair is thin, his eyes are blue, his nose is large, he has a
small moustache, and a square jaw. Everybody knows Brisbane,
and when he asked for a cigar everybody looked at him.

"It is a very singular thing," said Brisbane.

Everybody stopped talking. Brisbane's voice was not loud,
but possessed a peculiar quality of penetrating general conversation, and cutting it like a knife. Everybody listened. Brisbane,
perceiving that he had attracted their general attention, lit his

cigar with great equanimity.

"It is very singular," he continued, "that thing about ghosts. People are always asking whether anybody has seen a ghost. I have."

"Bosh! What, you? You don't mean to say so, Brisbane? Well, for a man of his intelligence!"

A chorus of exclamations greeted Brisbane's remarkable statement. Everybody called for cigars, and Stubbs, the butler, suddenly appeared from the depths of nowhere with a fresh bottle of dry champagne. The situation was saved; Brisbane was going to tell a story.

I am an old sailor, said Brisbane, and as I have to cross the Atlantic pretty often, I have my favourites. Most men have their favourites. I have seen a man wait in a Broadway bar for three-quarters of an hour for a particular car which he liked. I believe the bar-keeper made at least one-third of his living by that man's preference. I have a habit of waiting for certain ships when I am obliged to cross that duck-pond. It may be a prejudice, but I was never cheated out of a good passage but once in my life. I remember it very well; it was a warm morning in June, and the Custom House officials, who were hanging about waiting for a steamer already on her way up from the Quarantine, presented a peculiarly hazy and thoughtful appearance.

I had not much luggage—I never have. I mingled with the crowd of passengers, porters, and officious individuals in blue coats and brass buttons, who seemed to spring up like mushrooms from the deck of a moored steamer to obtrude their unnecessary services upon the independent passenger. I have often noticed with a certain interest the spontaneous evolution of these fellows. They are not there when you arrive; five minutes after the pilot has called 'Go ahead!' they, or at least their blue coats and brass buttons, have disappeared from deck and gangway as completely as though they had been consigned to that locker which tradition ascribes to Davy Jones. But, at the moment of starting, they are there, clean shaved, blue coated, and ravenous for fees. I hastened on board.

The *Kamtschatka* was one of my favourite ships. I say was, because she emphatically no longer is. I cannot conceive of any inducement which could entice me to make another voyage in her. Yes, I know what you are going to say. She is uncommonly clean in the run aft, she has enough bluffing off in the bows to keep her dry, and the lower berths are most of them double. She has a lot of advantages, but I won't cross in her again. Excuse the digression. I got on board. I hailed a steward, whose red nose and redder whiskers were equally familiar to me.

"One hundred and five, lower berth," said I, in the business-like tone peculiar to men who think no more of crossing the Atlantic than taking a whisky cocktail at down-town Delmonico's.

The steward took my portmanteau, greatcoat, and rug. I shall never forget the expression on his face. Not that he turned pale. It is maintained by the most eminent divines that even miracles cannot change the course of nature. I have no hesitation in saying that he did not turn pale; but, from his expression, I judged that he was either about to shed tears, to sneeze, or to drop my portmanteau. As the latter contained two bottles of particularly fine old sherry presented to me for my voyage by my old friend Snigginson van Pickyns, I felt extremely nervous. But the steward did none of these things.

"Well, I'm d——d!" said he in a low voice, and led the way.

I supposed my Hermes, as he led me to the lower regions, had had a little grog, but I said nothing, and followed him. One hundred and five was on the port side, well aft. There was nothing remarkable about the state-room. The lower berth, like most of those upon the *Kamtschatka*, was double. There was plenty of room; there was the usual washing apparatus, calculated to convey an idea of luxury to the mind of a North American Indian; there were the usual inefficient racks of brown wood, in which it is more easy to hand a large-sized umbrella than the common tooth-brush of commerce. Upon the uninviting mattresses were carefully bolded together those blankets which a great modern humorist has aptly compared to cold buckwheat cakes.

The question of towels was left entirely to the imagination. The glass decanters were filled with a transparent liquid faintly tinged with brown, but from which an odourless faint, but not more pleasing, ascended to the nostrils, like a far-off sea-sick reminiscence of oily machinery. Sad-coloured curtains half-closed the upper berth. The hazy June daylight shed a faint illumination upon the desolate little scene. Ugh! how I hate that state-room!

The steward deposited my traps and looked at me, as though he wanted to get away—probably in search of more passengers and more fees. It is always a good plan to start in favour with those functionaries, and I accordingly gave him certain coins there and then.

"I'll try and make yer comfortable all I can," he remarked, as he put the coins in his pocket. Nevertheless, there was a doubtful intonation in his voice which surprised me. Possibly his scale of fees had gone up, and he was not satisfied; but on the whole I was inclined to think that, as he himself would have expressed it, he was "the better for a glass". I was wrong, however, and did the man injustice.

2

Nothing especially worthy of mention occurred during that day. We left the pier punctually, and it was very pleasant to be fairly under way, for the weather was warm and sultry, and the motion of the steamer produced a refreshing breeze. Everybody knows what the first day at sea is like. People pace the decks and stare at each other, and occasionally meet acquaintances whom they did not know to be on board. There is the usual uncertainty as to whether the food will be good, bad, or indifferent, until the first two meals have put the matter beyond a doubt; there is the usual uncertainty about the weather, until the ship is fairly off Fire Island. The tables are crowded at first, and then suddenly thinned. Pale-faced people spring from their seats and precipitate themselves towards the door, and each old sailor breathes more freely as his sea-sick neighbour rushes from his side, leaving him plenty of elbow-room and an unlimited command over the mustard.

One passage across the Atlantic is very much like another, and we who cross very often do not make the voyage for the sake of novelty. Whales and icebergs are indeed always objects of interest, but, after all, one whale is very much like another whale, and one rarely sees an iceberg at close quarters. To the majority of us the most delightful moment of the day on board an ocean steamer is when we have taken our last turn on deck, have smoked our last cigar, and having succeeded in tiring ourselves, feel at liberty to turn in with a clear conscience. On that first night of the voyage I felt particularly lazy, and went to bed in one hundred and five rather earlier than I usually do. As I turned in, I was amazed to see that I was to have a companion. A portmanteau, very like my own, lay in the opposite corner, and in the upper berth had been deposited a neatly-folded rug, with a stick and umbrella. I had hoped to be alone, and I was disappointed; but I wondered who my room-mate was to be, and I determined to have a look at him.

Before I had been long in bed he entered. He was, as far as I could see, a very tall man, very thin, very pale, with sandy hair and whiskers and colourless grey eyes. He had about him, I thought, an air of rather dubious fashion; the short of man you might see in Wall Street, without being able precisely to say what he was doing there—the sort of man who frequents the *Café Anglais,* who always seems to be alone and who drinks champagne; you might meet him on a racecourse, but he would never appear to be doing anything there either. A little over-dressed—a little odd. There are three or four of his kind on every ocean steamer. I made up my mind that I did not care to make his acquaintance, and I went to sleep saying to myself that I would study his habits in order to avoid him. If he rose early, I would rise late; if he went to bed late, I would go to bed early. I did not care to know him. If you once know people of that kind they are always turning up. Poor fellow! I need not have taken the trouble to come to so many decisions about him, for I never saw him again after that first night in one hundred and five.

I was sleeping soundly when I was suddenly waked by a loud noise. To judge from the sound, my room-mate must have sprung with a single leap from the upper berth to the floor. I heard him fumbling with the latch and bolt of the door, which opened almost immediately, and then I heard his footsteps as he ran at full speed down the passage, leaving the door open behind him. The ship was rolling a little, and I expected to hear him stumble or fall, but he ran as though he were running for his life. The door swung on its hinges with the motion of the vessel, and the sound annoyed me. I got up and shut it, and groped my way back to my berth in the darkness. I went to sleep again; but I have no idea how long I slept.

When I awoke it was still quite dark, but I felt a disagreeable sensation of cold, and it seemed to me that the air was damp. You know the peculiar smell of a cabin which has been wet with sea-water. I covered myself up as well as I could and dozed off again, framing complaints to be made the next day, and selecting the most powerful epithets in the language. I could hear my room-mate turn over in the upper berth. He had probably returned while I was asleep. Once I thought I heard him groan, and I argued that he was sea-sick. That is particularly unpleasant when one is below. Nevertheless I dozed off and slept till early daylight.

The ship was rolling heavily, much more than on the previous evening, and the grey light which came in through the porthole changed in tint with every movement according as the angle of the vessel's side turned the glass seawards or skywards. It was very cold—unaccountably so for the month of June. I turned my head and looked at the porthole, and saw to my surprise that it was wide open and hooked back. I believe I swore audibly. Then I got up and shut it. As I turned back I glanced at the upper berth. The curtains were drawn close together; my companion had probably felt cold as well as I. It struck me that I had slept enough. The state-room was uncomfortable, though, strange to say, I could not smell the dampness which had an-

372

noyed me in the night. My room-mate was still asleep—excellent opportunity for avoiding him, so I dressed at once and went on deck. The day was warm and cloudy, with an oily smell on the water. It was seven o'clock as I came out—much later than I had imagined. I came across the doctor, who was taking his first sniff of the morning air. He was a young man from the West of Ireland—a tremendous fellow, with black hair and blue eyes, already inclined to be stout; he had a happy-go-lucky, healthy look about him which was rather attractive.

"Fine morning," I remarked, by way of introduction.

"Well," said he, eyeing me with an air of ready interest, "it's a fine morning and it's not a fine morning. I don't think it's much of a morning."

"Well, no—it is not so very fine," said I.

"It's just what I call fuggly weather," replied the doctor.

"It was very cold last night, I thought," I remarked. "However, when I looked about, I found that the porthole was wide open. I had not noticed it when I went to bed. And the stateroom was damp, too."

"Damp!" said he. "Whereabouts are you?"

"One hundred and five——"

To my surprise the doctor started visibly, and stared at me.

"What is the matter?" I asked.

"Oh—nothing," he answered; "only everybody has complained of that state-room for the last three trips."

"I shall complain too," I said. "It has certainly not been properly aired. It is a shame!"

"I don't believe it can be helped," answered the doctor. "I believe there is something—well, it is not my business to frighten passengers."

"You need not be afraid of frightening me," I replied. "I can stand any amount of damp. If I should get a bad cold I will come to you."

I offered the doctor a cigar, which he took and examined very critically.

"It is not so much the damp," he remarked. "However, I dare

say you will get on very well. Have you a room-mate?"

"Yes; a deuce of a fellow, who bolts out in the middle of the night, and leaves the door open."

Again the doctor glanced curiously at me. Then he lit the cigar and looked grave.

"Did he come back?" he asked presently.

"Yes. I was asleep, but I waked up, and heard him moving. Then I felt cold and went to sleep again. This morning I found the porthole open."

"Look here," said the doctor quietly, "I don't care much for this ship. I don't care a rap for her reputation. I tell you what I will do. I have a good-sized place up here. I will share it with you, though I don't know you from Adam."

I was very much surprised at the proposition. I could not imagine why he should take such a sudden interest in my welfare. However, his manner as he spoke of the ship was peculiar.

"You are very good, doctor," I said. "But, really, I believe even now the cabin could be aired, or cleaned out, or something. Why do you not care for the ship?"

"We are not superstitious in our profession, sir," replied the doctor, "but the sea makes people so. I don't want to prejudice you, and I don't want to frighten you, but if you will take my advice you will move in here. I would as soon see you overboard," he added earnestly, "as know that you or any other man was to sleep in one hundred and five."

"Good gracious! Why?" I asked.

"Just because on the last three trips the people who have slept there actually have gone overboard," he answered gravely.

The intelligence was startling and exceedingly unpleasant, I confess. I looked hard at the doctor to see whether he was making game of me, but he looked perfectly serious. I thanked him warmly for his offer, but told him I intended to be the exception to the rule by which everyone who slept in that particular state-room went overboard. He did not say much, but looked as grave as ever, and hinted that, before we got across, I should probably reconsider his proposal. In the course of time we went to breakfast, at which only an inconsiderable number of passengers assembled. I noticed that one or two of the officers who breakfasted with us looked grave. After breakfast I went into my state-room in order to get a book. The curtains of the upper berth were still closely drawn. Not a word was to be heard. My room-mate was probably still asleep.

As I came out I met the steward whose business it was to look after me. He whispered that the captain wanted to see me, and then scuttled away down the passage as if very anxious to avoid any questions. I went toward the captain's cabin, and found him waiting for me.

"Sir," said he, "I want to ask a favour of you."

I answered that I would do anything to oblige him.

"Your room-mate had disappeared," he said. "He is known to have turned in early last night. Did you notice anything extraordinary in his manner?"

The question coming, as it did, in exact confirmation of the fears the doctor had expressed half an hour earlier, staggered me.

"You don't mean to say he has gone overboard?" I asked.

"I fear he has," answered the captain.

"This is the most extraordinary thing----" I began.

"Why?" he asked.

"He is the fourth, then?" I exclaimed. In answer to another question from the captain, I explained, without mentioning the doctor, that I had heard the story concerning one hundred and five. He seemed very much annoyed at hearing that I knew of it. I told him what had occurred in the night.

"What you say," he replied, "coincides almost exactly with what was told me by the room-mates of two of the other three. They bolt out of bed and run down the passage. Two of them were seen to go overboard by the watch; we stopped and lowered boats, but they were not found. Nobody, however, saw or heard the man who was lost last night—if he is really lost. The steward, who is a superstitious fellow, perhaps, and expected something to go wrong, went to look for him, this morning, and found his berth empty, but his clothes lying about, just as he had left them. The steward was the only man on board who knew him by sight, and he has been searching everywhere for him. He has disappeared! Now, sir, I want to beg you not to mention the circumstance to any of the passengers; I don't want the ship to get a bad name, and nothing hangs about an ocean-goer like stories of suicides. You shall have your choice of any one of the officers' cabins you like, including my own, for the rest of the passage. Is that a fair bargain?"

"Very," said I; "and I am much obliged to you. But since I am alone, and have the state-room to myself, I would rather not move. If the steward will take out that unfortunate man's things, I would as leave stay where I am. I will not say anything about the matter, and I think I can promise you that I will not follow my room-mate."

The captain tried to dissuade me from my intention, but I preferred having a state-room alone to being the chum of any officer on board. I do not know whether I aced foolishly, but if I had taken his advice I should have had nothing more to tell. There would have remained the disagreeable coincidence of several suicides occurring among men who had slept in the same cabin, but that would have been all.

That was not the end of the matter, however, by any means. I obstinately made up my mind that I would not be disturbed by such tales, and I even went so far as to argue the question with the captain. There was something wrong about the state-room, I said. It was rather damp. The porthole had been left open last night. My room-mate might have been ill when he came on board, and he might have become delirious after he went to bed. He might even now be hiding somewhere on board, and might be found later. The place ought to be aired and the fastening on the port looked to. If the captain would give me leave, I would see that what I thought necessary were done immediately.

"Of course you have a right to stay where you are if you please," he replied, rather petulantly; "but I wish you would turn out and let me lock the place up, and be done with it."

I did not see it in the same light, and left the captain, after promising to be silent concerning the disappearance of my companion. The latter had had no acquaintances on board, and was not missed in the course of the day. Towards evening I met the doctor again, and he asked me whether I had changed my mind. I told him I had not.

"Then you will before long," he said, very gravely.

3

We played whist in the evening, and I went to bed late. I will confess now that I felt a disagreeable sensation when I entered my state-room. I could not help thinking of the tall man I had seen on the previous night, who was now dead, drowned, tossing about in the long swell, two or three hundred miles astern. His face rose very distinctly before me as I undressed, and I even went so far as to draw back the curtains of the upper berth, as though to persuade myself that he was actually gone. I also bolted the door of the state-room. Suddenly I became aware that the porthole was open, and fastened back. This was more than I could stand. I hastily threw on my dressing-gown and went in search of Robert, the steward of my passage. I was very angry, I remember, and when I found him I dragged him roughly to the door of one hundred and five, and pushed him towards the open porthole.

"What the deuce do you mean, you scoundrel, by leaving that port open every night? Don't you know it is against the regulations? Don't you know that if the ship heeled and the water began to come in, ten men could not shut it? I will report you to the captain, you blackguard, for endangering the ship!"

I was exceedingly wroth. The man trembled and turned pale, and then began to shut the round glass plate with the heavy brass fittings.

"Why don't you answer me?" I said roughly.

"If you please, sir," faltered Robert, "there's nobody on board as can keep this 'ere port shut at night. You can try it yourself, sir. I ain't a-going to stop hany longer on board o' this vessel, sir;

I ain't, indeed. But if I was you, sir, I'd just clear out and go and sleep with the surgeon, or something, I would. Look 'ere, sir, is that fastened what you may call securely, or not, sir? Try it, sir, see if it will move a hinch."

I tried the port, and found it perfectly tight.

"Well, sir," continued Robert triumphantly, "I wager my reputation as a A1 steward that in 'arf an hour it will be open again; fastened back, too, sir, that's the horful thing—fastened back!"

I examined the great screw and the looped nut that ran on it.

"If I find it open in the night, Robert, I will give you a sovereign. It is not possible. You may go."

"Soverin' did you say, sir? Very good, sir. Thank ye, sir. Goodnight, sir. Pleasant reepose, sir, and all manner of hinchantin' dreams, sir."

Robert scuttled away, delighted at being released. Of course, I thought he was trying to account for his negligence by a silly story, intended to frighten me, and I disbelieved him. The consequence was that he got his sovereign, and I spent a very peculiarly unpleasant night.

I went to bed, and five minutes after I had rolled myself up in my blankets the inexorable Robert extinguished the light that burned steadily behind the ground-glass pane near the door. I lay quite still in the dark trying to go to sleep, but I soon found that impossible. It had been some satisfaction to be angry with the steward, and the diversion had banished that unpleasant sensation I had at first experienced when I thought of the drowned man who had been my chum; but I was no longer sleepy, and I lay awake for some time, occasionally glancing at the porthole, which I could just see from where I lay, and which, in the darkness, looked like a faintly-luminous soup-plate suspended in blackness. I believe I must have lain there for an hour, and, as I remember, I was just dozing into sleep when I was roused by a draught of cold air, and by distinctly feeling the spray of the sea blown upon my face. I started to my feet, and not having allowed in the dark for the motion of the ship, I was instantly thrown violently across the state-room upon the couch which was placed beneath the port-hole. I recovered myself immediately, however, and climbed upon my knees. The port-hole was again wide open and fastened back!

Now these things are facts. I was wide awake when I got up, and I should certainly have been waked by the fall had I still been dozing. Moreover, I bruised my elbows and knees badly, and the bruises were there on the following morning to testify to the fact, if I myself had doubted it. The porthole was wide open and fastened back—a thing so unaccountable that I remember very well feeling astonishment rather that fear when I discovered it. I at once closed the plate again, and screwed down the loop nut with all my strength. It was very dark in the state-room. I reflected that the port had certainly been opened within an hour after Robert had at first shut it in my presence, and I determined to watch it, and see whether it would open again. Those brass fittings are very heavy and by no means easy to move; I could not believe that the clamp had been turned by the shaking of the screw. I stood peering out through the thick glass at the alternate white and grey streaks of the sea that foamed beneath the ship's side. I must have remained there a quarter of an hour.

Suddenly, as I stood, I distinctly heard something moving behind me in one of the berths, and a moment afterwards, just as I turned instinctively to look—though I could, of course, see nothing in the darkness—I heard a very faint groan. I sprang across the state-room, and tore the curtains of the upper berth aside, thrusting in my hands to discover if there were any one there. There was someone.

I remember that the sensation as I put my hands forward was as though I were plunging them into the air of a damp cellar, and from behind the curtains came a gust of wind that smelled horribly of stagnant sea-water. I laid hold of something that had the shape of a man's arm, but was smooth, and wet, and icy cold. But suddenly, as I pulled, the creature sprang violently forward against me, a clammy oozy mass, as it seemed to me, heavy and wet, yet endowed with a sort of supernatural strength. I reeled across the state-room, and in an instant the door opened and the thing rushed out. I had not had time to be frightened, and quickly recovering myself, I sprang through the door and gave chase at the top of my speed, but I was too late. Ten yards before me I could see—I am sure I saw it—a dark shadow moving in the dimly lighted passage, quickly as the shadow of a fast horse thrown before a dog-cart by the lamp on a dark night. But in a moment it had disappeared, and I found myself holding on to the polished rail that ran along the bulkhead where the passage turned towards the companion. My hair stood on end, and the cold perspiration rolled down my face. I am not ashamed of it in the least: I was very badly frightened.

Still I doubted my senses, and pulled myself together. It was absurd, I thought. The Welsh rarebit I had eaten had disagreed with me. I had been in a nightmare. I made my way back to my state-room, and entered it with an effort. The whole place smelled of stagnant sea-water, as it had when I had waked on the previous evening. It required my utmost strength to go in, and grope among my things for a box of wax lights. As I lighted a railway reading lantern which I always carry in case I want to read after the lamps are out, I perceived that the porthole was again open, and a sort of creeping horror began to take possession of me which I never felt before, nor wish to feel again. But I got a light and proceeded to examine the upper berth, expecting to find it drenched with sea-water.

But I was disappointed. The bed had been slept in, and the smell of the sea was strong; but the bedding was as dry as a bone. I fancied that Robert had not had the courage to make the bed after the accident of the previous night—it had all been a hideous dream. I drew the curtains back as far as I could and examined the place very carefully. It was perfectly dry. But the porthole was open again. With a sort of dull bewilderment of horror I closed it and screwed it down, and thrusting my heavy stick through the brass loop, wrenched it with all my might, till the thick metal began to bend under the pressure. Then I hooked my reading lantern into the red velvet at the head of the couch, and sat down to recover my senses if I could. I sat there all night, unable to think of rest—hardly able to think at all. But the porthole remained closed, and I did not believe it would now open again without the application of a considerable force.

The morning dawned at last, and I dressed myself slowly, thinking over all that had happened in the night. It was a beautiful day and I went on deck, glad to get out into the early, pure sunshine, and to smell the breeze from the blue water, so different from the noisome, stagnant odour of my state-room. Instinctively I turned aft, towards the surgeon's cabin. There he stood, with a pipe in his mouth, taking his morning airing precisely as on the preceding day.

"Good-morning," said he quietly, but looking at me with evident curiosity.

"Doctor, you were quite right," said I. "There is something wrong about that place."

"I thought you would change your mind," he answered, rather triumphantly. "You have had a bad night, eh? Shall I make you a pick-me-up? I have a capital recipe."

"No, thanks," I cried. "But I would like to tell you what happened."

I then tried to explain as clearly as possible precisely what had occurred, not omitting to state that I had been scared as I had never been scared in my whole life before. I dwelt particularly on the phenomenon of the porthole, which was a fact to which I could testify, even if the rest had been an illusion. I had closed it twice in the night, and the second time I had actually bent the brass in wrenching it with my stick. I believe I insisted a good deal on this point.

"You seem to think I am likely to doubt the story," said the doctor, smiling at my detailed account of the state of the porthole. "I do not doubt in the least. I renew my invitation to you. Bring your traps here, and take half my cabin."

"Come and take half of mine for one night," I said. "Help me to get at the bottom of this thing."

"You will get to the bottom of something else if you try," answered the doctor.

"What?" I asked.

"The bottom of the sea. I am going to leave this ship. It is not canny."

"Then you will not help me to find out----"

"Not I," said the doctor quickly. "It is my business to keep my wits about me—not to go fiddling about with ghosts and things."

"Do you really believe it is a ghost?" I enquired, rather contemptuously. But as I spoke I remembered very well the horrible sensation of the supernatural which had got possession of me during the night. The doctor turned sharply on me—

"Have you any reasonable explanation of these things to offer?" he asked. "No; you have not. Well, you say you will find an explanation. I say that you won't, sir, simply because there is not any."

"But, my dear sir," I retorted, "do you, a man of science, mean to tell me that such things cannot be explained?"

"I do," he answered stoutly. "And, if they could, I would not be concerned in the explanation."

I did not care to spend another night alone in the stateroom, and yet I was obstinately determined to get at the root of the disturbances. I do not believe there are many men who would have slept there alone, after passing two such nights. But I made up my mind to try it, if I could not get anyone to share a watch with me. The doctor was evidently not inclined for such an experiment. He said he was a surgeon, and that in case any accident occurred on board he must be always in readiness. He could not afford to have his nerves unsettled. Perhaps he was quite right, but I am inclined to think that his precaution was prompted by his inclination. On enquiry, he informed me that there was no one on board who would be likely to join me in my investigations, and after a little more conversation I left him. A little later I met the captain, and told him my story. I said that, if no one would spend the night with me, I would ask leave to have the light burning all night, and would try it alone.

"Look here," said he, "I will tell you what I will do. I will share your watch myself, and we will see what happens. It is my belief that we can find out between us. There may be some fellow skulking on board, who steals a passage by frightening the passengers. It is just possible that there may be something queer in the carpentering of that berth."

I suggested taking the ship's carpenter below and examining the place; but I was overjoyed at the captain's offer to spend the night with me. He accordingly sent for the workman and ordered him to do anything I required. We went below at once. I had all the bedding cleared out of the upper berth, and we examined the place thoroughly to see if there was a board loose anywhere, or a panel which could be opened or pushed aside. We tried the planks everywhere, tapped the flooring, unscrewed the fittings of the lower berth and took it to pieces—in short, there was not a square inch of the state-room which was not searched and tested. Everything was in perfect order, and we put everything back in its place. As we were finishing our work, Robert came to the door and looked in.

"Well, sir—find anything, sir?" he asked, with a ghastly grin.

"You were right about the porthole, Robert," I said, and I gave him the promised sovereign. The carpenter did his work silently and skilfully, following my directions. When he had done he spoke.

"I'm a plain man, sir," he said. "But it's my belief you had better just turn out your things, and let me run half a dozen four-inch screws through the door of this cabin. There's no good never came o' this cabin yet, sir, and that's all about it. There's been four lives lost out o' here to my own remembrance, and that is four trips. Better give it up, sir—better give it up!"

"I will try it for one night more," I said.

"Better give it up, sir—better give it up! It's a precious bad job," repeated the workman, putting his tools in his bag and leaving the cabin.

But my spirits had risen considerably at the prospect of having the captain's company, and I made up my mind not to be prevented from going to the end of this strange business. I abstained from Welsh rare-bits and grog that evening, and did not even join in the customary game of whist. I wanted to be quite sure of my nerves, and my vanity made me anxious to make a good figure in the captain's eyes.

4

The captain was one of those splendidly tough and cheerful specimens of seafaring humanity whose combined courage, hardihood, and calmness in difficulty leads them naturally into high positions of trust. He was not the man to be led away by an idle tale, and the mere fact that he was willing to join me in the investigation was proof that he thought there was something seriously wrong, which could not be accounted for on ordinary theories, nor laughed down as a common superstition. To some extent, too, his reputation was at stake, as well as the reputation of the ship. It is no light thing to lose passengers overboard, and he knew it.

About ten o'clock that evening, as I was smoking a last cigar, he came up to me, and drew me aside from the beat of the other passengers who were patrolling the deck in the warm darkness.

"This is a serious matter, Mr. Brisbane," he said. "We must make up our minds either way—to be disappointed or to have a pretty rough time of it. You see I cannot afford to laugh at the affair, and I will ask you to sign your name to a statement of whatever occurs. If nothing happens tonight we will try it again tomorrow and next day. Are you ready?"

So we went below, and entered the state-room. As we went in I could see Robert the steward, who stood a little further down the passage, watching us, with his usual grin, as though certain that something dreadful was about to happen. The captain closed the door behind us and bolted it.

"Supposing we put your portmanteau before the door," he suggested. "One of us can sit on it. Nothing can get out then. Is the port screwed down?"

I found it as I had left it in the morning. Indeed, without using a lever, as I had done, no one could have opened it. I drew back the curtains of the upper berth so that I could see well into it. By the captain's advice I lighted my reading lantern, and placed it so that it shone upon the white sheets above. He insisted upon sitting on the portmanteau, declaring that he wished to be able to swear that he had sat before the door.

Then he requested me to search the state-room thoroughly, an operation very soon accomplished, as it consisted merely in looking beneath the lower berth and under the couch below the porthole. The spaces were quite empty.

"It is impossible for any human being to get in," I said, "or for any human being to open the port."

"Very good," said the captain calmly. "If we see anything now, it must be either imagination or something supernatural."

I sat down on the edge of the lower berth.

"The first time it happened," said the captain, crossing his legs and leaning back against the door, "was in March. The passenger who slept here, in the upper berth, turned out have been a lunatic—at all events, he was known to have been a little touched, and he had taken his passage without the knowledge of his friends. He rushed out in the middle of the night, and threw himself overboard, before the officer who had the watch could stop him. We stopped and lowered a boat; it was a quiet night, just before that heavy weather came on; but we could not find him. Of course his suicide was afterwards accounted for on the ground of his insanity."

"I suppose that often happens?" I remarked, rather absently.

"Not often—no," said the captain; "never before in my experience, though I have heard of it happening on board of other ships. Well, as I was saying, that occurred in March. On the very next trip——What are you looking at?" he asked, stopping suddenly in his narration.

I believe I gave no answer. My eyes were riveted upon the porthole. It seemed to me that the brass loop-nut was beginning to turn very slowly upon the screw—so slowly, however, that I was not sure it moved at all. I watched it intently, fixing its position in my mind, and trying to ascertain whether it changed. Seeing where I was looking, the captain looked too.

"It moves!" he exclaimed, in a tone of conviction. "No, it does not," he added, after a minute.

"If it were the jarring of the screw," said I, "it would have opened during the day; but I found it this evening jammed tight as I left it this morning."

I rose and tried the nut. It was certainly loosened, for by an effort I could move it with my hands.

"The queer thing," said the captain, "is that the second man who was lost is supposed to have got through that very port. We had a terrible time over it. It was in the middle of the night, and the weather was very heavy; there was an alarm that one of the ports was open and the sea running in. I came below and found everything flooded, the water pouring in every time she rolled, and the whole port swinging from the top bolts—not the porthole in the middle. Well, we managed to shut it, but the water did some damage. Ever since that the place smells of sea-water from time to time. We supposed the passenger had thrown himself out, though the Lord only knows how he did it. The steward kept telling me that he cannot keep anything shut here. Upon my word—I can smell it now, cannot you?" he enquired, sniffing the air suspiciously.

"Yes—distinctly," I said, and I shuddered as that same odour of stagnant sea-water grew stronger in the cabin. "Now, to smell like this, the place must be damp," I continued, "and yet when I examined it with the carpenter this morning everything was perfectly dry. It is most extraordinary—hallo!"

My reading lantern, which had been placed in the upper berth, was suddenly extinguished. There was still a good deal of light from the pane of ground glass near the door, behind which loomed the regulation lamp. The ship rolled heavily, and the curtain of the upper berth swung far out into the state-room and back again. I rose quickly from my seat on the edge of the bed, and the captain at the same moment started to his feet with a loud cry of surprise. I had turned with the intention of taking down the lantern to examine it, when I heard his exclamation, and immediately afterwards his call for help.

I sprang towards him. He was wrestling with all his might with the brass loop of the port. It seemed to turn against his hands in spite of all his efforts. I caught up my cane, a heavy oak stick I always used to carry, and thrust it through the ring and bore on it with all my strength. But the strong wood snapped suddenly and I fell upon the couch. When I rose again the port was wide open, and the captain was standing with his back against the door, pale to the lips.

"There is something in that berth!" he cried, in a strange voice, his eyes almost starting from his head. "Hold the door, while I look—it shall not escape us, whatever it is!"

But instead of taking his place, I sprang upon the lower bed, and seized something which lay in the upper berth.

It was something ghostly, horrible beyond words, and it moved in my grip. It was like the body of a man long drowned, and yet it moved, and had the strength of ten men living; but I gripped it with all my might—the slippery, oozy, horrible thing—the dead white eyes seemed to stare at me out of the dusk; the putrid odour of rank sea-water was about it, and its shiny hair hung in foul wet curls over its dead face. I wrestled with the dead thing; it thrust itself upon me and forced me back and nearly broke my arms; it wound its corpse's arms about my neck, the living death, and overpowered me, so that I, at last, cried aloud and fell, and left my hold.

As I fell the thing sprang across me, and seemed to throw itself upon the captain. When I last saw him on his feet his face was white and his lips set. It seemed to me that he struck a violent blow at the dead being, and then he, too, fell forward upon his face, with an inarticulate cry of horror.

The thing paused an instant, seeming to hover over his prostrate body, and I could have screamed again for very fright, but I had no voice left. The thing vanished suddenly, and it seemed to my disturbed senses that it made its exit through the open port, though how that was possible, considering the smallness of the aperture, is more than anyone can tell. I lay a long time on the floor, and the captain lay beside me. At last I partially recovered my senses and moved, and instantly I knew that my arm was broken—the small bone of my left forearm near the wrist.

I got upon my feet somehow, and with my remaining hand I tried to raise the captain. He groaned and moved, and at last came to himself. He was not hurt, but he seemed badly stunned.

Well, do you want to hear any more? There is nothing more. That is the end of my story. The carpenter carried out his scheme of running half a dozen four-inch screws through the door of one hundred and five; and if ever you take a passage in the *Kamtschatka*, you may ask for a berth in that state-room. You will be told that it is engaged—yes—it is engaged by that dead thing.

I finished the trip in the surgeon's cabin. He doctored my broken arm, and advised me not to "fiddle about with ghosts and things" any more. The captain was very silent, and never sailed again in that ship, though it is still running. And I will not sail in her either. It was a very disagreeable experience, and I was very badly frightened, which is a thing I do not like. That is all. That is how I saw a ghost—if it was a ghost. It was dead, anyhow.

The Mysterious Lodger

By J. Sheridan le Fanu

PART 1

About the year 1822 I resided in a comfortable and roomy old house, the exact locality of which I need not particularise, further than to say that it was not very far from Old Brompton, in the immediate neighbourhood, or rather continuity (as even my *Connemara* readers perfectly well know), of the renowned city of London.

Though this house was roomy and comfortable, as I have said, it was not, by any means, a handsome one. It was composed of dark red brick, with small windows, and thick white sashes; a porch, too—none of your flimsy trellis-work, but a solid projection of the same vermillion masonry—surmounted by a leaded balcony, with heavy, half-rotten balustrades, darkened the hall-door with a perennial gloom. The mansion itself stood in a walled enclosure, which had, perhaps, from the date of the erection itself, been devoted to shrubs and flowers. Some of the former had grown there almost to the dignity of trees; and two dark little yews stood at each side of the porch, like swart and inauspicious dwarfs, guarding the entrance of an enchanted castle.

Not that my *domicile* in any respect deserved the comparison: it had no reputation as a haunted house; if it ever had any ghosts, nobody remembered them. Its history was not known to me: it may have witnessed plots, cabals, and forgeries, bloody suicides and cruel murders. It was certainly old enough to have become acquainted with iniquity; a small stone slab, under the balustrade, and over the arch of the porch I mentioned, had the date 1672, and a half-effaced coat of arms, which I might have deciphered any day, had I taken the trouble to get a ladder, but always put it off. All I can say for the house is, that it was well stricken in years, with a certain air of sombre comfort about it; contained a vast number of rooms and closets; and, what was of far greater importance, was got by me a dead bargain.

Its individuality attracted me. I grew fond of it for itself, and for its associations, until other associations of a hateful kind first disturbed, and then destroyed, their charm. I forgave its dull red brick, and pinched white windows, for the sake of the beloved and cheerful faces within: its ugliness was softened by its age; and its sombre evergreens, and moss-grown stone flower-pots, were relieved by the brilliant hues of a thousand gay and graceful flowers that peeped among them, or nodded over the grass.

Within that old house lay my life's treasure! I had a darling little girl of nine, and another little darling—a boy—just four years of age; and dearer, unspeakably, than either—a wife—the prettiest, gayest, best little wife in all London. When I tell you that our income was scarcely L380 a-year, you will perceive that our establishment cannot have been a magnificent one; yet, I do assure you, we were more comfortable than a great many lords, and happier, I dare say, than the whole peerage put together.

This happiness was not, however, what it ought to have been. The reader will understand at once, and save me a world of moralising circumlocution, when he learns, bluntly and nakedly, that, among all my comforts and blessings, I was an infidel.

I had not been without religious training; on the contrary, more than average pains had been bestowed upon my religious instruction from my earliest childhood. My father, a good, plain, country clergyman, had worked hard to make me as good as himself; and had succeeded, at least, in training me in godly habits. He died, however, when I was but twelve years of age; and fate had long before deprived me of the gentle care of a mother. A boarding-school, followed by a college life, where nobody having any very direct interest in realising in my behalf the ancient blessing, that in fullness of time I should "die a good old man," I was left very much to my own devices, which, in truth, were none of the best.

Among these were the study of Voltaire, Tom Paine, Hume, Shelley, and the whole school of infidels, poetical as well as prose. This pursuit, and the all but blasphemous vehemence with which I gave myself up to it, was, perhaps, partly reactionary. A somewhat injudicious austerity and precision had indissolubly associated in my childish days the ideas of restraint and gloom with religion. I bore it a grudge; and so, when I became thus early my own master, I set about paying off, after my own fashion, the old score I owed it. I was besides, like every other young infidel whom it has been my fate to meet, a conceited coxcomb.

A smattering of literature, without any real knowledge, and a great assortment of all the cut-and-dry flippancies of the school I had embraced, constituted my intellectual stock in trade. I was, like most of my school of philosophy, very proud of being an unbeliever; and fancied myself, in the complacency of my wretched ignorance, at an immeasurable elevation above the church-going, Bible-reading herd, whom I treated with a good-humoured superciliousness which I thought vastly indulgent.

My wife was an excellent little creature and truly pious. She had married me in the full confidence that my levity was merely put on, and would at once give way before the influence she hoped to exert upon my mind. Poor little thing! she deceived herself. I allowed her, indeed, to do entirely as she pleased; but for myself, I carried my infidelity to the length of an absolute superstition. I made an ostentation of it. I would rather have been in a "hell" than in a church on Sunday; and though I did not prevent my wife's instilling her own principles into the minds of our children, I, in turn, took especial care to deliver mine upon all occasions in their hearing, by which means I trusted to sow the seeds of that unprejudiced scepticism in which I prided myself, at least as early as my good little partner dropped those of her own gentle "superstition" into their infant minds. Had I had my own absurd and impious will in this matter, my children should have had absolutely no religious education whatsoever, and been left wholly unshackled to choose for themselves among all existing systems, infidelity included, precisely as chance, fancy, or interest might hereafter determine.

It is not to be supposed that such a state of things did not afford her great uneasiness. Nevertheless, we were so very fond of one another, and in our humble way enjoyed so many blessings, that we were as entirely happy as any pair can be without the holy influence of religious sympathy.

But the even flow of prosperity which had for so long gladdened my little household was not destined to last forever. It was ordained that I should experience the bitter truth of more than one of the wise man's proverbs, and first, especially, of that which declares that "he that hateth suretyship is sure." I found myself involved (as how many have been before) by a "d——d good-natured friend," for more than two hundred pounds. This agreeable intelligence was conveyed to me in an attorney's letter, which, to obviate unpleasant measures, considerately advised my paying the entire amount within just one week of the date of his pleasant epistle. Had I been called upon within that time to produce the Pitt diamond, or to make title to the Buckingham estates, the demand would have been just as easily complied with.

I have no wish to bore my reader further with this little worry—a very serious one to me, however—and it will be enough to mention, that the kindness of a friend extricated me from the clutches of the law by a timely advance, which, however, I was bound to replace within two years. To enable me to fulfil this engagement, my wife and I, after repeated consultations, resolved upon the course which resulted in the odd and unpleasant consequences which form the subject of this narrative.

We resolved to advertise for a lodger, with or without board, &c.; and by resolutely submitting, for a single year, to the economy we had prescribed for ourselves, as well as to the annoyance of a stranger's intrusion, we calculated that at the end of that term we should have liquidated our debt.

Accordingly, without losing time, we composed an advertisement in the most tempting phraseology we could devise, consistently with that economic laconism which the cost per line in the columns of the *Times* newspaper imposes upon the rhetoric of the advertising public.

Somehow we were unlucky; for although we repeated our public notification three times in the course of a fortnight, we had but two applications. The one was from a clergyman in ill health—a man of great ability and zealous piety, whom we both knew by reputation, and who has since been called to his rest. My good little wife was very anxious that we should close with his offer, which was very considerably under what we had fixed upon; and I have no doubt that she was influenced by the hope that his talents and zeal might exert a happy influence upon my stubborn and unbelieving heart. For my part, his religious character displeased me. I did not wish my children's heads to be filled with mythic dogmas—for so I judged the doctrines of our holy faith—and instinctively wished him away. I therefore declined his offer; and I have often since thought not quite so graciously as I ought to have done. The other offer—if so it can be called—was so very inadequate that we could not entertain it.

I was now beginning to grow seriously uneasy—our little project, so far from bringing in the gains on which we had calculated, had put me considerably out of pocket; for, independently of the cost of the advertisement I have mentioned, there were sundry little expenses involved in preparing for the meet reception of our expected inmate, which, under ordinary circumstances, we should not have dreamed of. Matters were in this posture, when an occurrence took place which immediately revived my flagging hopes.

As we had no superfluity of servants, our children were early obliged to acquire habits of independence; and my little girl, then just nine years of age, was frequently consigned with no other care than that of her own good sense, to the companionship of a little band of playmates, pretty similarly circumstanced, with whom it was her wont to play. Having one fine summer afternoon gone out as usual with these little companions, she did not return quite so soon as we had expected her; when she did so, she was out of breath, and excited.

"Oh, papa," she said, "I have seen such a nice old, kind gentleman, and he told me to tell you that he has a particular friend who wants a lodging in a quiet place, and that he thinks your house would suit him exactly, and ever so much more; and, look here, he gave me this."

She opened her hand, and shewed me a sovereign.

"Well, this does look promisingly," I said, my wife and I having first exchanged a smiling glance.

"And what kind of gentleman was he, dear?" inquired she. "Was he well dressed—whom was he like?"

"He was not like any one that I know," she answered; "but he had very nice new clothes on, and he was one of the fattest men I ever saw; and I am sure he is sick, for he looks very pale, and he had a crutch beside him."

"Dear me, how strange!" exclaimed my wife; though, in truth there was nothing very wonderful in the matter. "Go on, child," I said; "let us hear it all out."

"Well, papa, he had such an immense yellow waistcoat!—I never did see such a waistcoat," she resumed; "and he was sitting or leaning, I can't say which, against the bank of the green lane; I suppose to rest himself, for he seems very weak, poor gentleman!"

"And how did you happen to speak to him?" asked my wife.

"When we were passing by, none of us saw him at all but I suppose he heard them talking to me, and saying my name; for he said, 'Fanny—little Fanny—so, that's your name—come here child, I have a question to ask you.'"

"And so you went to him?" I said.

"Yes," she continued, "he beckoned to me, and I did go over to him, but not very near, for I was greatly afraid of him at first."

"Afraid! dear, and why afraid?" asked I.

"I was afraid, because he looked very old, very frightful, and as if he would hurt me."

"What was there so old and frightful about him?" I asked.

She paused and reflected a little, and then said—

"His face was very large and pale, and it was looking upwards: it seemed very angry, I thought, but maybe it was angry from pain; and sometimes one side of it used to twitch and tremble for a minute, and then to grow quite still again; and all the time he was speaking to me, he never looked at me once, but always kept his face and eyes turned upwards; but his voice was very soft, and he called me little Fanny, and gave me this pound to buy toys with; so I was not so frightened in a little time, and then he sent a long message to you, papa, and told me if I forgot it he would beat me; but I knew he was only joking, so that did not frighten me either."

"And what was the message, my girl?" I asked, patting her pretty head with my hand.

"Now, let me remember it all," she said, reflectively; "for he told it to me twice. He asked me if there was a good bedroom at the top of the house, standing by itself—and you know there is, so I told him so; it was exactly the kind of room that he described. And then he said that his friend would pay two hundred pounds a-year for that bedroom, his board and attendance; and he told me to ask you, and have your answer when he should next meet me."

"Two hundred pounds!" ejaculated my poor little wife; "why that is nearly twice as much as we expected."

"But did he say that his friend was sick, or very old; or that he had any servant to be supported also?" I asked.

"Oh! no; he told me that he was quite able to take care of himself, and that he had, I think he called it, an asthma, but nothing else the matter; and that he would give no trouble at all, and that any friend who came to see him, he would see, not in the house, but only in the garden."

"In the garden!" I echoed, laughing in spite of myself.

"Yes, indeed he said so; and he told me to say that he would pay one hundred pounds when he came here, and the next hundred in six months, and so on," continued she.

"Oh, ho! half-yearly in advance—better and better," said I.

"And he bid me say, too, if you should ask about his character, that he is just as good as the master of the house himself," she added; "and when he said that, he laughed a little."

"Why, if he gives us a hundred pounds in advance," I answered, turning to my wife, "we are safe enough; for he will not find half that value in plate and jewels in the entire household, if he is disposed to rob us. So I see no reason against closing with the offer, should it be seriously meant—do you, dear?"

"Quite the contrary, love," said she. "I think it most desirable—indeed, most *providential.*"

"Providential! my dear little bigot!" I repeated, with a smile. "Well, be it so. I call it *lucky* merely; but, perhaps, you are happier in your faith, than I in my philosophy. Yes, you are *grateful* for the chance that I only rejoice at. You receive it as a proof of a divine and tender love—I as an accident. Delusions are often more elevating than truth."

And so saying, I kissed away the saddened cloud that for a moment overcast her face.

"Papa, he bid me be sure to have an answer for him when we meet again," resumed the child. "What shall I say to him when he asks me?"

"Say that we agree to his proposal, my dear—or stay," I said, addressing my wife, "may it not be prudent to reduce what the child says to writing, and accept the offer so? This will prevent misunderstanding, as she may possibly have made some mistake."

My wife agreed, and I wrote a brief note, stating that I was willing to receive an inmate upon the terms recounted by little Fanny, and which I distinctly specified, so that no mistake could possibly arise owing to the vagueness of what lawyers term a parole agreement. This important memorandum I placed in the hands of my little girl, who was to deliver it whenever the old gentleman in the yellow waistcoat should chance to meet her. And all these arrangements completed, I awaited the issue of the affair with as much patience as I could affect. Meanwhile, my wife and I talked it over incessantly; and she, good little soul, almost wore herself to death in settling and unsettling the furniture and decorations of our expected inmate's apartments.

Days passed away—days of hopes deferred, tedious and anxious. We were beginning to despond again, when one morning our little girl ran into the breakfast-parlour, more excited even than she had been before, and fresh from a new interview with the gentleman in the yellow waistcoat. She had encountered him suddenly, pretty nearly where she had met him before, and the result was, that he had read the little note I have mentioned, and desired the child to inform me that his friend, *Mr. Smith*, would take possession of the apartments I proposed setting, on the terms agreed between us, that very evening.

"This evening!" exclaimed my wife and I simultaneously—*I* full of the idea of making a first instalment on the day following; *she*, of the hundred-and-one preparations which still remained to be completed.

"And so Smith is his name! Well, that does not tell us much," said I; "but where did you meet your friend on this occasion, and how long is it since?"

"Near the corner of the wall-flower lane (so we indicated one which abounded in these fragrant plants); he was leaning with his back against the old tree you cut my name on, and his crutch was under his arm."

"But how long ago?" I urged.

"Only this moment; I ran home as fast as I could," she replied.

"Why, you little blockhead, you should have told me that at first," I cried, snatching up my hat, and darting away in pursuit of the yellow waistcoat, whose acquaintance I not unnaturally coveted, inasmuch as a man who, for the first time, admits a stranger into his house, on the footing of permanent residence, desires generally to know a little more about him than that his name is Smith.

The place indicated was only, as we say, a step away; and as yellow waistcoat was fat, and used a crutch, I calculated on easily overtaking him. I was, however, disappointed; crutch, waistcoat, and all had disappeared. I climbed to the top of the wall, and from this commanding point of view made a sweeping observation—but in vain. I returned home, cursing my ill-luck, the child's dullness, and the fat old fellow's activity.

I need hardly say that Mr. Smith, in all his aspects, moral, social, physical, and monetary, formed a fruitful and interesting topic of speculation during dinner. How many phantom Smiths, short and long, stout and lean, ill-tempered and well-tempered— rich, respectable, or highly dangerous merchants, spies, forgers, nabobs, swindlers, danced before us, in the endless mazes of fanciful conjecture, during that anxious *tete-a-tete*, which was probably to be interrupted by the arrival of the gentleman himself.

My wife and I puzzled over the problem as people would over the possible *denouement* of a French novel; and at last, by mutual consent, we came to the conclusion that Smith could, and would turn out to be no other than the good-natured valetudinarian in the yellow waistcoat himself, a humorist, as was evident enough, and a millionaire, as we unhesitatingly pronounced, who had no immediate relatives, and as I hoped, and my wife "was certain," taken a decided fancy to our little Fanny; I patted the child's head with something akin to pride, as I thought of the magnificent, though remote possibilities, in store for her.

Meanwhile, hour after hour stole away. It was a beautiful autumn evening, and the amber lustre of the declining sun fell softly upon the yews and flowers, and gave an air, half melancholy, half cheerful, to the dark-red brick piers surmounted with their cracked and grass-grown stone urns, and furnished with the light foliage of untended creeping plants. Down the short broad walk leading to this sombre entrance, my eye constantly wandered; but no impatient rattle on the latch, no battering at the gate, indicated the presence of a visited, and the lazy bell hung dumbly among the honey-suckles.

"When will he come? Yellow waistcoat promised *this evening*! It has been evening a good hour and a half, and yet he is not here. When will he come? It will soon be dark—the evening will have passed—will he come at all?"

Such were the uneasy speculations which began to trouble us. Redder and duskier grew the light of the setting sun, till it saddened into the mists of night. Twilight came, and then darkness, and still no arrival, no summons at the gate. I would not admit even to my wife the excess of my own impatience. I could, however, stand it no longer; so I took my hat and walked to the gate, where I stood by the side of the public road, watching every vehicle and person that approached, in a fever of expectation. Even these, however, began to fail me, and the road grew comparatively quiet and deserted.

Having kept guard like a sentinel for more than half an hour, I returned in no very good humour, with the punctuality of an expected inmate—ordered the servant to draw the curtains and secure the hall-door; and so my wife and I sate down to our disconsolate cup of tea. It must have been about ten o'clock, and we were both sitting silently—she working, I looking moodily into a paper—and neither of us any longer entertaining a hope that anything but disappointment would come of the matter, when a sudden tapping, very loud and sustained, upon the window pane, startled us both in an instant from our reveries.

I am not sure whether I mentioned before that the sitting-room we occupied was upon the ground-floor, and the sward came close under the window. I drew the curtains, and opened the shutters with a revived hope; and looking out, saw a very tall thin figure, a good deal wrapped up, standing about a yard before me, and motioning with head and hand impatiently towards the hall-door. Though the night was clear, there was no moon, and therefore I could see no more than the black outline, like that of an *ombre chinoise* figure, signing to me with mop and moe. In a moment I was at the hall-door, candle in hand; the stranger stept in—his long fingers clutched in the handle of a valise, and a bag which trailed upon the ground behind him.

The light fell full upon him. He wore a long, ill-made, black *surtout*, buttoned across, and which wrinkled and bagged about his lank figure; his hat was none of the best, and rather broad in the brim; a sort of white woollen muffler enveloped the lower part of his face; a pair of prominent green goggles, fenced round with leather, completely concealed his eyes; and nothing of the genuine man, but a little bit of yellow forehead, and a small transverse segment of equally yellow cheek and nose, encountered the curious gaze of your humble servant.

"You are—I suppose"—I began; for I really was a little doubtful about my man.

"Mr. Smith—the same; be good enough to show me to my bedchamber," interrupted the stranger, brusquely, and in a tone which, spite of the muffler that enveloped his mouth, was sharp and grating enough.

"Ha!—Mr. Smith—so I supposed. I hope you may find everything as comfortable as we desire to make it—"

I was about making a speech, but was cut short by a slight bow, and a decisive gesture of the hand in the direction of the staircase. It was plain that the stranger hated ceremony.

Together, accordingly, we mounted the staircase; he still pulling his luggage after him, and striding lightly up without articulating a word; and on reaching his bedroom, he immediately removed his hat, showing a sinister, black scratch-wig underneath, and then began unrolling the mighty woollen wrapping of his mouth and chin.

"Come," thought I, "we *shall* see something of your face after all."

This something, however, proved to be very little; for under his muffler was a loose cravat, which stood up in front of his chin and upon his mouth, he wore a respirator—an instrument which I had never seen before, and of the use of which I was wholly ignorant.

There was something so excessively odd in the effect of this piece of unknown mechanism upon his mouth, surmounted by the huge goggles which encased his eyes, that I believe I should have laughed outright, were it not for a certain unpleasant and peculiar impressiveness in the *tout ensemble* of the narrow-chested, long-limbed, and cadaverous figure in black. As it was, we stood looking at one another in silence for several seconds.

"Thank you, sir," at last he said, abruptly. "I shan't want anything whatever tonight; if you can only spare me this candle."

I assented; and, becoming more communicative, he added—

"I am, though an invalid, an independent sort of fellow enough. I am a bit of a philosopher; I am my own servant, and, I hope, my own master, too. I rely upon myself in matters of the body and of the mind. I place valets and priests in the same category—fellows who live by our laziness, intellectual or corporeal. I am a Voltaire, without his luxuries—a Robinson Crusoe, without his Bible—an anchorite, without a superstition—in short, my indulgence is asceticism, and my faith infidelity. Therefore, I shan't disturb your servants much with my bell, nor yourselves with my psalmody. You have got a rational lodger, who knows how to attend upon himself."

During this singular address he was drawing off his ill-fitting black gloves, and when he had done so, a bank-note, which had been slipped underneath for safety, remained in his hand.

"Punctuality, sir, is one of my poor pleasures," he said; "will you allow me to enjoy it now? Tomorrow you may acknowledge this; I should not rest were you to decline it."

He extended his bony and discoloured fingers, and placed the note in my hand. Oh, Fortune and Plutus! It was a *L*100 bank-note.

"Pray, not one word, my dear sir," he continued, unbending still further; "it is simply done pursuant to agreement. We shall know one another better, I hope, in a little time; you will find me always equally punctual. At present pray give yourself no further trouble; I require nothing more. Good night."

I returned the valediction, closed his door, and groped my way down the stairs. It was not until I had nearly reached the hall, that I recollected that I had omitted to ask our new inmate at what hour he would desire to be called in the morning, and so I groped my way back again. As I reached the lobby on which his chamber opened, I perceived a long line of light issuing from the partially-opened door, within which stood Mr. Smith, the same odd figure I had just left; while along the boards was creeping towards him across the lobby, a great, big-headed, buff-coloured cat. I had never seen this ugly animal before; and it had reached the threshold of his door, arching its back, and rubbing itself on the post, before either appeared conscious of my approach, when, with an angry growl, it sprang into the stranger's room.

"What do you want?" he demanded, sharply, standing in the doorway.

I explained my errand.

"I shall call myself," was his sole reply; and he shut the door with a crash that indicated no very pleasurable emotions.

I cared very little about my lodger's temper. The stealthy rustle of his banknote in my waistcoat pocket was music enough to sweeten the harshest tones of his voice, and to keep alive a cheerful good humour in my heart; and although there was, indisputably, something queer about him, I was, on the whole, very well pleased with my bargain.

The next day our new inmate did not ring his bell until noon. As soon as he had had some breakfast, of which he very sparingly partook, he told the servant that, for the future, he desired that a certain quantity of milk and bread might be left outside his door; and this being done, he would dispense with regular meals. He desired, too, that, on my return, I should be acquainted that he wished to see me in his own room at about nine o'clock; and, meanwhile, he directed that he should be left undisturbed. I found my little wife full of astonishment at Mr. Smith's strange frugality and seclusion, and very curious to learn the object of the interview he had desired with me. At nine o'clock I repaired to his room.

I found him in precisely the costume in which I had left him—the same green goggles—the same muffling of the mouth, except that being now no more than a broadly-folded black silk handkerchief, very loose, and covering even the lower part of the nose, it was obviously intended for the sole purpose of concealment. It was plain I was not to see more of his features than he had chosen to disclose at our first interview. The effect was as if the lower part of his face had some hideous wound or sore. He closed the door with his own hand on my entrance, nodded slightly, and took his seat. I expected him to begin, but he was so long silent that I was at last constrained to address him.

I said, for want of something more to the purpose, that I hoped he had not been tormented by the strange cat the night before.

"What cat?" he asked, abruptly; "what the plague do you mean?"

"Why, I certainly did see a cat go into your room last night," I resumed.

"Hey, and what if you did—though I fancy you dreamed it-I'm not afraid of a cat; are you?" he interrupted, tartly.

At this moment there came a low growling mew from the closet which opened from the room in which we sat.

"Talk of the devil," said I, pointing towards the closet. My companion, without any exact change of expression, looked, I thought, somehow still more sinister and lowering; and I felt for a moment a sort of superstitious misgiving, which made the rest of the sentence die away on my lips.

Perhaps Mr. Smith perceived this, for he said, in a tone calculated to reassure me—

"Well, sir, I think I am bound to tell you that I like my apartments very well; they suit me, and I shall probably be your tenant for much longer than at first you anticipated."

I expressed my gratification.

He then began to talk, something in the strain in which he had spoken of his own peculiarities of habit and thinking upon the previous evening. He disposed of all classes and denominations of superstition with an easy sarcastic slang, which for me was so captivating, that I soon lost all reserve, and found myself listening and suggesting by turns—acquiescent and pleased-sometimes hazarding dissent; but whenever I did, foiled and floored by a few pointed satirical sentences, whose sophistry, for such I must now believe it, confounded me with a rapidity which, were it not for the admiration with which he had insensibly inspired me, would have piqued and irritated my vanity not a little.

While this was going on, from time to time the mewing and growling of a cat within the closet became more and more audible. At last these sounds became so loud, accompanied by scratching at the door, that I paused in the midst of a sentence, and observed—

"There certainly is a cat shut up in the closet?"

"Is there?" he ejaculated, in a surprised tone; "nay, I do not hear it."

He rose abruptly and approached the door; his back was towards me, but I observed he raised the goggles which usually covered his eyes, and looked steadfastly at the closet door. The angry sounds all died away into a low, protracted growl, which again subsided into silence. He continued in the same attitude for some moments, and then returned.

"I do not hear it," he said, as he resumed his place, and taking a book from his capacious pocket, asked me if I had seen it before? I never had, and this surprised me, for I had flattered myself that I knew, at least by name, every work published in England during the last fifty years in favour of that philosophy in which we both delighted. The book, moreover, was an odd one, as both its title and table of contents demonstrated.

While we were discoursing upon these subjects, I became more and more distinctly conscious of a new class of sounds proceeding from the same closet. I plainly heard a measured and heavy tread, accompanied by the tapping of some hard and heavy substance like the end of a staff, pass up and down the floor—first, as it seemed, stealthily, and then more and more unconcealedly. I began to feel very uncomfortable and suspicious. As the noise proceeded, and became more and more unequivocal, Mr. Smith abruptly rose, opened the closet door, just enough to admit his own lath-like person, and steal within the threshold for some seconds. What he did I could not see—I felt conscious he had an associate concealed there; and though my eyes remained fixed on the book, I could not avoid listening for some audible words, or signal of caution. I heard, however, nothing of the kind. Mr. Smith turned back—walked a step or two towards me, and said—

"I fancied I heard a sound from that closet, but there is nothing—nothing—nothing whatever; bring the candle, let us both look."

I obeyed with some little trepidation, for I fully anticipated that I should detect the intruder, of whose presence my own ears had given me, for nearly half an hour, the most unequivocal proofs. We entered the closet together; it contained but a few chairs and a small spider table. At the far end of the room there was a sort of grey woollen cloth upon the floor, and a bundle of something underneath it. I looked jealously at it, and half thought I could trace the outline of a human figure; but, if so, it was perfectly motionless.

"Some of my poor wardrobe," he muttered, as he pointed his lean finger in the direction. "It did not sound like a cat, did it—hey—did it?" he muttered; and without attending to my answer, he went about the apartment, clapping his hands, and crying, "Hish—hish—hish!"

The game, however, whatever it was, did not start. As I entered I had seen, however, a large crutch reposing against the wall in the corner opposite to the door. This was the only article in the room, except that I have mentioned, with which I was not familiar. With the exception of our two selves, there was not a living creature to be seen there; no shadow but ours upon the bare walls; no feet but our own upon the comfortless floor.

I had never before felt so strange and unpleasant a sensation.

"There is nothing unusual in the room but that crutch," I said.

"What crutch, you dolt? I see no crutch," he ejaculated, in a tone of sudden but suppressed fury.

"Why, *that* crutch," I answered (for somehow I neither felt nor resented his rudeness), turning and pointing to the spot where I had seen it. It was gone!—it was neither there nor anywhere else. It must have been an illusion—rather an odd one, to be sure. And yet I could at this moment, with a safe conscience, *swear* that I never saw an object more distinctly than I had seen it but a second before.

My companion was muttering fast to himself as we withdrew; his presence rather scared than reassured me; and I felt something almost amounting to horror, as, holding the candle above his cadaverous and sable figure, he stood at his threshold, while I descended the stairs, and said, in a sort of whisper—

"Why, but that I am, like yourself, a philosopher, I should say that your house is—is—a—ha! ha! ha!—HAUNTED!"

"You look very pale, my love," said my wife, as I entered the drawing-room, where she had been long awaiting my return. "Nothing unpleasant has happened?"

"Nothing, nothing, I assure you. Pale!—*do* I look pale?" I answered. "We are excellent friends, I assure you. So far from having had the smallest disagreement, there is every prospect of our agreeing but too well, as you will say; for I find that he holds all my opinions upon speculative subjects. We have had a great deal of conversation this evening, I assure you; and I never met, I think, so scholarlike and able a man."

"I am sorry for it, dearest," she said, sadly. "The greater his talents, if such be his opinions, the more dangerous a companion is he."

We turned, however, to more cheerful topics, and it was late before we retired to rest. I believe it was pride—perhaps only vanity—but, at all events, some obstructive and stubborn instinct of my nature, which I could not overcome—that prevented my telling my wife the odd occurrences which had disturbed my visit to our guest. I was unable or ashamed to confess that so slight a matter had disturbed me; and, above all, that any accident could possibly have clouded, even for a moment, the frosty clearness of my pure and lofty scepticism with the shadows of superstition.

Almost every day seemed to develop some new eccentricity of our strange guest. His dietary consisted, without any variety or relief, of the monotonous bread and milk with which he started; his bed had not been made for nearly a week; nobody had been admitted into his room since my visit, just described; and he never ventured down stairs, or out of doors, until after nightfall, when he used sometimes to glide swiftly round our little enclosed shrubbery, and at others stand quite motionless, composed, as if in an attitude of deep attention. After employing about an hour in this way, he would return, and steal up stairs to his room, when he would shut himself up, and not be seen again until the next night—or, it might be, the night after that—when, perhaps, he would repeat his odd excursion.

Strange as his habits were, their eccentricity was all upon the side least troublesome to us. He required literally no attendance; and as to his occasional night ramble, even *it* caused not the slightest disturbance of our routine hour for securing the house and locking up the hall-door for the night, inasmuch as he had invariably retired before that hour arrived.

All this stimulated curiosity, and, in no small degree, that of my wife, who, notwithstanding her vigilance and her anxiety to see our strange inmate, had been hitherto foiled by a series of cross accidents. We were sitting together somewhere about ten o'clock at night, when there came a tap at the room-door. We had just been discussing the unaccountable Smith; and I felt a sheepish consciousness that he might be himself at the door, and have possibly even overheard our speculation—some of them anything but complimentary, respecting himself.

"Come in," cried, I, with an effort; and the tall form of our lodger glided into the room. My wife was positively frightened, and stood looking at him, as he advanced, with a stare of manifest apprehension, and even recoiled mechanically, and caught my hand.

Sensitiveness, however, was not his fault: he made a kind of stiff nod as I mumbled an introduction; and seating himself unasked, began at once to chat in that odd, off-hand, and sneering style, in which he excelled, and which had, as he wielded it, a sort of fascination of which I can pretend to convey no idea.

My wife's alarm subsided, and although she still manifestly felt some sort of misgiving about our visitor, she yet listened to his conversation, and, spite of herself, soon began to enjoy it. He stayed for nearly half an hour. But although he glanced at a great variety of topics, he did not approach the subject of religion. As soon as he was gone, my wife delivered judgment upon him in form. She admitted he was agreeable; but then he was such an unnatural, awful-looking object: there was, besides, something indescribably frightful, she thought, in his manner—the very tone of his voice was strange and hateful; and, on the whole, she felt unutterably relieved at his departure.

A few days after, on my return, I found my poor little wife agitated and dispirited. Mr. Smith had paid her a visit, and brought with him a book, which he stated he had been reading, and which contained some references to the Bible which he begged of her to explain in that profounder and less obvious sense in which they had been cited. This she had endeavoured to do; and affecting to be much gratified by her satisfactory exposition, he had requested her to reconcile some discrepancies which he said had often troubled him when reading the Scriptures. Some of them were quite new to my good little wife; they startled and even horrified her.

He pursued this theme, still pretending only to seek for information to quiet his own doubts, while in reality he was sowing in her mind the seeds of the first perturbations that had ever troubled the sources of her peace. He had been with her, she thought, no more than a quarter of an hour; but he had contrived to leave her abundant topics on which to ruminate for days. I found her shocked and horrified at the doubts which this potent Magus had summoned from the pit—doubts which she knew not how to combat, and from the torment of which she could not escape.

"He has made me very miserable with his deceitful questions.

I never thought of them before; and, merciful Heaven! I cannot answer them! What am I to do? My serenity is gone; I shall never be happy again."

In truth, she was so very miserable, and, as it seemed to me, so disproportionately excited, that, inconsistent in me as the task would have been, I would gladly have explained away her difficulties, and restored to her mind its wonted confidence and serenity, had I possessed sufficient knowledge for the purpose. I really pitied her, and heartily wished Mr. Smith, for the nonce, at the devil.

I observed after this that my wife's spirits appeared permanently affected. There was a constantly-recurring anxiety, and I thought something was lying still more heavily at her heart than the uncertainties inspired by our lodger.

One evening, as we two were sitting together, after a long silence, she suddenly laid her hand upon my arm, and said—

"Oh, Richard, my darling! would to God you could pray for me!"

There was something so agitated, and even terrified, in her manner, that I was absolutely startled. I urged her to disclose whatever preyed upon her mind.

"You can't sympathise with me—you can't help me—you can scarcely compassionate me in my misery! Oh, dearest Richard! Some evil influence has been gaining upon my heart, dulling and destroying my convictions, killing all my holy affections, and—and absolutely transforming me. I look inward upon myself with amazement, with terror—with—oh, God!—with actual despair!"

Saying this, she threw herself on her knees, and wept an agonised flood of tears, with her head reposing in my lap.

Poor little thing, my heart bled for her! But what could I do or say?

All I could suggest was what I really thought, that she was unwell—hysterical—and needed to take better care of her precious self; that her change of feeling was fancied, not real; and that a few days would restore her to her old health and former spirits and serenity.

"And sometimes," she resumed, after I had ended a consolatory discussion, which it was but too manifest had fallen unprofitably upon her ear, "such dreadful, impious thoughts come into my mind, whether I choose it or not; they come, and stay, and return, strive as I may; and I can't pray against them. They are forced upon me with the strength of an independent will; and oh!—horrible—frightful—they blaspheme the character of God himself. They upbraid the Almighty upon his throne, and I can't pray against them; there is something in me now that resists prayer."

There was such a real and fearful anguish in the agitation of my gentle companion, that it shook my very soul within me, even while I was affecting to make light of her confessions. I had never before witnessed a struggle at all like this, and I was awe-struck at the spectacle.

At length she became comparatively calm. I did gradually succeed, though very imperfectly, in reassuring her. She strove hard against her depression, and recovered a little of her wonted cheerfulness.

After a while, however, the cloud returned. She grew sad and earnest, though no longer excited; and entreated, or rather implored, of me to grant her one special favour, and this was, to avoid the society of our lodger.

"I never," she said, "could understand till now the instinctive dread with which poor Margaret, in *Faust*, shrinks from the hateful presence of Mephistopheles. I now feel it in myself. The dislike and suspicion I first felt for that man—Smith, or whatever else he may call himself—has grown into literal detestation and terror. I hate him—I am afraid of him—I never knew what anguish of mind was until he entered our doors; and would to God—would to God he were gone."

I reasoned with her—kissed her—laughed at her; but could not dissipate, in the least degree, the intense and preternatural horror with which she had grown to regard the poor philosophic invalid, who was probably, at that moment, poring over some metaphysical book in his solitary bedchamber.

The circumstance I am about to mention will give you some notion of the extreme to which these excited feelings had worked upon her nerves. I was that night suddenly awakened by a piercing scream—I started upright in the bed, and saw my wife standing at the bedside, white as ashes with terror. It was some seconds, so startled was I, before I could find words to ask her the cause of her affright. She caught my wrist in her icy grasp, and climbed, trembling violently, into bed. Notwithstanding my repeated entreaties, she continued for a long time stupified and dumb.

At length, however, she told me, that having lain awake for a long time, she felt, on a sudden, that she could pray, and lighting the candle, she had stolen from beside me, and kneeled down for the purpose. She had, however, scarcely assumed the attitude of prayer, when somebody, she said, clutched her arm violently near the wrist, and she heard, at the same instant, some blasphemous menace, the import of which escaped her the moment it was spoken, muttered close in her ear. This terrifying interruption was the cause of the scream which had awakened me; and the condition in which she continued during the remainder of the night confirmed me more than ever in the conviction, that she was suffering under some morbid action of the nervous system.

After this event, which *I* had no hesitation in attributing to fancy, she became literally afraid to pray, and her misery and despondency increased proportionately.

It was shortly after this that an unusual pressure of business called me into town one evening after office hours. I had left my dear little wife tolerably well, and little Fanny was to be her companion until I returned. She and her little companion occupied the same room in which we sat on the memorable evening which witnessed the arrival of our eccentric guest. Though usually a lively child, it most provokingly happened upon this night that Fanny was heavy and drowsy to excess. Her mamma would have sent her to bed, but that she now literally feared to be left alone; although, however, she could not so far overcome her horror of solitude as to do this, she yet would not persist in combating the poor child's sleepiness.

Accordingly, little Fanny was soon locked in a sound sleep, while her mamma quietly pursued her work beside her. They had been perhaps some ten minutes thus circumstanced, when my wife heard the window softly raised from without—a bony hand parted the curtains, and Mr. Smith leaned into the room.

She was so utterly overpowered at sight of this apparition, that even had it, as she expected, climbed into the room, she told me she could not have uttered a sound, or stirred from the spot where she sate transfixed and petrified.

"Ha, ha!" he said gently, "I hope you'll excuse this, I must admit, very odd intrusion; but I knew I should find you here, and could not resist the opportunity of raising the window just for a moment, to look in upon a little family picture, and say a word to yourself. I understand that you are troubled, because for some cause you cannot say your prayers—because what you call your 'faith' is, so to speak, dead and gone, and also because what *you* consider bad thoughts are constantly recurring to your mind. Now, all that is very silly. If it is really impossible for you to believe and to pray, what are you to infer from that? It is perfectly plain your Christian system can't be a true one—faith and *prayer* it everywhere represents as the conditions of grace, acceptance, and salvation; and yet your Creator will not *permit* you either to believe or pray.

"The Christian system is, forsooth, a *free* gift, and yet he who formed *you* and *it*, makes it absolutely impossible for you to accept it. *Is* it, I ask you, from your own experience—is it a free gift? And if your own experience, in which you can't be mistaken, gives its pretensions the lie, why, in the name of common sense, will you persist in believing it? I say it is downright blasphemy to think it has emanated from the Good Spirit—assuming that there is one. It tells you that you must be tormented hereafter in a way only to be made intelligible by the image of eternal fires—pretty strong, we must all allow—unless you comply with certain conditions, which it pretends are so easy that it is a positive pleasure to embrace and perform them; and yet, for the life of you, you can't—physically *can't*—do either. Is this truth and mercy?—or is it swindling and cruelty? Is it the part of the Redeemer, or that of the tyrant, deceiver, and tormentor?"

Up to that moment, my wife had sate breathless and motionless, listening, in the catalepsy of nightmare, to a sort of echo of the vile and impious reasoning which had haunted her for so long. At the last words of the sentence his voice became harsh and thrilling; and his whole manner bespoke a sort of crouching and terrific hatred, the like of which she could not have conceived.

Whatever may have been the cause, she was on a sudden disenchanted. She started to her feet; and, freezing with horror though she was, in a shrill cry of agony commanded him, in the name of God, to depart from her. His whole frame seemed to darken; he drew back silently; the curtains dropped into their places, the window was let down again as stealthily as it had just been raised; and my wife found herself alone in the chamber with our little child, who had been startled from her sleep by her mother's cry of anguish, and with the fearful words, "tempter," "destroyer," "devil," still ringing in her ears, was weeping bitterly, and holding her terrified mother's hand.

There is nothing, I believe, more infectious than that species of nervousness which shows itself in superstitious fears. I began—although I could not bring myself to admit anything the least like it—to partake insensibly, but strongly of the peculiar feelings with which my wife, and indeed my whole household, already regarded the lodger up stairs. The fact was, beside, that the state of my poor wife's mind began to make me seriously uneasy; and, although I was fully sensible of the pecuniary and other advantages attendant upon his stay, they were yet far from outweighing the constant gloom and frequent misery in which the protracted sojourn was involving my once cheerful house.

I resolved, therefore, at whatever monetary sacrifice, to put an end to these commotions; and, after several debates with my wife, in which the subject was, as usual, turned in all its possible and impossible bearings, we agreed that, deducting a fair proportion for his five weeks' sojourn, I should return the remainder of his L100, and request immediate possession of his apartments. Like a man suddenly relieved of an insufferable load, and breathing freely once more, I instantly prepared to carry into effect the result of our deliberations.

In pursuance of this resolution, I waited upon Mr. Smith. This time my call was made in the morning, somewhere about nine o'clock. He received me at his door, standing as usual in the stealthy opening which barely admitted his lank person. There he stood, fully equipped with goggles and respirator, and swathed, rather than dressed, in his puckered black garments.

As he did not seem disposed to invite me into his apartment, although I had announced my visit as one of business, I was obliged to open my errand where I stood; and after a great deal of fumbling and muttering, I contrived to place before him distinctly the resolution to which I had come.

"But I can't think of taking back any portion of the sum I have paid you," said he, with a cool, dry emphasis.

"Your reluctance to do so, Mr. Smith, is most handsome, and I assure you, appreciated," I replied. "It is very generous; but, at the same time, it is quite impossible for me to accept what I have no right to take, and I must beg of you not to mention that part of the subject again."

"And why should *I* take it?" demanded Mr. Smith.

"Because you have paid this hundred pounds for six months, and you are leaving me with nearly five months of the term still unexpired," I replied. "I expect to receive fair play myself, and always give it."

"But who on earth said that I was going away so soon?" pursued Mr. Smith, in the same dry, sarcastic key. "*I* have not said so—because I really don't intend it; I mean to stay here to the last day of the six months for which I have paid you. I have no notion of vacating my hired lodgings, simply because you say, *go*. I shan't quarrel with you—I never quarrel with anybody.

I'm as much your friend as ever; but, without the least wish to disoblige, I can't do this, positively I cannot. Is there anything else?"

I had not anticipated in the least the difficulty which thus encountered and upset our plans. I had so set my heart upon effecting the immediate retirement of our inauspicious inmate, that the disappointment literally stunned me for a moment. I, however, returned to the charge: I urged, and prayed, and almost besought him to give up his apartments, and to leave us. I offered to repay every farthing of the sum he had paid me—reserving nothing on account of the time he had already been with us. I suggested all the disadvantages of the house. I shifted my ground, and told him that my wife wanted the rooms; I pressed his gallantry—his good nature—his economy; in short, I assailed him upon every point—but in vain, he did not even take the trouble of repeating what he had said before—he neither relented, nor showed the least irritation, but simply said—

"I can't do this; here I am, and here I stay until the half-year has expired. You wanted a lodger, and you have got one—the quietest, least troublesome, least expensive person you could have; and though your house, servants, and furniture are none of the best, I don't care for that. I pursue my own poor business and enjoyments here entirely to my satisfaction."

Having thus spoken, he gave me a sort of nod, and closed the door.

So, instead of getting rid of him the next day, as we had hoped, we had nearly five months more of his company in expectancy; I hated, and my wife dreaded the prospect. She was literally miserable and panic-struck at her disappointment—and grew so nervous and wretched that I made up my mind to look out for lodgings for her and the children (subversive of all our schemes of retrenchment as such a step would be), and surrendering the house absolutely to Mr. Smith and the servants during the remainder of his term.

Circumstances, however, occurred to prevent our putting this plan in execution. My wife, meanwhile, was, if possible, more depressed and nervous every day. The servants seemed to sympathise in the dread and gloom which involved ourselves; the very children grew timid and spiritless, without knowing why—and the entire house was pervaded with an atmosphere of uncertainty and fear. A poorhouse or a dungeon would have been cheerful, compared with a dwelling haunted unceasingly with unearthly suspicions and alarms. I would have made any sacrifice short of ruin, to emancipate our household from the odious mental and moral thraldom which was invisibly established over us—overcasting us with strange anxieties and an undefined terror.

About this time my wife had a dream which troubled her much, although she could not explain its supposed significance satisfactorily by any of the ordinary rules of interpretation in such matters. The vision was as follows.

She dreamed that we were busily employed in carrying out our scheme of removal, and that I came into the parlour where she was making some arrangements, and, with rather an agitated manner, told her that the carriage had come for the children. She thought she went out to the hall, in consequence, holding little Fanny by one hand, and the boy—or, as we still called him, "baby,"—by the other, and feeling, as she did so, an unaccountable gloom, almost amounting to terror, steal over her. The children, too, seemed, she thought, frightened, and disposed to cry.

So close to the hall-door as to exclude the light, stood some kind of vehicle, of which she could see nothing but that its door was wide open, and the interior involved in total darkness. The children, she thought, shrunk back in great trepidation, and she addressed herself to induce them, by persuasion, to enter, telling them that they were only "going to their new home." So, in a while, little Fanny approached it; but, at the same instant, some person came swiftly up from behind, and, raising the little boy in his hands, said fiercely, "No, the baby first"; and placed him in the carriage. This person was our lodger, Mr. Smith, and was gone as soon as seen. My wife, even in her dream, could not act or speak; but as the child was lifted into the carriage-door, a man, whose face was full of beautiful tenderness and compassion, leaned forward from the carriage and received the little child, which, stretching his arms to the stranger, looked back with a strange smile upon his mother.

"He is safe with me, and I will deliver him to you when you come."

These words the man spoke, looking upon her, as he received him, and immediately the carriage-door shut, and the noise of its closing wakened my wife from her nightmare.

This dream troubled her very much, and even haunted my mind unpleasantly too. We agreed, however, not to speak of it to anybody, not to divulge any of our misgivings respecting the stranger. We were anxious that neither the children nor the servants should catch the contagion of those fears which had seized upon my poor little wife, and, if truth were spoken, upon myself in some degree also. But this precaution was, I believe, needless, for, as I said before, everybody under the same roof with Mr. Smith was, to a certain extent, affected with the same nervous gloom and apprehension.

And now commences a melancholy chapter in my life. My poor little Fanny was attacked with a cough which soon grew very violent, and after a time degenerated into a sharp attack of inflammation. We were seriously alarmed for her life, and nothing that care and medicine could effect was spared to save it. Her mother was indefatigable, and scarcely left her night or day; and, indeed, for some time, we all but despaired of her recovery.

One night, when she was at the worst, her poor mother, who had sat for many a melancholy hour listening, by her bedside, to those plaintive incoherences of delirium and moanings of fever, which have harrowed so many a fond heart, gained gradually from her very despair the courage which she had so long wanted, and knelt down at the side of her sick darling's bed to pray for her deliverance.

With clasped hands, in an agony of supplication, she prayed that God would, in his mercy, spare her little child—that, justly as she herself deserved the sorest chastisement his hand could inflict, he would yet deal patiently and tenderly with her in this one thing. She poured out her sorrows before the mercy-seat—she opened her heart, and declared her only hope to be in his pity; without which, she felt that her darling would only leave the bed where she was lying for her grave.

Exactly as she came to this part of her supplication, the child, who had grown, as it seemed, more and more restless, and moaned and muttered with increasing pain and irritation, on a sudden started upright in her bed, and, in a thrilling voice, cried—

"No! no!—the baby first."

The mysterious sentence which had secretly tormented her for so long, thus piercingly uttered by this delirious, and, per-haps, dying child, with what seemed a preternatural earnestness and strength, arrested her devotions, and froze her with a feeling akin to terror.

"Hush, hush, my darling!" said the poor mother, almost wildly, as she clasped the attenuated frame of the sick child in her arms; "hush, my darling; don't cry out so loudly—there—there—my own love."

The child did not appear to see or hear her, but sate up still with feverish cheeks, and bright unsteady eyes, while her dry lips were muttering inaudible words.

"Lie down, my sweet child—lie down, for your own moth-er," she said; "if you tire yourself, you can't grow well, and your poor mother will lose you."

At these words, the child suddenly cried out again, in pre-cisely the same loud, strong voice—"No! no! the baby first, the baby first"—and immediately afterwards lay down, and fell, for the first time since her illness into a tranquil sleep.

My good little wife sate, crying bitterly by her bedside. The child was better—*that* was, indeed, delightful. But then there was an omen in the words, thus echoed from her dream, which she dared not trust herself to interpret, and which yet had seized, with a grasp of iron, upon every fibre of her brain.

"Oh, Richard," she cried, as she threw her arms about my

neck, "I am terrified at this horrible menace from the unseen world. Oh! poor, darling little baby, I shall lose you—I am sure I shall lose you. Comfort me, darling, and say he is not to die."

And so I did; and tasked all my powers of argument and persuasion to convince her how unsubstantial was the ground of her anxiety. The little boy was perfectly well, and, even were he to die before his sister that event might not occur for seventy years to come. I could not, however, conceal from myself that there was something odd and unpleasant in the coincidence; and my poor wife had grown so nervous and excitable, that a much less ominous conjecture would have sufficed to alarm her.

Meanwhile, the unaccountable terror which our lodger's presence inspired continued to increase. One of our maids gave us warning, solely from her dread of our queer inmate, and the strange accessories which haunted him. She said—and this was corroborated by her fellow-servant—that Mr. Smith seemed to have constantly a companion in his room; that although they never heard them speak, they continually and distinctly heard the tread of two persons walking up and down the room together, and described accurately the peculiar sound of a stick or crutch tapping upon the floor, which my own ears had heard.

They also had seen the large, ill-conditioned cat I have mentioned, frequently steal in and out of the stranger's room; and observed that when our little girl was in greatest danger, the hateful animal was constantly writhing, fawning, and crawling about the door of the sick room after nightfall. They were thoroughly persuaded that this ill-omened beast was the foul fiend himself, and I confess I could not—sceptic as I was—bring myself absolutely to the belief that he was nothing more than a "harmless, necessary cat." These and similar reports—implicitly believed as they palpably were by those who made them—were certainly little calculated to allay the perturbation and alarm with which our household was filled.

The evenings had by this time shortened very much, and darkness often overtook us before we sate down to our early tea. It happened just at this period of which I have been speaking, after my little girl had begun decidedly to mend, that I was sitting in our dining-parlour, with my little boy fast asleep upon my knees, and thinking of I know not what, my wife having gone up stairs, as usual, to sit in the room with little Fanny. As I thus sate in what was to me, in effect, total solitude, darkness unperceived stole on us.

On a sudden, as I sate, with my elbow leaning upon the table, and my other arm round the sleeping child, I felt, as I thought, a cold current of air faintly blowing upon my forehead. I raised my head, and saw, as nearly as I could calculate, at the far end of the table on which my arm rested, two large green eyes confronting me. I could see no more, but instantly concluded they were those of the abominable cat. Yielding to an impulse of horror and abhorrence, I caught a water-croft that was close to my hand, and threw it full at it with all my force. I must have missed my object, for the shining eyes continued fixed for a second, and then glided still nearer to me, and then a little nearer still. The noise of the glass smashed with so much force upon the table called in the servant, who happened to be passing. She had a candle in her hand, and, perhaps, the light alarmed the odious beast, for as she came in it was gone.

I had had an undefined idea that its approach was somehow connected with a designed injury of some sort to the sleeping child. I could not be mistaken as to the fact that I had plainly seen the two broad, glaring, green eyes. Where the cursed animal had gone I had not observed: it might, indeed, easily have run out at the door as the servant opened it, but neither of us had seen it do so; and we were every one of us in such a state of nervous excitement, that even this incident was something in the catalogue of our ambiguous experiences.

It was a great happiness to see our darling little Fanny every day mending, and now quite out of danger: this was cheering and delightful. It was also something to know that more than two months of our lodger's term of occupation had already expired; and to realise, as we now could do, by anticipation, the unspeakable relief of his departure.

My wife strove hard to turn our dear child's recovery to good account for me; but the impressions of fear soon depart, and those of religious gratitude must be preceded by religious faith. All as yet was but as seed strewn upon the rock.

Little Fanny, though recovering rapidly, was still very weak, and her mother usually passed a considerable part of every evening in her bedroom—for the child was sometimes uneasy and restless at night. It happened at this period that, sitting as usual at Fanny's bedside, she witnessed an occurrence which agitated her not a little.

The child had been, as it seems, growing sleepy, and was lying listlessly, with eyes half open, apparently taking no note of what was passing. Suddenly, however, with an expression of the wildest terror, she drew up her limbs, and cowered in the bed's head, gazing at some object; which, judging from the motion of her eyes, must have been slowly advancing from the end of the room next the door.

The child made a low shuddering cry, as she grasped her mother's hand, and, with features white and tense with terror, slowly following with her eyes the noiseless course of some unseen spectre, shrinking more and more fearfully backward every moment.

"What is it? Where? What is it that frightens you, my darling?" asked the poor mother, who, thrilled with horror, looked in vain for the apparition which seemed to have all but bereft the child of reason.

"Stay with me—save me—keep it away—look, look at it—making signs to me—don't let it hurt me—it is angry—Oh! mamma, save me, save me!"

The child said this, all the time clinging to her with both her hands, in an ecstasy of panic.

"There—there, my darling," said my poor wife, "don't be afraid; there's nothing but me—your own mamma—and little baby in the room; nothing, my darling; nothing indeed."

"Mamma, mamma, don't move; don't go near him"; the child continued wildly. "It's only his back now; don't make him turn again; he's untying his handkerchief. Oh! baby, baby; he'll *kill* baby! and he's lifting up those green things from his eyes; don't you see him doing it? Mamma, mamma, why does he come here? Oh, mamma, poor baby—poor little baby!"

She was looking with a terrified gaze at the little boy's bed, which lay directly opposite to her own, and in which he was sleeping calmly.

"Hush, hush, my darling child," said my wife, with difficulty restraining an hysterical burst of tears; "for God's sake don't speak so wildly, my own precious love—there, there—don't be frightened—there, darling, there."

"Oh! poor baby—poor little darling baby," the child continued as before; "will no one save him—tell that wicked man to go away—oh—there—why, mamma—don't—oh, sure you won't let him—don't—don't—he'll take the child's life—will you let him lie down that way on the bed—save poor little baby—oh, baby, baby, waken—his head is on your face."

As she said this she raised her voice to a cry of despairing terror which made the whole room ring again.

This cry, or rather yell, reached my ears as I sate reading in the parlour by myself, and fearing I knew not what, I rushed to the apartment; before I reached it, the sound had subsided into low but violent sobbing; and, just as I arrived at the threshold I heard, close at my feet, a fierce protracted growl, and something rubbing along the surbase. I was in the dark, but, with a feeling of mingled terror and fury, I stamped and struck at the abhorred brute with my feet, but in vain. The next moment I was in the room, and heard little Fanny, through her sobs, cry—

"Oh, poor baby is killed—that wicked man has killed him—he uncovered his face, and put it on him, and lay upon the bed and killed poor baby. I knew he came to kill him. Ah, papa, papa, why did you not come up before he went?—he is gone, he went away as soon as he killed our poor little darling baby."

I could not conceal my agitation, quite, and I said to my wife—

"Has he, Smith, been here?"

"No."

"What is it, then?"

"The child has seen *someone*."

"Seen whom? Who? Who has been here?"

"I did not see it; but—but I am sure the child saw—that is, *thought* she saw *him*;—the person you have named. Oh, God, in mercy deliver us! What shall I do—what shall I do!"

Thus saying, the dear little woman burst into tears, and crying, as if her heart would break, sobbed out an entreaty that I would look at baby; adding, that she herself had not courage to see whether her darling was sleeping or dead.

"Dead!" I exclaimed. "Tut, tut, my darling; you must not give way to such morbid fancies—he is very well, I see him breathing;" and so saying, I went over to the bed where our little boy was lying. He was slumbering; though it seemed to me very heavily, and his cheeks were flushed.

"Sleeping tranquilly, my darling—tranquilly, and deeply; and with a warm colour in his cheeks," I said, rearranging the coverlet, and retiring to my wife, who sate almost breathless whilst I was looking at our little boy.

"Thank God—thank God," she said quietly; and she wept again; and rising, came to his bedside.

"Yes, yes—alive; thank God; but it seems to me he is breathing very short, and with difficulty, and he looks—*does* he not look hot and feverish? Yes, he *is* very hot; feel his little hand-feel his neck; merciful heaven! he is burning."

It was, indeed, very true, that his skin was unnaturally dry and hot; his little pulse, too, was going at a fearful rate.

"I do think," said I—resolved to conceal the extent of my own apprehensions—"I do think that he is just a *little* feverish; but he has often been much more so; and will, I dare say, in the morning, be perfectly well again. I dare say, but for little Fanny's *dream*, we should not have observed it at all."

"Oh, my darling, my darling, my darling!" sobbed the poor little woman, leaning over the bed, with her hands locked together, and looking the very picture of despair. "Oh, my darling, what has happened to you? I put you into your bed, looking so well and beautiful, this evening, and here you are, stricken with sickness, my own little love. Oh, you will not—you cannot, leave your poor mother!"

It was quite plain that she despaired of the child from the moment we had ascertained that it was unwell. As it happened, her presentiment was but too truly prophetic. The apothecary said the child's ailment was "suppressed smallpox"; the physician pronounced it "typhus." The only certainty about it was the issue—the child died.

To me few things appear so beautiful as a very young child in its shroud. The little innocent face looks so sublimely simple and confiding amongst the cold terrors of death—crimeless, and fearless, that little mortal has passed alone under the shadow, and explored the mystery of dissolution. There is death in its sublimest and purest image—no hatred, no hypocrisy, no suspicion, no care for the morrow ever darkened that little face; death has come lovingly upon it; there is nothing cruel, or harsh, in his victory. The yearnings of love, indeed, cannot be stifled; for the prattle, and smiles, and all the little world of thoughts that were so delightful, are gone forever. Awe, too, will overcast us in its presence—for we are looking on death; but we do not fear for the little, lonely voyager—for the child has gone, simple and trusting, into the presence of its all-wise Father; and of such, we know, is the kingdom of heaven.

And so we parted from poor little baby. I and his poor old nurse drove in a mourning carriage, in which lay the little coffin, early in the morning, to the churchyard of ———. Sore, indeed, was my heart, as I followed that little coffin to the grave! Another burial had just concluded as we entered the churchyard, and the mourners stood in clusters round the grave, into which the sexton was now shovelling the mould.

As I stood, with head uncovered, listening to the sublime and touching service which our ritual prescribes, I found that a gentleman had drawn near also, and was standing at my elbow. I did not turn to look at him until the earth had closed over my darling boy; I then walked a little way apart, that I might be alone, and drying my eyes, sat down upon a tombstone, to let the confusion of my mind subside.

While I was thus lost in a sorrowful reverie, the gentleman who had stood near me at the grave was once more at my side. The face of the stranger, though I could not call it handsome, was very remarkable; its expression was the purest and noblest I could conceive, and it was made very beautiful by a look of such compassion as I never saw before.

"Why do you sorrow as one without hope?" he said, gently.

"I *have* no hope," I answered.

"Nay, I think you have," he answered again; "and I am sure you will soon have more. That little child for which you grieve, has escaped the dangers and miseries of life; its body has perished; but he will receive in the end the crown of life. God has given him an early victory."

I know not what it was in him that rebuked my sullen pride, and humbled and saddened me, as I listened to this man. He was dressed in deep mourning, and looked more serene, noble, and sweet than any I had ever seen. He was young, too, as I have said, and his voice very clear and harmonious. He talked to me for a long time, and I listened to him with involuntary reverence. At last, however, he left me, saying he had often seen me walking into town, about the same hour that he used to go that way, and that if he saw me again he would walk with me, and so we might reason of these things together.

It was late when I returned to my home, now a house of mourning.

PART 2

Our home was one of sorrow and of fear. The child's death had stricken us with terror no less than grief. Referring it, as we both tacitly did, to the mysterious and fiendish agency of the abhorred being whom, in an evil hour, we had admitted into our house, we both viewed him with a degree and species of fear for which I can find no name.

I felt that some further calamity was impending. I could not hope that we were to be delivered from the presence of the malignant agent who haunted, rather than inhabited our home, without some additional proofs alike of his malice and his power.

My poor wife's presentiments were still more terrible and overpowering, though not more defined, than my own. She was never tranquil while our little girl was out of her sight; always dreading and expecting some new revelation of the evil influence which, as we were indeed both persuaded, had bereft our darling little boy of life. Against an hostility so unearthly and intangible there was no guarding, and the sense of helplessness intensified the misery of our situation. Tormented with doubts of the very basis of her religion, and recoiling from the ordeal of prayer with the strange horror with which the victim of hydrophobia repels the pure water, she no longer found the consolation which, had sorrow reached her in any other shape, she would have drawn from the healing influence of religion. We were both of us unhappy, dismayed, DEMON-STRICKEN.

Meanwhile, our lodger's habits continued precisely the same. If, indeed, the sounds which came from his apartments were to be trusted, he and his agents were more on the alert than ever. I can convey to you, good reader, no notion, even the faintest, of the dreadful sensation always more or less present to my mind, and sometimes with a reality which thrilled me almost to frenzy—the apprehension that I had admitted into my house the incarnate spirit of the dead or damned, to torment me and my family.

It was some nights after the burial of our dear little baby; we had not gone to bed until late, and I had slept, I suppose, some hours, when I was awakened by my wife, who clung to me with the energy of terror. She said nothing, but grasped and shook me with more than her natural strength. She had crept close to me, and was cowering with her head under the bedclothes.

The room was perfectly dark, as usual, for we burned no night-light; but from the side of the bed next her proceeded a voice as of one sitting there with his head within a foot of the curtains—and, merciful heavens! it was the voice of our lodger.

He was discoursing of the death of our baby, and inveighing, in the old mocking tone of hate and suppressed fury, against the justice, mercy, and goodness of God. He did this with a terrible plausibility of sophistry, and with a resolute emphasis and precision, which seemed to imply, "I have got something to tell you, and, whether you like it or like it not, I *will* say out my say."

To pretend that I felt anger at his intrusion, or emotion of any sort, save the one sense of palsied terror, would be to depart from the truth. I lay, cold and breathless, as if frozen to death—unable to move, unable to utter a cry—with the voice of that demon pouring, in the dark, his undisguised blasphemies and temptations close into my ears. At last the dreadful voice ceased—whether the speaker went or stayed I could not tell- the silence, which he might be improving for the purpose of some hellish strategem, was to me more tremendous even than his speech.

We both lay awake, not daring to move or speak, scarcely even breathing, but clasping one another fast, until at length the welcome light of day streamed into the room through the opening door, as the servant came in to call us. I need not say that our nocturnal visitant had left us.

The magnanimous reader will, perhaps, pronounce that I ought to have pulled on my boots and inexpressibles with all available despatch, run to my lodger's bedroom, and kicked him forthwith downstairs, and the entire way moreover out to the public road, as some compensation for the scandalous affront put upon me and my wife by his impertinent visit. Now, at that time, I had no scruples against what are termed the laws of honour, was by no means deficient in "pluck," and gifted, moreover, with a somewhat excitable temper. Yet, I will honestly avow that, so far from courting a collision with the dreaded stranger, I would have recoiled at his very sight, and given my eyes to avoid him, such was the ascendancy which he had acquired over me, as well as everybody else in my household, in his own quiet, irresistible, hellish way.

The shuddering antipathy which our guest inspired did not rob his infernal homily of its effect. It was not a new or strange thing which he presented to our minds. There was an awful subtlety in the train of his suggestions. All that he had said had floated through my own mind before, without order, indeed, or shew of logic. From my own rebellious heart the same evil thoughts had risen, like pale apparitions hovering and lost in the fumes of a necromancer's cauldron. His was like the summing up of all this—a reflection of my own feelings and fancies—but reduced to an awful order and definiteness, and clothed with a sophistical form of argument. The effect of it was powerful. It revived and exaggerated these bad emotions—it methodised and justified them—and gave to impulses and impressions, vague and desultory before, something of the compactness of a system.

My misfortune, therefore, did not soften, it exasperated me. I regarded the Great Disposer of events as a persecutor of the human race, who took delight in their miseries. I asked why my innocent child had been smitten down into the grave?—and why my darling wife, whose first object, I knew, had ever been to serve and glorify her Maker, should have been thus tortured and desolated by the cruellest calamity which the malignity of a demon could have devised? I railed and blasphemed, and even in my agony defied God with the impotent rage and desperation of a devil, in his everlasting torment.

In my bitterness, I could not forbear speaking these impenitent repetitions of the language of our nightly visitant, even in the presence of my wife. She heard me with agony, almost with terror. I pitied and loved her too much not to respect even her weaknesses—for so I characterised her humble submission to the chastisements of heaven. But even while I spared her reverential sensitiveness, the spectacle of her patience but enhanced my own gloomy and impenitent rage.

I was walking into town in this evil mood, when I was overtaken by the gentleman whom I had spoken with in the churchyard on the morning when my little boy was buried. I call him *gentleman*, but I could not say *what* was his rank—I never thought about it; there was a grace, a purity, a compassion, and a grandeur of intellect in his countenance, in his language, in his mien, that was beautiful and kinglike. I felt, in his company, a delightful awe, and an humbleness more gratifying than any elation of earthly pride.

He divined my state of feeling, but he said nothing harsh. He did not rebuke, but he reasoned with me—and oh! how mighty was that reasoning—without formality—without effort—as the flower grows and blossoms. Its process was in harmony with the successions of nature—gentle, spontaneous, irresistible.

At last he left me. I was grieved at his departure—I was wonder-stricken. His discourse had made me cry tears at once sweet and bitter; it had sounded depths I knew not of, and my heart was disquieted within me. Yet my trouble was happier than the resentful and defiant calm that had reigned within me before.

When I came home, I told my wife of my having met the same good, wise man I had first seen by the grave of my child. I recounted to her his discourse, and, as I brought it again to mind, my tears flowed afresh, and I was happy while I wept.

I now see that the calamity which bore at first such evil fruit, was good for me. It fixed my mind, however rebelliously, upon God, and it stirred up all the passions of my heart. Levity, inattention, and self-complacency are obstacles harder to be overcome than the violence of evil passions—the transition from hate is easier than from indifference, to love. A mighty change was making on my mind.

I need not particularise the occasions upon which I again met my friend, for so I knew him to be, nor detail the train of reasoning and feeling which in such interviews he followed out; it is enough to say, that he assiduously cultivated the good seed he had sown, and that his benignant teachings took deep root, and flourished in my soul, heretofore so barren.

One evening, having enjoyed on the morning of the same day another of those delightful and convincing conversations, I was returning on foot homeward; and as darkness had nearly closed, and the night threatened cold and fog, the footpaths were nearly deserted.

As I walked on, deeply absorbed in the discourse I had heard on the same morning, a person overtook me, and continued to walk, without much increasing the interval between us, a little in advance of me. There came upon me, at the same moment, an indefinable sinking of the heart, a strange and unaccountable fear. The pleasing topics of my meditations melted away, and gave place to a sense of danger, all the more unpleasant that it was vague and objectless. I looked up. What was that which moved before me? I stared—I faltered; my heart fluttered as if it would choke me, and then stood still. It was the peculiar and unmistakeable form of our lodger.

Exactly as I looked at him, he turned his head, and looked at me over his shoulder. His face was muffled as usual. I cannot have seen its features with any completeness, yet I felt that his look was one of fury. The next instant he was at my side; and my heart quailed within me—my limbs all but refused their office; yet the very emotions of terror, which might have overcome me, acted as a stimulus, and I quickened my pace.

"Hey! what a pious person! So I suppose you have learned at last that 'evil communications corrupt good manners'; and you are absolutely afraid of the old infidel, the old blasphemer, hey?"

I made him no answer; I was indeed too much agitated to speak.

"You'll make a good Christian, no doubt," he continued; "the independent man, who thinks for himself, reasons his way to his principles, and sticks fast to them, is sure to be true to whatever system he embraces. You have been so consistent a philosopher, that I am sure you will make a steady Christian. You're not the man to be led by the nose by a sophistical mumbler. *You* could never be made the prey of a grasping proselytism; *you* are not the sport of every whiff of doctrine, nor the facile slave of whatever superstition is last buzzed in your ear. No, no: you've got a masculine intellect, and think for yourself, hey?"

I was incapable of answering him. I quickened my pace to escape from his detested persecution; but he was close beside me still.

We walked on together thus for a time, during which I heard him muttering fast to himself, like a man under fierce and malignant excitement. We reached, at length, the gateway of my dwelling; and I turned the latch-key in the wicket, and entered the enclosure. As we stood together within, he turned full upon me, and confronting me with an aspect whose character I felt rather than saw, he said—

"And so you mean to be a Christian, after all! Now just reflect how very absurdly you are choosing. Leave the Bible to that class of fanatics who may hope to be saved under its system, and, in the name of common sense, study the Koran, or some less ascetic tome. Don't be gulled by a plausible slave, who wants nothing more than to multiply *professors* of his theory. Why don't you *read* the Bible, you miserable, puling poltroon, before you hug it as a treasure? Why don't you read it, and learn out of the mouth of the founder of Christianity, that there is one sin for which there is *no* forgiveness—blasphemy against the Holy Ghost, hey?—and that sin I myself have heard you commit by the hour—in my presence—in my room. I have heard you commit it in our free discussions a dozen times. The Bible seals against you the lips of mercy. If *it* be true, you are this moment as irrevocably damned as if you had died with those blasphemies on your lips."

Having thus spoken, he glided into the house. I followed slowly.

His words rang in my ears—I was stunned. What he had said I feared might be true. Giant despair felled me to the earth. He had recalled, and lighted up with a glare from the pit, remembrances with which I knew not how to cope. It was true I had spoken with daring impiety of subjects whose sacredness I now began to appreciate. With trembling hands I opened the Bible. I read and re-read the mysterious doom recorded by the Redeemer himself against blasphemers of the Holy Ghost—monsters set apart from the human race, and damned and dead, even while they live and walk upon the earth. I groaned—I wept. Henceforward the Bible, I thought, must be to me a dreadful record of despair. I dared not read it.

I will not weary you with all my mental agonies. My dear little wife did something toward relieving my mind, but it was reserved for the friend, to whose heavenly society I owed so much, to tranquillise it once more. He talked this time to me longer, and even more earnestly than before. I soon encountered him again. He expounded to me the ways of Providence, and showed me how needful sorrow was for every servant of God. How mercy was disguised in tribulation, and our best happiness came to us, like our children, in tears and wailing. He showed me that trials were sent to call us up, with a voice of preter-natural power, from the mortal apathy of sin and the world. And then, again, in our new and better state, to prove our patience and our faith—

"The more trouble befalls you, the nearer is God to you. He visits you in sorrow—and sorrow, as well as joy, is a sign of his presence. If, then, other griefs overtake you, remember this—be patient, be faithful; and bless the name of God."

I returned home comforted and happy, although I felt assured that some further and sadder trial was before me.

Still our household was overcast by the same insurmountable dread of our tenant. The same strange habits characterised him, and the same unaccountable sounds disquieted us—an atmosphere of death and malice hovered about his door, and we all hated and feared to pass it.

Let me now tell, as well and briefly as I may, the dreadful circumstances of my last great trial. One morning, my wife being about her household affairs, and I on the point of starting for town, I went into the parlour for some letters which I was to take with me. I cannot easily describe my consternation when, on entering the room, I saw our lodger seated near the window, with our darling little girl upon his knee.

His back was toward the door, but I could plainly perceive

that the respirator had been removed from his mouth, and that the odious green goggles were raised. He was sitting, as it seemed, absolutely without motion, and his face was advanced close to that of the child.

I stood looking at this group in a state of stupor for some seconds. He was, I suppose, conscious of my presence, for although he did not turn his head, or otherwise take any note of my arrival, he readjusted the muffler which usually covered his mouth, and lowered the clumsy spectacles to their proper place.

The child was sitting upon his knee as motionless as he himself, with a countenance white and rigid as that of a corpse, and from which every trace of meaning, except some vague character of terror, had fled, and staring with a fixed and dilated gaze into his face.

As it seemed, she did not perceive my presence. Her eyes were transfixed and fascinated. She did not even seem to me to breathe. Horror and anguish at last overcame my stupefaction.

"What—what is it?" I cried; "what ails my child, my darling child?"

"I'd be glad to know, myself," he replied, coolly; "it is certainly something very queer."

"What is it, darling?" I repeated, frantically, addressing the child.

"What is it?" he reiterated. "Why it's pretty plain, I should suppose, that the child is ill."

"Oh merciful God!" I cried, half furious, half terrified—"You have injured her—you have terrified her. Give me my child- give her to me."

These words I absolutely shouted, and stamped upon the floor in my horrid excitement.

"Pooh, pooh!" he said, with a sort of ugly sneer; "the child is nervous—you'll make her more so—be quiet and she'll probably find her tongue presently. I have had her on my knee some minutes, but the sweet bird could not tell what ails her."

"Let the child go," I shouted in a voice of thunder; "let her go, I say—let her go."

He took the passive, death-like child, and placed her standing by the window, and rising, he simply said—

"As soon as you grow cool, you are welcome to ask me what questions you like. The child is plainly ill. I should not wonder if she had seen something that frightened her."

Having thus spoken, he passed from the room. I felt as if I spoke, saw, and walked in a horrid dream. I seized the darling child in my arms, and bore her away to her mother.

"What is it—for mercy's sake what is the matter?" she cried, growing in an instant as pale as the poor child herself.

"I found that—that *demon*—in the parlour with the child on his lap, staring in her face. She is manifestly terrified."

"Oh! gracious God! she is lost—she is killed," cried the poor mother, frantically looking into the white, apathetic, meaningless face of the child.

"Fanny, darling Fanny, tell us if you are ill," I cried, pressing the little girl in terror to my heart.

"Tell your own mother, my darling," echoed my poor little wife. "Oh! darling, darling child, speak to your poor mother."

It was all in vain. Still the same dilated, imploring gaze—the same pale face—wild and dumb. We brought her to the open window—we gave her cold water to drink—we sprinkled it in her face. We sent for the apothecary, who lived hard by, and he arrived in a few moments, with a parcel of tranquillising medicines. These, however, were equally unavailing.

Hour after hour passed away. The darling child looked upon us as if she would have given the world to speak to us, or to weep, but she uttered no sound. Now and then she drew a long breath as though preparing to say something, but still she was mute. She often put her hand to her throat, as if there was some pain or obstruction there.

I never can, while I live, lose one line of that mournful and terrible portrait—the face of my stricken child. As hour after hour passed away, without bringing the smallest change or amendment, we grew both alarmed, and at length absolutely terrified for her safety.

We called in a physician toward night, and told him that we had reason to suspect that the child had somehow been frightened, and that in no other way could we at all account for the extraordinary condition in which he found her.

This was a man, I may as well observe, though I do not name him, of the highest eminence in his profession, and one in whose skill, from past personal experience, I had the best possible reasons for implicitly confiding.

He asked a multiplicity of questions, the answers to which seemed to baffle his attempts to arrive at a satisfactory diagnosis. There was something undoubtedly anomalous in the case, and I saw plainly that there were features in it which puzzled and perplexed him not a little.

At length, however, he wrote his prescription, and promised to return at nine o'clock. I remember there was something to be rubbed along her spine, and some medicines beside.

But these remedies were as entirely unavailing as the others. In a state of dismay and distraction we watched by the bed in which, in accordance with the physician's direction, we had placed her. The absolute changelessness of her condition filled us with despair. The day which had elapsed had not witnessed even a transitory variation in the dreadful character of her seizure. Any change, even a change for the worse, would have been better than this sluggish, hopeless monotony of suffering.

At the appointed hour the physician returned. He appeared disappointed, almost shocked, at the failure of his prescriptions. On feeling her pulse he declared that she must have a little wine. There had been a wonderful prostration of all the vital powers since he had seen her before. He evidently thought the case a strange and precarious one.

She was made to swallow the wine, and her pulse rallied for a time, but soon subsided again. I and the physician were standing by the fire, talking in whispers of the darling child's symptoms, and likelihood of recovery, when we were arrested in our conversation by a cry of anguish from the poor mother, who had never left the bedside of her little child, and this cry broke into bitter and convulsive weeping.

The poor little child had, on a sudden, stretched down her little hands and feet, and died. There is no mistaking the features of death: the filmy eye and dropt jaw once seen, are recognised whenever we meet them again. Yet, spite of our belief, we cling to hope; and the distracted mother called on the physician, in accents which might have moved a statue, to say that her darling was not dead, not quite dead—that something might still be done—that it could not be all over. Silently he satisfied himself that no throb of life still fluttered in that little frame.

"It is, indeed, all over," he said, in tones scarce above a whisper; and pressing my hand kindly, he said, "comfort your poor wife"; and so, after a momentary pause, he left the room.

This blow had smitten me with stunning suddenness. I looked at the dead child, and from her to her poor mother. Grief and pity were both swallowed up in transports of fury and detestation with which the presence in my house of the wretch who had wrought all this destruction and misery filled my soul. My heart swelled with ungovernable rage; for a moment my habitual fear of him was neutralised by the vehemence of these passions. I seized a candle in silence, and mounted the stairs. The sight of the accursed cat, flitting across the lobby, and the loneliness of the hour, made me hesitate for an instant. I had, however, gone so far, that shame sustained me. Overcoming a momentary thrill of dismay, and determined to repel and defy the influence that had so long awed me, I knocked sharply at the door, and, almost at the same instant, pushed it open, and entered our lodger's chamber.

He had had no candle in the room, and it was lighted only by the "darkness visible" that entered through the window. The candle which I held very imperfectly illuminated the large apartment; but I saw his spectral form floating, rather than walking, back and forward in front of the windows.

At sight of him, though I hated him more than ever, my instinctive fear returned. He confronted me, and drew nearer and nearer, without speaking. There was something indefinably fearful in the silent attraction which seemed to be drawing him to me. I could not help recoiling, little by little, as he came toward me, and with an effort I said—

"You know why I have come: the child—she's dead!"

"Dead—ha!—*dead*—is she?" he said, in his odious, mocking tone.

"Yes—dead!" I cried, with an excitement which chilled my very marrow with horror; "and *you* have killed her, as you killed my other."

"How?—I killed her!—eh?—ha, ha!" he said, still edging nearer and nearer.

"Yes; I say you!" I shouted, trembling in every joint, but possessed by that unaccountable infatuation which has made men invoke, spite of themselves, their own destruction, and which I was powerless to resist—"deny it as you may, it is you who killed her—wretch!—FIEND!—no wonder she could not stand the breath and glare of HELL!"

"And you are one of those who believe that not a sparrow falls to the ground without your Creator's consent," he said, with icy sarcasm; "and this is a specimen of Christian resignation-hey? You charge his act upon a poor fellow like me, simply that you may cheat the devil, and rave and rebel against the decrees of heaven, under pretence of abusing me. The breath and flare of hell!—eh? You mean that I removed this and these (touching the covering of his mouth and eyes successively) as I *shall* do now again, and show you there's no great harm in that."

There was a tone of menace in his concluding words not to be mistaken.

"Murderer and liar from the beginning, as you are, I defy you!" I shouted, in a frenzy of hate and horror, stamping furiously on the floor.

As I said this, it seemed to me that he darkened and dilated before my eyes. My senses, thoughts, consciousness, grew horribly confused, as if some powerful, extraneous will, were seizing upon the functions of my brain. Whether I were to be mastered by death, or madness, or possession, I knew not; but hideous destruction of some sort was impending: all hung upon the moment, and I cried aloud, in my agony, an adjuration in the name of the three persons of the Trinity, that he should not torment me.

Stunned, bewildered, like a man recovered from a drunken fall, I stood, freezing and breathless, in the same spot, looking into the room, which wore, in my eyes, a strange, unearthly character. Mr. Smith was cowering darkly in the window, and, after a silence, spoke to me in a croaking, sulky tone, which was, however, unusually submissive.

"Don't it strike you as an odd procedure to break into a gentleman's apartment at such an hour, for the purpose of railing at him in the coarsest language? If you have any charge to make against me, do so; I invite inquiry and defy your worst. If you think you can bring home to me the smallest share of blame in this unlucky matter, call the coroner, and let his inquest examine and cross-examine me, and sift the matter—if, indeed, there is anything to *be* sifted—to the bottom. Meanwhile, go you about your business, and leave me to mine. But I see how the wind sits; you want to get rid of me, and so you make the place odious to me. But it won't do; and if you take to making criminal charges against me, you had better look to yourself; for two can play at that game."

There was a suppressed whine in all this, which strangely contrasted with the cool and threatening tone of his previous conversation.

Without answering a word I hurried from the room, and scarcely felt secure, even when once more in the melancholy chamber, where my poor wife was weeping.

Miserable, horrible was the night that followed. The loss of our child was a calamity which we had not dared to think of. It had come, and with a suddenness enough to bereave me of reason. It seemed all unreal, all fantastic. It needed an effort to convince me, minute after minute, that the dreadful truth was so; and the old accustomed feeling that she was still alive, still running from room to room, and the expectation that I should hear her step and her voice, and see her entering at the door, would return.

But still the sense of dismay, of having received some stunning, irreparable blow, remained behind; and then came the horrible effort, like that with which one rouses himself from a haunted sleep, the question, "What disaster is this that has befallen?"— answered, alas! but too easily, too terribly! Amidst all this was perpetually rising before my fancy the obscure, dilated figure of our lodger, as he had confronted me in his malign power that night. I dismissed the image with a shudder as often as it recurred; and even now, at this distance of time, I have felt more than I could well describe in the mere effort to fix my recollection upon its hated traits, while writing the passages I have just concluded.

This hateful scene I did not recount to my poor wife. Its horrors were too fresh upon me. I had not courage to trust myself with the agitating narrative; and so I sate beside her, with her hand locked in mine: I had no comfort to offer but the dear love I bore her.

At last, like a child, she cried herself to sleep—the dull, heavy slumber of worn-out grief. As for me, the agitation of my soul was too fearful and profound for repose. My eye accidentally rested on the holy volume, which lay upon the table open, as I had left it in the morning; and the first words which met my eye were these—*For our light affliction, which is but for a moment, worketh for us a far more exceeding and eternal weight of glory.* This blessed sentence riveted my attention, and shed a stream of solemn joy upon my heart; and so the greater part of that mournful night, I continued to draw comfort and heavenly wisdom from the same inspired source.

Next day brought the odious incident, the visit of the undertaker—the carpentery, upholstery, and millinery of death. Why has not civilisation abolished these repulsive and shocking formalities? What has the poor corpse to do with frills, and pillows, and napkins, and all the equipage in which it rides on its last journey? There is no intrusion so jarring to the decent grief of surviving affection, no conceivable mummery more derisive of mortality.

In the room which we had been so long used to call "the nursery," now desolate and mute, the unclosed coffin lay, with our darling shrouded in it. Before we went to our rest at night we visited it. In the morning the lid was to close over that sweet face, and I was to see the child laid by her little brother. We looked upon the well-known and loved features, purified in the sublime serenity of death, for a long time, whispering to one another, among our sobs, how sweet and beautiful we thought she looked; and at length, weeping bitterly, we tore ourselves away.

We talked and wept for many hours, and at last, in sheer exhaustion, dropt asleep. My little wife awaked me, and said—

"I think they have come—the—the undertakers."

It was still dark, so I could not consult my watch; but they were to have arrived early, and as it was winter, and the nights long, the hour of their visit might well have arrived.

"What, darling, is your reason for thinking so?" I asked.

"I am sure I have heard them for some time in the nursery," she answered. "Oh! dear, dear little Fanny! Don't allow them to close the coffin until I have seen my darling once more."

I got up, and threw some clothes hastily about me. I opened the door and listened. A sound like a muffled knocking reached me from the nursery.

"Yes, my darling!" I said, "I think they have come. I will go and desire them to wait until you have seen her again."

And, so saying, I hastened from the room.

Our bedchamber lay at the end of a short corridor, opening from the lobby, at the head of the stairs, and the nursery was situated nearly at the end of a corresponding passage, which opened from the same lobby at the opposite side As I hurried along I distinctly heard the same sounds. The light of dawn had not yet appeared, but there was a strong moonlight shining through the windows. I thought the morning could hardly be so far advanced as we had at first supposed; but still, strangely as it now seems to me, suspecting nothing amiss, I walked on in noiseless, slippered feet, to the nursery-door. It stood half open; someone had unquestionably visited it since we had been there. I stepped forward, and entered. At the threshold horror arrested my advance.

The coffin was placed upon tressles at the further extremity of the chamber, with the foot of it nearly towards the door, and a large window at the side of it admitted the cold lustre of the moon full upon the apparatus of mortality, and the objects immediately about it.

At the foot of the coffin stood the ungainly form of our lodger. He seemed to be intently watching the face of the corpse, and was stooped a little, while with his hands he tapped sharply, from time to time at the sides of the coffin, like one who designs to awaken a slumberer. Perched upon the body of the child, and nuzzling among the grave-clothes, with a strange kind of ecstasy, was the detested brute, the cat I have so often mentioned.

The group thus revealed, I looked upon but for one instant; in the next I shouted, in absolute terror—

"In God's name! what are you doing?"

Our lodger shuffled away abruptly, as if disconcerted; but the ill-favoured cat, whisking round, stood like a demon sentinel upon the corpse, growling and hissing, with arched back and glaring eyes.

The lodger, turning abruptly toward me, motioned me to one side. Mechanically I obeyed his gesture, and he hurried hastily from the room.

Sick and dizzy, I returned to my own chamber. I confess I had not nerve to combat the infernal brute, which still held possession of the room, and so I left it undisturbed.

This incident I did not tell to my wife until sometime afterwards; and I mention it here because it was, and is, in my mind associated with a painful circumstance which very soon afterwards came to light.

That morning I witnessed the burial of my darling child. Sore and desolate was my heart; but with infinite gratitude to the great controller of all events, I recognised in it a change which nothing but the spirit of all good can effect. The love and fear of God had grown strong within me—in humbleness I bowed to his awful will—with a sincere trust I relied upon the goodness, the wisdom, and the mercy of him who had sent this great affliction. But a further incident connected with this very calamity was to test this trust and patience to the uttermost.

It was still early when I returned, having completed the last sad office. My wife, as I afterwards learned, still lay weeping upon her bed. But somebody awaited my return in the hall, and opened the door, anticipating my knock. This person was our lodger.

I was too much appalled by the sudden presentation of this abhorred spectre even to retreat, as my instinct would have directed, through the open door.

"I have been expecting your return," he said, "with the design of saying something which it might have profited you to learn, but now I apprehend it is too late. What a pity you are so violent and impatient; you would not have heard me, in all probability, this morning. You cannot think how cross-grained and intemperate you have grown since you became a saint—but that is your affair, not mine. You have buried your little daughter this morning. It requires a good deal of that new attribute of yours, *faith*, which judges all things by a rule of contraries, and can never see anything but kindness in the worst afflictions which malignity could devise, to discover benignity and mercy in the torturing calamity which has just punished you and your wife for *nothing*!

"But I fancy that it will be harder still when I tell you what I more than suspect—ha, ha. It would be really ridiculous, if it were not heart-rending; that your little girl has been actually buried *alive*; do you comprehend me?—alive. For, upon my life, I fancy she was not dead as she lay in her coffin."

I knew the wretch was exulting in the fresh anguish he had just inflicted. I know not how it was, but any announcement of *disaster* from his lips, seemed to me to be necessarily true. Half-stifled with the dreadful emotions he had raised, palpitating between hope and terror, I rushed frantically back again, the way I had just come, running as fast as my speed could carry me, toward the, alas! distant burial-ground where my darling lay.

I stopped a cab slowly returning to town, at the corner of the lane, sprang into it, directed the man to drive to the church of ——, and promised him anything and everything for despatch. The man seemed amazed; doubtful, perhaps, whether he carried a maniac or a malefactor. Still he took his chance for the promised reward, and galloped his horse, while I, tortured with suspense, yelled my frantic incentives to further speed.

At last, in a space immeasurably short, but which to me was protracted almost beyond endurance, we reached the spot. I halloed to the sexton, who was now employed upon another grave, to follow me. I myself seized a mattock, and in obedience to my incoherent and agonised commands, he worked as he had never worked before. The crumbling mould flew swiftly to the upper soil—deeper and deeper, every moment, grew the narrow grave—at last I sobbed, "Thank God—thank God," as I saw the face of the coffin emerge; a few seconds more and it lay upon the sward beside me, and we both, with the edges of our spades, ripped up the lid.

There was the corpse—but not the tranquil statue I had seen it last. Its knees were both raised, and one of its little hands drawn up and clenched near its throat, as if in a feeble but agonised struggle to force up the superincumbent mass. The eyes, that I had last seen closed, were now open, and the face no longer serenely pale, but livid and distorted.

I had time to see all in an instant; the whole scene reeled and darkened before me, and I swooned away.

When I came to myself, I found that I had been removed to the vestry-room. The open coffin was in the aisle of the church, surrounded by a curious crowd. A medical gentleman had examined the body carefully, and had pronounced life totally extinct. The trepidation and horror I experienced were indescribable. I felt like the murderer of my own child. Desperate as I was of any chance of its life, I dispatched messengers for no less than three of the most eminent physicians then practising in London. All concurred—the child was now as dead as any other, the oldest tenant of the churchyard.

Notwithstanding which, I would not permit the body to be reinterred for several days, until the symptoms of decay became unequivocal, and the most fantastic imagination could no longer cherish a doubt. This, however, I mention only parenthetically, as I hasten to the conclusion of my narrative. The circumstance which I have last described found its way to the public, and caused no small sensation at the time.

I drove part of the way home, and then discharged the cab, and walked the remainder. On my way, with an emotion of ecstasy I cannot describe, I met the good being to whom I owed so much. I ran to meet him, and felt as if I could throw myself at his feet, and kiss the very ground before him. I knew by his heavenly countenance he was come to speak comfort and healing to my heart.

With humbleness and gratitude, I drank in his sage and holy discourse. I need not follow the gracious and delightful exposition of God's revealed will and character with which he cheered and confirmed my faltering spirit. A solemn joy, a peace and trust, streamed on my heart. The wreck and desolation there, lost their bleak and ghastly character, like ruins illuminated by the mellow beams of a solemn summer sunset.

In this conversation, I told him what I had never revealed to any one before—the absolute terror, in all its stupendous and maddening amplitude, with which I regarded our ill-omened lodger, and my agonised anxiety to rid my house of him. My companion answered me—

"I know the person of whom you speak—he designs no good for you or any other. He, too, knows me, and I have intimated to him that he must now leave you, and visit you no more. Be firm and bold, trusting in God, through his Son, like a good soldier, and you will win the victory from a greater and even worse than he—the *unseen* enemy of mankind. You need not see or speak with your evil tenant any more. Call to him from your hall, in the name of the Most Holy, to leave you bodily, with all that appertains to him, this evening. He knows that he must go, and will obey you. But leave the house as soon as may be yourself; you will scarce have peace in it. Your own remembrances will trouble you and *other minds have established associations within its walls and chambers too.*"

These words sounded mysteriously in my ears.

Let me say here, before I bring my reminiscences to a close, a word or two about the house in which these detested scenes occurred, and which I did not long continue to inhabit. What I afterwards learned of it, seemed to supply in part a dim explanation of these words.

In a country village there is no difficulty in accounting for the tenacity with which the sinister character of a haunted tenement cleaves to it. Thin neighbourhoods are favourable to scandal; and in such localities the reputation of a house, like that of a woman, once blown upon, never quite recovers. In huge London, however, it is quite another matter; and, therefore, it was with some surprise that, five years after I had vacated the house in which the occurrences I have described took place, I learned that a respectable family who had taken it were obliged to give it up, on account of annoyances, for which they could not account, and all proceeding from the apartments formerly occupied by our "lodger." Among the sounds described were footsteps restlessly traversing the floor of that room, accompanied by the peculiar tapping of the crutch.

I was so anxious about this occurrence, that I contrived to have strict inquiries made into the matter. The result, however, added little to what I had at first learned—except, indeed, that our old friend, the cat, bore a part in the transaction as I suspected; for the servant, who had been placed to sleep in the room, complained that something bounded on and off, and ran to-and-fro along the foot of the bed, in the dark. The same servant, while in the room, in the broad daylight, had heard the sound of walking, and even the rustling of clothes near him, as of people passing and repassing; and, although he had never seen anything, he yet became so terrified that he would not remain in the house, and ultimately, in a short time, left his situation.

These sounds, attention having been called to them, were now incessantly observed—the measured walking up and down the room, the opening and closing of the door, and the teasing tap of the crutch—all these sounds were continually repeated, until at last, worn out, frightened, and worried, its occupants resolved on abandoning the house.

About four years since, having had occasion to visit the capital, I resolved on a ramble by Old Brompton, just to see if the house were still inhabited. I searched for it, however, in vain, and at length, with difficulty, ascertained its site, upon which now stood two small, staring, bran-new brick houses, with each a gay enclosure of flowers. Every trace of our old mansion, and, let us hope, of our "mysterious lodger," had entirely vanished.

Let me, however, return to my narrative where I left it.

Discoursing upon heavenly matters, my good and gracious friend accompanied me even within the outer gate of my own house. I asked him to come in and rest himself, but he would not; and before he turned to depart, he lifted up his hand, and blessed me and my household.

Having done this, he went away. My eyes followed him till he disappeared, and I turned to the house. My darling wife was standing at the window of the parlour. There was a seraphic smile on her face—pale, pure, and beautiful as death. She was gazing with an humble, heavenly earnestness on us. The parting blessing of the stranger shed a sweet and hallowed influence on my heart. I went into the parlour, to my darling: childless she was now; I had now need to be a tender companion to her.

She raised her arms in a sort of transport, with the same smile of gratitude and purity, and, throwing them round my neck, she said—

"I have seen him—it is he—the man that came with you to the door, and blessed us as he went away—is the same I saw in my dream—the same who took little baby in his arms, and said he would take care of him, and give him safely to me again."

More than a quarter of a century has glided away since then; other children have been given us by the good God—children who have been, from infancy to maturity, a pride and blessing to us. Sorrows and reverses, too, have occasionally visited us; yet, on the whole, we have been greatly blessed; prosperity has long since ended all the cares of the *res angusta domi*, and expanded our power of doing good to our fellow-creatures. God has given it; and God, we trust, directs its dispensation. In our children, and—would you think it?—our *grand*-children, too, the same beneficent God has given us objects that elicit and return all the delightful affections, and exchange the sweet converse that makes home and family dearer than aught else, save that blessed home where the Christian family shall meet at last.

The dear companion of my early love and sorrows still lives, blessed be Heaven! The evening tints of life have fallen upon her; but the dear remembrance of a first love, that never grew cold, makes her beauty changeless for me. As for your humble servant, he is considerably her senior, and looks it: time has stolen away his raven locks, and given him a *chevelure* of snow instead. But, as I said before, I and my wife love, and, I believe, *admire* one another more than ever; and I have often seen our elder children smile archly at one another, when they thought we did not observe them, thinking, no doubt, how like a pair of lovers we two were.

Green Tea

By J. Sheridan le Fanu

PROLOGUE
MARTIN HESSELIUS, THE GERMAN PHYSICIAN

Though carefully educated in medicine and surgery, I have never practised either. The study of each continues, nevertheless, to interest me profoundly. Neither idleness nor caprice caused my secession from the honourable calling which I had just entered. The cause was a very trifling scratch inflicted by a dissecting knife. This trifle cost me the loss of two fingers, amputated promptly, and the more painful loss of my health, for I have never been quite well since, and have seldom been twelve months together in the same place.

In my wanderings I became acquainted with Dr. Martin Hesselius, a wanderer like myself, like me a physician, and like me an enthusiast in his profession. Unlike me in this, that his wanderings were voluntary, and he a man, if not of fortune, as we estimate fortune in England, at least in what our forefathers used to term "easy circumstances." He was an old man when I first saw him; nearly five-and-thirty years my senior.

In Dr. Martin Hesselius, I found my master. His knowledge was immense, his grasp of a case was an intuition. He was the very man to inspire a young enthusiast, like me, with awe and delight. My admiration has stood the test of time and survived the separation of death. I am sure it was well-founded.

For nearly twenty years I acted as his medical secretary. His immense collection of papers he has left in my care, to be arranged, indexed and bound. His treatment of some of these cases is curious. He writes in two distinct characters. He describes what he saw and heard as an intelligent layman might, and when in this style of narrative he had seen the patient either through his own hall-door, to the light of day, or through the gates of darkness to the caverns of the dead, he returns upon the narrative, and in the terms of his art and with all the force and originality of genius, proceeds to the work of analysis, diagnosis and illustration.

Here and there a case strikes me as of a kind to amuse or horrify a lay reader with an interest quite different from the peculiar one which it may possess for an expert. With slight modifications, chiefly of language, and of course a change of names, I copy the following. The narrator is Dr. Martin Hesselius. I find it among the voluminous notes of cases which he made during a tour in England about sixty-four years ago.

It is related in series of letters to his friend Professor Van Loo of Leyden. The professor was not a physician, but a chemist, and a man who read history and metaphysics and medicine, and had, in his day, written a play.

The narrative is therefore, if somewhat less valuable as a medical record, necessarily written in a manner more likely to interest an unlearned reader.

These letters, from a memorandum attached, appear to have been returned on the death of the professor, in 1819, to Dr. Hesselius. They are written, some in English, some in French, but the greater part in German. I am a faithful, though I am conscious, by no means a graceful translator, and although here and there I omit some passages, and shorten others, and disguise names, I have interpolated nothing.

CHAPTER 1
DR. HESSELIUS RELATES HOW HE MET THE REV. MR. JENNINGS

The Rev. Mr. Jennings is tall and thin. He is middle-aged, and dresses with a natty, old-fashioned, high-church precision. He is naturally a little stately, but not at all stiff. His features, without being handsome, are well formed, and their expression extremely kind, but also shy.

I met him one evening at Lady Mary Heyduke's. The modesty and benevolence of his countenance are extremely prepossessing.

We were but a small party, and he joined agreeably enough in the conversation, He seems to enjoy listening very much more than contributing to the talk; but what he says is always to the purpose and well said. He is a great favourite of Lady Mary's, who it seems, consults him upon many things, and thinks him the most happy and blessed person on earth. Little knows she about him.

The Rev. Mr. Jennings is a bachelor, and has, they say sixty thousand pounds in the funds. He is a charitable man. He is most anxious to be actively employed in his sacred profession, and yet though always tolerably well elsewhere, when he goes down to his vicarage in Warwickshire, to engage in the actual duties of his sacred calling, his health soon fails him, and in a very strange way. So says Lady Mary.

There is no doubt that Mr. Jennings' health does break down in, generally, a sudden and mysterious way, sometimes in the very act of officiating in his old and pretty church at Kenlis. It may be his heart, it may be his brain. But so it has happened three or four times, or oftener, that after proceeding a certain way in the service, he has on a sudden stopped short, and after a silence, apparently quite unable to resume, he has fallen into solitary, inaudible prayer, his hands and his eyes uplifted, and then pale as death, and in the agitation of a strange shame and horror, descended trembling, and got into the vestry-room, leaving his congregation, without explanation, to themselves. This occurred when his curate was absent. When he goes down to Kenlis now, he always takes care to provide a clergyman to share his duty, and to supply his place on the instant should he become thus suddenly incapacitated.

When Mr. Jennings breaks down quite, and beats a retreat from the vicarage, and returns to London, where, in a dark street off Piccadilly, he inhabits a very narrow house, Lady Mary says that he is always perfectly well. I have my own opinion about that. There are degrees of course. We shall see.

Mr. Jennings is a perfectly gentlemanlike man. People, however, remark something odd. There is an impression a little ambiguous. One thing which certainly contributes to it, people I think don't remember; or, perhaps, distinctly remark. But I did, almost immediately. Mr. Jennings has a way of looking sidelong upon the carpet, as if his eye followed the movements of something there. This, of course, is not always. It occurs now and then. But often enough to give a certain oddity, as I have said, to his manner, and in this glance travelling along the floor there is something both shy and anxious.

A medical philosopher, as you are good enough to call me, elaborating theories by the aid of cases sought out by himself, and by him watched and scrutinised with more time at command, and consequently infinitely more minuteness than the ordinary practitioner can afford, falls insensibly into habits of observation, which accompany him everywhere, and are exercised, as some people would say, impertinently, upon every subject that presents itself with the least likelihood of rewarding inquiry.

There was a promise of this kind in the slight, timid, kindly, but reserved gentleman, whom I met for the first time at this agreeable little evening gathering. I observed, of course, more than I here set down; but I reserve all that borders on the technical for a strictly scientific paper.

I may remark, that when I here speak of medical science, I do so, as I hope someday to see it more generally understood, in a much more comprehensive sense than its generally material treatment would warrant. I believe the entire natural world is but the ultimate expression of that spiritual world from which, and in which alone, it has its life. I believe that the essential man is a spirit, that the spirit is an organised substance, but as different in point of material from what we ordinarily understand by matter, as light or electricity is; that the material body is, in the most literal sense, a vesture, and death consequently no interruption of the living man's existence, but simply his extrication from the natural body—a process which commences at the moment of what we term death, and the completion of which, at furthest a few days later, is the resurrection "in power."

The person who weighs the consequences of these positions will probably see their practical bearing upon medical science. This is, however, by no means the proper place for displaying the proofs and discussing the consequences of this too generally unrecognized state of facts.

In pursuance of my habit, I was covertly observing Mr. Jennings, with all my caution—I think he perceived it—and I saw plainly that he was as cautiously observing me. Lady Mary happening to address me by my name, as Dr. Hesselius, I saw that he glanced at me more sharply, and then became thoughtful for a few minutes.

After this, as I conversed with a gentleman at the other end of the room, I saw him look at me more steadily, and with an interest which I thought I understood. I then saw him take an opportunity of chatting with Lady Mary, and was, as one always is, perfectly aware of being the subject of a distant inquiry and answer.

This tall clergyman approached me by-and-by; and in a little time we had got into conversation. When two people, who like reading, and know books and places, having travelled, wish to discourse, it is very strange if they can't find topics. It was not accident that brought him near me, and led him into conversation. He knew German and had read my Essays on Metaphysical Medicine which suggest more than they actually say.

This courteous man, gentle, shy, plainly a man of thought and reading, who moving and talking among us, was not altogether of us, and whom I already suspected of leading a life whose transactions and alarms were carefully concealed, with an impenetrable reserve from, not only the world, but his best beloved friends—was cautiously weighing in his own mind the idea of taking a certain step with regard to me.

I penetrated his thoughts without his being aware of it, and was careful to say nothing which could betray to his sensitive vigilance my suspicions respecting his position, or my surmises about his plans respecting myself.

We chatted upon indifferent subjects for a time but at last he said:

"I was very much interested by some papers of yours, Dr. Hesselius, upon what you term Metaphysical Medicine—I read them in German, ten or twelve years ago—have they been translated?"

"No, I'm sure they have not—I should have heard. They would have asked my leave, I think."

"I asked the publishers here, a few months ago, to get the book for me in the original German; but they tell me it is out of print."

"So it is, and has been for some years; but it flatters me as an author to find that you have not forgotten my little book, although," I added, laughing, "ten or twelve years is a considerable time to have managed without it; but I suppose you have been turning the subject over again in your mind, or something has happened lately to revive your interest in it."

At this remark, accompanied by a glance of inquiry, a sudden embarrassment disturbed Mr. Jennings, analogous to that which makes a young lady blush and look foolish. He dropped his eyes, and folded his hands together uneasily, and looked oddly, and you would have said, guiltily, for a moment.

I helped him out of his awkwardness in the best way, by appearing not to observe it, and going straight on, I said: "Those revivals of interest in a subject happen to me often; one book suggests another, and often sends me back a wild-goose chase over an interval of twenty years. But if you still care to possess a copy, I shall be only too happy to provide you; I have still got two or three by me—and if you allow me to present one I shall be very much honoured."

"You are very good indeed," he said, quite at his ease again, in a moment: "I almost despaired—I don't know how to thank you."

"Pray don't say a word; the thing is really so little worth that I am only ashamed of having offered it, and if you thank me any more I shall throw it into the fire in a fit of modesty."

Mr. Jennings laughed. He inquired where I was staying in London, and after a little more conversation on a variety of subjects, he took his departure.

Chapter 2

The Doctor Questions Lady Mary, and She Answers

"I like your vicar so much, Lady Mary," said I, as soon as he was gone. "He has read, travelled, and thought, and having also suffered, he ought to be an accomplished companion."

"So he is, and, better still, he is a really good man," said she. "His advice is invaluable about my schools, and all my little undertakings at Dawlbridge, and he's so painstaking, he takes so much trouble—you have no idea—wherever he thinks he can be of use: he's so good-natured and so sensible."

"It is pleasant to hear so good an account of his neighbourly virtues. I can only testify to his being an agreeable and gentle companion, and in addition to what you have told me, I think I can tell you two or three things about him," said I.

"Really!"

"Yes, to begin with, he's unmarried."

"Yes, that's right—go on."

"He has been writing, that is he *was*, but for two or three years perhaps, he has not gone on with his work, and the book was upon some rather abstract subject—perhaps theology."

"Well, he was writing a book, as you say; I'm not quite sure what it was about, but only that it was nothing that I cared for; very likely you are right, and he certainly did stop—yes."

"And although he only drank a little coffee here tonight, he likes tea, at least, did like it extravagantly."

"Yes, that's *quite* true."

"He drank green tea, a good deal, didn't he?" I pursued.

"Well, that's very odd! Green tea was a subject on which we used almost to quarrel."

"But he has quite given that up," said I.

"So he has."

"And, now, one more fact. His mother or his father, did you know them?"

"Yes, both; his father is only ten years dead, and their place is near Dawlbridge. We knew them very well," she answered.

"Well, either his mother or his father—I should rather think his father, saw a ghost," said I.

"Well, you really are a conjurer, Dr. Hesselius."

"Conjurer or no, haven't I said right?" I answered merrily.

"You certainly have, and it *was* his father: he was a silent, whimsical man, and he used to bore my father about his dreams, and at last he told him a story about a ghost he had seen and talked with, and a very odd story it was. I remember it particularly, because I was so afraid of him. This story was long before he died—when I was quite a child—and his ways were so silent and moping, and he used to drop in sometimes, in the dusk, when I was alone in the drawing-room, and I used to fancy there were ghosts about him."

I smiled and nodded.

"And now, having established my character as a conjurer, I think I must say goodnight," said I.

"But how *did* you find it out?"

"By the planets, of course, as the gipsies do," I answered, and so, gaily we said goodnight.

Next morning I sent the little book he had been inquiring after, and a note to Mr. Jennings, and on returning late that evening, I found that he had called at my lodgings, and left his card. He asked whether I was at home, and asked at what hour he would be most likely to find me.

Does he intend opening his case, and consulting me "professionally," as they say? I hope so. I have already conceived a theory about him. It is supported by Lady Mary's answers to my parting questions. I should like much to ascertain from his own lips. But what can I do consistently with good breeding to invite a confession? Nothing. I rather think he meditates one. At all events, my dear Van L., I shan't make myself difficult of access; I mean to return his visit tomorrow. It will be only civil in return for his politeness, to ask to see him. Perhaps something may come of it. Whether much, little, or nothing, my dear Van L., you shall hear.

Chapter 3

Dr. Hesselius Picks Up Something in Latin Books

Well, I have called at Bank Street.

On inquiring at the door, the servant told me that Mr. Jennings was engaged very particularly with a gentleman, a clergyman from Kenlis, his parish in the country. Intending to reserve my privilege, and to call again, I merely intimated that I should try another time, and had turned to go, when the servant begged my pardon, and asked me, looking at me a little more attentively than well-bred persons of his order usually do, whether I was Dr. Hesselius; and, on learning that I was, he said, "Perhaps then, sir, you would allow me to mention it to Mr. Jennings, for I am sure he wishes to see you."

The servant returned in a moment, with a message from Mr. Jennings, asking me to go into his study, which was in effect his back drawing-room, promising to be with me in a very few minutes.

This was really a study—almost a library. The room was lofty, with two tall slender windows, and rich dark curtains. It was much larger than I had expected, and stored with books on every side, from the floor to the ceiling. The upper carpet—for to my tread it felt that there were two or three—was a Turkey carpet. My steps fell noiselessly. The bookcases standing out, placed the windows, particularly narrow ones, in deep recesses. The effect of the room was, although extremely comfortable, and even luxurious, decidedly gloomy, and aided by the silence, almost oppressive. Perhaps, however, I ought to have allowed something for association. My mind had connected peculiar ideas with Mr. Jennings. I stepped into this perfectly silent room, of a very silent house, with a peculiar foreboding; and its darkness, and solemn clothing of books, for except where two narrow looking-glasses were set in the wall, they were everywhere, helped this sombre feeling.

While awaiting Mr. Jennings' arrival, I amused myself by looking into some of the books with which his shelves were laden. Not among these, but immediately under them, with their backs upward, on the floor, I lighted upon a complete set of Swedenborg's *Arcana Caelestia*, in the original Latin, a very fine folio set, bound in the natty livery which theology affects, pure vellum, namely, gold letters, and carmine edges. There were paper markers in several of these volumes, I raised and placed them, one after the other, upon the table, and opening where these papers were placed, I read in the solemn Latin phraseology, a series of sentences indicated by a pencilled line at the margin. Of these I copy here a few, translating them into English.

> When man's interior sight is opened, which is that of his spirit, then there appear the things of another life, which cannot possibly be made visible to the bodily sight. . . .
>
> By the internal sight it has been granted me to see the things that are in the other life, more clearly than I see those that are in the world. From these considerations, it is evident that external vision exists from interior vision, and this from a vision still more interior, and so on. . . .
>
> There are with every man at least two evil spirits. . . .
>
> With wicked *genii* there is also a fluent speech, but harsh and grating. There is also among them a speech which is not fluent, wherein the dissent of the thoughts is perceived as something secretly creeping along within it. . . .
>
> The evil spirits associated with man are, indeed from the hells, but when with man they are not then in hell, but are taken out thence. The place where they then are, is in the midst between heaven and hell, and is called the world of spirits—when the evil spirits who are with man, are in that world, they are not in any infernal torment, but in every thought and affection of man, and so, in all that the

man himself enjoys. But when they are remitted into their hell, they return to their former state. . . .

If evil spirits could perceive that they were associated with man, and yet that they were spirits separate from him, and if they could flow in into the things of his body, they would attempt by a thousand means to destroy him; for they hate man with a deadly hatred. . . .

Knowing, therefore, that I was a man in the body, they were continually striving to destroy me, not as to the body only, but especially as to the soul; for to destroy any man or spirit is the very delight of the life of all who are in hell; but I have been continually protected by the Lord. Hence it appears how dangerous it is for man to be in a living consort with spirits, unless he be in the good of faith. . . .

Nothing is more carefully guarded from the knowledge of associate spirits than their being thus conjoint with a man, for if they knew it they would speak to him, with the intention to destroy him. . . .

The delight of hell is to do evil to man, and to hasten his eternal ruin. . . .

A long note, written with a very sharp and fine pencil, in Mr. Jennings' neat hand, at the foot of the page, caught my eye. Expecting his criticism upon the text, I read a word or two, and stopped, for it was something quite different, and began with these words, *Deus misereatur mei*—"May God compassionate me." Thus warned of its private nature, I averted my eyes, and shut the book, replacing all the volumes as I had found them, except one which interested me, and in which, as men studious and solitary in their habits will do, I grew so absorbed as to take no cognisance of the outer world, nor to remember where I was.

I was reading some pages which refer to "representatives" and "correspondents," in the technical language of Swedenborg, and had arrived at a passage, the substance of which is, that evil spirits, when seen by other eyes than those of their infernal associates, present themselves, by "correspondence," in the shape of the beast (*fera*) which represents their particular lust and life, in aspect direful and atrocious. This is a long passage, and particularises a number of those bestial forms.

CHAPTER 4
FOUR EYES WERE READING THE PASSAGE

I was running the head of my pencil-case along the line as I read it, and something caused me to raise my eyes.

Directly before me was one of the mirrors I have mentioned, in which I saw reflected the tall shape of my friend, Mr. Jennings, leaning over my shoulder, and reading the page at which I was busy, and with a face so dark and wild that I should hardly have known him.

I turned and rose. He stood erect also, and with an effort laughed a little, saying:

"I came in and asked you how you did, but without succeeding in awaking you from your book; so I could not restrain my curiosity, and very impertinently, I'm afraid, peeped over your shoulder. This is not your first time of looking into those pages. You have looked into Swedenborg, no doubt, long ago?"

"Oh dear, yes! I owe Swedenborg a great deal; you will discover traces of him in the little book on Metaphysical Medicine, which you were so good as to remember."

Although my friend affected a gaiety of manner, there was a slight flush in his face, and I could perceive that he was inwardly much perturbed.

"I'm scarcely yet qualified, I know so little of Swedenborg. I've only had them a fortnight," he answered, "and I think they are rather likely to make a solitary man nervous—that is, judging from the very little I have read—I don't say that they have made me so," he laughed; "and I'm so very much obliged for the book. I hope you got my note?"

I made all proper acknowledgments and modest disclaimers.

"I never read a book that I go with, so entirely, as that of yours," he continued. "I saw at once there is more in it than is quite unfolded. Do you know Dr. Harley?" he asked, rather abruptly.

In passing, the editor remarks that the physician here named was one of the most eminent who had ever practised in England.

I did, having had letters to him, and had experienced from him great courtesy and considerable assistance during my visit to England.

"I think that man one of the very greatest fools I ever met in my life," said Mr. Jennings.

This was the first time I had ever heard him say a sharp thing of anybody, and such a term applied to so high a name a little startled me.

"Really! and in what way?" I asked.

"In his profession," he answered.

I smiled.

"I mean this," he said: "he seems to me, one half, blind—I mean one half of all he looks at is dark—preternaturally bright and vivid all the rest; and the worst of it is, it seems *wilful*. I can't get him—I mean he won't—I've had some experience of him as a physician, but I look on him as, in that sense, no better than a paralytic mind, an intellect half dead. I'll tell you—I know I shall some time—all about it," he said, with a little agitation. "You stay some months longer in England. If I should be out of town during your stay for a little time, would you allow me to trouble you with a letter?"

"I should be only too happy," I assured him.

"Very good of you. I am so utterly dissatisfied with Harley."

"A little leaning to the materialistic school," I said.

"A *mere* materialist," he corrected me; "you can't think how that sort of thing worries one who knows better. You won't tell anyone—any of my friends you know—that I am hippish; now, for instance, no one knows—not even Lady Mary—that I have seen Dr. Harley, or any other doctor. So pray don't mention it; and, if I should have any threatening of an attack, you'll kindly let me write, or, should I be in town, have a little talk with you."

I was full of conjecture, and unconsciously I found I had fixed my eyes gravely on him, for he lowered his for a moment, and he said:

"I see you think I might as well tell you now, or else you are forming a conjecture; but you may as well give it up. If you were guessing all the rest of your life, you will never hit on it."

He shook his head smiling, and over that wintry sunshine a black cloud suddenly came down, and he drew his breath in, through his teeth as men do in pain.

"Sorry, of course, to learn that you apprehend occasion to consult any of us; but, command me when and how you like, and I need not assure you that your confidence is sacred."

He then talked of quite other things, and in a comparatively cheerful way and after a little time, I took my leave.

CHAPTER 5
DR. HESSELIUS IS SUMMONED TO RICHMOND

We parted cheerfully, but he was not cheerful, nor was I. There are certain expressions of that powerful organ of spirit—the human face—which, although I have seen them often, and possess a doctor's nerve, yet disturb me profoundly. One look of Mr. Jennings haunted me. It had seized my imagination with so dismal a power that I changed my plans for the evening, and went to the opera, feeling that I wanted a change of ideas.

I heard nothing of or from him for two or three days, when a note in his hand reached me. It was cheerful, and full of hope. He said that he had been for some little time so much better—quite well, in fact—that he was going to make a little experiment, and run down for a month or so to his parish, to try whether a little work might not quite set him up. There was in it a fervent religious expression of gratitude for his restoration, as he now almost hoped he might call it.

A day or two later I saw Lady Mary, who repeated what his note had announced, and told me that he was actually in Warwickshire, having resumed his clerical duties at Kenlis; and she added, "I begin to think that he is really perfectly well, and that there never was anything the matter, more than nerves and fancy; we are all nervous, but I fancy there is nothing like a little hard work for that kind of weakness, and he has made up his mind to try it. I should not be surprised if he did not come back for a year."

Notwithstanding all this confidence, only two days later I had this note, dated from his house off Piccadilly:

Dear Sir,—I have returned disappointed. If I should feel at all able to see you, I shall write to ask you kindly to call. At present, I am too low, and, in fact, simply unable to say all I wish to say. Pray don't mention my name to my friends. I can see no one. By-and-by, please God, you shall hear from me. I mean to take a run into Shropshire, where some of my people are. God bless you! May we, on my return, meet more happily than I can now write.

About a week after this I saw Lady Mary at her own house, the last person, she said, left in town, and just on the wing for Brighton, for the London season was quite over. She told me that she had heard from Mr. Jenning's niece, Martha, in Shropshire. There was nothing to be gathered from her letter, more than that he was low and nervous. In those words, of which healthy people think so lightly, what a world of suffering is sometimes hidden!

Nearly five weeks had passed without any further news of Mr. Jennings. At the end of that time I received a note from him. He wrote:

I have been in the country, and have had change of air, change of scene, change of faces, change of everything— and in everything—but *myself*. I have made up my mind, so far as the most irresolute creature on earth can do it, to tell my case fully to you. If your engagements will permit, pray come to me today, tomorrow, or the next day; but, pray defer as little as possible. You know not how much I need help.

I have a quiet house at Richmond, where I now am. Perhaps you can manage to come to dinner, or to luncheon, or even to tea. You shall have no trouble in finding me out. The servant at Blank Street, who takes this note, will have a carriage at your door at any hour you please; and I am always to be found. You will say that I ought not to be alone. I have tried everything. Come and see.

I called up the servant, and decided on going out the same evening, which accordingly I did.

He would have been much better in a lodging-house, or hotel, I thought, as I drove up through a short double row of sombre elms to a very old-fashioned brick house, darkened by the foliage of these trees, which overtopped, and nearly surrounded it. It was a perverse choice, for nothing could be imagined more triste and silent.

The house, I found, belonged to him. He had stayed for a day or two in town, and, finding it for some cause insupportable, had come out here, probably because being furnished and his own, he was relieved of the thought and delay of selection, by coming here.

The sun had already set, and the red reflected light of the western sky illuminated the scene with the peculiar effect with which we are all familiar. The hall seemed very dark, but, getting to the back drawing-room, whose windows command the west, I was again in the same dusky light.

I sat down, looking out upon the richly-wooded landscape that glowed in the grand and melancholy light which was every moment fading. The corners of the room were already dark; all was growing dim, and the gloom was insensibly toning my mind, already prepared for what was sinister. I was waiting alone for his arrival, which soon took place. The door communicating with the front room opened, and the tall figure of Mr. Jennings, faintly seen in the ruddy twilight, came, with quiet stealthy steps, into the room.

We shook hands, and, taking a chair to the window, where there was still light enough to enable us to see each other's faces, he sat down beside me, and, placing his hand upon my arm, with scarcely a word of preface began his narrative.

CHAPTER 6

HOW MR. JENNINGS MET HIS COMPANION

The faint glow of the west, the pomp of the then lonely woods of Richmond, were before us, behind and about us the darkening room, and on the stony face of the sufferer—for the character of his face, though still gentle and sweet, was changed—rested that dim, odd glow which seems to descend and produce, where it touches, lights, sudden though faint, which are lost, almost without gradation, in darkness. The silence, too, was utter: not a distant wheel, or bark, or whistle from without; and within the depressing stillness of an invalid bachelor's house.

I guessed well the nature, though not even vaguely the particulars of the revelations I was about to receive, from that fixed face of suffering that so oddly flushed stood out, like a portrait of Schalken's, before its background of darkness.

"It began," he said, "on the 15th of October, three years and eleven weeks ago, and two days—I keep very accurate count, for every day is torment. If I leave anywhere a chasm in my narrative tell me.

"About four years ago I began a work, which had cost me very much thought and reading. It was upon the religious metaphysics of the ancients.'

"I know," said I, "the actual religion of educated and thinking paganism, quite apart from symbolic worship? A wide and very interesting field."

"Yes, but not good for the mind—the Christian mind, I mean. Paganism is all bound together in essential unity, and, with evil sympathy, their religion involves their art, and both their manners, and the subject is a degrading fascination and the Nemesis sure. God forgive me!

"I wrote a great deal; I wrote late at night. I was always thinking on the subject, walking about, wherever I was, everywhere. It thoroughly infected me. You are to remember that all the material ideas connected with it were more or less of the beautiful, the subject itself delightfully interesting, and I, then, without a care."

He sighed heavily.

"I believe, that everyone who sets about writing in earnest does his work, as a friend of mine phrased it, *on* something—tea, or coffee, or tobacco. I suppose there is a material waste that must be hourly supplied in such occupations, or that we should grow too abstracted, and the mind, as it were, pass out of the body, unless it were reminded often enough of the connection by actual sensation. At all events, I felt the want, and I supplied it. Tea was my companion—at first the ordinary black tea, made in the usual way, not too strong: but I drank a good deal, and increased its strength as I went on. I never experienced an uncomfortable symptom from it. I began to take a little green tea. I found the effect pleasanter, it cleared and intensified the power of thought so, I had come to take it frequently, but not stronger than one might take it for pleasure.

"I wrote a great deal out here, it was so quiet, and in this room. I used to sit up very late, and it became a habit with me to sip my tea—green tea—every now and then as my work proceeded. I had a little kettle on my table, that swung over a lamp, and made tea two or three times between eleven o'clock and two or three in the morning, my hours of going to bed. I used to go into town every day. I was not a monk, and, although I spent an hour or two in a library, hunting up authorities and looking out lights upon my theme, I was in no morbid state as far as I can judge. I met my friends pretty much as usual and enjoyed their society, and, on the whole, existence had never been, I think, so pleasant before.

"I had met with a man who had some odd old books, German editions in mediaeval Latin, and I was only too happy to be permitted access to them. This obliging person's books were in the City, a very out-of-the-way part of it. I had rather out-stayed my intended hour, and, on coming out, seeing no cab near, I was tempted to get into the omnibus which used to drive past this house. It was darker than this by the time the 'bus had reached an old house, you may have remarked, with four poplars at each side of the door, and there the last passenger but myself got out. We drove along rather faster. It was twilight now. I leaned back in my corner next the door ruminating pleasantly.

"The interior of the omnibus was nearly dark. I had observed in the corner opposite to me at the other side, and at the end next the horses, two small circular reflections, as it seemed to me of a reddish light. They were about two inches apart, and about the size of those small brass buttons that yachting men used to put upon their jackets. I began to speculate, as listless men will, upon this trifle, as it seemed. From what centre did that faint but deep red light come, and from what—glass beads, buttons, toy decorations—was it reflected? We were lumbering along gently, having nearly a mile still to go. I had not solved the puzzle, and it became in another minute more odd, for these two luminous points, with a sudden jerk, descended nearer and nearer the floor, keeping still their relative distance and horizontal position, and then, as suddenly, they rose to the level of the seat on which I was sitting and I saw them no more.

"My curiosity was now really excited, and, before I had time to think, I saw again these two dull lamps, again together near the floor; again they disappeared, and again in their old corner I saw them.

"So, keeping my eyes upon them, I edged quietly up my own side, towards the end at which I still saw these tiny discs of red.

"There was very little light in the 'bus. It was nearly dark. I leaned forward to aid my endeavour to discover what these little circles really were. They shifted position a little as I did so. I began now to perceive an outline of something black, and I soon saw, with tolerable distinctness, the outline of a small black monkey, pushing its face forward in mimicry to meet mine; those were its eyes, and I now dimly saw its teeth grinning at me.

"I drew back, not knowing whether it might not meditate a spring. I fancied that one of the passengers had forgot this ugly pet, and wishing to ascertain something of its temper, though not caring to trust my fingers to it, I poked my umbrella softly towards it. It remained immovable—up to it—*through* it. For through it, and back and forward it passed, without the slightest resistance.

"I can't, in the least, convey to you the kind of horror that I felt. When I had ascertained that the thing was an illusion, as I then supposed, there came a misgiving about myself and a terror that fascinated me in impotence to remove my gaze from the eyes of the brute for some moments. As I looked, it made a little skip back, quite into the corner, and I, in a panic, found myself at the door, having put my head out, drawing deep breaths of the outer air, and staring at the lights and tress we were passing, too glad to reassure myself of reality.

"I stopped the 'bus and got out. I perceived the man look oddly at me as I paid him. I dare say there was something unusual in my looks and manner, for I had never felt so strangely before."

CHAPTER 7
THE JOURNEY: FIRST STAGE

"When the omnibus drove on, and I was alone upon the road, I looked carefully round to ascertain whether the monkey had followed me. To my indescribable relief I saw it nowhere. I can't describe easily what a shock I had received, and my sense of genuine gratitude on finding myself, as I supposed, quite rid of it.

"I had got out a little before we reached this house, two or three hundred steps. A brick wall runs along the footpath, and inside the wall is a hedge of yew, or some dark evergreen of that kind, and within that again the row of fine trees which you may have remarked as you came.

"This brick wall is about as high as my shoulder, and happening to raise my eyes I saw the monkey, with that stooping gait, on all fours, walking or creeping, close beside me, on top of the wall. I stopped, looking at it with a feeling of loathing and horror. As I stopped so did it. It sat up on the wall with its long hands on its knees looking at me. There was not light enough to see it much more than in outline, nor was it dark enough to bring the peculiar light of its eyes into strong relief. I still saw, however, that red foggy light plainly enough. It did not show its teeth, nor exhibit any sign of irritation, but seemed jaded and sulky, and was observing me steadily.

"I drew back into the middle of the road. It was an unconscious recoil, and there I stood, still looking at it. It did not move.

"With an instinctive determination to try something—anything, I turned about and walked briskly towards town with askance look, all the time, watching the movements of the beast. It crept swiftly along the wall, at exactly my pace.

"Where the wall ends, near the turn of the road, it came down, and with a wiry spring or two brought itself close to my feet, and continued to keep up with me, as I quickened my pace. It was at my left side, so close to my leg that I felt every moment as if I should tread upon it.

"The road was quite deserted and silent, and it was darker every moment. I stopped dismayed and bewildered, turning as I did so, the other way—I mean, towards this house, away from which I had been walking. When I stood still, the monkey drew back to a distance of, I suppose, about five or six yards, and remained stationary, watching me.

"I had been more agitated than I have said. I had read, of course, as everyone has, something about 'spectral illusions,' as you physicians term the phenomena of such cases. I considered my situation, and looked my misfortune in the face.

"These affections, I had read, are sometimes transitory and sometimes obstinate. I had read of cases in which the appearance, at first harmless, had, step by step, degenerated into something direful and insupportable, and ended by wearing its victim out. Still as I stood there, but for my bestial companion, quite alone, I tried to comfort myself by repeating again and again the assurance, 'the thing is purely disease, a well-known physical affection, as distinctly as smallpox or neuralgia. Doctors are all agreed on that, philosophy demonstrates it. I must not be a fool. I've been sitting up too late, and I daresay my digestion is quite wrong, and, with God's help, I shall be all right, and this is but a symptom of nervous dyspepsia.' Did I believe all this? Not one word of it, no more than any other miserable being ever did who is once seized and riveted in this satanic captivity. Against my convictions, I might say my knowledge, I was simply bullying myself into a false courage.

"I now walked homeward. I had only a few hundred yards to go. I had forced myself into a sort of resignation, but I had not got over the sickening shock and the flurry of the first certainty of my misfortune.

"I made up my mind to pass the night at home. The brute moved close beside me, and I fancied there was the sort of anxious drawing toward the house, which one sees in tired horses or dogs, sometimes as they come toward home.

"I was afraid to go into town, I was afraid of any one's seeing and recognizing me. I was conscious of an irrepressible agitation in my manner. Also, I was afraid of any violent change in my habits, such as going to a place of amusement, or walking from home in order to fatigue myself. At the hall door it waited till I mounted the steps, and when the door was opened entered with me.

"I drank no tea that night. I got cigars and some brandy and water. My idea was that I should act upon my material system, and by living for a while in sensation apart from thought, send myself forcibly, as it were, into a new groove. I came up here to this drawing-room. I sat just here. The monkey then got upon a small table that then stood *there*. It looked dazed and languid. An irrepressible uneasiness as to its movements kept my eyes always upon it. Its eyes were half closed, but I could see them glow. It was looking steadily at me. In all situations, at all hours, it is awake and looking at me. That never changes.

"I shall not continue in detail my narrative of this particular night. I shall describe, rather, the phenomena of the first year, which never varied, essentially. I shall describe the monkey as it appeared in daylight. In the dark, as you shall presently hear, there are peculiarities. It is a small monkey, perfectly black. It had only one peculiarity—a character of malignity—unfathomable malignity. During the first year it looked sullen and sick. But this character of intense malice and vigilance was always underlying that surly languor. During all that time it acted as if on a plan of giving me as little trouble as was consistent with watching me. Its eyes were never off me. I have never lost sight of it, except in my sleep, light or dark, day or night, since it came here, excepting when it withdraws for some weeks at a time, unaccountably.

"In total dark it is visible as in daylight. I do not mean merely its eyes. It is *all* visible distinctly in a halo that resembles a glow of red embers, and which accompanies it in all its movements.

"When it leaves me for a time, it is always at night, in the dark, and in the same way. It grows at first uneasy, and then furious, and then advances towards me, grinning and shaking, its paws clenched, and, at the same time, there comes the appearance of fire in the grate. I never have any fire. I can't sleep in the room where there is any, and it draws nearer and nearer to the chimney, quivering, it seems, with rage, and when its fury rises to the highest pitch, it springs into the grate, and up the chimney, and I see it no more.

"When first this happened, I thought I was released. I was now a new man. A day passed—a night—and no return, and a blessed week—a week—nother week. I was always on my knees, Dr. Hesselius, always, thanking God and praying. A whole month passed of liberty, but on a sudden, it was with me again."

Chapter 8
The Second Stage

"It was with me, and the malice which before was torpid under a sullen exterior, was now active. It was perfectly unchanged in every other respect. This new energy was apparent in its activity and its looks, and soon in other ways.

"For a time, you will understand, the change was shown only in an increased vivacity, and an air of menace, as if it were always brooding over some atrocious plan. Its eyes, as before, were never off me."

"Is it here now?" I asked.

"No," he replied, "it has been absent exactly a fortnight and a day—fifteen days. It has sometimes been away so long as nearly two months, once for three. Its absence always exceeds a fortnight, although it may be but by a single day. Fifteen days having past since I saw it last, it may return now at any moment."

"Is its return," I asked, "accompanied by any peculiar manifestation?"

"Nothing—no," he said. "It is simply with me again. On lifting my eyes from a book, or turning my head, I see it, as usual, looking at me, and then it remains, as before, for its appointed time. I have never told so much and so minutely before to anyone."

I perceived that he was agitated, and looking like death, and he repeatedly applied his handkerchief to his forehead; I suggested that he might be tired, and told him that I would call, with pleasure, in the morning, but he said:

"No, if you don't mind hearing it all now. I have got so far, and I should prefer making one effort of it. When I spoke to Dr. Harley, I had nothing like so much to tell. You are a philosophic physician. You give spirit its proper rank. If this thing is real—"

He paused looking at me with agitated inquiry.

"We can discuss it by-and-by, and very fully. I will give you all I think," I answered, after an interval.

"Well—very well. If it is anything real, I say, it is prevailing, little by little, and drawing me more interiorly into hell. Optic nerves, he talked of. Ah! well—there are other nerves of communication. May God Almighty help me! You shall hear.

"Its power of action, I tell you, had increased. Its malice became, in a way, aggressive. About two years ago, some questions that were pending between me and the bishop having been settled, I went down to my parish in Warwickshire, anxious to find occupation in my profession. I was not prepared for what happened, although I have since thought I might have apprehended something like it. The reason of my saying so is this—"

He was beginning to speak with a great deal more effort and reluctance, and sighed often, and seemed at times nearly overcome. But at this time his manner was not agitated. It was more like that of a sinking patient, who has given himself up.

"Yes, but I will first tell you about Kenlis, my parish.

"It was with me when I left this place for Dawlbridge. It was my silent travelling companion, and it remained with me at the vicarage. When I entered on the discharge of my duties, another change took place. The thing exhibited an atrocious determination to thwart me. It was with me in the church—in the reading-desk—in the pulpit—within the communion rails. At last, it reached this extremity, that while I was reading to the congregation, it would spring upon the book and squat there, so that I was unable to see the page. This happened more than once.

"I left Dawlbridge for a time. I placed myself in Dr. Harley's hands. I did everything he told me. He gave my case a great deal of thought. It interested him, I think. He seemed successful. For nearly three months I was perfectly free from a return. I began to think I was safe. With his full assent I returned to Dawlbridge.

"I travelled in a chaise. I was in good spirits. I was more—I was happy and grateful. I was returning, as I thought, delivered from a dreadful hallucination, to the scene of duties which I longed to enter upon. It was a beautiful sunny evening, everything looked serene and cheerful, and I was delighted. I remember looking out of the window to see the spire of my church at Kenlis among the trees, at the point where one has the earliest view of it. It is exactly where the little stream that bounds the parish passes under the road by a culvert, and where it emerges at the road-side, a stone with an old inscription is placed. As we passed this point, I drew my head in and sat down, and in the corner of the chaise was the monkey.

"For a moment I felt faint, and then quite wild with despair and horror. I called to the driver, and got out, and sat down at the roadside, and prayed to God silently for mercy. A despairing resignation supervened. My companion was with me as I re-entered the vicarage. The same persecution followed. After a short struggle I submitted, and soon I left the place.

"I told you," he said, "that the beast has before this become in certain ways aggressive. I will explain a little. It seemed to be actuated by intense and increasing fury, whenever I said my prayers, or even meditated prayer. It amounted at last to a dreadful interruption. You will ask, how could a silent immaterial phantom effect that? It was thus, whenever I meditated praying; It was always before me, and nearer and nearer.

"It used to spring on a table, on the back of a chair, on the chimney-piece, and slowly to swing itself from side to side, looking at me all the time. There is in its motion an indefinable power to dissipate thought, and to contract one's attention to that monotony, till the ideas shrink, as it were, to a point, and at last to nothing—and unless I had started up, and shook off the catalepsy I have felt as if my mind were on the point of losing itself. There are other ways," he sighed heavily; "thus, for instance, while I pray with my eyes closed, it comes closer and closer, and I see it. I know it is not to be accounted for physically, but I do actually see it, though my lids are closed, and so it rocks my mind, as it were, and overpowers me, and I am obliged to rise from my knees. If you had ever yourself known this, you would be acquainted with desperation."

CHAPTER 9
THE THIRD STAGE

"I see, Dr. Hesselius, that you don't lose one word of my statement. I need not ask you to listen specially to what I am now going to tell you. They talk of the optic nerves, and of spectral illusions, as if the organ of sight was the only point assailable by the influences that have fastened upon me—I know better. For two years in my direful case that limitation prevailed. But as food is taken in softly at the lips, and then brought under the teeth, as the tip of the little finger caught in a mill crank will draw in the hand, and the arm, and the whole body, so the miserable mortal who has been once caught firmly by the end of the finest fibre of his nerve, is drawn in and in, by the enormous machinery of hell, until he is as I am. Yes, Doctor, as *I* am, for a while I talk to you, and implore relief, I feel that my prayer is for the impossible, and my pleading with the inexorable."

I endeavoured to calm his visibly increasing agitation, and told him that he must not despair.

While we talked the night had overtaken us. The filmy moonlight was wide over the scene which the window commanded, and I said:

"Perhaps you would prefer having candles. This light, you know, is odd. I should wish you, as much as possible, under your usual conditions while I make my diagnosis, shall I call it-otherwise I don't care."

"All lights are the same to me," he said; "except when I read or write, I care not if night were perpetual. I am going to tell you what happened about a year ago. The thing began to speak to me."

"Speak! How do you mean—speak as a man does, do you mean?"

"Yes; speak in words and consecutive sentences, with perfect coherence and articulation; but there is a peculiarity. It is not like the tone of a human voice. It is not by my ears it reaches me—it comes like a singing through my head.

"This faculty, the power of speaking to me, will be my undoing. It won't let me pray, it interrupts me with dreadful blasphemies. I dare not go on, I could not. Oh! Doctor, can the skill, and thought, and prayers of man avail me nothing!"

"You must promise me, my dear sir, not to trouble yourself with unnecessarily exciting thoughts; confine yourself strictly to the narrative of *facts*; and recollect, above all, that even if the thing that infests you be, you seem to suppose a reality with an actual independent life and will, yet it can have no power to hurt you, unless it be given from above: its access to your senses depends mainly upon your physical condition—this is, under God, your comfort and reliance: we are all alike environed. It is only that in your case, the *'paries,'* the veil of the flesh, the screen, is a little out of repair, and sights and sounds are transmitted. We must enter on a new course, sir,—be encouraged. I'll give to-night to the careful consideration of the whole case."

"You are very good, sir; you think it worth trying, you don't give me quite up; but, sir, you don't know, it is gaining such an influence over me: it orders me about, it is such a tyrant, and I'm growing so helpless. May God deliver me!"

"It orders you about—of course you mean by speech?"

"Yes, yes; it is always urging me to crimes, to injure others, or myself. You see, Doctor, the situation is urgent, it is indeed. When I was in Shropshire, a few weeks ago" (Mr. Jennings was speaking rapidly and trembling now, holding my arm with one hand, and looking in my face), "I went out one day with a party of friends for a walk: my persecutor, I tell you, was with me at the time. I lagged behind the rest: the country near the Dee, you know, is beautiful.

"Our path happened to lie near a coal mine, and at the verge of the wood is a perpendicular shaft, they say, a hundred and fifty feet deep. My niece had remained behind with me—she knows, of course nothing of the nature of my sufferings. She knew, however, that I had been ill, and was low, and she remained to prevent my being quite alone.

"As we loitered slowly on together, the brute that accompanied me was urging me to throw myself down the shaft. I tell you now—oh, sir, think of it!—the one consideration that saved me from that hideous death was the fear lest the shock of witnessing the occurrence should be too much for the poor girl. I asked her to go on and walk with her friends, saying that I could go no further. She made excuses, and the more I urged her the firmer she became. She looked doubtful and frightened. I suppose there was something in my looks or manner that alarmed her; but she would not go, and that literally saved me. You had no idea, sir, that a living man could be made so abject a slave of Satan," he said, with a ghastly groan and a shudder.

There was a pause here, and I said, "You *were* preserved nevertheless. It was the act of God. You are in His hands and in the power of no other being: be therefore confident for the future."

Chapter 10

Home

I made him have candles lighted, and saw the room looking cheery and inhabited before I left him. I told him that he must regard his illness strictly as one dependent on physical, though *subtle* physical causes. I told him that he had evidence of God's care and love in the deliverance which he had just described, and that I had perceived with pain that he seemed to regard its peculiar features as indicating that he had been delivered over to spiritual reprobation. Than such a conclusion nothing could be, I insisted, less warranted; and not only so, but more contrary to facts, as disclosed in his mysterious deliverance from that murderous influence during his Shropshire excursion. First, his niece had been retained by his side without his intending to keep her near him; and, secondly, there had been infused into his mind an irresistible repugnance to execute the dreadful suggestion in her presence.

As I reasoned this point with him, Mr. Jennings wept. He seemed comforted. One promise I exacted, which was that should the monkey at any time return, I should be sent for immediately; and, repeating my assurance that I would give neither time nor thought to any other subject until I had thoroughly investigated his case, and that tomorrow he should hear the result, I took my leave.

Before getting into the carriage I told the servant that his master was far from well, and that he should make a point of frequently looking into his room. My own arrangements I made with a view to being quite secure from interruption.

I merely called at my lodgings, and with a travelling-desk and carpet-bag, set off in a hackney carriage for an inn about two miles out of town, called "The Horns," a very quiet and comfortable house, with good thick walls. And there I resolved, without the possibility of intrusion or distraction, to devote some hours of the night, in my comfortable sitting-room, to Mr. Jennings' case, and so much of the morning as it might require.

(There occurs here a careful note of Dr. Hesselius' opinion upon the case, and of the habits, dietary, and medicines which he prescribed. It is curious—some persons would say mystical. But, on the whole, I doubt whether it would sufficiently interest a reader of the kind I am likely to meet with, to warrant its being here reprinted. The whole letter was plainly written at the inn where he had hid himself for the occasion. The next letter is dated from his town lodgings.)

I left town for the inn where I slept last night at half-past nine, and did not arrive at my room in town until one o'clock this afternoon. I found a letter in Mr. Jennings' hand upon my table. It had not come by post, and, on inquiry, I learned that Mr. Jennings' servant had brought it, and on learning that I was not to return until today, and that no one could tell him my address, he seemed very uncomfortable, and said his orders from his master were that that he was not to return without an answer.

I opened the letter and read:

DEAR DR. HESSELIUS.—It is here. You had not been an hour gone when it returned. It is speaking. It knows all that has happened. It knows everything—it knows you, and is frantic and atrocious. It reviles. I send you this. It knows every word I have written—I write. This I promised, and I therefore write, but I fear very confused, very incoherently. I am so interrupted, disturbed.

> Ever yours,
>   sincerely yours,
>   Robert Lynder Jennings.

"When did this come?" I asked.

"About eleven last night: the man was here again, and has been here three times today. The last time is about an hour since."

Thus answered, and with the notes I had made upon his case in my pocket, I was in a few minutes driving towards Richmond, to see Mr. Jennings.

I by no means, as you perceive, despaired of Mr. Jennings' case. He had himself remembered and applied, though quite in a mistaken way, the principle which I lay down in my Metaphysical Medicine, and which governs all such cases. I was about to apply it in earnest. I was profoundly interested, and very anxious to see and examine him while the "enemy" was actually present.

I drove up to the sombre house, and ran up the steps, and knocked. The door, in a little time, was opened by a tall woman in black silk. She looked ill, and as if she had been crying. She curtseyed, and heard my question, but she did not answer. She turned her face away, extending her hand towards two men who were coming down-stairs; and thus having, as it were, tacitly made me over to them, she passed through a side-door hastily and shut it.

The man who was nearest the hall, I at once accosted, but being now close to him, I was shocked to see that both his hands were covered with blood.

I drew back a little, and the man, passing downstairs, merely said in a low tone, "Here's the servant, sir."

The servant had stopped on the stairs, confounded and dumb at seeing me. He was rubbing his hands in a handkerchief, and it was steeped in blood.

"Jones, what is it? what has happened?" I asked, while a sickening suspicion overpowered me.

The man asked me to come up to the lobby. I was beside him in a moment, and, frowning and pallid, with contracted eyes, he told me the horror which I already half guessed.

His master had made away with himself.

I went upstairs with him to the room—what I saw there I won't tell you. He had cut his throat with his razor. It was a frightful gash. The two men had laid him on the bed, and composed his limbs. It had happened, as the immense pool of blood on the floor declared, at some distance between the bed and the window. There was carpet round his bed, and a carpet under his dressing-table, but none on the rest of the floor, for the man said he did not like a carpet on his bedroom. In this sombre and now terrible room, one of the great elms that darkened the house was slowly moving the shadow of one of its great boughs upon this dreadful floor.

I beckoned to the servant, and we went downstairs together. I turned off the hall into an old-fashioned panelled room, and there standing, I heard all the servant had to tell. It was not a great deal.

"I concluded, sir, from your words, and looks, sir, as you left last night, that you thought my master was seriously ill. I thought it might be that you were afraid of a fit, or something. So I attended very close to your directions. He sat up late, till past three o'clock. He was not writing or reading. He was talking a great deal to himself, but that was nothing unusual. At about that hour I assisted him to undress, and left him in his slippers and dressing-gown. I went back softly in about half-an-hour. He was in his bed, quite undressed, and a pair of candles lighted on the table beside his bed. He was leaning on his elbow, and looking out at the other side of the bed when I came in. I asked him if he wanted anything, and he said No.

"I don't know whether it was what you said to me, sir, or something a little unusual about him, but I was uneasy, uncommon uneasy about him last night.

"In another half hour, or it might be a little more, I went up again. I did not hear him talking as before. I opened the door a little. The candles were both out, which was not usual. I had a bedroom candle, and I let the light in, a little bit, looking softly round. I saw him sitting in that chair beside the dressing-table with his clothes on again. He turned round and looked at me. I thought it strange he should get up and dress, and put out the candles to sit in the dark, that way. But I only asked him again if I could do anything for him. He said, No, rather sharp, I thought. I asked him if I might light the candles, and he said, 'Do as you like, Jones.' So I lighted them, and I lingered about the room, and he said, 'Tell me truth, Jones; why did you come again—you did not hear anyone cursing?' 'No, sir,' I said, wondering what he could mean.

"'No,' said he, after me, 'of course, no;' and I said to him, 'Wouldn't it be well, sir, you went to bed? It's just five o'clock;' and he said nothing, but, 'Very likely; goodnight, Jones.' So I went, sir, but in less than an hour I came again. The door was fast, and he heard me, and called as I thought from the bed to know what I wanted, and he desired me not to disturb him again. I lay down and slept for a little. It must have been between six and seven when I went up again. The door was still fast, and he made no answer, so I did not like to disturb him, and thinking he was asleep, I left him till nine. It was his custom to ring when he wished me to come, and I had no particular hour for calling him. I tapped very gently, and getting no answer, I stayed away a good while, supposing he was getting some rest then. It was not till eleven o'clock I grew really uncomfortable about him—for at the latest he was never, that I could remember, later than half-past ten. I got no answer. I knocked and called, and still no answer. So not being able to force the door, I called Thomas from the stables, and together we forced it, and found him in the shocking way you saw."

Jones had no more to tell. Poor Mr. Jennings was very gentle, and very kind. All his people were fond of him. I could see that the servant was very much moved.

So, dejected and agitated, I passed from that terrible house, and its dark canopy of elms, and I hope I shall never see it more. While I write to you I feel like a man who has but half waked from a frightful and monotonous dream. My memory rejects the picture with incredulity and horror. Yet I know it is true. It is the story of the process of a poison, a poison which excites the reciprocal action of spirit and nerve, and paralyses the tissue that separates those cognate functions of the senses, the external and the interior. Thus we find strange bed-fellows, and the mortal and immortal prematurely make acquaintance.

CONCLUSION
A WORD FOR THOSE WHO SUFFER

My dear Van L——, you have suffered from an affection similar to that which I have just described. You twice complained of a return of it.

Who, under God, cured you? Your humble servant, Martin Hesselius. Let me rather adopt the more emphasised piety of a certain good old French surgeon of three hundred years ago: "I treated, and God cured you."

Come, my friend, you are not to be hippish. Let me tell you a fact. I have met with, and treated, as my book shows, fifty-seven cases of this kind of vision, which I term indifferently "sublimated," "precocious," and "interior."

There is another class of affections which are truly termed-though commonly confounded with those which I describe-spectral illusions. These latter I look upon as being no less simply curable than a cold in the head or a trifling dyspepsia.

It is those which rank in the first category that test our promptitude of thought. Fifty-seven such cases have I encountered, neither more nor less. And in how many of these have I failed? In no one single instance. There is no one affliction of mortality more easily and certainly reducible, with a little patience, and a rational confidence in the physician. With these simple conditions, I look upon the cure as absolutely certain.

You are to remember that I had not even commenced to treat Mr. Jennings' case. I have not any doubt that I should have cured him perfectly in eighteen months, or possibly it might have extended to two years. Some cases are very rapidly curable, others extremely tedious. Every intelligent physician who will give thought and diligence to the task, will effect a cure.

You know my tract on *The Cardinal Functions of the Brain*. I there, by the evidence of innumerable facts, prove, as I think, the high probability of a circulation arterial and venous in its mechanism, through the nerves. Of this system, thus considered, the brain is the heart. The fluid, which is propagated hence through one class of nerves, returns in an altered state through another, and the nature of that fluid is spiritual, though not immaterial, any more than, as I before remarked, light or electricity are so.

By various abuses, among which the habitual use of such

agents as green tea is one, this fluid may be affected as to its quality, but it is more frequently disturbed as to equilibrium. This fluid being that which we have in common with spirits, a congestion found upon the masses of brain or nerve, connected with the interior sense, forms a surface unduly exposed, on which disembodied spirits may operate: communication is thus more or less effectually established.

Between this brain circulation and the heart circulation there is an intimate sympathy. The seat, or rather the instrument of exterior vision, is the eye. The seat of interior vision is the nervous tissue and brain, immediately about and above the eyebrow. You remember how effectually I dissipated your pictures by the simple application of iced *eau-de-cologne*. Few cases, however, can be treated exactly alike with anything like rapid success. Cold acts powerfully as a repellent of the nervous fluid. Long enough continued it will even produce that permanent insensibility which we call numbness, and a little longer, muscular as well as sensational paralysis.

I have not, I repeat, the slightest doubt that I should have first dimmed and ultimately sealed that inner eye which Mr. Jennings had inadvertently opened. The same senses are opened in delirium tremens, and entirely shut up again when the over-action of the cerebral heart, and the prodigious nervous congestions that attend it, are terminated by a decided change in the state of the body. It is by acting steadily upon the body, by a simple process, that this result is produced—and inevitably produced—I have never yet failed.

Poor Mr. Jennings made away with himself. But that catastrophe was the result of a totally different malady, which, as it were, projected itself upon the disease which was established. His case was in the distinctive manner a complication, and the complaint under which he really succumbed, was hereditary suicidal mania. Poor Mr. Jennings I cannot call a patient of mine, for I had not even begun to treat his case, and he had not yet given me, I am convinced, his full and unreserved confidence. If the patient do not array himself on the side of the disease, his cure is certain.

The Death Mask

By Mrs. H. D. Everett

"Yes, that is a portrait of my wife. It is considered to be a good likeness. But of course she was older-looking towards the last."

Enderby and I were on our way to the smoking-room after dinner, and the picture hung on the staircase. We had been chums at school a quarter of a century ago, and later on at college; but I had spent the last decade out of England. I returned to find my friend a widower of four years' standing. And a good job too, I thought to myself when I heard of it, for I had no great liking for the late Gloriana. Probably the sentiment, or want of sentiment, had been mutual: she did not smile on me, but I doubt if she smiled on any of poor Tom Enderby's bachelor cronies. The picture was certainly like her. She was a fine woman, with aquiline features and a cold eye. The artist had done the features justice—and the eye, which seemed to keep a steely watch on all the comings and goings of the house out of which she had died.

We made only a brief pause before the portrait, and then went on. The smoking-room was an apartment built out at the back of the house by a former owner, and shut off by double doors to serve as a nursery. Mrs. Enderby had no family, and she disliked the smell of tobacco. So the big room was made over to Tom's pipes and cigars; and if Tom's friends wanted to smoke, they must smoke there or not at all. I remembered the room and the rule, but I was not prepared to find it still existing. I had expected to light my after dinner cigar over the dessert dishes, now there was no presiding lady to consider.

We were soon installed in a couple of deep-cushioned chairs before a good fire. I thought Enderby breathed more freely when he closed the double doors behind us, shutting off the dull formal house, and the staircase and the picture. But he was not looking well; there hung about him an unmistakable air of depression. Could he be fretting after Gloriana? Perhaps during their married years, he had fallen into the way of depending on a woman to care for him. It is pleasant enough when the woman is the right sort; but I shouldn't myself have fancied being cared for by the late Mrs. Enderby. And, if the fretting was a fact, it would be easy to find a remedy. Evelyn has a couple of pretty sisters, and we would have him over to stay at our place.

"You must run down and see us," I said presently, pursuing this idea. "I want to introduce you to my wife. Can you come next week?"

His face lit up with real pleasure.

"I should like it of all things," he said heartily. "But a qualification came after. The cloud settled back over him and he sighed. "That is, if I can get away."

"Why, what is to hinder you?"

"It may not seem much to stay for, but I—I have got in the way of stopping here—to keep things together." He did not look at me, but leaned over to the fender to knock the ash off his cigar.

"Tell you what, Tom, you are getting hipped living by yourself. Why don't you sell the house, or let it off just as it is, and try a complete change?"

"I can't sell it. I'm only the tenant for life. It was my wife's."

"Well, I suppose there is nothing to prevent you letting it? Or if you can't let it, you might shut it up."

"There is nothing *legal* to prevent me—!" The emphasis was too fine to attract notice, but I remembered it after.

"Then, my dear fellow, why not? Knock about a bit, and see the world. But, to my thinking, the best thing you could do would be to marry again."

He shook his head drearily.

"Of course it is a delicate matter to urge upon a widower. But you have paid the utmost ceremonial respect. Four years, you know. The greatest stickler for propriety would deem it ample.

"It isn't that. Dick, I—I've a great mind to tell you rather a queer story." He puffed hard at his smoke, and stared into the red coals in the pauses. "But I don't know what you'd think of it. Or think of me."

"Try me," I said. "I'll give you my opinion after. And you know I'm safe to confide in."

"I sometimes think I should feel better if I told it. It's—it's queer enough to be laughable. But it hasn't been any laughing matter to me."

He threw the stump of his cigar into the fire, and turned to me. And then I saw how pale he was, and that a dew of perspiration was breaking out on his white face.

"I was very much of your opinion, Dick: I thought I should be happier if I married again. And I went so far as to get engaged. But the engagement was broken off, and I am going to tell you why.

"My wife was some time ailing before she died, and the doctors were in consultation. But I did not know how serious her complaint was till the last. Then they told me there was no hope, as coma had set in. But it was possible, even probable, that there would be a revival of consciousness before death, and for this I was to hold myself ready.

"I daresay you will write me down a coward, but I dreaded the revival: I was ready to pray that she might pass away in her sleep. I knew she held exalted views about the marriage tie, and I felt sure if there were any last words she would exact a pledge. I could not at such a moment refuse to promise, and I did not want to be tied. You will recollect that she was my senior. I was about to be left a widower in middle life, and in the natural course of things I had a good many years before me. You see?"

"My dear fellow, I don't think a promise so extorted ought to bind you. It isn't fair!—"

"Wait and hear me. I was sitting here, miserable enough, as you may suppose, when the doctor came to fetch me to her room. Mrs. Enderby was conscious and had asked for me, but he particularly begged me not to agitate her in any way, lest pain should return. She was lying stretched out in the bed, looking already like a corpse.

"'Tom,' she said, 'they tell me I am dying, and there is something I want you to promise.'

"I groaned in spirit. It was all up with me, I thought. But she went on.

"'When I am dead and in my coffin, I want you to cover my face with your own hands. Promise me this.'

"It was not in the very least what I expected. Of course I promised.

"'I want you to cover my face with a particular handkerchief on which I set a value. When the time comes, open the cabinet to the right of the window, and you will find it in the third drawer from the top. You cannot mistake it, for it is the only thing in the drawer.'

"That was every word she said, if you believe me, Dick. She just sighed and shut her eyes as if she was going to sleep, and she never spoke again. Three or four days later they came again to ask me if I wished to take a last look, as the undertaker's men were about to close the coffin.

"I felt a great reluctance, but it was necessary I should go. She looked as if made of wax, and was colder than ice to touch. I opened the cabinet, and there, just as she said, was a large handkerchief of very fine cambric, lying by itself. It was embroidered with a monogram device in all four corners, and was not of a sort I had ever seen her use. I spread it out and laid it over the dead face; and then what happened was rather curious. It seemed to draw down over the features and cling to them, to nose and mouth and forehead and the shut eyes, till it became a perfect mask. My nerves were shaken, I suppose; I was seized with horror, and flung back the covering sheet, hastily quitting the room. And the coffin was closed that night.

"Well, she was buried, and I put up a monument which the neighbourhood considered handsome. As you see, I was bound by no pledge to abstain from marriage; and, though I knew what would have been her wish, I saw no reason why I should regard it. And, some months after, a family of the name of Ashcroft came to live at The Leasowes, and they had a pretty daughter.

"I took a fancy to Lucy Ashcroft the first time I saw her, and it was soon apparent that she was well inclined to me. She was a gentle, yielding little thing; not the superior style of woman. Not at all like——"

(I made no comment, but I could well understand that in his new matrimonial venture Tom would prefer a contrast.)

"——But I thought I had a very good chance of happiness with her; and I grew fond of her: very fond of her indeed. Her people were of the hospitable sort, and they encouraged me to go to The Leasowes, dropping in when I felt inclined: it did not seem as if they would be likely to put obstacles in our way. Matters progressed, and I made up my mind one evening to walk over there and declare myself. I had been up to town the day before, and came back with a ring in my pocket: rather a fanciful design of double hearts, but I thought Lucy would think it pretty, and would let me put it on her finger. I went up to change into dinner things, making myself as spruce as possible, and coming to the conclusion before the glass that I was not such a bad figure of a man after all, and that there was not much grey in my hair. Ay, Dick, you may smile: it is a good bit greyer now.

"I had taken out a clean handkerchief, and thrown the one carried through the day away crumpled on the floor. I don't know what made me turn to look at it as it lay there, but, once it caught my eye, I stood staring at it as if spell-bound. The handkerchief was moving—Dick, I swear it—rapidly altering in shape, puffing up here and there as if blown by wind, spreading and moulding itself into the features of a face. And what face should it be but that death-mask of Gloriana, which I had covered in the coffin eleven months before!

"To say I was horror-stricken conveys little of the feeling that possessed me. I snatched up the rag of cambric and flung it on the fire, and it was nothing but a rag in my hand, and in another moment no more than blackened tinder on the bar of the grate. There was no face below."

"Of course not," I said. "It was a mere hallucination. You were cheated by an excited fancy."

"You maybe be sure I told myself all that, and more; and I went downstairs and tried to pull myself together with a dram. But I was curiously upset, and, for that night at least, I found it impossible to play the wooer. The recollection of the death-mask was too vivid; it would have come between me and Lucy's lips.

"The effect wore off, however. In a day or two I was bold again, and as much disposed to smile at my folly as you are at this moment. I proposed, and Lucy accepted me; and I put on the ring. Ashcroft *père* was graciously pleased to approve of the settlements I offered, and Ashcroft *mère* promised to regard me as a son. And during the first forty-eight hours of our engagement, there was not a cloud to mar the blue.

"I proposed on a Monday, and on Wednesday I went again to dine and spend the evening with just their family party. Lucy and I found our way afterwards into the back drawing-room, which seemed to be made over to us by tacit understanding. Any way, we had it to ourselves; and as Lucy sat on the settee, busy with her work, I was privileged to sit beside her, close enough to watch the careful stitches she was setting, under which the pattern grew.

"She was embroidering a square of fine linen to serve as a tea-cloth, and it was intended for a present to a friend; she was anxious, she told me, to finish it in the next few days, ready for despatch. But I was somewhat impatient of her engrossment in the work; I wanted her to look at me while we talked, and to be permitted to hold her hand. I was making plans for a tour we would take together after Easter; arguing that eight weeks spent in preparation was enough for any reasonable bride. Lucy was easily entreated; she laid aside the linen square on the table at her elbow. I held her fingers captive, but her eyes wandered from my face, as she was still deliciously shy.

"All at once she exclaimed. Her work was moving, there was growing to be a face in it: did I not see?

"I saw, indeed. It was the Gloriana death-mask, forming there as it had formed in my handkerchief at home: the marked nose and chin, the severe mouth, the mould of forehead, almost complete. I snatched it up and dropped it over the back of the couch. 'It did look like a face,' I allowed. 'But never mind it, darling; I want you to attend to me.' Something of this sort I said, I hardly know what, for my blood was running cold. Lucy pouted; she wanted to dwell on the marvel, and my impatient action had displeased her. I went on talking wildly, being afraid of pauses, but the psychological moment had gone by. I felt I did not carry her with me as before: she hesitated over my persuasions; the forecast of a Sicilian honeymoon had ceased to charm. By-and-bye she suggested that Mrs. Ashcroft would expect us to rejoin the circle in the other room. And perhaps I would pick up her work for her—still with a slight air of offence.

"I walked round the settee to recover the luckless piece of linen; but she turned also, looking over the back, so at the same instant we both saw.

"There again was the Face, rigid and severe; and now the corners of the cloth were tucked under, completing the form of the head. And that was not all. Some white drapery had been improvised and extended beyond it on the floor, presenting the complete figure laid out straight and stiff, ready for the grave. Lucy's alarm was excusable. She shrieked aloud, shriek upon shriek, and immediately an indignant family of Ashcrofts rushed in through the half-drawn *portières* which divided the two rooms, demanding the cause of her distress.

"Meanwhile I had fallen upon the puffed-out form, and destroyed it. Lucy's embroidery composed the head; the figure was ingeniously contrived out of a large Turkish bath-sheet, brought in from one of the bedrooms, no one knew how or when. I held up the things protesting their innocence, while the family were stabbing me through and through with looks of indignation, and Lucy was sobbing in her, mother's arms. She might have been foolish, she allowed; it did seem ridiculous now she saw what it was. But at the moment it was too dreadful: it looked so like—so like! And here a fresh sob choked her into silence.

"Peace was restored at last, but plainly the Ashcrofts doubted me. The genial father stiffened, and Mrs. Ashcroft administered indirect reproofs. She hated practical joking, so she informed me; she might be wrong, and no doubt she was old-fashioned, but she had been brought up to consider it in the highest degree ill-bred. And perhaps I had not considered how sensitive Lucy was, and how easily alarmed. She hoped I would take warning for the future, and that nothing of this kind would occur again.

"Practical joking—oh, ye gods! As if it was likely that I, alone with the girl of my heart, would waste the precious hour in building up effigies of sham corpses on the floor! And Lucy ought to have known that the accusation was absurd, as I had never for a moment left her side. She did take my part when more composed; but the mystery remained, beyond explanation of hers or mine.

"As for the future, I could not think of that without a failing heart. If the Power arrayed against us were in truth what my superstition feared, I might as well give up hope at once, for I knew there would be no relenting. I could see the whole absurdity of the thing as well as you do now; but, if you put yourself in my place, Dick, you will be forced to confess that it was tragic too.

"I did not see Lucy the next day, as I was bound to go again to town; but we had planned to meet and ride together on the Friday morning. I was to be at The Leasowes at a certain hour, and you may be sure I was punctual. Her horse had already been brought round, and the groom was leading it up and down. I had hardly dismounted when she came down the steps of the porch; and I noticed at once a new look on her face, a harder set about that red mouth of hers which was so soft and kissable. But she let me put her up on the saddle and settle her foot in the stirrup, and she was the bearer of a gracious message from her mother. I was expected to return to lunch, and Mrs. Ashcroft begged us to be punctual, as a friend who had stayed the night with them, would be leaving immediately after.

"'You will be pleased to meet her, I think,' said Lucy, leaning forward to pat her horse. 'I find she knows you very well. It is Miss Kingsworthy.'

"Now Miss Kingsworthy was a schoolfriend of Gloriana's, who used now and then to visit us here. I was not aware that she and the Ashcrofts were acquainted; but, as I have said, they had only recently come into the neighbourhood as tenants of The Leasowes. I had no opportunity to express pleasure or the reverse, for Lucy was riding on, and putting her horse to a brisk pace. It was some time before she drew rein, and again admitted conversation. We were descending a steep hill, and the groom was following at a discreet distance behind, far enough to be out of earshot.

"Lucy looked very pretty on horseback; but this is by the way. The mannish hat suited her, and so did the habit fitting closely to her shape.

"'Tom,' she said; and again I noticed that new hardness in her face. 'Tom, Miss Kingsworthy tells me your wife did not wish you to marry again, and she made you promise her that you would not. Miss Kingsworthy was quite astonished to hear that you and I were engaged. Is this true?'

"I was able to tell her it was not: that my wife had never asked, and I had never given her, any such pledge. I allowed she disliked second marriages—in certain cases, and perhaps she had made some remark to.that effect to Miss Kingsworthy; it was not unlikely. And then I appealed to her. Surely she would not let a mischief-maker's tittle-tattle come between her and me?

"I thought her profile looked less obdurate, but she would not let her eyes meet mine as she answered:

"'Of course not, if that was all. And I doubt if I would have

491

heeded it, only that it seemed to fit in with—something else. Tom, it was very horrible, what we saw on Wednesday evening. And—and—don't be angry, but I asked Miss Kingsworthy what your wife was like. I did not tell her why I wanted to know.'

"'What has that to do with it?' I demanded—stoutly enough; but, alas! I was too well aware.

She told me Mrs. Enderby was handsome, but she had very marked features, and was severe-looking when she did not smile. A high forehead, a Roman nose, and a decided chin. Tom, the face in the cloth was just like that. Did you not see?'

"Of course I protested.

"'My darling, what nonsense! I saw it looked a little like a face, but I pulled it to pieces at once because you were frightened. Why, Lucy, I shall have you turning into a spiritualist if you take up these fancies.'

"'No,' she said, 'I do not want to be anything foolish. I have thought it over, and if it happens only once I have made up my mind to believe it a mistake and to forget. But if it comes again—if it goes on coming!' Here she shuddered and turned white. 'Oh Tom, I could not—I could not!'

"That was the ultimatum. She liked me as much as ever; she even owned to a warmer feeling; but she was not going to marry a haunted man. Well, I suppose I cannot blame her. I might have given the same advice in another fellow's case, though in my own I felt it hard.

"I am close to the end now, so I shall need to tax your patience very little longer. A single chance remained. Gloriana's power, whatever its nature and however derived, might have been so spent in the previous efforts that she could effect no more. I clung to this shred of hope, and did my best to play the part of the light-hearted lover, the sort of companion Lucy expected, who would shape himself to her mood; but I was conscious that I played it ill.

"The ride was a lengthy business. Lucy's horse cast a shoe, and it was impossible to change the saddle on to the groom's hack or my own mare, as neither of them had been trained to the habit. We were bound to return at a foot-pace, and did not reach The Leasowes until two o'clock. Lunch was over: Mrs. Ashcroft had set out for the station driving Miss Kingsworthy; but some cutlets were keeping hot for us, so we were informed, and could be served immediately.

"We went at once into the dining-room, as Lucy was hungry; and she took off her hat and laid it on a side-table: she said the close fit of it made her head ache. The cutlets had been mis-represented: they were lukewarm; but Lucy made a good meal off them and the fruit-tart which followed, very much at her leisure. Heaven knows I would not have grudged her so much as a mouthful; but that luncheon was an ordeal I cannot readily forget.

"The servant absented himself, having seen us served; and then my troubles began. The tablecloth seemed alive at the corner which was between us; it rose in waves as if puffed up by wind, though the window was fast shut against any wandering airs. I tried to seem unconscious; tried to talk as if no horror of apprehension was filling all my mind, while I was flattening out the bewitched damask with a grasp I hardly dared relax. Lucy rose at last, saying she must change her dress. Occupied with the cloth, it had not occurred to me to look round, or keep watch on what might be going on in another part of the room. The hat on the side-table had been tilted over sideways, and in that position it was made to crown another presentation of the Face. What it was made of this time I cannot say; probably a serviette, as several lay about. The linen material, of whatever sort, was again moulded into the perfect form; but this time the mouth showed humour, and appeared to relax in a grim smile.

"Lucy shrieked, and dropped into my arms in a swoon: a real genuine fainting-fit, out of which she was brought round with difficulty, after summoned help of doctors.

"I hung about miserably till her safety was assured, and then went as miserably home. Next morning I received a cutting little note from my mother-in-law elect, in which she returned the ring, and informed me the engagement must be considered at an end.

"Well, Dick, you know now why I do not marry. And what have you to say?"

The Last of Squire Ennismore
By Mrs J. H. Riddell

'Did I see it myself? No, sir; I did not see it: and my father before me did not see it; or his father before him, and he was Phil Regan, just the same as myself. But it is true, for all that; just as true as that you are looking at the very place where the whole thing happened. My great-grandfather (and he did not die till he was ninety-eight) used to tell, many and many's the time, how he met the stranger, night after night, walking lonesome-like about the sands where most of the wreckage came ashore.'

'And the old house, then, stood behind that belt of Scotch firs?'

'Yes; a fine house it was, too. Hearing so much talk about it when a boy, my father said, made him often feel as if he knew every room in the building, though it had all fallen to ruin before he was born. None of the family ever lived in it after the Squire went away. Nobody else could be got to stop in the place. There used to be awful noises, as if something was being pitched from the top of the great staircase down into the hall; and then there would be a sound as if a hundred people were clinking glasses and talking all together at once. And then it seemed as if barrels wire rolling in the cellars; and there would be screeches, and howls, and laughing, fit to make your blood run cold. They say there is gold hid away in those cellars; but not one has ever ventured to find it. The very children won't come here to play; and when the men are ploughing the field behind, nothing will make them stay in it, once the day begins to change. When the night is coming on, and the tide creeps in on the sand, more than one thinks he has seen mighty queer things on the shore there.'

'But what is it really they think they see? When I asked my landlord to tell me the story from beginning to end, he said he could not remember it; and, at any rate, the whole rigmarole was nonsense, put together to please strangers.'

'And what is he but a stranger himself? And how should he know about the doings of real quality like the Ennismores? For they were gentry, every one of them—good old stock; and as for wickedness, you might have searched Ireland through and not found their match. It is a sure thing, though, that if Riley can't tell you the story, I can; for, as I said, my own people were in it, of a manner of speaking. So, if your honour will rest yourself off your feet, on that bit of a bank, I'll set down my creel and give you the whole pedigree of how Squire Ennismore went away from Ardwinsagh.'

It was a lovely day, in the early part of June; and, as the Englishman cast himself on a low ridge of sand, he looked over Ardwinsagh Bay with a feeling of ineffable content. To his left lay the Purple Headland; to his right, a long range of breakers, that went straight out into the Atlantic till they were lost from sight; in front lay the Bay of Ardwinsagh, with its bluish-green water sparkling in the summer sunlight, and here and there breaking over some sunken rock, against which the waves spent themselves in foam.

'You see how the currents set, sir? That is what makes it dangerous, for them as doesn't know the coast, to bathe here at any time, or walk when the tide is flowing. Look how the sea is creeping in now, like a race-horse at the finish. It leaves that tongue of sand bare to the last, and then, before you could look round, it has you up to the middle. That is why I made bold to speak to you; for it is not alone on the account of Squire Ennismore the bay has a bad name. But it is about him and the old house you want to hear. The last mortal being that tried to live in it, my great-grandfather said, was a creature, by name Molly

Leary; and she had neither kith nor kin, and begged for her bite and sup, sheltering herself at night in a turf cabin she had built at the back of a ditch. You may be sure she thought herself a made woman when the agent said, "Yes: she might try if she could stop in the house; there was peat and bog-wood," he told her, "and half-a-crown a week for the winter, and a golden guinea once Easter came," when the house was to be put in order for the family; and his wife gave Molly some warm clothes and a blanket or two; and she was well set up.

'You may be sure she didn't choose the worst room to sleep in; and for a while all went quiet, till one night she was wakened by feeling the bedstead lifted by the four corners, and shaken like a carpet. It was a heavy four-post bedstead, with a solid top: and her life seemed to go out of her with the fear. If it had been a ship in a storm off the Headland, it couldn't have pitched worse; and then, all of a sudden, it was dropped with such a bang as nearly drove the heart into her mouth.

'But that, she said, was nothing to the screaming and laughing, and hustling and rushing that filled the house. If a hundred people had been running hard along the passages and tumbling downstairs, they could not have made a greater noise.

'Molly never was able to tell how she got clear of the place; but a man coming late home from Ballycloyne Fair found the creature crouched under the old thorn there, with very little on her —saving your honour's presence. She had a bad fever, and talked about strange things, and never was the same woman after.'

'But what was the beginning of all this? When did the house first get the name of being haunted?'

'After the old Squire went away: that was what I purposed telling you. He did not come here to live regularly till he had got well on in years. He was near seventy at the time I am talking about; but he held himself as upright as ever, and rode as hard as the youngest; and could have drunk a whole roomful under the table, and walked up to bed as unconcerned as you please at the end of the night.

'He was a terrible man. You couldn't lay your tongue to a wickedness he had not been in the fore-front of—drinking, du-elling, gambling—all manner of sins had been meat and drink to him since he was a boy almost. But at last he did something in London so bad, so beyond the beyonds, that he thought he had best come home and live among people who did not know so much about his goings on as the English. It was said he wanted to try and stay in this world for ever; and that he had got some secret drops that kept him well and hearty. There was something wonderful queer about him, anyhow.

'He could hold foot with the youngest; and he was strong, and had a fine fresh colour in his face; and his eyes were like a hawk's; and there was not a break in his voice—and him near upon threescore and ten!

'At long and at last it came to be the March before he was seventy—the worst March ever known in all these parts—such blowing, sleeting, snowing, had not been experienced in the memory of man; when one blusterous night some foreign vessel went to bits on the Purple Hleadland. They say it was an awful sound to hear the death-cry that went up high above the noise of the wind; and it was as bad a sight to see the shore there strewed with corpses of all sorts and sizes, from the little cabin boy to the grizzled seaman.

'They never knew who they were or where they came from, but some of the men had crosses, and beads, and such like, so the priest said they belonged to him, and they were all buried decently in the chapel graveyard.

'There was not much wreckage of value drifted on shore. Most of what is lost about the Head stays there; but one thing did come into the bay—a queer thing—a puncheon of bran-dy.

'The Squire claimed it; it was his right to have all that came on his land, and he owned this sea-shore from the Head to the breakers—every foot—so, in course, he had the brandy; and there was sore ill-will because he gave his men nothing—not even a glass of whiskey.

'Well, to make a long story short, that was the most wonderful liquor anybody ever tasted. The gentry came from far and near to take share, and it was cards and dice, and drinking and story-telling night after night—week in, week out. Even on Sundays, God forgive them! the officers would drive over from Ballyclone, and sit emptying tumbler after tumbler till Monday morning came, for it made beautiful punch.

'But all at once people quit coming—a word went round that the liquor was not all it ought to be. Nobody could say what ailed it, but it got about that in some way men found it did not suit them.

'For one thing, they were losing money very fast.

'They could not make head against the Squire's luck, and a hint was dropped the puncheon ought to have been towed out to sea, and sunk in fifty fathoms of water.

'It was getting to the end of April, and fine, warm weather for the time of year, when first one, and then another, and then another still, began to take notice of a stranger who walked the shore alone at night. He was a dark man, the same colour as the drowned crew lying in the chapel graveyard, and had rings in his ears, and wore a strange kind of hat, and cut wonderful antics as he walked, and had an ambling sort of gait, curious to look at. Many tried to talk to him, but he only shook his head; so, as nobody could make out where he came from or what he wanted, they felt sure he was the spirit of some poor wretch who was tossing about the Head, longing for a snug corner in holy ground.

'The priest went and tried to get some sense out of him.

'"Is it Christian burial you're wanting?" asked his reverence; but the creature only shook his head.

'"Is it word sent to the wives and daughters you've left orphans and widows, you'd like?" but no; it wasn't that.

'"Is it for sin committed you're doomed to walk this way? Would masses comfort ye? There's a heathen," said his reverence; "did you ever hear tell of a Christian that shook his head when masses were mentioned?"

'"Perhaps he doesn't understand English, Father," says one of the officers who was there; "try him with Latin."

'No sooner said than done. The priest started off with such a string of *aves* and *paters* that the stranger fairly took to his heels and ran.

'"He is an evil spirit," explained the priest, when he had stopped, tired out, "and I have exorcised him."

'But the next night my gentleman was back again, as unconcerned as ever.

'"And he'll just have to stay." said his reverence, "for I've got lumbago in the small of my back, and pains in all my joints—never to speak of a hoarseness with standing there shouting; and I don't believe he understood a sentence I said."

'Well, this went on for a while, and people got that frightened of the man, or appearance of a man, they would not go near the sands; till in the end Squire Ennismore, who had always scoffed at the talk, took it into his head he would go down one night, and see into the rights of the matter himself. He, maybe, was feeling lonesome, because, as I told your honour before, people had left off coming to the house, and there was nobody for him to drink with.

'Out he goes, then, as bold as brass; and there were a few followed him. The man came forward at sight of the Squire and took off his hat with a foreign flourish, Not to be behind in civility, the Squire lifted his.

'"I have come, sir," he said, speaking very loud, to try to make him understand, "to know if you are looking for anything, and whether I can assist you to find it."

'The man looked at the Squire as if he had taken the greatest liking to him, and took off his hat again.

'"Is it the vessel that was wrecked you are distressed about?"

'There came no answer, only a forbye mournful shake of the head.

'"Well, *I* haven't your ship, you know; it went all to bits months ago; and as for the sailors, they are snug and sound enough in consecrated ground."

'The man stood and looked at the Squire with a queer sort of smile on his lace.

"What *do* you want?" asked Mr Ennismore, in a bit of a passion. "If anything belonging to you went down with the vessel it's about the Head you ought to be looking for it, not here—unless, indeed, it's after the brandy you're fretting."

'Now, the Squire had tried him in English and French, and was now speaking a language you'd have thought nobody could understand; but, faith, it seemed natural as kissing to the stranger.

"'Oh! that's where you are from, is it?" said the Squire. "Why couldn't you have told me so at once. I can't give you the brandy, because it's mostly drunk; but come along, and you shall have as stiff a glass of punch as ever crossed your lips." And without more to-do off they went, as sociable as you please, jabbering together in some outlandish tongue that made moderate folks' jaws ache to hear.

'That was the first night they conversed together, but it wasn't the last. The stranger must have been the height of good company, for the Squire never tired of him. Every evening, regularly, he came up to the house, always dressed the same, always smiling and polite, and then the Squire called for brandy and hot water, and they drank and played cards till cock-crow, talking and laughing into the small hours.

'This went on for weeks and weeks, nobody knowing where the man came from, or where he went; only two things the old housekeeper did know—that the puncheon was nearly empty, and that the Squire's flesh was wasting off him; and she felt so uneasy she went to the priest, but he could give her no manner of comfort.

'She got so concerned at last that she felt bound to listen at the dining-room door; but they always talked in that foreign gibberish, and whether it was blessing or cursing they were at she couldn't tell.

'Well, the upshot of it came one night in July—on the eve of the Squire's birthday—there wasn't a drop of spirit left in the puncheon—no, not as much as would drown a fly. They had drunk the whole lot clean up—and the old woman stood trembling, expecting every minute to hear the bell ring for more brandy, for where was she to get more if they wanted any?

'All at once the Squire and the stranger came out into the hall. It was a full moon, and light as day.

"I'll go home with you tonight by way of a change," says the Squire.

"'Will you so?" asked the other.

"'That I will," answered the Squire.

"'It is your own choice, you know."

"'Yes; it is my own choice: let us go."

'So they went. And the housekeeper ran up to the window on the great staircase and watched the way they took. Her niece lived there as housemaid, and she came and watched too; and, after a while, the butler as well. They all turned their faces this way, and looked after their master walking beside the strange man along these very sands. Well, they saw them walk out and out to the very ebb-line—but they didn't stop there—they went on, and on, and on, and on, till the water took them to their knees, and then to their waists, and then to their armpits, and then to their heads; but long before that the women and the butler were running out on the shore as fast as they could, shouting for help.'

'Well?' said the Englishman.

'Living or dead, Squire Ennismore never came back again. Next morning, when the tide ebbed again, one walking over the sand saw the print of a cloven foot—that he tracked to the water's edge. Then everybody knew where the Squire had gone, and with whom.'

'And no more search was made?'

'Where would have been the use searching?'

'Not much, I suppose. It's a strange story, anyhow.'

'But true, your honour—every word of it.'

'Oh! I have no doubt of that,' was the satisfactory reply.

The Man With the Nose

By Rhoda Broughton

[The details of this little story are of course imaginary, but the main incidents are, to the best of my belief, facts. They happened twenty, or more than twenty years ago.]

CHAPTER 1

"Let us get a map and see what places look pleasantest?" says she.

"As for that," reply I, "on a map most places look equally pleasant."

"Never mind; get one!"

I obey.

"Do you like the seaside?" asks Elizabeth, lifting her little brown head and her small happy white face from the English sea-coast along which her forefinger is slowly travelling.

"Since you ask me, distinctly *no,*" reply I, for once venturing to have a decided opinion of my own, which during the last few weeks of imbecility I can be hardly said to have had. "I broke my last wooden spade five and twenty years ago. I have but a poor opinion of cockles—sandy red-nosed things, are not they? and the air always makes me bilious."

"Then we certainly will not go there," says Elizabeth, laughing. "A bilious bridegroom! alliterative but horrible! None of our friends show the least eagerness to lend us their country house."

"Oh that God would put it into the hearts of men to take their wives straight home, as their fathers did" say I, with a cross groan.

"It is evident, therefore, that we must go somewhere," returns she, not heeding the aspiration contained in my last speech, making her forefinger resume its employment, and reaching Torquay.

"I suppose so," say I, with a sort of sigh; "for once in our lives we must resign ourselves to having the finger of derision pointed at us by waiters and landlords."

"You shall leave your new portmanteau at home, and I will leave all my best clothes, and nobody will guess that we are bride and bridegroom; they will think that we have been married—oh, ever since the world began" (opening her eyes very wide).

I shake my head. "With an old portmanteau and in rags we shall still have the mark of the beast upon us."

"Do you mind much? do you hate being ridiculous ?' asks Elizabeth, meekly, rather depressed by my view of the case; "because if so, let us go somewhere out of the way, where there will be very few people to laugh at us."

"On the contrary," return I, stoutly, "we will betake ourselves to some spot where such as we do chiefly congregate where we shall be swallowed up and lost in the multitude of our fellow-sinners." A pause devoted to reflection. "What do you say to Killarney?" say I, cheerfully.

"There are a great many fleas there, I believe," replies Elizabeth, slowly; "fleabites make large lumps on me; you would not like me if I were covered with large lumps."

At the hideous ideal picture thus presented to me by my little beloved I relapse into inarticulate idiocy; emerging from which by-and-by, I suggest "The Lakes?" My arm is round her, and I feel her supple body shiver though it is mid July, and the bees are booming about in the still and sleepy noon garden outside.

"Oh—no—no—not *there!*"

"Why such emphasis?" I ask gaily; "more fleas? At this rate, and with this *sine quâ non*, our choice will grow limited."

"Something dreadful happened to me there," she says, with another shudder. "But indeed I did not think there was any harm in it—I never thought anything would come of it."

"What the devil was it?" cry I, in a jealous heat and hurry; "what the mischief *did* you do, and why have not you told me about it before ?"

"I did not *do* much," she answers meekly, seeking for my hand, and when found kissing it in timid deprecation of my wrath;"but I was ill—very ill—there; I had a nervous fever. I was in a bed hung with a chintz with a red and green fern-leaf pattern on it. I have always hated red and green fern-leaf chintzes ever since."

"It would be possible to avoid the obnoxious bed, would not it?" say I, laughing a little. "Where does it lie? Windermere? Ulleswater? Wastwater? Where "

"We were at Ulleswater," she says, speaking rapidly, while a hot colour grows on her small white cheeks—"Papa, mamma, and I; and there came a mesmeriser to Penrith, and we went to see him—everybody did—and he asked leave to mesmerise me—he said I should be such a good medium—and—and I did not know what it was like. I thought it would be quite good fun—and—and I let him."

She is trembling exceedingly; even the loving pressure of my arms cannot abate her shivering.

"Well?"

"And after that I do not remember anything—I believe I did all sorts of extraordinary things that he told me—sang and danced, and made a fool of myself—but when I came home I was very ill, very—I lay in bed for five whole weeks, and—and was off my head, and said odd and wicked things that you would not have expected me to say—that dreadful bed! shall I ever forget it?"

"We will *not* go to the Lakes," I say, decisively, "and we will not talk any more about mesmerism."

"That is right," she says, with a sigh of relief, "I try to think about it as little as possible; but sometimes, in the dead black of the night, when God seems a long way off, and the devil near, it comes back to me so strongly—I feel, do not you know, as if he were *there*—somewhere in the room, and I *must* get up and follow him."

"Why should not we go abroad" suggest I, abruptly turning the conversation.

"Why, indeed," cries Elizabeth, recovering her gaiety, while her pretty blue eyes begin to dance. "How stupid of us not to have thought of it before; only *abroad* is a big word, *What* abroad?"

"We must be content with something short of Central Africa," I say, gravely, "as I think our one hundred and fifty pounds would hardly take us that far."

"Wherever we go, we must buy a dialogue book," suggests my little bride elect, "and I will learn some phrases before we start."

"As for that, the Anglo-Saxon tongue takes one pretty well round the world," reply I, with a feeling of complacent British swagger, putting my hands in my breeches pockets.

"Do you fancy the Rhine?" says Elizabeth, with a rather timid suggestion; "I know it is the fashion to run it down nowadays, and call it a cocktail river; but—but after all it cannot be so *very* contemptible, or Byron could not have said such noble things about it."

The castled crag of Drachenfels
Frowns o'er the wide and winding Rhine,
Whose breast of waters broadly swells
Between the banks which bear the vine,

. . . .say I, spouting. "After all, that proves nothing, for Byron could have made a silk purse out of a sow's ear."

"The Rhine will not do then?" says she, resignedly, suppressing a sigh.

"On the contrary, it will do admirably: it *is* a cocktail river, and I do not care who says it is not," reply I, with illiberal positiveness; "but everybody should be able to say so from their own experience, and not from hearsay: the Rhine let it be, by all means."

So the Rhine it is.

CHAPTER 2

I have got over it; we have both got over it tolerably, creditably; but after all, it is a much severer ordeal for a man than a woman, who, with a bouquet to occupy her hands, and a veil to gently shroud her features, need merely be prettily passive. I am alluding, I need hardly say, to the religious ceremony of marriage, which I natter myself I have gone through with a stiff sheepishness not unworthy of my country. It is a three-days-old event now, and we are getting used to belonging to one another, though Elizabeth still takes off her ring twenty times a day to admire its bright thickness; still laughs when she hears herself called "*Madame.*" Three days ago, we kissed all our friends, and left them to make themselves ill on our cake, and criticise our bridal behaviour, and now we are at Brussels, she and I, feeling oddly, joyfully free from any chaperone. We have been mildly sight-seeing—very mildly, most people would say, but we have resolved not to take our pleasure with the railway speed of Americans, or the hasty sadness of our fellow Britons. Slowly and gaily we have been taking ours.

Today we have been to visit Wiertz's pictures. Have you ever seen them, oh reader? They are known to comparatively few people, but if you have a taste for the unearthly terrible—if you wish to sup full of horrors, hasten thither. We have been peering through the appointed peep-hole at the horrible cholera picture—the man buried alive by mistake, pushing up the lid of his coffin, and stretching a ghastly face and livid hands out of his winding sheet towards you, while awful grey-blue coffins are piled around, and noisome toads and giant spiders crawl damply about. On first seeing it, I have reproached myself for bringing one of so nervous a temperament as Elizabeth to see so haunting and hideous a spectacle; but she is less impressed than I expected—less impressed than I myself am.

"He is very lucky to be able to get his lid up," she says, with a half-laugh; "we should find it hard work to burst our brass nails, should not we? When you bury me, dear, fasten me down very slightly, in case there may be some mistake."

And now all the long and quiet July evening we have been prowling together about the streets. Brussels is the town of towns for *flâner*-ing—have been flattening our noses against the shop windows, and making each other imaginary presents. Elizabeth has not confined herself to imagination, however; she has made me buy her a little bonnet with feathers "in order to look married," as she says, and the result is such a delicious picture of a child playing at being grown up, having practised a theft on its mother's wardrobe, that for the last two hours I have been in a foolish ecstasy of love and laughter over her and it. We are at the "Bellevue," and have a fine suite of rooms, *au premier*, evidently specially devoted to the English, to the gratification of whose well-known loyalty the Prince and Princess of Wales are simpering from the walls.

Is there anyone in the three kingdoms who knows his own face as well as he knows the faces of Albert Victor and Alexandra? The long evening has at last slidden into night—night far advanced—night melting into earliest day. All Brussels is asleep. One moment ago I also was asleep, soundly as any log. What is it that has made me take this sudden, headlong plunge out of sleep into wakefulness? Who is it that is clutching at and calling upon me? What is it that is making me struggle mistily up into a sitting posture, and try to revive my sleep-numbed senses? A summer night is never wholly dark; by the half light that steals through the closed *persiennes* and open windows I see my wife standing beside my bed; the extremity of terror on her face, and her fingers digging themselves with painful tenacity into my arm.

"Tighter, tighter!" she is crying, wildly. "What are you thinking of? You are letting me go!"

"Good heavens!" say I, rubbing my eyes, while my muddy brain grows a trifle clearer. "What is it? What has happened? Have you had a nightmare?"

"You saw him," she says, with a sort of sobbing breathlessness; "you know you did! You saw him as well as I."

"I!" cry I, incredulously—"not I. Till this second I have been fast asleep. *I* saw nothing."

"You did!" she cries, passionately. "You know you did. Why do you deny it? You were as frightened as I?"

"As I live," I answer, solemnly, "I know no more than the dead what you are talking about; till you woke me by calling me and catching hold of me, I was as sound asleep as the seven sleepers."

"Is it possible that it can have been a *dream?*" she says, with a long sigh, for a moment loosing my arm, and covering her face with her hands. "But no—in a dream I should have been somewhere else, but I was here—*here*—on that bed, and he stood *there*," pointing with her forefinger, "just *there*, between the foot of it and the window!"

She stops, panting.

"It is all that brute Wiertz," say I, in a fury. "I wish I had been buried alive myself, before I had been fool enough to take you to see his beastly daubs."

"Light a candle," she says, in the same breathless way, her teeth chattering with fright. "Let us make sure that he is not hidden somewhere in the room."

"How could he be?" say I, striking a match; "the door is locked."

"He might have got in by the balcony," she answers, still trembling violently.

"He would have had to have cut a very large hole in the *persiennes*," say I, half-mockingly. "See, they are intact and well fastened on the inside."

She sinks into an armchair, and pushes her loose soft hair from her white face.

"It was a *dream* then, I suppose?"

She is silent for a moment or two, while I bring her a glass of water, and throw a dressing-gown round her cold and shrinking form.

"Now tell me, my little one," I say, coaxingly, sitting down at her feet, "what it was what you thought you saw?"

"*Thought* I saw!" echoes she, with indignant emphasis, sitting upright, while her eyes sparkle feverishly. "I am as certain that

I saw him standing there as I am that I see that candle burning that I see this chair that I see you."

"*Him!* but who is *him?*"

She falls forward on my neck, and buries her face in my shoulder.

"That dreadful man!" she says, while her whole body is one tremor.

"*What* dreadful man?" cry I, impatiently.

She is silent.

"Who was he?"

"I do not know."

"Did you ever see him before ?"

"Oh, no—no, never! I hope to God I may never see him again!"

"What was he like?"

"Come closer to me," she says, laying hold of my hand with her small and chilly fingers; "stay *quite* near me, and I will tell you,"—after a pause—"he had a *nose!*"

"My dear soul," cry I, bursting out with a loud laugh in the silence of the night, "do not most people have noses? Would not he have been much more dreadful if he had had *none?*"

"But it was *such* a nose!" she says, with perfect trembling gravity.

"A bottle nose?" suggest I, still cackling.

"For heaven's sake, don't laugh!" she says, nervously; "if you had seen his face, you would have been as little disposed to laugh as I."

"But his nose?" return I, suppressing my merriment; "what kind of nose was it? See, I am as grave as a judge."

"It was very prominent," she answers, in a sort of awe-struck half-whisper, "and very sharply chiselled; the nostrils very much cut out." A little pause. "His eyebrows were one straight black line across his face, and under them his eyes burnt like dull coals of fire, that shone and yet did not shine; they looked like dead eyes, sunken, half extinguished, and yet sinister."

"And what did he do?" ask I, impressed, despite myself, by

her passionate earnestness; "when did you first see him?"

"I was asleep," she said "at least I thought so and suddenly I opened my eyes, and he was *there—there*"—pointing again with trembling finger—"between the window and the bed."

"What was he doing? Was he walking about?"

"He was standing as still as stone I never saw any live thing so still—*looking* at me; he never called or beckoned, or moved a finger, but his eyes *commanded* me to come to him, as the eyes of the mesmeriser at Penrith did." She stops, breathing heavily. I can hear her heart's loud and rapid beats.

"And you?" I say, pressing her more closely to my side, and smoothing her troubled hair.

"I *hated* it," she cries, excitedly; "I loathed it—abhorred it. I was ice-cold with fear and horror, but—I *felt* myself going to him."

"Yes?"

"And then I shrieked out to you, and you came running, and caught fast hold of me, and held me tight at first—quite tight— but presently I felt your hold slacken—slacken—and though I *longed* to stay with you, though I was *mad* with fright, yet I felt myself pulling strongly away from you—going to him; and he— he stood there always looking—looking and then I gave one last loud shriek, and I suppose I awoke—and it was a dream!"

"I never heard of a clearer case of nightmare," say I, stoutly; "that vile Wiertz! I should like to see his whole *Musée* burnt by the hands of the hangman tomorrow."

She shakes her head. "It had nothing to say to Wiertz; what it meant I do not know, but—"

"It meant nothing," I answer, reassuringly, "except that for the future we will go and see none but good and pleasant sights, and steer clear of charnel-house fancies."

CHAPTER 3

Elizabeth is now in a position to decide whether the Rhine is a cocktail river or no, for she is on it, and so am I. We are sitting, with an awning over our heads, and little wooden stools under our feet. Elizabeth has a small sailor's hat and blue ribbon on her head. The river breeze has blown it rather awry; has tangled her plenteous hair; has made a faint pink stain on her pale cheeks. It is some fete day, and the boat is crowded. Tables, countless camp-stools, volumes of black smoke pouring from the funnel, as we steam along. "Nothing to the Caledonian Canal!" cries a burly Scotchman in leggings, speaking with loud authority, and surveying with an air of contempt the eternal vine-clad slopes, that sound so well, and look so *sticky* in reality. "Cannot hold a candle to it!" A rival bride and bridegroom opposite, sitting together like love-birds under an umbrella, looking into each other's eyes instead of at the Rhine scenery.

"They might as well have stayed at home, might not they?" says my wife, with a little air of superiority. "Come, we are not so bad as that, are we?"

A storm comes on: hailstones beat slant-wise and reach us—stone and sting us right under our awning. Everybody rushes down below, and takes the opportunity to feed ravenously. There are few actions more disgusting than eating *can* be made. A handsome girl close to us—her immaturity evidenced by the two long tails of black hair down her back—is thrusting her knife half way down her throat.

"Come on deck again," says Elizabeth, disgusted and frightened at this last sight. "The hail was much better than this!"

So we return to our camp-stools, and sit alone under one mackintosh in the lashing storm, with happy hearts and empty stomachs.

"Is not this better than any luncheon?" asks Elizabeth, triumphantly, while the raindrops hang on her long and curled lashes.

"Infinitely better," reply I, madly struggling with the umbrella to prevent its being blown inside out, and gallantly ignoring a species of gnawing sensation at my entrails.

The squall clears off by and by, and we go steaming, steaming on past the unnumbered little villages by the water's edge with church spires and pointed roof, past the countless rocks with their little pert castles perched on the top of them, past the tall, stiff poplar rows. The church bells are ringing gaily as we go by. A nightingale is singing from a wood. The black eagle of Prussia droops on the stream behind us, swish-swish through the dull green water. A fat woman who is interested in it, leans over the back of the boat, and by some happy effect of crinoline, displays to her fellow-passengers two yards of thick white cotton legs. She is, fortunately for herself, unconscious of her generosity.

The day steals on; at every stopping place more people come on. There is hardly elbow room; and, what is worse, almost everybody is drunk. Rocks, castles, villages, poplars, slide by, while the paddles churn always the water, and the evening draws greyly on. At Bingen a party of big blue Prussian soldiers, very drunk, "glorious" as Tam o'Shanter, come and establish themselves close to us. They call for Lager Beer; talk at the tip-top of their strong voices; two of them begin to spar; all seem inclined to sing. Elizabeth is frightened. We are two hours late in arriving at Biebrich. It is half an hour more before we can get ourselves and our luggage into a carriage and set off along the winding road to Wiesbaden. "The night is chilly, but not dark." There is only a little shabby bit of a moon, but it shines as hard as it can. Elizabeth is quite worn out, her tired head droops in uneasy sleep on my shoulder. Once she wakes up with a start.

"Are you sure that it meant nothing?" she asks, looking me eagerly in my face; "do people often have such dreams?"

"Often, often," I answer, reassuringly.

"I am always afraid of falling asleep now," she says, trying to sit upright and keep her heavy eyes open, "for fear of seeing him standing there again. Tell me, do you think I shall? Is there any chance, any probability of it?"

"None, none!"

We reach Wiesbaden at last, and drive up to the Hôtel des Quatre Saisons. By this time it is full midnight. Two or three men are standing about the door. Morris, the maid, has got out—so have I, and I am holding out my hand to Elizabeth, when I hear her give one piercing scream, and see her with ash-white face and starting eyes point with her fore-finger—

"There he is!—there!—there!"

I look in the direction indicated, and just catch a glimpse of a tall figure, standing half in the shadow of the night, half in the gas-light from the hotel. I have not time for more than one cursory glance, as I am interrupted by a cry from the bystanders, and turning quickly round, am just in time to catch my wife, who falls in utter insensibility into my arms. We carry her into a room on the ground floor; it is small, noisy, and hot, but it is the nearest at hand. In about an hour she reopens her eyes. A strong shudder makes her quiver from head to foot.

"Where is he?" she says, in a terrified whisper, as her senses come slowly back. "He is somewhere about—somewhere near. I feel that he is!"

"My dearest child, there is no one here but Morris and me," I answer, soothingly. "Look for yourself. See."

I take one of the candles and light up each corner of the room in succession.

"You saw him!" she says, in trembling hurry, sitting up and clenching her hands together. "I know you did—I pointed him out to you—you *cannot* say that it was a dream *this* time."

"I saw two or three ordinary looking men as we drove up," I answer, in a commonplace, matter-of-fact tone. "I did not notice anything remarkable about any of them; you know the fact is, darling, that you have had nothing to eat all day, nothing but a biscuit, and you are overwrought, and fancy things."

"Fancy!" echoes she, with strong irritation. "How you talk! Was I ever one to fancy things? I tell you that as sure as I sit here—as sure as you stand there—I saw him—*him*—the man I saw in my dream, if it was a dream. There was not a hair's breadth of difference between them—and he was looking at me—looking—"

She breaks off into hysterical sobbing.

"My dear child!" say I, thoroughly alarmed, and yet half angry, "for God's sake do not work yourself up into a fever: wait till tomorrow, and we will find out who he is, and all about him;

you yourself will laugh when we discover that he is some harmless bagman."

"Why not *now?*" she says, nervously; "why cannot you find out *now—this minute?*"

"Impossible! Everybody is in bed! Wait till tomorrow, and all will be cleared up."

The morrow comes, and I go about the hotel, inquiring. The house is so full, and the data I have to go upon are so small, that for some time I have great difficulty in making it understood to whom I am alluding. At length one waiter seems to comprehend.

"A tall and dark gentleman, with a pronounced and very peculiar nose? Yes; there has been such a one, certainly, in the hotel, but he left at *grand matin* this morning; he remained only one night."

"And his name?"

The *garçon* shakes his head. "That is unknown, *monsieur*; he did not inscribe it in the visitor's book."

"What countryman was he?"

Another shake of the head. "He spoke German, but it was with a foreign accent."

"Whither did he go?"

That also is unknown. Nor can I arrive at any more facts about him.

CHAPTER 4

A Fortnight has passed; we have been hither and thither; now we are at Lucerne. Peopled with better inhabitants, Lucerne might well do for Heaven. It is drawing towards eventide, and Elizabeth and I are sitting hand in hand on a quiet bench, under the shady linden trees, on a high hill up above the lake. There is nobody to see us, so we sit peaceably hand in hand. Up by the still and solemn monastery we came, with its small and narrow windows, calculated to hinder the holy fathers from promenading curious eyes on the world, the flesh, and the devil, tripping past them in blue gauze veils: below us grass and green trees, houses with high-pitched roofs, little dormer-windows, and shutters yet greener than the grass; below us the lake in its rippleless peace, calm, quiet, motionless as Bethesda's pool before the coming of the troubling angel.

"I said it was too good to last," say I, doggedly, "did not I, only yesterday? Perfect peace, perfect sympathy, perfect freedom from nagging worries—when did such a state of things last more than two days?"

Elizabeth's eyes are idly fixed on a little steamer, with a stripe of red along its side, and a tiny puff of smoke from its funnel, gliding along and cutting a narrow white track on Lucerne's sleepy surface.

"This is the fifth false alarm of the gout having gone to his stomach within the last two years," continue I, resentfully. "I declare to Heaven, that if it has not really gone there this time, I'll cut the whole concern."

Let no one cast up their eyes in horror, imagining that it is my father to whom I am thus alluding; it is only a great uncle by marriage, in consideration of whose wealth and vague promises I have dawdled professionless through twenty-eight years of my life.

"You *must* not go," says Elizabeth, giving my hand an imploring squeeze. "The man in the Bible said, '*I have married a wife, and therefore I cannot come;*' why should it be a less valid excuse now a days?"

"If I recollect rightly, it was considered rather a poor one even then," reply I, dryly.

Elizabeth is unable to contradict this, she therefore only lifts two pouted lips (Monsieur Taine objects to the redness of English women's mouths, but I do not) to be kissed, and says, "Stay." I am good enough to comply with her unspoken request, though I remain firm with regard to her spoken one.

"My dearest child," I say, with an air of worldly experience and superior wisdom, "kisses are very good things—in fact there are few better—but one cannot live upon them."

"Let us try," she says, coaxingly.

"I wonder which would get tired first?" I say, laughing. But she only goes on pleading, "Stay, stay."

"How *can* I stay?" I cry, impatiently; "you talk as if I *wanted* to go! Do you think it is any pleasanter to me to leave you than to you to be left? But you know his disposition, his rancorous resentment of fancied neglects. For the sake of two days' indulgence, must I throw away what will keep us in ease and plenty to the end of our days?"

"I do not care for plenty," she says, with a little petulant gesture. "I do not see that rich people are any happier than poor ones. Look at the St. Glairs; they have £40,000 a-year, and she is a miserable woman, perfectly miserable, because her face gets red after dinner."

"There will be no fear of *our* faces getting red after dinner," say I, grimly, "for we shall have no dinner for them to get red after."

A pause. My eyes stray away to the mountains. Pilatus on the right, with his jagged peak and slender snow-chains about his harsh neck; hill after hill rising silent, eternal, like guardian spirits standing hand in hand around their child, the lake. As I look, suddenly they have all flushed, as at some noblest thought, and over all their sullen faces streams an ineffable rosy joy—a solemn and wonderful effulgence, such as Israel saw reflected from the features of the Eternal in their prophet's transfigured eyes. The unutterable peace and stainless beauty of earth and sky seem to lie softly on my soul. "Would God I could stay! Would God all life could be like this!" I say, devoutly, and the aspiration has the reverent earnestness of a prayer.

"Why do you say, '*Would God!*'" she cries, passionately, "when it lies with yourself? Oh my dear love," gently sliding her hand through my arm, and lifting wetly-beseeching eyes to my face, "I do not know why I insist upon it so much—I cannot tell you myself—I dare say I seem selfish and unreasonable—but I feel as if your going now would be the end of all things—as if—."

She breaks off suddenly.

"My child," say I, thoroughly distressed, but still determined to have my own way, "you talk as if I were going for ever and a day; in a week, at the outside, I shall be back, and then you will thank me for the very thing for which you now think me so hard and disobliging."

"Shall I?" she answers, mournfully. "Well, I hope so."

"You will not be alone, either; you will have Morris."

"Yes."

"And every day you will write me a long letter, telling me every single thing that you do, say, and think."

"Yes."

She answers me gently and obediently; but I can see that she is still utterly unreconciled to the idea of my absence.

"What is it that you are afraid of?" I ask, becoming rather irritated. "What do you suppose will happen to you?"

She does not answer; only a large tear falls on my hand, which she hastily wipes away with her pocket handkerchief, as if afraid of exciting my wrath.

"Can you give me any good reason why I *should* stay?" I ask, dictatorially.

"None—none—only—stay—stay!"

But I am resolved *not* to stay. Early the next morning I set off.

CHAPTER 5

This time it is not a false alarm; this time it really has gone to his stomach, and, declining to be dislodged thence, kills him. My return is therefore retarded until after the funeral and the reading of the will. The latter is so satisfactory, and my time is so fully occupied with a multiplicity of attendant business, that I have no leisure to regret the delay. I write to Elizabeth, but receive no letters from her. This surprises and makes me rather angry, but does not alarm me. "If she had been ill, if anything had happened, Morris would have written. She never was great at writing, poor little soul. What dear little babyish notes she used to send me during our engagement; perhaps she wishes to punish me for my disobedience to her wishes. Well, *now* she will see who was in the right." I am drawing near her now; I am walking up from the railway station at Lucerne. I am very joyful as I march along under an umbrella, in the grand broad shining of the summer afternoon. I think with pensive passion of the last glimpse I had of my beloved—her small and wistful face looking out from among the thick fair fleece of her long hair—winking away her tears and blowing kisses to me.

It is a new sensation to me to have anyone looking tearfully wistful over my departure. I draw near the great glaring Schweizerhof, with its colonnaded, tourist-crowded porch; here are all the pomegranates as I left them, in their green tubs, with their scarlet blossoms, and the dusty oleanders in a row. I look up at our windows; nobody is looking out from them; they are open, and the curtains are alternately swelled out and drawn in by the softly-playful wind. I run quickly upstairs and burst noisily into the sitting-room. Empty, perfectly empty! I open the adjoining door into the bedroom, crying "Elizabeth! Elizabeth!" but I receive no answer. Empty too. A feeling of indignation creeps over me as I think, "Knowing the time of my return, she might have managed to be indoors."

I have returned to the silent sitting-room, where the only noise is the wind still playing hide-and-seek with the curtains. As I look vacantly round my eye catches sight of a letter lying on the table. I pick it up mechanically and look at the address. Good heavens! what can this mean? It is my own, that I sent her two days ago, unopened, with the seal unbroken. Does she carry her resentment so far as not even to open my letters? I spring at the bell and violently ring it. It is answered by the waiter who has always specially attended us.

"Is *madame* gone out?"

The man opens his mouth and stares at me.

"*Madame!* Is *monsieur* then not aware that *madame* is no longer at the hotel?"

"*What?*"

"On the same day as *monsieur, madame* departed."

"*Departed!* Good God! what are you talking about?"

"A few hours after *monsieur's* departure—I will not be positive as to the exact time, but it must have been between one and two o'clock as the midday *table d'hôte* was in progress—a gentleman came and asked for *madame*—"

"Yes—be quick."

"I demanded whether I should take up his card, but he said 'No,' that was unnecessary, as he was perfectly well known to *madame*; and, in fact, a short time afterwards, without saying anything to anyone, she departed with him."

"And did not return in the evening?"

"No, *monsieur; madame* has not returned since that day."

I clench my hands in an agony of rage and grief. "So this is it!" With that pure child-face, with that divine ignorance—only three weeks married—this is the trick she has played me!" I am recalled to myself by a compassionate suggestion from the *garçon*.

"Perhaps it was the brother of *madame*."

Elizabeth has no brother, but the remark brings back to me the necessity of self-command. "Very probably," I answer, speaking with infinite difficulty. "What sort of looking gentleman was he?"

"He was a very tall and dark gentleman with a most peculiar nose—not quite like any nose that I ever saw before—and most singular eyes. Never have I seen a gentleman who at all resembled him."

I sink into a chair, while a cold shudder creeps over me as I think of my poor child's dream—of her fainting fit at Wiesbaden—of her unconquerable dread of and aversion from my departure. And this happened twelve days ago! I catch up my hat, and prepare to rush like a madman in pursuit.

"How did they go?" I ask incoherently; "by train?—driving?—walking?"

"They went in a carriage."

"What direction did they take? Whither did they go?"

He shakes his head. "It is not known."

"It *must* be known," I cry, driven to frenzy by every second's delay. "Of course the driver could tell; where is he? where can I find him ?"

"He did not belong to Lucerne, neither did the carriage; the gentleman brought them with him."

"But *madame's* maid," say I, a gleam of hope flashing across my mind; "did she go with her?"

"No, *monsieur*, she is still here; she was as much surprised as monsieur at *madame's* departure."

"Send her at once," I cry eagerly; but when she comes I find that she can throw no light on the matter. She weeps noisily and says many irrelevant things, but I can obtain no information from her beyond the fact that she was unaware of her mistress's departure until long after it had taken place, when, surprised at not being rung for at the usual time, she had gone to her room and found it empty, and on inquiring in the hotel, had heard of her sudden departure; that, expecting her to return at night, she had sat up waiting for her till two o'clock in the morning, but that, as I knew, she had not returned, neither had anything since been heard of her.

Not all my inquiries, not all my cross-questionings of the whole staff of the hotel, of the visitors, of the railway officials, of nearly all the inhabitants of Lucerne and its environs, procure me a jot more knowledge. On the next few weeks I look back as on a hellish and insane dream. I can neither eat nor sleep; I am unable to remain one moment quiet; my whole existence, my nights and my days, are spent in seeking, seeking. Everything that human despair and frenzied love can do is done by me. I advertise, I communicate with the police, I employ detectives; but that fatal twelve days' start for ever baffles me. Only on one occasion do I obtain one tittle of information. In a village a few miles from Lucerne the peasants, on the day in question, saw a carriage driving rapidly through their little street. It was closed, but through the windows they could see the occupants—a dark gentleman, with the peculiar physiognomy which has been so often described, and on the opposite seat a lady lying apparently in a state of utter insensibility. But even this leads to nothing.

Oh, reader, these things happened twenty years ago; since then I have searched sea and land, but never have I seen my little Elizabeth again.

The Tapestried Chamber

A.K.A. THE LADY IN THE SACQUE

By Sir Walter Scott[1]

About the end of the American war, when the officers of
Lord Cornwallis's army, which surrendered at York-town, and
others, who had been made prisoners during the impolitic and
ill-fated controversy, were returning to their own country, to
relate their adventures and repose themselves after their fatigues,
there was amongst them a general officer, to whom Miss S. gave
the name of Browne, but merely, as I understood, to save the
inconvenience of introducing a nameless agent in the narrative.
He was an officer of merit, as well as a gentleman of high consideration for family and attainments.

Some business had carried General Browne upon a tour
through the western counties, when, in the conclusion of a
morning stage, he found himself in the vicinity of a small country town, which presented a scene of uncommon beauty, and of
a character peculiarly English.

The little town, with its stately old church, whose tower bore
testimony to the devotion of ages long past, lay amidst pasture

---

1. The present writer heard the following events related, more than twenty years
since, by the celebrated Miss Seward of Litchfield, who to her numerous ac-
complishments added, in a remarkable degree, the power of narrative in private
conversation. In its present form the tale must necessarily lose all the interest which
was attached to it by the flexible voice and intelligent features of the gifted narrator.
Yet still, read aloud to an undoubting audience by the doubtful light of the closing
evening, or in silence by a decaying taper, and amidst the solitude of a half-lighted
apartment, it may redeem its character as a good ghost story.

and cornfields of small extent, but bounded and divided with hedgerow timber of great age and size. There were few marks of modern improvement. The environs of the place intimated neither the solitude of decay nor the bustle of novelty; the houses were old, but in good repair; and the beautiful little river murmured freely on its way to the left of the town, neither restrained by a dam nor bordered by a towing-path.

Upon a gentle eminence nearly a mile to the southward of the town were seen, amongst many venerable oaks and tangled thickets, the turrets of a castle as old as the wars of York and Lancaster, but which seemed to have received important alterations during the age of Elizabeth and her successors. It had not been a place of great size; but whatever accommodation it formerly afforded was, it must be supposed, still to be obtained within its walls; at least such was the inference which General Browne drew from observing the smoke arise merrily from several of the ancient wreathed and carved chimney-stalks. The wall of the park ran alongside of the highway for two or three hundred yards; and, through the different points by which the eye found glimpses into the woodland scenery, it seemed to be well stocked. Other points of view opened in succession, now a full one of the front of the old castle, and now a side glimpse at its particular towers; the former rich in all the *bizarrerie* of the Elizabethan school, while the simple and solid strength of other parts of the building seemed to show that they had been raised more for defence than ostentation.

Delighted with the partial glimpses which he obtained of the castle through the woods and glades by which this ancient feudal fortress was surrounded, our military traveller was determined to inquire whether it might not deserve a nearer view, and whether it contained family pictures or other subjects of curiosity worthy of a stranger's visit; when, leaving the vicinity of the park, he rolled through a clean and well-paved street, and stopped at the door of a well-frequented inn.

Before ordering horses to proceed on his journey, General Browne made inquiries concerning the proprietor of the *château* which had so attracted his admiration, and was equally surprised and pleased at hearing in reply a nobleman named whom we shall call Lord Woodville. How fortunate! Much of Browne's early recollections, both at school and at college, had been connected with young Woodville, whom, by a few questions, he now ascertained to be the same with the owner of this fair domain. He had been raised to the peerage by the decease of his father a few months before, and, as the General learned from the landlord, the term of mourning being ended, was now taking possession of his paternal estate in the jovial season of merry autumn, accompanied by a select party of friends to enjoy the sports of a country famous for game.

This was delightful news to our traveller. Frank Woodville had been Richard Browne's fag at Eton, and his chosen intimate at Christ Church; their pleasures and their tasks had been the same; and the honest soldier's heart warmed to find his early friend in possession of so delightful a residence, and of an estate, as the landlord assured him with a nod and a wink, fully adequate to maintain and add to his dignity. Nothing was more natural than that the traveller should suspend a journey which there was nothing to render hurried, to pay a visit to an old friend under such agreeable circumstances.

The fresh horses, therefore, had only the brief task of conveying the General's travelling carriage to Woodville Castle. A porter admitted them at a modern Gothic lodge, built in that style to correspond with the castle itself, and at the same time rang a bell to give warning of the approach of visitors. Apparently the sound of the bell had suspended the separation of the company bent on the various amusements of the morning; for, on entering the court of the *château*, several young men were lounging about in their sporting dresses, looking at and criticising the dogs which the keepers held in readiness to attend their pastime. As General Browne alighted, the young lord came to the gate of the hall, and for an instant gazed, as at a stranger, upon the countenance of his friend, on which war, with its fatigues and its wounds, had made a great alteration. But the uncertainty lasted no longer than till the visitor had spoken, and the hearty greeting which followed was such as can only be exchanged betwixt those who have passed together the merry days of careless boyhood or early youth.

"If I could have formed a wish, my dear Browne," said Lord Woodville, "it would have been to have you here, of all men, upon this occasion, which my friends are good enough to hold as a sort of holiday. Do not think you have been unwatched during the years you have been absent from us. I have traced you through your dangers, your triumphs, your misfortunes, and was delighted to see that, whether in victory or defeat, the name of my old friend was always distinguished with applause."

The General made a suitable reply, and congratulated his friend on his new dignities, and the possession of a place and domain so beautiful.

"Nay, you have seen nothing of it as yet," said Lord Woodville, "and I trust you do not mean to leave us till you are better acquainted with it. It is true, I confess, that my present party is pretty large, and the old house, like other places of the kind, does not possess so much accommodation as the extent of the outward walls appears to promise. But we can give you a comfortable old-fashioned room; and I venture to suppose that your campaigns have taught you to be glad of worse quarters."

The General shrugged his shoulders and laughed. "I presume," he said, "the worst apartment in your *chateau* is considerably superior to the old tobacco-cask in which I was fain to take up my night's lodging when I was in the Bush, as the Virginians call it, with the light corps. There I lay, like Diogenes himself, so delighted with my covering from the elements that I made a vain attempt to have it rolled on to my next quarters; but my commander for the time would give way to no such luxurious provision, and I took farewell of my beloved cask with tears in my eyes."

"Well, then, since you do not fear your quarters," said Lord Woodville, "you will stay with me a week at least. Of guns, dogs, fishing-rods, flies, and means of sport by sea and land we have enough and to spare; you cannot pitch on an amusement but we will pitch on the means of pursuing it. But if you prefer the gun and pointers, I will go with you myself, and see whether you have mended your shooting since you have been amongst the Indians of the back settlements."

The General gladly accepted his friendly host's proposal in all its points. After a morning of manly exercise, the company met at dinner, where it was the delight of Lord Woodville to conduce to the display of the high properties of his recovered friend, so as to recommend him to his guests, most of whom were persons of distinction. He led General Browne to speak of the scenes he had witnessed; and as every word marked alike the brave officer and the sensible man, who retained possession of his cool judgment under the most imminent dangers, the company looked upon the soldier with general respect, as on one who had proved himself possessed of an uncommon portion of personal courage, that attribute, of all others, of which everybody desires to be thought possessed.

The day at Woodville Castle ended as usual in such mansions. The hospitality stopped within the limits of good order; music, in which the young lord was a proficient, succeeded to the circulation of the bottle; cards and billiards, for those who preferred such amusements, were in readiness; but the exercise of the morning required early hours, and not long after eleven o'clock the guests began to retire to their several apartments.

The young lord himself conducted his friend, General Browne, to the chamber destined for him, which answered the description he had given of it, being comfortable, but old-fashioned. The bed was of the massive form used in the end of the seventeenth century, and the curtains of faded silk, heavily trimmed with tarnished gold. But then the sheets, pillows, and blankets looked delightful to the campaigner, when he thought of his mansion, the cask. There was an air of gloom in the tapestry hangings, which, with their worn-out graces, curtained the walls of the little chamber, and gently undulated as the autumnal breeze found its way through the ancient lattice-window, which pattered and whistled as the air gained entrance. The toilet, too, with its mirror, turbaned after the manner of the beginning of the century with a *coiffure* of murrey-coloured silk, and its hundred strange-shaped boxes, providing for arrangements which had been obsolete for more than fifty years, had an antique, and in so far a melancholy, aspect. But nothing could blaze more brightly and cheerfully than the two large wax candles; or, if aught could rival them, it was the flaming bickering faggots in the chimney, that sent at once their gleam and their warmth through the snug apartment; which, notwithstanding the general antiquity of its appearance, was not wanting in the least convenience that modern habits rendered either necessary or desirable.

"This is an old-fashioned sleeping apartment, General," said the young lord; "but I hope you will find nothing that makes you envy your old tobacco-cask."

"I am not particular respecting my lodgings," replied the General; "yet, were I to make any choice, I would prefer this chamber by many degrees to the gayer and more modern rooms of your family mansion. Believe me, that when I unite its modern air of comfort with its venerable antiquity, and recollect that it is your lordship's property, I shall feel in better quarters here than if I were in the best hotel London could afford."

"I trust—I have no doubt—that you will find yourself as comfortable as I wish you, my dear General," said the young nobleman; and once more bidding his guest goodnight, he shook him by the hand and withdrew.

The General again looked round him, and internally congratulating himself on his return to peaceful life, the comforts of which were endeared by the recollection of the hardships and dangers he had lately sustained, undressed himself, and prepared himself for a luxurious night's rest.

Here, contrary to the custom of this species of tale, we leave the General in possession of his apartment until the next morning.

The company assembled for breakfast at an early hour, but

without the appearance of General Browne, who seemed the guest that Lord Woodville was desirous of honouring above all whom his hospitality had assembled around him. He more than once expressed surprise at the General's absence, and at length sent a servant to make inquiry after him. The man brought back information that General Browne had been walking abroad since an early hour of the morning, in defiance of the weather, which was misty and ungenial.

"The custom of a soldier," said the young nobleman to his friends; "many of them acquire habitual vigilance, and cannot sleep after the early hour at which their duty usually commands them to be alert."

Yet the explanation which Lord Woodville thus offered to the company seemed hardly satisfactory to his own mind, and it was in a fit of silence and abstraction that he awaited the return of the General. It took place near an hour after the breakfast-bell had rung. He looked fatigued and feverish. His hair, the powdering and arrangement of which was at this time one of the most important occupations of a man's whole day, and marked his fashion as much as in the present time the tying of a cravat or the want of one, was dishevelled, uncurled, void of powder, and dank with dew. His clothes were huddled on with a careless negligence, remarkable in a military man, whose real or supposed duties are usually held to include some attention to the toilet; and his looks were haggard and ghastly in a peculiar degree.

"So you have stolen a march upon us this morning, my dear General," said Lord Woodville; "or you have not found your bed so much to your mind as I had hoped and you seemed to expect. How did you rest last night?"

"Oh, excellently well! remarkably well! never better in my life," said General Browne rapidly, and yet with an air of embarrassment which was obvious to his friend. He then hastily swallowed a cup of tea, and, neglecting or refusing whatever else was offered, seemed to fall into a fit of abstraction.

"You will take the gun today, General?" said his friend and host, but had to repeat the question twice ere he received the abrupt answer, "No, my lord; I am sorry I cannot have the honour of spending another day with your lordship; my post-horses are ordered, and will be here directly."

All who were present showed surprise, and Lord Woodville immediately replied, "Post-horses, my good friend! what can you possibly want with them, when you promised to stay with me quietly for at least a week?"

"I believe," said the General, obviously much embarrassed, "that I might, in the pleasure of my first meeting with your lordship, have said something about stopping here a few days; but I have since found it altogether impossible."

"That is very extraordinary," answered the young nobleman. "You seemed quite disengaged yesterday, and you cannot have had a summons today; for our post has not come up from the town, and therefore you cannot have received any letters."

General Browne, without giving any further explanation, muttered something of indispensable business, and insisted on the absolute necessity of his departure in a manner which silenced all opposition on the part of his host, who saw that his resolution was taken, and forbore further importunity.

"At least, however," he said, "permit me, my dear Browne, since go you will or must, to show you the view from the terrace, which the mist, that is now rising, will soon display."

He threw open a sash window, and stepped down upon the terrace as he spoke. The General followed him mechanically, but seemed little to attend to what his host was saying, as, looking across an extended and rich prospect, he pointed out the different objects worthy of observation. Thus they moved on till Lord Woodville had attained his purpose of drawing his guest entirely apart from the rest of the company, when, turning round upon him with an air of great solemnity, he addressed him thus: "Richard Browne, my old and very dear friend, we are now alone. Let me conjure you to answer me upon the word of a friend and the honour of a soldier. How did you in reality rest during last night?"

"Most wretchedly indeed, my lord," answered the General in

the same tone of solemnity; "so miserably, that I would not run the risk of such a second night, not only for all the lands belonging to this castle, but for all the country which I see from this elevated point of view."

"This is most extraordinary," said the young lord, as if speaking to himself; "then there must be something in the reports concerning that apartment." Again turning to the General, he said, "For God's sake, my dear friend, be candid with me, and let me know the disagreeable particulars which have befallen you under a roof where, with consent of the owner, you should have met nothing save comfort."

The General seemed distressed by this appeal, and paused a moment before he replied. "My dear lord," he at length said, "what happened to me last night is of a nature so peculiar and so unpleasant that I could hardly bring myself to detail it even to your lordship, were it not that, independent of my wish to gratify any request of yours, I think that sincerity on my part may lead to some explanation about a circumstance equally painful and mysterious. To others the communication I am about to make might place me in the light of a weak-minded, superstitious fool, who suffered his own imagination to delude and bewilder him; but you have known me in childhood, and youth, and will not suspect me of having adopted in manhood the feelings and frailties from which my early years were free."

Here he paused, and his friend replied, "Do not doubt my perfect confidence in the truth of your communication, however strange it may be," replied Lord Woodville; "I know your firmness of disposition too well to suspect you could be made the object of imposition, and am aware that your honour and your friendship will equally deter you from exaggerating whatever you may have witnessed."

"Well, then," said the General, "I will proceed with my story as well as I can, relying upon your candour, and yet distinctly feeling that I would rather face a battery than recall to my mind the odious recollections of last night."

He paused a second time, and then, perceiving that Lord

Woodville remained silent and in an attitude of attention, he commenced, though not without obvious reluctance, the history of his night's adventures in the Tapestried Chamber.

"I undressed and went to bed so soon as your lordship left me yesterday evening; but the wood in the chimney, which nearly fronted my bed, blazed brightly and cheerfully, and, aided by a hundred exciting recollections of my childhood and youth, which had been recalled by the unexpected pleasure of meeting your lordship, prevented me from falling immediately asleep. I ought, however, to say that these reflections were all of a pleasant and agreeable kind, grounded on a sense of having for a time exchanged the labour, fatigues, and dangers of my profession for the enjoyments of a peaceful life, and the reunion of those friendly and affectionate ties which I had torn asunder at the rude summons of war.

"While such pleasing reflections were stealing over my mind, and gradually lulling me to slumber, I was suddenly aroused by a sound like that of the rustling of a silken gown and the tapping of a pair of high-heeled shoes, as if a woman were walking in the apartment. Ere I could draw the curtain to see what the matter was, the figure of a little woman passed between the bed and the fire. The back of this form was turned to me, and I could observe from the shoulders and neck it was that of an old woman, whose dress was an old-fashioned gown which, I think, ladies call a *sacque*; that is, a sort of robe completely loose in the body, but gathered into broad plaits upon the neck and shoulders, which fall down to the ground and terminate in a species of train.

"I thought the intrusion singular enough, but never harboured for a moment the idea that what I saw was anything more than the mortal form of some old woman about the establishment, who had a fancy to dress like her grandmother, and who, having perhaps (as your lordship mentioned that you were rather straitened for room) been dislodged from her chamber for my accommodation, had forgotten the circumstance, and returned by twelve to her old haunt. Under this persuasion I moved myself in bed and coughed a little, to make the intruder sensible of my being in possession of the premises. She turned slowly round, but, gracious Heaven! my lord, what a countenance did she display to me! There was no longer any question what she was, or any thought of her being a living being. Upon a face which wore the fixed features of a corpse were imprinted the traces of the vilest and most hideous passions which had animated her while she lived.

"The body of some atrocious criminal seemed to have been given up from the grave and the soul restored from the penal fire, in order to form for a space a union with the ancient accomplice of its guilt. I started up in bed, and sat upright, supporting myself on my palms, as I gazed on this horrible spectre. The hag made, as it seemed, a single and swift stride to the bed where I lay, and squatted herself down upon it, in precisely the same attitude which I had assumed in the extremity of horror, advancing her diabolical countenance within half a yard of mine, with a grin which seemed to intimate the malice and the derision of an incarnate fiend.'

Here General Browne stopped, and wiped from his brow the cold perspiration with which the recollection of his horrible vision had covered it.

"My lord," he said, "I am no coward. I have been in all the mortal dangers incidental to my profession, and I may truly boast that no man ever knew Richard Browne dishonour the sword he wears; but in these horrible circumstances, under the eyes and, as it seemed, almost in the grasp of an incarnation of an evil spirit, all firmness forsook me, all manhood melted from me like wax in the furnace, and I felt my hair individually bristle. The current of my life-blood ceased to flow, and I sank back in a swoon, as very a victim to panic terror as ever was a village girl or a child of ten years old. How long I lay in this condition I cannot pretend to guess.

"But I was roused by the castle clock striking one, so loud that it seemed as if it were in the very room. It was some time before I dared open my eyes, lest they should again encounter the horrible spectacle. When, however, I summoned courage to look up, she was no longer visible. My first idea was to pull my bell, wake the servants, and remove to a garret or a hay-loft, to be insured against a second visitation. Nay, I will confess the truth, that my resolution was altered, not by the shame of exposing myself, but by the fear that, as the bell-cord hung by the chimney, I might, in making my way to it, be again crossed by the fiendish hag, who, I figured to myself, might be still lurking about some corner of the apartment.

"I will not pretend to describe what hot and cold fever-fits tormented me for the rest of the night, through broken sleep, weary vigils, and that dubious state which forms the neutral ground between them. A hundred terrible objects appeared to haunt me; but there was the great difference betwixt the vision which I have described and those which followed, that I knew the last to be deceptions of my own fancy and over-excited nerves.

"Day at last appeared, and I rose from my bed ill in health and humiliated in mind. I was ashamed of myself as a man and a soldier, and still more so at feeling my own extreme desire to escape from the haunted apartment, which, however, conquered all other considerations; so that, huddling on my clothes with the most careless haste, I made my escape from your lordship's mansion, to seek in the open air some relief to my nervous system, shaken as it was by this horrible *rencontre* with a visitant—for such I must believe her—from the other world. Your lordship has now heard the cause of my discomposure, and of my sudden desire to leave your hospitable castle. In other places I trust we may often meet; but God protect me from ever spending a second night under that roof!"

Strange as the General's tale was, he spoke with such a deep air of conviction that it cut short all the usual commentaries which are made on such stories. Lord Woodville never once asked him if he was sure he did not dream of the apparition, or suggested any of the possibilities by which it is fashionable to explain supernatural appearances, as wild vagaries of the fancy or deceptions of the optic nerves. On the contrary, he seemed deeply impressed with the truth and reality of what he had heard, and after a considerable pause regretted, with much appearance of sincerity, that his early friend should in his house have suffered so severely.

"I am the more sorry for your pain, my dear Browne," he continued, "that it is the unhappy, though most unexpected, result of an experiment of my own! You must know that, for my father and grandfather's time at least, the apartment which was assigned to you last night had been shut on account of reports that it was disturbed by supernatural sights and noises. When I came, a few weeks since, into possession of the estate, I thought the accommodation which the castle afforded for my friends was not extensive enough to permit the inhabitants of the invisible world to retain possession of a comfortable sleeping apartment. I therefore caused the Tapestried Chamber, as we call it, to be opened; and, without destroying its air of antiquity, I had such new articles of furniture placed in it as became the modern times.

"Yet, as the opinion that the room was haunted very strongly prevailed among the domestics, and was also known in the neighbourhood and to many of my friends, I feared some prejudice might be entertained by the first occupant of the Tapestried Chamber, which might tend to revive the evil report which it had laboured under, and so disappoint my purpose of rendering it a useful part of the house. I must confess, my dear Browne, that your arrival yesterday, agreeable to me for a thousand reasons besides, seemed the most favourable opportunity of removing the unpleasant rumours which attached to the room, since your courage was indubitable, and your mind free of any preoccupation on the subject. I could not, therefore, have chosen a more fitting subject for my experiment."

"Upon my life," said General Browne somewhat hastily, "I am infinitely obliged to your lordship very particularly indebted indeed. I am likely to remember for some time the consequences of the experiment, as your lordship is pleased to call it."

"Nay, now you are unjust, my dear friend," said Lord Woodville. "You have only to reflect for a single moment, in order to be convinced that I could not augur the possibility of the pain to which you have been so unhappily exposed. I was yesterday morning a complete sceptic on the subject of supernatural appearances. Nay, I am sure that, had I told you what was said about that room, those very reports would have induced you, by your own choice, to select it for your accommodation. It was my misfortune, perhaps my error, but really cannot be termed my fault, that you have been afflicted so strangely."

"Strangely indeed!" said the General, resuming his good temper; "and I acknowledge that I have no right to be offended with your lordship for treating me like what I used to think myself—a man of some firmness and courage. But I see my post-horses are arrived, and I must not detain your lordship from your amusement."

"Nay, my old friend," said Lord Woodville, "since you cannot stay with us another day, which, indeed, I can no longer urge, give me at least half-an-hour more. You used to love pictures, and I have a gallery of portraits, some of them by Vandyke, representing ancestry to whom this property and castle formerly belonged. I think that several of them will strike you as possessing merit."

General Browne accepted the invitation, though somewhat unwillingly. It was evident he was not to breathe freely or at ease till he left Woodville Castle far behind him. He could not refuse his friend's invitation, however; and the less so that he was a little ashamed of the peevishness which he had displayed towards his well-meaning entertainer.

The General, therefore, followed Lord Woodville through several rooms into a long gallery hung with pictures, which the latter pointed out to his guest, telling the names and giving some account of the personages whose portraits presented themselves in progression. General Browne was but little interested in the details which these accounts conveyed to him. They were, indeed, of the kind which are usually found in an old family gallery. Here was a Cavalier who had ruined the estate in the royal cause; there a fine lady who had reinstated it by contracting a match with a wealthy Roundhead. There hung a gallant who had been in danger for corresponding with the exiled court at Saint Germains; here one who had taken arms for William at the Revolution; and there a third that had thrown his weight alternately into the scale of Whig and Tory.

While Lord Woodville was cramming these words into his guest's ear "against the stomach of his sense," they gained the middle of the gallery, when he beheld General Browne suddenly start, and assume an attitude of the utmost surprise, not unmixed with fear, as his eyes were caught and suddenly riveted by a portrait of an old lady in a *sacque*, the fashionable dress of the end of the seventeenth century.

"There she is!" he exclaimed; "there she is, in form and features, though inferior in demoniac expression to the accursed hag who visited me last night!"

"If that be the case," said the young nobleman, "there can remain no longer any doubt of the horrible reality of your apparition. That is the picture of a wretched ancestress of mine, of whose crimes a black and fearful catalogue is recorded in a family history in my charter-chest. The recital of them would be too horrible; it is enough to say that in yon fatal apartment incest and unnatural murder were committed. I will restore it to the solitude to which the better judgment of those who preceded me had consigned it; and never shall any one, so long as I can prevent it, be exposed to a repetition of the supernatural horrors which could shake such courage as yours."

Thus the friends, who had met with such glee, parted in a very different mood, Lord Woodville to command the Tapestried Chamber to be unmantled and the door built up, and General Browne to seek in some less beautiful country, and with some less dignified friend, forgetfulness of the painful night which he had passed in Woodville Castle.

Dickon the Devil

By J. Sheridan le Fanu

About thirty years ago I was selected by two rich old maids to visit a property in that part of Lancashire which lies near the famous forest of Pendle, with which Mr. Ainsworth's *Lancashire Witches* has made us so pleasantly familiar. My business was to make partition of a small property, including a house and de-mesne, to which they had a long time before succeeded as co-heiresses.

The last forty miles of my journey I was obliged to post, chiefly by cross-roads, little known, and less frequented, and pre-senting scenery often extremely interesting and pretty. The pic-turesqueness of the landscape was enhanced by the season, the beginning of September, at which I was travelling.

I had never been in this part of the world before; I am told it is now a great deal less wild, and, consequently, less beautiful.

At the inn where I had stopped for a relay of horses and some dinner—for it was then past five o'clock—I found the host, a hale old fellow of five-and-sixty, as he told me, a man of easy and garrulous benevolence, willing to accommodate his guests with any amount of talk, which the slightest tap sufficed to set flowing, on any subject you pleased.

I was curious to learn something about Barwyke, which was the name of the demesne and house I was going to. As there was no inn within some miles of it, I had written to the steward to put me up there, the best way he could, for a night.

The host of the "Three Nuns," which was the sign under

which he entertained wayfarers, had not a great deal to tell. It was twenty years, or more, since old Squire Bowes died, and no one had lived in the Hall ever since, except the gardener and his wife.

"Tom Wyndsour will be as old a man as myself; but he's a bit taller, and not so much in flesh, quite," said the fat innkeeper.

"But there were stories about the house," I repeated, "that they said, prevented tenants from coming into it?"

"Old wives' tales; many years ago, that will be, sir; I forget 'em; I forget 'em all. Oh yes, there always will be, when a house is left so; foolish folk will always be talkin'; but I hadn't heard a word about it this twenty year."

It was vain trying to pump him; the old landlord of the "Three Nuns," for some reason, did not choose to tell tales of Barwyke Hall, if he really did, as I suspected, remember them.

I paid my reckoning, and resumed my journey, well pleased with the good cheer of that old-world inn, but a little disappointed.

We had been driving for more than an hour, when we began to cross a wild common; and I knew that, this passed, a quarter of an hour would bring me to the door of Barwyke Hall.

The peat and furze were pretty soon left behind; we were again in the wooded scenery that I enjoyed so much, so entirely natural and pretty, and so little disturbed by traffic of any kind. I was looking from the chaise-window, and soon detected the object of which, for some time, my eye had been in search. Barwyke Hall was a large, quaint house, of that cage-work fashion known as "black-and-white," in which the bars and angles of an oak framework contrast, black as ebony, with the white plaster that overspreads the masonry built into its interstices. This steep-roofed Elizabethan house stood in the midst of park-like grounds of no great extent, but rendered imposing by the noble stature of the old trees that now cast their lengthening shadows eastward over the sward, from the declining sun.

The park-wall was grey with age, and in many places laden with ivy. In deep grey shadow, that contrasted with the dim fires of evening reflected on the foliage above it, in a gentle hollow, stretched a lake that looked cold and black, and seemed, as it were, to skulk from observation with a guilty knowledge.

I had forgot that there was a lake at Barwyke; but the moment this caught my eye, like the cold polish of a snake in the shadow, my instinct seemed to recognize something dangerous, and I knew that the lake was connected, I could not remember how, with the story I had heard of this place in my boyhood.

I drove up a grass-grown avenue, under the boughs of these noble trees, whose foliage, dyed in autumnal red and yellow, returned the beams of the western sun gorgeously.

We drew up at the door. I got out, and had a good look at the front of the house; it was a large and melancholy mansion, with signs of long neglect upon it; great wooden shutters, in the old fashion, were barred, outside, across the windows; grass, and even nettles, were growing thick on the courtyard, and a thin moss streaked the timber beams; the plaster was discoloured by time and weather, and bore great russet and yellow stains. The gloom was increased by several grand old trees that crowded close about the house.

I mounted the steps, and looked round; the dark lake lay near me now, a little to the left. It was not large; it may have covered some ten or twelve acres; but it added to the melancholy of the scene. Near the centre of it was a small island, with two old ash trees, leaning toward each other, their pensive images reflected in the stirless water. The only cheery influence in this scene of antiquity, solitude, and neglect was that the house and landscape were warmed with the ruddy western beams. I knocked, and my summons resounded hollow and ungenial in my ear; and the bell, from far away, returned a deep-mouthed and surly ring, as if it resented being roused from a score years' slumber.

A light-limbed, jolly-looking old fellow, in a barracan jacket and gaiters, with a smile of welcome, and a very sharp, red nose, that seemed to promise good cheer, opened the door with a promptitude that indicated a hospitable expectation of my arrival.

There was but little light in the hall, and that little lost itself in darkness in the background. It was very spacious and lofty, with a gallery running round it, which, when the door was open, was visible at two or three points. Almost in the dark my new acquaintance led me across this wide hall into the room destined for my reception. It was spacious, and wainscoted up to the ceiling. The furniture of this capacious chamber was old-fashioned and clumsy. There were curtains still to the windows, and a piece of Turkey carpet lay upon the floor; those windows were two in number, looking out, through the trunks of the trees close to the house, upon the lake.

It needed all the fire, and all the pleasant associations of my entertainer's red nose, to light up this melancholy chamber. A door at its farther end admitted to the room that was prepared for my sleeping apartment. It was wainscoted, like the other. It had a four-post bed, with heavy tapestry curtains, and in other respects was furnished in the same old-world and ponderous style as the other room. Its window, like those of that apartment, looked out upon the lake.

Sombre and sad as these rooms were, they were yet scrupulously clean. I had nothing to complain of; but the effect was rather dispiriting. Having given some directions about supper—a pleasant incident to look forward to—and made a rapid toilet, I called on my friend with the gaiters and red nose (Tom Wyndsour) whose occupation was that of a "bailiff," or under-steward, of the property, to accompany me, as we had still an hour or so of sun and twilight, in a walk over the grounds.

It was a sweet autumn evening, and my guide, a hardy old fellow, strode at a pace that tasked me to keep up with.

Among clumps of trees at the northern boundary of the demesne we lighted upon the little antique parish church. I was looking down upon it, from an eminence, and the park-wall interposed; but a little way down was a stile affording access to the road, and by this we approached the iron gate of the churchyard. I saw the church door open; the sexton was replacing his pick, shovel, and spade, with which he had just been digging a grave in the churchyard, in their little repository under the stone stair of the tower. He was a polite, shrewd little hunchback, who was very happy to show me over the church. Among the monuments was one that interested me; it was erected to commemorate the very Squire Bowes from whom my two old maids had inherited the house and estate of Barwyke. It spoke of him in terms of grandiloquent eulogy, and informed the Christian reader that he had died, in the bosom of the Church of England, at the age of seventy-one.

I read this inscription by the parting beams of the setting sun, which disappeared behind the horizon just as we passed out from under the porch.

"Twenty years since the Squire died," said I, reflecting as I loitered still in the churchyard.

"Ay, sir; 'twill be twenty year the ninth o' last month."

"And a very good old gentleman?"

"Good-natured enough, and an easy gentleman he was, sir; I don't think while he lived he ever hurt a fly," acquiesced Tom Wyndsour. "It ain't always easy sayin' what's in 'em though, and what they may take or turn to afterwards; and some o' them sort, I think, goes mad."

"You don't think he was out of his mind?" I asked.

"He? La! no; not he, sir; a bit lazy, mayhap, like other old fellows; but a knew devilish well what he was about."

Tom Wyndsour's account was a little enigmatical; but, like old Squire Bowes, I was "a bit lazy" that evening, and asked no more questions about him.

We got over the stile upon the narrow road that skirts the churchyard. It is overhung by elms more than a hundred years old, and in the twilight, which now prevailed, was growing very dark. As side-by-side we walked along this road, hemmed in by two loose stone-like walls, something running towards us in a zigzag line passed us at a wild pace, with a sound like a frightened laugh or a shudder, and I saw, as it passed, that it was a human figure. I may confess now, that I was a little startled. The dress of this figure was, in part, white: I know I mistook it at first

542

for a white horse coming down the road at a gallop. Tom Wyndsour turned about and looked after the retreating figure.

"He'll be on his travels tonight," he said, in a low tone. "Easy served with a bed, *that* lad be; six foot o' dry peat or heath, or a nook in a dry ditch. That lad hasn't slept once in a house this twenty year, and never will while grass grows."

"Is he mad?" I asked.

"Something that way, sir; he's an idiot, an awpy; we call him 'Dickon the devil,' because the devil's almost the only word that's ever in his mouth."

It struck me that this idiot was in some way connected with the story of old Squire Bowes.

"Queer things are told of him, I dare say?" I suggested.

"More or less, sir; more or less. Queer stories, some."

"Twenty years since he slept in a house? That's about the time the Squire died," I continued.

"So it will be, sir; and not very long after."

"You must tell me all about that, Tom, tonight, when I can hear it comfortably, after supper."

Tom did not seem to like my invitation; and looking straight before him as we trudged on, he said,

"You see, sir, the house has been quiet, and nout's been troubling folk inside the walls or out, all round the woods of Barwyke, this ten year, or more; and my old woman, down there, is clear against talking about such matters, and thinks it best—and so do I—to let sleepin' dogs be."

He dropped his voice towards the close of the sentence, and nodded significantly.

We soon reached a point where he unlocked a wicket in the park wall, by which we entered the grounds of Barwyke once more.

The twilight deepening over the landscape, the huge and solemn trees, and the distant outline of the haunted house, exercised a sombre influence on me, which, together with the fatigue of a day of travel, and the brisk walk we had had, disinclined me to interrupt the silence in which my companion now indulged.

A certain air of comparative comfort, on our arrival, in great measure dissipated the gloom that was stealing over me. Although it was by no means a cold night, I was very glad to see some wood blazing in the grate; and a pair of candles aiding the light of the fire, made the room look cheerful. A small table, with a very white cloth, and preparations for supper, was also a very agreeable object.

I should have liked very well, under these influences, to have listened to Tom Wyndsour's story; but after supper I grew too sleepy to attempt to lead him to the subject; and after yawning for a time, I found there was no use in contending against my drowsiness, so I betook myself to my bedroom, and by ten o'clock was fast asleep.

What interruption I experienced that night I shall tell you presently. It was not much, but it was very odd.

By next night I had completed my work at Barwyke. From early morning till then I was so incessantly occupied and hard-worked, that I had not time to think over the singular occurrence to which I have just referred. Behold me, however, at length once more seated at my little supper-table, having ended a comfortable meal. It had been a sultry day, and I had thrown one of the large windows up as high as it would go. I was sitting near it, with my brandy and water at my elbow, looking out into the dark. There was no moon, and the trees that are grouped about the house make the darkness round it supernaturally profound on such nights.

"Tom," said I, so soon as the jug of hot punch I had supplied him with began to exercise its genial and communicative influence; "you must tell me who beside your wife and you and myself slept in the house last night."

Tom, sitting near the door, set down his tumbler, and looked at me askance, while you might count seven, without speaking a word.

"Who else slept in the house?" he repeated, very deliberately. "Not a living soul, sir"; and he looked hard at me, still evidently expecting something more.

"That *is* very odd," I said returning his stare, and feeling really a little odd. "You are sure *you* were not in my room last night?"

"Not till I came to call you, sir, this morning; *I* can make oath of that."

"Well," said I, "there was someone there, *I* can make oath of that. I was so tired I could not make up my mind to get up; but I was waked by a sound that I thought was someone flinging down the two tin boxes in which my papers were locked up violently on the floor. I heard a slow step on the ground, and there was light in the room, although I remembered having put out my candle. I thought it must have been you, who had come in for my clothes, and upset the boxes by accident. Whoever it was, he went out and the light with him.

"I was about to settle again, when, the curtain being a little open at the foot of the bed, I saw a light on the wall opposite; such as a candle from outside would cast if the door were very cautiously opening. I started up in the bed, drew the side curtain, and saw that the door *was* opening, and admitting light from outside. It is close, you know, to the head of the bed. A hand was holding on the edge of the door and pushing it open; not a bit like yours; a very singular hand. Let me look at yours."

He extended it for my inspection.

"Oh no; there's nothing wrong with your hand. This was differently shaped; fatter; and the middle finger was stunted, and shorter than the rest, looking as if it had once been broken, and the nail was crooked like a claw. I called out 'Who's there?' and the light and the hand were withdrawn, and I saw and heard no more of my visitor."

"So sure as you're a living man, that was him!" exclaimed Tom Wyndsour, his very nose growing pale, and his eyes almost starting out of his head.

"Who?" I asked.

"Old Squire Bowes; 'twas *his* hand you saw; the Lord a' mercy on us!" answered Tom. "The broken finger, and the nail bent like a hoop. Well for you, sir, he didn't come back when you called, that time. You came here about them Miss Dymock's business,

545

and he never meant they should have a foot o' ground in Bar-wyke; and he was making a will to give it away quite different, when death took him short. He never was uncivil to no one; but he couldn't abide them ladies. My mind misgave me when I heard 'twas about their business you were coming; and now you see how it is; he'll be at his old tricks again!"

With some pressure and a little more punch, I induced Tom Wyndsour to explain his mysterious allusions by recounting the occurrences which followed the old Squire's death.

"Squire Bowes of Barwyke died without making a will, as you know," said Tom. "And all the folk round were sorry; that is to say, sir, as sorry as folk will be for an old man that has seen a long tale of years, and has no right to grumble that death has knocked an hour too soon at his door. The Squire was well liked; he was never in a passion, or said a hard word; and he would not hurt a fly; and that made what happened after his decease the more surprising.

"The first thing these ladies did, when they got the property, was to buy stock for the park.

"It was not wise, in any case, to graze the land on their own account. But they little knew all they had to contend with.

"Before long something went wrong with the cattle; first one, and then another, took sick and died, and so on, till the loss began to grow heavy. Then, queer stories, little by little, began to be told. It was said, first by one, then by another, that Squire Bowes was seen, about evening time, walking, just as he used to do when he was alive, among the old trees, leaning on his stick; and, sometimes when he came up with the cattle, he would stop and lay his hand kindly like on the back of one of them; and that one was sure to fall sick next day, and die soon after.

"No one ever met him in the park, or in the woods, or ever saw him, except a good distance off. But they knew his gait and his figure well, and the clothes he used to wear; and they could tell the beast he laid his hand on by its colour—white, dun, or black; and that beast was sure to sicken and die. The neighbours grew shy of taking the path over the park; and no one liked to walk in the woods, or come inside the bounds of Barwyke: and the cattle went on sickening and dying as before.

"At that time there was one Thomas Pyke; he had been a groom to the old Squire; and he was in care of the place, and was the only one that used to sleep in the house.

"Tom was vexed, hearing these stories; which he did not believe the half on 'em; and more especial as he could not get man or boy to herd the cattle; all being afeared. So he wrote to Matlock in Derbyshire, for his brother, Richard Pyke, a clever lad, and one that knew nout o' the story of the old Squire walking.

"Dick came; and the cattle was better; folk said they could still see the old Squire, sometimes, walking, as before, in openings of the wood, with his stick in his hand; but he was shy of coming nigh the cattle, whatever his reason might be, since Dickon Pyke came; and he used to stand a long bit off, looking at them, with no more stir in him than a trunk o' one of the old trees, for an hour at a time, till the shape melted away, little by little, like the smoke of a fire that burns out.

"Tom Pyke and his brother Dickon, being the only living souls in the house, lay in the big bed in the servants' room, the house being fast barred and locked, one night in November.

"Tom was lying next the wall, and he told me, as wide awake as ever he was at noonday. His brother Dickon lay outside, and was sound asleep.

"Well, as Tom lay thinking, with his eyes turned toward the door, it opens slowly, and who should come in but old Squire Bowes, his face lookin' as dead as he was in his coffin.

"Tom's very breath left his body; he could not take his eyes off him; and he felt the hair rising up on his head.

"The Squire came to the side of the bed, and put his arms under Dickon, and lifted the boy—in a dead sleep all the time—and carried him out so, at the door.

"Such was the appearance, to Tom Pyke's eyes, and he was ready to swear to it, anywhere.

"When this happened, the light, wherever it came from, all on a sudden went out, and Tom could not see his own hand before him.

"More dead than alive, he lay till daylight.

"Sure enough his brother Dickon was gone. No sign of him could he discover about the house; and with some trouble he got a couple of the neighbours to help him to search the woods and grounds. Not a sign of him anywhere.

"At last one of them thought of the island in the lake; the little boat was moored to the old post at the water's edge. In they got, though with small hope of finding him there. Find him, nevertheless, they did, sitting under the big ash tree, quite out of his wits; and to all their questions he answered nothing but one cry—'Bowes, the devil! See him; see him; Bowes, the devil!' An idiot they found him; and so he will be till God sets all things right. No one could ever get him to sleep under roof-tree more. He wanders from house to house while daylight lasts; and no one cares to lock the harmless creature in the workhouse. And folk would rather not meet him after nightfall, for they think where he is there may be worse things near."

A silence followed Tom's story. He and I were alone in that large room; I was sitting near the open window, looking into the dark night air. I fancied I saw something white move across it; and I heard a sound like low talking that swelled into a discordant shriek—"Hoo-oo-oo! Bowes, the devil! Over your shoulder. Hoo-oo-oo! ha! ha! ha!" I started up, and saw, by the light of the candle with which Tom strode to the window, the wild eyes and blighted face of the idiot, as, with a sudden change of mood, he drew off, whispering and tittering to himself, and holding up his long fingers, and looking at the tips like a "hand of glory."

Tom pulled down the window. The story and its epilogue were over. I confess I was rather glad when I heard the sound of the horses' hoofs on the courtyard, a few minutes later; and still gladder when, having bidden Tom a kind farewell, I had left the neglected house of Barwyke a mile behind me.

Bagnell Terrace

By E F Benson

I had been for ten years an inhabitant of Bagnell Terrace, and, like all those who have been so fortunate as to secure a footing there, was convinced that for amenity, convenience, and tranquillity it is unrivalled in the length and breadth of London. The houses are small; we could, none of us, give an evening party or a dance, but we who live in Bagnell Terrace do not desire to do anything of the kind. We do not go in for sounds of revelry at night, nor, indeed, is there much revelry during the day, for we have gone to Bagnell Terrace in order to be anchored in a quiet little backwater. There is no traffic through it, for the terrace is a *cul-de-sac*, closed at the far end by a high brick wall, along which, on summer nights, cats trip lightly on visits to their friends. Even the cats of Bagnell Terrace have caught something of its discretion and tranquillity, for they do not hail each other with long-drawn yells of mortal agony like their cousins in less well-conducted places, but sit and have quiet little parties like the owners of the houses in which they condescend to be lodged and boarded.

But, though I was more content to be in Bagnell Terrace than anywhere else, I had not got, and was beginning to be afraid I never should get, the particular house which I coveted above all others. This was at the top end of the terrace adjoining the wall that closed it, and in one respect it was unlike the other houses, which so much resemble each other. The others have little square gardens in front of them, where we have our bulbs abloom in the spring, when they present a very gay appearance, but the gardens are too small, and London too sunless to allow of any very effective horticulture. The house, however, to which I had so long turned envious eyes, had no garden in front of it; instead, the space had been used for the erection of a big, square room (for a small garden will make a very well-sized room) connected with the house by a covered passage. Rooms in Bagnell Terrace, though sunny and cheerful, are not large, and just one big room, so it occurred to me, would give the final touch of perfection to those delightful little residences.

Now, the inhabitants of this desirable abode were something of a mystery to our neighbourly little circle, though we knew that a man lived there (for he was occasionally seen leaving or entering his house), he was personally unknown to us. A curious point was that though we had all (though rarely) encountered him on the pavements, there was a considerable discrepancy in the impression he had made on us. He certainly walked briskly, as if the vigour of life was still his, but while I believed that he was a young man, Hugh Abbot, who lived in the house next his, was convinced that, in spite of his briskness, he was not only old, but very old. Hugh and I, life-long bachelor friends, often discussed him in the ramble of conversation when he had dropped in for an after-dinner pipe, or I had gone across for a game of chess. His name was not known to us, so, by reason of my desire for his house, we called him Naboth. We both agreed that there was something odd about him, something baffling and elusive.

I had been away for a couple of months one winter in Egypt; the night after my return Hugh dined with me, and after dinner I produced those trophies which the strongest-minded are unable to refrain from purchasing, when they are offered by an engaging *burnoused* ruffian in the Valley of the Tombs of the Kings. There were some beads (not quite so blue as they had appeared there), a *scarab* or two, and for the last I kept the piece of which I was really proud, namely, a small *lapis-lazuli* statuette, a few inches high, of a cat. It sat square and stiff on its haunches, with upright forelegs, and, in spite of the small scale, so good were the proportions and so accurate the observation of the artist, that it gave the impression of being much bigger. As it stood on Hugh's palm, it was certainly small, but if, without the sight of it, I pictured it to myself, it represented itself as far larger than it really was."

"And the odd thing is," I said, "that though it is far and away the best thing I picked up, I cannot for the life of me remember where I bought it. Somehow I feel that I've always had it."

He had been looking very intently at it. Then he jumped up from his chair and put it down on the chimney-piece.

"I don't think I quite like it," he said, "and I can't tell you why. Oh, a jolly bit of workmanship; I don't mean that. And you can't remember where you got it, did you say? That's odd. . . . Well, what about a game of chess."

We played a couple of games, without much concentration or fervour, and more than once I saw him glance with a puzzled look at my little image on the chimney-piece. But he said nothing more about it, and when our games were over, he gave me the discursive news of the terrace. A house had fallen vacant and been instantly snapped up.

"Not Naboth's?" I asked.

"No, not Naboth's. Naboth is in possession still. Very much in possession; going strong."

"Anything new?" I asked.

"Oh, just bits of things. I've seen him a good many times lately, and yet I can't get any clear idea of him. I met him three days ago, as I was coming out of my gate, and had a good look at him, and for a moment I agreed with you and thought he was a young man. Then he turned and stared me in the face for a second, and I thought I had never seen anyone so old. Frightfully alive, but more than old, antique, primeval."

"And then?" I asked.

"He passed on, and I found myself, as has so often happened before, quite unable to remember what his face was like. Was he old or young? I didn't know. What was his mouth like, or his nose? But it was the question of his age which was the most baffling."

Hugh stretched his feet out towards the blaze, and sank back in his chair, with one more frowning look at my *lapis lazuli* cat.

"Though after all, what is age?" he said. "We measure age by time, we say 'so many years,' and forget that we're in eternity here and now, just as we say we're in a room or in Bagnell Terrace, though we're much more truly in infinity."

"What has that got to do with Naboth?" I asked.

Hugh beat his pipe out against the bars of the grate before he answered.

"Well, it will probably sound quite cracked to you," he said, "unless Egypt, the land of ancient mystery, has softened your rind of materialism, but it struck me then that Naboth belonged to eternity much more obviously than we do. We belong to it, of course, we can't help that, but he's less involved in this error or illusion of time than we are. Dear me, it sounds amazing nonsense when I put it into words."

I laughed.

"I'm afraid my rind of materialism isn't soft enough yet," I said. "What you say implies that you think Naboth is a sort of apparition, a ghost, a spirit of the dead that manifests itself as a human being, though it isn't one!"

He drew his legs up to him again.

"Yes; it must be nonsense," he said. "Besides he has been so much in evidence lately, and we can't all be seeing a ghost. It doesn't happen. And there have been noises coming from his house, loud and cheerful noises, which I've never heard before. Somebody plays an instrument like a flute in that big, square room you envy so much, and somebody beats an accompaniment as if with drums. Odd sort of music; it goes on often now at night. . . . Well, it's time to go to bed."

Again he glanced up at the chimney-piece.

"Why, it's quite a little cat," he said.

This rather interested me, for I had said nothing to him about the impression left on my mind that it was bigger than its actual dimensions.

"Just the same size as ever," I said.

"Naturally. But I had been thinking of it as life-size for some reason," said he.

I went with him to the door, and strolled out with him into the darkness of an overcast night. As we neared his house, I saw that big patches of light shone into the road from the windows of the square room next door. Suddenly Hugh laid his hand on my arm.

"There!" he said. "The flutes and drums are at it tonight."

The night was very still, but, listen as I would, I could hear nothing but the rumble of traffic in the street beyond the terrace.

"I can't hear it," I said.

Even as I spoke, I heard it, and the wailing noise whisked me back to Egypt again. The boom of the traffic became for me the beat of the drum, and upon it floated just that squeal and wail of the little reed pipes which accompany the Arab dances, tuneless and rhythmless, and as old as the temples of the Nile.

"It's like the Arab music that you hear in Egypt," I said.

As we stood listening it ceased to his ears as well as mine, as suddenly as it had begun, and simultaneously the lights in the windows of the square room were extinguished.

We waited a moment in the roadway opposite Hugh's house, but from next door came no sound at all, nor glimmer of illumination from any of its windows. . . .

I turned; it was rather chilly to one lately arrived from the South.

"Goodnight," I said, "we'll meet tomorrow sometime."

I went straight to bed, slept at once, and woke with the impress of a very vivid dream on my mind. There was music in it, familiar Arab music, and there was an immense cat somewhere. Even as I tried to recall it, it faded, and I had but time to recognise it as a hash-up of the happenings of the evening before I went to sleep again.

The normal habits of life quickly reasserted themselves. I had work to do, and there were friends to see; all the minute events of each day stitched themselves into the tapestry of life. But somehow a new thread began to be woven into it, though at the time I did not recognise it as such. It seemed trivial and extraneous that I should so often hear a few staves of that odd music from Naboth's house, or that as often as it fixed my attention it was silent again, as if I had imagined, rather than actually heard it. It was trivial, too, that I should so often see Naboth entering or leaving his house. And then one day I had a sight of him, which was unlike any previous experience of mine.

I was standing one morning in the window of my front room. I had idly picked up my *lapis lazuli* cat, and was holding it in the splash of sunlight that poured in, admiring the soft texture of its surface which, though it was of hard stone, somehow suggested fur. Then, quite casually, I looked up, and there a few yards in front of me, leaning on the railings of my garden, and intently observing not me, but what I held, was Naboth. His eyes, fixed on it, blinked in the April sunshine with some purring sensuous content, and Hugh was right on the question of his age; he was neither old nor young, but timeless.

The moment of perception passed; it flashed on and off my mind like the revolving beam of some distant lighthouse. It was just a ray of illumination, and was instantly shut off again, so that it appeared to my conscious mind like some hallucination. He suddenly seemed aware of me, and turning, walked briskly off down the pavement.

I remember being rather startled, but the effect soon faded, and the incident became to me one of those trivial little things that make a momentary impression and vanish. It was odd, too, but in no way remarkable, that more than once I saw one of those discreet cats of which I have spoken sitting on the little balcony outside my front room, and gravely regarding the interior. I am devoted to cats, and several times I got up in order to open the window and invite it to enter, but each time on my movement it jumped down and slunk away. And April passed into May.

I came back after dining out one night in this month, and

found a telephone message from Hugh that I should ring him up on my return. A rather excited voice answered me.

"I thought you would like to know at once," he said. "An hour ago a board was put up on Naboth's house to say that the freehold was for sale. Martin and Smith are the agents. Good-night; I'm in bed already."

"You're a true friend," I said.

Early next morning, of course, I presented myself at the house-agent's. The price asked was very moderate, the title perfectly satisfactory. He could give me the keys at once, for the house was empty, and he promised that I could have a couple of days to make up my mind, during which time I was to have the prior right of purchase if I was disposed to pay the full price asked. If, however, I only made an offer, he could not guarantee that the trustees would accept it. . . . Hot-foot, with the keys in my pocket, I sped back up the terrace again.

I found the house completely empty, not of inhabitants only, but of all else. There was not a blind, not a strip of drugget, not a curtain-rod in it from garret to cellar. So much the better, thought I, for there would be no tenants' fixtures to take on. Nor was there any debris of removal, of straw and waste paper; the house looked as if it was prepared for an occupant instead of just rid of one. All was in apple-pie order, the windows clean, the floors swept, the paint and woodwork bright; it was a clean and polished shell ready for its occupier. My first inspection, of course, was of the big built-out room, which was its chief attraction, and my heart leaped at the sight of its plain spaciousness. On one side was an open fireplace, on the other a coil of pipes for central heating, and at the end, between the windows, a niche let into the wall, as if a statue had once stood there; it might have been designed expressly for my bronze Perseus. The rest of the house presented no particular features; it was on the same plan as my own, and my builder, who inspected it that afternoon, pronounced it to be in excellent condition.

"It looks as if it had been newly done up, and never lived in," he said, "and at the price you mention is a decided bargain."

The same thing struck Hugh when, on his return from his office, I dragged him over to see it.

"Why, it all looks new," he said, "and yet we know that Naboth has been here for years, and was certainly here a week ago. And then there's another thing. When did he remove his furniture? There have been no vans at the house that I have seen."

I was much too pleased at getting my heart's desire to consider anything except that I had got it.

"Oh, I can't bother about little things like that," I said. "Look at my beautiful big room. Piano there, bookcases all along the wall, sofa in front of the fire, Perseus in the niche. Why, it was made for me."

Within the specified two days the house was mine, and within a month papering and distempering, electric fittings, and blinds and curtain rods were finished, and my move began. Two days were sufficient for the transport of my goods, and at the close of the second my old house was dismantled, except for my bedroom, the contents of which would be moved next day. My servants were installed in the new abode, and that night, after a hurried dinner with Hugh, I went back for a couple more hours' work of hauling and tugging and arranging books in the large room, which it was my purpose to finish first. It was a chilly night for May, and I had had a log-fire lit on the hearth, which from time to time I replenished, in intervals of dusting and arranging. Eventually, when the two hours had lengthened themselves into three, I determined to give over for the present, and, much tired, sat down for a recuperative pause on the edge of my sofa and contemplated with satisfaction the result of my labours. At that moment I was conscious that there was a stale, but aromatic, smell in the room that reminded me of the curious odour that hangs about an Egyptian temple. But I put it down to the dust from my books and the smouldering logs.

The move was completed next day, and after another week I was installed as firmly as if I had been there for years. May slipped by, and June, and my new house never ceased to give me a vivid pleasure: it was always a treat to return to it. Then came a certain afternoon when a strange thing happened.

The day had been wet, but towards evening it cleared up: the pavements soon dried, but the road remained moist and miry. I was close to my house on my way home, when I saw form itself on the paving-stones a few yards in front of me the mark of a wet shoe, as if someone invisible to the eye had just stepped off the road. Another and yet another briskly imprinted themselves going up towards my house. For the moment I stood stock still, and then, with a thumping heart I followed. The marks of these strange footsteps preceded me right up to my door: there was one on the very threshold faintly visible.

I let myself in, closing the door, I confess, very quickly be-hind me. As I stood there I heard a resounding crash from my room, which, so to speak, startled my fright from me, and I ran down the little passage, and burst in. There, at the far end of the room was my bronze Perseus fallen from its niche and lying on the floor. And I knew, by what sixth sense I cannot tell, that I was not alone in the room and that the presence there was no human presence.

Now fear is a very odd thing: unless it is over-mastering and overwhelming, it always produces its own reaction. Whatever courage we have rises to meet it, and with courage comes anger that we have given entrance to this unnerving intruder. That, at any rate, was my case now, and I made an effective emotional re-sistance. My servant came running in to see what the noise was, and we set Perseus on his feet again and examined into the cause of his fall. It was clear enough: a big piece of plaster had broken away from the niche, and that must be repaired and strengthened before we reinstated him. Simultaneously my fear and the sense of an unaccountable presence in the room slipped from me. The footsteps outside were still unexplained and I told myself that if I was to shudder at everything I did not understand, there would be an end to tranquil existence for ever.

I was dining with Hugh that night: he had been away for the last week, only returning today, and he had come in before these slightly agitating events happened to announce his arrival and suggest dinner. I noticed that as he stood chatting for a few minutes, he had once or twice sniffed the air but he had made no comment, nor had I asked him if he perceived the strange faint odour that every now and then manifested itself to me. I knew it was a great relief to some secretly-quaking piece of my mind that he was back, for I was convinced that there was some psychic disturbance going on, either subjectively in my mind, or a real invasion from without. In either case his presence was comforting, not because he is of that stalwart breed which believes in nothing beyond the material facts of life, and pooh-poohs these mysterious forces which surround and so strangely interpenetrate existence, but because, while thoroughly believing in them, he has the firm confidence that the deadly and evil powers which occasionally break through into the seeming security of existence are not really to be feared, since they are held in check by forces stronger yet, ready to assist all who realise their protective care. Whether I meant to tell him what had occurred today I had not fully determined.

It was not till after dinner that such subjects came up at all, but I had seen there was something on his mind of which he had not spoken yet.

"And your new house," he said at length, "does it still remain as all your fancy painted?"

"I wonder why you ask that," I said.

He gave me a quick glance.

"Mayn't I take any interest in your well-being?" he said.

I knew that something was coming, if I chose to let it.

"I don't think you've ever liked my house from the first," I said. "I believe you think there's something queer about it. I allow that the manner in which I found it empty was odd."

"It was rather," he said. "But so long as it remains empty, except for what you've put in it, it is all right."

I wanted now to press him further.

"What was it you smelt this afternoon in the big room?" I said. "I saw you nosing and sniffing. I have smelt something, too. Let's see if we smelt the same thing."

"An odd smell," he said. "Something dusty and stale, but aromatic."

"And what else have you noticed?" I asked.

He paused a moment.

"I think I'll tell you," he said. "This evening from my window I saw you coming up the pavement, and simultaneously I saw, or thought I saw, Naboth cross the road and walk on in front of you. I wondered if you saw him, too, for you paused as he stepped on to the pavement in front of you, and then you followed him."

I felt my hands grow suddenly cold, as if the warm current of my blood had been chilled.

"No, I didn't see him," I said, "but I saw his step."

"What do you mean?"

"Just what I say. I saw footprints in front of me, which continued on to my threshold."

"And then?"

"I went in, and a terrific crash startled me. My bronze Perseus had fallen from his niche. And there was something in the room,"

There was a scratching noise at the window. Without answering, Hugh jumped up and drew aside the curtain. On the sill was seated a large grey cat, blinking in the light. He advanced to the window, and on his approach the cat jumped down into the garden. The light shone out into the road, and we both saw, standing on the pavement just outside, the figure of a man. He turned and looked at me, and then moved away towards my house, next door.

"It's he," said Hugh.

He opened the window and leaned out to see what had become of him. There was no sign of him anywhere, but I saw that light shone from behind the blinds of my room.

"Come on," I said. "Let's see what is happening. Why is my room lit?"

I opened the door of my house with my latch-key, and followed by Hugh went down the short passage to the room. It was perfectly dark, and when I turned the switch, we saw that it was empty. I rang the bell, but no answer came, for it was already late, and doubtless my servants had gone to bed.

"But I saw a strong light from the windows two minutes ago," I said, "and there has been no one here since."

Hugh was standing by me in the middle of the room. Suddenly he threw out his arm as if striking at something. That thoroughly alarmed me.

"What's the matter?" I asked. "What are you hitting at?"

He shook his head.

"I don't know," he said. "I thought I saw——But I'm not sure. But we're in for something if we stop here. Something is coming, though I don't know what."

The light seemed to me to be burning dim; shadows began to collect in the corner of the room, and though outside the night had been clear, the air here was growing thick with a foggy vapour, which smelt dusty and stale and aromatic. Faintly, but getting louder as we waited there in silence, I heard the throb of drums and the wail of flutes As yet I had no feeling that there were other presences in the place beyond ours, but in the growing dimness I knew that something was coming nearer. Just in front of me was the empty niche from which my bronze had fallen, and looking at it, I saw that something was astir. The shadow within it began to shape itself into a form, and out of it there gleamed two points of greenish light. A moment more and I saw that they were eyes of antique and infinite malignity.

I heard Hugh's voice in a sort of hoarse whisper.

"Look there!" he said. "It's coming! Oh, my God, it's coming!"

Sudden as the lightning that leaps from the heart of the night it came. But it came not with blaze and flash of light, but, as it were, with a stroke of blinding darkness, that fell not on the eye, or on any material sense, but on the spirit, so that I cowered under it in some abandonment of terror. It came from those eyes which gleamed in the niche, and which now I saw to be set in the face of the figure that stood there. The form of it, naked, but for a loin-cloth, was that of a man, the head seemed now human, now to be that of some monstrous cat. And as I looked, I knew that if I continued looking there I should be submerged and drowned in that flood of evil that poured from it. As in some catalepsy of nightmare I struggled to tear my eyes from it, but still they were riveted there, gazing on incarnate hate. Again I heard Hugh's whisper. "Defy it," he said. "Don't yield an inch." A swarm of disordered and hellish images were buzzing in my brain, and now I knew as surely as if actual words had been spoken to us that the presence there told me to come to it.

"I've got to go to it," I said. "It's making me go." I felt his hand tighten on my arm. "Not a step," he said. "I'm stronger than it is. It will know that soon. Just pray—pray."

Suddenly his arm shot out in front of me, pointing at the presence.

"By the power of God," he shouted. "By the power of God."

There was dead silence. The light of those eyes faded, and then came dawn on the darkness of the room. It was quiet and orderly, the niche was empty, and there on the sofa by me was Hugh, his face white and streaming with sweat.

"It's over," he said, and without pause fell fast asleep. Now we have often talked over together what happened that evening. Of what seemed to happen, I have already given the account, which anyone may believe or not, precisely as they please. He, as I, was conscious of a presence wholly evil, and he tells me that all the time that those eyes gleamed from the niche, he was trying to realise what he believed, namely, that only one power in the world is Omnipotent, and that the moment he gained that realisation the presence collapsed. What exactly that presence was it is impossible to say. It looks as if it was the essence or spirit of one of those mysterious Egyptian cults, of which the force survived, and was seen and felt in this quiet terrace. That it was embodied in Naboth seems (among all these incredibilities) possible, and Naboth certainly has never been seen again. Whether or not it was connected with the worship and cult of cats might occur to the mythological mind, and it is perhaps worthy of record that I found next morning my little *lapis lazuli* image, which stood on the chimneypiece, broken into fragments. It was too badly damaged to mend, and I am not sure that, in any case, I should have attempted to have it restored.

Finally, there is no more tranquil and pleasant room in London than the one built out in front of my house in Bagnell Terrace.

The Wife of Usher's Well

Anonymous

There lived a wife at Usher's Well,
And a wealthy wife was she;
She had three stout and stalwart sons,
And sent them over the sea.

They hadna been a week from her,
A week but barely ane,
Whan word came to the carline wife,
That her three sons were gane.

They hadna been a week from her,
A week but barely three,
Whan word came to the carlin wife
That her three sons were gone.

"I wish the wind may never cease,
Nor fashes in the flood,
Till my three sons come hame to me,
In earthly flesh and blood."

It befell about the Martinmass,
When nights are long and mirk,
The carlin wife's three sons came hame,
And their hats were o the birk.

It neither grew in syke nor ditch,
Nor yet in ony sheugh;
But at the gates o Paradise,

That birk grew fair enough

"Blow up the fire my maidens,
Bring water from the well;
For a' my house shall feast this night,
Since my three sons are well."

And she has made to them a bed,
She's made it large and wide,
And she's taen her mantle her about,
Sat down at the bedside.

Up then crew the red, red, cock,
And up the crew the gray;
The eldest to the youngest said,
'Tis time we were away.

The cock he hadna crawed but once,
And clappd his wings at a',
When the youngest to the eldest said,
Brother, we must awa.

The cock doth craw, the day both daw,
The cahannerin worm doth chide;
Gin we be mist out o our place,
A sair pain we maun bide.

"Fare ye weel, my mother dear!
Fareweel to barn and byre!
And fare ye weel, the bonny lass
That kindles my mother's fire!"

A List of The Stories Appearing in This Anthology Series